PS   Blacker, Irwin   85115
561   The Old West In Fiction
B5
1961

$10.

DATE DUE

NOV 1 0 1989			
2/21/04			
3/1 /oil			

The Old West in Fiction

THE
OLD WEST
IN FICTION

Edited by

IRWIN R. BLACKER

IVAN OBOLENSKY, INC.

New York

ACKNOWLEDGMENTS

Grant of Kingdom by Harvey Fergusson, Copyright 1950 by The Curtis Publishing Company, reprinted by permission of William Morrow and Company, Inc.

"The Buffalo," from *The Long Rifle,* by Stewart Edward White, Copyright 1931 by Stewart Edward White, Copyright renewed 1959 by N. Rugee White, reprinted by permission of Brandt & Brandt. The book was originally published by Doubleday & Company, Inc.

"Rendezvous," from *The Big Sky,* by A. B. Guthrie, reprinted by permission of Houghton Mifflin Company.

"The Raid," from *The Searchers,* by Alan LeMay, Copyright 1954 by Alan LeMay, Copyright 1954 by The Curtis Publishing Company, reprinted by permission of Harper & Bros.

"Flame on the Frontier," from *Indian Country,* by Dorothy Johnson, published by Ballantine Books, reprinted by permission of McIntosh and Otis, Inc.

"The Wind and the Snow of Winter," from *The Watchful Gods and Other Stories,* by Walter Van Tilburg Clark, Copyright 1944 by Walter Van Tilburg Clark, reprinted by permission of Random House, Inc.

"Early Marriage," from *Early Americana,* by Conrad Richter, Copyright 1935, 1936 by The Curtis Publishing Company, reprinted by permission of Alfred A. Knopf, Inc.

"The Fool's Heart" by Eugene Manlove Rhodes, reprinted by permission of the Literary Executor of the Estate of E. M. Rhodes.

The "Gunsmoke" television script by John Meston, reprinted by permission of Columbia Broadcasting System, Inc.

"Stage to Lordsburg," from *Rope and Lead,* by Ernest Haycox, Copyright 1937 by Ernest Haycox, reprinted by permission of Little, Brown & Company.

"Open Winter," from *Team Bells Woke Me and Other Stories,* by H. L. Davis, Copyright 1939 by H. L. Davis, reprinted by permission of William Morrow and Company, Inc.

"The Leader of the People," from *The Red Pony,* by John Steinbeck, Copyright 1938 by John Steinbeck, reprinted by permission of The Viking Press, Inc.

For
Frank, Harry, and Jack

It takes all kinds.

NOTES FOR A PREFACE

For many reasons there have been no overall histories of the literature of the West. High among these reasons is the low regard in which Western literature has been held for many years by university faculties across the country. While this is no attempt to compare it with the great writing of a Shakespeare or a Chaucer, there is sufficient cause to believe that it warrants consideration in its own right and that, indeed, the literature of the West may be coming into its own. One of the proofs of this is that critics have begun to recognize that it is better than has been generally believed and that it has its own quality as a native genre.

Many years ago a young J. Frank Dobie, fresh off a Texas ranch, showed his English professors a collection of songs he had gathered on the range; and he was told that this was worthless stuff, not worth keeping. A more perceptive Harvard faculty member, realizing what had been discarded, sent Dobie back to start collecting again. Today even the most conservative Milton scholar would hesitate to call the range songs of the West worthless. More likely, he would rush the student over to that younger member of the faculty who is working in that still questionable field known as folklore. Something then is happening to our recognition of the West. Not enough has happened, however. The fiction, the tales and novels, which recreate that period loosely called the Old West, still live in a half-shadow world in the university English departments across the country.

Perhaps the chief factor underlying this non-acceptance is the general inability of all who study the Old West to really define it. When scholars look at what is termed the Matter of Troy or the Matter of Britain, they know just what they are speaking about. The Matter of Troy is pretty specifically all of the Greek tales which have to do with those persons who were involved in one way or another with the Trojan War—the Homeric epics and certain plays, while the matter of Britain concerns those members of King Arthur's Court who fought for that vague, almost mythical character. But the Matter of the Old West does not define so simply. Does the literature include all of the tales which are set in the land west of the Mississippi—Across the Wide Missouri? Is it that area west of the 100th meridian where there is less than twenty annual inches of rainfall? That section on the map marked by the census office as a frontier line which disappeared about 1890? Or is the Old West more a place at the edge of things, that vast area where the law came late? If the latter definition—a most romantic one—were to be used, then James Fenimore Cooper and Walter D. Edmonds would have to be considered Western writers, and there are few who would be willing to call them that. Under this romantic, and not very serviceable definition, that the West is the edge of things, the place where the law came late—or just a state of mind, almost anything can be included, from the tales of a fanciful Fray Marcos who first told of seeing the Seven Cities of Gold to John Steinbeck's *A Leader of the People* which looks back with sadness to the loss of that state of mind. President Kennedy was prepared to view the West as a state of mind when he referred to the country's need for a New Frontier. And the writers who think of it in this way easily shift their focus from the Pacific—that Western border which so abruptly closed the dream—to the northern reaches to include Alaska.

If one falls back on the definition of the West as a desert area where the rain falls less than a specified number of inches a year, the literature of the Oregon Trail does not qualify: *The Covered Wagon, The Way West, Westering, The Shining Mountain,* and many other tales as well as the factual accounts such as Joel Palmer's Journal and Parkman's *The Oregon Trail.*

In short, the West is a little too vast to be roped and branded by any simple turn of phrase. This very largeness itself must be part of any serious attempt to understand just what the Old West is.

If we have trouble defining the geography of the Old West, we have just as much trouble defining it in time. The first white men to wander over the American West were the Spaniards. And in a culture developed and perpetuated largely by our great Eastern universities, which have looked toward England as the source of their history and literature, the Spanish of the borderlands have had little place. Fray Marcos pressed northward from Culiacan while the great captain Hernan Cortes was still alive. The castaway, Cabeza de Vaca, had already journeyed from Florida to the Pacific and left a detailed account of his travels. Fray Marcos probably went into what is now Arizona and New Mexico and left his letters to describe the country. Several of those who traveled the route from the Pacific to the Kansas River with Coronado left records of their journey. Intermittently the Spaniards returned to the Southwest until Onate came to stay near the end of the sixteenth century. In the center of the city of Santa Fe, New Mexico, sits the Palace of the Governors, built by those who came with Onate. It was lost in 1680 to an Indian rebellion which was perhaps the greatest massacre of civilians by Indians on this continent, a massacre which ended in a retreat out of New Mexico and the settlement of what is now Juarez, Mexico, and El Paso, Texas. The Spaniards came back thirteen years later and remained until they were forced out over a century later by the aggressive pioneers from the United States. Is it possible to define the Old West in such a way as to leave out that empire which stretched across the whole southwest from Texas to California? Many people have, many historians do not take it into account, most literary scholars do not consider these tales and histories a part of the literature of the Old West. But no one reading Cabeza de Vaca will find his writings any less a record of the land than those of Lewis and Clark. Kit Carson is certainly a part of the American West. He guided General Fremont into what were believed to be new lands. But Carson married into the Spanish culture and must have learned part of his craft and knowledge from his wife's people. The best novel written of Carson's times is probably *Death Comes for the Archbishop* by Willa Cather. She wrote of that Spanish culture and its legends. Very few scholars would call it a novel of the Old West. Granting it is more than that, it is also that.

If we limit the Old West chauvinistically and forget that men of other cultures were here first, we have simplified the dating, but we are still left with problems in defining a history. Do we begin that history with Lewis and Clark? Most scholars would hesitate to include the novels of their journey as part of the literature. Do we begin with the crossing of the country by the first settlers into Oregon with Marcus Whitman? This would exclude the Mountain Men who left their mark on the land, opened the first trails and left behind their own legends. It would also exclude the tales of Texas: the Austins, the Alamo, the earlier settlers. To some scholars and writers the history of the Old West is only that brief period of the open range when the cattlemen built the great herds and moved them to market. This period would neatly begin at about the time of the Civil War and end with the closing of the ranges. It would neatly include the cattle wars of Lincoln and Johnson Counties and would exclude the rest of the history of the frontier. It would include the great body of literature about the cowboys—mostly without their cows—the bad men, the cattle drives and the shoot down, but it would not include the miners, the railroaders, or most of the captivity narratives. If the Old West is difficult to define geographically, it is just as difficult to define historically. Any arbitrary dates would exclude some part of the literature, unless one began with the early Spanish incursions into the areas west of the Mississippi.

The Western Writers Association which annually give their Golden Spur awards to the best writers of the West have separated the fiction of the Old West into two major categories—the myth (which they do not label as that) and the historical novel. In this way they recognize that there are actually two Wests being written about. The West of the myth is replete with all of its own readily recognized symbols: the hero and the villain, the clear-cut differences between good and evil, the shoot-down, the six gun, the Stetson hat, the horse, the code of honor, the unkissed heroine. With these simple devices, the writer who works in the myth

West is able to tell almost any story. In recent years traditional tales from any culture have been reset in the West. *Antigone,* the Homeric tales, *The School for Scandal, Great Expectations,* and *Hamlet* have all been shifted to the Western locale and dressed up in the trappings of the myth.

But what is the myth and what is its source? Chasing down a myth is more difficult than following the traces a bird leaves in a clear sky. The basic elements described above all have their roots in fact. The Stetson was a popular and practical hat for drinking, watering a horse and keeping the sun off a man's head on a long ride. The horse certainly was the best means of transportation. The Colt revolver was created so that the man on horseback could fire more than once without dismounting to reload. It was carried as a weapon as well as a working tool on a ranch. Shoot-downs actually did take place. The gunfight at the OK corral is an historic incident. Billy the Kid was a part of the Lincoln County War. Abilene was the end of a cattle drive. The drovers did take cattle over the Chisholm and other trails. The heroine probably was kissed, however. The confusion of the virgin land and the woman was added after the fact, along with the clear-cut differences between good and evil.

But how did the clear-cut differences between good and evil grow so strongly into the myth? To the men who drifted westward with the frontier, to the restless, the failures, the ones who moved to the edges of civilization leaving behind them bankruptcy, bad farms, poverty, criminal records, or merely responsibilities, the West became a kind of dream. It was the place where a man could begin again, where there was a rebirth and a new kind of democracy in which only what he was meant anything. In the long trek westward over the Oregon Trail, where the dead averaged seventeen to the mile, the journey was a long trying-out in the sense of a rendering down. The strong survived, and it did not make any difference if they had been good or evil. The same was true of the settlers throughout the whole vague area. So that in the end, the ones who remained, both the good men and the bad, were strong and free in the wild life, and the moral *images* of these men became sharper. It is doubtful, of course, if the *actual differences* were.

Early in the last century an ancient idea became confused or linked with the actual character of those who lived on the wild frontier. When the Spaniards first began their conquest in the New World, the argument raged over the character of the Indians. Were they noble savages? Were they men without sin, men who did not understand the idea of sin itself, true innocents of nature, natural beings without the façades which civilization imposes? By the nineteenth century this very concept of the noble savage began to attach itself to the white men of the frontier. Daniel Boone was so described by those who wrote of him. Walt Whitman wrote, "The friendly and flowing savage . . . Wherever he goes men and women accept and desire him." He has "behavior lawless as snowflakes, words simple as grass, uncombed head, laughter and naivete, slow-stepping feet, common features . . . ." This Nature's Nobleman had already been equated with the Indian slayer by the flood of dime novels which flowed off the presses in the middle of the nineteenth century. It was a simple thing to unconsciously shift the character onto the cowboy in *The Virginian*. The entire concept of the Western hero as the Noble Savage, the Innocente, was soon so fixed that his character could only be all white and his enemy's all black.

The Noble Savage was a non-wanter, a man who treasured only his freedom, the chance to do his good deed and ride on unencumbered by property. The villain was almost always the wanter of range or water or cattle or money or the woman he should not have. And so fictionally a marriage was made between the actual character of the Westerner, strong and capable of survival, and the concept of the Noble Savage, a marriage which gave birth to the mythical Western hero as we find him today.

But the Western hero as we know him today is also part of a great tradition. He has found his place in literature beside the men of King Arthur's court. The Knights of the Round Table were also noble creatures. They, too, rode out, helped the innocent and punished the evil. But there is a sophistication in the Arthurian tales not generally found in the popular Western tale. They may have the duel in common—a sword in place of a six gun—as well as a fine horse and standard pieces of clothing, but they do not all have the same attitude toward women. Lancelot was the lover of his best friend's wife. Tristram ran off with his uncle's spouse. And Gawaine was almost seduced by the wife of the Green Knight. Here the innocence is almost gone except in the special case of Galahad who alone was so innocent he could see the Holy Grail. The Matter of the West parts ways with the Matter of Britain because the hero of Britain was a much worldlier figure. However, the Arthurian tales were not always sophisticated, as the musty volumes of the Early English Text Society will testify. The change in character came later as the stories matured out of the chronicles in the hands of those who used the materials as a means of saying something important—the tragedy of the dying world which was Arthur's, the morality tale of Galahad, and the tale of Lancelot whose sins destroyed those he loved most and brought down the very world for which he had fought. The same change is beginning to take place as the Western myth frame is used for serious ideas. It has been said that a writer must be a consummate artist to be able to use the Western myth in such a way that his story is not judged out of hand to be a Western in the popular sense of the word—a tale of two dimensional figures moving without motivation through a series of violent incidents to destroy an obvious evil. But the change is taking place more rapidly than one might have expected. Though there had been bits and pieces of sophisticated Arthurian materials earlier, over five hundred years elapsed between the first references to Arthur and Malory's weaving the myth into a meaningful work of art. By any historical definition of the Old West, we are less than a century away from its demise. Perhaps the change is coming faster because of the vast flood of materials poured out to a literate audience which has already begun to demand certain standards. Perhaps the change from naive to purposeful use of the myth elements has begun because the audience knows all of the possible variations of the simpler uses of the material. However, these answers may be too pat. There is no question that the Western myth is developing into the materials for serious and possibly great works of art. At the same time, the very primitive form which has been dominant since the Western took its place in the catalogues of Beadle's Dime Novels is as popular as it has ever been—and perhaps even more so. A television series of the westering, *Wagon Train* is one of the most popular in England, while another, *Gunsmoke,* dubbed with native dialogue, is the most popular program in Japan. The same year that the motion picture *The Big Country* was a box office failure in the United States, it turned out to be the most successful film of the year in literate England.

And so the Western myth tale is splitting into two parts. The old form continues to be used in the old ways, telling and retelling the same story of the fight for justice, against rustlers, gunfighting bullies, covetous bankers and empire builders. At the same time, co-existing with it, the new literature uses the very same elements to tell stories with significant meanings.

Though never as popular as the myth in its sweep through the mass media, there has always been a completely different western genre which is possibly best called the historical novel of the West. This is a straight historical novel set in the western areas. Whether or not any of these books is included in the literature of the West depends upon how wide or narrow one sets the geographic and historical boundaries. These works are less readily identifiable as they lack the obvious signposts of the myth tales. The historical novel of the West really is no different from the historical novel of any other place or time. The central characters may be drawn directly from history or may be fictional, meeting men who actually roamed the West. Some authors, such as A. B. Guthrie, Jr., and Stewart Edward White use historical figures in their novels, while others do not. It is easier to evaluate the Western historical novel than the Western myth tale because writers of the former are in an historic tradition in which it is generally accepted that great works of art have been written. "Generally accepted" is used because the scholars who write the histories and critiques of our literature find the historical novel in America suspect. They will recognize the validity of a *War and Peace,* a *A Tale of Two Cities,* a *The Cloister and the Hearth,* but they are not quite sure what they should do with the historical novel written in the United States and covering a portion of our national history. They may be accused of chauvinism if they praise it. Uneducated to the genre, they are unable to tell at a glance the difference between the serious historical novel and a costume romance designed to titillate. Most critics and scholars play it safe and avoid the field entirely. But this does not mean that the books have not been written and accepted by the general public. Nor does it mean that the basic qualities of many of these books go unnoticed. Year after year major literary awards are given to authors who write historical novels of the West. And at the same time almost no serious critique of American literature would include these very same works.

A good historical novel of the West has the same basic elements as any good novel. It tries to say something worth saying as well as to recapture the emotions and ideas of those persons who lived in a recreated time and place. Its degree of importance is in direct relationship to the extent it achieves these goals. The historical novel may be the accurate recreation of actual persons in an historical incident and be based directly on a moment of history, or it may be purely fictional, telling a fictional tale set in a past time. Whichever it is, it must be judged against the other works of literature which strive for the same goals. There have been some nationalistic efforts to relax the standards of literature and accept books for more than their intrinsic value because they belonged to a particular region or represented elements of a national culture. Lowering literary standards merely to satisfy the national ego can only detract from those works of honestly attempted art in which the creative writer has set himself the highest goals. In the long run the chaff falls away and only works of importance remain. Too often the regional critic and bibliographer tends to be kind to the book written about his own section of the country. This has probably happened more often than it should in relationship to historical novels of the West. Too often have works been accepted as being significant because they appear to capture a nostalgic past in moldy dialect. If the literature of the Western myth is judged on its popularity and the way in which it has reached the largest number of persons and made an entire world aware of its symbols, the serious historical novel must be judged against the best books of any country written in any time or place. While they must have, as the Western myth tale has had, a universality, they must reach it on a completely different level, the level of human experience and not symbol.

From the very first time a man rode his horse alongside a railroad train, jumped aboard and robbed that train in *The Great Train Robbery* the motion picture screen has been the most popular means of spreading the stories of the Old West. Year after year, Hollywood has produced Westerns for mass consumption. In many cases the producers have not bothered to use the stories written by novelists, but instead have turned to the scriptwriter who has become one of the most skilled practitioners in the manipulation of the stock symbols. In some instances the scriptwriter has taken a single hero and written him into tale after tale, creating new deeds of derring-do. In some instances he has fallen back on the classic pattern of the peripatetic tale, the incidents of adventure which take place upon a journey, and he has given his hero a companion. The Sancho Panza of the Western serves his own purpose. He is usually the leit-motif and at the same time he is the buffer off whom the hero bounces his ideas. No camera is small enough to get inside the hero's brain, and so the only way that the scriptwriter can let us know what the hero is thinking is to have him talk to a person who will not get in the way of the action. This secondary figure is always loyal, always ready to do and die, always prepared to express his appreciation of the hero's courage and wisdom. But at the same time, he is wise enough in his own right never to interfere with the hero's victory or to take any of the credit away from Nature's Nobleman. In recent years some changes have taken place in the presentation of the film hero of the Western myth. In a *Gunfighter, Stagecoach,* or *Red River,* the hero is no longer simon-pure. In fact, he may be a killer viewed with sympathy or a ruthless empire builder. In short, the film Western has kept pace with the Western in books and the same changes are already taking place in the use of the myth for serious purposes. And as with the book, at the same time there remains the traditional and unsullied use of the myth symbols without any intention other than the most primitive one of storytelling. The television screen offered the Western something which it never had had before—a proper length. The simplicity of the Western tale was generally stretched beyond reasonable lengths to fit the needs of theater owners, but the short hour (50 minutes) and the shorter half hour (26 minutes) required by television seems to perfectly meet the needs of the story writer. The simplicity of the stories is sharply evident in the recurring theme of the quest. The hero for one reason or another rides into a town in true knightly fashion, solves the problems of the townfolk and rides on again. In the event the hero is a lawman, the villain rides into town at the show's opening and is defeated and killed by the show's end. The quest pattern is so obviously that of the Medieval knight tale that one of the most popular Westerns on television has even named its hero Paladin after one of the twelve knights in attendance on Charlemagne. In the past half decade more Western tales were probably written for television than were ever written for all other media in the past century.

The Western has begun to grow up. It is going to continue to grow toward maturity. At the same time it does not seem to be any less virile than it was over a half century ago when over forty Western titles were to be found in Beadle's catalogue of Dime Novels. It is an American genre though the English have written and filmed Westerns and Hollywood has had no trouble changing the Japanese *The Seven Samurai* into *The Magnificent Seven.* The parts are interchangeable and timeless. And every so often a serious work of art will emerge, be lost for a short time in the flood of Western myth tales, and then slowly find its place in the world's serious literature.

EDITOR'S NOTE

The selections made for this anthology cover most of the forms of the fiction of the Old West. Two novels are included intact, as well as parts of other novels, and numerous short stories. There is one television script and one short story which was the basis for what many consider to be the finest motion picture of the West. Some of the items were picked because of their intrinsic quality, some for sheer entertainment. Some are popular, some serious works of art which will hold their own with any literature. Some were written by men who knew the West, some by strangers to it. Some are truthful tales and some purest dream stuff. Many worthwhile pieces had to be omitted for lack of space. An *Ox-Bow Incident* is not easily passed over, nor is Willa Cather's *Death Comes for the Archbishop*. One is, however, readily available while the author of the other placed restrictions against most of her work being extracted, used in anthologies, or dramatized. Perhaps the most important book in the history of Western fiction writing, Owen Wister's *The Virginian*—which set many elements of the Western myth, including cow-less cowboys and the shoot-down—is not here because it can be found in numerous editions elsewhere. Similar problems pertain to a few other pieces which might have been included. But a book has to close with its back cover and there must be some limits set on the materials between. The general preface is really intended to be no more than it is labeled—Notes for a Preface.

Some serious thinking has been done on the subject of Western writing by such men as W. Prescott Webb, J. Frank Dobie, Bernard DeVoto, Henry Nash Smith, B. A. Botkin, Frederick Jackson Turner, Lawrence Clark Powell and others. And there are some scattered histories of sections of Western fiction. The cowboy has probably come in for more literary study than the mountain man, for example, but there is still a great deal to be done, a lot of scholarly arrowheads to be collected, before someone can really do more than jot down some notes.

Irwin R. Blacker
May 7, 1961

CONTENTS

The Mountain Men

GRANT OF KINGDOM

A Novel by

HARVEY FERGUSSON

Probably no novel covers the whole wide sweep of Western history better than does Grant of Kingdom, *and few novels have been written about the West by men who have known it better than Harvey Fergusson. Centering his story about the Lucien Maxwell Land Grant of 1,750,000 acres, Fergusson has told not only of those who possessed the land and those who wanted it, but also of the land itself. From his poetic novel* Wolf Song *to his evocative tragedy of* The Conquest of Don Pedro, *Fergusson has tried to wed the Spanish West to the rest of Western history. No one else has succeeded half so well.*

CONTENTS

FOREWORD

More than twenty years ago I visited a beautiful valley at the foot of the Rocky Mountains and found there the crumbling ruin of a great house. Its walls were then still standing a few feet high, with great roof beams rotting in the rubble. I could count the rooms and there were thirty-eight of them, including a dining hall that might have seated a hundred guests.

When I learned that a man had ridden into a wilderness where no human habitation had ever stood before, had built that great house, founded a society and ruled it as long as he lived, my imagination was stirred. I began talking to old-timers and reading old books, slowly reconstructing an episode which began about 1850, shortly after the American occupation of New Mexico, and ended in the late seventies, just before the completion of the Santa Fe railroad brought the epoch of primary pioneering to an end.

The valley had been the heart of one of the old Spanish Royal Land Grants, and it had been truly a grant of kingdom, not merely to one man but to four, each of whom had achieved his moment of power in that dominion and by reason of that royal grant, as though the prerogative of empire had reached across space and time to quicken his life and test his qualities.

During the many years it has occupied my imagination, that episode has been largely transformed, and so have all of the men and women who played their parts in it. This book is a fiction and neither its characters nor its incidents are to be identified with real ones. In fact each of its four principal figures is based upon a study of various men in the effort to make them true products of a period and a region and at the same time, as I see them, figures of a wider significance. For I am indebted to the actual episode for my theme. Here, it seemed to me, was a struggle for power in a small but complete society, isolated by distance and wilderness, which had much in common with the greater power struggles that periodically shake the world. Here were the benevolent autocrat creating order, the power-hungry egoist destroying it, the warrior tragically bound to his weapon, the idealist always in conflict with an irrational world, struggling to save his own integrity.

7

The chief purpose of the book is to portray these four men, each in his turn and in his moment of crisis—to trace him back to his origins and see him in the making, to show the form and meaning of his destiny. Two women stand beside the men as major characters because they shared in the same indomitable quality, the same spectacle of life sustained by courage. These six and all the others, men and women, who played a part in their destinies, have lived for me. If they live also for the reader I have accomplished all I hoped.

PART ONE

THE CONQUEROR

JEAN BALLARD

The hot spring lay in a little glade at the head of a shallow canyon where the scattering piñon of the lower slopes gave way to the tall timber. In this month of May the glade was green with new grass and sprinkled with bright small flowers, white and red. East of it the forest was dark and tall but fringed with slim white aspens bearing pale new leaves. The Truchas peaks, still covered with snow, rose sharp and white above the trees. To the west the country tumbled steeply to purple depths where the Rio Grande crawled through lava gorges, then rose again to a pale blue horizon of distant ranges.

The spring had been dug out and walled with rock, no one knew when or by whom, so that it was wide enough to hold several men and chin-deep when they sat. It had been a place of resort for generations, perhaps for centuries, and for many kinds of men. Pueblos, Apaches, Utes and Arapahoe came this way, crossing the mountains, and always stopped to bathe. Mexicans came from Taos and Talpa and sometimes much farther south. Mountain men always camped there when they could and soaked their hard-used hides in hot water. To Indians the spring was sacred and the faint mist that wavered over its face was the breath of a living spirit. To all men the pale green water, with its tickling bottom of bubbling sand, was a healing caress in a rocky and dangerous world. In an informal way, the spring was a place of sanctuary. Men stopped here to relax and met to trade rather than to fight. So far as the record ran, no one had lost his hair here and sea shells had traveled through many hands from the Gulf to be swapped here for turquoise and buffalo robes. Every April a great grizzly bear came down from the peaks to scratch his mark as high as he could reach on a near-by tree and soak himself in the spring. More than one man had seen him heave his bulk out of the water, shake himself like a great wet dog and amble off into the timber, but no one had ever shot at him. In those days of muzzle loaders a grizzly was more dangerous than a man.

Jean Ballard and Ed Hicks had come to the spring to bathe and loaf for a week. They had made their camp in the edge of the timber under a great fir that would shed water like a tent. Each had spread for his bed a heavy prime buffalo robe and a Navajo blanket. They had built a rock fireplace for their cooking, driven sharp pegs into the trunk of the tree to hold their gear, and they had all the home they needed. Ballard had cilmbed up to the edge of the snow and killed a two-year-old mountain ram, the best meat in the mountains. They had brought bread and coffee and brown sugar from Taos, but to them meat was primary and they ate it three times a day, buttered with its own fat.

Now when the sun was high and warm they stripped to bathe. Ballard was a stocky, powerful man, round in chest and limb, with a ruddy face and black curly hair, as thick on his chest as on his head. He had dark blue eyes and was a handsome man in a massive fashion, but wholly unconscious of his appearance except that he was vain of the hair on his chest. When he was in town around women he liked to wear a scarlet shirt open at the throat to show his plumage.

Ed Hicks, ten years older, was by contrast a lean and stringy figure with a face as deeply riven as the mountains that had claimed his whole life. He was one of those restless, driven men, common on the frontier, who stayed in towns only as long as he was drunk, would leave his bones beside a trail, and knew it. This was not true of Ballard. At thirty-three he had been on the move for thirteen years, because he lived in a moving world, but he had always felt sure he had a destination, that his time would come to settle and build.

They eased themselves into the water a little at a time. They were not used to hot water and this was about as hot as the human skin could stand. When finally he was in it to his neck, Ballard settled back with a sigh of beatific relief, leaning his head against a rock and closing his eyes. For ten minutes he was conscious of nothing but the soothing warmth of the spring and the wind-whispering hush of the wilderness. Then he came suddenly upright and his eyes met those of his companion. Both of them had heard the same thing—the clink of shod hoofs striking rock far down the trail in the canyon. Both of them knew what it meant. Since the horses were shod it couldn't be Indians and it was not likely to be mountain men at this time of the year. It must be Mexicans from Taos. The sound grew louder.

"Five or six horses," Hicks said.

Ballard nodded and rose dripping from his bath.

"Come on, get out of there," he said.

"To hell with them greasers," Hicks protested.

"Get out, I tell you," Ballard repeated as he reached for his shirt. "There'll be women in that outfit, a whole family. They come up here the first warm days to cook the misery out of their bones."

"To hell with them," Hicks repeated. "It's getting so the whole country is full of people and a man can't have no peace." Nevertheless he climbed out of the spring and started dressing. He always did what Ballard said.

They were dressed but still squeezing the water out of their hair when the Mexican outfit came in sight, emerging from the steep canyon, and stopped politely a hundred yards away, all strung out in single file on the narrow trail. In the lead was an old man, lean and erect in his saddle, with white whiskers decorating a dark, weathered face. A younger man followed, then two women riding on great pillowy sidesaddles, two younger girls of twelve or thirteen, a heavily laden pack horse and at the rear another man, obviously a peon. These people never moved far without a servant. All of them rode good horses, even the peon, and the old man in front sat a splendid sorrel on a silver-mounted saddle.

Ballard walked slowly toward them, raising his right-hand palm forward in a slight and casual gesture, which it was customary always to make when approaching strangers in the mountains—a gesture which meant he bore no weapon and came as a friend. The two men dismounted to meet him. He knew the old man by sight as Don Tranquilino Coronel, one of the three or four richest Mexicans in Taos, who owned about fifty thousand little scrubby sheep, a great house and wide irrigated lands in the valley. The younger man was doubtless one of his sons. The Don stood with calm dignity, waiting to be approached, as befitted one born to power and command.

Ballard, long trained to quick and accurate notice, surveyed the whole group as he came near. His eyes came to rest on the younger woman, directly behind the two men and clearly revealed when they dismounted. She would have captured the eyes of almost any man. She was a large girl and a pretty one, with heavy dark hair about her shoulders. On horseback her figure was in part a mystery, but Ballard was sharply aware of the full round pressure of her breasts against her white linen bodice and the beauty of her half-bare arms and her hands, one of which now fluttered self-consciously about her hair. He was aware especially of her lovely coloring. Many Mexican girls had sallow skins or swarthy ones, but hers was like the petal of a flower, all pink and white with a dusky underflush. Her eyes were a light, conspicuous hazel under long black lashes. As he drew near she smiled at him, slowly and deliberately, as Mexican women always smile at strangers, over the shoulders of her protecting menfolk.

"We intrude," the Don said quietly, as he gave the brief limp handshake of his kind. "We will wait. . . . There is much time."

Ballard knew his Spanish well. He was a polite man and Spanish is a polite language.

"A thousand times no," he protested. "It would be a great sorrow if we delayed you. We have a camp in the pines, we stay for a week. The spring is yours."

He bowed his head and made a sweeping gesture with his right hand, consigning the whole country irrevocably to the newcomers. The Don thanked him with dignity. Ballard smiled, bowed, withdrew, feeling triumphantly that he had mastered a delicate situation.

Back in camp he pulled down the meat from where it hung in the shade, unwrapped it and began slicing the back-strap, choicest part of the kill. He threaded round bits of meat on an iron ramrod, with bits of fat between. Skewered over the coals, this was the best eating he knew. Hicks regarded him with a sardonic and suspicious eye.

"You're cuttin' enough meat for a crowd," he observed.

"Maybe we'll have company," Ballard said.

Hicks snorted.

"Them rich greasers won't eat with you," he said. "They hate your guts and you ought to know it."

Ballard smiled and went on cutting meat. He never argued or quarreled. He knew Hicks was probably right. Mexicans were always polite but the rich Mexicans had hated the gringos ever since the wagons began crossing the plains. They hated them more than ever since Kearney had taken over in Santa Fe a few years before. Moreover, Taos had always been the headquarters of that hatred. It was in Taos that rebellion had broken out the year after the conquest. The Taos rebellion had been a bloody fiasco with Indians and a few peons running amock and killing Americans until the army under Price drove them into Taos Pueblo and slaughtered them. Most of the rich Mexicans had taken no open part in that business, but everyone believed the all-powerful Padre Martinez of Taos had organized it and then disowned it when it failed. And everyone knew that what the Padre did had the backing of all the old families. He was their political boss as well as their spiritual adviser.

Down in Sante Fe, some of the ricos had begun to smile upon the Americans, and even in Taos, Kit Carson had married one of the Jaramillo girls, but most of the few rich Mexicans in Taos Valley expressed their quiet hatred by ignoring the existence of their conquerors, and none more completely than the Coronels. Probably no American had ever passed the heavy front door of their great adobe house, with its barred windows and hidden courtyards. They had all been polite, but only the girl had smiled at him. Mexican girls often smiled at Americans, and that was one more reason the men hated them.

After he had finished his work, Ballard went to the spring and washed his hands. Then he dug into his duffle for a bright red shirt he had bought in Santa Fe, put it on and combed his hair carefully with the aid of a bit of mirror—both the hair on his head and that on his chest. Like most of the mountain men he was smooth-shaven, and he was glad he had shaved that morning.

Hicks, sitting in the shade with a pipe in his mouth, rumbled a growing disgust.

"Puttin' on your wenchin' clothes, are you?" he queried. "That shirt's enough to scare a horse but it won't do you no good with that gal. You got no more chance to lay a hand on her than you have to pat a deer on the rump."

Ballard grinned and went on with his toilet, wholly untroubled. He knew the girl was probably beyond his reach, but he had a hunch and a plan, and he always followed his hunches. When he was satisfied with his appearance, he sat down in the shade and watched the Mexicans, as he might have watched distant game he was planning to stalk. He knew Mexicans well and he knew what they would do because they always did everything the same way. He had seen Mexican women bathe outdoors before, both at hot springs and in rivers. Women of the upper class, such as these, would never bathe in a river, and only once or twice a year would they visit a hot spring, strictly for the purposes of health. The procedure was always the same. They came accompanied by their menfolk, who were always armed. The men sat down at a certain distance, about a hundred yards from the spring, as the Don and his son did now. The women brought great white robes, such as the Taos Indians wore in summer. Each of them tented herself under one of these, adroitly shed her few clothes and emerged in a long white cotton shift reaching to her ankles, so that she would be more completely dressed in the water than out.

Ballard knew all the etiquette of this occasion and he knew his hope of success lay in observing it exactly. He waited until the women were all in the water, showing only as a row of dark heads in a cloud of steam, bobbing to a medley of squeals and giggles. This was a rare and exciting occasion to them for they seldom got beyond the walls of their own house. When he saw they had made a bowl of amole-root suds and set it on the rim of the spring, he knew they were all going to wash their hair. That would keep them busy quite a while.

Now it was quite appropriate, he knew, since amenities had been exchanged, to join the menfolk for a little platicando, which is the Mexican word for polite chat about everything that is not important or personal. Not only would this now be permissible, but it was the only possible approach. To pass or go near the spring from any other direction would be a breach of etiquette, and to go even one step closer to it than the men sat would be a cause of war.

He strolled casually toward the Coronels, followed by the half-reluctant Hicks, and was politely received, as he had known he would be. Don Tranquilino produced a tiny horn, just like a powder horn but much smaller, which was filled with native tobacco and a roll of cigarette papers made from corn husks. Each of the four rolled a cigarette, the Mexicans with great skill and the Americans awkwardly, because they were pipe smokers. The Don then clapped his hands. The peon had made a small fire near by and he now came running with a live coal skillfully caught between two splinters of fat pine. He waved it into flame, lit each of the cigarettes, bowed and withdrew.

Talk was slow at first, but developed a growing momentum. Hicks had nothing to say until the Don mentioned the trouble he had encountered in getting sheep herds across the Rio Grande north of Taos. Hicks knew all about that country. He presently smoothed a piece of bare ground with the palm of his hand and began drawing a map with a little stick, as country-wise men always did in those days. In just a little while all four of them had sticks and were making contributions to the problem of getting across the Rio Grande gorge. They were no longer conscious of difference and antagonism, they had found their common ground.

All of them were completely absorbed in their talk and their map except Ballard. He made a few marks, too, but his mind was not on the subject and he was soon watching the women again. The girl was already out of the water, statuesque and erect in her white robe, shaking and fluffing her heavy black hair in the sun. She was looking straight at him. Although she was too far away for him to read her face, he felt sure she was just as much aware of him as he was of her. He wished he had never taken his eyes off her. There must have been a revealing moment when she climbed out of the spring with her wet shift clinging to her body. . . . But presently there was another moment, an almost incredible moment. With a single swift gesture, like a great bird flapping its wings, she flung the robe wide for an instant, then gathered it tightly about her again, at the same time throwing her head back, as though in laughter. For just a fraction of a second he saw her naked—the perfect bowls of her breasts, the dark triangle between her thighs. . . . Maybe a gust of wind had caught the robe, maybe it had slipped in her wet hand. It could have been a wholly accidental gesture. But he refused to believe so. She had known he was watching her and no one else was. Improbable as it seemed, he felt sure she had flung him a challenge and a signal, offered herself in the only way she could. Whether she had planned it or not she had certainly jolted him. He had felt the impact of that glimpse as keenly as though she had reached out and touched him. He couldn't get his eyes or his mind off her. In months of hard work away from women he had almost forgotten them, as so often before. Now he found himself watching one with an eager helpless fascination he half resented.

A little later all of the women and girls were dressed and sitting on a great red blanket in the sun, drying their hair, over on the other side of the spring where the peon had unpacked their baggage. The Don and his son rose, turned to the others. This was the moment Ballard had been waiting for.

"We have much meat," he said, as the Don extended his hand. "A two-year-old cimarron, very fat. It would be a great honor if you would eat with us."

As he spoke he was watching the Don's eyes. Ballard had faced a great many men when something was at stake—in trades, in fights, in poker games—and he had learned to watch a man's eyes and his mouth and to go by what he saw there. The Don's mouth was hidden behind his magnificent whiskers, but before this unexpected challenge his eyes wavered and fell. He was too polite to say no and he didn't want to say yes. He fumbled for words.

"It would be a great pleasure," he lied. "But it grows late. . . ." He looked over his shoulder at the son. He jerked a thumb at the women. "The Señora . . . I will ask what she wishes. . . ." He turned to go.

Ballard stood watching him, feeling sure that now his fate depended on the women and probably on the Doña. It was customary in such a matter for a man to consult his wife, as a matter of form, but the male head of a Mexican household was supposed to be second only to God. His word was final. The decision was supposed to be the Don's. But Ballard shrewdly doubted that any man ruled his women as absolutely as he was supposed to do, and he doubted especially that Don Tranquilino truly dominated anything. That wavering look he had seen in the eyes of many Mexican men in recent years. They were being overwhelmed by a rush of energy from the East, which they could neither stop nor deal with, and they were losing confidence.

Ballard did not despise Mexicans as all Texans and most mountain men professed to do. These people had come into the country when it was wilder than now. They had built great houses and churches and good solid towns. They had learned how to irrigate the valleys and raise sheep on the open range. It was more than the gringos had done. Ballard had deep respect for men who built things and established order, and the Mexicans had done it—a long time ago. Years of easy authority, of leisure and fat living, had softened them, made them fearful of all invaders.

The Don was evidently not exercising any easy authority just then. He was in a close huddle with his wife and son and daughter and it was plain to see that everybody had something to say. In particular the girl seemed to be something less than the perfectly submissive creature she was supposed to be, for she was talking with both hands as well as her mouth, her silver bracelets flashing in the sun.

The Don finally left the others and returned slowly to where Ballard and Hicks waited. He bowed his head and spoke gravely.

"It will be a great pleasure," he said. "We will share your meat."

The Navajo blanket was spread in the shade. Ballard and Hicks were busy with their skewers, Hicks serving skillfully as chief cook, while Ballard solicitously served his guests. The peon brought forth round Mexican loaves, honey in the comb, cheese made of goat's milk, candy that had come north a thousand miles in trade and stone crocks of preserved fruits. He set a great jug of native wine on the blanket and a smaller one of brandy. Coffee was brewing on the fire. It was a feast.

Everyone ate with polite restraint, watching everyone else narrowly, eager to help, groping for words, as people always do when they are a little afraid of each other. Silver cups of heavy purple wine helped to loosen tongues, but it was Choppo, the tiny Chihuahua dog, who truly saved the occasion for he alone was wholly unembarrassed. A nimble little creature with a restless pink tongue, he had been taught to sit up and beg. The smell of all that good meat set him wild with eagerness, so that he ran from one to another, begging morsels from each, catching them when they were tossed in the air, barking his sharp demands when he was kept waiting. Consuelo—now he had learned her name—threw her head back and laughed with delight, then brought her eyes down to meet Ballard's. The others laughed at Choppo, but these two laughed together, looking at each other with shining eyes, as though they had shared a secret of great joy.

When cigarettes had been smoked over coffee, the Don rose and all of the others rose too, with perfect decorum. This, Ballard knew, was the second decisive moment, but he had no doubt of what was coming. When a Mexican has accepted your hospitality, he always offers you his in return, and always in the same words. The Don spoke gravely again, as he extended his hand.

"When you are in Taos," he said, "my house is yours."

"I thank you," Ballard replied and he had never meant it more profoundly.

The Don's words, of course, did not mean what they said. Ballard knew he would not be likely ever to see Consuelo alone, that it might not be easy to see her at all. But at least, when he went to the formidable great front door and lifted the iron knocker, the portero would let him in. Nothing was sure, but a barrier had been crossed.

He stood watching as the Mexicans mounted and started away, both of the men saluting him as they turned their horses. Just before they disappeared down the canyon, Consuelo swung halfway round in her saddle, snatched the bright blue shawl off her shoulders and waved it high over her head in a splendid gesture of triumph and farewell.

Ballard started breaking camp right away, while Hicks, grumbling, went to catch the horses.

"I thought we was here for a week," he said.

"You can stay if you want to," Ballard told him. "I've got business in Taos right now."

They rode down the canyon, over a high shoulder of the foothills and descended toward the valley of Taos. It was a triangular splotch of bright cultivated green, spread like a shining robe across the dull gray and purple of sage and lava. Three bright clear streams, coming down from the mountains to meet and plunge into the Rio Grande, gave it the water of life, and it shimmered and quivered and sang with life in the May sunshine. The fields were all green with new-sprung crops and the cottonwoods along the ditches waved new leafage in the breeze. The bright abundant water of the spring thaw flashed like silver stitching in all the ditches, and their banks were heavy with the white fragrant blossom of the wild plum. The valley was filled with voices of birds as are all places where men have long lived and cultivated the ground. Few birds sing in a wilderness. Their abundant song is truly a voice of human being.

Ballard was little aware of birds, but he always noticed them when he first rode into Taos Valley, especially the meadow larks, bulging from the tops of walls and bushes, their voices seemingly full of triumph, and the turtledoves, soft and urgent, crooning desire from every tree.

All of this Ballard had heard and seen many times before, and with pleasure, for almost every year of his trapping he had come back to Taos in the spring, and always he had been glad of the first glimpse of this green and singing valley. But never before had he ridden into it so joyfully as now, so filled with a hope that seemed foolish but would not down. He felt as though he rode to music, and beauty was spread before his feet.

— 2 —

The Ballards were long settled in Rockbridge County, Virginia, where the great valley is narrow and fertile between the Blue Ridge and the Allegheny. They had lived there nearly a hundred years when Jean's father was born.

This part of Virginia had little in common with the tidewater region of great plantations and silk-stockinged aristocrats. It was settled by Scotch-Irish immigrants who moved south from Pennsylvania in colonial days and were all hardworking farmers. Three Ballard brothers bought land there and established families so that they became a powerful and numerous clan. They owned a few Negroes but worked hard in their own fields, raising wheat and apples, a few good cattle and many hogs which ran half-wild in their wooded uplands. They lived in good brick houses and set a table heavy with prime meats, fresh and cured, with home-grown vegetables and homemade preserves. Any man could ride up to their picket fences, rest his saddle and stay for dinner. On Sundays they drove behind fat teams to a Presbyterian church, uncomfortable in broad-cloth coats and high stocks they never wore any other time except when they were married and buried. They went to Lexington about once a month to buy supplies and always attended court. In town they drank white corn liquor and talked politics. The young men went to dances and sometimes got into rough-and-tumble fights but held no grudges. They were confident men, secure and independent, who saw their abundant living come up out of their own land every spring—men who could not imagine either want or subservience.

William Ballard, Jean's grandfather, had three sons, of whom Samuel, his father, was the youngest, the best looking, and commonly called the "wildest." This meant that Samuel spent too much time hunting and chasing girls, that he had a restless foot and a quick temper. The other two sons stayed in Rockbridge County, living on the land they inherited, but

Sam sold his share, bought a wagon and team and went through the Cumberland Gap to Kentucky. There he bought land near the headwaters of the Kentucky River, built a cabin and cleared enough ground to raise a crop of corn. But Sam, still unmarried, couldn't stay anywhere. He built a boat, floated down the Kentucky to the Ohio, a great brown waterway cleaving the massive and virginal forest which then covered all that part of America. He hunted and trapped all the way down the Ohio to the Wabash, then laboriously worked his way north to Vincennes and sold his furs for good money. Vincennes was the center of civilization for all that region, the capital of Indiana territory, already an old town where the French had been settled for three generations. With money in his pocket, Sam dressed up and did the town. He emerged from a month of social excitement standing in a Catholic church with a bride on his arm. She was Jeannette Bissot, of an old and well-educated French family—a small, pretty girl with large brown eyes and delicate hands. She knew of her husband only that he came of a good Virginia family, that he was very handsome and that she was happy and helpless in his arms.

Her ordeal began when they left Vincennes. Despite the fact that she had grown up in a wild country, she was a wholly civilized woman, for the French carried civilization wherever they went. She was afraid of the wilderness. She wept when she saw the Kentucky farm with its two-room cabin standing in a stump-studded clearing, the forest threatening it from every side. Nevertheless she went to work to make a home of it and had some success for about two years. Then Sam felt the urge to move again. He was in love with the wild country of the Ohio Valley, and soon he was building another boat. The Kentucky land was sold and they went down the great river again, to settle near its banks where it marked the line between Indiana and Kentucky. Jean then was a baby in his mother's arms. Sam built on his new holding what was called a "half-faced camp" —a shelter of poles and brush—and went to work again clearing forest. It was a year before he got a cabin built and made a crop of corn—a year when he lived by hunting and his wife struggled with cold and dirt and an open fire, also with malaria and dysentery.

Sam Ballard was undergoing a deterioration of a kind not uncommon in that day. Gradually he shed every trait and property that linked him with the society he had left. He sold his good coat to an Indian because he never wore it. His fine linen shirts were cut to bits to make patches for rifle bullets. He was now dressed always in buckskin, greased and polished by the constant wiping of his hunting knife. He was a man of the frontier and primarily of the forest, a man of rifle, ax and hoe, who loved the rifle better than the ax and the ax better than the hoe. Although he was a farmer after a fashion, most of his living came out of the forest, in wild meat and fur, in wild honey, ginseng and buckskin. To his wife the forest was a wall that cut her off from the world, through which her husband disappeared, sometimes to be gone for days at a time. To him it was a place of refuge and excitement, more and more the only place he felt at home.

Jeannette Ballard bore two daughters after Jean, both of them in a log cabin with a dirt floor and only a local midwife to help. It seemed only luck that she survived those first few years in the forest. Her lot became a little easier as her children grew. Both girls helped around the house from an early age, and Jean's life became a struggle to realize his mother's ideal of order and cleanliness. For although she never triumphed, she never surrendered. She had brought from Vincennes a few dishes of fine china and a little china clock of French make. The dishes were never used. They and the clock were set on a shelf, often washed and dusted, kept by her as a shrine to civilized living. Pioneer cabins of that day were nearly all dirty, with dirt floors, and often infested by vermin. Jeannette finally achieved a puncheon floor and she fought dirt without compromise as long as she lived. She was not an unsocial woman but she shrank from the pioneer society of log-rolling and husking-bee and camp meeting, full of hearty joy and stinking of corn liquor. All the few neighbors she knew spoke a dialect which became almost standard in the Mississippi Basin of that day, and she longed to save her children from it. Carefully she taught Jean to read and write and to speak correct English. Her only scoldings came when he said "mought" for might or "fit" for fought, or used a double negative.

From the age of eight or nine, Jean toiled in the fields with his father and helped his mother whenever he could. He became a hunter when he was so small he could not shoot the long Kentucky rifle without resting it in a forked stick, and when the old English double-barreled shotgun kicked him off his feet every time he pulled the trigger. He was a better shot than his father, and he too learned to love the forest. Often he would crawl out of his corn-shuck bed in the attic before daylight and tiptoe out of the house with a gun, to prowl through a dawn-gray forest where the oaks were ten feet thick, the hickories a hundred feet high and the great ropes of the wild grape laced the trees together. Soft-footed on the dew-wet leaf mold, he would surprise a deer on its way to water, or slip quietly beneath a tree where wild turkeys roosted and bring a great gobbler crashing down to earth.

He loved the forest, but his first allegiance was always to his mother and to the house. She had little time to give him but often at night she came and sat beside his bed. His hands in winter were always chapped and split to the red from working in the fields without gloves and setting traps in cold water for otter, mink and muskrat. She would bring a saucer of warm deer tallow and gently anoint his aching knuckles. It was a kind of lovemaking, the only tenderness she ever bestowed. With her hand gentle upon his, she talked always of great cities where men and women walked in silk and satin and rode in carriages and life moved to music. She had been to New Orleans once in her girlhood and the greatness and beauty of Paris she knew from old people who had lived there. Her voice was soft with longing when she talked of these things. The world she talked about was only half real to her and to him it was a fairyland for he had never seen anything like it. But always she made him understand that life can be order and beauty, and always she kept for him a small refuge of tenderness in a world of toil and hardship and much brutality. She never succeeded in planting civilization in the forest but she planted the idea of it and the feeling for it in the consciousness of her son.

Jean was twenty when she died. In fact, she had been dying slowly for years for the malaria had never left her. Year by year he had seen her once-beautiful face shrivel and yellow until only her great brown eyes remained the same. Her small once-pretty hands had become clawlike—human pothooks worn by an endless struggle with heavy iron skillets and Dutch ovens. She had been sick so much of the time that her husband thought nothing of it, but Jean had a fateful intuition about this illness and stayed as close to her as he could for both of his sisters had then married, the youngest at fifteen.

It was March, with snow on the ground and a cold wind keening around the eaves much of the time. All of the frontier people were deeply superstitious—about black cats across your path, and Friday, and walking under ladders and especially about a dog howling when someone was going to die. No dog howled that March, but almost every evening when he sat beside her bed, a timber wolf somewhere across the river lifted his muzzle to the sky and gave the deep-throated howl which is the most mournful far-carrying sound in the American wild. Jeannette had always despised superstition and she had taught Jean to despise it, but she heard the voice of the wolf with despair in her eyes. It was to her truly the voice of doom, the voice of the wilderness that had killed her.

Jean had to run and call his father when he saw that she was struggling for breath. Only when they sat on either side of her, holding her hands, did Sam become aware of crisis. In a few minutes she was dead. Begetter and begotten, the two now faced each other across the body of their victim, then bowed their heads and wept.

When spring broke after his mother's death, Jean would go down to the river almost every evening and sit there alone on the bank, listening to the soft deep voice of the flood-swollen current and watching the night slowly bury the forest on the other side. After a few weeks he began building a boat. His father watched him uneasily but said nothing. He knew Jean was going away. He did not want him to go but knew he could not stop him. Both he and Jeannette had known for several years that this quiet, thick-bodied boy was far more than a match for his father. Jean moved slowly and only after long thought but he was as hard to stop as a freshet or a landslide.

So when the time came for him to go, there were no arguments and no tears. His father gave him a rifle. His sisters came home and prepared much food for him, mostly jerked meat and corn meal and salt and a little sugar. He had a bale of furs of his own trapping and these were currency in the world of that day. He pushed his flat boat into the current and turned once to wave at the watching three before he disappeared around a bend. All of them knew it was probably a final parting but all over America young men were heading West with little chance of return. Jean was carried by the current of his time no less than by the great Ohio.

At first he felt a little lost but the farther he went the more he was sustained by a feeling that he went to meet his necessary destiny and by the excitement of penetrating the unknown. He rounded every bend with eager interest and poked into the forest where he camped every night, taking his meat where he found it. He saw a few other boats and passed landings where crude roads led inland but most of the time he floated through a wilderness, where deer came down to drink, wild turkeys sailed across the river on set wings and the sky was filled with thunderous clouds of pigeons and wild fowl night and morning.

When he reached the Mississippi he took passage on a steamboat from New Orleans and worked his way upstream to St. Louis. There for the first time he knew he had emerged from the world of his youth. St. Louis then was only a town of about fifteen thousand but it was one of the nerve centers of American life. White steamboats with great housed paddle wheels made a forest of their tall smokestacks on the water front, which was filled with the smash and rumble of moving freight and the shouts and singing of the Negroes who loaded and unloaded the boats. In bars and stores frock-coated gentlemen and gamblers off the river boats lined up with long-haired buckskinned men from farther west and traders and merchants, flush with silver money, draping heavy gold watch chains across their gaudy vests. Back from the river were old brick houses, some of which had already sheltered two generations, where Negro coachmen held horses while ladies in great ballooning silk skirts were helped into coaches. All of this Jean stared at with eager, hungry eyes. He was seeing something like the world his mother had described, but he had only half believed in its existence. Houses that were something more than shelter from the weather, houses built for beauty and comfort, were strange and a little incredible to him, and so were women with lovely arms and hands and flowerlike skins and great masses of soft hair—women who were not drudges but creatures of beauty and mystery for the delight of men. Houses and women and prancing sleek horses made him ache with envy and longing, with a feeling he had entered a world in which he had no share. None of these people seemed even aware of his existence. He had never been before where he could not hail any man he saw or knock on any door if he was hungry. He felt a quick resentment toward these people who walked apart and ignored him and would not share what they had.

But the sight of the city stimulated him too. It made him aware of great energies and great appetites stirring within him. He felt denied but he also felt curiously confident.

Jean was moving west like a migrating animal, following his instinct and his nose, moved by a collective urge that was in the air of his time. He had heard only vaguely of the Santa Fe Trail, but now he talked to wagon men and trappers and learned all about Santa Fe and the big money in beaver. He asked many questions, listened carefully and remembered all he heard.

He did not consider and decide that he would cross the plains, but just became slowly sure that he would do so. He began making himself over in the image of the men he met, buying a rifle of heavy caliber, a wide felt hat and boots. Independence, where the wagons started, was only a few miles away, and hard jobs were to be had for the asking. He started as every greenhorn did, walking beside a team of oxen with a long prod, eating the dust of the prairie summer, burning his skin beneath the prairie sun. The forest he had fought all his life scattered and thinned and fell back like a beaten army and the earth seemed wide and empty as never before.

Jean reached Santa Fe at a time when the boom in beaver fur had begun to wane, although it was still to engage many men for years, while the wagon trade across the prairies was steadily growing. Beaver had been boomed by the fashionable vogue of the beaver hat. That oppressive ornament of male vanity now was going out of style and beaver fur was dropping in price, while many of the best streams had been nearly trapped out. Nevertheless Jean became a beaver trapper first because it was an easy thing for him to do. He had been a trapper from the age of eight as had almost every backwoods boy west of the Allegheny. He had grown up in a world where peltries were currency, where a coonskin bought a jug of whisky and a prime otter was good for a hundred pounds of meal, where men were dressed mostly in the skins of animals and only women wore fabrics they wove on hand looms. Jean had a lore and technique he could now turn into money. He knew all about land-sets and water-sets—how to anchor a beaver trap to a sliding pole so it would drown its victim, how to make scent that would bring quarry from afar, how to case and stretch and flesh a pelt, which was most important, for every man was known by the skill with which he prepared his furs for market. The men who rode the beaver trails were men of his own kind, nearly all of whom had come from Virginia, Pennsylvania, Kentucky and Tennessee, floating down rivers as he had done, changing from boat to horse when they passed the Mississippi. It was not hard for him to become one of them. For a while he worked for wages in one of the organized outfits that still went north to the Platte and Red River country, but in a few years he had become a free trapper, one of the mountain men. These traveled in small gangs, usually of five or six men, starting in early fall, trapping until heavy snow fell, or all winter on the southern streams, such as the Gila and the lower Rio Grande, emerging in the spring to sell furs in Taos or Santa Fe, at Bent's Fort on the Arkansas or at the great rendezvous on Green River, now past its best days. Each man had a saddle horse and a pack horse for his dunnage, a rifle and six traps. When they started they usually had some meal or flour, sometimes coffee and sugar, but before they saw a town or a trader again they became as carnivorous as wolves, eating straight meat three times a day, except for wild berries and fruits. Most of them saw times in the dry south when they had to eat rattlesnake and prairie dog and were glad to get it.

These gangs appointed no leader, and no man was bound to obey another, or even to stay with the outfit if he wanted to leave. They had only one rule, which was never all to fire at once when they got into trouble with Indians. But almost always, on the long trails, one man became informally a leader, just as one horse always became the bell horse and led all the others when they were turned loose to graze. So one man always came to ride at the head of the gang as they traveled single file over the faint trails Indians had followed for years, but no white men before these. One man they all turned and looked at when it was a question of this way or that, of whether to go ahead in the face of a storm or hole up, of whether to trap a certain stream or look for better. Jean Ballard became one of those informal leaders even when most of the men he rode with were years his senior. He looked older than he was, he kept his mouth shut except when it was necessary to say something, and he was completely unflustered no matter what struck. Moreover, he was never lost. His sense of direction seemed never to fail him. This he had known for years, and the Rocky Mountains, with their heavily marked topography, were easy going for him after the flat forests of his youth, where many men had to blaze the trees in order to get back home, but he had always just followed his nose. This was a part of his native gift, his genius, and another part was that he had intuitions of a singular certainty. He was a man who noticed everything and he never knew how much he went by what he noticed and how much was pure hunch, but he believed in pure hunches. More than once he grew suddenly cautious when Indians were ahead, although neither he nor anyone else had seen a track or a wisp of smoke or heard a sound. One such time he remembered that his old yellow buckskin horse had suddenly pointed his ears against the wind. He always watched his horse's ears. A horse heard and smelled things a long way off and always pointed his ears toward whatever worried him. Anyway, he often knew trouble was ahead when no one else did, and this had been true so often that those who knew him would always listen to him.

So Jean became a greatly respected man in his own world, and he moved through it with more ease and certainty and less damage to himself than most. It was a violent world with a violent rhythm which men came to love if they could stand it at all. For five to eight months, and sometimes longer, they lived like wild animals, seeing neither house nor woman. Then for two months or three they were in a settlement with heavy bags of silver money to spend. When it was gone they were eager to take the trails again. Each phase had its own intense excitement and each was an escape and a relief from the other. Most of them were forever unfitted for any other way of life.

In the mountains they all lived and worked alike, disciplined by the hard necessities of food and fur and safety, but in Taos and Santa Fe especially, every man went to hell in his own way. Many of them stayed drunk, more or less, the whole time they were in town, ending in a sleep that might last for two or three days. There were men who had to have a fight after a certain number of drinks and went around challenging all comers until they got one. Most of these were rough-tumble fights, the aboriginal form of human combat, with men rolling over and over in fighting fury like tomcats, sometimes biting off ears and noses and. gouging eyes. There were duels with hunting knives and a few with rifles which were usually fatal. Most men also gambled and games of poker and high-low-jack and the game kept going for days and nights, with men squatting around a blanket piled with silver Mexican dollars and gold slugs and all kinds of personal property.

A few held aloof from women, for some of them had lost all interest in the sex, but most men acquired a girl when they struck town and kept her until they left or got too drunk to do anything with her. In either Taos or Santa Fe a man could often buy a common Mexican girl for about twenty dollars, and Indian women were for sale for less than that. Many of them were Navajo women the Mexicans had captured and kept as slaves, but there were also men who made a business of catching Ute and Digger women and driving them into Santa Fe like sheep, letting them forage along the way, selling them for what they could get. Some became regular prostitutes, but most were to be bought like a horse.

Jean Ballard drank but he never got drunk, for he was a watchful man who had no desire to lose consciousness or fog his eyes. He spent long hours playing poker and almost always won, if only because he was sober and most of his opponents were drunk. He loved to bluff, watching a man's eyes, playing his hunches. The money he won never meant much because there was nothing to do with it. There were no banks or places of safekeeping and it was too heavy to carry on the trail. Often, when it came time to leave he gave away whatever dollars he had left. He had no conception of money as a form of power which can destroy both those who have it and others.

He had few fights because he was not one who loved fighting for its own sake. Most of the fighting was among men who made a sport of it and had a reputation to sustain. A man seldom had to fight if he minded his own business and Jean always did that.

Women interested him more than anything else in the towns, and he had many Mexican girls during his trapping years. All of them were girls of the common people. As a trapper among trappers he saw the aristocrats only at a distance. They truly lived apart from all others, looked and acted like a separate race. The common Mexicans were mostly the peons who worked the great estates and followed the sheep herds across the mesas, although some of them were small freeholders, owning a few acres of soil. They were the most oppressed and helpless people Jean had ever seen, living in tiny adobe houses, cooking their beans and chile over a corner fire, seldom seeing a whole dollar, completely at the mercy of their masters. Yet they were kind and friendly people. Many of them never married because they could not pay the fees of the church. They just set up housekeeping and lived together. So it was not hard for a Mexican mother to let her daughter go away with a gringo who had bags of silver money to spend. Any man could find a Mexican girl. There were professional panderers who could arrange such matters for a price. But Jean never did business so crudely. He went about his wenching, as he did everything else, with patience, deliberation and adroitness. He wanted to perfect his Spanish and to learn about Mexican people. When he saw a girl who took his eyes he would call on the family, bringing always gifts, first of food and tobacco, later, at just the right moment, presents of money. He spent long hours platicando. He squatted with huge families about their bowls of chile con carne, learned to scoop up his food gracefully in a tortilla and to swallow the burning hot chile without gagging or wiping his eyes. He always addressed himself to the grandmother first, if there was one, and then to the mother, working his way down through the generations. By the time he got to the girl, he usually had the whole family eating out of his hand and that quite literally.

Some of these Mexican girls took a powerful hold upon his flesh. Many of them were pretty and they had a soft and voluptuous quality, a completeness of submission and response that made them wholly different from the shrill and nervous women, laborious and full of malaria, he had known in Indiana. But always Jean rode away in the fall. Always he promised to return and sometimes he did and sometimes not. His time had not yet come to stay anywhere or stick to anything.

For eight years he rode the beaver trail, with prices falling and fur becoming scarce. Then, just before the conquest, he turned to the growing wagon trade and traveled between Santa Fe and Independence for several years. Here, as anywhere, he became a man of responsibility. After three years he had charge of a wagon train for a wealthy Jew who owned a store and two saloons in Santa Fe, and he was making big money. But he grew weary of the dust and sweat of the great road. He had come to love the mountains. Knowing now much of Indians and Indian languages, he became a trader with Ed Hicks for his assistant. They traded with the Utes across the Rio Grande, and came to know that tribe as well as any white man could. Then they made a trip south into the Apache country, a precarious operation, for Apaches wanted to trade but could not be trusted. Nevertheless, they came back to Santa Fe with a herd of mules and horses the Apaches had stolen in Sonora and sold to the white men for beads, knives, powder and lead. It was a profitable operation.

In this fateful thirty-third year of his life, he and Hicks had come to Taos for the summer, planning another Apache trip in the fall. Taos was quiet now, with few trappers there, no big money, no fights, no three-day poker games. So the two mountain men had ridden to the hot spring, men of leisure, taking their ease, glad of peace and running water and tall timber.

After thirteen years in the mountains, Jean Ballard owned nothing but his outfit and as much cash as he could pack around on a horse, but he was a man of reputation, and also, in the lore and skill of his own world, a man of learning. He knew Spanish as well as he did English and he spoke them both with careful correctness, though slowly and with no great fluency. He knew enough of three Indian languages—Ute, Arapahoe and Apache—for purposes of trade. He knew the difficult sign language perfectly and could talk in nimble-fingered silence with any Indian. He was known also as a "good man with Indians" who could win their confidence and keep it. He lived in a world of incessant movement, and he was an expert on transportation. He was a master packer who not only could throw a diamond hitch, but could load a barebacked horse with a squaw hitch that would hold. He was a good judge of both horses and mules, who had only to look at teeth and feel shins and knees to know what an animal was worth. He had learned the wagon business and almost every mile of road that a wagon could travel west of the Mississippi. He knew an immense territory, from Sonora in the south to the Platte in the north, and from the Buffalo plains all the way across the mountains to the Great Salt Lake.

It was no common trapper Consuelo Coronel had flirted with at the hot spring. Whether by luck or by intuition she had picked a man of power, one who was born to command other men, and also one who felt deeply the need of woman, not merely as a complement to his flesh, but as an anchor to the earth and a center of his being. For man alone may be a conqueror but everything that lasts is built around a woman. And Jean Ballard was destined to be a builder.

THE HOUSE OF CORONEL

The Coronel place stood on a low hill at the western edge of town, and was known therefore as La Loma. It looked almost as though it had been carved from the earth, or upthrust from it by some subterranean force— a great angular block of earthen wall, golden brown, plastered smooth, glinting in the sun with tiny bits of mica. Its windows were few, opaque with oiled paper and barred with wrought iron. A long narrow veranda ran across the front but no one ever sat there. The front entrance was a double door, iron-barred from within, which would have resisted a battering-ram. Behind the house was a square enclosed by adobe walls as high as the house itself, with cactus growing along its top. A solid double carriage gate, ten feet high, was the only way in from the rear. The house of Coronel was a very old house, a house of immense strength and stability, which kept its life secret and secluded, presented to the world a passive, impenetrable resistance.

For months Jean Ballard had felt that resistance as he had never felt resistance before in his life. He was a man with an appetite for difficulty, a love of struggle, but the house of Coronel offered him nothing to struggle with. It just let him sit. It also let him look at Consuelo, across a room, under the watchful eyes of at least one and sometimes two other women, and it let him say trivial things to her. Once in a long while he was left alone with her for a matter of minutes, and then they exchanged quick eager words. But there had been no word of hope. The correct procedure was for him to ask her father for her hand, but she had told him it was no use. She had been engaged since the age of six to a second cousin who lived in Santa Fe. This betrothal had been arranged by the parents of both, as was customary among the rich Mexicans. It meant a great deal to both families. It would unite two large estates, and had something of the necessity and importance of a marriage of royal persons. It had been endorsed by the great and autocratic Padre Martinez. It did not mean much either to Consuelo or to her affianced, for they had met only a few times, mostly at great Christmas gatherings, and their marriage had been unhappily delayed when he went south on a trading trip and was wounded by an Apache arrow. But for that she would have been married a year ago.

Consuelo had gone to her father, had tried to tell him of her love for the gringo. All Jean knew of that interview was conveyed to him in a shrug, a gesture of spreading both her beautiful hands, a single sentence.

"He won't listen to me," she said.

For many hours now these two had sat looking at each other, saying one thing in words and another with their eyes. They had talked a little in English. She had asked him to teach her English and this had given them a game to play and a little more private communication, though not much. For the most part they made only small talk. They chatted as though they were the most casual of acquaintances, and their chatter covered a tension of mutual need that had grown ever since the day they met. Jean had no doubt about his own feeling, nor yet of hers. She had given herself with her eyes and lips a dozen times, yet she was as much beyond his reach as if he had looked at her only through glass.

For the first time in his life he felt the massive, inert resistance of old established things, of a people fortified by wealth and custom and tradition, by a way of life stronger than they were, a social pattern which was a power in itself. They did not hate him as a person but they hated anything alien. Family was everything to them. Their whole society was a great family and it was organized to repel intrusion. They did not have to insult him or reject him or even close a door to him. They could freeze him out and wait him out. He might come and sit and sip chocolate for months and even for years and never pass any of the barriers of custom and manner that were set up against him.

He felt no hope—or almost none. There was something about Consuelo that slightly renewed his hope every time he saw her. She was a creature watched and guarded like a thousand-dollar horse, yet she never gave the impression of being helpless. She had a most unmistakable feeling of power about her—in the sweep of her walk, the tone of her voice, the toss of her head. He had noticed the same thing about a good many Mexican women. The men had gone to pot on too much easy living, but the women remained as lively and eager as ever. They had no rights but they had vitality.

Consuelo inspired confidence and she did not seem hopeless herself, but what could she do against the organized power of family and church, the trammels of custom that held her fast? Moreover, his time in Taos was growing short. Within the month he and Hicks must start for the south. They had bought all their supplies and trade goods and he had given his word. It was hard to go and still harder to tell her he was going. But he couldn't sit there all winter. Nor could he endure either the tension or the idleness much longer.

Always before he had forgotten women in the mountains. Something told him the image of this one was going to follow him down the trail, but even so, he knew he must go.

He tied his horse to one of the hitching posts in front of the house, as he had done so often before, and lifted the heavy knocker on the great front door. It was opened by the portero, a little old bearded man, one of the most trusted servants, whose whole use and destiny was to be guardian of that door and to know the exact right and status of everyone who knocked. The portero spoke a soft greeting, bowing with averted eye, and led him into the great sala. As always, no one was there but the little dog. Choppo was the only member of the household who felt free to show enthusiasm. He liked Jean, always barked a greeting and leaped to caress his hand with a soft pink tongue.

The sala was a long room, running all the way across the front of the house, with a low heavy-raftered ceiling and walls washed white with gypsum. There were two fireplaces in opposite corners, both banked in this hot season with fragrant boughs of juniper. Some of the wealthy families now were beginning to buy furniture from St. Louis, but not the conservative Coronels. Their house remained as it had been for three generations. Along the walls were couches made by folding mattresses and covering them with great Navajo blankets in large patterns of black and red. A light red cotton cloth was hung against the lower part of the walls to keep the white wash from rubbing off. There was no other furniture except a few homemade chairs with rawhide seats and two low tables of excellent workmanship. Two windows covered with oiled paper admitted a dim light, shadowed by the iron bars without. The place was never warm, even on the hottest days, and it was almost soundproof. It created an atmosphere of its own, a block of cool sequestered silence. Coming in from the glare and heat of the August afternoon, Jean always felt as though he had entered a cave.

He sat down on one of the couches and relaxed. Almost always he had a long wait. In the past few months he had learned the habits of the family in great detail, and those habits never varied except that everyone seemed to have a vague sense of time. The same things always happened, but sooner or later and generally later. So chocolate was served in this room every afternoon some time between four and six. Anyone who had access to the house might come and be admitted and sit down. In due course the visitor would be given chocolate and would be greeted by some part of the family. The women always appeared first, the men later, or sometimes not at all if they had ridden out to supervise a shearing or the irrigation of their crops. Most of the visitors came on certain days of the week and Jean had learned to avoid these.

He was desperately hoping this day to see Consuelo alone for a few minutes. It was never for more than a few minutes, and whether he saw her alone at all depended upon who presided over their meeting. Any married woman of the family who was older than Consuelo might act as her chaperon, but so far only two other women had appeared. One of these was the Doña Anastasia, her mother, and the other was a widowed aunt, who lived with the family, known as Señora Catalina Romero y Salazar.

The Doña Anastasia was a woman of enormous weight, and to Jean an enigma of some importance. She was the most uncertain factor in the situation. He knew the men regarded him as an intruder who had to be tolerated for the sake of politeness until he went his way. He knew also that the aunt contemplated him with hostility and suspicion. She was a tall, lean, angular woman, somewhere in her forties he thought, who had lost her husband in the Navajo wars years ago and had never found another. Neither had she any children, a great sorrow to any Mexican. Perhaps she had been soured by her misfortunes. At any rate, toward the gringo suitor she had an uncompromising resentment. When it was her turn to guard the family virgin she always appeared first, gave him a perfunctory hand with a barely perceptible smile, sat down on one of the straight-backed chairs and remained there, silent, erect and watchful, until he departed. She always reminded him of a hungry hawk perched on a pine stub.

The Doña Anastasia was wholly different. She was slow and heavy on her feet and at this time of day she had but recently emerged from the profound slumbers of her siesta. Perhaps this was the only reason her daughter so often beat her to the reception room when Jean came to call. But he cherished a hopeful suspicion that the Doña, if not an ally, was at least not unfriendly. He had also an impression, dating back to that first encounter at the hot spring, that the women of this family were in league against the men.

He had studied the Doña's face for confirmation of his hopes but without achieving any assurance. Padded with fat, her wide, placid countenance was unrevealing as an egg. Her smile was habitual, and fell upon all, like the sunshine. Only the shrewd, kindly look in her small, half-buried eyes gave him the impression that he was in the presence of something cunning, subtle and perhaps not wholly averse to his desire—that and the fact that she always came in late and subsided into a corner, her hands folded across a great, smooth stomach, and seemed to pay no attention to the talk, whether it was in English or in Spanish. Often she nodded, and a few times she apparently dozed. One such time, sitting near Consuelo, longing to touch her willing flesh, he had started impulsively toward her. The girl had warned him with a quick lift of the hand and he had turned to see the mother's small, shrewd eyes suddenly wide open, watchful, enigmatic —the eyes of an old woman who had spent a long life watching people, prevailing by cunning and patience if she prevailed at all. He suspected the Doña had feigned sleep to see what he would do. He had learned long since that an old Mexican woman is often tricky as a pet coon. It was no wonder that among the common people so many of them were considered witches and suspected of working spells.

This day he knew Consuelo was coming first and alone, because he knew her step so well. He rose to meet her and she gave him both her hands. He resisted an impulse to seize her, to know the feel of her body and the taste of her lips at least once before he left her. There would be only a few minutes and he had to blurt his message.

"I must go," he told her. "You know that . . ."

The pain in her eyes stopped him.

"Two more weeks," she begged. "Wait two more weeks!"

"But of what use?" he asked.

"Two more weeks," she repeated, breathless with haste and eagerness. "It is all I ask of you. Promise me!"

"Very well," he said. "I would promise you anything. But why?"

Consuelo took a deep breath and smiled. She turned and seated herself with great composure.

"My cousin, Adelita Otero, is coming from Albuquerque for a long visit," she explained. Her voice now was chatty and easy as it had been before. "She will stay for the Fiesta of San Geronimo in September."

"Yes," he assented.

"I want you to meet her," Consuelo explained. "I am sure you will find her very sympathetic."

Muy sympatico. It was a polite and invariable formula. So he would tarry two more weeks to meet the very sympathetic cousin. It made no sense but he had promised. And the Doña Anastasia forestalled any further explanations by rolling heavily into the room, offering a limp, plump hand, murmuring a greeting so soft it seemed almost confidential.

The first meeting with Adelita left him even more bewildered. The two women came into the room together, Consuelo leading her cousin by the hand, while Adelita hung back, shy and giggling. She was a plump young matron, very dark, with a mass of coarse black hair and a small, round, pretty face. She gave Jean her hand with a faint pressure, averting her eyes, flushed and flustered. He felt at once that Adelita was friendly but timid and he worked to put her at her ease. When she found that he could speak Spanish as well as she could she visibly relaxed, conquered her childish giggle and began to prattle about her trip. Jean pretended a great interest in the road to Santa Fe. He was going south himself in a few weeks. He knew every foot of it, as a matter of fact, but he bombarded her with polite questions, and she responded with the profuse and irrelevant detail which encumbers simple minds.

Later the whole family came in, and several visitors, evidently come to meet Adelita. Each of them took him by the hand, greeted him and then ignored him almost completely. Now and then a word was tossed in his direction for the sake of politeness, but most of their talk was about their own friends and doings. He felt, as he always had felt in these gatherings, that he was an intruder and an alien.

Chocolate arrived in a tall pitcher of hand-hammered silver and was served in silver cups that were hot to the lips by an old woman who devoted her whole life to making thick chocolate, beating it into a perfect froth with a wooden beater she spun between her hands. It was heavy, cloying chocolate, almost a liquid candy, and he always found it hard to down. A little later he rose and bowed himself out to a chorus of faint farewells, eloquent of polite indifference.

He returned a few days later, because Consuelo had bade him return, but with a feeling of futility and defeat. Somewhat to his surprise, Adelita came in first, but Consuelo joined them almost immediately.

Because he had watched her so long and so intently he had become acutely aware of her moods, and he knew at once that she was filled with excitement, flushed and quick on her feet. He could see too that she had dressed as though for a special occasion. She always wore a bodice of white linen, which left her arms and shoulders bare and just revealed the cleft of her breasts, and a short red skirt, only a little below her knees. Her legs were bare, too, and she wore homemade slippers, so fragile that one night of dancing would ruin a pair. This bodice and skirt were the house dress of all Mexican girls and much alike in all classes. Consuelo was to be known as a person of quality by her fine linen but chiefly by her shawls and her jewelry. No Mexican woman was ever without a shawl, and her shawl revealed both her wealth and her taste. It was also the most expressive part of her costume. She could draw it about her in a way that expressed aversion or coquetry or dissent, and she could fling it off in a gesture of challenge or invitation. A Mexican girl was always doing something with her shawl and one of a wealthy family would have a shawl for every kind of occasion. He had seen at least a dozen different ones about Consuelo's shoulders. All of them were of silk, in bright colors; some had come all the way from Spain and some were worth a hundred dollars or more.

This day Consuelo wore a vivid shawl of bright yellow silk, worked with a design of scarlet flowers. She wore also a red flower in her hair and earrings which were disks of soft, pure gold, each set with a single pearl. She had never looked more beautiful, he thought, and her beauty made him acutely uncomfortable. He was a calm man, but for once his calm was failing him. Never had he looked so longingly at anything so completely beyond his reach.

Conversation limped and stalled. Consuelo played with her shawl, even twisted it in her hands, revealing a nervous tension he had never seen in her before. Adelita seemed to feel the tension too, watching Consuelo uneasily, giggling without reason. It was evident that she both feared and adored her gorgeous and strong-minded cousin.

Consuelo at last fixed her eye upon the uncomfortable girl.

"Adelita!" she said. Her voice was restrained but monitory, as though Adelita had been guilty of some nameless dereliction. Adelita giggled without mirth and squirmed in her seat. She looked pathetically young and helpless—a weak personality caught between two strong ones.

"Adelita!" Consuelo's voice now had an edge like a knife.

Adelita was plainly in misery, the victim of some painful inner conflict. She hesitated a moment longer, then rose. Her politeness did not fail her. She nodded to each of them.

"With your permission," she said. Then she turned and fairly fled from the room as though she had been pushed by an invisible hand.

Consuelo's eyes followed her to the door and watched it close. Then she dropped her shawl from her shoulders and leaned toward him.

"I want you to make me one more promise," she said. "That you will come back in three months, as surely as you live."

"I will always come back, as long as you are here," he told her. "You know that. But what then?"

"Do not ask me," she said. "And do not come to the house. But let it be known that you are in town."

All this mystified him.

"I am yours to command," he said. It was another form of politeness, but he was aware that he meant it exactly.

"If you do not come," she said, "I am lost."

"But I give you my word. . . ."

"You may be killed," she reminded him. He had noticed again and again that Mexicans always thought of death, often mentioned death. He never thought of it. He could not imagine his own extinction. He laughed.

"I never get killed," he assured her.

"Your life now is mine," she said, "for I am yours."

Even then, at first, he did not understand. For so long he had looked at her across impassable barriers. . . . It was her face that made her meaning clear. It seemed suddenly transformed. Her eyes were larger and deeper, they were all pupil. Her cheeks were flushed and her mouth, soft as a flower, was an open invitation.

He rose and went to her, aware of the tremor of his hands and the thunder of his blood. It seemed a rash, an almost incredible moment, but after he had found her lips, he knew there was no stopping. Their union was for him a fulfillment so intense it blotted out awareness of everything except the receiving warmth of her body, the clasp of her arms, her half-smothered cry of willing pain. . . . Afterward there was a brief moment of peace, of quiet triumph—then suddenly she pushed him away and the moment dissolved into comedy. She was sitting up again, both hands playing around her hair, while he was retreating to his chair in very bad order.

"Act as though nothing had happened!" she said breathlessly.

From where he sat he could see the red marks of his fingers on her bare shoulders.

"Your reboso!" he said, making a gesture of drawing a shawl about his shoulders.

"Your hair!" she said, as she obeyed him, while he smoothed his heavy mop with trembling fingers.

Then both of them began to laugh. They laughed together, looking into each other's eyes, as they had laughed that day at the hot spring. They were laughing when Adelita came back into the room. She resumed her seat and looked from one to the other of them.

"Tell me," she begged, "what is so funny?"

Consuelo shook her head, struggling to control her laughter, which was so much more than mirth and had filled her eyes with tears.

"Forgive me, dear cousin," she said at last, wiping her eyes. "There is no joke. We laugh because we are happy."

— 2 —

When Jean Ballard returned to Taos the mountains were faintly powdered with the first light snow, streams tinkled and gleamed with ice and a cold wind whispered across bare fields, tore the last dead papery leaves from the cottonwoods, whipped blue wood smoke away from the chimneys of adobe houses.

He rode alone. He had left Hicks in Santa Fe to dispose of a herd of mules and a load of furs they had brought from the Gila country.

In Santa Fe he had made careful preparations. He had no idea what he faced or what he was going to do, but he wanted to look, feel and be strong and ready. He had thought first of a horse for a horse to him was a part of his personality. The pack and saddle stock he had used on his southern trip was gaunt and shaggy. This time he would not ride into Taos on a trail-worn cayuse, as he had done so often before. Instead he bought from an army officer for three hundred dollars a chestnut gelding, seventeen hands high—a single-footer that rocked him gently with a feeling of latent speed and power. He bought also a suit of buckskin, dyed black, well-cut by a Mexican tailor and trimmed with silver buttons—such clothing as the ricos had always worn before the wagons came, and such as many of them still wore. He paid forty dollars for a pair of boots that came from St. Louis and half as much for a wide black felt hat with a flat crown. He was no dandy but just now he was more acutely conscious of how he looked than ever before. He put on these clothes as a man might put on armor in preparation for battle. He bought also a small percussion-lock pistol he could wear inside the band of his trousers. It would never do to appear armed—or not to be so.

About a mile from Taos on the Questa road was a deserted one-room adobe house which had a good fireplace in one corner and a roof that would shed the weather. There was a spring near by and good winter-cured grass and piñon wood on the slope behind it. Water, grass and wood were the essentials of life to him. On the earthen floor he spread his robe and blanket. He had used the place before, and it was home enough for a trail-faring man. He never liked to be inside a town at night. Years in the mountains give a man an aversion to close human huddles.

The next day he dressed himself with care, saddled his new horse and rode into town. She had told him to let it be known he was there, and he made no mistake about that. He rode slowly about the streets, knowing his fine mount alone would draw many eyes, waving a greeting to friends, nearly all of whom were poor people he had known for years, buying supplies in a store and drinking native brandy in the small cantina where the mountain men had always gathered. None of them were there now. It was no time for a mountain man to be in Taos. He was probably the only gringo in town and therefore conspicuous. He did not even go near the house of Coronel.

Then his trial by patience began. He had nothing to do but go back to his camp and wait. It was the hardest of all things for him to do. He longed to take his rifle and go hunting. He knew there were good fat bucks in the piñon less than a mile away. But he did not dare to go that far from his camp. He might miss something. So he took an ax instead and cut firewood, much more than he needed, stacking it neatly in a corner, as though he were preparing to spend a month. At night he sat and stared at his fire, not lonely but restless and uneasy.

He was not a man to engage in useless speculations. He felt profoundly sure that something was going to happen but he could not guess what or when, and he did not try. He was painfully conscious he had lost his freedom for the first time since his mother's death. He knew he would wait all winter if necessary.

The second day a Mexican woodcutter came to his door. He knew the man, Enrique Lopez, as one who made a living peddling firewood in the town. He had two burros loaded high with split fat pine, as only a Mexican could load it. He invited Enrique into his house, gave him a drink of brandy, filled him up with hot meal and chile, chatted with him for an hour. The man might have been an emissary but apparently he was not. He had nothing to offer but a large appetite and a great many idle words. He might have questioned Enrique, too, might have found out at least whether Consuelo was at home. But he shrewdly refrained. If the man was not a messenger he might be a spy. He knew he was dealing with a cunning people and that he had probably created a situation big with trouble. So he asked nothing.

The next day a woman came by his door. He was on the sheltered side of the house in welcome autumn sunshine, squatting on his heels against the wall, smoking his pipe. He saw the woman in the distance, wrapped in the great black shawl all the common women wore. In the chilly morning wind it was hooded over her head and gathered tightly about her body. When she came near she spoke a soft, "Como le va," and when he responded she stopped and dropped her shawl about her shoulders so that he could see her broadly smiling face. He noticed too that she glanced quickly up and down the road to be sure that no one was in sight. He knew that she would have come into his house if he had asked her. She had heard of the gringo camped alone and she was interested. But he only exchanged a few words with her, and she commended him to God and went her way.

In the next few days several others passed his door. Each of them greeted him, stopped and chatted. Each of them raised his hopes a little, for any one of them might have been the bearer of a message. But he had been there nearly a week before the message came. It was brought by a boy of about twelve who accepted an invitation to eat, and ate in shy silence. Just before he left he took a letter out of the front of his shirt, handed it to Jean and departed.

The letter was from the abogado, Don Solomon Sandoval, a man he knew by reputation. It requested him, in terms of formal politeness, to call on the lawyer that afternoon at four and to drink a copita with him. In form it was only a social gesture, but Jean knew that now he was going to learn his fate.

Sandoval was a somewhat unusual figure in Taos in that he was not native-born but had come from Mexico City a good many years before. He was said to be not a Mexican but a Spaniard who had been brought by his father from Madrid and educated for the law. His legend was that he had been a brilliant practitioner, with a gift for intrigue, who had found it advisable to leave the capital for reasons not wholly to his credit. It was difficult otherwise to account for the presence of such a man in this country, which had been for two hundred years a remote and neglected outpost of the Spanish power. In Taos the abogado found little practice in the courts, but he nevertheless had become a man of power, chiefly because of his association with the great and all-powerful Padre Martinez. No one knew exactly what his relation was to the Padre. Padre Martinez had many agents and henchmen, not only in Taos but all over the territory. Although it was believed that he had conspired to drive the Americans out of New Mexico after the conquest, he had not lost in prestige since then. The Padre was a man of truly great intelligence as well as one who loved power for its own sake. He had always hated gringos but he was too intelligent not to accept inevitable change. He was also too astute not to see that power can be won under one government as well as another. For thirty years he had held more power in New Mexico than any one man because he not only dominated the Church and all of the great land-owning families, but also commanded the allegiance of the poor, and especially of the Penitentes Hermanos, the bloody brotherhood, who crucified one of their own number every Good Friday. They were the only organized power among the poor. It was known that he preached in many of their Moradas. He also periodically protested the heavy tithes which the Church laid upon the poor. The tithes had never been lifted but the Padre had always stood forth as a defender of the poor, and as one to whom they could always come for help.

A man who commands the allegiance of both high and low is a man to fear and the Padre was feared. Moreover, a man who commands numbers as well as money has in his hands the making of a first-class political power in the best American model. The Padre had not overlooked that fact either. Of late he had betrayed a strange friendliness toward some Americans.

Jean Ballard, who had a natural gift for keeping his ear close to the ground and listening to the rumble of rumor, was aware of all this, but not at all sure how it bore upon his own destiny. He knew the abogado would very likely be speaking for the Padre as well as for the Coronels, that what happened now might well be a matter of policy as well as a family affair. He was aware that he, Jean Ballard, was now in some sense a part of a conquering power. But he could not imagine what weighty conferences might have taken place, what decisions might have been reached. Whether he faced a warning or a welcome was any man's guess. As he saddled his horse for the trip to town he was tense with the feeling that he went to meet one of the decisive moments of his life.

The abogado was formally known as Licenciado Don Solomon Sandoval, but to a great many who did not like him he was known behind his back as El Coyote. A coyote, in Mexican parlance, is a negotiator, one who arranges difficult matters and always for a price. All Mexican society abounds in coyotes and of many different kinds and degrees. For the Mexicans are not a direct people, they are deviously and elaborately indirect. They love both ceremony and intrigue for their own sakes, and they hate the blunt and the obvious. So the professional go-between has a large part in their lives. Jean Ballard had learned long since that almost anything may be arranged in a Mexican town if you can find the right coyote. If you see a girl in the plaza who gives you a meaning smile, it would be a rank breach of etiquette to approach her, but a perfectly correct procedure to make discreet inquiries about her. A long series of such inquiries might very well lead to someone who could arrange something very interesting. Jean Ballard had anointed the palms of a good many coyotes in the course of his social life and he had also had some business dealings with them. Before the American occupation it had been against the law for Americans to trap beaver in Mexican streams. All of the streams were trapped, of course, but this was always arranged by an elaborate system of briberies in which one never saw the final recipient of the bribe. Silver traveled from hand to hand, dwindling on its way, until it got to the right place. Because he spoke Spanish so well and was so patient and polite, Jean had arranged these matters for most of the trapping expeditions in which he had taken part. So he knew much about coyotes in general, but he had never dealt with such a mighty and subtle coyote as this Sandoval, who might indeed be a very high-class pimp on occasion, but on other occasions was nothing less than a minor ambassador. Only God and perhaps Padre Martinez knew what the abogada was about.

Jean knew that Consuelo Coronel was not the first girl of high family who had bestowed herself informally upon the man of her choice. In theory such a thing was impossible, but in practice it was known to happen.

It was in fact the only mode of rebellion open to women in a society where they had no rights, where their destinies were arranged for them, sometimes when they were still in the cradle. The fact that the women were set to watch each other left a perceptible loophole in a wall of custom that was supposed to be impassable. When it was found that a girl of important family had improbably and shockingly violated the most important of all proprieties, there was a great disturbance within the afflicted family but never any open scandal. Those great earthen houses kept their secrets well. The matter was likely to come to the attention of the Padre but not of anyone else. For every marriage had to be sanctioned by the Church. If the union was suitable, marriage would usually be arranged. The bride would be likely to go away for a long visit and to return with her first-born in her arms. It was never good form to inquire about the age of a baby in any case. When the marriage was not deemed suitable the girl was even more sure to disappear for a while. It would be known that she had entered a convent, usually in Durango or Chihuahua. Sometimes a girl never came back. She became the bride of Christ. More often she did return, a more dutiful daughter, and there was one more child in a great household swarming with children, in a society where adoption was common custom. All of these things were well and discreetly managed. There was a method and precedent for almost everything.

In this instance the unprecedented thing, as he well understood, was that a gringo trapper had penetrated to the holiest of all holy places—that an alien seed had been planted in the sacred flesh of the right people, who had so long guarded their blood from such contamination that by this time almost all of them were blood relations. It was only by chance and daring that he had come among them, and his presence in the house of Coronel had doubtless been a subject of comment and suspicion for months. So it was not hard for him to imagine that he was about to receive bad news.

What he feared most was that Consuelo had already been sent away. In that case it might be impossible even to discover where she was. He might be politely informed that it would be useless for him ever to try to see her again, and that any inquiries about her would be rather more than indiscreet. For all of this to be conveyed to him in graceful hints, over a drink, with many good wishes—that would be typical of this people who loved good form and hated invaders, whether they came with guns or with exigent desires. . . . He could also imagine the abogado might be playing a game of his own, wholly unauthorized. He had no idea how corrupt the man might be, nor yet how much he knew. Without knowing more than he could infer from gossip he might be planning something like blackmail. When it came to creating a situation full of vague promise and polite delay, the Mexicans were artists. In this respect, as in others, there was something feminine about all of them.

So Jean went to face the abogado, alert, tense and suspicious, but determined to be polite and patient. He knew a rash word, a premature demand, a touch of irritation now could ruin everything. He knew also that he was about to hear a great many words. The abogado was famous for his eloquence. Like many cunning men he was fundamentally reticent and superficially verbose. Jean knew he would have to extract a fateful meaning from a cloud of vague and beautiful language.

At the abogado's house he was admitted as always by a portero, who led him across a courtyard and into a small square room which was plainly an office, a place of business. It was furnished only with a heavy homemade table of pine and two small chairs. Shelves against the wall held great heavy books, bound in leather and covered with a fine dust, which suggested that the labors of the abogado were not primarily intellectual.

As he expected he had a long interval in which to stretch his legs and listen to the buzz of a few flies. Then a woman entered and placed upon the table a fine glass decanter, filled with amber El Paso brandy, and two small silver cups without handles. There was another brief interval before the abogado made his entrance, beaming, hand outstretched. He was a short stout man in his fifties, very dark, bald on top of his head, with a fine rudder of a nose, faintly empurpled by the brandy he drank on all occasions, and small dark eyes under coarse heavy brows. He wore a coat of blue broadcloth with brass buttons and a high black stock—a formal and somewhat unusual attire for that country.

"You give me great pleasure," he announced. "Please to be seated."

After a few polite inquiries he poured two cups of brandy, offered one to Jean with a gesture across the table, and took the other himself. He gazed at it fixedly, as old topers often do, for a long thoughtful moment. It was customary seldom to lift a cup without a toast, especially when greeting a stranger, and the abogado was doubtless considering one.

"To health and money and the time to enjoy them," he proposed. It was a common toast, widely used. Jean nodded his thanks and they drank, the abogado taking his liquor with a single, swift gulp.

"By the way," he inquired, "how much money have you?"

Jean was a little surprised by the blunt directness of this attack. But he thought he understood. He was now wholly at the mercy of Sandoval. The abogado wanted to make this clear in the beginning, and also that his services were not to be had for nothing. Even if the news was all bad it was going to cost something. It would never do to resent this, to betray any suspicion, to bargain. Jean laughed with an affectation of great good humor, pulled out a small buckskin bag full of silver and tossed it on the table.

"I have only a few pesos here," he said, "but you know I can get more."

The abogado nodded solemnly several times.

"Yes," he agreed. "I know that. I know a great deal about you because I have made it my business to learn. I know that in Santa Fe you are highly regarded—by the merchants, by the freighters, by the army—by all who have dealt with you. I know that many men would give you money for the asking and take your word as bond. It is fortunate for you that I know these things."

Jean nodded his thanks.

"Your words give me the greatest of pleasure," he said. And this time he was not lying.

"For the service I am about to render you," the abogado spoke gravely, "money is no recompense. It is a mere token—the souvenir of a great occasion. What I count upon is your enduring friendship."

Again Jean nodded with the slow motion of solemn assent.

"My friendship is yours," he said, "and my purse is at your disposal."

"Let us say two hundred pesos in gold," the abogado proposed. "I ask no more than your word. I am a professional man and I live by the services I render my friends."

"You have my word," Jean assured him, "and you shall have the money as soon as I can get it. My compadre is even now selling mules and peltries in Santa Fe."

The abogado dismissed the crudities of financial consideration with a careless wave of the hand. He refilled the two cups with brandy and again, for a portentous interval, he gazed into the amber depths of his potion, as though searching for suitable words. Again he lifted his drink and this time his eyes were raised in reverence above the face of his guest, as though he addressed himself to the divine as well as the human.

"I drink to the welfare of your soul," he intoned, "to your repose in the bosom of God, to your eternal bliss in paradise."

This burst of pious eloquence made Jean blink at his brandy in sudden surprise, left him without a reply. But the next words of the abogado enlightened him and also warmed him with new hope.

"Are you a member of the Church?" he inquired.

Jean knew well that if he ever married Consuelo it would be in a Catholic church and as a member of it. The Church meant nothing to him, but he was perfectly willing to join anything if only he could also join Consuelo. He shook his head slowly as one who expresses a deep regret.

"I have lived far from churches," he said. "But my beloved mother was a French Catholic."

This last was evidently a fortunate word and a fortunate circumstance. For the first time he saw in the eyes of Sandoval something like a genuine response.

"Then you truly belong to the Holy Faith by birth and by right," he said. "The church of your mother is forever the home of your soul."

Jean bowed his head as one receiving a benediction, wholly unable to match the abogado's words but completely alert to all of his meanings.

Sandoval now poured brandy for a third time, and Jean watched him with a feeling that fateful words impended as the abogado lifted his cup.

"I drink to the prosperity of your family, to the health of your children, to the beauty of your wife."

He delivered this one with a broad smile.

"But I am not a married man," Jean objected, giving grin for grin.

"No," the abogado agreed, looking thoughtfully at his empty cup. "But you are going to be, as surely as you live." His words, spoken slowly, contained the delicate implication of a double meaning. They were followed by a long pause. Jean felt that for the first time it was his lead.

"You speak the very words of my hope," he said, feeling his way with caution. "I have truly longed for a family, for a beautiful wife, for one whom you may know . . . "

The abogado nodded his approval, at the same time lifting a hand, as though to intimate that enough had been said.

"I am aware," he replied, "that during the summer you paid court to the Señorita Consuelo Coronel, but wholly without success."

"I waited upon the Señorita long and wholly in vain," Jean agreed.

"The Señorita herself perhaps was unable to make up her mind," the abogado suggested.

"She remained completely undecided." Jean spoke with the gravity of one who had borne a great disappointment.

"Her parents, perhaps, did not look with complete favor upon your suit," the abogado continued.

"The sentiments of her esteemed parents were not made known to me," Jean told him.

"You departed, no doubt, without hope, but with a great longing in your heart," the abogado prompted, as though the case had to be completely stated in terms of the most perfect propriety.

"You read my heart like a book," Jean replied, his face rigid with a determination to play this comedy as long as necessary. "Have you any word of hope for me?" he ventured.

The abogado again executed his solemn nod.

"I am authorized to inform you that if you should renew your suit, it might be more favorably considered, both by the Señorita and by her parents, my very esteemed friends."

At this point Jean gave way to his one weakness as a man of manner— an irrepressible propensity to laugh in moments of relief and triumph. His laugh shocked and startled a good many people. It was a deep, explosive laugh that sprang from the bottom of his belly and went off like a clap of thunder, shaking him all over, turning his face red and bringing tears to his eyes. It revealed suddenly a latent power which was generally masked in caution and patience.

His whole relation to Consuelo had been a series of laughing triumphs and this, he knew, was the final triumph. Now he knew that she had won her battle. His laughter relieved a tension that had held him for months, and he was wholly unable to restrain it, although he could see that it shocked the abogado as though a gun had gone off in his face. It destroyed suddenly the perfect propriety, the solemn pretense of their interview. It seemed to make a mockery of the whole business. The abogado looked hurt and astounded, but even so it was seconds before Jean could control his voice.

"I ask your pardon," he said at last, and for the first time he spoke with honesty. "I have suffered long from doubt and anxiety. Your words give me great joy. I thank you and I ask your advice. How should I proceed?"

The abogado looked somewhat mollified. He rose and extended his hand, indicating that the interview was over.

"You are at liberty to call upon the Señorita whenever you wish," he said. "I can assure you of a welcome."

— 3 —

Jean Ballard dismounted before the house of Coronel and tied his horse, just as he had done so often before. The old portero greeted him without the faintest note of surprise in his voice and Choppo barked and leaped to lick his hand. Again he sat down alone in the great sala, which was just as it had been except that now a bright new fire of fat pine blazed red in each of the two corner fireplaces.

He heard her step and rose to meet her. For a moment they stood staring at each other as though neither could quite believe in the reality of this meeting. Then she rushed into his arms, laid her face upon his chest and burst into tears. He could feel the bulge of his unborn child pressing against his body.

"Oh, Juanito!" she cried when she had regained control of her voice. "It has not been easy! They tried to tell me you would not return. . . . I told them you would return if you lived. . . ."

He held her off, looking at her with admiration.

"What else did you tell them?" he asked.

"I told them I would marry you if I had to climb over walls to do it," she replied. "And I also told them that if they harmed you I would scratch their eyes out."

The lovers were left alone for only a few minutes. This was now a family occasion, a ceremonial one, with exact and invariable requirements. The Doña made her entrance next and there was no hesitation about her and no sign of either grief or embarrassment. She waddled right up to him, enfolded him in her great arms and received his kiss upon her brow.

"My son!" she said, and she said it with a possessive warmth and finality which made him sure he had had one friend at court.

The rest of the family then came trooping in, the younger girls first, the Don and his two sons bringing up the rear. The girls walked into his

arms and received his kiss with untroubled grace and not the slightest reluctance, but the men looked as unhappy as though they had faced a
firing squad. For the Don, especially, this was visibly a painful occasion.
He swallowed hard, smiled rigidly, and his Adam's apple ran up and
down his throat like a frightened squirrel. Nevertheless, he knew the requirements of the occasion and he was not a man to shirk his ceremonial
duty. He embraced Jean, patted him on the back and kissed him twice,
once on each cheek. Then each of the sons stepped forward and went
through the same performance with the same stiff reluctance. Afterward
there was a moment of embarrassed silence. All the necessary gestures had
been made and no one knew what to do next.

Jean Ballard looked all around the room.

"What?" he demanded. "No one else to be kissed?"

His eyes fell upon the little dog standing at his feet, his eager tail
seeming to wag his whole body. Jean stooped and picked him up in one
hand.

"Choppo!" he exclaimed, "I almost forgot you!"

He lifted the dog to his face and Choppo caressed his nose with a quick
pink tongue. Everyone laughed and the tension and uneasiness seemed
to dissolve in their laughter. Then the Doña clapped her hands, a woman
came in with steaming chocolate, and Jean Ballard sat down as a member
of the house of Coronel.

VIRGIN EARTH

The watershed of the Dark River lies on the eastern slope of the southern Rockies, where the mountains reach down from their bald rocky
summits in long wooded ridges to the edge of the great plains. Rio Oscuro,
the Mexicans named it, and so it was known when Ballard first saw it, but
the Americans changed the name to Dark River. It could be called a
river only in the Southwest, where any stream that carries water all the
year around is a river. In fact, it is only a large trout stream which runs
about twenty-five miles from its source to the foot of the mountains and
then sinks back into the earth. It rises in a little lake at the foot of a peak
above timber line, beginning as a bright thread of water creeping among
the roots of the grass, then plunging suddenly into a long, dark, narrow
canyon, alternately foaming through rocky gorges and disappearing into
forests of spruce so dense that sunlight barely touches the water. This
long dark cleft in the country is what gave the river its name. But below
the box canyon, as the mountain men called such a gorge, the river
emerges into a valley that widens as it falls toward the plain, the ridges
dwindling and parting on either hand, the spruce giving way to tall forests

of yellow pine, the stream running under a covert of wind-rippled willow, through open meadows, with here and there a tall perfect fir offering shade and shelter.

In this month of September, after the heavy rains of late summer, the country was at its best. On the upland meadows the short grass was so thick it felt like a heavy-piled carpet under the feet, and it was richly colored with the late blooming flowers of the high country. Down in the valley the wild oats would brush the belly of a deer and the river ran full and clear, with feeding trout marking perfect circles on the smooth green pools. The wild turkeys with their well-grown broods had come down into the canyons to hunt grasshoppers in the tall grass. Up on the ridges the black-tail bucks were thrashing the velvet off their new-grown antlers, getting ready for the season of lust and battle. Higher up in thick timber the bull elk were beginning to bugle. Black bears were feeding like pigs in the berry patches, turning over logs and rocks in search of ants and grubs, laying on fat against the winter sleep. The whole country was astir with the autumn business of feeding and breeding, in the last warm days of the year and under the full September moon.

This was a country that would look good to any man who loved country for its own sake, who wanted only to spread his blankets under a tree and take his meat where he found it. And it would also look good to any man who knew the value of things and wanted to own them and use them, for here was timber enough to build a city and a thousand acres of rich bottom land that could be plowed and irrigated, and range on the lower ridges and down on the flats for thousands of cattle and sheep and horses. Whether a man was looking for peace or for power, whether he loved the earth as it was or wanted to seize it and make it over in the image of his restless desire, this was a country that would stir his blood.

Jean Ballard rode over the divide from the other side of the mountains, crossing the summit twelve thousand feet above sea level, where wild sheep with great curling horns snorted and ran for the peaks, and a golden eagle, on rigid wings, wheeled around the sun. He rode alone, for this was a venture he would not ask anyone to share. He was mounted on his big chestnut and led a pack horse with a light load. His rifle was across the saddle before him and his long knife hung at his belt. For the first time in a year he was back on the trail, feeling alert and alive and glad of solitude and hazard. He rode across the alpine meadows, his horses sinking to their fetlocks in the lush, damp sod, and out upon a rocky spur from which he could overlook the whole of the watershed, spread at his feet like a great map in massive relief. There he pulled up and dismounted and sat down on a rock to look. A rare excitement pounded in his blood. He felt big and tense with hope and desire. For the momentous, the incredible thing was that all he saw, clear down to the wide valley and the vague spread of the plain, was his dominion if he could take and use it.

— 2 —

For nearly a year he had lived in Taos, in a house his father-in-law had given him, with more servants than he needed and all the easy comfort of a way of life long established. During that period he had learned two things very surely. He had learned that he was profoundly married, for Consuelo held him, flesh and spirit. She had set limits to his life, made him a man who must spend his energy in the narrow circle of a binding attachment rather than scatter it all over the country.

He had also learned that he had married much besides a woman—an estate and a way of life and a social position. He could see that if he stayed in Taos he would become simply a part of the Coronel family and the Coronel domain. He could see also that in the course of years he might become the dominating figure in that great loose aggregation of people and lands and livestock which had grown slowly for generations. The Don was old and neither of his sons was a man of much ability. All three of them had begun by ignoring him with a politeness that covered a certain antagonism, but he had gradually won their confidence. He had made something of the slow conquest which the strong always make over the weak, which begins in resentment and ends in dependence.

In particular, they had begun to turn to him in time of emergency. The routine of their lives and the business they managed well enough. In fact, their great estate, as he had come to understand, almost managed itself. Everything was done according to habits and customs which had been established for nearly a hundred years. Every spring the great sheep herds were gathered and sheared and then driven to the mountains for summer range. Every fall they were brought back down to the flats for the winter, moving just ahead of the snow. Every spring also the irrigating ditches were dug out clean and the water gates were repaired and the fields were plowed and planted. Every fall there was a period of reaping with long rows of men swinging their scythes across the fields and others binding the grain and loading it into carts. Then came the ancient ritual of threshing, still done here as it had been done for a thousand years, with horses and mules driven round and round a circular threshing floor to beat the grain from the straw, and men and women tossing it into the wind to winnow it clean. It was a slow and laborious business which required a great many horses and mules and men and women and boys, and it might now have been somewhat improved, but there was no need to improve it, for these people had more peons and slaves than they knew what to do with. Moreover, tradition was sacred. This whole great aggregation, from top to bottom, was imbued with the love of the past and moved by the power of habit. No one wanted to suffer the pain of change, nor yet the sweat of hurry.

Not that the Coronels were idle people. All three of the men were much
in the saddle, riding over their great domain, shouting orders to men
who scampered like rabbits at the sound of their voices, knelt at their
feet in supplication when they were displeased. On their splendid horses
they were striking figures, erect and assured, exercising a godlike power
over their henchmen and sometimes a godlike and condescending mercy.
But Jean had come to understand that if they had stayed quietly at home
everything would have gone on much the same, not only because everything was done at a certain time and in a certain way according to immutable custom, but also because the important men in the organization
were a few trusted and able peons. All of these were organized like an
army with definite rank, hard won and jealously guarded. So all of the
sheep were under one man who was responsible only to the Don and
needed few orders from him. He was the Mayodomo, the commander-in-
chief. Under him was a certain number of caporals, each of whom had
charge of three herds, and each herd was under an ayudante, who in turn
had a couple of boys to assist him. It was an ancient hierarchy, in which
men began as boys and worked their way up according to their seniority
and their ability. The men of high rank were truly experts in their own
way and they were supported by a great tradition. They had a loyalty to
sheep which was second only to their loyalty to God. Many a caporal had
laid down his life rather than desert his herds in a snowstorm, and many
of them also had lost their lives to marauding Apaches.

It was the Mescalero Apaches who first gave Jean Ballard a chance
to show his usefulness. Almost every fall, when the fat sheep came down
from the mountains, the Mescaleros would make a raid, sometimes killing
a man or two and always running off with a small herd of fat wethers.
They openly boasted that they took what they needed. What could anyone do? You never knew when the Apaches would strike, and no one
could catch an Apache in the mountains. Moreover, this sort of thing had
been going on, like everything else, for about a hundred years. Every year
a certain number of sheep were lost to the Apaches, just as a certain
number were lost to wolves. It was in the nature of things. But Jean Ballard knew a great deal about Apaches, he was itching for action, and he
regarded nothing as immutable. The sheep herders were armed only with
bows and arrows and slingshots. Jean armed half a dozen carefully chosen
men with good guns, which was in itself against all precedent, for the
peons had always been kept unarmed. He did this on his own account and
despite some feeble expostulation on the part of the Don. He knew about
when the Apaches would strike. He learned that they had struck within a
few weeks of the same time every year since the fall of the Spanish Empire. He then further violated custom by going out and camping with his
carefully planted herd of sheep, sharing the beans and tortillas of his men,
keeping all arms carefully concealed, setting a watch every night. When
the Apaches struck at dawn, as they always did, they met a roar of rifle

fire. Three of them fell and were scalped by the delighted peons, who had been thirsting for Apache blood all their lives.

This feat made a deep impression, not only on the Coronels but on the whole of Taos. "Killing Apaches" had long been a proverbial metaphor for telling boastful lies. Many men claimed to have killed an Apache but hardly anyone could produce an authentic Apache scalp to prove it. A man who truly killed Apaches, and brought home their hair, was a man of might. Jean found that he had suddenly grown in importance, and not only among the aristocrats. The peons began coming to him instead of to the Don when they needed help. They had discovered that he had the peculiarity of doing what he said he would do, and immediately. They also began calling him Don Juan Ballárd, with the accent on the last syllable.

Don Juan Ballárd! The name would stick. He would lose his very identity. He would cease to be Jean Ballard and become a Mexican gentleman, riding the family acres, shouting commands to scampering men. His life had always been a thing of change and hazard, a continuous thrust against the unknown. Now he found himself staring down a long straight corridor of years without hope of struggle or surprise. The comfortable happiness of his marriage had been invaded by a growing boredom and restlessness.

— 3 —

The Don had moved rather slowly in the matter of a dowry. There would of course be a dowry. The daughter of a great family would always bring something to her husband, even if he too was a person of property. When she had married a man who did not own an acre, some sort of endowment was deemed a necessity. So the Don had given the young couple a house and a small amount of land in the valley.

Concerning the provisions he had made for his daughter and his son-in-law he was at once a little vague and a little apologetic, but Jean did not find it hard to understand the Don's intention and feeling. He wanted his daughter to be secure and there would never be any doubt about that. Jean would have his part in the management of the estate as a whole and his share in its abundant proceeds. It produced grain and mutton and wool enough for all and to spare. But the Don wanted above all for his great house and his valley lands and his sheep herds to descend to his sons, and most of it to his eldest son. Both Spanish and Mexican law would have made this compulsory under the rule of primogeniture. Since the American conquest, it was no longer so, but the Don had no intention of deviating from ancient custom or impairing the might and importance of his dynasty. He would bequeath his daughter nothing and give her little, so far as the Taos estate was concerned. But there was another part of the family heritage which had long lain unused. In fact neither the Don nor his sons had ever even seen it, and neither of the younger men was likely ever to make any use of it. This was a royal grant of lands on the other side of the mountains, which had been bestowed upon the family in the late eighteenth century, when the Don was a child. In a conference with Jean, he produced the deed to the grant, embossed on parchment, bearing the royal seal, with a certain pride and flourish. It was proof of the great and ancient importance of his family. He explained how the grant had been confirmed, after the revolution of 1821, by the Mexican government, and now, only a year before, by the American government. Governments come and go but property is sacred.

This grant was one of a series of similar grants which His Most Catholic Majesty, the King of Spain, had bestowed upon certain loyal subjects in New Mexico, only about thirty years before those loyal subjects had revolted against him and set up the Mexican Republic. At the time the grants were made the Spanish Empire was already a tottering power, both in Europe and in America. In America it was menaced from the east, both by the wild tribes and by the growing power of the United States on the eastern seaboard. It had been foreseen that sooner or later the enterprising Americans would cross the plains, first as traders and then, most probably, with an army. The plan was to establish on the eastern side of the mountains a long line of great haciendas which would act as a buffer against both wild Indians and even more dreaded whites.

Had the Spanish power survived and thriven, this plan might have been carried out. There would then have been garrisons of Spanish troops to protect the settlers. But the Spanish power had fallen and the government of the Mexican Republic had been nothing but a series of revolutions, so frequent and sudden that even a well-informed man seldom knew who was president at a given moment. New Mexico was a remote province and it had become almost a forgotten one. Who was going to cross the mountains and settle these lands, without military protection or escort, without in fact any kind of governmental backing whatsoever? Manifestly, no one. None of the owners of these grants had ever seen them. Their very existence was half-forgotten. Stretching all the way from the Cimarron in the north to the Capitan in the south, they remained just a part of the wilderness. To their owners each of them was only a beautiful sheet of parchment, enscrolled in three colors, signed by a monarch, worth in cash exactly nothing.

The Don was candid about all this. He made it perfectly clear that he did not expect his son-in-law to do anything with the grant or even to look at it. That whole country had long been a hunting ground for the most dangerous savages. A man could hardly hope to enter and come back with his hair.

Just now the grant was without use, but the Don expatiated eloquently on its future possibilities. The Santa Fe Trail passed only a few miles east of the foot of the mountains. Settlers were coming to New Mexico in greater numbers every year. In ten years or in twenty these lands might acquire value. Even if Jean never saw them they would be a magnificent bequest for his children.

Jean listened and nodded his dignified thanks. He understood perfectly what the Don thought he was doing. He was keeping the farm for his sons and giving his gringo son-in-law the briar patch.

Jean betrayed no emotion then or later but he felt a sudden stirring conviction that his destiny had been revealed to him. Ever since his marriage he had felt as though he were waiting for something. Now he was suddenly sure it had come. For he knew the Dark River country where the grant was located. He had camped once, nearly ten years before, in the lower valley, and had seen those great rich meadows along the stream and the stands of virgin pine on either side. The limits of the grant were vague, for they were designated only by reference to peaks and watercourses, but it was clear at least that the lower valley and the pine forests and the rich grazing lands were included, and this was the vital heart of the region. Here was truly a royal gift if a man could use it. And Jean felt a calm confidence that if any man in the Southwest could go into the Dark River Valley and stay there, he was that man. For he not only knew the country but he knew as much as any white man did about the Ute Indians, who claimed the valley as their hunting ground.

When it came to making any use of the grant, the Indians were of course the problem. Whichever way you turned, in the New Mexico of that day, the Indians were the problem, and this had been true for more than two hundred years. When the Spaniards first came to the valley they had fought a great war with the Pueblos and had conquered them, but that had been the last as well as the first of their conquests over the Indians. The Pueblos had long since become a part of the valley civilization, owning their own lands, supplying the province with fruit and pottery. Within the valley, life had become fairly secure for the great landowners in their great houses. The wild tribes had no need or desire to assault these. But neither government nor conquest had ever been extended so much as five miles beyond the valley and a few other bits of arable land. New Mexico was, in fact, only a narrow green strip of civilization in a vast wilderness dominated by savages. The Apaches and Navajos to the south, the Utes and Arapahoe in the north, contained it in a kind of loose, informal siege. The northern Indians, for the most part, stayed away in the wilderness, making only an occasional raid, but also making the high mountains of the north an impassable barrier. The Apaches and Navajos, on the other hand, had become proud and powerful peoples, who levied tribute rather than made war, and went in for rape, murder and kidnaping as incident and sport. The Navajos had been stealing Mexican sheep for over a century and had founded large sheep herds of their own with stolen stock. They boasted that they took what they wanted and left the rest for seed. The

Apaches made annual raids into Chichuahua, stealing herds of mules and horses, which they brought north and sold in New Mexico. Often the same stock was stolen again and sold in the south. The Apaches laughed at Mexicans, and some of them had grown rich in silver and blankets. Both they and the Navajos had captured many Mexican women and children. Some of these had become good Indians and some had been ransomed for heavy prices in silver and livestock. It was all a disgraceful situation and it had become worse since the fall of the Spanish power. Nor had the American army so far done anything to make it better. The American soldiers stayed in Santa Fe, playing Monte and courting Mexican girls.

What Jean Ballard proposed to himself, then, was a revolutionary move, a major feat in pioneering. He proposed to do what the Spanish government had intended, when it made those royal grants. He proposed to carry civilization across the mountains and plant it on the edge of the great plains, which must some day become a part of it.

He did not put the matter to himself in such terms. He was not a man of words nor yet one with a conviction of personal importance. But he did feel that quickening of the whole being, that jump of blood and clutch of gut which every man feels when he faces a major challenge of his destiny. For this task, it seemed, had been presented to him by a most improbable fate. And for this task, it seemed, he had been training for years. Only a mountain man, such as he, could go into that country at all. The beaver trappers were the only men who had traversed the mountains, had learned how to travel and live in them, which was no small art in itself. But the mountain men had built nothing and conquered nothing. They had fought Indians when necessary but most of the time they had made friends with Indians, gone to bed with Indian women. Many of them had become more than half Indian themselves. They had penetrated the wilderness and the wilderness had made them its own. They had found the way but that was all.

Jean Ballard was one of those who had found the way. But more than that, he was one of the few men who knew the Ute language, who had lived and traded with the Utes. All of this did not make it easy for him to go into the Dark River country, much less to settle there. The Utes were as elusive as deer and as unpredictable as summer rain. Moreover, he knew that they had left their ancient range, devasted by American whisky and Mexican smallpox, in search of a place where they might be let alone. They were not going to welcome any intruder. But at least he could hope to parley with them if he could reach their camp, and he had great confidence in his ability to deal with Indians. He felt as though a job had been laid in his lap for which he was especially qualified, and at a time when all of his energies yearned for use.

This conspiracy of circumstance, with everything pointing one way, was what thrilled and moved him. It was the unformulated philosophy of his life to wait patiently for the ripe moment and then seize it. And the ripe moment he had always known, not so much by careful consideration, as by a slow and steady gathering of impulse and conviction—a growing, undeniable need of action. So he had felt when he launched his boat on the Ohio and again when he started across the plains. So he felt now. The springs of action were tightening within him. The finger of destiny again pointed the way.

It was characteristic of him that he moved slowly and said little. He waited until early fall because he knew then it would be easiest to find the Indians. He broached the subject to the Don in the most casual manner. He was going on a little trip into the mountains, he said. He might be gone a month. Where was he going? He might drop across the divide and have a look at the grant. Since it was his, he felt curious about it.

The Don was at once uneasy. By this time he was quite friendly to Jean, but always a little afraid of him. He instinctively knew his son-in-law for the kind of man who is apt to do new and startling things. The Don lived for the loving repetition of the familiar. He did not like new ideas of any kind. Moreover, like all Mexicans, he feared the mountains. He was a creature of the valley. Mountains were mystery and danger. He was in favor of leaving them alone. Of what use, he inquired, to make such a trip?

Jean did not want to alarm anyone or commit himself to anything. It would be useful at least to take a look at the country. No one knew even what was there.

"But you cannot go alone," the Don objected. "If you must go, take a dozen men with rifles, as you did when you met the Apaches."

Jean smiled and shook his head. He knew that if he went into the country with an armed band, he would never even see the Utes, unless they felt strong enough to drive him out. He reminded the Don he had been going about the mountains for thirteen years. He knew what he was doing. Mountain travel was his profession. This was just a casual jaunt to him.

The Don was far from satisfied but he did not know what to say or do. In this situation he inevitably confided in his wife and his sons. Inevitably the matter led to a family conference, for to the Coronels everything was a family matter. Jean found himself facing them all, alone against the field, painfully conscious that he would never be truly one of them—that he had married into an alien race. They did not sympathize at all with his restlessness, his curiosity, his need of action and conquest. But that was not all. He knew what worried them most. They were afraid he might take their darling daughter and go into that wild country to live—or try to live. That, of course, was exactly what he hoped to do, but he hated to disclose his whole intention to anyone until it became necessary to do so. If he went into the Dark River country and could not find the Utes, or if he found himself dodging arrows and riding for his life, then it was useless to go back—at least for the present. He had hoped to play carefully and keep his cards close to his chest. But he knew now they were going to force his hand. It was the Doña, a far more formidable person than her husband, who took the offensive.

"You know you cannot go to that country and live," she told him. "So what is the use of going at all?"

He could not quibble any longer.

"If I can find the Utes and make an agreement with them," he said, "I can go back and build a house—and I will."

"But that is impossible!" Her voice was tremulous with rising emotion. "For a man it is bad enough, but to take a woman with a young child in her arms. . . . No! It is too much!"

Jean sat silent and miserable but unyielding. Everyone looked very grave. The Doña gulped her tears and resumed the attack.

"I called you my son!" she wailed. "I took you to my heart as a son! And now, and now. . . . No! I cannot bear it!" She buried her face in her hands, wept gently for a moment, then wiped her eyes and sat stubbornly shaking her head.

Everyone was looking at Consuelo. It became suddenly clear to all that the issue was hers to decide. No one knew it better than Jean. He had told her only that he planned a short trip across the mountains to look at the grant. She had said only, "But that would be dangerous." He had told her no, it would not be dangerous. She had not questioned him. She had learned that his reticence was often impenetrable. But now she knew what he intended. And now, once more, she held his destiny in her hands.

He could go ino the Dark River Valley alone. She could not stop him. He could even compel her to go along if he decided to settle there. But to drag a reluctant woman into that country would be worse than fighting Utes every day. Moreover, he knew that he was not going to drag Consuelo anywhere, be his rights what they might. Like many another strong man, he felt equal to almost any kind of opposition except that of his wife. If the Dark River Valley was conquered, it would be as much her conquest as his. So he sat looking at her now, knowing his fate was for her to decide, just as he had sat looking at her in this same room, over a year ago, waiting for the moment that only she could create.

Consuelo knew her power and she loved it. That he had learned more than once. She also loved a dramatic situation. So now she was in no hurry. She let them all wait for a long moment. She wanted them all to know that she was the heroine of this occasion. Then she rose and went to stand by his side, facing her parents.

"The land is ours," she reminded them. "You gave it to us." She laid her hand upon her husband's shoulder. "Where he goes, I go!"

Her few words knocked the argument dead in its tracks. No Mexican would deny the right and obligation of a woman to follow her husband, even if he were going toward certain death. They had hoped she would side with them, try to dissuade him. They had hoped she was more a Mexican than a wife. Now they knew they were beaten. The conference broke up in silence, and the two elders went away shaking their heads, as old people have always shaken their heads at the young, in futile dissent.

When they were gone Jean took his wife in his arms.

"You are truly my consolation," he said.

"And you?" she replied, her voice a curious mingling of tenderness and asperity. "You are my Juanito, my little boy who cannot sit still. . . . All the time you are gone I will worry. But this is the last time you go alone. If you return, I go with you!"

— 4 —

From where he sat, just below the top of the divide, Jean could see about a thousand square miles of steep and wooded country. Somewhere in it was a little band of Indians, which he had to find, and these, he knew, were the most elusive Indians in the Southwest. For the Utes were supremely the mountain Indians—the only ones who lived almost wholly in the mountains, ranging to the very summits in summer, descending to the sheltered canyons when the deep snows fell. The great tilted ranges west of the Rio Grande had been their home long before the Spaniards came. There they had lived as a secluded, almost an unknown people. Navajos and Apaches attacked them rarely and never followed them into the high country, for no one could catch a Ute in the mountains. It was like trying to catch a deer by the tail. Far from all routes of travel, they had come into contact with white men little, either in peace or in war, but they had been quick to resent any intrusion. They lived in small, scattered bands. Even a Ute of another band, it was said, did not dare to approach a Ute camp unannounced. The only way to find a Ute was to let him find you.

In the years before the conquest few traders had ever reached the Utes. Jean had been one of those few and that fact was all that made his present quest a hopeful one. Three years in succession he had ridden into the San Juan country with two horseloads of trade goods, had found the Moache band, camped with them for part of a summer, come out with profitable loads of Indian-tanned furs. Jean Ballard was known to the Utes as a good trader, and since his visits to them they had learned much about bad traders. Jean had taken them good iron pots and skillets, knives, cotton cloth, powder and lead—things they needed. He had taken no whisky. He had learned something of their language and had made some friends among them. In particular, he had made a friend of one somewhat unusual Indian, the young chief known as Kenyatch.

Making a friend of an Indian, he had long since learned, was a difficult and peculiar business. You never knew an Indian as you knew a white man. He neither confided in you nor asked you any questions. He did not reveal himself. He did not, in fact, seem to have a self as a white man has one. He existed only as part of a tribe. But an Indian who had not been ruined by contact with dishonest white men was always a good friend in two ways. He would never forget you, any more than a dog or a horse will forget you, and he would keep his word. Each year, when he had left the Moache Utes, Kenyatch had said: "Next year, when the moon is full in July, I will meet you there." And he would designate a certain camping place. Ten months later he would be waiting there, and business would be picked up where it had been dropped ten months before.

Kenyatch, he knew, would remember him—in fact, would remember every swap they had made, almost every word they had exchanged. Moreover, Kenyatch was a man of some power among his own people, and an Indian of unusual experience, for he had lived among the Mexicans. It was said that for a long time the Utes used to trade their own children to the Spaniards for horses. This was not because they did not love their children. All Indians are devoted to their children. But the Utes were poor and they were among the last Indians to acquire horses. They had nothing that was worth as much as a horse except a human being. So they had traded human flesh for horse flesh. Whether Kenyatch had truly been traded for a horse or captured in battle, it was certain that he had belonged for some years to a Mexican family living near Penasco, that he had served them as a sheep herder, and that when he was about sixteen he had stolen their best horse, run away and rejoined his people. As an Indian who knew Mexicans and could speak Spanish, he was a great man to his own people. Whether he was the leader of the Moache band or not, he was a man of influence among them. Jean strongly suspected it was the cunning Kenyatch who had led them into the Dark River country, after the great misfortunes which had befallen them.

Of these misfortunes he knew only by hearsay. He knew that a band of Indian traders of the worst kind had moved into the little Mexican settlement of Abiquiu, on the edge of the Ute country. These traders had sold whisky to the Utes. Whisky was deadly to all Indians, but especially so to these, who had never tasted alcohol. There had been terrible drunken orgies in which Ute had killed Ute. Their leaders had warned the traders away, but young men of the Moaches had sneaked into Abiquiu and bought whisky. Moreover, one of them, returning to his own people, had brought smallpox, probably caught from a Mexican woman. Mexicans had an epidemic of smallpox almost every year. Some of them died but most recovered. Most of the peon Mexicans were deeply pitted by the disease. But few Indians ever recovered from it. More than half of the Moache Utes had died, all in about a week. The survivors had made a great pile of their tepees and blankets and burned them in a huge bonfire. Then they had ridden away across the Rio Grande, in search of a new home, in flight not from battle but from smallpox and whisky—from a civilization which to them was more poisonous than a rattlesnake.

They had gone into the Dark River country because no Indians claimed

it and no white man or Mexican ever went there. It had been only a summer hunting ground for various tribes and a place where small hunting
parties fought each other when they met. There the Utes would live in
constant dread of the Arapahoe. There they would find the winters hard
and dangerous. A large band could not have hoped to survive, but this
handful of mountain dwellers could do so.

Jean knew these Utes wanted no intruders of any kind. He knew any
Mexican who crossed that summit would be a dead Mexican. He knew
no trader would dare to cross it. But he also knew that if he could ride
into the main Ute camp with his right hand lifted in sign of peace, Kenyatch would greet him as a friend.

He was sure he could find that camp if he were given a few days to look
for it. Indians in summer made tiny fires, but a wisp of smoke would show.
Also he could find Indian tracks. They would be the tracks of wandering
hunters, but any track would lead finally to the camp. In a few days he
could find them—but he was not going to have a few days to search. The
Utes would find him long before he could find them.

It was amazing how a few Indians could guard a great country. They
watched from the high points and nothing moved without their knowledge.
They watched the trails for tracks—and there was only one way across
the summit. You could no more enter their country undetected than you
could walk into a white man's front yard without his knowledge.

Jean knew that hidden eyes would be watching him long before he
could reach the lower valley. The Indians were like wild animals in that
respect. A man rode through the wilderness, perhaps seeing little life, but
the wilderness was always aware of him. A grizzly lifted his sensitive
muzzle to sample the wind and moved quietly into the timber. A mountain lion crossed his trail and turned and followed on silent pads, just to
watch this strange, noisy mammal on its way. Buzzards spotted him from
a thousand feet in the air and came and circled above him to see if he
would lie down and die or if something would kill him. Deer and elk
knew he was coming long before he appeared. The beat of hoofs tele-
graphed his approach to exquisitely sensitive ears and the wind carried
his identity to noses that were better than eyes.

The Utes would spot him as quickly and almost as far as a buzzard or
an eagle. They would find his tracks and know as much as though he had
sent them a message. Like other wild things, they would follow and watch,
but being men, they would also consider. To a hunting party of young
Utes, usually not more than three, he would be a tempting prize, with
his two good horses and his rifle. And some of these young men had
learned to hate white flesh, and to see it as poison. If they could get close
enough, one arrow might do their work. This would probably be against
the warnings of their leaders. A white man killed would likely mean more
white men coming. But young men are eager and reckless.

More likely, the news of his presence would travel fast and would reach the main camp. He would be followed and watched while his fate was debated. If he only passed through on his way to the plains, perhaps they would let him pass, and he would no more see Indians than he would see ghosts. But if he stayed in the country they would reveal themselves, one way or another. And he was going to stay until they did. He had come on an errand of peace and diplomacy, and his pack horse was loaded with gifts, but he knew that he could not count on peace. He was taking a calculated risk.

This situation made him alert and tense. He was aware of suspense and he knew the suspense would intensify until something happened, but he also knew he could stand it because it was a familiar thing to him.

Most of his trapping years had been spent in Indian country, and often his situation had been just about what it was now. He would know that Indians were watching and would not know whether they were dangerous or not. So he knew exactly what he had to do. First of all, he had to stay in the open and as far from cover as possible. An Indian arrow was seldom effective beyond sixty yards. They might have a rifle or two, but these Moaches were very poor people, would have little powder or lead. Moreover, they were poor rifle shots, chiefly because they got no practice. . . . Stay in the open and keep moving. Ultimately they could come into the open too. And then? Well, it seemed a precarious enterprise but he felt curiously confident. He was a confident man, who always expected to have his way, and also a patient one. If not this time, then some other time. This was his dominion now and he meant to have it.

Before he started down the long drop to the valley he planned his route with care. He was above timber line at first and could see for miles in every direction. Then he reached the Dark River and followed it down a wide, shallow canyon which slowly narrowed and deepened. Presently there was a growth of short dense spruce on either side, but a hundred yards away, so that he still felt safe. As he lost altitude the canyon narrowed and deepened and the spruce crowded closer on either hand, as though it were preparing an ambush for him.

He had begun the descent about noon, and by three o'clock he felt sure he was spotted and watched. It was the old intuitive feeling of danger or presence he had known so often before, but as always he soon saw evidence to confirm his hunch. He saw where a frightened deer had run across the trail, hoofs spread wide and dew claws deep in the soft earth. Something had scared that deer out of the timber on the other side of the canyon. Then far below him, where the first tall timber appeared, he saw a small bunch of turkeys run to the top of a point, launch themselves one by one with a running start and sail beautifully across the open. Turkeys seldom took wing for any animal but a man.

By late afternoon, with the sun already touching the high summits, he was in the last wide open before the river plunged into its deep and

wooded gorge. It was too late now to go farther and this was the last
safe place to camp. He made his bed under a tree that stood alone in
the middle of the open. His horses he hobbled and sat with his rifle in
his lap watching them crop thick, ripe grass until dark. Then he tethered
them under the tree. They had not fed long enough, but he knew it was
"better to count their ribs than their tracks," as the Mexicans say. Even
an Indian who wouldn't kill would steal a horse. He made no fire, but
chewed dried beef and drank cold mountain water for supper. Afterward
he sat with his back against the tree and smoked his pipe. The stream sang
and chuckled and seemed to have human voices in it, as mountain water
always does to a man who sits alone. A vesper sparrow tinkled his song
in the aspen. Far away, down toward the plain, he heard the long, sad
howl of a wolf, and briefly remembered back to the rolling Ohio and his
mother dying, as he always did when he heard that sound.

Most men would have been crushed by the weight of this black, in-
human solitude, full of hidden eyes hostile or frightened, astir with life
that cared nothing for his own. But he was used to it. As long as he could
remember he had known moments like this. After months of talk and
people and the warm clinging huddle of love, he was even quietly glad
of it.

He sat there living in his ears as the light died. After a while he heard
the hoot of a great horned owl on one side of the canyon and an answer
from the other side. He knew he was probably not hearing owls. Indians
used that call for a signal at night. They had been on either side of him
all day long and they were with him still. . . . He knocked the ashes out
of his pipe and went to bed. Indians never moved at night. They were
truly afraid of the dark. But he must wake well before daylight, and he
knew that he would, for he could set his mind to end his sleep at any hour.

It seemed only a moment later that he was wide awake, feeling the
tingle of the cold hour before the dawn. The big dipper and the North
Star told him the time. He was saddled and packed as soon as he could
see the sharp tops of the spruce on the ridge above him, and he was
climbing out of the canyon by the first full daylight, his horses humping
and grunting up the steep grade. For he had to climb far above the canyon
now, to get around the gorge, before he could drop into the comparative
safety of the meadows below. This was the dangerous part of the journey,
and he was almost painfully alert. He was not frightened but he could
feel the growing tension in his muscles and his bowels. He began to wish
something would happen soon—or at least soon after he got back into the
open. Days of this riding with hidden eyes on either side with the sense
of something impending, would wear down any man. He had known men
to go into a panic in Indian country, without having seen or heard a
thing, and ride madly for the open, smashing through brush and timber
like a frightened bear. So he held himself carefully in check. Now and

again, when the terrain permitted, he made a wide swing to right or left
and then came back to his line of travel, watching his back track at every
turn, just as does a wary old buck who knows he is hunted.

By noon he was out of the timber, with a feeling of great relief, and
riding through the open meadows at the head of the lower valley. But he
was also worried. It began to look as though the Indians might watch him
all the way through to the foot of the mountains without showing themselves. He rode swinging his gaze from right to left and all the way
around the horizon, watching the ground for tracks, too. He might have
to turn in and hunt them on foot. . . . Then, suddenly, he looked to his
right where a low grassy ridge lay on the edge of the valley. There, just
below the crest, three Indians sat their horses, watching, still as so many
rocks. They were true wilderness Indians, such as he had seen long ago
on trapping trips, naked to the waist, riding bareback, with full quivers
sticking up over their shoulders. They were poised there, like wary wild
animals, ready to disappear over the ridge if he made a hostile move.

A warm wave of elation and relief went through his body. He was not
at all afraid now, for he understood the situation at a glance. They had
been watching him for nearly twenty-four hours. Undoubtedly word of his
presence had gone to the main camp, and these men had been sent to
bring him in—if he was friendly. They would not make the first move.
They were ready for anything.

He swung his horse about, facing them, lifting his right hand in sign
of peace. One of the Indians lifted a hand in response, rode forward fifty
yards alone, and stopped. Jean rode to meet him, greeted him in his own
tongue, saw the quick flicker of surprise and pleasure in his eyes.

"Come and eat," Jean invited, making a gesture toward the level open
beside the creek. The Indian grinned and nodded, beckoned to his fellows.
Jean turned and rode to his chosen camping place, dismounted and unpacked, started his fire, all without so much as looking at the Indians,
just as though this were a meeting long expected—which it was on his
part. He was well prepared for this occasion. Shoot if you have to but
feed them if you possibly can. That had been his method of dealing with
Indians for years. Those who eat together truly become one. There might
be white men who would share your food and knife you in the back, but
not Indians.

He dug out bread and salt and brown sugar, dried beef and chile for
a quick stew, above all coffee. Almost all Indians had learned to love
coffee. He brewed a big pot, making it strong, and he cooked enough
meat and chile for six white men. These bucks probably hadn't eaten since
yesterday. Like all primitive men, they could go days without eating and
eat enough at a sitting to last for days. They ate now swiftly and skillfully, licking their fingers clean. They did not talk. For the time being
they lived in their bellies. Afterward Jean produced tobacco and corn-
husk wrappers and they all smoked. Then the leader rose, pointing to the

sun, and they helped him pack. Jean asked only: "Is Kenyatch there?" and the leader nodded. He led the way, Jean following, and the other two behind him. In single file they went up and up, by a route only an Indian could have followed, dropped into the upper canyon of a tributary to the Dark River, followed it clear above timber line. When they topped a low rise, Jean saw the camp in the distance. It was the prettiest Indian camp he had seen in years. There were only a dozen tepees, which meant not more than fifty or sixty Indians—all that was left of the Moaches. The camp was on the far side of a small lake at the foot of a rocky peak, the tepees mirrored in the still blue water, fat horses grazing on the rich upland pasture, brown children playing beside the lake, women working over hides pegged out on the grass. There was no sign of the dirt and rags, the general squalor, that invade an Indian camp so soon when it is near to white men.

The leader shouted and every Indian in sight lifted and turned his head but there was no evidence of surprise. When he dismounted, Kenyatch came forward, holding out his hand in grave welcome.

"You have come to trade?" he inquired.

"No," Jean replied, "I have come bringing gifts and I have come to talk. I have much to tell you."

Kenyatch nodded.

"Will you eat first?" he asked.

"I am not hungry," Jean replied.

Kenyatch led the way to a spot in front of one of the tepees, probably his own. He shouted an order and women came and spread tanned buckskins and a Navajo blanket on the ground. A dozen other men gathered, including three very old, toothless men. All of them greeted him and all sat down. Most of these, he knew, he had seen before. He knew also that these old men would have much to say, not to him, but in private council, for the Utes have great respect for the aged. But he felt more than ever sure that Kenyatch was the top man and this encouraged him. He knew too that he could speak to Kenyatch in Spanish, which most of the others would not understand. Afterward there would be a tribal council. If he could persuade Kenyatch, the young chief might have power enough to persuade the others.

He began quietly, feeling his way, by reminding Kenyatch of his visits to the Moache camp on the other side of the Rio Grande, of those good summers on the great pine-covered mesas, of an elk hunt they had taken together, and a great feast they prepared. Kenyatch nodded, his face curiously sad, like that of a wistful child.

"Those camps and that life are all gone now," he said. "Everything moves on and is lost. Nothing is left of those days now but my words and yours."

"Everything is change," Jean agreed. "And now change is quick. Down there, beyond the foot of the mountains, is the great road·from the east.

I have been working on it. A few years ago the wagons came in tens. Now they come in hundreds, bringing men who want to stay—farmers and miners and men driving cattle. Go where you will, men are coming, men by the thousand."

"That is why we have come here to the high mountains," Kenyatch said. "The mountains have always belonged to the Utes. We have always been able to live where others would starve or die in the snow. Here we hope to be left alone."

"You will not be left alone," Jean told him. "Men will come even to the high peaks looking for gold. They will drive cattle and sheep into the valleys and cut down the timber on the mesas. There will be fires and the game will be driven out. You have seen it happen before. Unless someone can stop them, it will happen again."

Kenyatch nodded, his face unmoving, except that his mouth set in a hard line.

"Perhaps we can stop them," he said. "We are not afraid to fight."

"You are brave men," Jean agreed. "But you cannot stop them. Where have the Indians ever stopped the Americans? They have stopped the Mexicans, yes, but never the men from the east. The great road down there is like a river. It cannot stop and nothing can stop it."

Kenyatch looked like a man listening to the word of doom.

"What you say is true," he admitted. "We are a lost people. We are not many, like the Navajos and the Apaches, and we do not live behind deserts where white men are afraid to go. The earth is good and it is large, and yet there seems to be no room for us. We are caught here between the valley on one side and the great road on the other. Where can we go? What can save us?"

Kenyatch was truly thinking aloud now, carried away by his own feelings. Jean was quick to seize his opportunity.

"I can save you," he said quietly. "I have come to save you. All this country of the Dark River, from the peaks down to the plains and on both sides of the water, belongs to my father-in-law, Don Tranquilino Coronel. It is a grant to him from the king of Spain. He has sent me to take possession."

Having lived among Mexicans, and being a smart Indian, Kenyatch knew about grants and even about the king of Spain and how he bestowed lands upon his subjects, but like all Indians he found this business of owning the earth a little hard to understand.

"How does your father-in-law own it?" he demanded. "He could not come here and stay alive as we can. No Mexican would dare to come here. The Mexicans all are women. It takes a man to live in the mountains."

Jean had known this would be the sticking point in the argument, and he was prepared for it.

"You are right," he said. "The mountains belong to the Utes because they have always lived in the mountains. I do not want to take the mountains away from you. I want only to build a home in the valley, to pasture cattle on the plains. Because I can claim all of this land I can keep other white men out. I can stand between you and them. I can say to you, here is your hunting ground and it shall be yours always. When the Arapahoe come up from the plains, we will fight them together. When the deep snows fall in the winter, my beef will be yours. I offer you my friendship and I ask for yours. This is my word and you know my word is good."

Kenyatch sat silent for a long moment. His face was more than grave, it was sad. Jean knew well enough what the Indian was thinking. He knew the Utes did not want any white man to enter their country. They wanted only to be left alone. But he knew also that his argument was unanswerable. They would not be left alone. And they knew he would keep his word. That was his whole strength. They distrusted and feared the world of white men, but they trusted him.

Kenyatch rose and held out his hand, indicating that the conference was over.

"We will talk tonight," he said, with a gesture toward the others. "We will give you our word in the morning."

He then led Jean to a small tepee which had been prepared for him, and left him with a grave good night. A little later a woman came bringing an earthen pot filled with a steaming stew of venison and wild turkey. Jean ate largely and stretched out on his blankets, pillowing his head on his pack, puffing his pipe, feeling completely at ease for the first time since he had crossed the crest of the mountains. Although nothing was decided yet, he felt sure that he had won.

It was only half a personal triumph and he was aware of this. Kenyatch belonged to a dying world; he could hope for nothing but mercy. Jean Ballard belonged to a growing one, young, lusty and ruthless. He was strong because of what stood behind him, filled with the hope and power of those who ride on the wave of change. He was a man who belonged to the moment and the moment belonged to him.

In the morning the matter was quickly concluded, as Jean had felt sure it would be. Kenyatch assembled his little council again and once more Jean stood before it.

"We have talked," Kenyatch said, "and this is our word. If you build a house in the valley, we will be your friends. In return we ask only that you will let no one else settle on the lands you claim, that you will let no other traders come to us, and that you will sell no whisky to our young men. As for food, we will bring you gifts when we have plenty and you may give us what you will."

Jean held out his hand.

"You have spoken well," he said, "and you have my word for all you ask."

Then he turned to his pack and brought out a good rifle, powder and lead, which he presented to Kenyatch. For the others there were knives, beads and iron pots and skillets. Kenyatch gave him in return a beautifully tanned prime buffalo robe. Afterwards, young Indians brought his horses, helped him saddle and pack, and he rode away toward the rising sun.

He rode wholly relaxed now; suspense and struggle were over. It had been easy after all, once the Indians were found. Now he knew they were just a part of his responsibilities, as much so as the cattle he would bring into the valley. They would cost him a certain number of fat beefs every year, they would become more and more dependent upon him, but they would also be his watch dogs—against the Arapahoe, against all invaders.

In the wake of easy triumph came a moment of unwonted depression. For over a year now, everything had come his way, everything had yielded to his touch and his voice. Life had suddenly widened before him. Something in him distrusted all this bounty of fortune. He was a hard-bitten man and knew that life is hard. He felt safest when he saw danger and felt resistance. He knew they were always there.

Once more he rode down into the valley of the Dark River, past the place where he had met the Indians and on down into the wide meadows that lay below. Here his spirits rose again. It was the first time he had looked upon this country in five years and he saw now that it was even better than he had remembered. He had long been a wandering man without house or woman, but he came of a race of men who owned the earth, and he knew its value. He saw now a thousand acres that could be plowed and planted, more than he had thought. He saw how the straight, clean boles of the pine forest marched down a gentle slope to the edge of the valley, and how the flat lands farther down were tinged with the purple of ripe grama grass, the richest forage in the world. Where the stream reached the level prairie there were a few acres of high flat ground fifty feet or so above it. It was a place that might have been designed for the site of a house—as great a house as man might wish to build.

He rode to the top of the little plateau, reined in his horse and feasted his eyes upon potential dominion. His eager imagination fenced and planted and builded. This bit of the earth would become whatever he could make it, and here would be no law except his word. He felt again the same thrill of wonder and desire he had known when first he looked over the valley from the crest of the mountains. For what had fallen into his hands was not merely a place to live and cultivate. It was the vital heart of a whole region, a place where men would gather as surely as he made it safe, a place to be ruled as well as owned, a means to power as surely as he had power in him. By chance almost beyond belief a king in Spain had granted him a kingdom.

PART TWO

THE AUTOCRAT

THE RECOLLECTIONS OF
JAMES LANE MORGAN

A traveler by stagecoach over the Old Santa Fe Trail in the seventies first saw the Ballard establishment from the crest of a rolling ridge which bounded the Dark River Valley on the north. I think nearly everyone must have seen it, as I did, with a surprise that was almost incredulity. For seven days and nights I had been bumping across a prairie wilderness, jammed into a coach with six other tortured human beings, over a road which was not a road at all but only a terrible scar on the face of the earth, still hub-deep in mud this month of May, with wrecked vehicles rotting beside the wheel tracks and dead mules bloating in the mudholes, with stagecoaches, freight wagons, buckboards and carts fighting their way westward to a chorus of curses, shouts and whips cracking over the sweat-streaked backs of straining animals. Every twenty to fifty miles horses were changed at a station where passengers were given twenty minutes to gobble hardtack and salt pork drowned in its own grease, and to drink coffee black as tar and bitter as defeat. The land we crossed, especially the eastern part of it, looked rich and ripe for the plow, but no one stopped to claim it or cultivate it. In the whole prairie country no one had built anything that was meant to last. The stage stations were shacks or dugouts, just as the track-end towns were literally built in a week and deserted in a year. The impression, especially to one who had known the rather placid beauty of nineteenth century Europe, was that of enormous energy and vitality, but also of a kind of collective insanity. Everyone was rushing frantically somewhere—to Colorado or California or Santa Fe —in search of gold or a quick profit, cursing every delay, sparing neither man nor beast, fighting the very earth as a prostrate but unyielding enemy. No one seemed ever to relax or rest. Life roared, rattled and cursed by day and exploded into drunken laughter and the crash of gunfire at night. Only the prairie, where it rolled away from the road in green billows of waving grass, and the blue mountains that looked over the horizon, seemed to have anything of dignity or permanence.

Then suddenly half a mile away I saw a great house topping a low hill beside a stream—a house large enough to be called a castle, with heavy earthen walls, steep shingled roofs and dormer windows, giving it a resemblance, which many had remarked, to some of the chateaux of northern France. A grove of graceful mountain cottonwoods spread their shade around it and over its walls. Hollyhocks were pink and white behind the picket fence of its dooryard and a plume of blue wood smoke wavered away from its great kitchen chimney. At the foot of the hill many other buildings, mostly of adobe, were strung out along a road that paralleled the stream. The valley both above and below the village was green with well-sprung crops of oats and hay, and riven by the clear, quick stream, flashing among the willows. To the east the mountains lifted heavily wooded shoulders to sheer faces of rock and finally to peaks still tipped and streaked with snow. The place owed its beauty chiefly to the splendid roll and lift and color of the country, but what made it so surprising, gave it somewhat the quality of a dream or a vision at a first and distant look, was simply that someone here had stopped and built and planted, had imagined something and brought it into being, had peopled the wilderness without destroying it.

— 2 —

My own presence at the Ballard grant that day is soon explained.

A New Yorker by birth, I had been educated for the law at Harvard and had afterward spent more than a year in England and on the Continent, indulging a taste for history, which has always rivaled the law in my own interest. My father was a prosperous commission merchant, and when I returned to New York I entered his office as a legal adviser, expecting to spend the rest of my life there. A bad case of pneumonia developed into tuberculosis and brought my business career to a sudden end. I made a partial recovery but my physician assured me the dry air of the Southwest was my only hope of a complete cure. I was determined not to be idle, and my father's business connections in Kansas City enabled him to find me a place of a sort. It was learned that Jean Ballard, the owner of a large and heavily encumbered property in northern New Mexico, required the services of a resident lawyer. After some correspondence, it was agreed that I should visit the Ballard establishment as a guest with the hope that some lasting arrangement might be made.

In that spring of 1878, Ballard had been established in his great house beside the Santa Fe Trail for nearly twenty years. I knew a good deal about his business affairs from my own investigations in Kansas City, but nothing about those years of struggle and success and even less about the strange community they had created. The chief purpose of this memoir is to describe the Ballard kingdom—for it was no less than that—and to bring out its history much as I discovered it, so that the community and its making may be seen as one. Before I left the grant I felt that I understood both Ballard's triumph and his tragedy, and that understanding is what I hope to communicate here.

— 3 —

I was the only passenger who left the stage at the Ballard grant that day. No one appeared to meet me or took any notice of me, although I was aware of a hum and bustle of human activity, of talking and singing voices somewhere in the great house, of moving figures down among the minor buildings, of the distant thud of an ax, the beat of hoofs, the bleat and bellow of livestock. But I was much more aware at first of the painful state of my own anatomy. I stood there before the long front porch kicking the kinks out of my knees, stretching my arms, feeling my ribs, filling my lungs with air. A man released from the stocks or from a strait jacket would not have felt a greater or more needed relief. Then I heard a laugh and looked up and saw a man sitting alone on the porch, with his chair tilted back, his feet on the railing and a cigar between his fingers.

"It's a rough ride," he remarked as he rose and came to meet me, holding out his hand. "You must be Morgan. I'm Ballard."

I had been warned that Ballard was a sick man, afflicted with the stone, and that when his pains were upon him he was sometimes a bit explosive. But there was nothing about Ballard's appearance or manner to suggest that he was either sick or troubled. I saw a heavy, powerful-looking man of middle height, a little too thick in the middle but limber and well carried, wearing a red woolen shirt, blue trousers and fine cowboy half-boots. His face was ruddy, his eyes dark blue, his black hair thick, curly and tipped with silver. His shirt was open at the neck to show a hairy chest which was also brightly grizzled. The effect was one of striking color and vitality, of slow-moving, soft-spoken confidence and power. I have observed that some unusual men take on a protective look of insignificance, but not so Ballard. There was nothing pretentious about him but he looked like a ruler, stood out in any group and commanded attention without trying.

"Your room will be ready in an hour or so," he said as we sat down on the porch and he offered me a cigar. He was almost never seen without one, and they were the finest of Havanas. A Mexican boy of about sixteen appeared when he clapped his hands, took an order in Spanish and brought a bottle of imported cognac and glasses on a heavy hand-hammered silver tray. Ballard proposed my health with great courtesy and took his own liquor at a gulp instead of savoring it as a good brandy deserves.

The hour stretched into nearly two as we chatted casually while shadows mantled the mountains and lengthened under the trees. I was afterwards aware that Ballard had questioned me about a good many things—the condition of the road, the amount of traffic on it, business in the East—and I suspect that he was sizing me up in his own way, but at the time it all seemed easy, pleasant talk. He asked me nothing about myself, told me nothing about his own affairs and never mentioned the business that had brought me to his door. Nothing was accomplished, from my point of view, except that I became aware of a certain spontaneous sympathy between us. Ballard and I had nothing much in common, except that both of us had felt the stab of mortal illness, but I nevertheless felt sure that he and I would get along and that whether I could serve his purpose or not, he was glad of my presence. As I sat there looking at the mountains through the smoke of a good cigar, I felt curiously and unexpectedly at home.

When the boy came to lead me to my quarters, I asked Ballard rather bluntly what he wanted me to do.

"Look around," he said, waving his cigar in a wide inclusive gesture. "Take your time. Can you ride?"

I told him I could ride well enough to get over the ground.

"Go down to the corral in the morning and pick out a horse. There's a blue buckskin mare I think you'll like. She's a single-footer, easy as a rocking chair. But pick out any horse you like. Ride around. It'll take you a while to know this place. I told Joe Ankers down at the store to answer any questions you want to ask. Come and see me whenever you get ready."

For a man presumably threatened by death and bankruptcy, Ballard certainly showed a magnificent unconcern.

— 4 —

I had come west in the belief that I was rather well-informed about Ballard and his affairs. I had been told that he owned a large ranch, deriving its title from a royal Spanish grant, on which he raised both cattle and sheep. I knew he had made a great deal of money just before and during the Civil War and it was easy to understand how this had happened. The discovery of gold in California had created a huge market at high prices. Ballard had sent herds and flocks all the way across the desert, and had sold stock to others who made the long drive. Then the war had created a great government demand for beef, at Fort Union, at Fort Marcey in Santa Fe and for the newly created Indian agencies, where several thousand retired braves were eating government rations. For a decade money had poured in upon Ballard in fabulous sums, and he had evidently regarded it as a perennial flow, for he had spent it all and a great deal more. He had gone heavily in debt to wholesalers in St. Louis and Dodge City, and had borrowed from several banks when cash began to be scarce. As a merchant he had extended an unlimited credit and as a host he offered the most complete and indiscriminate hospitality I ever saw. Anyone, Mexican, white or Indian, could eat at the Ballard table, or at one of the many Ballard tables, so long as he behaved himself.

Then had come the panic of seventy-three. Prices of everything fell, and especailly the prices of beef and wool. Cattle were not worth what it cost to drive them to market. Ballard's potential assets were enormous, but all of his creditors were pressing him for cash, and cash was the only thing he lacked. The whole country was in much the same situation. It was rich in resource and running over with food, but nearly everyone was poor because money was scarce. And money was a terrible weapon in the hands of those who had it.

All of this information I had obtained from businessmen in St. Louis, and it was correct as far as it went, but it failed-completely to take account of the actual character of the Ballard dominion. For Ballard had established not merely a property but a society, small but complete and organic. He was in fact the absolute ruler of a minor kingdom, strictly feudal in its social structure. For nearly twenty years it had grown slowly, as independent and self-sufficient as any principality in Europe. Ballard had not planned it, yet it was wholly a creation of his power and personality. When society is unorganized, personal allegiance always takes the place of law, and the force of individual personality is the only thing that can hold men together and create order. Ballard had established safety and a source of supply in a wilderness, and men had gathered about him. His dominion had grown out of the frontier chaos just as the walled towns of Europe grew out of the Dark Ages. As an example of the way social forms spring from conditions it was a fascinating study, but as a business problem I think it would have given any lawyer a headache. The farther I pursued my investigations, the more bewildered I became. Here I am trying to describe the Ballard dominion as I see it in retrospect, rather than to tell the long story of my own inquiries.

— 5 —

As nearly as I could estimate, about fifteen hundred human beings, Mexican, white and Indian, lived on and about the Ballard grant. At any one time about a third of them were Ballard's employees, but all of these and all of the others were permanently in debt to him. They were at once completely dependent upon him and completely at his mercy. Certainly it had been a mercy liberal to a fault. No one had ever gone hungry in the Ballard dominion, whether he worked or not. Ballard had been completely tolerant of almost everything except violence and theft. The penalty for these crimes was simple and primitive: it was expulsion from the kingdom. If a man misbehaved once he might get a warning. If he repeated the offense, he disappeared between dark and daylight. There was no legal apparatus whatsoever and none had ever been needed. So far as felonies and misdemeanors were concerned, Ballard had established something like Utopia. No doors were locked and nothing was guarded, but neither was anything ever stolen, except that children of three races were always pilfering food from the kitchen.

The most famous symbol of Ballard's achievement as a ruler was the cash drawer in his combined office and council chamber. It was the bottom drawer in a huge chest of drawers and was known to every traveler who passed that way, for many of them had seen Ballard dip into it for a handful of cash whenever he needed it. This unlocked drawer was said to contain seldom less than ten or fifteen dollars in bills and silver, but it was just as safe as any vault.

Much more impressive, in my opinion, was Ballard's way of handling dangerous characters, for it must be remembered that almost every man then wore some kind of weapon, and that the frontier produced a class of professional fighting men, jealous of their reputations. All the mining camps and track-end towns were plagued by them. Some six-shooter artist would periodically ride into town, announce that he was the boss and issue a challenge to all comers, including the officers of the law. He seldom lasted long, but he always burned gunpowder and shed blood. A good many of these difficult gentlemen had passed through the Ballard grant and some of them had tried to stay. They were of course easily identified, and each of them presently met Ballard in a seemingly casual way. Ballard never wore a weapon and there were never any witnesses to these meetings who were near enough to hear what was said. It was known only that Ballard stood very close to his man and talked to him in a low voice. Most of these trouble-makers were gone next day, but a few stayed and became good cowboys.

Despite the fact that his manner was easy and genial most of the time, Ballard's voice and presence carried an irresistible authority. Men were afraid of him and of his power, as they had reason to be, but no one could say that he ruled by fear. His power rested firmly upon the fact that he had established peace and security in a world where both were rare.

The farther I pursued my inquiries the more I was impressed by Ballard's instinctive gift and power as a leader and organizer and by the way his personal influence permeated the whole of his dominion, making it truly something created in his own image, but I was also appalled by his shortcomings as a businessman. In this respect he certainly belonged to the past and not to the future. From the standpoint of a lawyer the most disconcerting fact was that Ballard did not know what he owned. I had studied the ancient Spanish document from which his title derived, and it was incredibly vague, bounding his lands by peaks and canyons which were often hard to identify. All of these royal grants had been confirmed by the treaty of Guadalupe Hidalgo between the United States and Mexico.

A surveyor-general had been appointed by the president, and the owners of any grant could procure a survey and a clear title by demanding it. Ballard as sole owner might have had his lands surveyed at any time, and it seemed to me at first almost incredible that he had not done so. No lawyer would have overlooked the fact there were dangerous possibilities of corruption in such a survey, especially since the surveyors were paid by the mile for running the lines. It seemed to me that Ballard might have claimed almost anything, up to a couple of thousand square miles, but the worst of the situation was the obvious temptations it presented to anyone who might see an opportunity to force him out.

It was clear enough from his papers that Ballard owned the arable part of the Dark River Valley and the watersheds on either side, but what the grant included beyond that was somewhat a question of opinion and still more an opportunity for fraud. For there was only one other bit of land in the whole region to which any other had had clear title. This was a small "community grant" a few miles north of the Dark River. Community grants had been made by the Spanish Crown to groups of poor Mexicans who farmed small individual allotments and held in common fifteen or twenty square miles of grazing land. This one was evidently designed to give the owners of the great estate an assured labor supply, and so it had worked for Ballard. After he had made life safe from the Indians on that side of the mountains, a typical Mexican village had been built on the community lands wtih its tiny plaza, its flat adobe houses clustered about a church which saw a circuit-riding priest perhaps twice a year, and its Morada on a near-by hilltop—a sinister, windowless adobe block, with a great cross planted before it, where the Penitentes Hermanos, the flagellant religious sect of the common people, held its bloody rites. Every Good Friday a procession of half-naked men marched out of the Morada, their backs ripped with flint, bloody to the heels, whipping each other across the snowy mountains in bleak spring weather to the scream of a primitive flute and the rumble of their own chanting.

Most of the few hundred inhabitants of this primitive village with its goat herds and chile patches belonged to a single great family named Royball, and it was ruled by an old man, Anastasio Royball, who held the office of village Alcalde and was also Hermano Mayor or chief of the Penitentes. Anastasio was an absolute ruler in his own little kingdom, no less so than Ballard, and a good deal more deadly, for the Penitentes had a way of disposing of all rebels and dissidents, quietly and finally.

The family and state of Royball supplied Ballard with all of his sheep herders and they were experts, with Anastasio as Mayodomo. In return the whole village got its supplies at his store and all of its inhabitants were always in debt to him—a type of relationship to which their kind had been accustomed for centuries. Plaza Royball contained a good many Mexicans who were handy with a knife and some who lived there because their reputations on the other side of the mountains were not good, but Bal-

lard's sheep were a sacred trust to them. On the morning after Good
Friday, when Royball-town was full of sore backs, Ballard always sent
Anastasio a gallon of horse liniment and a gallon of whisky, which went
far both to ease the pains of the mortified flesh and to sustain the feudal
spirit. Moreover, all of these people had an almost religious devotion to
Ballard's wife, who was a powerful but inconspicuous influence in his kingdom. She, more than Ballard, was to the Mexicans the symbol and representative of the ancient aristocracy which had always ruled them. It was
to her their women went when children were sick and every baby born
in the village got a present from La Patrona. When she went among them,
they stood with heads uncovered, just as they did when the priest came
to town.

This was the traditional part of the Ballard kingdom, which he had
taken over from the Spanish background, with all of its conventions and
relationships resting upon ancient use and wont. But it was only half of
his dominion and his problem. The Meixcans handled his fifty thousand
sheep, but his cattle herds, numbering at least ten thousand head, and his
thousand or more of horses were in charge of hard-riding, gun-toting
Americans, mostly from Texas. It was an impressive part of Ballard's
achievement that he had kept peace between these men of two races who
then had a traditional enmity, going clear back to the fall of the Alamo.
A Texas cattleman was of a human species as definite and true to type as
an English bulldog or a thoroughbred horse. All of them talked with the
same twang, wore their guns low on their hips and customarily referred
to Mexicans as greasers or yellow bellies. But this prejudice they had to lay
aside when they entered the Ballard dominion. His Mexican village and
the handful of Ute Indians who lived up the canyon were his special pets.
He stood between them and the whole world.

The Texans constituted no such definite and established society as the
Mexicans did. Just as the Mexicans instinctively huddled together and
built a town, so the cattlemen seemed to want to get as far apart as they
could. Fiercely self-sufficient men, they wanted room and isolation and no
intruders. They had drifted into the country, one by one, somewhat mysteriously, after Ballard had made it safe. Wherever permanent water
sprang and good grass grew within twenty or thirty miles of the Ballard
store, some lank horseman had built a little house of adobe, or of logs if
he was near enough to timber, and a circular pole corral with a snubbing
post in its center. Usually he came driving a small herd of cattle and it
would have been the worst of bad manners to inquire where he got them.
Maybe he had picked up cripples and strays in the wake of the great
drives from Texas to the railheads at Dodge City and Abilene. Maybe
he had roped and branded wild longhorns in the brush country along the
lower Rio Grande. Maybe he was just lucky at finding mavericks wherever
he went. A man who was good with a rope and a running iron could
always get a start in life in those days. Some of these men bunked alone

but usually if you rode to the door of one of the ranch houses a slim blonde woman would appear, with two or three tow-headed kids peering from behind her skirts, and tell you her man would be home about sundown.

All of these ranchers, in their own opinion, were squatters or homesteaders on the public domain, although I think few of them had filed any papers. None of them was located in the Dark River watershed and that was all Ballard apparently claimed as his own. Moreover, he had welcomed these men, for he wanted to people the country. He had given all of them credit at his store and taken their fat steers in trade. They almost all worked for him more or less, on his roundups, with his trail drives to market, as broncobusters and horse wranglers. He knew them for what they were—rustlers and gunmen, more than one of whom had killed a man in the cowtown brawls. He did not trust them, but he knew he could depend upon them because they had to depend upon him. His cattle herds were among the safest in the West, not only because these men respected his brand but because they would have made short work of anyone who did not. The only thing a good rustler feared was another good rustler.

Ballard was not exactly a cynic. He was too good-humored and tolerant to fit the word. But he certainly did not rely upon the higher nature of man. He would hire a known horse thief if one came to his door. A good horse thief often had a special gift for handling horses, and if he needed a little watching, how many men did not? Ballard never asked a man any questions, never intruded on his private life and never offered any charity. He practiced only one form of benevolence and that was toward children. If a man brought his wife and kids to town, the kids were always fed while their mothers shopped. Ballard would not tolerate a bawling brat. He would always send someone to put something in its mouth, usually a long red and white stick of candy. I think Ballard truly liked children but he also knew that the hardest man on earth is apt to be soft about his offspring.

— 6 —

All my investigations of the Ballard dominion led me to the heart of it, the place where everyone else came, the thing which held it together—and that was the store. Although he now seldom entered his store himself, Ballard was a major merchant, and trade was the lifeblood of his dominion. For many years he had freighted all his own goods over the Santa Fe Trail in his own wagons. Now most of it came by established freight lines, but his store was still the only considerable point of supply between Santa Fe and the Raton Pass. To me it was the most fascinating part of his establishment. I was something of a merchant myself, my father was a trader, my grandfather had run a country store in upstate New York.

Merchandise was in my blood. I loved the smell of a store, the palaver of sales talk, the clink of money, the mingling of men brought together by their shared necessities. The give and take of trade has been the making of nations, and here I saw it in a patriarchal and elemental form.

The store building was a long low adobe with iron-barred windows, a high-walled wagon yard at one side, a hitch rack in front where ponies dozed on three legs, a front porch with benches where cowboys rested their spurs on the railing, Mexicans puffed tiny brown cigarettes, Indians sat wrapped in blankets and in the long immobility of primitive men to whom time is nothing. Within, the store smelled richly of coffee, tobacco and whisky, of hides, pelts, leather and dry goods, and of the mixed human throng that poured through its door. On Saturday afternoons and nights it was crowded and kept eight or ten clerks hopping. All of these were Mexicans who spoke fair English, a little Ute and enough sign language for business purposes. They made much better clerks than Americans, who generally lacked patience, politeness and the gift of tongues.

At the far end of the store was a small office where, for twelve hours a day, Joseph Ankers, the genius of the place, bent over his great ledgers and conferred with his clerks, seldom appearing in the store himself except when some large deal was in the making. Ankers was a tall, lean, pink old man, with thin white hair and thick white whiskers, with fine ascetic features and a great dignity. He was in his early sixties but looked older. A man of small education who spoke a strictly American English, he was nevertheless a good businessman and a good bookkeeper. He had been in Ballard's employ for fifteen years and was one of perhaps three men Ballard undoubtedly trusted.

The store was as much Ankers' creation as Ballard's, and its stock was truly a creation—a thing perfected through years by trial and error, a major feat in memory and judgment. Its items were numbered in thousands, for Ankers had to supply all the needs of a whole community, anything a man might want from a dose of quinine to a shotgun or a plow, and he had to buy in a market eight hundred miles away. Moreover, only a small part of his business was done for cash. He had to receive everything the region produced and credit it against his sales. Only deals for livestock on the hoof were made by Ballard. Everything else was appraised and credited by Ankers. He was a man of high professional pride and almost painful conscience. He could make a rather large profit without compunction, but it gave him genuine pain to be unable to supply any human need or to refuse any article in trade that might conceivably be negotiable. Mostly he took in hides and furs, beans and chile, but many exotic items claimed his attention first and last. He had to weigh gold nuggets and estimate the value of turquoise. He once turned a handsome profit on three Apache scalps, which finally reached a museum in Europe. One of his most embarrassing deals was for two live bear cubs, which grew to weigh a hundred pounds each and occupied a pen in the wagon yard for more than a year before they went east in a crate and fulfilled their commercial destiny under a circus tent.

Ankers welcomed me as a fellow merchant and one who knew something of accounts, which few did in the West of that day. From his books and his talk I finally gained a clear picture of the Ballard dilemma, even though I never quite reduced it to a balance sheet. Ballard in effect had a mortgage on everything in his dominion. By simply demanding payment of the debts on his books he could have taken every ranch and waterhole and every head of stock within fifty miles. It was easy to understand that he would be reluctant to do so, but such a drastic measure would not have solved his problem in any case. There was not enough cash market for anything. He was not fairly a bankrupt but any concerted action on the part of his creditors could force him to sell his holdings, drive him out of his kingdom.

How could Ballard and his dominion be saved? That was my problem and it was a bewildering one. It seemed hopeless to raise a loan, both because Ballard's credit was already strained and because a mortgage on his holdings would be a danger. I could see only one way to keep him solvent and in power. That was to procure a survey of his holdings, incorporate the grant, cut up the rich lands of the valley into small allotments and put them on the market. With settlers pouring west and a railroad building, I believed the lands could be sold fast enough to carry the debt and would ultimately pay it.

At first the scheme made no great appeal to me, nor did I feel sure that Ballard would accept it, but when I began to explore its possibilities, it grew upon me strongly. I remember well that one morning I climbed a high hill south of the river, from which I could survey the whole of the valley and its surrounding lands, spread before me like a great map. I may truly say that on a hilltop I saw a vision and came down an inspired man. For it struck me suddenly that the potentialities of the Dark River itself had never been exploited or even considered. At the head of the valley was a perfect natural site, where a dam would create a deep lake of several square miles, impounding flood waters that now were lost in the sands. A great area east of the valley could then be irrigated, one much larger than the valley itself. Moreover, the dam would furnish water power more than enough for a flour mill and for a sawmill with several hundred square miles of virgin pine timber at its door.

It must be remembered that I was young and that this was a day of dreams and schemes, when the unused and unconquered earth challenged the imagination. I found it easy to picture a city in the valley and the plains plowed and planted all the way to the eastern horizon. The railroad would reach the settlement in three or four years. No one knew its exact route but it could not possibly ignore a growing town. Land values would rise steadily as it approached. There would be a boom in town lots as well as in farm lands. The place would rival Denver, might well replace it as the metropolis of the Rocky Mountains.

Briefly I tasted the ecstasy of vision, the lust to create and transform. I could imagine how Ballard must have felt when first he looked upon the Dark River country as a savage wilderness and resolved that he would claim it for civilization. He had seen a vision and had made it real. He had been a great pioneer. In this new development he would become, of course, something of a figurehead. His authority over his people would be of the greatest value, but the actual administration would require one who was both a lawyer and a businessman.

The longing for power is strong in us all. I truly wanted to serve Ballard, to keep his dominion intact, but I could not escape the conviction that my own destiny had suddenly been revealed to me. I knew that Ballard trusted me and that he trusted few. I knew that his day was nearly over. How right and inevitable it all seemed! Ballard had taken the first step. He had created a walled town—walled by the wilderness, depending upon its isolation for its integrity. The wall had been breached, the turbulent vanguard of civilization was pouring in. Someone must meet it and deal with it. Someone must preserve the order he had created, extend his conquest, master the new forces of money and machinery which were transforming the whole world. . . . I felt suddenly full of energy, as though new life had been poured into me. As I went down from the hill, my heart was pounding, partly from exertion but mostly from excitement.

I felt bound to lay my plan before Joseph Ankers first, since he was my only appointed consultant. I expounded it to him at length, and I believe with some eloquence. In fact, I was surprised at my own flow of words. I built an imaginary city for the old man, who sat patiently puffing and tamping his pipe until I had done. Then he spoke shortly.

"I don't believe he'll do it," he said.

"But why not?" I demanded. "It's the only way."

"The Utes, for one thing," Ankers said. "When Ballard moved in here he made an agreement with them that he wouldn't let anyone else settle in the valley. Of course, if he lives long enough, he'll finally have to sell the grant as a whole, and then the crowd will come. But he's never sold a separate acre and I don't believe he ever will—not while the Utes are here."

"But the Utes!" I expostulated. "They're just a handful of beggars, good for nothing. They'll end up on a reservation somewhere anyway. . . ."

"Yep," Ankers agreed with his invariable sweetness. "You can't save the Indians and they ain't worth a damn now. But they was good men once and he ain't forgot it. When he first come here, before he built the big house, the Arapahoe from down on the plains took a crack at him.

They wanted to wipe him out before he got any stronger. About fifty warriors charged down out of the timber one morning just after dawn. Ballard had only his wife and about six Mexicans on the place. The Indians killed a couple of his men and drove the rest into the little adobe house where he lived, all but one Mexican boy that took to the brush and sneaked up the canyon to where Kenyatch and his Utes was camped. The Arapahoe thought they had Ballard dead to rights. He and his men had three rifles and they killed a few Indians, shooting through the windows. They say the Doña loaded guns for the men and knocked an Indian off his horse with a shotgun. But they couldn't get out and they couldn't get water. It looked like just a matter of time. Then, along about sunset, Kenyatch and his braves came tearing down the canyon, yipping like a pack of coyotes, all riding bareback, in a dead run, stripped to their breechclouts with their faces painted black. They had rifles Ballard had given them and a few old horse pistols. They went through the Arapahoes like a dose of salts through a mule, shooting under their horses' necks. Then they split into two bunches, tore up onto the high ground, on both sides of the river, piled off their horses and poured in the lead. The Arapahoe had Utes all around them and Ballard and his men in the middle. It didn't last long. Only about half the Arapahoe got out of there alive and they never tried it again."

Ankers paused to light his pipe.

"An army officer told me the Utes was the best light cavalry he ever seen," he went on. "They maneuvered like a flock of ducks on the wing and they could shoot off the back of a running horse the way only buffalo hunters can. . . . Like you say, they ain't worth a damn now. They got nothing to do but eat government beef and beg whisky. A man with nothing to do ain't no man at all."

Ankers' little story left me silent for minutes. It seemed to recreate a lost world, doubtless the one where Ballard's memories lived, where his obligations were rooted. I understood a little better about the Utes, but I still did not see how they could stand in the way of necessary change.

"Anyhow," I said, a little weakly, "I've got to put it up to him. There's no other way."

"Yep," Ankers agreed. "I reckon you've got to put it up to him."

My enthusiasm had been temporarily depressed but it rapidly recovered. A man loves nothing so much as his own idea and I became more and more infatuated with mine. I even worked out a scheme for giving the Utes an allotment of the farmland I proposed to create, teaching them to plow and plant, making them over into good hustling Americans. I began to see myself as a benefactor of all concerned. I could hardly wait to lay my plan before Ballard. I knew I faced difficulties, but I felt the logic of the situation was irresistible. The historical process was on my side. "Manifest destiny" had been a political catchword of the years since the war with Mexico. It seemed to me the manifest destiny of the Dark River Valley to become an expanding center of civilization, and I felt that I had a fateful part to play in the sweep of change.

— 7 —

It was easy enough to see Ballard but not at all easy to talk business with him. I knew that by common report. A good many men had found a business interview with Ballard almost as hard to arrange as an audience with the Pope. Controlling vast resources as he did, and sitting on the main line of travel, Ballard had long been the object of a great many plans and solicitations. Men came to the Ballard grant with all sorts of projects to lay before him. All of them were welcomed, fed and housed, some of them hung around for weeks, but few of them ever saw Ballard alone.

During the period of his great expansion Ballard had traveled widely and spent much time in the saddle, but at this stage of his life he lived by a simple routine. His mornings were spent in his office, transacting such business as he considered necessary. He took his midday meal alone and always followed it with a siesta. In this as in other respects, he lived like a Mexican gentleman of the old regime. About four in the afternoon, in warm weather, he almost always appeared on the front porch and sat there, with his cigar in his mouth and his feet on the railing for a couple of hours. If he did not appear it meant he was ill. No one ever saw Ballard when he was ill unless his pains struck him suddenly. He had never been known even to admit that he was an ailing man, and I think few knew he was.

Anyone could join Ballard on the front porch and he received all comers with the same good-humored courtesy. On quiet days sometimes Kenyatch, the old Ute chief, would come and sit with him for an hour. Kenyatch was a ridiculous figure, addicted to begging drinks and afflicted with a passion for wearing white men's clothes. Sometimes he would appear in an old army coat with gilt epaulets, and again in a seedy frock coat and a beaver top hat, which he adorned with an eagle feather. Ballard permitted no one to sell liquor to the Indians, but he would always give Kenyatch a drink and they would hold pow-wows in a mixture of Ute and Spanish, mostly about the days of danger and excitement they had shared. Daniel Laird, the builder, was another who often came when Ballard sat alone, but never stayed when a crowd formed, as it often did. For when Ballard had many guests, his afternoon on the porch became an informal reception, with two or three boys serving drinks, and army officers, scouts and traders making a picturesque and noisy company. Ballard seemed to enjoy a throng, and he could tell a good story, although he was more a listener than a talker. But it was a strict convention of these social gatherings that business could not be discussed. Anyone then might ask Ballard for an interview. If he was willing to give it, he would always say: "Come to my office in the morning." Otherwise he simply said no. No one ever pleaded or argued with him. He had the great gift of calm and absolute refusal.

Ballard had told me to let him know when I was ready to talk, so that I felt entirely justified in asking him for an interview. He smiled and nodded. "I'm busy these days," he said. "I'll send you word when I have time." I contained my bulging ideas for three weeks, and then ventured to approach him again. He didn't resent my insistence in the least and neither was he moved by it. "Take it easy, Morgan," he said. "There's plenty of time."

I didn't believe there was plenty of time, and this stalling was not at all in keeping with the Ballard tradition. He was famous for his quick and final decisions, but I could not escape the impression that now he was evading.

At first I felt a good deal of youthful pique. It seemed to me I was not being taken seriously. I even thought of serving Ballard with an ultimatum, of demanding that my plans be considered, and of going away if he refused. Fortunately this mood evaporated, partly because Ballard made obvious effort to show that he appreciated my presence. When he had important guests he always introduced me as his lawyer, his right-hand man. I was present at most of his afternoon gatherings, and as I sat watching him, I began to consider the situation a little more from his point of view and less from my own.

Ballard always remained an enigma to me. He never revealed or explained himself and there was nothing obvious about him, but during these last months I came to believe that his apparent serenity was that of a man who knew his day was nearly over and had the courage to face the fact. He had lived through a period of spectacular change. He knew the destroying power of change and he knew he sat in its path. It promised him nothing he wanted. I think what he loved was the past, as do most men over fifty. Moreover, he must have known the future for him was short in any case. Perhaps he had a good deal of the fatalism which often belongs to men of action. A man who has faced gunfire, heard the whisper of a bullet in his ear, has none of the comfortable illusion of security and permanence that most men cultivate all their lives, never acknowledging death even on their deathbeds. . . . I think Ballard had also an enormous egotism, too assured to need any assertion. He didn't in the least believe anyone else could take over his kingdom and rule it. It was the body of his being and with him it would go.

All this was largely speculation on my part, but it had at least the value of relieving my impatience, of letting my own dream of conquest quietly subside. I was never an ambitious man, but only one with an in-

flammable imagination. Did I truly want to destroy this place and this
moment, let in the rabble of the track-end towns, imprison the river and
turn loose a screaming buzz saw on the ancient forest? In the idle and
reflective mood that now possessed me, I knew that I did not.

— 8 —

Early autumn now had touched the mountains, splashing the ridges
with the brilliant yellow of the aspen, filling the heads of the canyons with
the rusty red of scrub oak. Days were cool and bright and made for riding.
Nights were chilly enough so that fire glowed red on the hearth at the
great house and in the big-bellied stove down at the store.

This last Indian summer I spent in the Dark River Valley lives in my
memory as one of those enchanted periods we all know, when some brief
and accidental harmony falls upon our lives, when we are at peace with
ourselves and the world seems to come smiling with gifts in its hands.

I had not done much for the Ballard dominion, but I began to understand that it had done much for me. I had stopped coughing and gained
ten pounds. I had ridden until I was more at home on a horse than on my
own feet. The sun had burned me to the color of a Mexican, and I had
learned enough Spanish so that I could often sound like one. I wore cowboy half-boots and blue jeans, a faded shirt and a wide hat. I rolled little
brown cigarettes and blew smoke through my nose. I had taken on the
color of the country so completely that I was no longer a stranger in it
anywhere. I went to all the Saturday night dances and mastered the choppy
Mexican waltz to the complete satisfaction of the nimble brown girls who
were my partners. I had sat by the stove in the store until I had become
accepted as a part of the coterie that gathered around it almost every
night to swap gossip and tall tales. I seemed everywhere welcome and
everywhere at home. I experienced the rare delight, possible only in youth,
of becoming part of a new environment, living a new life, seeming to
myself another person.

Part of the charm of this life, to me, lay in its rare combination of
society and solitude, of easy human contact and easy escape. Almost
every day I would ride into the mountains with a rifle across my saddle,
alert for a shot at a buck or a turkey but bent primarily on losing myself
in that beautiful wilderness where a forest a thousand years old talked
softly to the wind, and the waters ran clear, and the wild things turned to
stare as though I had been the first human intruder. Almost always I could
find a new canyon to explore or reach a summit from which I could see
new country. I saw the elk herds break and run, their great antlers laid
back along their necks, their hoofs clicking like castanets. I watched
a grizzly at his laborious business of turning over stones and logs in search
of grubs and ants, I jumped blacktail bucks out of their high windy beds

and saw them go bouncing down the slopes in twenty-foot leaps. In that unspoiled country one could still see big game by hundreds of head in a day. Often I did not fire a shot, and when I did, the roar of my rifle seemed to violate the ancient peace of a prehuman world. More than once I got well lost and trusted my horse to bring me home, as he always would if I gave him his head. Sometimes darkness would fall before I saw the great house far below me, alive with light and fire, dwarfed by the heights I rode. Then I would spur forward, eager for a drink and dinner, for the warm human huddle of the great dining room, the clasp and laughter of dancing girls.

The evening meal at the house of Ballard was always a social event. Seldom did less than twenty men sit down to the great table. Sometimes there were nearly a hundred, and those of minor importance had to wait for a second serving. A truly astonishing variety of human beings passed through that great dining room, for almost everyone who crossed the plains stopped at the Ballard grant. There I met Kit Carson, the most famous scout of his day, a stocky, bowlegged little man with a high small voice and a modest manner, who nevertheless gave a most unmistakable impression of strength. Lord Dunraven, the famous British sportsman, who had faced charging lions in Africa, spent a week at the grant and killed a grizzly bear. A young German ethnologist, named Bandelier, was another visitor. He pumped Ballard by the hour with systematic questions about the Indians, and Ballard, to my surprise, endured this cross-examination with the most perfect patience. He always seemed to know a good man when he saw one. Bandelier was wholly unknown then, but he became famous before he died.

All such distinguished visitors sat down at the same long table with cowboys and trappers and casual travelers, but important guests were seated near the head of the table and were always served first. The fare was of a patriarchal abundance, with game and beef in great haunches and sides, with trout from the creek and vegetables from the garden. Powerful corn whisky from Turley's still at Taos and good red El Paso wine were free for all. Everyone was served on hand-hammered silver plates, which had long been the standard service of the Mexican ricos. There was no china and little glass. Mexican boys did all the work of serving and clearing. In fact, most of the visitors to the Ballard dominion seldom saw a woman, unless at a distance.

This regime was somewhat surprising until you understood that the Ballard household was a Mexican household, designed in a tradition that went clear back to the Moorish regime in Spain. Ballard ruled his grant, or at least the masculine half of it, but his wife ruled the house, and it was a house divided strictly into masculine and feminine parts. There were, in fact, two separate structures, connected by high adobe walls and a small courtyard. The front structure contained the great dining and receiving rooms, and the quarters for all male guests. The rear structure was a feminine world where, I am sure, Ballard himself never intruded without his wife's permission. She also ruled the kitchen and all the women who worked in it, but her influence did not stop at the door. All the Mexican women on the grant came to her when they were in trouble, especially when children were sick. She had a long line of petitioners before her door every day. She dispensed simple remedies, gave away enormous quantities of food, and often let her visitors kneel and pray in her private chapel, which was said to be a room of great beauty. All of her part of the house was reputed to be as luxuriously furnished as the masculine part of it was bare and simple, but a male person could know of this only by hearsay.

This strict separation of the masculine and feminine spheres was common to all of the aristocratic Mexican houses, but in most of them the whole family dined together except when there were many male guests. Only intimate friends and relatives would sit at the family table. Ballard, during all of his later years, had enjoyed no privacy except in the solitude of his own rooms, so that the traditional division of the household had become almost complete. Only three or four times in a year did the Doña Consuelo appear in public, generally at formal receptions in the great front hall. These usually took place when distinguished visitors, especially army officers, were accompanied by their wives. The ladies always were housed in the feminine half of the establishment and had their meals with the Doña, but after dinner a reception was held at which they appeared in the most formal costumes they possessed and the officers were in full military dress. Even Ballard then donned a coat and necktie, which had almost the effect of a disguise.

To these gatherings the Doña Consuelo always came late and she always made a most effective entrance. Once I saw her flanked by both of her daughters, but usually they were away and had been most of the time for years. The elder had married an army officer and her sister then was in a convent in St. Louis. The two girls, I learned, had been tutored by their mother until it had become necessary to send them away to school. Obviously, the grant was no place for them after a certain age and their absence must have been a trial for both their parents. The younger sister was a beautiful girl and must have been almost an image of her mother's youth, for she had the same hazel eyes and rose-petal skin. She bore her mother's name and was said to be a great favorite with her father, but he treated her always with an almost formal courtesy, as though he did not quite trust his own emotions—a trait which marked all of his personal relations. I remember that when little Consuelo came for a brief visit that first summer, she brought him for a present an immense beaver hat, then considered the very summit of male elegance. Ballard accepted the two-pound headpiece with grave courtesy, but I think he never put it on. After his daughter had left he presented it to Kenyatch, who wore it on important occasions as long as he lived.

When his wife appeared, Ballard would always go to meet her, bend over her hand with formal courtesy, lead her into the room and present her to all of his guests. She was a large woman and somewhat stout, but it was easy to see that in her youth she must have been a spectacular beauty. In fact, she still had beauty—the beauty of perfect carriage and bearing, of gracious self-assurance without any trace of pretension or hauteur. I am no believer in the value of the aristocratic tradition, but generations of security and assured social status do give some men, and even more, some women, an almost perfect manner, and the Doña was a striking example of the fact.

I wondered, as many others must have done, what sort of relation existed between these two proud people. Except at these gatherings, they were never seen together. Some said that the Doña had withdrawn from her husband as completely as she had withdrawn from the world, that her whole life was bound up in her religious devotions and her charities, but this may have been merely a part of the legend that gossip creates.

The romance of their marriage was a famous one, touched with scandal. It was said that her family had permitted her to cross the mountains with her husband partly because her first child was born a little too early for the strict conventions of her class. Even better attested was the mutual devotion of their early days in the wilderness when they built their first small house in the Dark River Valley and lived there at peril from the Indians in a long isolation before the great highway came to their door. It was said the Doña, defying the custom of her kind, rode astride like a man and followed Ballard on the trail and the roundup. It was told of her too that she went out and found him once when he was lost in a blizzard, taking food and blankets, resolved to bring back her husband or die with him. There may have been much romantic invention about all this, but Mexican women are famous for a kind of fiercely possessive devotion which seems peculiar to their blood. . . . It was not hard to imagine that his sudden success had come between them. It had certainly taken him away from her, for he was a great traveler in those days, managing his own own wagon trains and trail herds, covering thousands of miles in the saddle, riding relays of blooded horses. At this period of his life he was reputed to have been a man of many affairs, who had girls wherever he went, from Santa Fe to St. Louis. No one seemed to be able to name any of these mistresses but that did not disprove their existence. Ballard had a singular gift for keeping his private life private.

It was obvious that the Doña had played a most unusual part in his career. The grant had come to him through his marriage. All that he possessed and all that he had done was based upon it, and his kingdom was as much her creation as his. Watching them at one of the great receptions, I noticed that his eyes followed her as long as she remained in the room— that he seemed to be completely absorbed by the consciousness of her presence. Whatever their relations may have become, I somehow felt sure that she remained the dominating influence of his life.

— 9 —

The great house was a spectacular thing and a unique one, but it was more a hotel than a home and singularly apart from the life of the community. That was centered elsewhere, chiefly in the store and in the community hall where dances and all other public gatherings were held, and it came to interest me far more than the picturesque processions of strangers I saw at the great house. In fact, I discovered in myself a strong and surprising tendency to go native. Nothing pleased me more than to be taken for a cowpuncher or to be invited to dinner at one of the houses in Royball-town. I went to the dance hall almost every Saturday night, and also again on Sunday, if it happened to be one of those Sundays when its presiding genius, Daniel Laird, was present to lead the singing and turn loose his magnificent voice in a recitation from the Bible.

Next to Ballard himself, Laird was the most prominent man in the community and this despite the fact that he certainly did not court prominence. He was a shy and solitary fellow who lived alone in a log house of his own building a mile or more from the valley. He had no intimates and was almost always seen alone except when he performed a public function. He was generally called "the preacher" behind his back, but never to his face, because he did not care to be known as a preacher, and in fact he was a preacher only incidentally and almost accidentally. His peculiar position in the community had been imposed upon him by public need and demand and by his own qualities and powers. I never saw a man who made fewer claims for himself or took his leadership in a more modest and casual spirit.

A tall, lean man in his middle thirties, with long arms and powerful shoulders, he was a Tennessee mountaineer by origin and a builder by profession—a hard-working man who had built almost everything on the Ballard property except the great house itself and the one who kept all the corrals and outbuildings in repair. Like all men of his type, he was an axman primarily, who could build a house with no other tools than an ax and a drawknife and without an ounce of iron, using wooden dowels and pins in place of nails. But he could also make good planks with a pitsaw and had provided the Ballard establishment with its first wooden floors. Later he had built a small sawmill, powered by a water wheel and capable of producing a thousand board feet a day. More than that, he had mastered adobe construction and bossed half a dozen Mexicans when adobe walls had to be built or plastered. He was also foreman of the gang that supplied the establishment with all its firewood, swinging a six-pound double-bitted ax himself, chiefly because he loved the tool.

I had once spent several months in the southern highlands in search of health and I could see that in all of his aptitudes and talents Laird was a typical product of the region. He came of the pioneering strain that produced Daniel Boone and carried civilization across the Allegheny barrier. His amateur preaching, his singing of hymns and folk songs, his scratchy fiddling of "Turkey in the Straw" and "Old Dan Tucker," his mastery of the primitive arts of healing were all common accomplishments of hillbilly tradition. The southern mountains abounded in unordained preachers, most of whom were also singers and often herb doctors as well. I learned that Laird's father had been such a primitive master of the Word, a minor backwoods revivalist, and doubtless Daniel had learned all of his tricks at home. He was essentially a hillbilly preacher gone west, but he was by no means to be explained wholly in terms of his origins. He was a remarkable man, as I think his subsequent career abundantly proved, and he bore a somewhat unusual relation to his fellows, standing apart from them and yet dominating them without effort whenever they gathered around him. There was a kind of power in him which was hard to explain, but certainly his voice, more than anything else, had determined his destiny. Without his great vocal powers, I feel sure, he would have been a contented recluse. As it was, he had only to open his mouth to command attention. He sang at his work and he sang as he walked the hills. Men could hear him coming a quarter of a mile away, and almost always they would stop to listen. His singing voice was powerful and true, if limited in range, but his speaking voice was almost perfect. It filled a room without effort and people always turned to look when they heard it.

It was his voice which had made him the moving spirit of all the gatherings that took place in the town meeting hall—a long, low adobe structure which had been built as a warehouse for wool, and later converted to public purposes, chiefly because it had a good wooden floor. Laird first had been called upon to preside at funerals and weddings, chiefly by the wives of the ranchmen—lonely women, starved for any kind of social life. Later he had been persuaded to hold meetings on Sunday mornings, and these were strictly in the tradition of his background. He simply recited passages from the Bible, interspersed occasionally with original remarks, and then led his congregation in the singing of hymns.

I attended these gatherings without fail and they were much like typical backwoods meeting-house performances, but of an unusual quality. Laird had discovered several good voices among his feminine followers, and the singing at its best was superb. But his own recitation of the Holy Word was the most impressive thing. Whether he loved God I do not know, but he most assuredly loved the Bible. Although his speech had the inflection of the mountain dialect, so that he said "cheer" for chair, and "hyar" for here, he yet spoke the language of the Bible, simply because he had soaked himself in it. He was a natural lover of words, and to him, I think, the Bible was the whole of literature, the only book he truly knew. But more than that, it was also a perfect vehicle for his voice and there is no doubt that Laird loved to hear his own voice. I noticed repeatedly that as he recited the great Biblical poetry he always threw back his head, looked up and over his auditors, seeming wholly unaware of their presence, making word-music for its own sake, fairly hypnotizing himself. All of his favorite passages he recited wtih peculiar emphasis, seeming always to give them a new meaning and value. So in the Twenty-third Psalm, he always emphasized the personal pronouns, announcing with eloquent conviction, "The Lord is *my* shepherd, *I* shall not want. He maketh *me* to lie down in green pastures. He leadeth *me* beside the still waters." And when he intoned Ecclesiastes, proclaiming "Vanity, vanity, *all* is vanity," that resounding *all* seemed to reduce all human effort and pretension to eternal futility. It was an impressive demonstration of the power which sound can add to sense.

Sometimes Laird would half scandalize his audience by reciting a passage from the Song of Songs, and in this rich poetry his great voice seemed to be at its best. It did not bear so heavily upon certain words, although I noticed a tendency for his voice to linger with caressing eloquence upon anatomical details, giving his recitation a sensuous quality of which he was probably unaware.

> *Thy lips are like a thread of scarlet,*
> *And thy speech is comely;*
> *Thy temples are like a piece of pomegranate*
> *Within thy locks.*
> *Thy neck is like the tower of David builded*
> *For an armory,*
> *Whereon they hang a thousand bucklers,*
> *All shields of mighty men.*
> *Thy two breasts are like two young roes that are twins,*
> *Which feed among the lilies.*

While Laird softly boomed his chant of desire, lean ranchwomen in gingham dresses and sunbonnets, with hands reddened by dish water, watched him with adoring eyes, sometimes visibly swaying to the music of his voice, while the few menfolk who came to his meetings stared uncomfortably at the floor. I wondered whether he knew what he was doing, and I doubted it. But he kept his distance from women with the utmost care. He was never seen alone with one, and no woman was ever known to go to his house. He visited the ranch houses and the homes of the Mexicans only when he was sent for in case of sickness, and then he seldom ministered to women. There were several midwives in the settlement who also practiced a limited art of healing, but no doctor nearer than Fort Union. Laird had added to his traditional lore of herbs a limited knowledge of materia medica, but he relied mainly on heat and pressure. He was an expert of mustard plasters and hot compresses, and like all such frontier healers, he was supposed to have a gift of touch. He could "rub the misery out of your back." He was at his best with children and was credited with curing several cases of pneumonia.

After hearing him intone the sacred word on Sunday mornings, it was a little surprising to find Laird always at the dances on Saturday night and presiding over these most profane gatherings with the same easy authority he brought to his Sabbath congregations. But here, it appeared, his presence was official, in that Ballard had asked him to take charge of these explosive gatherings after several of them had ended in rather damaging fights.

The Mexican baile was then even more than now an institution all over the Southwest, and those in the Ballard dominion were typical. A Mexican orchestra of three pieces, led by an aged and blind fiddler, announced the dance by touring the settlement in the afternoon, the leader mounted on a white mule, fiddling as he went. Everyone, Mexican and gringo, was welcome, and all male persons paid a small price, which was usually tossed into a hat. No introductions were required. Any man could ask any girl to dance. This did not mean that he could talk to her or sit beside her, or claim her acquaintance off the dance floor, but he could dance with her in becoming silence and then return her to the side of her duenna. The girls and their chaperons sat in a long row all around the room and the men crowded about the doorway. Just as in Santa Fe and all of the other larger towns, these were always biracial gatherings. The girls from Royball-town in their white bodices and red petticoats, the young Mexicans from the sheep camps with their black hair heavily oiled, ranchmen bringing wives and daughters, cowboys from the Ballard bunkhouse, all crowded into the hall, made the sanded floor rasp in time to the fast and wheezy music. Guns were checked at the door and knives were supposed to be. No liquor was allowed inside the house. But in spite of these precautions, any baile was an explosive mixture of sex, corn whisky and racial antagonism. In fact, many young men felt that a baile which did not break up in a fight was a failure. In Taos the mountain men used to start a riot whenever they thought the party was getting dull. Ballard himself had been through many a dance-hall brawl, but he would not tolerate any of this traditional bellicosity on his own premises. With his sure instinct for all the means of power, he knew that mobs and factions are the enemies of authority, and that trouble between the two races would split the country. He was also quick to see the value of Laird's towering presence and commanding voice. So dances took place only when Laird was there. He was what they called in the cowtowns the official bouncer, but he seldom had to bounce anyone and he brought a good deal to the dances besides his long reach and resounding voice. He never waltzed, but he led and called all the square dances and sometimes joined the orchestra with his fiddle. I watched him with much interest, and I am sure he was quick to spot trouble in the making. Often he brought it to an end by calling for a square dance, dissolving the hot couples, the dangerous triangles, in a dancing, laughing crowd. The most impressive evidence of his power was the way he adjourned the dances, which he always did at midnight. He would pick up his wide black hat off the floor and stand with it in his hand until the music had come to an end. Then he would put it on his head and walk out, followed by the whole crowd. Of course, he had the power of Ballard behind him, but his person seemed to contain a certain authority by natural endowment.

Only once did I see Laird intervene to stop trouble. That time he saved young Bob Clarey from a knife, with the help and support of practically the whole crowd, white and Mexican. For young Bob was a favorite figure in the settlement and his romance with Adelita Royball had become something like a public institution—the leading subject of local gossip. Young Bob was the only son of a widower ranchman, known simply as Old Bob, who had the usual waterhole and corral and log house about twenty miles from the store, and the usual herd of about a hundred half-bred longhorns. Old Bob belonged to a type all too common in the frontier—a man driven by some obscure impulse of social avoidance, who had pursued solitude halfway across a continent—a lean, thin-lipped man with small eyes peering suspiciously from under thick brows. He was a good and honest cowman, but one who could not trust the world or his fellows. He came to town only about once a month for a wagonload of supplies and a mild spree. Young Bob, on the other hand, was around the place most of the time. His whole life and character seemed to be a reaction against the old man's taciturn seclusion. He had great social gifts and he used them. His self-assurance and good feeling were supported by his remarkably good looks, for he was handsome as an actor and wholly aware of the fact, with dark curly hair and blue eyes, a perfect build, an easy carriage, and a smile that never seemed to wear out. He rode a white pony which he washed carefully in the creek every few days, white goatskin chaps on Sunday, and a great white hat which must have cost him a month's savings. He carried a big Colt six-shooter low on his hip, but had never been known to shoot at anything but a mark or a coyote. He was a star of the local rodeos, a crack roper and broncobuster—a congenital showoff, but one with real courage. Everybody liked him and women adored him. As Waverly Buncombe remarked, when he rode down the street, you could hear the girls sigh like a rising wind. But he had only one girl, so far as anyone could learn, and that was the eighteen-year-old daughter of Old Man Royball himself—the tyrannical ruler of sheep and sheep herders. It seemed as though Bob's dramatic instinct had dictated his choice of a love as it did almost everything else in his life, for this affair was inevitably conspicuous and potentially dangerous. Old Bob was said to have threatened to disown his son if he married that coffee-colored wench, and old man Royball had retaliated by muttering that he would run young Bob out of the plaza if he ever came there to see her. What success these two had in meeting alone I do not know, although there was reason to believe they did not fail completely. But on the dance floor they got together with impressive grace and velocity, and there no one could deny them. For the dance floor in Mexican tradition is the sanctuary of lovers, and Bob and Adelita were a pair of gifted dancers. The swift choppy waltz, which was the product of rough and sanded floors, they could make into a thing of speed and grace, but the cuna or cradle waltz was their specialty. In this the two dancers seized each other by the shoulders, leaned far back and whirled round and round, making a cradle which was never bottomless. Bob and Adelita would waltz in a close embrace for a while, then go into their ecstatic spin, belly to belly, her long hair flying loose, while other couples circled the passionate whirlpool of their delight. Adelita was a slim, pretty girl, brown as an Indian, with an immense mane of black hair that seemed always to escape whatever discipline she tried to impose upon it, so that after an hour of dancing she looked like a happy young witch, peering through her own tresses, tossing them with a splendid gesture of abandon. It was a delight to watch them and they were both quite conscious of giving a good show.

Inevitably, Bob had a Mexican rival, and inevitably he came to the dance full of alcohol and with a hidden knife. The trouble started in the usual way, with both men claiming the same dance. Adelita lifted her pretty nose and glided into the arms of her beloved Bob. The Mexican snatched him by the shoulder, spun him free. Bob swung his right in good Anglo-Saxon fashion, the Mexican staggered and came back with a flashing blade drawn from his sock. Laird, watching from the platform, landed between them in one long bound, got them both by their collars and held them apart, dangling helpless at the ends of his mighty reach. It was an amazing show of strength—the strength of a man who has swung an ax all his life, building muscle all the way from wrist to shoulder. The whole crowd closed in on them, the Mexican was ejected by common consent, and in two minutes the dance was going on as though nothing had happened. There was a kind of quick crowd justice in the incident. The aggressor was known to all, and a sheep herder helped a cowboy boost him through the door.

I had observed Laird for months before I ever saw him alone, and it would never have happened then except for the fact that both of us were fishermen. Almost everyone collected a few grasshoppers and snatched a meal from the creek once in a while, but only Laird and I cared for trout fishing as a sport, following the creek with our long, limber willow poles, using horsehair leaders, angling for the big ones that lived in the deep holes. It was characteristic of Laird that he met me several times before he began to recognize me as the same fellow he had seen before. He was always smiling and pleasant, an evident lover of the human race, but he seemed to focus on individuals with a certain difficulty if not with reluctance. When we finally got into conversation one day he seemed sud-

denly to accept me as a friend and invited me to have dinner with him—
a distinction he conferred upon few.

He lived in a one-room cabin of squared timbers, standing alone in a
tall grove of yellow pine, with a deep brown carpet of needles covering
the ground. I was told that he had declined to live there as a squatter and
since Ballard sold no land he had laughingly deeded Laird half an acre.
Within, the cabin was bare and neat, furnished only with a long built-in
bunk, two homemade chairs and a table, shelves for his supplies and pegs
on the wall to hold his collection of axes, of all weights from two pounds
to six and all sharp and shining. A heavy rifle hung on a rack of elkhorn.
Laird was a hunter when he needed meat but never fired a shot near his
own place because he liked to see the wild things about.

He was shy yet self-possessed and fed me amazingly well on fried trout
and boiled potatoes, excellent biscuits, wild raspberries and cream, and
a big tin pot of strong coffee. He also poured me a generous slug of El
Paso brandy, but took none himself.

"I've drunk enough of that stuff to last me a lifetime," he explained
with an apologetic grin. The remark struck me as revealing, but it was the
only revealing one he made. He did not talk about himself at all, but he
questioned me at length about my travels—about New York and Europe
and ships and the ocean, which he had never seen. He sat listening with
an intent, abstracted look, as though trying to imagine a world wholly
beyond his experience, making me feel that I was in the presence of a
starved intellectual curiosity, a mind of power and appetite which had
never even discovered its own need. Yet the man seemed at peace with
himself. He had a long, angular ruddy face, deeply lined for one of his age,
with thick sandy hair and bright gray eyes under heavy brows—eyes as
keen and steely as a blade. But his wide, slow-spreading grin was full of
peace and good feeling.

It was a warm evening and after supper we sat a little while on a bench
in front of his cabin smoking our pipes. From his doorway you could see
nothing but the great pines, now spreading their long wavering shadows
on the carpet of needles that covered the earth, and there was no sound
but a breath of evening breeze and the tinkling song of a vesper sparrow.
Any man, I thought, might find peace in a place such as this, if he was
a man who could live with his own mind—and if the world would leave
him in peace.

— 10 —

I never heard but one man say anything against Laird and that man
was his chief, if not his only, rival as a public character—a peculiar individual bearing the musical name of Waverly Buncombe. According to the
legend he had bestowed upon himself, Buncombe was the errant scion of

a wealthy and prominent family in South Carolina, who preferred the wild, free life of the frontier to the aristocratic ease and luxury he might have claimed as his own. It was true, at least, that a county in South Carolina was named for the Buncombe family, and that Waverly had been born there, but the stories he told about himself, like those he told about others, seemed to contain a large element of romantic invention. For Waverly was a storyteller and a gossip by avocation, one who had dedicated his life to spreading the news, whether it was any credit to anyone or not, and to lending it the embellishment of his imagination, which was lively, and also of his wit, which was irreverent, sometimes malicious and often obscene. Nobody professed much respect for Waverly, but everyone listened to him and many feared him. Moreover, as I came to understand, he performed a genuine and necessary social function, for he took the place of a newspaper. He made it his business to know everything about everybody and to tell everybody else. I believe that every primitive community harbors such a semi-professional carrier of the word, and Waverly was a talented example. To give him his due, he was a shrewd man and a gifted observer, but even these talents did not fully account for his unfailing knowledge of what was going on. He seemed to sense events in the making, to know what men were going to do before they did it. In a word, like all gifted gossips, he had a touch of genius. And where news travels only by word of mouth, gossip has an enormous importance. In such a community everyone has his legend and Waverly was the keeper if not the creator of legend. Everyone's reputation was to some extent at his mercy, and he was not always merciful, but he was always entertaining. Moreover, he had a philosophy of a kind—a profoundly skeptical philosophy. He did not believe at all in anyone's pretensions and very little in anyone's virtues. If he did some men, and also some women, a grave injustice, he also punctured a great many false fronts. I cannot say that I admired Waverly, but I enjoyed him, and I listened to him with the mingled feeling of guilt and delight which we all bring to the tongue of gossip. Moreover, I did not find it hard to justify myself. If I heard a good many dubious stories from Waverly, I also learned some useful things about the little world I had set myself to understand.

Waverly's favorite hangout and listening post, at this time of year, was the big iron stove in the front of the store. It was also mine, and by this time I had become an accepted member of the group which gathered there in the evening to swap news and tell stories, with Waverly supplying the greater part of both. In personal appearance, he did not quite fulfill the ideal of southern aristocracy from which he claimed descent. He was a man of moderate stature, with a long hatchet face, a long nose, notably sloping shoulders and long arms. As I heard a cowpuncher remark, he looked as though he had been built to crawl through a knothole. The only thing that marred his tapering symmetry was the huge wad of chewing tobacco he almost always wore in the left side of his cheek. It seemed to interfere not at all with his gifted utterance, and like all veteran lovers of the plug, he could hold his juice for an incredible length of time. When he did spit, he had impressive accuracy. Not only could he hit a cuspidor infallibly at four feet, but he could drown a fly perched on the edge of it.

By profession, Waverly was a cow-camp cook, and to all accounts a good one. In those days of the open range and the long drives, his calling was an important and a well-paid one. A camp cook not only cooked but bought supplies, drove the chuck wagon, was the practical and moral equivalent of the quartermaster in an army. He had to feed crowds of hungry men on short notice, in all kinds of weather, often getting breakfast for twenty cowpunchers long before daylight in a pouring rain. Waverly discharged this difficult function on all the local roundups and whenever Ballard sent a trail herd to Fort Union or Santa Fe, but his work was sporadic in the nature of the case. Most of the time he was a gentleman of leisure and of language.

I do not believe that Daniel Laird was much aware of Waverly, but Waverly was acutely aware of the preacher. Laird could not be called a pretentious man but he was one who stood apart from his fellows, had no share in their quarrels and scandals, kept his own life to himself. He was the shining mark gossip is supposed to love and Waverly certainly loved to shoot at him. Nothing about the preacher had his approval. As a singer he considered Laird "just a good hog caller where there ain't no hogs," and he put no faith in the man's ministrations to the sick. "Sure, he'll cure you if he can do it with a dose of salts or a bucket of hot water, and if he can't he'll bury you right nice." But what annoyed him most was the apparent austerity and purity of Laird's life. Waverly believed not at all in the value of chastity and very little in its existence. Moreover, it had small place in the customs of a country which abounded in willing brown women and had a long tradition of erotic license. Perhaps if he had been able to discover the preacher in some weakness of the flesh, he would have been more tolerant of him, but Laird was one man whom scandal had never touched.

The subject came up one evening when Seth Larrick, foreman of Ballard's cowpunchers, remarked upon the fact that Laird seemed "downright skeered of a skirt." When called upon to attend the sick, he declined ever to be left alone with a woman.

"There ain't no mystery about it," Waverly remarked. "You can't chase women and play Jesus at the same time. He's afraid some gal will tumble him off his high horse."

I thought the remark showed insight as well as malice, and this was true of much that Waverly said. On this and other occasions I had the uncomfortable feeling that my friends and neighbors were being stripped naked for my inspection, but sometimes Waverly dispensed information that was truly useful. So it was Waverly who called my attention to Major Arnold Newton Blore, a man destined to play a rather large part in the subsequent history of the Dark River Valley. I had met Blore at the dinner table, but to me he was just one of the many guests who accepted Ballard's hospitality for a few days or a few weeks. I did not in the least suspect his fateful importance, but Waverly did.

"I don't know what he's up to yet," he told me. "But he ain't here for fun. I can tell that by the way he noses around."

Major Blore was a Confederate veteran who had risen from the ranks in Lee's command to become an artillery officer of exceptional skill. Of his present occupation nothing was known except that he made his headquarters in Denver, and like nearly everyone else in the Denver of that day had "mining interests," which probably meant that he was a promoter and dealer in mining stocks. He had very markedly the soft speech and elaborate courtesy of a Virginian, and contrived to invert himself with an air of importance, slightly touched by the kind of pomposity which is so often the weakness of men deficient in stature. For Blore was a very short man and obviously conscious of the fact. I doubt that he would have been more than three inches over five feet in his socks, but no one ever saw him that way. He wore upon all occasions riding boots of the most expensive make with very high heels, and he further extended himself at the other end by means of a large felt hat with a high crown. His carriage also had something lofty about it. The appearance of a man, and especially the first impression you get of it, has always seemed highly revealing to me. Major Blore seemed to be always engaged in lifting himself, and doing it with a certain aggressive confidence, which was expressed in the bulge of his barrel chest and confident carriage of his rather large head. Seated behind a desk or at a table, he might have been taken for a large man. His features were handsome, dominated by a Roman nose and decorated with a silky blond mustache which effectively concealed his mouth. His eyes were bright blue, prominent, and curiously unrevealing. I did not like him, but he gave an unmistakable impression of personal power, nourished on a habit of command.

My next news of him came also from Waverly. It appeared that Blore had promoted a horse race in which a nag of his own was to be matched with Ballard's favorite three-mile horse, the celebrated Fly. Waverly mentioned this matter only to Seth Larrick and myself, and he did so in a portentously confidential tone.

"If you want to make some easy money," he told us, "bet on Blore's horse. He's putting something over on the old man, sure as hell."

Blore had arrived at the Ballard place alone in a buckboard—a light two-horse rig which was then the favorite means of rapid transit when any baggage had to be carried. The buckboard was drawn by a pair of chestnut geldings which were gaunt from hard driving when he arrived, streaked with sweat and caked with dust. No one paid much attention to them and no one had seen anything of them since Blore's arrival. Blore had used one of Ballard's saddle horses for his rides about the grant. Only

Waverly had noticed that Blore tended his team himself, grooming them daily, taking them out of the stable only briefly in the evening for a little exercise, measuring the oats he fed them with the utmost care.

"He takes care of 'em like a couple of babies," Waverly reported. "And they're worth it. They're Kentucky thoroughbreds, sure as I'm a foot high. Hardly anybody out here knows a thoroughbred when he sees one but I seen a lot of 'em back home."

Waverly was right about that. Horse racing was the commonest of all sports in the West of that day, but it was not a sport of professionals and thoroughbreds. Cowboys raced their ponies, almost always for a stake. Every ranchman had at least one horse in his remuda that he would bet a few dollars on. Ballard loved a horse race and had a small stable of running horses he used for nothing else, but even these were native stock, mostly mustangs of exceptional speed and power, or crosses between a native mare and a blooded stallion. Thoroughbreds were too delicate for a frontier world and endurance was valued more than speed. A good horse was one that could outrun pursuing Indians or overtake a herd of buffalo and keep his rider in their midst long enough for a kill. Races were always over long distances, at least two miles and often three. There were no circular tracks. Any long straight stretch of road would serve the purpose, such as the one that paralleled the river near Ballard's house. When a race was to be run the course was carefully inspected for gopher holes and loose rocks, starters and judges took their positions at either end and all was ready.

As became evident later, Major Blore was not merely interested in winning a horse race. Like many others who had come to the grant with a plan and a purpose, he had found Ballard cordial but also supremely elusive and he had used his horses with notable cunning as a means of approach to the royal presence. Evidently he had heard of Fly and of Ballard's pride in the black stallion, and he had asked to see the animal, explaining that he was a bit of a horseman himself. Pedro Gonzales, a skinny little Mexican about forty years old who was Ballard's jockey and chief hostler, reported the result to Waverly, who gave it wide currency.

Pedro brought the stallion out of his stall, mounted him bareback, and rode him up and down for Blore's inspection. Fly was a horse of magnificent appearance—a mustang which had been caught wild on the prairies east of the grant. All of this wild stock was of course descended from horses the Spaniards had imported in the sixteenth century. Much of it was of the finest Barb and Arabian blood, the same strains from which our own thoroughbreds are descended. Most of it had deteriorated as a result of interbreeding and crossing with all kinds of range stock, but an occasional mustang was found which seemed a perfect specimen of the original Arabian type, and such was Fly. He had the small pointed head, the tiny ears, the powerful arched neck and deep barrel of the Arabian, and also the perfect grace of movement—a horse far more beautiful than any of a more specialized type.

Major Blore watched the horse for some minutes, had the boy bring him to a stop, inspected his forelegs with a practiced hand, viewed the wide spread of his chest from in front, opened his mouth with the easy touch of an expert, and carefully considered his teeth.

"That's a fine horse, Ballard," he said finally. "But he's not a running horse. I'm surprised you should think he is. He's too short-coupled and too heavy in the rear."

Ballard laughed with delight.

"Major Blore," he said, "if you can find anything that can beat that horse for two miles I'll make it worth a thousand dollars to you."

"Why, for the matter of that, Ballard," Blore replied, "I'll take one of those nags of mine right out of harness, ride him myself, and make your mustang look through a cloud of dust. That boy of yours is twenty pounds lighter than I am, but I think that much of a handicap is no more than fair."

"You've got yourself a race right now," Ballard told him. "I never looked at your horses, but I've been backing Fly against all comers, sight unseen, for four years. He's never lost but one race and that time he threw shoe."

Ballard was no innocent where horses were concerned. He knew Fly was not fast by eastern track standards, but he had complete confidence in the courage and bottom of his horse. Another horse often led the stallion for more than half the distance and sometimes took a long lead, but on the home stretch Fly would run his opponent down like a hound, seeming stronger at the finish than when he started.

A crowd of several hundred gathered to watch the race. Most of those who had money tried to bet it on Fly. Only Waverly bet all he had and all he could borrow on Blore's horse.

When I saw Blore mounted I knew at once I was looking at a man to whom horses must have been a profession, one who had in all probability been a jockey. At this time he was in his late thirties, and had doubtless put on some weight. It was easy to imagine that ten or fifteen years earlier he had looked like a typical track professional. It was significant that he had his own racing saddle and his seat was the one that only jockeys use, with his knees up around the mount's withers. Most of those present had never seen such a rider and some of them laughed at him. Pedro Gonzales was a picturesque contrast. Like most of his breed he was more than half Navajo and he rode stripped to a breech-clout, as all Indians do, with only a blanket and surcingle on the horse's back.

I took my stand with the judges and saw the two horses come down the course with Fly slightly in the lead and Blore hanging on his flank. It was easy to see Blore had chosen that position and was saving his mount with perfect control. When they were not more than a hundred yards from the finish, Blore rose in his stirrups, laid on the quirt and gave the rebel yell. He shot ahead two full lengths and finished with Pedro dodging clods from the flying hoofs of the thoroughbred. The little Mexican was a bewildered and heartbroken man. He turned the stallion and rode back toward the stables without meeting an eye or saying a word.

Ballard was a perfect loser. He extended his hand to Blore with a broad grin.

"You've got a good horse," he said, "and you know how to ride him. It was worth a thousand dollars to see you. Come to my office in the morning and we'll settle up."

That final word, I have no doubt, was what Blore had been working for.

— 11 —

I had a premonition, based partly on Waverly's delicate hints, that this first private meeting between Ballard and the Major might be an important one, but I was a little surprised when Ballard sent for me the next day about noon. As I crossed the porch on my way to Ballard's office, I met Blore leaving the house. The little man was flushed, his bulging blue eyes were bright with excitement and he walked with a kind of strut, like a victorious gamecock leaving the pit. He gave me a smile, a nod and a quick appraising look.

I found Ballard seated behind the long heavy table at which he transacted all his business. It was a bare table except for a big inkpot, a few pens and a wide Pueblo bowl which Ballard used for an ash tray. During the past twenty years, hundreds of thousands of dollars had flowed across that table, both ways, most of it in silver, for everyone liked heavy money in those days. Ballard was famous for the way he would go to his cash drawer, take out a huge canvas bag of silver dollars and count out what he owed, tossing the coins onto the table in handfuls. He had always dealt lightly with money. If he was buying a herd of sheep from a poor Mexican, he would always toss a few extra dollars and say: "That's for the dog." First and last he had tossed a lot of money to the dogs. I don't think he had much respect for money. He had a sharp eye for land and livestock, for water, fur and timber, but the importance of money had always eluded him.

Ballard was leaning back in his big homemade chair with its rawhide seat and wide arms. He looked tired and a little grim, but he was perfectly composed. He greeted me with a smile, and waved me to the chair Blore had just left. There was no sign of disturbance about him except that the cigar he took out of his mouth was almost chewed to pieces, and the bowl before him was piled high with ashes and with badly chewed cigars.

When he was serene Ballard smoked a cigar slowly and carefully, without getting his teeth into it. If he chewed the weed to pieces, you could be sure he was disturbed.

He was silent for several minutes after I sat down, and when he spoke it was very quietly.

"Morgan," he said, "Major Blore has made me an offer for the grant. He represents a syndicate of mining men in Denver. . . . The offer is pretty good."

He sat looking at the end of his cigar for a long time.

"You don't want to sell," I ventured finally.

Ballard shifted in his seat, plowed his hand through his hair.

"No," he said, and his voice took on a certain intensity, while he continued to stare at his dying cigar. I felt that he was talking as much to himself as to me. "I never wanted to sell anything. I always wanted to hang on, to hold things together, to make things work. When I came in here I promised the Utes I would never let in any settlers as long as I controlled the valley. That agreement doesn't bar me from selling the place as a whole. I have a right to sell." He paused a long time. "And I've got to sell," he said finally.

I asked him only if he was sure there was no alternative. He nodded slowly.

"I've got to be frank with you now, Morgan," he said. "I've kept you waiting for months, but the time hasn't been wasted. You've been learning about the grant and I've been learning about you. I've seen this moment coming for years. I knew I would need a lawyer and that he would need to know all about this place. I knew I would need a man I could trust and I can't trust a man until I've watched him a long time."

He paused again, and I knew this confession was costing him an effort. It was no part of his habit to confide.

"About three years ago, when the market for beef went flat, I went back to St. Louis. I talked to bankers and I talked to doctors—two kinds of men I don't like. All the news they gave was bad." He said it calmly, as though he were talking about someone else, but when he spoke again there was a stir of power, a note of belligerent pride in his voice.

"If I had another ten years," he said, "I would give myself the pleasure of telling Major Blore to go to hell. No man could come in here and take this place over unless I would let him—I don't care how much money he might have." He looked a long time at the end of his cigar. "But I haven't got ten years, nor anywhere near it. A man is a fool to start what he can't finish. And I've got to think of my family. This way they'll be safe."

I knew I was listening to a man who had heard a sentence of death and accepted it. Ballard's affliction now is often cured by surgery, but then it was considered incurable. I could understand well enough the temptation he had resisted—the temptation to fight and to go down fighting, to use his power to the last ounce and the last moment, be the result what it might. He knew that peace and order in the Dark River Valley were his creation. He knew his power over his own people. A great deal of Eastern and some British capital was invested in the Western cattle business in those first decades after the war, and a great deal of it was lost. The herds of the strangers melted away. They fell prey to the lean riders with the ropes and the running irons. Ballard commanded all such men in a region nearly a hundred miles wide, and none of them had anything to gain by a change of masters. It was simple truth that he could have defied any usurper and also that his defiance would have meant something like war in the long run, both in the courts and on the ranges. . . . Ballard had decided against a fight he couldn't finish. He had decided a long time ago. He had fought out his battle with himself. It would have been impertinence to argue or advise, nor did his attitude invite any expression of sympathy.

"What do you want me to do?" I asked.

"I want you to dicker with Blore," he said. "This is a job for a lawyer. When you see his papers, you'll understand. He's a cunning little bastard and no mistake." He smiled, and there was a shrewd look in his eye.

"I didn't commit myself to a thing," he added. "I just told him that I would talk to my lawyer. You've got a clear field and you have my permission to say what you please. Boost the price if you can. But there's only one thing I've got to have. I've got to have a year—I think it's all I'll need."

— 12 —

When I faced Blore across a table two days later and examined his papers, I knew at once that the situation was hopeless, so far as saving the grant for Ballard was concerned, and the fact is even more evident in the long retrospect than it was then. While I had been dreaming of myself as an agent of the future in the Dark River Valley, Blore had been cleverly at work for more than a year. He had begun by forming a syndicate of capitalists in Denver. Six men of money were represented in it, but the chief of these was one Colonel Alonzo Tweedale, like Blore a Confederate veteran, and one who had made a great deal of money in the Pike's Peak mining boom. Tweedale was president of the organization and he was a millionaire or somewhere near it. It was called the Rocky Mountain Land and Cattle Company, but its stated purposes were inclusive—to buy and sell both lands and cattle, to erect sawmills and build dams and irrigation works, to lay out town sites, to develop mining claims. No specific lands were mentioned in the charter, but it was aimed primarily at the Spanish land grants of the Southwest, with the Ballard grant as its first victim. Blore had other papers covering this phase of the plan. In short, he had gone secretly to all of Ballard's creditors and had promised each of them payment in full, provided a sale was consummated. He had asked each of them in return to agree to file suit against Ballard in the event that Ballard refused to sell. Not all of them had agreed, but enough had done so to make Ballard's resistance futile in the long run.

What, I asked myself, could Ballard have done if he had been granted that ten years of life and health he longed for? He could have made a great deal of trouble, but he would have been like a man standing in the path of a flood that grows slowly from a rill to a torrent. For I knew then and I see even more clearly now that I was looking at a blueprint for empire—the empire of property, of ownership, of money. Settlers were pouring west in a picturesque throng. That was the obvious, the spectacular thing. But behind the settlers was coming a stream of money, of organized capital. It was invisible, but it was the potent, the irresistible thing. Money was the new conqueror, the power destined to triumph and rule for generations.

The West for fifty years had been truly a world of free wealth. It is hard for anyone who did not see it to understand that world. Men drove their wagons across hundreds of miles of rich black soil without ever a thought of settlement or ownership. The cattle range was one vast communal pasture where any man might graze his herd. The forests stood waiting the ax and no one thought them worth seizing. Gold and silver and fur were there for the taking. The problem was not to find wealth but to hold it and defend it and find a market for it. It seemed as though there was more of everything than men could ever use.

With the thrust of rails across the continent, free wealth was doomed, although only a few were shrewd enough to know it. The world of money and monopoly then was in the making—the world of fences and titles and mortgages, the world of the few who have and the many who want. Money worked a vast and inevitable transformation in the West—I do not belittle it—but it destroyed one kind of man and created another. The men such as Ballard, who conquered the West, were reckless men with a touch of the heroic about them. Some of them were good men and some were deadly men, with blood upon their hands. But money is never reckless and never heroic. Money is cunning and it finds and uses and creates cunning men. Money has a long arm. It may kill but it seldom faces its victim.

Blore was the agent of money. His strength was not in his right arm, nor in his personal power, but in his complete and devious scheme, and in the money that lay behind him. If Blore had died or vanished another would have come to take his place. I know now that Ballard's day was over, and I think he knew it too. Ballard was a shrewd man, but not a man of money or of financial schemes. Money had been only a plaything to him—a counter he tossed across a table with a lavish hand. Money was his nemesis as surely as rifles and whisky had been the nemesis to the Indians.

As I sat looking at Blore, I knew I faced a cunning man, and I proposed to practice a little cunning myself. I came of a race of traders, of men who win their victories on the pages of a ledger, who fear nothing but the figures in red. I knew that business is business and that making a bargain is an imaginative art. In a word, I proposed to bluff. I had no doubt that Blore was a gifted liar, and I did not propose to be outdone in the arts of invention.

Our meeting was cordial in the extreme. It had an atmosphere of mutual esteem which was somewhat bogus and of mutual confidence which was wholly so. We trusted each other as do a couple of tomcats maneuvering for position before a fight but nothing of this showed in our manners. We drank our brandies and lit our cigars as though this were the friendliest occasion anyone could imagine. I complimented Blore on his horsemanship. He in turn, it appeared, had heard of me and of my father and was delighted to find himself dealing with a man who knew the necessities of business and also its amenities. We were delighted with each other and each of us was busily engaged in trying to spot the weakness in the other. I began by saying that I personally favored the sale, regarded it as a good necessary thing. In effect, I was working for Blore, trying to expedite his business. But my principal, I indicated, was a bit difficult. He did not understand finance. For him possession had always been rather more than nine-tenths of the law. What he believed in was personal power, and of this, I felt bound to make it clear, he had a great deal.

I knew well that what Blore and his backers most feared was the lawless men and the lawless spirit which then infested the West. The fact is that the notion of private property, as something sacred and inviolable, had never been established west of the Mississippi. A man who built his house and corral beside a waterhole felt that he owned it because he used it, but he would not deny the right of anyone else to share the surrounding range. Livestock on the range had a way of changing hands in a most informal fashion. The feeling was general that a calf belonged to whoever put his brand upon it, and few thought it a crime to shoot a calf when they needed beef, without any regard to the brand under which it was born. Only a horse thief was truly a social outcast because to steal a man's saddle horse was often to leave him helpless. For twenty years the cattle barons fought a war with rustlers who were not truly criminals but only men who had never learned a proper respect for vested interest. In the Rocky Mountain country that war was just beginning, but I knew men such as Blore and Tweedale were aware they proposed to invade a lawless world, and they were afraid of it—for money is always timid. So I placed a gentle and diplomatic emphasis upon the fact that the men who surrounded the Ballard grant and dealt at the Ballard store were all lawless men, rustlers by origin if not by profession, men who wore their guns whenever they wore their clothes. I made it clear that Ballard controlled them and that it was not going to be easy for anyone else to do so without his good will.

All this, of course, was true enough. But I contrived a delicate implication that Ballard's mood was a defiant one, that his good will was worth a great deal, that it might be won with my expert assistance, but it was going to cost something.

While I held forth, Blore sat watching me with those bright, bulging eyes of his. They were as unrevealing as a couple of polished doorknobs. I have never trusted men with eyes of that kind. Feeling betrays itself in the muscles around the eyes, in a twitching corner or a mobile lid, but a pop-eyed man has little of this expressive play. He has the steady stare of an owl or a lynx. . . . Blore's face did not give him away, but I noticed that as he listened he kept crossing and uncrossing his legs, as I could tell by the shift of his body, and this, I knew, is always a sign of nervousness. I had him worried and I had him guessing. I paused to relight my cigar and sat waiting for him to lead. He shifted his pins twice before he spoke.

"All right, Morgan," he said. "What do you want?"

I knew then that I had the advantage. After all, I had had it from the first, so far as bargaining was concerned. I knew a great deal more about Ballard and the grant than he did. No doubt he and his backers were irresistible in the long run, but they could have a great deal of trouble and I was in a position to make trouble. So now I made my major bluff. I told him that I thought the sale might be arranged provided Ballard was left in charge as manager. I knew, of course, that Ballard would accept no such arrangement, but I felt almost equally sure that Blore would not. The shake of his head was emphatic—a quick, nervous reaction.

"I'm afraid my principals wouldn't agree to that," he said shortly.

I nodded gravely. I pointed out that the administration of such a property would be an exacting job. I thought the identity of the manager was a legitimate consideration in the making of the deal. Whom, I inquired, did he have in mind for the position?

Blore did not hesitate for an instant.

"I expect to take it myself," he said. He spoke with a finality, a confidence, an intensity, which revealed the man at last. I knew now, what I had suspected all along, that Blore was a power-hungry man. I have no doubt that the first article of his own private agreement with Tweedale was that he should rule. He wanted to move into the great house, sit in the place of absolute authority. The power that Ballard had built was the thing he had bargained for, dreamed of, coveted. Doubtless he had also imagined a great expansion, as I had done. I faced a man with a vision, backed by a passionate desire. I knew he would not renounce it, and I also knew he would pay for it. I felt sure that now I was in a position to dictate. I boosted the price about fifty thousand dollars and specified that Ballard must have a year to put his affairs in order. On these terms, I told Blore, I would do my best to persuade Ballard that he must sell.

Blore sat silent for a moment, which contained a good deal of suspense for me, although I knew well enough what he was thinking. He was wondering how much of my talk was bluff, how much power I had with Ballard. He could refuse my terms and still force Ballard out—in the long run. But it might be a very long run and a very hard one and that was just what he didn't want. It had taken him many months to perfect his scheme and to get Ballard's ear. He couldn't afford to let the moment pass without a decision. He nodded slowly, smiled. Like all cunning men he was infallibly smooth.

"Agreed," he said lightly, as though we had been bargaining for apples. "Fifty thousand dollars more or less is not important in a deal of this size. The year is more than I had expected, but I'll agree to that too, provided Ballard will sign within a week."

The signing was a brief occasion but an impressive one to me, for I knew that I was watching a ruler abdicate and a man resign his life. I had gone all over the papers with Ballard before we called Blore in. There was nothing more to say. Ballard took a pen and signed his name slowly and carefully in his large upright hand with its powerful downstrokes. He pushed the paper across the table to Blore.

"All right, Major," he said quietly, "it's all yours. . . . And God help you!"

CONSUELO

During his last summer in the Dark River Valley Jean Ballard seldom appeared on his porch in the afternoon, as he had done for so many years, but he often went there late in the evening and sometimes sat alone far into the night. Because he had been alone so much in his youth it was easy for him to go back to solitude now. In his early years of mountain wandering he had sat alone beside a thousand campfires, and like all solitary outdoor men he had learned to live upon his own mind, without benefit of printed page, simply ruminating upon his own experience, licking the wounds it had given him, savoring the flavor of its good. After he had come to the valley, for many years his life had been driven and crowded and his thought had all looked ahead, facing exigent necessity. . . . All that was over now. Now he sat alone again as the night deepened and the life about him disappeared and went to sleep. For a while he saw lights scattered all up and down the valley road and heard talk and laughter and the tinkle of music. One by one the lights died, the voices fell silent, the night seemed to swallow the human world. It seemed to blot out all he had built and done in so many years, leaving him alone once more with stars and mountains, with the voices of wind and water—and with all his former selves. Now that his life was leaving him he seemed to possess it more completely than ever before, to see it whole and clear for the first time. He remembered now all the blunders of his younger years, all the times he had seemed blind to the value of things, but he also remembered much of peace and much of passionate delight. There were many things to regret, but even so, the night was crowded with the ghosts of good moments, as though all of them were coming back to say good-by. He was one who had loved life and to such men memory is kind.

— 2 —

There in the dark Consuelo came back to him. It was the first time in years she had come to him, but he was not wholly surprised and she came quietly and confidently, as though this had been a tryst long appointed, as though both of them had known that in the end she would return, and he laid his hand upon hers to let her know she was welcome. Evening after evening they sat silent for the most part. Even in the years when they had been so close they had not talked much except of trivial things and necessary things. They had never tried to explain themselves to each other. Their relation had rested upon wordless understanding and especially upon her intuitive understanding of the fact that he could not communicate much of himself, even to those he loved, that he was a man shut up in a reticence deeply rooted in his past. Ever since boyhood, life had called upon him for cunning and caution, for alertness. He had grown up in a wilderness and had kept all his life something of the silent watchfulness of the wild. For many years he had been an armed man watching his back track. Then for many years he had been a man of power who had learned over and over that safety lies not in trusting men but in seeing them for exactly what they are. He had learned how to live and triumph, he had grown strong enough to be merciful, but he had never opened his mind to anyone.

It was Consuelo who began to speak of the past as though she knew instinctively his mind was ranging back among the years. She spoke quietly and casually of little things, of moments and details, and he listened and nodded and sometimes chuckled. Her voice was truly the voice of the past for it had never changed. There in the dark she was the past come alive and speaking. She spoke mostly of the first years, the hardest years, before they built the big house and before the great road came to their door. Then it had been three days on a good horse to Taos when the weather was open, and no human habitation was nearer. When the deep snows fell it might as well have been a thousand miles to anywhere. They were locked away from the whole world.

It was not pioneering as he had known it in his youth. They had come to the valley with cattle and sheep and fifty good horses and six peons. They built a house of squared timbers there where the great one stood now and quarters down along the river for their followers and corrals and a barn. They were ricos and Consuelo created at once a bit of the world that had produced her, with servants that came when she clapped her hands and a good cook and chocolate, wine and sugar, the luxuries of her kind. But the wilderness did not know they were important people. The wolves almost wiped out their first band of sheep, mountain lions killed their colts and calves. Even before the Arapahoe tried to destroy them, little war parties of young Indians were always sneaking in, stealing a beef or trying to stampede a herd of sheep. For a long time it looked as though this had been a crazy adventure, just as everyone had said it would be. After three years they had less stock than when they started across the mountains. That fall the Apaches were known to be raiding all over the territory from the Gila in the south to the Brazos in the north, and it was followed by a winter when the snow almost buried their house. A rumor spread in Taos that they had both been killed, that an Apache had tried to sell Ballard's scalp, and another rumor had it that Consuelo had been taken captive and was to be held for a ransom. In the spring, the Don, old and sick as he was, led an armed party across the mountains to look for their bones. Followed by fifteen young men armed with bell-mouthed buffalo guns and horse pistols, he came riding down the valley and found Jean Ballard planting oats and shearing his few remaining sheep and Consuelo bossing her kitchen and singing to her child. They gave a great feast for the visitors, killed a beef and barbecued it, poured out the last drop of their wine and said no, they were not going back, they were never going back. They stood together in their doorway and waved long farewells to the departing riders, watched them out of sight, then turned and embraced each other and laughed.

Those were the best years, the hard years, when they lived in a little world of their own creation, bounded by mountains, admitting no intruders, living wholly for each other. But were they really hard years? That was a simple life with a simple discipline. Wolves and mountain lions and thieving Indians were nothing to what came later. Work and physical danger are simple things to deal with. What makes life hard is the bewilderment of change and complication, the rush of people and money, the impact of unexpected things, the swelling current of destiny that sweeps a man along even though he rides it successfully, that sweeps people apart, that wipes out whole patterns of living and creates new ones. This he had come to understand, though he could not say it, and he hoped she understood it too. Now in the long retrospect he understood what had happened to him and he wished he could explain it to her. He remembered so well the barren poverty of his boyhood, the great hungers of his youth, the avid longing with which he looked upon the wealth of St. Louis and of the ricos in Santa Fe and Taos. For so long he had been a landless man, a homeless man, a wandering man always in danger, one who lived on the meat he killed like a wild animal and went for months without seeing a woman or sleeping in a bed. Much of that life had been good to live and much of it was good to remember, but it had been a life of danger and denial, outside the warm circle of love and safety and secure possession. Marriage had been his first taste of tenderness since his mother died, his first taste of security in the possession of anything. He had been happy in the early years in the valley, would have asked nothing better, had expected nothing very different. But then had come the sudden burst of fortune, the flood of money. He had discovered in himself great powers and great appetites that might otherwise have slept all his life. He had long been a leader in a small way, one who had ridden at the head of a band and told others what to do, but he had never dreamed that he could command so much, that so many would bow to his will and jump at his word. Now that it was over he could see that for years he had been drunk on power and money, never quite losing his head, always quick and cunning, but driven by a lust of command and possession and by a great restlessness that sent him back and forth between the mountains and the railroad towns. The women he had taken had been nothing more than fruits of triumph, like the splendid horses he rode in relays. He had learned how desire sprouts in the moment of triumph and how women long to yield to any form of power they can feel. He had never meant to turn away from Consuelo and none had ever taken her place, but he had lived for years in a fever of success that grew on its own triumphs, and when it began to subside he had learned, as everyone learns, that he could not go back to the past, that he had been destroying one thing while he was building another. He saw all this, like a picture on a wall, but he had not the words to tell it. He could only repeat a phrase over and over.

"I was a fool, Carita," he said. "I never meant to go away from you. . . . I was a fool."

She wanted only to comfort him now as she might have comforted a child.

"I do not blame you, Juanito," she told him. "It was my fault too."

"I had been so poor," he said. "I had wanted so much. You cannot understand that. You always had everything. . . ."

"Yes, I can understand," she said. "And you finally had so much more than I. You had the whole world to deal with and I had nothing but you, especially after the girls had gone away to school. As long as they were little and I could teach them, it was different, but the world seems to claim everything, to take everything away. . . ."

"I never meant to leave you," he repeated.

"It was my fault as much as yours," she told him. "If I could have remained beautiful it might have been different. Oh, my beloved, I could never admit this before, but I was a vain woman! I could not bear to grow old. I turned away from you because I could not bear to be less beautiful in your eyes. . . . I must confess, Juanito! I was jealous even of my own daughter that she had my beauty and I had it no longer, that your eyes were all for her. . . . It was then I turned to God. . . . For the love of God! For the love of God! For the love of God I turned away from you because I could no longer be to you what I had been before. I spent long hours on my knees, staring at my lighted candles, my little ivory Jesus with his painted wounds, my Virgin of Guadalupe in her niche with her folded hands and her eyes rolling at Heaven. I wanted to love something that would never change, I wanted to lose myself. For long hours I lost myself. Time fell away from me and a day died in a moment. But I did not see God. I saw only pictures of the beloved past. I did not yearn for Heaven. I wanted only my own lost beauty and the moment of our love. . . ."

"I never knew . . ." He fumbled for the words that came so easily to her. "If I had only known!"

"I understand that, Juanito," she said. "I did not blame you then. I do not blame you now. I am sorry only for my own vanity. . . . May God forgive me!"

Her voice was a music moving to the high pitch of her feeling—a music that carried him all the way back to the first moment of their love. Her voice was the music of the unforgotten past, the perfect and finished past, of all the vivid moments that can never be again. He remembered them just as vividly as she did but he had not her gift of words. He too was filled with a great, troubled warmth of feeling but he could not utter it.

"I have come back to you now, Carita," he said gravely. "Nothing else now seems to be worth anything. . . . If God will not forgive us, we can forgive each other."

REQUIEM

At his own request Jean Ballard was buried in a grove of yellow pine on the crest of a knoll overlooking the Dark River Valley and at his own request the only service was there beside the grave. Nearly a thousand people, the largest gathering ever held in the valley, followed his body to the hilltop and banked the slopes. Nearly all of the Mexicans from Roy-ball-town were there, most of the cattlemen who had traded at the Ballard store and ridden the Ballard range, a group of officers from Santa Fe and Fort Union, and the wives of all these kinds of men, nearly all of them in black, the Mexican women hooding their faces under their great black shawls, looking like figures of death in a frieze. Only the Utes did not come to the grave side. Down at the foot of the hill they had set up a great lodge, made of buffalo hides, a relic of the days of their power, and there they gathered to mourn Ballard in their own way.

It was also Ballard's wish that his friend Daniel Laird should preside at his funeral. The big mountaineer stood up with his hat in his hand and recited the prayer for the dead. Afterward he was silent for a long moment, as though embarrassed or tongue-tied, and a faint rustle of uneasiness ran through the crowd. Then Laird delivered one of his rare speeches.

"The man we have come here to bury was a friend to all of us, and one we will long miss," he said slowly, and his great voice at once commanded the crowd. "Here in the Dark River Valley there has been peace among men for many years and that peace was made and kept by him. In all the years I have lived here no man has ever gone hungry. His table was set for all humanity. In all of those years there has never been a thief or a beggar among us, because no man felt his need denied. We have all sheltered under the strength of our friend, far more than most of us know. Now that he is gone we will learn that he was great, and some of us will learn in pain and trouble."

He paused for a long moment and then began again, even more slowly.

"We mourn that our friend is dead," he said, "but let us not have sorrow only, for death is kind. Let us rejoice that his long pain is over, that all suffering has an end, that he now can lie down and sleep in the earth he loved, the earth that gave him being—that he shall have rebirth in new forms of life, that tree and grass and flower shall take up his fallen clay and lift it once more to the sun."

When he had finished a sound of chanting came up from the valley and the whole crowd turned to look. The Utes had emerged from their tepee and formed a long column, all of them stripped to their breech-clouts, with their faces painted black. They moved in a slow dance to a deep booming chant, their feet and their voices both in perfect time. It was their ancient dance of mourning for a fallen chief, and in it they seemed to regain some long lost power and dignity, so that all stood and watched them in reverent silence until they disappeared into the forest and their chanting grew faint and was lost in the wind. Then the clods fell, the tall woman in black gave one great sobbing cry, the people turned away and began to talk again.

PART THREE
THE USURPERS

MAJOR ARNOLD NEWTON BLORE

Arnold Blore did not feel the war as a personal defeat until he rode home after Lee's surrender. Not until he saw his house and his father did he understand that the only world he knew had been destroyed and that he had to seek a new one.

For him the war had been a triumph so absorbing that he had thought little of anything except his own fortunes. He had gone through it all unwounded. He had tasted power for the first time. He had commanded hundreds and destroyed thousands. For most men war was misery and horror but for some it was a great fulfillment, releasing energies and desires they had never known they possessed, and Blore was one of these. His swift rise from the ranks was almost incredible to himself. His knowledge of horses and his rare gift for managing them was his first asset, and it gained him quick promotion to the rank of sergeant, but he soon discovered that he had also a gift for command and a talent for maneuver and for artillery fire. His opportunity came in the long wilderness battle, when both the commissioned officers of his battery were killed and command fell upon him by right of rank. In a swift and daring maneuver he brought his guns to a hilltop, flanked an enemy column, saw men stumble and fall in the sweep of his fire, saw a regiment break and scatter and turn into a futile mob. He got his commission promptly. In war nothing counted but ability.

Arnold Blore loved artillery, although he had never thought of himself as a fighting man. In all his life he had never wanted to fight with his own hands. But he loved the roar of the great guns, the flame and smoke of destruction. He loved a power that struck like a thunderbolt when he spoke the word. Battle filled him with a great elation, almost an ecstasy, and this feeling was always associated with the thunder of a battery, which was the very voice of battle to him. He was never confused or frightened. The only thing that gave him pain was the sight and sound of wounded horses. He did not mind seeing men fall. This surprised him at first but he accepted it rather easily because it was a great advantage in battle not to feel any personal shock.

106

He never understood how much the war had meant to him until it was over. When the guns fell silent, life seemed suddenly tame and flat. He felt small again, riding home alone, with no command behind him, no battle before.

— 2 —

He did not have far to ride. The Blores lived on the Virginia side of the Potomac, north of Washington, in a region that had been horse country since colonial days—a country of rolling hills and good grass. His grandfather, Edward Blore, had bought the place and established a stud farm there when he was an old man, and his father, William, had built the red brick house with the white-pillared porch—a house which expressed a social aspiration long denied.

Arnold rode down a rutted lane bordered by massive junipers and very old cherry trees which had been planted by birds that perched on the rotting rail fences on either side. In this month of May the cherry trees were in bloom, bobwhites whistled from the fence posts and wind rippled the grass in wide pastures. The house stood in a grove of forest trees with thick woodland climbing the hill behind it and pastures sloping down to the river in front.

As soon as he saw the place he had an impression of neglect and decay. The lawn had grown into long grass with broom sedge and even a few briars creeping in. The rose bushes on either side of the driveway had spread into an unkempt bramble, and a startled grouse went whirring out of their cover, making him feel as though he rode into a wilderness—as though the woodland and the wild were creeping up on the old house, now that the power had gone out of it. He could see white paint peeling off the pillars and green paint peeling off the shutters and the heavy-odored honeysuckle had almost buried the porch.

Arnold's mother had died before the war and his sister had married and gone to live in Maryland. The old man was living there alone now, except for a few Negroes who had stayed because they didn't know what else to do. At the height of their fortunes the Blores had owned about a dozen slaves—house servants and stable hands and a couple of men who tended a garden and a small orchard. The Blores raised nothing but horses and truck for their own table.

Arnold knew that his father had not been well, that the war had destroyed the market for horses, that the Negroes were a net loss. He had been prepared for hard times but not for the air of desolation and decay that possessed the place. He felt as though he had come back to something dead. The house was silent as a deserted house and it remained silent for a long moment after he knocked. Then he heard faint movement within, the door swung open and there stood old Cora, the great, fat, chocolate-colored woman who had been the family cook for about eighteen years, had fed him and wiped his nose when he was a child. She stood staring at him for a moment with her mouth open, as though she couldn't quite believe in his existence. Then she came forward and put her arms around him and said over and over, "You is home again! You is home again!"

Cora was one human he had always counted on and he felt something of the warmth and security of childhood in the pressure of her great soft body. He had always liked Negroes, as he liked horses, because they were submissive. He could guess that Cora now was doing more than anyone else to keep the household going. But he was staring over her shoulder at a large, shapely, full-bosomed yellow girl of about sixteen who had followed Cora into the hall and now stood giggling self-consciously. Cora released him, looked from one to the other of them, seemed to unite them in her broad smile.

"Don't you know little Milly?" she demanded. Then he knew this was Cora's daughter, who had been just a dirty child around the kitchen when he rode away. She was clean now in blue calico and a red headcloth and she came forward and gave him a soft, slavish hand and giggled at him again and purred something inarticulate in her musical Negro voice. He felt a sudden unwilling stir of desire toward her as he took her hand—a certainty that her soft yellow flesh was waiting for him, that he could sink into it and be mired there, in a way of life that had lost its hope and promise but still had a powerful hold upon him because all the roots of his being were in it. In the presence of these two women with their clean Negro smell, their caressing voices, he sensed what had happened. They had moved in on the old man, moved in on the house and taken it over, just as the woodland had moved into the grounds. He could feel them reaching out for him, wanting to capture him, suck him down into this easy half-rotten world.

"Yoah Pappy ain't right well today," Cora murmured as she led him toward the sitting room and opened the door.

The light was dim in there but it was enough to show a disorder of scattered papers and tobacco pipes, bottles and glasses. William Blore was seated behind a heavy table and when he rose Arnold could see that he was quite drunk. He lifted himself with both hands on the table and tottered forward—a short bowlegged man of sixty with powerful shoulders like all the Blores. Although they loved and married big women, they all bred true to the same type in the male line, as though an inexorable providence had designed them all to be jockeys.

"By God, my boy, I'm glad to see you! Have a drink. Pour him a drink, Cora. By God, everything will be all right now!"

He retreated to his chair and slumped back into it with heavy relief. Cora poured whisky and water, and turned to Arnold.

"Now I's gonna get you the best dinner you's et since you went away," she told him. "Chicken an' yams an' snaps and biscuits. . . ." She swept out of the room, laughing happily, possessive and assured. She had food and woman to offer and she could conceive of no other need or desire.

When they were alone, William Blore pushed his glass away from him with sudden resolution, shook his head, seemed to lift himself out of his stupor by conscious effort.

"Arnold, my boy," he said, "I lied to you just now. Nothing is all right. Nothing is worth a damn. This country is ruined. Racing is all over and money is all gone and you can't sell a two-year-old for what it costs to raise him. What am I now? Just a goddam nigger-loving poor white! . . . Arnold, my boy, I hate to see you go, but you've got to go. I've been making up my mind to that ever since I heard it was all over. There's nothing I can do for you here, and nothing you can do for me. There's two good colts in the pasture. That's all I've got to give you but they'll take you anywhere a horse can travel. . . ."

— 3 —

The house of Blore was founded on a horse and it had been associated with almost the entire history of thoroughbred racing stock in the South. The Virginians especially had always loved racing, but the quarter horse, short coupled and fast for a few hundred yards, had been the race horse of colonial days and racing had been only an informal sport. Not many thoroughbreds were imported until early in the nineteenth century. The famous stallion Fenwick, whose blood was to run through American racing lines for many generations, was one of the first of them. He was imported by Wade Hampton who went to London to make the purchase. At the same time he employed Edward Blore, the British jockey, who had trained the great stallion and ridden him to all his victories on the British turf. Blore proved to be an even better investment than Fenwick. He served the Hampton family as head trainer and jockey for twenty years and won much money for his master. He saved his wages, married a big girl from the mountain country of western Virginia, and established a stud farm of his own about 1830. His son William came into the property in 1845 when racing in Virginia was at the highest point of its development. Almost every great estate had its private track and there were public courses at Fairfield, Broad Rock, New Market and Tree Hill, where the ruling families of three states came together every year for a racing season. The racing balls of those days were the most exclusive and elaborate gatherings in the South.

It was William Blore who bred the famous stallion Timoleon, and Timoleon founded the family fortune. No stallion in American racing history had ever sired so many winning colts. Mares were sent to him from all over Virginia and South Carolina and as far south as New Orleans. He had a prodigious fertility. In one year he covered nearly two hundred mares at a hundred dollars a leap. His loins were a gold mine. They enlarged the Blore acres, built the red brick house with the white columns, bought the slaves which gave William Blore all the trapping and service of a Virginia gentleman. Moreover, Timoleon brought many of the most famous gentlemen of Virginia to his house. They treated him with distinguished courtesy but they did not invite him to their houses. They came to see Timoleon, who had breeding in every sense of the word. William Blore welcomed them and took their good money and began quietly hating them.

In the course of three generations the Blores underwent a peculiar social evolution. Edward Blore was the happiest of the three because he had the training of an English servant. All his life he dropped his H's and took off his cap or pulled his forelock when he approached his betters. He had the indestructible, inborn cockney feeling for caste. Moreover, he was too completely absorbed in horses to care much for human society. He raised a famous mare called Creeping Kate who won him much money on the Virginia track, and she became the love of his later years. It was said he never bred her because he was jealous of the stud.

William Blore looked almost exactly like his father, but he had a different speech and manner. He never quite mastered the soft southern inflection but neither did he speak like a cockney Englishman. He had a deferent manner in all his dealings with his proud customers but it was an uneasy deference that covered a resentment. He resented his own uneasiness as much as he resented the perfect manners of his patrons who were fortified by a snobbery so complete that they were not conscious of it as such. William Blore was a shrewd little man with a keen mind. He knew he was more intelligent than many of these gentlemen. During his best years he was also more secure and prosperous than most of them. In these last two decades before the war the Virginian aristocracy had renounced none of its pretensions but it lived upon a dying economy. Tobacco lands were worn out and Virginia planters lived more and more by selling Negroes to be sent to Alabama and Georgia where cotton was booming. William Blore knew that many of them were selling their own blood. He thought it more dignified to breed horses for the market than men. In his later years he drank a good deal. When he was mildly drunk and among his family he became a man his patrons would hardly have recognized, with a mouth full of earthy epithet and profanity whenever he talked about them.

In Arnold Blore the transformation of speech and manner became complete. He spoke exactly like a Virginia gentleman and he had southern courtesy in a form that was slightly exaggerated but good enough so that strangers always took him for a gentleman. But of course he was not a gentleman. He was a horse trader, a trainer, sometimes a jockey. And he was the grandson of a cockney servant in a society which worshiped ancestry and status. Arnold Blore learned from childhood how to be faultlessly polite to the men he dealt with and also how to despise them. Although he did not know it, he had toward these people the same attitude the Negroes had toward the whites—an attitude subtly compounded of hypocrisy, cunning, envy and contempt.

— 4 —

The Shadwells lived only a few miles from the Blores, but they lived in another world. They were related to the Washingtons on one side and the Pendletons on the other and their lands had been in the family for five generations. The estate contained about a thousand acres of which more than half was woodland, but the rest of it had once been good tobacco land and highly profitable. Most of this now was worn out and grown up to oldfield pine and broom sedge. A few hundred acres of corn and some garden truck were all their fields produced. They raised hogs which ran half wild in their woodlands and they made famous hams and bacons, or at least the old Negro who had charge of their smokehouse did. They still had about thirty-five Negroes, although once the estate had supported more than a hundred. Almost every year they sold a few, generally black field hands, but sometimes it became necessary to sell one of the yellow Negroes who worked around the house, and belonged to families the Shadwells had owned for generations. This always brought tears to the eyes of both slave and master, but Mark Shadwell was heavily in debt and Negroes were his most negotiable assets. He was a dignified gentleman in his late fifties, took his debts lightly and never let them curb his hospitality. The Shadwells could still entertain twenty at dinner and more than that at hunt breakfasts. Of course the place produced abundant food, including game from their own forests and hams from their own smokehouse. And there were only four of the Shadwells now—the old man, his fat and ailing wife, his son, Mark junior, who was charming and devoted his life to hunting, and his seventeen-year-old daughter, Gracie, who was already one of the best horsewomen in the country and could take a four-rail fence in her sidesaddle in perfect form. Gracie was a spontaneous, undisciplined creature, large and mature-looking for her years, who spent much of her time riding around the country alone, often taking a few fences just for the fun of it. She scandalized older women by her horsy talk and the freedom of her manners, but she went her way gaily and unconcerned. Gossip could not really damage a Shadwell, and everyone knew that Gracie was a fine girl but too much for her parents.

The Shadwells had several blooded mares which they bred to important stallions and once in a while they produced a colt that sold for large money. One of these colts brought Arnold Blore into somewhat intimate contact with the Shadwells, for the colt inevitably came to him for training. The Shadwells knew horses and could breed horses, but none of them could train a colt. The old man was past the age for such an undertaking and Mark junior had an unstable temper. He made horses nervous. Only Gracie had the real feeling for horses, the mysterious gift of hand and voice which horses seem to recognize almost instantly. Gracie might have been a trainer if she had been a man and not a Shadwell.

This colt, who was named Diomed after a famous stallion of colonial days, came to the Blore stables less than a year before the war, when Arnold was twenty-four. Arnold was already taking over much of his father's work, had trained several winners and had a reputation of his own. Diomed came to him wholly untaught. He put the colt through his first paces at the end of a long rope and in the sand pen, nailed his first shoes and saddled him for the first time. By that time he felt sure the colt was going to be a winner, and told his father so. They made the Shadwells a good offer for Diomed, but old Mark wouldn't sell. He said the colt belonged to Gracie, had been given her for a birthday present. This, of course, was mostly pretense. The colt was a family asset and would be sold at the right time, but Mark Shadwell was smart enough to know that if the Blores wanted to buy Diomed he was probably worth keeping until he was a two-year-old.

When the colt began to show his class, the old man and his son and Gracie all stopped at the Blore track, singly or together in a casual way, to watch Arnold work with him. The men soon lost interest, but not Gracie. She was a true horse lover and Diomed was her current love. He was a beautiful sorrel gelding with a coat that shone in the sun like new gold and the large full soft eye of the horse that is naturally gentle and never shows his whites to his masters. Gracie continued to stop at the Blore track every time she went for a ride and that was several times a week. At first she only stopped outside the fence, waved a greeting to Arnold and sat her horse to watch the colt go through his paces. But she could no more keep her hands off Diomed than she could keep her eyes off him. Soon she was riding into the paddock to examine his carefully wrapped ankles, to pat his neck, to feed him a carrot, and she and Arnold had several good talks, all about horses. This sort of visiting was an unusual thing for a woman to do in that time and place, but somehow not unusual for Gracie, who always went where she felt like going. When she was ready to leave, Arnold always cupped his two hands to hold her foot and boosted her onto her horse, for no woman could mount a sidesaddle unassisted.

After that first talk Gracie's visits became more frequent and Arnold began to anticipate her coming with eagerness. He spent more and more time with the colt, just in the hope that Gracie would come along. He was always watching for her, always saw her in the distance and waved to her and she waved back. She always dismounted now, and after the work-out was over they would sit side by side on a bench near the track and talk, sometimes for half an hour. They never talked about anything except horses in general and the colt in particular, as though it had been tacitly understood that this was their only common ground and that their relation must be strictly confined to it. But it was amazing how much they found to say, and how much they laughed together. Arnold felt sure that Gracie was happy with him and he was happy with her but she also gave him a growing feeling of insecurity. All his life he had lived inside the shell of his carefully cultivated manner, so far as almost everyone except the family was concerned. It was a manner he had inherited and perfected and he felt safe behind it. He had learned never to express his feelings. But he knew that with Gracie his defenses were in danger, especially when she sat beside him.

Gracie was not a beautiful girl but she was an attractive one. She was just a shade taller than Arnold and a little heavier. Her face was broad and good-humored, with large gray eyes, and a sprinkle of freckles across her nose. Her thick yellow hair was a little unkempt so that she was always tucking it up and brushing it back. She wore the long, voluminous riding skirt all horsewomen wore in those days, but in warm weather she never wore the jacket that went with it. Her blouse left her forearms bare and she had beautiful arms and hands—large, strong hands trained from childhood in a struggle with tugging bridle reins. To Arnold she looked perfect, as ripe fruit and newly blown flowers are perfect. He had never fallen in love before and he did not understand exactly what was happening to him. He talked horse and laughed and everything seemed to be all right, but all the time he was looking into her eyes and she was looking right back at him, never evading his steady, eager stare. His manner was holding up all right, but he was filled with a disturbing mixture of reverence and lust. He longed to serve Gracie, to do something heroic and astonishing for her, and he also longed to possess her large, soft, virginal body. The thrust and swell of his desire seemed a hidden, guilty threat to his careful manners, and when he cupped his hands to lift her into the saddle he was aware that they trembled a little. Once her horse swerved, throwing her leg hard against his body. She did not apologize but laughed happily and rode away, throwing him a smile over her shoulder, blushing but not at all confused. He knew then that a moment was coming, that there would have to be a climax.

It came one day when she had hoisted herself precariously to the top bar of a gate beside the track and perched there watching him work with the colt. When he had finished and turned Diomed over to the stable boy he came toward her and she held out both hands for him to help her down. She descended into his arms gracefully and easily, almost inevitably. He did not feel as though he had committed any aggression. She seemed to fall into his arms as a ripe peach falls into the hand that touches it. But when he had her there he could not let her go. He held her tightly and he could feel the beat of her heart against his ribs and the full, firm pressure of her breasts. He pushed her head back and kissed her hard on the lips. For a moment she was limp in his arms. He had a moment of triumph for her mouth was open and his tongue touched hers and he knew something in Gracie was answering to his desire. Then she pushed him away and stood staring at him with tears in her eyes and her lips trembling. She seemed suddenly transformed. In a moment a challenging, willing woman became a frightened, bewildered child. Then she covered her face with her hands and began to cry.

"Don't cry, Miss Gracie," he said, "I'm sorry."

He was more than sorry, he was sick. He stood before her, weak and helpless, until she dried her tears and walked over to her horse without looking at him. He cupped his hands and boosted her into the saddle, and she whirled her horse and rode away in a dead run, as though she had been overcome by an impulse of panic flight.

He never saw her again except a few times at a distance, and every time he did, he felt that same sickness in the pit of his stomach.

Mark Shadwell came over a few days later and took Diomed away. He was exceedingly polite and a little apologetic about it. He said they simply couldn't afford to go on with the training, at least not this year, with war threatening and the bottom dropping out of everything.

Even then, a few months before Sumter, many people in Virginia didn't believe there would be any war, and others thought it would not amount to anything. When it broke out, Arnold Blore enlisted at once, despite the protests of his father. William Blore didn't believe in secession or feel that he had any stake in the conflict. He felt that the war was an unnecessary disaster which had been brought on by these proud sons-of-bitches with their peculiar institution and their highfalutin talk. Arnold did not argue with his father. He was not interested in the issues of war either but he had a sure, intuitive conviction that war had meaning and value for him. He was full of war, and only half aware that Gracie Shadwell had sent him into battle.

— 5 —

When Arnold Blore left home again after Lee's surrender, he went first to St. Louis, driving the two young thoroughbreds his father had given him, hitched to a light wagon called a democrat. Almost everyone in the South who started west after the war went first to St. Louis, unless he was bound for Santa Fe by way of Independence. St. Louis was the boom city of the Mississippi Valley. It doubled its population ten years after the war and had almost two hundred thousand people when Arnold first saw it—a great overgrown town sprawling along the river where docks were multiplying to meet the greatest fleet of steamboats the river was ever to carry, and climbing the low hills from its turbulent roaring waterfront to the red brick dignity of its best residential streets. Because timber was scarce almost everything was built of brick, even the sidewalks, and for the same reason everyone burned soft coal, which darkly smudged the great red city and buried it under a black cloud when the wind was down. Americans were pouring into St. Louis from all over the South, but German immigrants of the first wave were coming even faster, creating the first large foreign colony of the West.

It was easy to make money in St. Louis and Arnold Blore made good money from the first. Inevitably he became a horse trader because horses were the only commodity he knew. He gained a capital by selling his two thoroughbreds for high prices, rented a small stable and began buying and selling horses. He had a sure eye for a colt that could be given style and sold at a fat profit, and he was also good at matching pairs and selling them to the carriage trade. Soon he was renting horses and equipage of all kinds, as well as selling them. His livery stable became one of the best in the city. But Arnold Blore was not content to stay there, and knew from the first he was not going to stay. In St. Louis he had become what his father had been—a purveyor of horse flesh to gentlemen. He did not know exactly what he wanted but he knew this was not it. He also knew that sooner or later he was going farther west. He was one of thousands of men who felt the same way. In those years men were drifting west in a vast unorganized migration. Many of them, like Arnold Blore, were unattached men with a tingle of excitement in their blood, carried over from the war. They were too restless to be easily captured by women and tied to a place. They tended to go from one boom town to another, and the country was full or talk about booms and big money. All through the years he spent in St. Louis, Arnold Blore was hearing more and more about Denver, which had grown in a few years from a mining camp to a city of more than fifty thousand with some of the finest bars and hotels in the West. When he got a good offer for his livery stable, he sold and set out for Denver, once more driving his own fine team, but this time with a substantial account behind him in a St. Louis bank. He was no longer a drifting veteran of the war. Now he was a capitalist.

On his way west he stopped briefly in Dodge City, which was then at the beginning of its brief career as a cattle-shipping point on the westward-crawling railroad. He struck the town in the spring and saw the bawling herds of longhorns pour into the shipping pens, saw the Texans take over the town and shoot it up, saw the bars and gambling joints take in money by the bucketful, saw men fight like wolves over the too few women who were shipped in by the carload from Kansas City and St. Louis. Blore loved the sound and smell of a boom town as he had loved the sound and smell of war, and he moved through it as he had moved through war, with quiet, efficient self-confidence. He never wore a gun and never got into trouble. He avoided women and drunks and looked for horses and bargains. The place abounded in both, and Blore left it richer than he had come, but he felt sure it was not a place to stay. It was doomed to dwindle as the rails reached westward.

In Denver he knew almost at once that he had found a home. Here was a town with a solid center of banks and hotels and wholesale houses, a town where money was piling up, a town that was going to last. He bought a livery stable and became a horse trader again, but soon his stable was only one of his interests and the one he talked least about. He invested discreetly in mining shares and also in real estate. Here too he had the curious experience of becoming a southern gentleman for the first time in his life. Here he was Major Blore, a Confederate veteran with a ·distinguished record. There were other men in Denver who had been Confederate officers and they constituted an informal club which met in the best bars, talked about the war over their whiskies and addressed each other with the utmost courtesy and always by their military titles. Some of them talked also about their families and the good old days before the war, but in the West it was bad manners to question a man about his past, and Major Blore did not talk about anything except the war.

The West was a belligerently democratic place, and at the same time it was busily founding a new aristocracy of money. In the West one man was just as good as another and ancestry counted for nothing, but already there was beginning to be a distinction between the few who accumulated money and the many who did not. For the West had a spendthrift tradition. Money was easy to make. A man might make a stake in a month or a year and throw it across the bars and the gambling tables in a few days. There was always more where that came from. It was customary for a lucky man to buy drinks for the house when the house might contain a hundred. Men lived in a world of waste and abundance and most of them could not imagine the end of it.

Arnold Blore could appear lavish when he thought it was necessary, but he held onto money instinctively. Money in the bank made him feel larger and stronger. It gave him the feeling of safety and power other men got from a weapon on the hip or in the pocket. Money, like the great guns of the war, was a weapon that reached a long way and worked without the sweat and strain of personal violence. Arnold Blore avoided men who went broke and wanted to borrow money, and he had an affinity for those who had money to lend, at good interest. In this way he became part of a little group which was beginning to gain control of Denver—those who owned most of the land it stood on, and most of the buildings and many of the mines. Town lots and mining claims were so far the chief forms of vested wealth.

When he had been there about five years, Major Blore was a well-known figure in Denver. He had no intimates but he had a great many acquaintances, all carefully chosen. He was infallibly smooth and polite, with a slight touch of pomposity which sometimes caused men to laugh at him behind his back, but never before his face. He had an especially charming and gallant manner with women, and women often liked him, despite his short stature, but the women he met socially found him elusive. No man ever had a more perfect and formal manner with the wives of his acquaintances. He knew that women set men against each other and that this is the most unprofitable and damaging kind of hostility. He had also learned that a woman can disarm a man and take him captive, and Major Blore did not propose to be taken captive. He did not feel safe with any woman he could not buy and pay for. Denver .abounded in women who could be had for a price, and he was a discreet and secretive connoisseur of such, judging woman-flesh with the same delicate feeling for form and action that he brought to horse flesh. Major Blore was not an ascetic but he was a dedicated man, as saints and poets are dedicated men. He wanted power and he sacrificed everything else to that end, not by a mighty effort of abnegation, but instinctively and shrewdly, with a quiet contempt for the emotional booby traps in which most men flounder.

— 6 —

The Spanish land grants of the Southwest came to his attention by accident, when he read in a newspaper about the Federal law which provided for a government survey whenever a majority of the owners requested it. His alert and hungry intelligence smelled opportunity in that brief item. He knew that those who own the earth rule it. He had always wanted to own land but so far he had seen no opportunity to acquire more than a few town lots, and these did not at all satisfy his desire.

Major Blore had imagination and he could imagine a man gaining control of something like an empire in the West. There it lay unused, by the millions of acres, but it was peculiarly difficult to gain title to any large part of it. East of the Mississippi land had been owned by the ruling families since colonial days in great tracts granted by the British crown, but the public domain of the West was now subject to the new Homestead Law, which provided that any man might have a quarter section, provided he lived on it and used it. The law was designed to create a world of small freeholders and the means of preventing this had not yet been perfected. Already there was beginning to be a business in "relinquishments," so that shrewd men might pick up homesteads here and there without effort, and some men hired others to homestead for them. But this was too slow and picayune a process to appeal to Major Blore. It was an exciting revelation to him that the Royal will had created ready-made empires in the Southwest, as well as in the East. Moreover, most of them were still in the hands of the Mexicans, a people who were rapidly losing power and property. He felt an intuitive conviction that he had discovered a great opportunity.

It was at this point that Major Blore became a true pioneer. So far he had been only a shrewd man following booms and picking up some of the easy money they put into circulation. Now he had an idea of his own and one that was eventually to be used by many others. He said nothing to anyone about what he was doing but he became a student of the Spanish Land Grants of the Southwest and one of the first. He had never been a student before, but he worked at this task with the concentrated intensity of a scientist bent on discovery. He learned enough Spanish so that he could read it with facility. He made two trips to Santa Fe and spent months poring over the records. For a long time his researches were wholly discouraging and a man with less confidence in his own ideas would have relinquished the project as hopeless. All of these grants had been held by Mexican families for generations and the families had been incredibly prolific. Most of them had so many heirs that to hunt them all out and procure a survey and a valid title seemed impossible. Then he came across the Coronel family and traced the history of its holdings on the eastern slope of the Rockies. Here was one great estate which had been captured and held by a single man. Like a hound on a hot trail he followed the story of Jean Ballard from Santa Fe to Taos, from Taos to the Dark River Valley, from there to St. Louis. He traced the man's rise and he saw the inevitability of his fall. Before he went to his friend, Colonel Tweedale, his scheme was complete to the last detail. There was no question he could not answer, no contingency he had not foreseen. He saw only one danger—that Ballard might not live to see a deal completed. For he had learned all about Ballard's health and knew the man might die any time, leaving his great estate in weak and scattered hands. He therefore urged upon Tweedale the need for haste and Tweedale did not hesitate. He set about organizing the syndicate in Denver while Blore was engaged in his delicate mission to the Dark River Valley.

— 7 —

During the year before he took charge of the grant, Major Blore was a busy man. He went first to Denver and reported to his principals, then to St. Louis where final arrangements had to be made with all Ballard's creditors. After that he went to work upon his bold plans for the exploitation of his prize. The necessary survey entailed a trip to Washington, and it also entailed a highly private and very delicate arrangement with the surveyor who was to make it. This, in fact, was the largest single outlay the syndicate had to make besides the purchase price. After receiving a rough estimate of his probable holdings, which would total nearly two thousand square miles, the Major prepared advertisements to be published in St. Louis, in Kansas City and even in eastern cities. These made it clear that a city was to be founded on the Dark River and that an auction sale of town lots was to be held on a certain stated date. The river was to be dammed, creating a vast area of irrigable land, and the advertisement contrived to imply that this was already an accomplished fact without quite saying so. A sawmill would make lumber for construction available on the spot in unlimited quantities. Investors were urged to waste no time if they wished to share in the first great boom of the empire which the United States had taken away from Mexico in 1849.

The Major's last stop was in Dodge City, Kansas, then at the height of its importance as a cattle-shipping point and track-end town. He knew that Dodge City was full of land-hungry men with guns on their hips. He knew also that it was a town whose boom days were nearly over. He proposed to acquire there certain employees, who would have to be carefully chosen, and also settlers who would be given special consideration in order to attach them to the interests of the syndicate. The Major knew what he faced and he knew it probably included some trouble.

BETTY WEISS

At the time of her murder in Dodge City, Dora Hand was perhaps the most famous woman between Kansas City and Santa Fe. Dora was a prostitute who belonged to a brief moment in American history that gave her profession something of the power and importance it had in the Renaissance and in the seventeenth century when Ninon de Lenclos ruled her court of lovers and courtesans seduced kings and prelates. Dora seduced mayors and town marshals and Texas cattle kings, who were the great men of her world, but she also became a valued and powerful member of her community and she seems truly to have charmed it. Men who had known her described her fifty years later as graciously beautiful and remembered her singing voice as the most lovely thing in a discordant world. Perhaps these oldtimers were a little in love with their own memories but there can be no doubt of the powerful impression that Dora made on her contemporaries. Neither can there be any doubt that, as one of them remarked, she elevated her profession considerably.

In general it had not been an elevated profession in the early West, nor in the early days of Dodge City. Dodge began as a shipping point for the buffalo hunters who destroyed the southern buffalo herd and shipped hides east in bales. Most of these men were of the toughest breed that ever forked a horse or pulled a trigger. They lived by wholesale slaughter and by way of relaxation they got drunk, fought rough-and-tumble and went to bed with almost anything that looked like a woman. They seldom washed and never bathed and when they lined up at a bar the last man to catch a louse on his own person had to pay for the drinks. The women who entertained them were brawny wenches, short-haired and painted like Indians—predatory bats who knew how to roll a drunk and seldom let a man get away with a dollar in his pocket.

When the cattle herds came streaming up the Chisholm Trail and three thousand cowboys hit the town, all this was changed. The Texans were violent but chivalrous men with cultivated tastes in women, horses and whisky. Often the outfit that brought a Texas herd over the trail was about half a family party of wild young men with pockets full of money. They wanted high-class women and they got them. Girls came from St. Louis and Kansas City in response to advertisements for waitresses and entertainers, and the whole town would be down at the station to look them over. They had to be pretty to make good and some of them were beautiful. Some of them were also smart and piled up money in banks and more than half of them eventually married. For these women were something more than whores. East of the river people had migrated in family parties, but west of it men went alone and the women who followed were the female pioneers, always a small minority, practicing an heroic polyandry. Often a pretty girl would become for a season the exclusive property of one Texas outfit and would be known to all as the sweetheart of the Turkey Track or the Bar-L-K. Nearly always one or more of the cowboys would offer to marry her, but these belles seldom married until their popularity began to wane with their looks. Nearly all of them preferred six or seven devoted lovers and much money to one husband and a job keeping house on a ranch.

These women always took charge of the town's charities and the sick and the down-and-out were their children. The celebrity of Dora Hand was due as much to her philanthropy as it was to her voice or her figure, which was a perfect specimen of the big-breasted, swivel-hipped blonde type men then admired. At night Dora wore gowns that just barely covered her nipples and the way she could switch her caboose was something men rode miles to see. But by day she wore calico and even a sunbonnet and was a hard and humorous Samaritan who gave what was needed and couldn't be fooled. Her singing had the same dual character. It was said she had sung in Grand Opera, which may be doubted, but she had a contralto of great power and some range. At night she could make cowboys weep into their chasers with her sentimental ballads, and on Sunday morning she always attended the one little Methodist chapel on North Side Hill and led the singing of hymns. The Reverend Dwight was her best friend and her chief assistant in her charitable work. Moreover, she packed his church, which might otherwise have been neglected. Some times she brought two or three of her girls with her and almost always, in the last year of her life, at least one, a slim girl named Betty Weiss, who also had a voice, though not one of such volume and authority as Dora's. The two of them standing up there in the choir loft, always dressed in black, lifting up their voices to God, were a sight men long remembered.

Dora's death was an accident, a simple case of mistaken identity, but it threw the town into a dither as no killing had done since its founding. Dora presided over the feminine adjunct of a large and lucrative establishment owned by Mayor Kelly, known as "Dog" Kelly because he was the first man to import greyhounds and cultivate the sport of chasing antelopes and coyotes with them. The Kelly joint, like many of its day and kind, included a bar, a restaurant, a long gambling room, a dance hall and bedrooms upstairs. It also included a two-room cottage at the rear where Mayor Kelly had lived until he rented it to Dora Hand. The mayor had a long-standing feud with the Texans, and especially with the great King and Kennedy outfit. The Kennedy cowboy who killed Dora Hand emptied his six-shooter late one night through the flimsy wall of the Kelly shack at the exact spot where the bed was known to stand, and then departed southward on a fast horse, confident he would be proclaimed a hero by his fellow Texans for killing the mayor. He had the honor of being trailed and captured by three of the greatest man hunters in the West—Bat Masterson, Bill Tilghman and Wyatt Earp—and he didn't learn that he had killed Dora Hand by mistake until Bat Masterson knocked him off his horse with a shot that shattered his right arm. When told what had happened he expressed his gentlemanly regret that his own wound had not been fatal.

The whole town mourned Dora Hand but the person most affected by her death was Betty Weiss. When someone came to the dance hall the day Dora was killed and wanted to know who was in charge, Betty stepped forward and said, "I am," in a tone that left no doubt in anyone's mind. She was, from then on. She had what it took to run things and she ran them, although she was only twenty-six and looked younger.

Betty was a contrast to the smooth and undulating Dora, being slim, nervous, quick and sharp, with dark brown hair and gray-green eyes, but she took over completely the dual role of her predecessor, managing the town charities in a very businesslike fashion and lending the church her moral and vocal support. She was also both more luxurious and more exclusive than Dora had been. She furnished her own quarters in a style such as Dodge had never seen before, with thick carpets, lace curtains and a beveled mirror in which she could contemplate her elegant person full length. She employed a Negro maid who announced all visitors, not all of whom were admitted. In fact, it was a mystery and a subject of speculation as to who achieved the ineffable favors of Betty Weiss and on what terms. Her public appearances as a singer were fewer than Dora's had been and more spectacular. She was much the best-dressed woman in Dodge, specializing in furs, always entering a room enveloped in mink or beaver, disclosing her slim white shoulders and pointed bosom with a certain grace and dramatic effect. In a few years she was almost as famous as Dora had been.

— 2 —

Betty Weiss was born in St. Louis of German Lutheran parents who came to the United States in the first wave of German immigration. Both of them died in one of the early outbreaks of cholera when the dead were hauled away in wagonloads and the city for a while was almost deserted. Betty was only a few years old at the time, and she spent most of her childhood in a Lutheran orphanage, where she wore a uniform and marched to meals and classes and to church on Sunday at the stroke of a bell. In the orphanage Betty learned to read and write and sing hymns and she also learned that she was an incorrigible rebel with an innate hatred of routine and authority. She ran away three times and was brought back by the police. Her mentors were as much relieved as Betty when she was adopted at the age of sixteen by a German family that ran a restaurant. They treated her strictly as an economic asset and put her to work as a waitress, but Betty was not slow to achieve her independence. Before she was eighteen she got a job at wages and defied her foster parents to bring her home. She also quickly made a place for herself in the kind of German society to which her parents had belonged—a society of small shopkeepers and of carpenters and bricklayers who prospered on the swift growth of the city. They were a thrifty, laborious, well-fed and prolific people, who spoke more German than English and had a social life of their own. Betty went to many balls and also to beer gardens where people came in family groups and the young folk danced and flirted while the elders drank beer and talked. On Sundays she went to the Lutheran church because she saw all her friends and acquaintances there and she sang in the choir because she liked to sing. She had many suitors and might have married almost any time, but she didn't. She was outrageously fickle and elusive. Whenever a nice German boy began to talk about marriage she would turn him down and shift her favor to another. Older women began to speak of her with disapproval.

Betty was a reticent girl. She did not confide in anyone nor argue with anyone but before she was nineteen she had a set of strong and definite convictions, acquired mostly by way of her senses which were exceptionally acute. She knew that she hated drudgery and especially the smell and the greasy feel of dish water which became for her the chief symbol of domesticity. She resented the complacent, domineering German male, reeking of beer and sauerkraut, who regarded it as his duty to keep his wife both pregnant and busy. She knew she would never submit herself to one of them. She knew also that she lusted after luxuries and especially after furs and fabrics. She spent a great deal of time staring at things in shop windows and well-dressed women, especially in silk and fur, were the only humans she envied. Her body longed for the caress of silk far more than it had ever longed for the weight and pressure of an amorous male. Betty knew that she was a greedy and undutiful girl, and she had some moments of guilt and doubt, but she had also the self-knowledge of the born adventurer, the instinctive certainty that she did not belong where she was, that her destiny was still undiscovered.

— 3 —

The man Betty married promised her everything she wanted and looked to her like the fulfillment of a dream. He was no part of the social world to which she belonged but a stranger, named Ronald Nelson, who came to the restaurant one day for a cup of coffee and returned almost every day for a long time because Betty worked there. He was tall and dark and superbly dressed with a pearl in his ascot tie and a diamond on his finger. He reminded her of an actor she had seen in *East Lynne* and in fact he was something of an actor, among other things. By profession he was a gambler who had been working the river boats between St. Louis and New Orleans, and who had decided upon a journey to California. But he did not tell Betty any of this. He told her a long and highly circumstantial story about a plantation in Louisiana which he had inherited. He did not begin by proposing marriage. He took her out to dinner and to shows and tried every time to persuade her to visit him in rooms he had rented over a store down on the water front. But Betty demurely refused. She thought she was being too smart for him, and when he put a diamond on her finger and told her he could wait no longer, they must be married that night, she felt sure of triumph. They were married all right by a justice of the peace and with a perfectly authentic license, and they went for their honeymoon to Kansas City, where urgent business required his attention before they could go south.

The honeymoon lasted a week and was a great success. It came to an end when Ronald Nelson simply walked out one morning and never returned. It took Betty a long time to understand and accept the fact that she had been deserted. For the first and for the last time she had been the victim of her own vanity. Even before the marriage she had been convinced that this man was her secure possession and afterward she had felt even more sure that his body belonged to her. When he failed to appear after twenty-four hours, she went to the Kansas City police in the firm belief that he must have met with foul play—a thing which could easily happen in Kansas City to a man who wore several hundred dollars' worth of jewelry. For that matter, there was never any proof that Ronald Nelson had not been murdered and thrown into the river, but the police quickly ascertained that he was not alive anywhere in town and their concern with him there ended. In those days men disappeared into the West as a wild animal disappears in a forest. But the police also knew a good deal about Ronald Nelson which they felt bound to tell his pale and shaken bride. They were able to ascertain that he had a very bad reputation as a gambler, that he had operated on the river under at least four different names and that he had been married under at least three of them.

During her days of uncertainty Betty had felt weak and crushed, for Ronald was an accomplished lover and he had revealed to Betty the fact that she was a passionate woman. But when she understood what had happened to her, her mood suddenly and significantly changed. She was filled with a great rage not only against Ronald Nelson but against the entire male half of the human race and against a world which could deal such a blow to her enormous pride. Rage seemed to run through her body like a hot liquid, filling her with furious power, with a longing for action and destruction. If she had been able to find his track she could have hunted Ronald Nelson with a gun. Briefly she enjoyed her rage almost as much as she had enjoyed some of her orgiastic moments in her lover's arms. When a detective tried to put his arm around her she slapped him with such emphasis that she knocked his cigar out of his mouth. Despite her bad manners, or perhaps partly because of them, the Kansas City police offered to pay her fare back to where she had come from. But Betty knew that whatever happened she was not going back. Nobody she knew was ever going to learn the story of her humiliation. Nor was it difficult to discover somewhere else to go. The great new wooden railroad station in Kansas City was crowded with people who were bound for the end of the rails, and it was also plastered with advertisements for waitresses to work in Dodge City at wages that seemed fabulous to Betty, and they included transportation. She landed in Dodge City two days later, badly shaken and rumpled, with a cinder in her eye, but nevertheless one of the best looking girls on the train. Men booted and spurred, with guns on their hips, were lined up four deep to watch her get off the train. For a moment she stood open-mouthed and bewildered. Then Dora Hand, almost motherly looking in her diurnal costume, came forward and put her arm around the girl and said, "Come with me, dearie."

— 4 —

Both Betty Weiss and Dodge City were at the highest point of their respective importance when Major Blore called upon her. Deborah, her Negro maid, brought Betty a card one evening which informed her that Major Blore would like to see her and that he represented the Rocky Mountain Land and Cattle Company. Betty sent back word that she saw gentlemen only by appointment. The Major in turn communicated the intelligence by way of Deborah that his call was of a purely business character, that his time in Dodge City was limited and that he would greatly appreciate a brief interview. Betty let him wait twenty minutes while she put on her most elegant gown and had Deborah do her hair. She felt nothing more than a mild curiosity about the Major but it was one of her two primary business principles always to make the best possible impression on a man. The other was never to trust him.

The Major wore the black frock coat, high-heeled riding boots and great white hat which then represented the height of frontier elegance. He could not have been more formal, more courteous or more respectful if he had been interviewing a queen. He accepted a chair, laid his great hat upon the floor bottom up, removed a map from a portfolio which he carried and proceeded to give Betty an illustrated lecture upon the properties, organization and intentions of the Rocky Mountain Land and Cattle Company. He was careful to explain that the syndicate commanded a capital of several million dollars and that he was prepared to offer bank references to prove it. Betty listened carefully, her green eyes narrow with amused suspicion.

"If you're trying to sell me real estate," she explained when the Major paused for breath, "it's no use. I never buy anything but clothes and liquor."

"I have nothing to sell you," the Major explained gravely. "I am soliciting your assistance in a great undertaking."

Betty received this announcement in silence. The Major uncrossed his legs, crossed them again and cleared his throat. It was evident that he was approaching the serious business of the interview and that it was also a somewhat delicate business.

"One of the company's enterprises," he explained, "will be a first-class hotel. It will include, of course, a bar and the usual games. I feel sure it will be the best establishment of its kind west of Kansas City. We would like to have you take charge of it. I am prepared to offer you a contract for a year and I feel sure the terms can be made satisfactory."

Betty considered this for a long moment.

"Why don't you get a man to run it?" she inquired. "I never heard of a joint that was really run by a woman."

The Major permitted himself to smile for the first time.

"We want to attract people to our town," he said. "I am sure you will be more of an attraction than any man we might employ. Of course, you will have whatever assistance you need."

"You mean you want me to be the two-story front," Betty suggested.

The Major raised a deprecatory hand.

"As you may imagine," he said, "I have made the fullest possible inquiries about you. I have no doubt at all of your business competence. Needless to say, your gifts as an entertainer are also a consideration."

Betty again paused before she spoke.

"I'll have to think it over," she said at last.

"Thank you," the Major replied. "May I suggest that you have nothing to lose? As a track-end town, Dodge City is near the end of its boom. I flatter myself that we have something more substantial to offer."

Betty nodded.

"I know this town can't last," she agreed. "I'll see you again before you go."

— 5 —

The next day Betty sent word to her friend Clay Tighe that she would like to consult him on important business. Tighe was at that time one of the half dozen most famous peace officers in the Southwest. He had been marshal of Hayes City and of Abilene, and was known as the man who tamed that refractory town. He had also been a deputy marshal in Dodge City. At the moment he was out of a job, due to a change in the city administration, but the services of Clay Tighe never went begging and they were worth anywhere from five hundred to a thousand dollars a month.

Betty Weiss trusted no man wholly, but she had more confidence in Tighe than in any other man she knew. For one thing, he had never shown the slightest interest in her as a woman. This piqued her vanity, but it gave her confidence that his advice was truly disinterested. For another thing, he never needed money. Finally, he had a reputation for honesty of a kind that was rare in the world they both inhabited. And she knew Clay Tighe would know something about Major Blore. It was part of his business to know about everybody in town.

"I don't trust that little shorthorn," she told him, after she had described the Major's visit. "He's too smooth. I'm afraid he's got something up his cuff."

"I don't trust him either," Clay said. "But there's no doubt that he's got the money and a clear title to about a million acres. I looked into that very carefully."

"Why so?" Betty inquired.

"Because he made me a proposition too," Clay explained. "He's here shopping for help and settlers. He'll take about half of Dodge City out there if he has his way."

"I suppose you'll be his trouble-shooter," Betty said.

Clay nodded.

"He's got a lot of squatters to deal with," he explained. "I don't like the proposition much, but there's big money in it and a chance to get hold of good range with water on it. . . . And somebody's got to do the job," he added.

"You took him up, then," Betty guessed.

"I told him I'd go out there and look it over," Clay said.

"Will you let me know what you think?" Betty asked.

"I'll write you a letter," Clay promised. "But I probably won't know any more about the Major then than I do now. He's as hard to figure out as a Chinaman in a poker game."

CLAY TIGHE

Clay Tighe put on his gun every morning as regularly as he put on his shirt and a great deal more carefully. After he had shaved and dressed he took his heavy gun belt off the post of his bed where he always hung it last thing at night, and buckled it around his waist, always exactly the same way, so that it rode aslant his body from just above his hip bone on the left side to just below it on the right, and slightly behind. He then drew his heavy frontier-model six-shooter, with its seven-inch barrel, from under his pillow—for he had slept upon it every night for fifteen years. He first unloaded it and then inserted it carefully in the holster, which had been molded to its form by soaking the leather in water and letting it dry on the well-greased gun. The holster had to hang so that his long slender fingers just reached the tip, and it was tied to his leg by a thong so that it could never flop or slide. When he felt sure the gun was perfectly placed he always practiced his draw several times. If there was a mirror in the room he practiced before the mirror so that he could study his own performance with the critical care which is the mark of the virtuoso. He would first execute his draw very slowly and perfectly. His hand traveled up the length of the holster in a long, smooth caress, his lower three fingers closed on the grip, his index finger curled around the emergent trigger, and the ball of his thumb at the same time drew back the hammer. In one long, smooth movement the gun swept upward to an exact horizontal and the hammer fell at that exact moment. After he had made his draw slowly and deliberately, he repeated it several times until he felt sure he had reached his maximum speed. He always knew whether his draw was working perfectly or not. If he had taken more than one drink the night before, and sometimes if he had been with a woman, he might be a fraction of a second slow at first. Then he would practice it until he felt sure it was perfect. This movement of hand and arm was as vital to him as his breathing or his digestion and for the same reason: his life depended on it. Clay Tighe's gun was the creator of his destiny, the instrument and symbol of his power. He was wedded to his gun and only death could part them.

His morning rehearsal was a small part of the time he devoted to his art. Unless urgent business interfered, he emptied his six-shooter at a mark every day, then carefully cleaned and reloaded it. He also fired a few shots with his short Winchester of the 1873 model, then the world's deadliest repeating arm. Tighe could shoot his rifle not only from the shoulder but also from the hip, holding the gun hard against his side and swinging his whole body.

Tighe was a man-killer, an expert in homicide. His life, his reputation and his earning capacity all depended upon the fact that he could kill more quickly and more surely than any but perhaps half a dozen men in the Southwest, and it is doubtful whether any of these was his superior. Yet he had killed but two men since the end of the Civil War, and both of those had shot at him and missed before he pulled a trigger. For Tighe had early reached that high degree of gunmanship which made his reputation his chief asset. He seldom shot because he seldom had to shoot. At least fifty times he had gotten the drop on his man before the other gun cleared its holster. Even more often he had arrested a man without even drawing a gun. It was said of him, as it had been said of many other supreme experts with the six-shooter, that he bore a charmed life. Tighe knew exactly what the charm was. It lay in the fact that the other fellow was always frightened. Sometimes he was too frightened to draw a gun and sometimes he was too frightened to hit anything. For fifteen years Clay Tighe had walked unscathed because men were afraid of him.

He walked unscathed but he did not walk at ease, for he was a marked man and a shining mark. A great many men would have liked to kill him. Some of these bore him a grudge because he had disarmed and arrested them—and to have your gun taken away from you was then supreme disgrace. More of them would have liked to kill him in fair fight simply for the glory of it. To kill Clay Tighe in fair fight would be not only high achievement but also the way to a reputation worth money. He knew a few men who would have shot him in the back if one had seen a safe chance. Few men were shot in the back in the West of that day because it was not a gesture that won social approval, but as Tighe was wont to remark in this and other connections: "There's always some son-of-bitch . . ."

Tighe was a striking figure of a man, a little over **six** feet tall, perfectly carried, wide in the shoulders and narrow in the hips, with a handsome aquiline face and deep-set gray eyes which carried a curious warning glint even when he smiled. He belonged to that order of athletes who combine great strength with a certain quick sensitivity, expressed in his long tapering fingers and the easy grace of his movement. He had nothing in common with the thick-skinned bull-like strength of the typical rough-and-tumble fighter or the man who loves a knife—the gouging, biting human brute who longs to destroy with his hands. Tighe had something of the artist about him and a little of the actor. He was a perfectionist who exercised a supreme skill for its own sake.

Walking down the street he looked to be relaxed and unconcerned but he was not. He was alert as a wild animal almost every minute of his waking life, except when he had wide space between himself and his fellow beings. He looked at every man he met and his glance was peculiarly keen and perceptive. He had been called cat-eyed. He had ears like a deer or a rabbit and he was habitually aware of the footfalls of a man behind him, and of any pause or change in his gait. One evening he met a cowboy who might have borne a grudge against him, nodded a smiling greeting and passed on, heard some slight, indefinable movement behind him and whirled with his hand on his gun. In the twilight he saw a bright flash from a hip pocket and his quick gun leaped to its deadly level, hammer raised. . . . He stayed his trigger finger just in time. The man had whipped out a white handkerchief to blow his nose and he never knew he had been within an instant of death.

When Tighe sat down in a room he always sat with his back to the wall and as close to it as he could get. If he went to the bar for a drink, which he seldom did, he always knew who was behind him.

Clay Tighe was a mighty man, one of the rulers of his world, and he walked with the knowledge of death and carried death in his hand.

— 2 —

Tighe grew up in Illinois in the forties and fifties—the green and placid Illinois where Abraham Lincoln rode the circuit and told his stories. Clay was a fighter from the age of six but he was never a bully or an undisciplined fighter. His father, Judge Tighe, saw to that. The judge was a moderately prosperous farmer and a country justice of the peace who achieved a local celebrity by reason of his strict and incorruptible sense of justice. He had jurisdiction only over minor civil cases and misdemeanors but this made him the judge and arbiter of many personal encounters. When a man was brought before him for disturbing the peace or charged with assault and battery, Judge Tighe worked long and hard and summoned all possible witnesses to ascertain who had started the trouble and how. His self-appointed mission in life was to suppress and punish transgressors and he had the courage to put prominent citizens in jail and to earn the enmity of men who were considered dangerous. He applied exactly the same principles to the education and upbringing of his son that he used in court. If Clay got into a fight and showed any signs of it, he had to prove that he had fought in self-defense. Otherwise the judge would always administer a rather severe thrashing with a doubled trunk strap, accompanied by a lecture on the principles of human justice and social order. "The old man gave me hell at both ends," was the way Clay Tighe described his early training.

Clay Tighe rebelled against his father's teachings and left home early but he lived to understand that the old man had provided him with a mission and an ethic he could not escape. A feeling for justice and order had been impressed upon his young mind and pounded into his young bottom. He became a deadly man but never a ruthless one. He spent his life stopping trouble, sometimes dead in its tracks.

Judge Tighe was a stout man with a great reverence for intellectual achievement and for Abraham Lincoln. He wanted his son to study law and to fulfill his own thwarted ambitions, but this lean and restless sprout of his loins was a creature of another kind. Clay longed for action, clean, deadly and precise. He was a hunter from the age of eight and could topple a squirrel out of a high hickory with a bullet through its head. By the time he was twelve he was one of the best shots in the county and won turkeys and beefs at shooting matches, competing with grown men. When he was only eighteen he left home against his father's wishes and headed west. The Tighe farm on the Illinois River was only about two hundred miles from the Kansas-Missouri border, where the prologue to the Civil War was being fought by pro-slavery settlers from the South and free-soil men from the North—a hard-riding, bushwhacking struggle in which men committed murder and larceny for the glory of God and in the name of freedom.

Clay Tighe said he was looking for land and work, and the Immigrant Society was offering both in an effort to build up the population of free-soil men against the southern raiders. But half consciously Tighe was hunting trouble—a young warrior with an itching trigger finger, moving instinctively toward the smell of powder and the thrill of battle. Inevitably he joined the Jayhawkers, riding with the famous Jim Montgomery who became a terror to the men from the South. Clay was a hot young partisan fighting for free soil and the ideals of Abraham Lincoln, but the Jayhawkers were only one degree removed from banditry. They burned fences and cabins, destroyed growing crops, stole horses and cattle, were not above lifting poultry off a roost or raiding fields for green corn and watermelons when provender was scarce. It was a warfare of ambuscade and running skirmish with a fine rattle and bang about it and little execution. This was the least creditable part of Tighe's career and the one he said least about in later years. It was chiefly significant as the time he first encountered the instrument of which he was to become one of the greatest masters. The border wars were fought largely with the old cap-and-ball six-shooter. Some of the Jayhawkers carried three and even four of these primitive revolvers in their belts and were famous for the way they could fill the landscape with smoke and lead. With the instinct of a master young Clay strove for speed and precision and had perfected a deadly draw before Colt became famous.

When the Civil War broke out Clay did not enlist. He was a shrewd young man with an aversion to military discipline and a sharp awareness of his own value in good hard dollars. He went to work for the Union army as a civilian teamster at several times a soldier's pay. Within two years he was a brigade wagon-master, commanding many men older than himself. His job was not merely to move supplies but to find routes that were safe from bushwhackers. He was so good at this that he became a master scout and sometimes a spy—one of those highly paid and expert men who were the eyes of the army. It was characteristic of Tighe that he came to the end of the war with money and a whole skin as well as a reputation.

Again he moved west only a few hundred miles from where his fighting career had begun. He was in Dodge City shortly after the railroad arrived and became one of the first of the hide hunters. Wherever he went work was waiting for his deadly hand and eye. Government is said to have secretly backed the buffalo hunters because the Indians could not be conquered until the wild meat was destroyed. Clay Tighe was a master buffalo hunter who owned his own team and outfit and hired three skinners. He shot a great Sharp's buffalo gun which was accurate at five hundred yards and weighed fourteen pounds. The trick of his trade was to kill buffalo dead in their tracks, so that the others wouldn't scare and run. Sometimes he killed thirty or forty from one position, shooting until his shoulder was pounded black and blue and his great rifle was too hot to handle. It was a mighty feat in wholesale slaughter and it paid big money while the herds lasted.

Then suddenly the buffalo were gone from the Kansas ranges. Almost at once, like the next act in a planned pageant, the first bawling longhorned herds of Texas cattle came pouring up from the South. The bales of buffalo hides vanished from the station platform, whitewashed cattle chutes were built beside the railroad track and a stream of beef on the hoof went rattling east to Kansas City and Chicago, while Texas cowboys, full of money and hard liquor, took over the town and almost tore it to pieces. It had neither law nor men to cope with this sudden invasion. Clay Tighe stood and watched them—a young man out of a job, but not for long.

The Civil War was over but almost every man in the West was still a touchy partisan and every town·was split into two factions. The Texans all were Confederates, hating Yankees and niggers with a proud, self-righteous and trigger-happy hatred. Since the war, killing niggers had been almost as much a legitimate sport in southeast Texas as killing Mexicans had been in the years after the fall of the Alamo.

There were always a few saloons run by Texas partisans but most of the men who owned Dodge City and tried to rule it were Northerners and many of them were Union veterans. In the face of this gun-toting, spur-jingling mob they were helpless. They had a town marshal and several deputies, but when the Texans decided to shoot up the town, these officers could only close the doors and lie low.

Shooting up the town was a sport that enjoyed a measure of social tolerance, but murder was not. Clay Tighe was standing on a street corner smoking a cigarette when he witnessed murder, ruthless and inexcusable. Across the street a Negro named Jeff Chandler was painting a sign on the two-story front of a new store. Jeff was a huge man, weighing over two hundred and fifty pounds, and one of three or four Negroes in the town. He was a good carpenter and painter, a respected and busy citizen, who wore no weapon and always sang at his work. Four Texas cowboys, all drunk, came tearing down the street at a fast gallop, reeling in their saddles as only a drunk can reel without falling, brandishing their six-shooters, firing a few shots into the air. Two of them suddenly swung their guns on the giant Negro, riddled him from behind, and dashed on down the street. All four of them brought their horses to a squatting stop in a cloud of dust before the Happy Hour saloon—a Texas stronghold— while Jeff Chandler fell from his scaffold like a shot bird and lay bleeding in the street.

Within three minutes the street was full of men—men of two factions, all wearing guns. Texans poured out of the Happy Hour, sized up the situation, hustled the guilty men inside, formed a solid rank before the door. Ben Gilroy, owner of the Happy Hour, came shouldering through the crowd with a cocked shotgun in his hands, took his stand in front of them. Across the street Jim Sellers, mayor of Dodge, assembled his marshal and two deputies. He ordered them to disarm Gilroy and arrest the two guilty men. The officers took one look at the assembled Texans and the Gilroy shotgun and declined the assignment. Ed Brown, chief marshal, suggested that just now was not a propitious time to make arrests. The attempt might touch off mob action, cost much human life.

The argument had merit. Gilroy was a famous killer, and especially handy with his high-grade, handmade shotgun. The street had suddenly become a no-man's land. Any armed men who tried to cross it might become a target at the first step. But Sellers, unarmed and fat, with glasses on his nose, was a man of nerve.

"If we let the bastards get away with this, we might as well give them the town," he said, addressing his police force. "You boys are fired!"

He spoke doubtless in the spirit of sincere disgust and without considering his next move, but his champion was at hand. Clay Tighe spoke quietly.

"I could take that gang," he remarked, studying the Texas tableau with a thoughtful eye. Mayor Sellers turned and looked at him. Sellers ran the largest store in town, owned about half of it, knew Clay Tighe as a customer and a buffalo hunter. He contemplated the young man for a long moment. Then he turned to his chief marshal, took the badge of office off his vest and pinned it on the man from Illinois.

"All right, Clay," he said. "You asked for it. Go to it."

Clay Tighe now started a short walk that carried him to fame and decided his destiny. He started it in a hush so complete that he could hear the hard breathing of excited men and his own soft footfalls in the dusty street as he stepped off the high board sidewalk.

Clay did not know why he had spoken, then or ever. He had heard his own quiet words with a kind of surprise. But he was not a man who thought much about his motives. He was one who always had his eye and his mind on the objects of his action. His eye just now was on the right hand of Ben Gilroy, where it grasped the stock of his shotgun. Gilroy held the gun diagonally across his body, like a hunter expecting a bird to flush. He could bring it into play with one swift movement. But Clay Tighe knew he could draw and fire before the long barrel of a shotgun could describe its arc. He knew also that he could see the beginning of that movement in the hand and wrist of the man who held the gun. He knew the cowboys crowded behind Gilroy were mostly drunk and too close together for effective action. So he walked slowly and confidently across the street with his hands at his sides, not touching his own weapon. Gilroy broke the silence.

"What do you want, Tighe?" he asked.

Clay stopped.

"I want you to throw that gun into the street and send those two boys out with their hands up and without their guns," he said quietly.

There was a long pause before the shotgun hit the dust, but after that everything was easy. The guilty cowboys were delivered to the law by their own partisans and Clay Tighe had become chief marshal of the hottest town in the West. His reign there was the beginning of law and order in the track-end cattle towns. They did not become quiet and peaceful places, but neither did the men from Texas ever again flout the government with impunity.

— 3 —

At thirty-nine, when he met Major Blore, Clay Tighe was a famous man, and like many another famous man he was beginning to feel the burden of his reputation. For a good many years he had truly enjoyed it. To be in danger, alert and unfrightened, is to be supremely alive. Clay Tighe had known the intensity of life as men who live in the mild boredom of perfect safety can never know it. But he had come a long way since he first rode west, tingling with the hope of battle, almost aching to use the skill and power he knew he had. He had grown from the wild boy who rode with the Jayhawkers to the man who could rule a town and do it without bloodshed. He was quick as ever, but the eagerness of his youth was gone. The long tension of incessant alertness had begun to tell. Something in him now longed for peace and safety—but battle and danger were his only trade. He could no more lay aside his gun than he could take off his skin.

Tighe was still erect and powerful but he looked old for his years. His black hair was brightly streaked with gray and the lines around his mouth had a hard and permanent set. His face in repose looked grim and a little sad, as do often the faces of men who have looked upon much violence. His deadly skill was still at its height and he knew it would decline. Few experts of the trigger finger were at their best much after forty. He had watched the careers of a good many such on both sides of the law. Some of them developed a ruthless hatred for their kind, began to kill for the love of killing. These never lasted long. Others he had known began to drink at a certain age, and these had even shorter lives.

During the past few years Tighe had spent more and more of his time alone, in a solitude that he enjoyed because it was safe. He felt best now when he rode across wide prairies where he could see a rider a mile away. Tighe was a man armed against his fellows and he liked a lot of space between himself and them.

He had never longed for possession. Money had come to him easily and he had never thought much about it. He had the adventurer's instinctive wish to remain unfettered. He had taken women lightly and he had never longed to own the earth. But out of his later mood had grown a dream of a wide, wild land he could call his own. It was not a home he longed for so much as a private wilderness to stand between him and a hostile world.

That longing, more than anything else, was what sent Clay Tighe to the Dark River Valley. He could have taken up a homestead anywhere, gathered a few cattle and a woman, become a settled man. But he wanted more than that. He wanted miles around him, not acres. He wanted a safe and private world.

Clay Tighe had seen the Dark River Valley once years before, when Ballard was at the height of his power. He had ridden from Abilene to Santa Fe, had stopped at the great house, talked to the great man, been invited to linger as long as he liked. He had stayed at the house only two nights but he had gone on a lone antelope hunt north of the valley and had camped at a spring near the foot of the mountains, called the Berenda Spring. It was a beautiful spring of clear, cold water, bubbling up out of white sand, flowing a steady stream, bowered by willows and lined with watercress, shaded by a few great mountain cottonwoods. He remembered the flat, wide mesa spreading westward, tinged purple by the ripe forage of early fall, where the white-rumped antelope skimmed the mirages like flying birds. Then the Berenda had been to him only a good place to camp. Now he thought of it as a refuge. And he also thought he was strong enough to take it. But that was not all that moved him toward the Dark River Valley. Tighe was a proud man and always aware of himself as a man with a mission. He felt sure trouble was making in the Dark River Valley and he thought if any man could keep the peace there he could do it.

Over and over, all his life, Clay Tighe had found himself riding toward trouble. Every man's life has a recurrent motif which is the beat and rhythm of his destiny, the thing he can never escape. Time and again he finds himself facing the same challenge, moving the same way.

Clay Tighe had ridden toward trouble a hundred times but this was the first time he had ever hoped it was the last.

— 4 —

Tighe was known by reputation all over the Southwest but few men in the Dark River Valley would be likely to know him by sight. So it was part of his canny plan to reach the valley after dark, to spend a day and a night asking questions, looking and listening. He wanted to know as much as he could before he faced the little Major.

Long before he reached the valley he saw a red glow in the sky, and when he was still a mile away he heard a wild, mechanical scream, which he knew for the voice of a buzz saw tearing its way through pitchy pine. When he topped the rise north of the valley he understood. They had been cutting down the forest on the mountainside beyond, the litter of tops and limbs had caught fire as they generally did in the wake of careless cutting, and the sawmill was working all night in the red glow of destruction. It shone on the faces of busy, sweating men and on the bare yellow lumber of new buildings going up on both sides of the road that paralleled the cheek. The little Major wasn't wasting any time. The drive of his nervous energy was already tearing down a forest and putting up a town.

Tighe remembered a summer night years before when all he could hear from the porch of the great house were a few low voices and the music of wind and water. Now he rode down a noisy, muddy street with two saloons and a store already running, all three of them one-story buildings with two-story fronts. It was all familiar to Clay Tighe—the cow ponies and buckboards at the hitch racks, the gun-belted men coming and going through the swinging doors of saloons, the rattle of bad piano music, the tattoo of boot heels on the new board walk, the rumble and guffaw of male voices. In effect he had spent about fifteen years patrolling this same street, for every frontier town took the same form, drew the same kinds of men, made the same noises. This was the seed and sprout of American civilization overleaping its own frontiers. This was the way it grew and spread, biting into the wilderness, setting up a town without law, a community of men each for himself and most of them armed to take what they wanted. Tighe knew this street for his business and his destiny. The little Major had built him a town. It was Clay Tighe's job to make it behave.

Down at the far end of the street he saw a sign he knew would be there. It too was painted on a high board front and it said "Livery Stable" in letters he could read a hundred yards away. He could have found it in the dark by its horsy odor and the steady munch and grind of feeding stock.

He rode through a wide door into a space between stalls where the light of a great lantern hanging from a roof beam shone on the polished rumps of stabled horses. A short, stocky, bowlegged man came to meet him, offered his hand as Tighe dismounted.

"I'm Ed Kelly," he said. "What can I do for you?"

"My name is Tighe," Clay replied, watching the man's eye for sign of recognition. He could see nothing there but a lively curiosity. "I'd like to leave my horse for a day or two, maybe longer."

"Aim to settle here?" Kelly inquired as he took the bridle rein. Curiosity about strangers was not good form but this was a polite and casual question.

"Hope to," Tighe replied. He pulled his rifle out of the saddle scabbard and started to loosen his cinches.

Kelly meditated a full minute before he asked another question. It was an impertinent and also a significant one.

"Pro-grant or anti-grant?" he asked.

"Neither," Tighe told him softly. "I'm just a poor cowboy looking for a waterhole."

Kelly surveyed Tighe's outfit thoughtfully—his three-hundred-dollar horse and his hundred-dollar saddle, his forty-dollar boots and the new Colt tied to his leg.

"Have it your own way," he said.

"Hope to," Tighe replied, as he turned away.

— 5 —

Outside the door of Blore's office, which had once been Ballard's sat a huge black man who answered to the name of Shad. He was now a famous figure in the Dark River Valley, simply because he was the first Negro who had ever appeared there. When he arrived the Mexicans, most of whom had never seen a Negro before, had come miles to look at him and follow him about the streets.

Shad was primarily a groom Blore had imported to care for the team of blooded trotters that drew his buckboard and the five-gaited Kentucky saddle horse he rode. But Shad seemed to be also a valet, a cook and a bodyguard. No one had ever seen him more than about fifty yards from the Major. When Blore rode abroad Shad rode behind him, exactly as an orderly rode behind a cavalary officer. All the Major's arrangements had something of the military about them.

Shad greeted Clay Tighe with a wide grin, a soft voice and a perfectly obsequious manner. He opened the door for him and bowed him through it. Tighe was expected and welcome.

The little Major sat behind a wide flat-topped desk at the far side of the great room, which had been transformed with heavy red curtains at the windows, red and black Navajo blankets on the floor, and shiny new furniture. He rose and greeted Tighe with a handshake, waved him to a chair, offered him a cigar. Tighe refused it, rolled a small brown cigarette with quick dexterity, blew a cloud of smoke, and waited calmly for the Major to open the proceedings.

"I think you'll agree that we have a fine development here, Mr. Tighe," he said, "and I'm delighted to have you join us."

"Thank you," Tighe replied with the perfect self-assurance of a man who knows his own value. "You have a very fine development and you also have the making of a fine little war."

The Major's eyes showed his surprise, but he was not at a loss.

"You seem to be well posted," he remarked. "Perhaps you know more about the situation here than I do."

"Maybe I do," Tighe replied. "I got here day before yesterday and I've been circulating around and picking up the news."

"I'll be very glad to have your impressions," the Major said.

"Well," Tighe spoke with slow deliberation, "my impression is that your survey takes in about four times as much territory as Ballard ever claimed. I don't know how you did it, but it's a government survey, on file in Washington. It's the law now and the law has got to be enforced."

"I'm glad you feel that way about it," the Major said.

"If I didn't I wouldn't be here," Tighe told him. "But a lot of these little ranchers that moved in and settled on what they thought was the public domain don't agree with me. They think they've been robbed."

The Major nodded easily.

"We have a little problem in law enforcement," he said. "I feel sure we can solve it."

"You haven't had much luck so far," Tighe informed him. "You made Happy Jack Marcos a deputy sheriff, and about two weeks ago you sent him out to the Bostwick ranch to serve a dispossess notice on Bill Bostwick. Is that right?"

The Major nodded.

"Your deputy found about twenty of the neighbors sitting in a row on the corral fence, each of them with a Winchester in his lap. Happy Jack just took one look and came back home with the papers in his pocket. Is that right?"

"Marcos isn't man enough for the job," the Major said. "That's why I sent for you."

"You didn't send any too soon," Tighe remarked. "A week ago you drove out to see Jack Shane at his ranch on the Rayado. Shane is your own man and you spent the night out there. When you got up in the morning your buckboard had been taken to pieces and one wheel was in the top of a tree and another was down in the creek and it took half a day to put it together again."

The Major laughed.

"I took it as a joke," he said.

"It was no joke," Tighe told him. "It was a hint and a warning. I suppose you know three or four of the boys have told around how much they'd like to get a shot at you."

"I'm used to being on a firing line," the Major remarked. He was obviously unfrightened and Tighe felt a half-reluctant respect for him.

"If you get yourself killed," he said, "it's going to be downright embarrassing."

"I'll try to be discreet," the Major told him. He scrutinized Tighe for a long moment. "May I assume, then, that you will join us here?" he inquired.

Tighe laughed.

"It's a fair question," he said. "I'll take the job if I can have it on my own terms."

"I don't think we'll have any trouble about the money," the Major replied.

"I'm not as much interested in money as I am in land," Tighe explained.

"We'll be glad to have you settle here, of course," the Major was quick to agree. Tighe nodded.

"I've got my eye on the Berenda Spring," he explained.

"That's one of the best locations on the grant," the Major remarked.

"I know it is," Tighe said. "That's why I want it. I want about ten sections on both sides of it. I'll pay your regular acre price and you can take it out of my wages."

The Major was thoughtful for a moment.

"We hadn't planned to sell holdings of that size," he said. "I'll have to consult my principals, but I believe it can be arranged. Meanwhile, I trust you'll accept a commission as deputy sheriff and take over. There's an office for you adjoining the new hotel."

"All right," Tighe said, and started to rise.

"Just a minute." The Major raised a delaying hand. "There are a few other things . . ."

"Shoot," Tighe said, relaxing in his chair and starting another cigarette.

"There's a character around here named Laird who seems to be making most of our trouble for us," the Major explained. "He did all of Ballard's building for him and he's some kind of a preacher, out of the Tennessee mountains."

"I heard him when I was here a few years ago," Tighe said. "He's got a voice like a range bull on the prod."

"Yes," the Major agreed, "and he can't keep it quiet. When the government survey was completed here about a month ago he got all the ranchers together and made them a speech. He gave them to understand the survey was—well, that the lines had been stretched. He claimed to know all about the original grant."

Tighe blew smoke and nodded.

"What did he tell them to do?" he inquired.

The Major hesitated a moment.

"I don't know that he gave them any specific advice," he said, a little uneasily. "But he worked up a lot of bad feeling against the company."

"Does he pack a gun?" Tighe inquired.

"No," the Major said, "I believe not."

"Well, he's got a right to shoot off his mouth." Tighe spoke with the finality of one who has no doubt about his principles. "If he tries anything else, I'll take care of him."

"Don't misunderstand me," the Major said smoothly. "I wouldn't want anything to happen to him. That might only make things worse. But I wish he would go somewhere else."

"I'm not going to start running people out of town," Tighe said. "That's not my way. It'll have to be understood I handle everything my own way here."

"Of course," the Major agreed. "I just wanted you to know about him."

"I know plenty about him," Tighe said. He started to rise again and again the Major raised a detaining hand.

"One other thing," he said. "We're having a little community celebration next Sunday. There will be an auction of town lots, and we've imported an auctioneer from Kansas City to hold it. After that we're going to have a barbecue and a rodeo, and probably a dance at night. . . ."

"That's about the worst thing you could do," Tighe interrupted quietly. "You've got two factions here now. All the old settlers are on one side, and all the men who have come to buy land from the company are on the other. They hope to see the old-timers dispossessed and then grab the good locations for themselves. It's a nice little mess and you ought to know it. If you bring them all together and let them get full of liquor, something can pop any minute."

The Major nodded imperturbably.

"I'm not suffering from any illusions," he remarked. "But this gathering can't be avoided." He paused a moment. "I thought you might open the exercises with a little exhibition of your trick shooting. I'm told you're one of the best performers in the West."

Tighe blew smoke and looked at the end of his cigarette. He knew the Major was proposing to put him to the test, and he knew that couldn't be avoided either.

"All right," he said at last. "If you're bound to have a show, I'll police it for you, and I'll show the boys how to handle a gun. But I want it understood that from now on you won't hold any celebrations without asking me. What we need is a spell of peace."

The Major laughed as he rose and held out his hand.

"I agree with you completely about that," he said.

Tighe walked slowly to his new office, shaking his head from time to time. "A smart little bastard," he said to himself, "if I ever saw one."

— 6 —

The auction day celebration drew a crowd of nearly three hundred, not counting Mexicans and Indians. They did not count, of course, either as potential customers or potential trouble-makers because they had no money, wore no guns and had nothing to fight about. Everyone ignored them.

Two men were conspicuously absent. The Major refrained from attending, thereby establishing a policy which governed him throughout his administration. He was seldom seen outside his own office and only a select few ever saw him there. When he traveled, he moved rapidly, sitting his big sorrel fox-trotter like the soldier he was, with the faithful Shad covering his rear.

Daniel Laird who had presided over almost all public gatherings before Ballard's death also stayed away, and Tighe was glad of that. He knew the preacher had a following and a man with a following was just what he didn't want around. Waverly Buncombe was the master of ceremonies on this occasion and Tighe had difficulty in recognizing him at first. He remembered Buncombe as a good chuck-wagon cook wearing jeans and a hickory shirt. Now he wore a long frock coat, a wide black hat, a high collar and a thick black tie—a costume which had become standard for gamblers, saloon keepers, mayors and other citizens of the first importance and dignity. It was generally understood that Waverly now worked for the company, although in exactly what capacity no one seemed to know. He was said to be one of the few who had regular access to the Major's office and it was easy for Tighe to guess that he supplied Blore with an extra pair of ears and eyes.

Waverly made a dignified and impressive master of ceremonies, superintending the four Mexicans who were roasting a whole beef over an open pit, discarding his enormous chew of tobacco to introduce Tighe as "the most famous peace officer west of Kansas City, who will now entertain you with a little exhibition of his skill in the use of that instrument of his profession and symbol of his authority—the Colt pacifier."

Tighe usually wore only a single gun, but he was one of the few men in the West who could shoot with both hands. For this occasion he wore a fancy two-gun belt of hand-carved leather, with the holsters built into the strap. He began by tossing a tin can thirty feet away and blasting it, first with one gun, then with the other, making it hop into the air like a live thing, hitting it again before it fell to the ground. He then gave a demonstration of the rare art of fanning, holding a gun in his left hand and beating the hammer spur with his right, delivering five shots in two seconds with enough accuracy to put them all in a tin bucket at ten yards. After that, he held out both guns butt first, as though he were surrendering them to an opponent, then reversed them with lightning speed by rolling the trigger guards around his fingers, delivering two accurate and simultaneous shots. But the final demonstration of his speed was the most impressive. He stood with his hands at his sides while a boy tossed a can into the air, then drew and hit it just as it reached the top of its arc. This final number got a round of applause from the assembled company, most of whom wore six-shooters themselves and all of whom knew they had seen the work of a master. Tighe bowed and withdrew, admitting to himself that the Major's idea might not have been such a bad one after all.

Throughout the rest of the afternoon he moved about among the crowd, receiving congratulations and making acquaintances. One of these was young Bob Clarey, who offered his hand and his wholly convincing tribute.

"Gosh!" he said. "I wish I could shoot like that!"

Tighe saw a chance to make a friend and he knew he was going to need friends.

"You can, son, if you'll practice," he said. "Look me up some day and I'll teach you what I know."

After the auction and the shooting match there were roping and bronco-riding contests. Bob Clarey won the latter by staying his time on top of a white outlaw called Twister, by reason of the terrific sidewise wrench he put into his bucking. Tighe was able to return the boy's congratulations with the utmost sincerity. Bob was a born rider with an infallible sense of balance—one of those who seem to dance with the frantic horse, anticipating his every plunge and turn.

When the crowd swarmed around the barbecue pit Tighe kept moving around among the guests, watching for signs of trouble, but he heard no arguments and saw no fights, although he could spot men of both factions and most of them wore guns. He was not greatly surprised at this. He knew tensions had not risen to the point of violence yet, and he knew his presence made a difference.

The only test of his authority came that night at the dance, when he stood at the door and held out his hand for every man's gun as he entered. A few hesitated briefly, as though about to question this procedure, but none of them refused and the dance was peaceful except for the usual fight between a cowboy and a Mexican over a Mexican girl. When the Mexican flashed a knife, Tighe neatly put him to sleep with a skillful tap of the gun barrel. It was an essential part of the practice of frontier police work, and the art of it lay in rolling the barrel as it struck, so that the man was stunned without breaking the skin or risking a fracture.

Young Clarey again was a star performer at the dance, doing the cradle waltz with his beautiful Adelita, practically monopolizing the floor for one number by the sheer speed and grace of their performance. This Bob Clarey, Tighe saw, was a young man with a gift for being in the middle of things.

Tighe got back to his combined office and living quarters about midnight, after he was sure the crowd had scattered and both saloons were closed, with the feeling that he had done a good and exhausting day's work. He pulled off his boots, sat down and poured himself a stiff drink. Just before going to bed was the only time he could take a drink with perfect safety. He was rolling a cigarette when he heard a light knock. He rose, stuck his gun in the band of his trousers and opened the door, standing far enough back to have room for action. The yellow bar of lamplight fell upon a short, plump Mexican with a smooth round face—a man of perhaps forty years. "Mr. Tighe," he said, "I am Ernesto Royball. I work in the store. May I talk with you?" He spoke softly, in excellent English with a slight Mexican accent. Tighe saw that he wore no gun. He extended his hand.

"Come in, Ernesto," he said. "Sit down and pour yourself a drink. What can I do for you?"

"Nothing, Mr. Tighe," the little man replied, as he helped himself to whisky. "I saw you shoot this afternoon. I have heard much about you. I think I can help you here."

Tighe was not at all surprised by this proposition. He had known that someone such as Ernesto would appear before long. In each of the towns he had tamed, men had come to him secretly, offering to serve him as spies and informers. He had long since learned that a man in a place of power always has such followers, as surely as a dog has fleas.

Tighe knew well enough that he was now part of a situation in which no one trusted anyone else. He had no doubt at all that Blore had his spies, that every move he made himself would be reported to the little Major and would also be known to the leaders of both factions among the cowmen. He knew he too needed someone to look and listen for him. He was essentially a policeman and no policeman can do without informers. Treachery begets treachery and espionage is a contagious disease. . . . The only question was whether he could trust the little Mexican.

"Tell me about yourself, Ernesto," he said. "I need friends here. Maybe we can work together."

"I went to the Brothers' School in Santa Fe," Ernesto told him. "Anastasio Royball—you know him?—he is my uncle. I worked in the store for Ballard and now I work in the company store. I know everybody. I hear a lot of talk."

Tighe reflected quickly that a Mexican might be his safest ally. A Mexican was on neither side in this struggle. He understood too the feeling of feudal loyalty a Mexican has for anyone whom he accepts as his patron. In this situation, he thought, he would rather trust a Mexican than one of his own breed.

Tighe judged men by their eyes. He knew the fighting eye and the veiled eye of treachery and the eye of the man who never reveals himself. He did not think about men or consciously classify them, but he trusted the impressions he got when he looked into their eyes. Ernesto had soft brown eyes—the eyes of devotion, the eyes of the born follower, of the eternal child in search of a father.

"All right, Ernesto," he said. "We'll make a deal. You know of course that you'll have to be careful how you come here."

Ernesto nodded and smiled faintly.

"You can trust me, Mr. Tighe," he said. "I know my way around." He paused a moment. "We had good times here in the old days," he spoke wistfully. "Ballard was a great patron. He knew how to keep the peace. Now the place is full of trouble. The old-timers meet almost every night in Ed Kelly's saloon. They all say they'll shoot before they'll move. They scared that Marcos right out of town. They say you won't last either."

Tighe nodded.

"There's been a plan to get rid of me most of the time for the last fifteen years," he remarked. "Who does most of the talking down there at Kelly's?"

"Old man Clarey, for one," Ernesto said. "He sounds pretty bad when he gets a few drinks in him."

"I think I can reach him through his kid," Clay said confidently. "The kid is all right."

"Yes," Ernesto agreed. "But if you try to serve papers on any of them, I think you'll have trouble right away."

"I'm not going to serve any papers—at least not for a long time," Clay said. "I'm not taking any orders from Blore. I'm going to try a lot of persuasion first. If I can get a few of the boys to sign up with the company the rest of them will probably come along."

After Ernesto had left, Tighe got out a map of the grant and tacked it up on the wall of his office. It showed the locations of all the ranches the survey had taken in. There were thirty-two of them, and he knew that each one was a potential trouble spot, and that most of them he would have to visit alone. It would be a long job but he faced it with some confidence. He knew all about the kind of men he had to deal with.

He began by giving himself a week to get acquainted with the town. Its heart and center was still the store—the one that Ballard had founded before the war, and that the company had taken over. But the company had built also a huge frame structure which was a combined hotel, restaurant and bar. This, apparently, was the place Betty Weiss was supposed to manage, when and if she arrived. Tighe had written her, saying simply there was a town all right and a lot of money going around. For the time being, Waverly Buncombe seemed to be functioning as a general manager at the hotel, although he circulated so widely, talked so much and told so little about his own business that he was a somewhat enigmatic figure. So far, Tighe observed, there were no public games in the company saloon and no girls except authentic waitresses. Evidently the Major wanted an orderly town if possible. But the hotel was crowded with strangers, some of whom Tighe could identify as professional gamblers and gunmen, the kind who had followed the tracks west and here had taken one jump ahead of them. They were waiting to see how big the town would boom. Like all such towns it was full of exciting rumors. Blore was said to be planning a dam across the narrow part of the Dark River Canyon which would irrigate the plains and bring in settlers by the thousands. The railroad was expected to reach the town within two years and it would probably become a division point. The company was said to have a huge contract for ties and bridge timbers. Prospectors were combing the near-by mountains and every few days there was a rumor of a rich gold or silver strike. The town now had an assay office and it was always busy. It also had a combined barber shop and undertaking parlor, a blacksmith shop, a butcher shop which often had a bear or a buck hung before its door. A lawyer had opened an office in a tent, and a small tent city was growing up across the creek like mushrooms after a rain.

Everyone agreed the town had a future, but so far it looked like a boom town only on Saturday nights when all the ranchers came to the store, as they had been doing for so many years, and joined the strangers in a buying and drinking spree. The newcomers all gathered at the company bar, but Tighe was quick to see that the old-timers shunned it completely and went to the little saloon that Ed Kelly ran as an adjunct to his livery stable. Already each faction had its headquarters and its leaders. Tighe knew his job was to keep them apart and slowly dissolve them. He circulated between the two bars, watching the eyes of men, making an acquaintance when he saw a chance, spotting those who went out of their way to avoid him. He found three ranchers he had known in the old days in Dodge City. Bill Bostwick was one of them and Tighe shook hands with him and said, "I'll be out to see you one of these days." "Glad to see you," Bostwick said, but he spoke uneasily.

Tighe found time also to give young Bob Clarey the shooting lesson he had promised, and quickly found that the boy had natural speed and dexterity. Thereafter young Bob wore his gun tied to his leg, exactly like Tighe's, even canted his hat at the same angle and gave his friends to understand that he too would become a peace officer, a ruler of towns and a tamer of bad men. Tighe could see that the boy had the makings of a crack shot, but not of an officer of the law in a lawless country. There was not enough iron in him or enough guile. He was still friends with everybody, too much absorbed in his girl and his horse to be aware of the growing tension.

— 7 —

Tighe timed his ride to the Bostwick ranch so that he could take a roundabout way and get there about sunset. He traveled roundabout, start-

ing in the wrong direction, because he didn't want anyone to know where
he was going, and he planned to arrive at sunset because he knew Bill
would get home about that time. He saw the ranch from the top of a low
hill, half a mile away—a pole corral, a long low house under cottonwoods with a blue plume of smoke going up from its rock chimney and
not another sign of human life clear to the wide horizons.

Bill was unsaddling his horse when Tighe rode up and they walked
together to the house where his Mary was frying venison in an iron skillet
and opening the oven door to look at a pan of browning biscuits, while
fragrant steam poured out of a tin coffeepot and the table was all set with
a pat of homemade butter and a jar of wild plum preserves. An invitation
to dinner was inevitable and Tighe had counted on that. He never talked
seriously to a man with an empty stomach if he could help it. All through
the meal he chatted about the early days in Dodge and Abilene, the trail
drives, the weather, an elk hunt they might take together when the first
snow fell—everything but business. Not until both of them had rolled and
lighted their cigarettes did he mention what had brought him there.

"Bill," he said, "you've got a nice little ranch here. I want to help you
hold it."

Bill was a tall lean man of about thirty with a permanently red face and
neck, a large Adam's apple and deep-set blue eyes—a kind of man you
nearly always found on a ranch twenty miles from a neighbor. It seemed
as though fat men always stayed in towns and these lean and quiet ones
were often stubborn and suspicious.

"I aim to hold it," Bill said bluntly. "I think that survey is a fraud."

"I don't know anything about the survey," Tighe told him. "That was
before my time. But what can you do about it? You can hire a lawyer
and it'll cost you more than to buy your quarter section from the company."

Bill sat silent, looking at the Winchester in the corner, and Tighe knew
he was thinking he didn't need a lawyer. He knew how fiercely these men
resented anything like invasion, how strong was their feeling that possession and use were the whole of the law. . . . He went on quickly to
outline the company's terms. They were fair terms, assuming that the
company had honest title to the land. They had doubtless come straight
from headquarters in Denver. The company was offering to sell any squatter the quarter-section he lived on, with its water rights, at a very moderate price per acre, or else to buy his improvements at a fair valuation.
Tighe argued now like a lawyer. It would be the easiest way in the long
run, he said, to get a clear title to the ranch. Otherwise there was a long
process of filing and waiting and proving up, even if the company was
ousted. He knew he was talking sense, and so did Bostwick.

"I'll think it over," the rancher said. That was all Tighe had hoped
for. He dropped the subject at once, talking a little while about trifles,
smoked a last cigarette and rose to go. Both the Bostwicks pressed him

to stay the night, but he knew when to make an exit. He rode away into starlit wilderness, feeling mildly triumphant and also more secure than he ever did in the light of day.

Most of his days now were devoted to such diplomatic missions. He visited first the men he had known farther east and those with whom he had established an acquaintanceship in the town. No doors were slammed in his face, no one refused to listen, most of the ranchers invited him to dinner. He knew well enough these were his easiest cases. There would be some die-hards who would bluster and threaten but he hoped to reduce them slowly to an isolated minority. He knew that most men will always follow the crowd.

Saturdays and Sundays he patrolled the town and visited both of the saloons every night before he went to bed. The company saloon was always crowded, with new faces present almost every night, and with a couple of private card games flourishing in the back room. But Ed Kelly's little joint seemed to have an ever-dwindling patronage, until finally one night he found the bowlegged proprietor all alone. He took a short beer for the sake of sociability.

"Where's your congregation tonight, Ed?" he inquired.

"Home, I reckon," Ed replied. "Most of 'em live quite a ways out."

This was true enough but it was also true that for weeks there had been a small gathering at Kelly's almost every night. Often he had noticed that conversation seemed to lag when he entered, but as long as the boys were all together there, he could watch them. Now he didn't know where they were. He went home slightly troubled.

Ernesto Royball confirmed the worst of his fears a few nights later. The little Mexican looked painfully worried. Tighe had learned long since that Ernesto was a true friend of peace—that he saw violence in the making and longed to prevent it—and this had greatly increased his faith in the man.

"The boys are riding every night," he told Tighe breathlessly. "Two of my cousins—they camp with their sheep on the Rayado—they saw them!"

Tighe nodded gravely. Night riders! He knew all about them. He had been a night rider himself in Kansas. When men banded together and rode in the dark, they were almost always a minority trying to beat other men into line by threat or violence.

"How many did they see?" he asked.

"At least ten," Ernesto reported. "Carlos said he thought they were headed for the Bostwick place."

"That's bad," Tighe said. "Did he recognize any of them?"

"No," Ernesto said. "Old man Clarey is probably one, and all that bunch that meet in Kelly's place. . . ."

"Do you think Laird is putting them up to this?" he asked.

"I don't think so," Ernesto said. "He is a good man. He cured my little boy when we thought he would die. Up at the plaza we all like him. Some of the women think he is a Cristo and has healing in his hands. He was always a peacemaker in the old days. He stopped lots of fights."

"But he did make a speech about the survey, so I heard," Tighe said.

"Yes, I heard him," Ernesto said. "He told them about the Royal Grant. He said Ballard had showed him the paper. He said it was hard to tell where the lines ran, but they couldn't possibly take in what the company claims. He told them they had a right to know."

"Was that all?" Tighe asked.

"Well, no." Ernesto spoke a little reluctantly. "He made quite a speech. You know how he can talk. He quoted from the Bible. I remember he said the earth belongs to those who plow it. Of course, we don't plow much around here, but he made the boys feel they had a right to their ranches."

"The hell of it is, he's probably right," Tighe said gravely. "Blore must have bought that surveyor. But what can you do? These poor suckers have got to buy or move and they ought to know it."

"The trouble is, some of them want to fight," Ernesto said. "There is always somebody who wants to fight. . . ."

"Yes," Tighe agreed, "and if they want a fight, they'll have to have one."

After Ernesto had gone Tighe sat long pondering a situation he didn't like. He had great confidence in his ability to deal with men one at a time. If a man had sense and courage he would almost always listen to reason, and if he was a fool and a coward you could almost always scare him. Like all frontier officers, what he dreaded was the mass movement—the mob and the gang. Every lawless town tended to produce them. Tighe knew the natural history of mobs. He knew it was possible to break one up in its early stages, but once it got moving it could not be scattered. You could only face it with a gun, then, pit your life against it. It was much the same with a night-riding gang. It started as a mob, gained leadership and organization as it went along. He knew the time to stop this one was early. He knew this gang was probably going to every rancher he had visited, trying to undo his work, whether by threat or persuasion. He knew if that continued he would have to start serving papers—and that might mean open war. Tighe had lost his taste for war. First he would face alone every man he could find. It would take time, but all of them came to town sooner or later.

He managed first to meet Bill Bostwick in the store.

"Bill," he said, "if anyone bothers you out there, I hope you'll let me know. I'm here to keep the peace."

Bostwick didn't meet his eye.

"I reckon I won't need any help," he said quietly, and then walked away.

Tighe knew that was bad, and he knew even better that things were going against him when another man he had visited crossed the street to avoid meeting him. For the first time in a good many years Clay Tighe could sense that his prestige was falling, that his authority and power were being defied. He was not the celebrity here that he had been in Dodge and Hays City and Abilene. Most of these men had heard of him but they had not seen him perform, except on a tin can. He had believed he could manage this situation without ever drawing a gun. With a slight tightening of the gut and tautening of the nerves he understood now that he was going to have to prove himself—how or when he still couldn't see.

Old man Clarey was the only member of the night-riding gang of whom he felt sure. He doubted that Clarey was the leader but he had been the chief talker for a long time. He had told several men that no goddam sheriff was ever going to run him off his own ranch. Tighe had encountered this loud-talking kind of man many times before. Almost always he proved to be more a bluff than a menace. The truly dangerous man seldom made much noise. Tighe had counted on Clarey to subside as others accepted the company offer. But now he knew he had to tackle Clarey, as being the only one of the enemy he could identify. He knew also that he had to meet him on the street, in the most casual way, and this took time. All of the ranchers necessarily came to the store, soon or late, but the old-timers seemed to be staying away from town as much as possible. Tighe could guess that they were meeting at some ranch house, laying their plans, making their midnight visits. . . . It was a week before he saw Clarey coming down the new board sidewalk past the company hotel, and he went to meet him.

He confronted the man squarely, brought him to a stop.

"Clarey," he said quietly, "I'm coming out to see you one of these days. I've got a little business to talk about."

"You've got no business with *me!*" Clarey said, his voice rising shrilly on the last word. "You've got no business on *my* ranch. I warn you now! If you don't want trouble, stay off *my* land!"

He glared at Tighe a moment, then pushed past him and went his way. Tighe stood staring after him a moment. "There would be one son-of-a-bitch . . ." he said to himself.

He carried back to his office a disturbing impression of small, bright, humorless eyes, with a spark of rage in them, under shaggy brows. They reminded him of the eyes of a wounded bear he had faced once, reared upon its hind legs, ready to charge. He remembered, too, the rising, strained inflection of the voice. He knew the type—the man who has violence bottled up inside him, who contrives crises half consciously because something in him always craves a crisis.

For once in his life Tighe spent days of indecision. He knew now that he had to make a move, but he didn't feel sure yet what he had to do. It was the indispensable Ernesto, making a cautious midnight call, who brought his doubts to an end.

"They are saying that Clarey has you bluffed," he reported. "They say you are afraid to go out there and take him."

"Just exactly who is saying that?" Tighe inquired.

"Buncombe, for one," Ernesto said. "When he starts talking about anything, it goes all over town. He's just a big mouth—that's all he is. He says Clarey has a buffalo gun right by his door. He's going to nail you when he sees you coming. . . . Of course you can't believe a word Waverly says."

"No," Tighe agreed, "but you can believe he has reason for saying it. Blore owns him, tooth and toenail."

After Ernesto had gone, Tighe sat thoughtful for a long time. Ruefully he faced the fact that the little Major had been too smart for him. Given time and no interference Tighe believed he could have reduced the rebels to a helpless minority who would sell out and move. He felt sure he could have settled the problem without ever serving a paper or drawing a gun. But the Major wanted quick action. He probably also wanted a show of force. Tighe spoke aloud to himself, as he always did when troubled.

"The hell of it is, he's going to get it. Now I've got to do something or else quit—and I can't quit."

He waited two more days. He spent them chiefly looking for young Bob Clarey, hoping he might yet reach the father through the son. But Bob was nowhere to be found and hadn't been seen in town for weeks. He was evidently sticking close to the home ranch, and doubtless that meant he was loyal to the old man.

—8—

On his decisive day, Tighe rose long before daylight. He inspected his six-shooter and tested his draw with care. He loaded his rifle and ran half a dozen shells through the action to be sure it was working smoothly. Then he mounted and rode out of town in the dark and solitude of the small hours.

Tighe's professional pride was deeply involved in this situation. He knew there was only one alternative to what he intended doing now—to admit he could not do the job alone and raise a posse to help him. That would be easy. Any of the newcomers who hung around the company bar would be glad to follow him. In effect, he would then be putting himself at the head of the other faction. He could ride to each of the disputed properties and serve a notice of dispossession by force of arms. Unless the night riders all were rank cowards they would then gather at one of the ranches and wait for him. There would be a pitched battle at short range with Winchesters.

Any fool could bring a tense situation to a climax, make a bloody mess of it. Most of the men Blore might have hired would have done just that, and done it in the first place. Clay Tighe was famous for the fact that he could dominate men, and even whole towns, without raising his voice, much less drawing his gun. He took pride in being a keeper of the peace. He still believed he could have kept the peace in the Dark River Valley if no one else had meddled. He still hoped he might regain his dominance without firing a shot. If he could serve papers on Clarey, or disarm him and bring him to town, he would at least have gained time.

Dawn was breaking when he got off his horse a quarter of a mile from the Clarey ranch, walked to the top of a low hill and studied the house from a screen of juniper and piñon, like a hunter stalking dangerous game. As the light widened in the east, he could see four saddle horses in the Clarey corral, feeding at a hayrack. Four men were more than he had expected but there was nothing for it. One of the horses was white and he knew that probably meant young Bob was at home. This also was bad news. A third horse, he knew, probably belonged to Bill McComas, a young cowboy who worked for Clarey from time to time. Bill was a harmless and simple young fellow, who wore a gun because it was customary, and he probably wouldn't fight. Tighe couldn't guess who the fourth man was.

He would have liked to catch the old man there alone, but he knew that would be pure luck, and he could not afford to wait and try again. He had to take the situation as he found it.

It was cold in the summer dawn. He stamped his feet and threshed his arms while he waited. He couldn't afford to be stiff or slow when he went to the door. . . . It was nearly an hour before he saw the signal he was waiting for—a thin blue wisp of smoke from the chimney. The men were awake and starting to cook breakfast. This was the traditional, the only right time to make an arrest. He mounted and rode slowly down toward the house, picking soft ground so there would be no sound of shod hoofs striking rock.

The Clarey house was a long low block of a structure, built of squared timbers, solid as a fort. The door was in the middle with a window on either side of it. Both windows still were closed by solid wooden shutters, and Tighe knew this was luck for him. Otherwise he might have had trouble approaching the house unseen. As it was he rode up within ten yards of the door and dismounted, turning his horse parallel to the house and dropping his bridle rein on the ground. The well-trained sorrel would stay right there until he got a signal to move. As he walked quietly to the door Tighe could just hear low voices within, a man whistling softly and the spat and sizzle of breakfast in a frying pan. He knocked loudly on the door. Instantly there was silence. He waited a minute that seemed very long and then knocked again. This time he heard a quick step and the door opened a few inches. For about three seconds he looked into the small, glaring, fanatical eyes of old man Clarey. Then the door closed with a bang, and without a word.

Tighe knew that meant war. He whipped out his six-shooter, covering the door with it, backed away swiftly and got behind his horse. There he holstered the revolver and drew his short Winchester from the saddle scabbard. Then he slapped the sorrel on the rump and the horse moved away, turning its head slightly so as not to step on the trailing bridle rein. Tighe stood rigid, the cocked rifle hard against his hip. Its muzzle was trained on the door. But he was watching both windows as well.

This was a feat of arms he had practiced often, but had used only once before when he had taken three Mexican horse thieves out of an adobe house. He knew that now, as then, it was his only chance. He could deliver a shot to the door or to either window, swinging the gun with his whole body, and do it far faster than he could level and shoot a revolver. Tense and ready he stood, a fair target. Clarey could have war now if he wanted it. The choice was his.

For three long minutes nothing happened except that Tighe could hear voices again. Then there was a terrific pounding on the inside of the door.

"Tighe, Tighe!" He knew the voice must be that of Bill McComas. "Don't shoot! I'm coming out. . . . I don't want no part of this!"

"All right!" Tighe called. "Come out with your hands up."

The door popped open, McComas popped out and the door slammed behind him. McComas stood visibly trembling, his mouth open, his hands high.

"Unbuckle your gun and let it drop," Tighe told him quietly. And then as the gun hit the ground, "Now go back in there and tell the rest of them to come out the same way."

"They won't do it!" McComas spoke in the strangulated voice of terror. "I argued with the old man. The damn fool won't move."

"All right, get going," Tighe said.

McComas jumped over his own gun and sprinted for the cover of the corral fence. Tighe's eyes never left the door. The strain of waiting lasted minutes longer, then the door jerked open a crack and he could see the muzzle of a gun in it. His rifle roared and spat flame. Blue smoke briefly obscured his vision but he knew he had hit his man. He could always call his shots.

He worked the lever of his rifle like lightning, and none too fast. He swung on a crack between the shutters of the left-hand window. A rifle barrel had poked them open, and this time the two shots were simultaneous, but Tighe still stood. Within he heard a thud and a groan. He stood fast, ready again, knowing two men were down but there must be a third to deal with.

For an intolerably long time nothing happened and he could hear no sound. There might be no third man after all, or one bullet might have struck two. . . . He had to do something. He strode up to the door and began kicking at it with all his strength, chancing a shot through the wood. The door crashed open and he jumped through it, rifle ready, almost falling over the body of old man Clarey, who lay on his back with arms outspread, a round, dark bullet hole between his eyes and a dark pool of blood widening beneath his head. Over by the window a second man knelt beside a fallen one, supporting his head. The kneeling man turned his head and Tighe recognized Daniel Laird.

"He's dying," Laird spoke in a tired, flat voice.

It was all over. Tighe suddenly felt all the tension drain out of him. He leaned his rifle against the wall and went and knelt on the other side of young Bob. The boy was shot through the lungs. Tighe knew that by the pinkish foam about his mouth and the sound of his breathing. Bob looked at Tighe with eyes wide in an expression of pained surprise.

"I wish, I wish, I wish . . ." he said. But no one ever knew what he wished for a great gout of blood welled up out of his mouth and he fell back and died. Laird covered his face and the two men rose and faced each other. There was no strain between them. They moved slowly, like old men, with the weariness of profound reaction.

"They're both dead," Laird said.

"Yes," Tighe agreed. "I had to do it. . . . They both had a shot at me."

Laird nodded.

"I've been out here with them three days," he said. "I tried to persuade them not to fight. I knew you would come."

They went out, closing the smashed door as best they could, and Tighe waited while Laird saddled his horse. They rode back toward town slowly, slumping a little in their saddles, and for a long time they rode in silence.

"I'm sure sorry I had to kill that boy," Tighe said at last, speaking as though to himself, looking at nothing.

"Yes," Laird said.

"The old man asked for it," Tighe said. "But I'm sure sorry about that boy."

Again they rode in silence for slow miles, and again Tighe spoke, as though from the depth of his own reflections.

"I guess I had to kill somebody," he said. "This will settle it. Nobody else will try anything now. If Clarey had killed me all hell would have broken loose."

Laird said nothing and they rode all the rest of the way in silence. As they neared the town Tighe could see a crowd gathered and growing on the sidewalk in front of the company saloon. He knew Bill McComas would have watched the fight, would have known the Clareys were both down when he saw Tighe enter the house. The news was there ahead of him and that was bad.

"You better cut for home," he told Laird. "I'll take this bunch alone."

Laird nodded and turned off across the creek toward his own cabin.

The crowd in front of the saloon was almost all company men and curious strangers, with a few Mexicans who had heard the news, and a few women. There was nothing hostile about it. As Tighe dismounted a few men came forward holding out their hands, but Tighe waved them away, shaking his head.

"I don't want any congratulations, boys," he said. "And I don't want a crowd. Break it up!"

Most of them were turning away when he saw Adelita coming. Her long hair was down around her shoulders, her face was a mask of agony and her great dark eyes were fixed upon his. They held him in his tracks and she came right up to him, her face within two feet of his.

"Is he dead?" she demanded. "Did you kill him?"

Tighe nodded grimly, dumb with distress.

"You killed him!" Her voice rose to a screaming pitch of grief. "Why did you kill him? What had he done to you?"

She covered her face with her hands for a moment, then looked up at him again, and this time he saw fury in her eyes.

"Murderer, murderer, murderer!" She hurled the words into his face like missiles. "You murdered him!"

She turned and walked slowly away, her face buried in her hands again, her heavy disheveled hair draping her shaken shoulders like a mourning veil.

Tighe went into the saloon and found it empty except for the bartender.

"Give me a double brandy," he said.

He lifted his drink and stared at it for a long moment, noticing that his hand trembled slightly for the first time in many years. He downed the brandy at a gulp and set down the glass.

"It takes a woman to make you feel things," he remarked.

PART FOUR

THE PROPHET

IN HIS OWN COUNTRY

After the killing of the Clareys, Daniel Laird was seldom seen on the streets of the town. He spent much of his time in the mountains with a rifle or a fishing rod. It was only in the mountains that he now had any feeling of peace, especially when he lay on the ground under the pines and listened to the long, deep breathing of the wind. This was a thing he had done ever since he could remember for he had always been a man of the forest. The great trees had often given him a feeling of peace and sometimes a kind of ecstasy. Sometimes he felt as though the wind was one with his breath and his body with the earth beneath him. Even now, when so much bitterness stirred inside him, he could walk himself tired and rest upon the earth and recover a moment of peace.

It was only a moment, for the whole way of his life in the Dark River Valley had been destroyed. There was much building in the valley but no work for him. He could not ask Blore for work and Blore was an absolute ruler. He never went near the meeting house now, for he knew no one would come to hear him. Dances still were held there every Saturday night and he saw the lights and heard the music and felt the cold weight of his exclusion. When he went to the store to buy supplies, men he had known for years refused to meet his eye or crossed the street to avoid him. He felt the eyes of strangers upon him, sometimes saw them pointing at him, always knew they were talking about him.

Only fragments of gossip had come to him, mostly through a few Mexicans who remained his friends because he had helped them when they were sick, but he knew what people were saying about him, as well as though he had heard their words. He knew they all blamed him for the killing of the Clareys, said he had persuaded the old man to fight, said there would have been open war if he had had his way. No one blamed Tighe for the killing. Everyone said Tighe had done only what he had to do. Tighe now was the great man of the Dark River Valley, the man who had brought peace with a gun. Everyone now had either signed up with the company or sold out and moved. Peace had come for everyone except Daniel Laird, the man who had wanted only to tell the truth and see justice done, the man who had longed to serve his fellows. . . . In his own mind he defended himself hotly, sometimes talking to himself as he strode along. This added a new phase to his legend, for many, especially among the newcomers, now said he was crazy.

He defended himself, he composed long soliloquies of self-justification, but it was all in vain. He was learning the painful fact that blame begets guilt, that no man can stand alone against the disapproval of his fellows. When he walked down the street he felt guilty in spite of himself, he peered suspiciously over his shoulder, he all but slunk through the town, hoping no one would notice his presence. Guilt hounded him, it drove him into the wilderness where the great trees spoke in soothing voices and the ancient earth received him into her bosom and let him rest. But only for a moment. . . . Worse than guilt was the longing for violence that had grown upon him. He could feel it in his breast as though it were a living, separate demon that had crept into his body. It poured a poison into his blood, changed the whole quality of his being, so that his great hands clenched as he walked. His muscles yearned for violence as a thirsty mouth for water. More than once he took an ax, just to relieve his feelings, felled a dead pine and reduced it to kindling, fighting it furiously until he was drenched with sweat and knew the passing relief of complete exhaustion. Such angers he had not tasted for years, not since the wild period of his youth when he had fought a few times in drunken fury and had known what it was to feel the warm blood of a man on his hands.

He did not blame most men now, those who turned away from him, but he despised them. What cowards they were! The ones who had listened to his words and agreed with him and offered to follow him now were afraid to be seen with him, afraid to meet his eye. The same men who had said they would chase Tighe out of the valley at the point of a gun now saluted Tighe when he walked down the street, paid him the craven homage of the yellow soul. Laird had persuaded himself once that he loved his fellow beings. Now suddenly he saw them as a pack of wolves who bit from behind and hunted in the dark and turned upon the fallen fellow. . . . But his rage, the rage that blinded his eyes and made his fingers writhe, was all against two men, Waverly Buncombe and Major Blore. He knew Blore was the man who had killed the Clareys, without ever lifting his hand, the one who had destroyed the peace. And he knew that Buncombe had played jackal to Blore's lion, had spread all the lies, had created the situation that made it necessary for Tighe to use a rifle. When he saw either of these men on the street he felt a rage that made him literally sick, so that he turned his eyes away. And both of them too had invaded his dreams. Not since his childhood had he known such vivid and terrible dreams. In one of them he was looking at Blore over the sights of a rifle. The Major was riding toward him from a great distance, growing slowly larger, while the bead of the front sight settled over his heart. Daniel awoke just before he pressed the trigger, with the feeling that he had been within an instant of murder. . . . The dream about Buncombe was even worse and it woke him repeatedly. He had Buncombe down on the ground and his fingers were around the man's throat, but he did not choke him. He pulled his head off, as he had seen a farmer pull the head off a chicken. Buncombe's neck stretched to an incredible length and then broke with a pop and a great spurt of blood. Daniel felt the warm blood all over him and woke to know that he was bathed in his own sweat.

He knew he was in a bad way, knew he ought to leave the valley, but a stubborn something in him would not let him leave. He had heard a rumor they were going to run him out—that Buncombe had boasted he would leave town on a rail if he didn't go pretty soon on his own horse. . . . Daniel Laird was not going to be run out of anywhere! He loved this country. It had been home to him for ten years. But maybe he would have gone if he hadn't heard that rumor. . . . Let them come! His hands clenched and his blood pounded when he thought about it. Let them come! He didn't care how many. . . .

— 2 —

As he went back to the mountains in search of peace, so he also went back to the past, reviewing his life as he had never done before, feeling the mystery of it, wondering how he had become what he was. And this too brought him a measure of peace, detached him from his own misery, gave him escape from the present, sent him all the way back to the Cumberland country where the little far-scattered farms lay in the coves beside bright leaping waters, and the mountains were clothed to their summits in virgin hardwood forest, the finest forest in the world, rich in timber, nuts and berries, fat with game. There men lived in log houses, raised corn with a hoe and ground it at watermills, made white liquor in their own stills, hunted for most of their meat and used buckskin for most of their clothing. It was the simplest, the most primitive and unchanging life that white men lived anywhere in America, and it was a hard life, but when he remembered it now, especially his childhood, he saw it all bathed in sunlight and moving to the music of singing voices—the singing of hymns in little mountain churches, the singing of folk songs that told long stories, his mother singing to the beat of a wooden churn.

Daniel Laird was raised on an ax and a rifle, a spelling book and a Bible. He knew many bits of the Bible by heart before he was fourteen because it was all he had to read, because he loved the sound and flavor of its words and also because it had been read to him, quoted to him, shouted at him, ever since he could remember. For the southern mountain country was truly vocal and vibrant with religion. It rocked and shouted and sang in the name of God. Religion was even more a social activity than a faith. Most public gatherings were religious gatherings. Every community had its little log church, and camp meetings brought people together from as far as you could ride a horse in a day. At the best and biggest camp meetings people went wild and rolled on the ground, men and women together and sin and salvation were sometimes part of the same occasion. Besides the main denominations, there were innumerable little sects, and almost any gifted preacher might found a sect of his own. Also, any man with a good voice might become a preacher, for most mountain preachers were unordained, farmed six days a week and preached on Sundays. Daniel's father was such a preacher and he was rated one of the best, chiefly because of the great and stirring power of his voice. The best preacher was the one who could get people to rocking and shouting the quickest, for to these mountain folk religion was a great communal excitement. They sobbed and bellowed and rolled and crawled but they truly achieved an escape from the limitations of self, a feeling of unity with Jesus and with each other.

In his boyhood Daniel knew much happiness of a simple, laborious kind, so that when he remembered it now it had almost the quality of an idyll. He worked hard with an ax and a hoe but he always had great strength and did his work easily. He was known as a "loner" who did not run much with other boys but liked to roam in the woods by himself when he was free. Every community had its loners and they were recognized and tolerated as such. Daniel was a good hunter and a first-class woodsman, who knew how to find wild honey and ginseng, and also all of the herbs the mountain people used in their doctoring. His mother had some reputation as a healer and he kept her supplied with herbs and learned something of her art. Like most solitary boys he stood somewhat apart from his family, escaping the tyranny of his two older brothers and of his father by taking to the timber like a woods-born shoat whenever the family atmosphere began to cramp him. He did not easily yield to the crowd feelings of church and camp meeting. He felt more at peace in the woods and more at one with the earth than with his fellows.

When he was seventeen he shot up suddenly to his full height and strength and the white stream of desire poured through his body, destroying the peace he had known in his best boyhood years. Then he began to join the gang of wild young men who gathered at the crossroads store. At first they would have none of him but he won his way by pinning each of them to the ground in a wrestling match. A few of these matches became fights when someone lost his temper and struck a blow. Daniel did not like to fight but he was terrible when he got started and he felt sick, win or lose, when it was over.

The gang Daniel went with attended every camp meeting they could reach, sometimes walking twenty miles, for these were the great excitements of their lives. They always had a jug of white corn liquor and they would lurk in the edge of the woods, a little way from the crowd, and prime their spirits with long burning swigs while they listened to the preaching and singing and shouting. They could tell by the noise the meeting made when it was reaching its highest point of excitement and then they would edge into the crowd, bellowng their hallelujahs as loud as the next fellow. All of them had the same idea, which was to get hold of some woman in a high state of excitement and edge her out of the crowd and get her down in the dark. There were always widow women who knew what was coming, and some married women who got away from their husbands, but it was dangerous business and sometimes there were terrible fights back in the shadows.

Some of the young fellows who came to camp meetings just to get drunk and chase women would be carried away by the preaching and singing and end up crawling toward the mourner's bench. Daniel never had that experience. By the time he was twenty-one he had been to many camp meetings, but he had never been saved, he had never come to Jesus. There was something in him that resisted the pull of the crowd, just as something in his body fought off the ague that shook most of his fellows. The better the camp meeting, the less he felt a part of it. If it was a good camp meeting the people always first began jigging and shouting, then fell on their faces and began to roll or crawl. Daniel's father remembered the great wave of revivals that swept over five states in the year 1802, when people gathered in thousands and sometimes fifteen preachers were working at once—all of them sweating to beat hell, some irreverent soul had said. In that great day hundreds fell all at once, like wheat before a scythe, his father had told him.

Daniel had never seen anything like that, but he had seen a good deal of jigging and crawling and he had never wanted to jig or crawl. At the best camp meeting he ever saw there were thirty or forty on the ground at once and some repentant sinners mounted the platform beside the preacher and shouted their confessions at the crowd. Daniel was full of corn liquor but still wholly unmoved when he climbed up on the platform and began bellowing in his great voice. He did not know or care what he was saying and neither did anyone else. They shouted hallelujah and praise God no matter what he said. "You can all go to hell!" he shouted at last, and they all answered him with a chorus of amen. Standing there above them, looking down on them, he felt more than ever detached from his fellows, but yet he longed for union with something. Presently he noticed a woman on the edge of the crowd who was going round and round with her eyes closed, dancing herself dizzy. She was a slim, blonde woman and a stranger to him—one who might have come from as much as twenty miles away, which was a long distance in the mountains. He went down to her and danced with her and caught her when she fell. Picking her up in his arms he carried her quickly into the shadows, and no one saw him or tried to stop him.

"Oh, for Christ's sake!" she murmured when he laid her on the ground, but she did not struggle, and afterwards he went heavily to sleep.

When he woke it was sunrise of a perfect June morning, with the slanting light silvering the leaves and a chorus of birdsong ringing softly
through the forest. The woman was gone, everyone was gone. Daniel had
a great thirst. He went down to the branch and took a deep drink and
bathed his head in the cool water. Then he lay down under the trees and
a feeling of great serenity and clarity came over him. It seemed as though
the woman had purified him of all desire, the alcohol in his blood had set
him free from his own body, and the peace of God had truly descended
upon this spot, now that all the people were gone. He felt like a disem-
bodied mind contemplating his own destiny with a new detachment. For
a long time he had been dissatisfied with his life and had thought of taking the long trail west. Some young men from the mountain settlements
went west every year, but not nearly so many as from other regions, for
these mountain people were passionately attached to their home country.
So Daniel had never made up his mind to go, but this morning he suddenly
felt sure he was going. He felt as though he were called to go, and also
as though the ties that bound him to a region had been all at once dissolved. He felt now that he could be at home anywhere on earth.

— 3 —

Daniel walked to Independence, Missouri, equipped with an ax and
one silver dollar. He got there with the same dollar and a few more.
Almost any farm would put him up for the night. Sometimes he chopped
wood to pay for his supper, but he was seldom asked to do so. When
he came to a sawmill he would stop for a few days and work at felling
timber, and sometimes he helped to raise a house or roof a barn. Everywhere populations were growing, men were building things, the country was
filled with the thud of axes, the whine of saws, the crash of falling timber.

He had no difficulty in getting a job as a teamster over the Santa Fe
Trail, for he moved westward with the first great wave of migration after
the war, but when he reached the high prairies in Kansas he almost wished
he could turn back. For the first time he saw a flat and treeless world, and
it made him acutely uncomfortable. He felt better when he reached the
Rocky Mountains, saw tall timber and clear running water again. He
stopped at Ballard's great house chiefly because of the fine forest and the
great mountains that rose behind it. He asked for a job and got one splitting firewood at the kitchen door. In a few months he had learned enough
Spanish to boss the gang of Mexicans who supplied the great house with
firewood, and within a year he had charge of all the building operations
on the grant. Ballard was quick to spot a useful man and one he could
trust. Daniel knew he owed his success almost wholly to Ballard's friendship. They were never intimates because neither of them had any intimates,
but he was one of the few men who went to Ballard's office whenever he

chose, and once in a while they sat and smoked together on the porch. Everyone knew that Ballard stood behind him and Daniel knew this made him a secure and privileged man, but he never understood how he came to occupy the peculiar position he did in the Dark River Valley. He had never intended to preach there, but he often sang at his work and his public career began when the women asked him to lead them in singing hymns. Neither had he wished to become an amateur doctor, but he began by patching up sick and injured Mexicans who worked for him, and this led to other calls for his services. Then Ballard asked him to take charge of the dance hall and keep order, and he became famous for his fiddling and his calling of square dances, which he had known all his life. So he became an important man—one who was listened to, obeyed and sent for in emergencies—and he enjoyed his importance.

He had acquired a role in the community and a legend, and he became more and more the creature and the prisoner of the part he had to play. It gave him authority over his fellows and it also set him apart from them, and especially from women. He went alone into houses where children were sick and it was known he could be trusted there. Had he begun to lay hands upon women he would have been quickly tangled in the briary bush of jealousy and desire. For the same reason he knew he could not afford ever to lose his temper. He never carried a weapon and no one wanted to fight him barehanded. He was known for the way he could boss his Mexicans without ever raising either his voice or his hand. He used his great strength only when he had to stop others from fighting. So he became a keeper of the peace in the community—but above all he kept the peace of his own separate being, and the need of his isolation grew upon him. In the best of his years in the valley he achieved a serenity he had never known before. He lived insulated from most of the shocks of human contact, from the muddle of lust and anger in which most men live, and this was nothing he had sought or chosen but a destiny which had befallen him.

When Ballard died after the grant was sold he knew a great grief for the first time in his life, and he had a sure premonition of trouble, but he had never imagined his own function and way of life would be destroyed as they had been. At first he had risen to a new importance. Men had flocked to hear him when he spoke in the meeting house about the grant and the fraudulent survey. They all felt a need of leadership and it seemed at first as though Daniel Laird had succeeded to some part of the power Ballard had held. He had planned to organize the ranchers, raise money and employ a lawyer, and for a while his plan had prospered. Then Blore had moved into the great house, and within a month everything was changed. Blore brought new settlers with him. Suddenly there were two factions and both sides were talking war. No one would listen to him after Tighe took over, and he became aware that Buncombe was working to destroy him. It was amazing how quickly the whole character and quality of life in the valley had changed, how men who long had lived at peace with each other suddenly began to quarrel, how tensions grew that made violence inevitable. It amazed Daniel Laird still more how the tension and the violence had invaded his own being. The man of peace had become a man of righteous anger.

— 4 —

Except for a few of the Mexicans there was not a man in the valley he could surely call his friend, but this was not true of the women. Now and then he met on the street the wives of some of the ranchers, the old-timers he had known for years, and these nearly always nodded and smiled. He had never had more than a nodding and smiling acquaintance with most of them, but they were grateful to him for the Sunday meetings he had held. Now he was grateful for their smiles as never before. One day Mother Fenton stopped him on the street, planting her bulk in his path so that he could not have avoided her if he wished. She was a great fat woman of sixty, who had raised a family of five boys, all of whom had scattered over the country in search of land and cattle. She and her husband, Bill Fenton, lived alone on a little ranch where they raised a few blooded cattle and horses. Fenton was a man of peace who would go to almost any length to avoid trouble. He had refused to get his dander up when the grant was sold. He had shrugged his shoulders and signed up with the company. Ma Fenton also declined to let anything disturb her serenity and good humor. The Fentons had stayed out on their ranch and tended to their stock while others fought and argued. Mother Fenton was one of the few who had called Daniel by his first name, and she addressed him now with the complete confidence of her all-embracing kindliness.

"Daniel," she demanded, "why don't you hold meeting any more? A little singing would do people a sight of good right now."

Daniel stood before her, feeling the blood mount into his ears, aware that he was blushing with pleasure and confusion.

"I'm afraid nobody would come, Missis Fenton," he said humbly, blurting the truth out of the depth of his despair. "I'm afraid nobody wants to hear me any more."

"Nonsense!" She spoke to him with good-humored severity, like a mother to her child. "You come down here next Sunday and open the doors and I'll have people here to listen. I promise you that!"

Daniel thanked her and hurried away, feeling pleased and shaken and not at all sure of himself. But he knew he would do it. The dance hall stood there empty every Sunday, and who was going to stop him? He would like to see anyone try to stop him! His anger began to rise again. But he went to the hall the following Sunday full of doubt.

Mother Fenton had assembled exactly eight women, five of whom were strangers to Daniel. But he recited to them from the Bible, led them in singing and discovered that two of the stranger women had good voices. Before the singing was over the crowd had more than doubled, and it included several men who were also strangers to him. All these people, he knew, had come simply because they heard the singing and were curious to know what was going on, but he felt better after the meeting than he had in weeks. He saw that he still had power to draw people together and make them listen to his voice. Maybe, after all, he still had a place here and something to do. He knew he would go to the hall now every Sunday as long as anyone would come to listen.

His second meeting was larger than his first and the third was still larger. Most of it was feminine but more men came each time. Few of the old-timers appeared but new people were coming to the valley every day and most of these cared nothing about the troubles of a few months ago. Daniel began to see that he might gather a wholly new following, and he longed for a following as never before.

He did not speak to these people in his own words at all. His method as a preacher was simply what he had learned from his father and all the other mountain preachers he had heard. All of them shouted passages of Holy writ at their hearers, then led them in song and then shouted again, working always toward a climax of crowd excitement. Daniel did not depart from this primitive pattern but neither did he try for any fervid response. He had never truly cared much about his hearers. Always he had chosen passages from the Bible which expressed his own mood of the moment—and every conceivable mood and notion seemed to be expressed somewhere in that great book. He combined passages to suit himself, even changed them a little, chanting their eloquent music in his great voice for the love of its sound and the release it gave to his feelings. So at his second meeting he recited only fragments from Ecclesiastes between the hymns.

"The words of the wise are heard more than the cry of him that ruleth among fools," he told them solemnly. "Wisdom is better than weapons of war; but one sinner destroyeth much good."

And at the end of the meeting he chanted lines that had been running through his head for weeks:

> Remember, the evil days come,
> And the years draw nigh,
> When thou shalt say, I have no pleasure in them.
> Because Man goeth to his lone home,
> And the mourners go about the streets,
> And the dust returneth to the earth, as it was,
> And the spirit returneth unto God, who gave it.

Then he took his hat and walked out, looking at no one, but several women stopped him and thanked him, and he got back to his cabin glowing with a sense of power, feeling sure he had moved these people.

It was at his third meeting that he first noticed Betty Weiss, and he felt sure it was the first time she had come, for she stood out from the crowd like a huckleberry in a bowl of milk. She was nothing like the other women, the wives of ranchmen. She was slim and elegant in a black dress which was open at the throat and tight about her small pointed breasts. She sat always near the middle of the hall and well up front. She looked at him steadily all through the meeting, and he could not keep his eyes away from her. He was acutely aware of her pale face, delicately rouged, of the dark mass of her hair, the curious green of her eyes, her shapely well-tended hands. He had never seen anything like her. She looked as exotic here as a cockatoo in a flock of barnyard hens. And she was a gifted singer. When he started a hymn he would nod to her and the two of them led and dominated the singing with great success. He felt as though she had come to help him, was trying to help him. . . . He knew little about her except that she ran the hotel and was a figure of mystery and a subject of gossip in the town. He knew some said she was Blore's woman—that he had imported her for his own amusement and made a job for her. He didn't care who or what she was. He knew only that she had moved into his imagination as soon as she entered the hall. He knew she was none of his business, he didn't want to think about her—but her image seemed to follow him home and stay with him, like an importunate and persistent ghost.

— 5 —

A few days after his third meeting Ernesto Royball came to his cabin, knocking timidly on the door, asking permission to enter. Ernesto was the first visitor who had come to him in months and he welcomed the man and gave him a drink. He had known Ernesto for years and once had treated him for a sprained back.

Ernesto was all friendliness and he talked for a long time about small and unimportant matters—about how late the rains were this year, and how many wild turkeys there were along Ute Creek, and that trade at the company store had nearly doubled. Daniel knew Mexicans well enough to be sure Ernesto was leading up to something. A Mexican always approached serious business indirectly, by way of a long preamble. Finally Ernesto got to it, obviously diffident and embarrassed.

"Those meetings you are holding, Mr. Laird," he said. "I'm afraid they may make trouble for you. I am your friend, Mr. Laird, that is why I tell you."

Daniel felt his anger rising again and he held it down with a conscious effort; he did not speak until he felt sure he could speak softly.

"Did Major Blore send you to tell me this, Ernesto?" he inquired.

"No, Mr. Laird!" Ernesto was emphatic. "Nobody sent me! I come because I am your friend and I don't want you to have trouble. I don't want anyone to have trouble. We have had too much trouble already. But I know the boss—he doesn't want meetings. He doesn't like to see people get together—I know that!"

Ernesto was fairly sweating with sincerity and embarrassment. Daniel felt sorry for him.

"Thank you, Ernesto," he said. "I know you are my friend."

He would not say any more than that. They chatted for a little longer and Ernesto refused an invitation to supper and went away. Daniel sat thoughtful for a long time after his visitor had gone, but he was not truly considering what he would do. He knew he would go on holding meetings, and if for no other reason, because he wanted to see Betty Weiss again, and hear her voice and feel her strange green eyes upon his own.

He had been hoping she might speak to him after a meeting or smile at him. She never did either, but the feeling that they were moving toward each other, that an intercourse had sprung up between them, grew stronger each time he saw her. It was easy for him to watch her, sitting there in front of him, without appearing to do so, and he became aware of every detail of her person—of the sprinkle of freckles across her nose, the slant of her eyebrows, especially of a faint pink birthmark upon her throat. It was an irregular splotch about the size of a dollar and looked like a pink map of Australia he remembered in an old schoolbook of geography. He noticed that when she sang with him this spot grew darker, becoming more vivid and visible with the play of her blood. Her expression told him nothing but it seemed as though this mark upon her throat betrayed the rise and fall of her feeling.

The longing to speak to her grew upon him, and then suddenly he found himself speaking to her in words he had known for years. He had spoken them many times before but never before had they meant anything to him. Now he found them the very music of his feeling.

> Thou art beautiful, O my love, as Tirzah,
> Comely as Jerusalem,
> Terrible as an army with banners.
> Turn away thine eyes from me,
>   For they have overcome me.

It was easy for him to utter this fragment, to speak it to her as directly as though they had been all alone in the hall, to build his whole recital about the Song of Songs, as he had often done before. Immediately afterward he started the singing again, drowning his own emotion in sound, covering up quickly his confession of love. He knew it had been that and he felt sure she knew it. For the little banner upon her throat flamed scarlet at his voice.

In spite of himself he spoke to her again, for it seemed as though the sacred words had been made for his speaking.

> *Thou hast ravished my heart, my sister,*
> *   my bride; thou hast ravished my heart*
> *With one look of thine eyes,*
> *With one chain of thy neck.*
> *How fair is thy love, my sister, my bride!*
> *How much better is thy love than wine!*

Again he sang, feeling as though he sang to her alone, and seeing again the flaming answer of her blood. He closed the meeting quickly and hurried home, feeling curiously weak and undone. He sat down in his great home-made chair and mopped sweat from his brow. It seemed as though all the disciplines and armors of his being had suddenly melted, so that he sat there helpless, obsessed, with her image dancing in his brain. No woman had ever disturbed him this way before. He knew that she had caught him in a vulnerable moment, that another time he might have dismissed her from his mind in a little while. But the fact remained that she had invaded his imagination—that he could not escape her any more than if she stood before him.

Finally he rose and poured himself a large jolt of Taos whisky, the first he had tasted in years. He cooked and ate his supper mechanically, then went and sat before his door as he had done so many other evenings. It was near the end of summer with the aspens just beginning to show a little yellow and the long, lush grass strident with the chirp of crickets, intoning their final chorus before the white death of winter fell upon them.

He had sat there many another summer evening, puffing his pipe, with a feeling of profound peace. Nearly always he had sat alone but he had never felt lonely. He had felt companioned by everything that grew and lived about him—by the music of crickets and of the wind in the trees and the evening song of vesper sparrows. He had sat apart from people, from the settlement, but he had been at peace with it, he had borne a good and necessary relation to it. He had never known how necessary that relation was until it had been destroyed. Now there were men in the town over the hill who hated him, who wished him ill, and their hatred flowed into him, filling him with their own malevolence, destroying his peace of mind as completely as though they had marched upon him in an armed band.

He was a shaken and troubled man now, full of conflicts he could not resolve. Something in him wanted to get away from this place, as far and as fast as he could. At moments he felt like rounding up his horse and striking out for the mountains. He didn't care where he went if only away from people. Something in him wanted to get away from the woman too— from the helpless and vulnerable feeling she caused him. But another part of him felt like going down to the town, hunting her up and offering himself to her. . . . He knew what rank folly that would be, but he was full of foolish notions. And he didn't truly want to run, either. He wanted to stay and fight—to defy and denounce and destroy. . . .

It was dark now and getting chilly, as late summer nights always did. He went inside and busied himself building a fire, using fat pine that threw a red bright light, against a log that would burn a long time. The red flame eagerly eating the pitch, purring softly into the log, was a companionable thing. He sat there for a long time, soothed a little by warmth and light, but with a disturbing conviction of approaching climax. All his life he had been a man of premonitions and now he knew he was waiting, with hope and yet with dread.

When her knock came at the door he didn't move for a full minute. Although he had not expected her so soon he felt almost sure it was she and he waited to get a better hold upon himself. Why, in the name of God, should he be so disturbed? He was not afraid of her, not afraid of anyone, yet if he had known a mortal enemy stood on his threshold he would not have been more shaken.

When he opened the door he saw a slim dark woman-figure, wrapped and hooded in a great black shawl such as all the Mexican women wore winter and summer. She dropped it about her shoulders and smiled at him.

"May I come in?" she asked. Her voice was casual and friendly as she entered, surveyed his quarters with evident curiosity, then seated herself in his only other chair. He sat down opposite her, tongue-tied for the moment, aware of his pounding blood. She looked him up and down with a quizzical smile. He felt as though she were looking clear through his clothes—felt sure she knew just how much she disturbed him and was enjoying her power.

"Nice little place you've got here," she remarked. "Nothing fancy, but nice and clean and quiet. I bet you like it."

"Yes," he said, "I used to like it."

"Before all these Texas billies turned against you," she said, as though perfectly confident she was speaking his mind.

"Well, yes," he admitted.

"They tell me you never have any women visitors," she said.

"That's right," he admitted. He got up and went and put another log on the fire, not because it needed wood but because he needed something to do.

"It's getting cold," he remarked.

"I thought it was about time you had one," she told him, declining to discuss the weather.

"It was kind of you to come," he said.

"But I didn't come just to keep you company." She spoke gravely now. "I came to warn you. That little shorthorn up in the big house—he's bound and determined to get rid of you one way or another. You ought to get out of here, and the sooner the better. I think you ought to know. . . ."

"Thank you," he said. "I know they've got it in for me."

"He wanted me to help." She blurted her confession in quick words, a little disturbed for the first time. "But I don't want to talk about that. . . . That bloody little shorthorn! I never did trust him. If I didn't have my own money tied up in that joint, I'd get out of here myself."

She paused, and he sat looking at her, making no reply. She went on hurriedly, moved by some confessional impulse, as though she wanted to strip her mind naked before him.

"I went down to that hall the first time just to look you over," she said. "I wasn't going to do what they wanted—honest I wasn't. But I wanted to look at you. I thought you must be some kind of a damn fool, and in some ways maybe you are, but you're a good man, too. I can tell that."

"Thank you," he said. He grinned for the first time. Her explosive candor made him feel easier.

"I know a lot about men," she said. "Men are my business. And you're the only good man I ever saw, except maybe that preacher in Dodge City, and he wasn't really a man. . . . I can tell about men, and mostly they're all alike. Some of them are worse than others, but when they get their shirts off they're all alike and you can't trust them from here to the door." She paused for breath. "But you're different!" she finished decisively. "I never saw anything like you before, but I know you're different."

He plowed a restless hand through his hair, bewildered by this flow of words.

"It was kind of you to come and tell me," he said.

She leaned toward him to emphasize her words.

"I'm telling you to get out of here," she said. "It ain't healthy for you around here. And I'd sure hate to see anything happen to you, honest I would."

Daniel sat looking at her, shaking his head. He didn't want to argue with her. He wished now she would go. He wanted to lay hands upon her and he knew he couldn't do that. Time had been when he had laid hands upon women easily but his long isolation from them had built up a wall he couldn't pass. She sat there almost within reach of his hand and yet wholly beyond his reach. He didn't want to argue with her. He wished she would leave.

"You won't go!" she said, reading his face.

"No!" He shook his head again. "Nobody can run me out."

She made a gesture and a mouth of mild exasperation.

"Just stubborn," she remarked.

He rose and held out his hand, hoping to be rid of her. He wanted her, but he wanted none of the soft and vulnerable feeling she gave him. He wanted to be hard, free and ready.

"I thank you for coming," he said, "and for giving me warning."

She rose too but she didn't take his hand. Instead she walked right up to him, with a slight swagger about her hips, smiling with perfect self-confidence.

"You want me to go, don't you?" she inquired. "But I'm not going. I can't go now, honest I can't."

She paused for a moment, spread her hands in a gesture that might have been invitation.

"I came to warn you," she said, "but that ain't all I came for, honest it ain't. Not after all those beautiful words you said. Nobody ever said such beautiful words to me before."

She stood a moment more, smiling up at him, wholly unabashed—then flung her arms around his neck and glued her mouth upon his in the full, wet, clinging kiss of the woman claiming her own.

He seized her by both shoulders, his fingers biting into her flesh, moved by a first impulse to fling her away, to free himself. Then he swept her up in his arms and laid her on his bunk, fumbling at her dress with clumsy, eager hands. Nothing existed for him now but her body.

She squirmed in his grasp, giggling with delight. She did not share his mood of enraptured confusion at all, nor yet his inner conflict. Something in him wanted to be free, but she wanted only union.

"Go easy," she advised him quietly. "You've got all night to do this. I'll undress if you'll let me."

With the red glow of the fire upon their bodies they faced each other in the final candor of nakedness. She was silent and easy in his arms when he picked her up again, and he was gentle now, in complete surrender to her and to his own desire. Into her willing body he poured the burden of his loneliness, the tension of his hatred, the pressure of his need for union with his kind, all the forces of his destiny uniting to drive him into her—aching, urgent flesh swelling to fill the void, limpid juice of life pouring into the void, eternal stream of life turning back to its source— lost fragment of life going back to its home, limp in the peace of its inevitable return.

— 6 —

It was near dawn when she prepared to leave him, dressing herself slowly, fussing with her hair before his fragment of a mirror, making a long business of it, while he sat watching her. Finally she turned to him, spreading her hands in a quick, questioning gesture.

"You know I can't come here any more," she said.

He made no reply.

"They would follow me and find out," she told him. "They wanted me to put you in a spot like that."

She stood looking at him for a long moment, and then she made her plea.

"Go away with me!" she begged. "Or meet me some place else—I don't care where. I don't care what we do. You're my man now—don't you see? I thought so before and now I know it. I can't let you go!"

He rose, shaking his head, knowing he was denying himself as surely as he was denying her, hating the hard thing within him that dictated this denial.

"I can't leave here," he said. "They would say I had run. They would think they had run me out. I can't do it!"

She stood looking at his rocklike face for a moment. Then she made another quick gesture with her eloquent hands—a gesture of angry assent —and turned and picked up her shawl and threw it around her shoulders. She stood before him again and her eyes softened. She kissed him lightly on the lips and gave him a pat on the cheek that was half a slap.

"You're just a damn fool after all, ain't you?" she said tenderly. Then she turned and went, closing the door firmly behind her.

Daniel sat down in his great chair and lit a pipe. He sat there for a long time, thinking nothing, staring at the familiar walls of his house, knowing now it would always be empty without her.

IN THE WILDERNESS

A crowd was forming in the company saloon and Ernesto Royball, who always had his nose in the wind, was there to watch it. He had known for days that Waverly Buncombe was at work on this project. He knew some men had been told that Daniel Laird was going to be run out of town— some said tarred and feathered—but most of them had been told only to be on hand, with a mysterious hint that there would be free drinks and excitement. Waverly was clever. There were nearly forty men in the room now and most of them didn't know what to expect, but all of them had been chosen carefully. Waverly knew the kind of a man who could be depended upon to join a mob. About half a dozen of those present Ernesto recognized as company henchmen. They were running the show, setting up the drinks, priming the crowd to exactly the right point, welding it into an instrument that would follow a leader. Waverly was behind the bar but he was not serving drinks. He was standing where he could watch the faces lined up on the other side. When he thought the moment was ripe he went around the end of the bar and shoved a table all the way across the room, to the far end of it, making a great rumpus about it, so that everyone turned and looked. Then, with an air of mock solemnity, he mounted a chair and from the chair he climbed to the top of the table, the whole crowd watching him. With a solemn face he lifted his right hand for silence, and all the voices died. Then he made a slow gesture with both hands as though he were opening a book and laying it on a table before him.

"Brethren and sistern," he intoned, in a portentous burlesque of Daniel's mighty voice. "The subject of our little discourse this evening is— Me and Jesus and how we can be told apart."

He raised his hand again to still a burst of laughter, then spoke in a wholly different tone.

"Boys," he began, "this town has got one citizen it doesn't need. . . ."

Ernesto Royball did not wait to hear more. He felt sure now it was going to happen. He slipped out the door and ran all the way to Tighe's office, a hundred feet down the street. Tighe came to the door in his carpet slippers, with a cigar between his fingers. He had been taking life easy for weeks. He took one look at Ernesto, wide-eyed and breathing hard, and shook his head.

"Come in," he said, "and sit down. I know you're full of bad news."

Ernesto nodded his head rapidly three times.

"Yes!" he gasped, "they're going after Mr. Laird. They're all down at the saloon, about forty of them. . . ."

Tighe showed neither surprise nor excitement. He asked a few questions, then sat thoughtful for a moment. He looked at his watch.

"Ten-thirty," he remarked. "They probably figure to find him in bed. That's about their speed!" He spoke with profound contempt. "Forty to one, and they hope to catch him asleep." He pulled on his boots now and took his gun belt off the head of his bed.

"I can't stop them down at the saloon," he said. "They've got a right to gang up. But I sure can stop them up at Laird's place."

He buckled on his gun, settling it carefully into place.

"That goddam little squirt of tobacco juice!" he remarked. "There's always some son-of-a-bitch. . . ."

— 2 —

Laird's cabin was dark, as he had expected, and he pounded long and hard before he saw the light of a lamp and heard the thud of bare feet. The door opened and the big man in his cotton nightshirt stood staring at him in amazement. Tighe did not waste any time in apologies.

"Get your clothes on," he said shortly. "I think you're going to have company."

Laird blinked and shook his head, still only half awake.

"What do you mean?" he demanded.

"I mean Waverly Buncombe is working up a mob down at the saloon," Tighe explained. "From what Ernesto told me I judge they plan to call on you."

Laird was wide awake instantly, as Tighe could tell by the quick change in his eyes, the tightening of the muscles about his jaws. Somewhat to Tighe's surprise, he looked almost eager. It took him no more than three minutes to splash cold water on his face, pull on his clothes and boots.

"Are they on their way?" he asked quietly.

"Not yet, I reckon," Tighe advised, "but it probably won't be long."

Laird had turned away and was standing before the row of six axes that hung between pegs against the wall at the far end of the room. They were the tools of a master axman, all of the blades shining clean from the expert touch of the whetstone. Laird stood looking at them a moment, then chose a five-pound, double-bited tool with a straight handle—a veritable battle-ax. He turned back to Tighe with the ax in his right hand and the trace of a grim smile about his mouth. Tighe, a specialist in fighting men, eyed him with interest and a growing respect. He sat down and stretched out his legs.

"You and I will be the reception committee," he suggested.

Laird shook his head firmly several times.

"I thank you for coming," he said, "but I don't want any help." He spoke with great finality.

Tighe rolled a cigarette and lit it before he spoke.

"I'm an officer of the law," he explained. "It's my job to keep order."

"I know," Laird said, "but this is my business. I don't want any help."

Tighe took a deep puff of smoke and sat looking at the end of his cigarette a moment before he spoke.

"Well." His tone was judicious. "I've always said a man has a right to make his own fight if he wants to. I never accepted any help myself."

He rose and held out his hand.

"Good luck," he said.

— 3 —

When Tighe had gone Daniel went out in front of his house and kindled a small fire. The ground was open there, with tall pines a hundred feet away, making a black wall of shadow beyond the red light of the blaze. He kept a pile of logs for firewood at the side of the cabin, and he now went to work furiously cutting and splitting, piling wood on the blaze, then building a pyramid of longer pieces until he had a bonfire that roared like an angry beast. Its quivering tongue of flame leaped ten feet in the air and sparks went dancing and dying as high as the treetops. Daniel went back to his cabin, put out the lamp and stood in the doorway, well back from the light of the fire, waiting. It was a dark night and the glare of the fire made it seem darker. Nothing was visible beyond the dance of shadows at the edge of the red stage he had set. He stood waiting, gripping his ax, aware of his quickened breathing, thinking nothing, knowing only that he was tense as the spring of a cocked rifle.

It seemed a long time but it was not more than ten minutes before he heard them coming—the shuffle of many feet in the trail, a few low voices and a cough. Then he glimpsed the wavering, small light of a single lantern, the only thing that broke the solid black of the night beyond the fire. The shuffle of feet came nearer and there were more voices for a moment— and then silence. He peered half blindly across his lighted arena. He could discern a few faces, but they seemed to recede rather than come nearer, and the light of the lantern went out. His muscles relaxed and he blew out his breath in a snort of disgust. The goddam yellow bellies! They were afraid to come into the light. . . . He waited a moment longer, then strode out into the open and stood beside the fire, holding his ax aloft, its blade red in the glow.

"Here I am!" he shouted. "I heard you were coming for me. . . . Here I am!"

He paused and peered again into the wall of darkness. He could see dimly a huddle of figures and light fell upon a few faces but not a sound came out of the darkness. . . . They were afraid! Suddenly he threw back his head and laughed, a great bellowing laugh that was a shout of defiance. He took three steps forward, holding the ax before him, shaking it in a vibrant tension of rage.

"Come on, you yellow bellies!" he shouted. "You came to get me, didn't you? I dare you to show your faces."

But there were no faces visible now and he was aware of the shuffle of feet again, far down the trail. He went forward cautiously, peering into the darkness, his eyes getting used to it. At first he thought all of them had gone, but then he saw a single figure, leaning against a tree with his feet crossed and his arms folded, in an attitude of negligent repose. He heard a low chuckle, went closer, recognized Tighe.

"I trailed along behind them," Tighe explained, "just to see the fun. They didn't know I was here."

Daniel suddenly felt limp in reaction. He stood shaking his head slowly.

"The goddam yellow bellies!" he said.

Tighe laughed again.

"You didn't have to kill any of 'em," he remarked, "but you damn near scared 'em to death. They didn't want any part of that ax. Their feet began to get cold as soon as they saw you."

He straightened up and made a gesture of respectful salute—the tribute of one unfrightened man to another.

"Good night, preacher," he said. "You put on a fine show."

— 4 —

Daniel went back into his cabin, filled and lit a pipe with hands that trembled a little. He sat down, suddenly weak in the knees. As always after a fight or a burst of rage, he felt a little sick—sick with guilt and fear, not fear of anyone else but of himself and of the violence inside him. For an awful moment he had hoped they would rush him, he had longed for battle, even for carnage. . . . He sat appalled before the image of what might have happened—if they had not been such cowards.

They had failed him as enemies even more completely than they had failed him as friends. But he knew they had succeeded in their purpose. They had run him out. He had sworn no one should run him out, but he knew now that he was going. He couldn't stay here now. He had to get away from this place in order to get away from his own feelings—from the anger and hatred that were eating him up.

He rose and began making his preparations, feeling a little better as soon as he was at work. He had no plan except to get away from this place, to be gone before morning, to bury himself in the mountains. He was vaguely aware that he was in flight, not only from this place but from human society. He wanted to get as far from people as he could.

He went through a familiar routine now, for he had made many trips of a few days or week. He pulled out from under his bunk the heavy canvas tarpaulin he used for camping, threw his blankets upon it and a few clothes and other possessions. Two rawhide paniers he filled with supplies —bacon and flour, coffee, sugar and salt, dried fruit, an iron skillet and a cup, cartridges for his rifle. He knew exactly what he needed. When he had finished packing he went out in the dark to find his horse, listening for the tinkle of the bell around its neck. He had only one horse, a big gray fourteen years old, slow but sure-footed on a trail. When he went into the mountain he always packed his horse and walked, after the fashion of a prospector. He was a footman by origin and habit, one who could walk thirty miles a day. Both he and the gray knew the trail up the canyon so well their feet could find it in the dark.

By the time the sun rose he was ten miles from town, near the summit of a high, bare ridge. Down the other side of it was a little branch canyon where he planned to make his first camp, and that was just as far as his knowledge of his destiny went. He stopped to rest, letting his horse crop the heavy grass, sat down and filled his pipe. From this spot for the last time he could see the town, miles away and three thousand feet below him. From where he sat it looked incredibly small and insignificant, a minor blemish on the face of the earth. The roads were scratches, the fields were angular scars, and a few faint blue wisps of smoke above the houses told that men and their fires were at work down there. Already he felt freed of the place and freed of the madness he had known the night before. He picked up the halter rope and set his face toward the mountains.

Late in the afternoon he saw the spot he had in mind a few hundred feet below him. The little stream there ran through an open level place two hundred yards long—what the mountain men called a park. Now in early September it bore heavy grass, sprinkled with the pink blossoms of wild cosmos. The stream was mostly hidden by a cover of willow and alder, but here and there flashed free in the sun. A few great fir trees were widely scattered over the open, each of them marking it with a long shadow. Below and above the open the canyon pinched narrow and impassable and the mountains rose steep and wooded on either side. The little park seemed made for a haven, a peaceful and sunny spot shut away from the rest of the world.

Daniel had been here before and knew exactly where he was going. He unpacked his horse under a big fir tree with a spread of twenty feet. The ground beneath it was bone dry for no rain could penetrate its lofty cone of evergreen foliage. It was safe to camp beneath a tree now that the lightning storms of summer were over. When storm came again it would be the first soft-footed invasion of the snow, creeping down from alpine summits. But first there would be days and maybe weeks of Indian summer, the best of all seasons in the high country.

He worked slowly, soothing his spirit by familiar tasks, by the exercise of easy skills which had always been associated with the peace of faraway quiet places. He hobbled and belled the gray and sat a moment watching him crop the rich forage. Then he made his bed under the tree, partly rolling it and propping it against the trunk so that it made a couch where he could lie and smoke his pipe. Like all men of long wayfaring in the mountains he knew how to be comfortable in camp. He built a rock fireplace with a good draft, drove pegs of hard, dry wood into the trunk of the tree to hold his gear, hung his paniers from convenient limbs, and his home was in order. He cooked his supper just before dark. An hour later a sudden, great weariness dragged at his eyelids and he went heavily to sleep.

— 5 —

For a week he enjoyed a feeling of peace such as he had not known for months before. It was the peace of life suddenly simplified, relieved of all the jolt and turmoil of human contact, of all the inner conflict that tears a man apart, makes his life a struggle for sanity. He felt as though he had gone back briefly to the uncomplicated happiness of childhood, and also as though he had returned to a familiar and beloved thing. The wilderness was one of his oldest friends and the wilderness is everywhere the same, with the same vast hush about it, the same feeling of an indestructible repose, of a soothing indifference to the nervous sputter of human being—of life become conscious and frightened, aware of time and death.

There were many men in the West who spent most of their lives alone in the mountains—prospectors and trappers who went away for months, sometimes for a year or more. A good many such men had come to the valley in Ballard's time to buy supplies at his store and hang around for a few days. Daniel had always looked at them with interest, talked to them if he had a chance. Some of them were surly men with a glint of suspicion in their eyes but others had a look of childlike sweetness and peace upon their faces. These often were eager to talk—for a little while. Then they would pack their burros and disappear again.

Daniel now played with the idea that he might become such a man. He knew he could find a living in the mountains and do it better than most. He did not plan, he merely let his imagination explore a possible destiny, for he felt sure he had left one life behind him and was on the way to another—what kind of a life he did not know. He did not want to plan or decide. He wanted to sleep and eat and live in his senses. He wanted to live as though tomorrow was none of his business.

It was not at all hard for him to spend his days. He explored his little region and became acquainted with all of its life. He knew the band of elk that came down to the creek at the upper end of the park to drink every morning, led by a bull with antlers like a picket fence. Morning and evening he heard the great bull bugle far up on the ridge. He knew the brood of blue grouse, nearly full grown now, which lived only a hundred yards from his camp. When he came near them they all fluttered into a tall spruce and sat there, craning their necks at him, curious but unafraid. "Fool hens" the gringos called them. Any creature that trusted a man was a fool. . . . A small black bear appeared every morning on the ridge where an old burn was red with ripe raspberries, and Daniel spent hours watching him gather the fruit, standing on his hind legs like a fat, awkward child, pulling the loaded bushes down into his mouth. Daniel did not kill any of these creatures. He did not want to shatter the peace with the roar of a gun. Most of his living he took from the creek which was alive with trout. Like most men in the mountains he carried a hook and line twisted around his hatband. He had only to cut a willow switch and catch as many grasshoppers as he needed fish. He could pick out the ones he wanted in the glass-clear pools, letting his bait drift over their waiting mouths.

Every day near noon, when the sun was warm, he stripped and bathed in the largest pool he could find, the icy water turning his body red with its tonic shock. Afterward he lay flat on the grass in the bright sun until he was dry. This reunion with earth and water was the high point of his day, the moment when peace seemed perfect. More than once he found his lips framing the words of the Twenty-third Psalm. "The Lord is my shepherd, I shall not want." For the moment he had transcended all want, had achieved the quiet ecstasy of merely being.

— 6 —

He became aware of the first rift in his contentment, after ten days of perfect solitude, when he found it hard to sleep and began lying awake listening to the voices of the running water. Ever since he reached the valley he had slept long, dreamless hours but now he woke before dawn and lay there listening. That he should hear voices in the running water was neither a new experience for him nor one peculiar to himself. All men who have slept much beside swift mountain streams know that running water in a rocky bed is full of voices. It makes an incredible variety of sounds, from indistinct murmurs and low chuckles, as of people talking apart, to loud laughter, and sometimes, when its volume is swollen by a storm, it shouts and roars. Often before Daniel had lain awake at night in the mountains listening to the talk and laughter of a stream, untroubled by it, but now the sound began to harass him and keep him awake. For the voice that emerged more and more distinctly was the voice of the woman, Betty Weiss, and with the sound of her voice came her image. His vivid imagination had been his curse more than once and now it was haunted by a single figure. He had hardly thought of her since leaving town and yet now the night seemed suddenly filled with her presence. First she would be away off there, somewhere in the dark, laughing at him in a mocking tone, and then she was beside him, naked and white, so vividly that he flung out his arm to grasp her. There in the dark in the wilderness he embraced a phantom that stirred all the longing of living flesh. He knew again the fragrance of her hair, the clasp of her thighs, the spastic roll and surge of her responsive body. And then she was gone again, she was away in the darkness, laughing at him, while he lay alone and tormented. More than once he rose before dawn and built a fire and made coffee, solely to escape this image that haunted and mocked him. His feeling toward her now was one of anger, of resentment. Everything else he had left behind— all the hatred and fury the town had stirred in him. Only this image of a naked woman had followed him into the wilderness, had caught up with him, as though it had been a living creature on his trail. A strange thing about it was that in imagination, in retrospect, she seemed more desirable, more perfect and necessary than she had seemed in the flesh. And always she was laughing at him, taunting him, that he had been fool enough to leave her. And he could see that he had been a fool. If he had gone away with her, if he had taken his fill of her, then he might have been free of this pursuing wraith, of the clinging memory of her flesh. As it was she had destroyed his peace completely.

After several tormented and sleepless nights he found himself one morning climbing the ridge, going back to the summit above the town. He sat there for a long time staring down at it but not truly seeing it. It was himself and his own destiny that he surveyed. It seemed to him that he was confronting himself and his own necessities now for the first time. He faced the fact that he wanted to go back down into the valley, hunt up the woman, offer himself to her, surrender completely to her and to his own desire. But it was not only the woman he had fled in vain. He knew that he needed to get back to people, any kind of people, that his dream of solitary escape had been pure illusion. It was as though the image of the woman had followed him to mock him, to make him aware of his own folly. He could understand too that he had tried to go back to his own childhood—to the remembered peace of long ago. He knew that because briefly he had succeeded. For days he had felt like a child again, alone in the beautiful forest, but that interlude was over.

He knew he was not going back to the valley. That was impossible. He knew in this moment of clarity that there is no going back to anything. And there was only one other way to go—across the mountains. He had started with the knowledge vaguely in the back of his mind that he must cross the mountains before the snow fell. He could not spend the winter in the high country. But he had started without a plan and now he had to make one.

Forty miles to the west, across bare alpine summits that rose twelve thousand feet above sea level, lay the Mexican settlements of the upper Rio Grande. Santa Fe was far to the south of them and Taos to the north. Between these two, the major settlements of the Spanish Southwest, were half a dozen little towns, each commanding a narrow mountain valley, where beans and chile grew and small herds of scrubby goats grazed on steep slopes above the fields. These were the most primitive and isolated communities in all the Southwest. The men who inhabited them were more than half Indian, of the same stock as the peons down in the main valley. But they were not peons. The ricos had taken all the good lands in the main valley and reduced all the common people there to peonage, but here in the mountains had grown up a small society of freeholders. They owned their houses and their tiny patches of farmland. They were poor but free and fiercely independent. Almost all of them belonged to the order of the Penitent Brothers, which was in fact a religious fraternity of the poor. Many of them were thieves as well, who went down into the valley to work now and then, picked up a stray ewe or a range horse when they had the chance, rating it a worthy enterprise to rob the rich, whom they hated.

Daniel knew all about these settlements by hearsay. He also knew the

old Indian trail across the mountains, as far as the summit, and he knew
he could find his way down the other side to one of the little mountain
towns. He knew the Mexicans would take him in. A poor Mexican would
take in any man who came to his door and asked for food and shelter and
would accept the guest as a sacred trust.

That was just as far ahead as Daniel could plan. He felt as though his
first and most urgent need was simply to regain a contact with his fellow
beings. For the first time he understood how completely he had exiled
himself. He had left the only life and the only society he knew. His destiny now was a thing to be discovered.

— 7 —

A change in the weather speeded his going. Next morning the sky was
dark and a strong, cold wind ruffled the grass and rippled the water, tearing yellow leaves off the aspens. As he turned his back on the little valley
and started up the spine of a long ridge leading to the crest of the range,
he knew that it might be snowing up there even now. At sunset he camped
just below timber line where the spruce grew thick and short and there
was hardly any forage for his horse. It was very cold that night and he
woke to see a light powdery snow falling.

Now he knew he ought to turn back. Snow would bury the trail which
was faint enough at best, a blizzard might blind him to every landmark,
drifts might pile up too deep to cross. He knew also it would be folly to
try to take a horse across the mountains. A horse traveling on grass needs
good forage and nearly eight hours a day to graze. Snow would bury the
grass and once he had started he must keep going until he had crossed the
divide and reached timber on the western slope.

He knew he ought to turn back but he also knew he was not going
to do so. He took the bell and hobbles off the gray and turned him loose
to find his way back to the valley. Then he rolled most of his outfit in the
tarpaulin and boosted it into the lower limbs of a spruce which he marked
with a large blaze. Maybe sometime he would come back and maybe not.
He took nothing but ax and rifle and one blanket in which he rolled a
small supply of bacon and flour, coffee and sugar. All of his preparations
were made with dispatch, with an exact knowledge of what he had to face.
Equally well he knew this was a fool expedition. It was not at all necessary for him to battle this storm. Snow would not hit the lower levels for
weeks yet. The sensible move would be to go back to the little valley or
even lower, and wait until the storm was over. Even if a foot of snow
fell on the divide it would be far easier to cross the mountains in clear
weather. But he knew he was not going back. He was in no mood to sit
down and wait for anything. Moreover, he was lifted now by a spirit of
elation, of relief, as though the struggle that lay before him was a needed

thing. He slung his rifle across his back by a thong he carried for the purpose, with his rolled blanket over the other shoulder like a soldier's field kit, took his ax in his right hand and set his face toward the high country. After a hundred yards of slow ascent he stopped and looked back. The gray stood staring after him, with lifted head and ears cocked in an expression of equine amazement that struck him as funny. He laughed aloud, turned and went on.

"He thinks I'm crazy," he remarked to himself. "And maybe I am, but here I go."

When he emerged upon the open country above timber line the snow was still a skimpy windblown thing. He could see the Truchas peaks a few miles to his left and he laid his course by them. He knew he had to pass along the foot of them and then drop off to his right into the head of a canyon called Quemado. A plain trail led down the canyon to a little town of the same name. There was no clear trail across the bare uplands but in bright weather the country was like a great topographic map. As the snow thickened later in the day the peaks were blotted out and the range of his vision steadily narrowed. He knew now he could keep a course only by using the utmost care. A man who has no bearings always feels that he is traveling in a straight line but he always in fact bears slowly to the left, will finally travel in a circle. So Daniel now would fix his eye on a rock or a tuft of grass, march straight to it and then select another objective.

As snow thickened in the air and deepened on the ground he traveled in a growing isolation for every wild creature goes to cover in a storm and the earth seems lifeless. Only the silent windblown snow seemed alive. It seemed to be surrounding him, steadily shrinking the circle of his vision, creeping along the ground in windy drifts both before and behind him, as though it were trying to bar his path and also keep him from turning back. It seemed a malevolent living thing, incessantly working against him.

Soon he found himself growing weary and his feet were wet and cold. He was going more and more slowly, wondering about his chances of getting across the divide before dark. For he had counted on getting across and reaching timber on the other side before the day was over. Once he reached timber he could build a great fire and spend the night safely. A man in timber with a good ax can survive the coldest weather. But here on top no timber grew—nothing but rare patches of arctic willow and of a kind of ground pine, which made a matted growth a few feet high, crouching before the winds and under the snow that no tree could withstand. If he had to spend the night here in the high country a patch of brush would be his only hope and it would be a poor one. He would have to spend the night grubbing out wood to keep a flame alive. And there was no assurance he could find enough timber even to do that.

He knew now his situation might become desperate but it was a curious fact that as he went on, more and more slowly, his anxiety seemed to die within him. A great somnolent weariness came over him, so that he dragged his feet and plunged into each new drift with a growing reluctance. He became aware that he wanted to stop and rest, to lie down in the snow and sleep. And all the time he knew that if he lay down now he would never get up again. He knew that death was right under his feet and it did not terrify him at all. It was as though the whispering snow had hypnotized him, lulled him into a mood of easy surrender. For the first time in his life he felt the temptation of death, the love of death, which is always hidden somewhere in the spirit of man, beneath the fear of death by which he lives. Death as violence is always frightening but death as easy sleep is sweet to the weary. It would be easy now to lie down and sleep in the great feather bed of the snow, the blowing, billowy snow, the gently caressing snow, the cold quiet lover that carries the kiss of death.

He wanted to lie down but he fought against his own desire—for he also wanted greatly to live. He had never known before how deeply he believed in living. Merely to stay on top of the snow and keep going seemed now a great assertion of faith in life. It would be so much easier to die. And he also wanted to defeat the storm, to elude the circling, treacherous snow. He knew he could do it if only he could find wood. He gave up trying to hold a straight course. Instead he traveled an erratic one, investigating every bulge and hollow that might conceal a patch of brush. It was hard hunting because he could only see about forty yards now.

Suddenly snow exploded before him in a roar of wings and a little band of ptarmigan, still in their brown summer plumage, went whirring away and vanished into the storm. He knew the birds lived on the arctic willow and he went plunging frantically in the direction they had taken. They never flew far. He found himself floundering up a little draw with a rill of water in it, bucking the deep snow it had gathered until he stumbled over a tangle of limbs and went sprawling in what he sought. On all fours he fumbled in the snow, breaking off dry willow twigs, scratching snow away with both hands, eager as a digging dog. He whittled shavings, struck a match with numb fingers, crouching over his tinder, saw red flame leap and glow. It was the very blossom of life to him. Man is a weak and naked creature but he owns the secret of fire and with fire he conquers the earth. For hours now he worked with his ax, chopping every bit of brush he could find, even grubbing up the roots. There was ground pine as well as willow and with that he built a windbreak to stop the drifting snow and reflect the heat of his fire. At last he could stop long enough to broil bacon on a twig and make the coffee in the pint cup he carried.

With hot meat and drink inside him he knew he had triumphed. His belly now was a fortress of defiant vitality in a hostile world. Toward morning he even dared to sleep a little while on the ground his fire had warmed. He woke very cold to revive his fire and see the sun rise in a clear sky.

With the peaks standing white against the blue it was easy to cross the summit and find the trail down the other side. Downhill going was easy too, and soon he was out of the snow, traveling through a pine forest where bluejays screamed at him and a few late flowers still bloomed. He walked with a long, swinging downhill stride feeling curiously light and free.

A little spike buck popped out of a patch of scrub oak and stopped to look when he whistled. He sat down, very slowly and carefully, resting both elbows on his knees, and shot the buck square between the forelegs. It went down like a poleaxed beef. He ran to it, drawing his knife, slit it open with one long clean stroke and spilled its guts on the ground in a steaming heap. Eagerly he fished out the liver, the only thing fit to eat with the body heat still in it. He washed it in a pool of rainwater, made a fire, heated a flat stone and cooked and ate it all. Then he lay flat and rested a long time, full as a tick and no more troubled. He had crossed the mountains, he had conquered the storm—he had crossed a barrier in his destiny.

IN EXILE

He saw the town first from a mile away and a thousand feet above. It was built on the tip of a long finger ridge, where the mountains broke and fell toward the Rio Grande—a tight little cluster of earthen houses about a plaza dominated by a small church. Perhaps three hundred Mexicans lived there and many of them, he knew, had never seen a man with a fair skin.

Now that he was about to face people again, he was suddenly overcome by a great self-consciousness. It was only two weeks since he had gone into the mountains, but he felt as though he had been alone for a long time, an indefinite time. The Dark River Valley, and everything that had happened there, seemed incredibly remote, as though in crossing the mountains he had left the past very far behind. He looked back upon the man he had been, the part he had played, with a detachment such as he had never known before, almost as though he were contemplating another person. And he felt curiously sure he would never become the same kind of man again—one who stood apart and addressed his fellows and commanded them. He did not know what he sought or what lay before him but he felt that it had to be something new, that he had left one self behind and was in search of another.

He knew it would not be wise to march into the town with arms in his hands. Ax and rifle he rolled in his blanket and carefully hid them under a shelving rock in a bed of dry oak leaves where he could easily find them again. Then he went down to the creek and bent over a smooth pool to wash. His image was faintly reflected in deep blue water and he saw it with a start. His face looked gaunt and long, his eyes large and bloodshot.

His hair was a matted mass and a reddish beard fringed his chin. His clothes were ragged, and dirt and soot and ashes were all over him. But there was also something strange in his expression, something fierce and intent. He looked like a wild man, as though a feral spirit had gotten into him there in the wilderness, in his struggle with it, and confronted him now in his own mirrored face. . . . He washed himself as best he could, then rose and went down the canyon, finding his legs a little weak—a great shambling figure of a man, an empty-handed fugitive in search of reunion with his kind.

— 2 —

When he walked into the plaza dogs greeted him first as they almost always do in a Mexican village. The poorer Mexicans are the more dogs they have. Daniel found himself beset on all sides by gaunt yapping curs, with more coming in response to the racket. He stood stock-still, knowing dogs will seldom attack a man who stands his ground with empty hands. Behind the dogs came children, about a dozen of them, dirty little brown brats of all ages up to fourteen. They stood and stared at him in round-eyed, open-mouthed amazement. After the children a woman came running in pursuit of her offspring. When she saw him she stopped, as though she had hit the end of a tether, and gave a shrill scream. It brought three more women, all on the run, and they all formed a black-shawled, whispering, suspicious group a little way behind the dogs and children. Presently one of them, a very old woman, came slowly forward, knelt before him, bowed her head and crossed herself.

Daniel knew Mexicans well enough to understand this gesture. These people were always looking for a messiah who would work miracles in their lives. A certain number of professional messiahs, most of them Mexicans from farther south, were always going about among the villages, professing to cure illness by incantation and the laying on of hands. He knew his strange and sudden appearance was perfectly calculated to strike a superstitious imagination. But there was nothing he wanted less to be than a messiah.

It would be terrible if these people set him apart, treated him as a demigod, brought him all their sick and asked him to work cures by magic. He wanted to be accepted simply as a human being in need.

When the old woman lifted her face he smiled at her and spoke gently in Spanish.

"I commend you to God, Madam," he said. "I am very hungry."

While she still knelt there, staring up at him, he saw a man coming rapidly across the plaza. He was a short, muscular, bowlegged man, and his very gait seemed to express purpose and authority. As he drew near Daniel became aware of a dark, square aquiline face, small deep-set shrewd-looking eyes and heavy black hair shot with gray. The man might have been fifty or more but he seemed to be of no particular age. He scattered the crowd, dogs, children and all, with a quick gesture, a few emphatic words, then turned his attention to Daniel, holding out his hand, smiling broadly.

"You are welcome, friend," he said. "My name is Solomon Valdez. I am the Alcalde here."

Daniel gave his name and thanked the man.

"You must be tired and hungry," the Alcalde said. "Come with me. My house is yours."

A little later Daniel found himself in a situation which had long been familiar to him in the Dark River Valley. He was seated on the floor with a whole Mexican family, gathered about a great steaming pot of beans cooked with red chile and a little goat meat, dipping up his hot food in a tortilla rolled to make a cup. It took a certain grace and skill to eat this way, and also an accustomed palate to swallow the burning chile, but Daniel was wholly equal to the occasion. This and his good command of Spanish made him an easy guest.

The Alcalde's wife was a large dark woman, and there were only two children, a pretty girl of sixteen and a boy a few years younger. These three were shy and silent but evidently trained to accept with submissive grace whatever Papa brought home, however strange it might look. The Alcalde, on the other hand, was a man of facile and voluminous discourse. He talked about the weather and the crops, the news from Santa Fe, the good hunting in the mountains and many other things, all trivial and insignificant. Like most Mexicans he was a master of the art of chatting. In all their conversation he asked Daniel not a single question, and Daniel understood perfectly the courtesy and convention of this attitude. He knew that many of these mountain Mexicans were bandits. They were not criminals in their own eyes. They had lived here for generations partly by preying on the flocks and herds of the ricos in the valley. To them the rich were legitimate objects of plunder. But they were a community of outlaws and outlaws do not ask questions of the fugitive stranger in any country or any language. So the Alcalde acted as if it were the most usual thing in the world for a giant gringo to walk across the mountains in two feet of snow and land upon his doorstep.

At a proper interval after the meal, Daniel rose and bowed, thanking first the wife and then the master of the house.

"But you cannot go," the Alcalde protested. "My house is yours as long as you wish to stay."

Daniel could see at a glance there was no room for him here.

"You are too kind," he protested. "Is there not an empty house or a room where I can make my bed?"

He knew that every Mexican village contains deserted houses, and he had expected to take up his abode in one of them, but the Alcalde could do better than that.

"There is a good room behind the church," he said. "The Padre stays there when he comes, but that is only a few times in a year. It is yours for as long as you want it."

So Daniel slept that night in the quarters reserved for priests—a little whitewashed room with a corner fireplace, a good pallet of sheep pelts with an old Navajo blanket spread over them, and a doll-like image of the Virgin of Guadelupe staring down at him from a niche in the wall.

— 3 —

Within a week Daniel had become as much a part of the town's life as though he had lived there a year. These people were just like children in that they contemplated him at first with suspicion and astonishment but when he had received the benison of the omnipotent Alcalde, and even more importantly, had proved himself a beneficent person, they accepted him without question as the gift of a just and provident God.

He was beneficent chiefly as a provider of good red meat. When he led the Alcalde up the canyon and showed him the Winchester he had hidden there, along with fifty cartridges, the man's eyes shone with delight and he fondled the weapon with reverent hands. Poor Mexicans were always meat-hungry. Their goats were primarily a milk herd. They made a good cheese and killed an occasional kid, but abundant meat they seldom had except when they stole it.

"We have not a single good gun in the village," the Alcalde explained. "Nothing but a few old trade muskets and hardly any powder for them. Now we can hunt!"

Hunt they did, in the laborious fashion of men to whom hunting is necessary business and meat is life. They drove four pack burros up into the heads of the canyons, where the deer always abounded and more had been driven down by the deep snow. It was easy to kill them and hard work to skin and butcher, cut up meat and pack it on the burros, standing blindfolded so that they would not run from the smell of blood. When they came back after three days in the mountains, meat was distributed to every house in town and many families sat up most of the night about bonfires, broiling bits of venison on sharp sticks, laughing and singing over their feast. Red meat seemed to put new life into the whole town and the bellies of children visibly bulged.

When men hunt and camp together, sharing action, work and hardship, matching their skills, they come to know each other well in a short time, and in the mountains Daniel and the Alcalde became good friends. At night they sat smoking and talking between their windbreak and a great red fire. The Alcalde did most of the talking. He still asked Daniel no questions but he was eager to talk about himself. Evidently he wanted

Daniel to know that he was no mere villager but a traveled man, a man of the world—at least of all the world that was anywhere within his reach and ken. When young he had repeatedly gone south as a packer with the conductas, the annual trading trips, all the way to the city of Chihuahua, and he also had been east on buffalo hunts as far as the staked plains of Texas. More than that, he had gone down into the valley to work as a sheep shearer, a business at which he had great skill, not merely to Taos and Santa Fe but as far south as Albuquerque. He knew all about the ricos, their great houses and their luxurious lives, their feuds and scandals. He regarded them with a humorous cynicism, and although he did not say so in plain words, it was evident that he considered their movable property as something to be appropriated whenever it was possible to do so with safety and discretion. It gradually became apparent that he regarded Daniel as a fellow spirit in this respect, and this was not surprising. A man would not walk across the mountains in a snowstorm just for fun. Obviously he must have been in rather urgent need of both departure and refuge. Having been himself often just one jump ahead of the law, the Alcalde could sympathize and understand. After the subtle fashion of his kind, he made it clear that he accepted Daniel as a fellow outlaw, and Daniel did not see how he could explain himself in any terms the Alcalde would understand. After all, he was a refugee, if not exactly of the kind the Alcalde supposed.

After they had returned to the village, the Alcalde continued to call upon him almost every day, and he became increasingly candid about himself and his position in the village. He was not only the Alcalde but also the Hermano Mayor of the local chapter of the Penitent Brothers, which made him in effect both the temporal and the spiritual ruler of his own small domain. For the Penitentes were the organized religion of all these mountain communities. Every man was a member. The great whips they used upon their own backs every Good Friday hung openly in the vestry of the church, and there too was the cart of death they used in their processions with its crude figure of a dark angel holding a drawn bow and arrow in his hand. This church belonged to the Penitentes no less than did the windowless Morada on the hill above the town and the great wooden cross where one of their number was every year crucified with ropes. Their domination of the community was obvious and it was a familiar fact to Daniel, yet it was rare for a Penitente even to mention his membership in the fraternity. The impression grew upon Daniel that the Alcalde must be telling him all this for a purpose—must be leading up to something important. His shrewd little eyes were full of friendliness but also of calculation. He still refrained from any direct questions but he was at pains to learn that Daniel was a literate man. The Alcalde could neither read nor write and neither could any of the others in the village, but he brought Daniel an old Santa Fe newspaper and asked him to translate an item in which he professed an interest. When he learned that Daniel could read and write both Spanish and English, it was plain to see that he was deeply impressed.

The impending revelation came during his next visit. After a little preliminary chat, he looked Daniel in the eye and spoke with great earnestness.

"My friend," he said, "I think God has sent you among us for a purpose. I have thought so ever since that day when you walked into the plaza. In a world ruled by a just God these things do not happen by chance."

Daniel nodded his head slowly several times. He knew this occasion called for the utmost in dignity and appreciation.

"You do me great honor," he said.

"I trust you," the Alcalde replied, "as I would trust my own brother. That is why I speak to you now. . . . You know that the Penitentes are many. Here in the upper river country we outnumber all others. Moreover, we act and think as one. In the town of Mora on the other side of the mountains we have our headquarters, and there lives the great brother who rules us all. There are no dissenters or traitors among us, for such cannot live."

He paused to let this revelation sink into his auditor's mind, but it was no revelation to Daniel. He had been dealing with Penitentes for years. He knew they had a tight and powerful organization, which was not merely a religious fraternity but also a league of poor men against the rich who had always oppressed them.

"I know that what you say is true," he replied.

"We are poor and ignorant," the Alcalde said. "Under the Mexican government all we could do was to care for our own, and also sometimes we could take care of our enemies. Those who are wise have always respected our power. But under the American government we might do much more. I am an ignorant man myself but I know that votes are power now and we have many votes. What we need is someone to speak for us in Santa Fe—someone who knows the written word and also the ways of the Americans. . . . My friend, I think God has appointed you to serve us!"

"You do me too much honor," Daniel protested. He was at a loss what else to say, for the Alcalde's proposal had stirred within him a conflict of feeling that surprised himself. He could not believe he was going to do this thing, and yet it made an appeal to his sympathies and his imagination that he could not deny. The Alcalde was vague about what could be done by this powerful advocate he wanted, but Daniel knew the man was not talking nonsense. He knew that anyone who had the Penitente vote in his pocket would be a man of power. He knew also just what it would mean to achieve that power. The Alcalde now was speaking his own thought.

"You would of course become one of us," he said. "You would take the vows of the Church as well as those of our Order. You would mingle your blood with ours. You would become our brother in the blood of Christ. . . ."

He would kneel in a little dark room and they would cut his bare back from neck to waist with a sharp flint. Perhaps they would lift him to a cross and bind him there. And when he came down he would be one of them and their power would be his.

"This is a grave matter, my friend," he said. "I must have time to think."

The Alcalde was quick to see that he had won an advantage. He knew when to stop.

"Surely," he said, "you must meditate. And we could do nothing until spring when the snows melt and we can go to Mora. . . . But I am sure this is your destiny in the eyes of God. You cannot refuse."

It was true, Daniel had to admit to himself. He could not refuse. At least not now. He was glad that nothing could be done for a matter of months, for he saw that once more, as so often, he faced a battle with himself.

— 4 —

Snow had fallen again and winter winds had stripped the last leaves off the willows along the creek when the Alcalde came to Daniel's room one evening, breathing hard with excitement.

"The sheriff in Taos is looking for you!" he blurted. "Pablo Gonzales was there today and they asked him if we had seen you. He said no, of course, but that makes no difference. The sheriff is a Mexican but he has a gringo deputy and that man is much too busy. He will be here surely. You must let us hide you. Believe me, we Penitentes know how to hide men. They will never find you, and these things are always forgotten. But there is no time to waste. . . ."

He was stopped by Daniel's incredulous expression.

"But I have done nothing wrong," Daniel said, shaking his head in bewilderment.

The Alcalde gave him a long look, his eyes shrewd and narrow, unbelieving but kindly.

"My friend," he said, "why do you not trust me? We are as brothers. Perhaps you had a fight and killed a man. There is no reason why you should hide that from me. Any man may kill in the heat of his blood. I have never killed a man but I have tried. At a dance one night in Taos a fellow tried to take a girl out of my arms. I had a knife for him. It took four men to hold me. Believe me, friend, I know what it is to lust for the blood of an enemy!"

"But I have never killed anyone," Daniel protested.

The Alcalde smiled.

"I didn't think you had," he admitted. "I have no doubt you stole.

Probably you stole cattle from those rich gringos in the Dark River Valley. You are not the only one. How is a poor man to live? The rich have everything except what you take away. I conceal nothing from you, my friend, and you should trust me. I have been stealing sheep for twenty years. When I worked for Don Augustin Romero in Taos I used to steal a few sheep from him every spring and sell them back to him in the fall. And why not? He had thousands and I had none. One old ewe I stole so often she used to bleat a greeting when she saw me coming."

"But I have not stolen anything," Daniel interrupted him to protest.

"Very well," the Alcalde said. "I believe you. If you have neither killed nor stolen, then it must be a woman!"

He paused, watching Daniel's expression with those acute and penetrating eyes. He saw a flicker of change there, for Daniel, badly puzzled, could think of but one human being who might be looking for him. It was hard to believe but it was possible.

. The Alcalde threw back his head and laughed. He was evidently relieved.

"Why should you deny that, of all things?" he demanded. " 'A sin of the flesh is no sin at all.' It is an old Spanish saying. But such sins can overtake a man and capture him. You must let me put you where she can never find you. This is no time for you to fall into the hands of a woman. If you want to marry later, I will take care of that. I will bring you a beautiful virgin with breasts like ripe melons. But we must let no one take you away from here now. We have work to do!"

Daniel sat shaking his head, smiling a little sadly. He knew it was going to be hard to make the Alcalde understand and he had a great regard for the man.

"If the sheriff is looking for me, I must go to Taos," he said. "I have done no wrong. It must be a mistake."

"It is no mistake," the Alcalde said firmly. "The deputy described you and there could be no other man like you."

He finally went away, shaking his head, evidently convinced that this strange man would not listen to sense.

When he returned next morning, Daniel was preparing to go. He refused the loan of a horse and handed the Alcalde his rifle and his ax.

"Keep these for me and use them," he said. "If I do not return they are yours. Let them remind you that we are friends."

The Alcalde was deeply moved by this gift but neither his gloom nor his disappointment was relieved.

"It is folly for you to go," he said sadly. "If the law does not get you, the woman will. But I see you cannot be dissuaded. Remember always that my house is yours."

They shook hands and Daniel set out on his thirty-mile walk, taking only the few dollars he owned and the small bundle of his belongings.

He turned once and looked back and waved his hand to the Alcalde, who stood watching him out of sight, and then went on his way, feeling curiously guilty, knowing that he had begotten a dream and a hope and was deserting them.

EPITHALAMIUM

Weary from long walking, Daniel crossed the dusty plaza in Taos and presented himself at the sheriff's office. Its chief functionary was an old cowpuncher named Shinburn a man of fifty, with a deeply lined, heavily weathered face and small deep-set blue eyes, lean in build and bowlegged from long years in the saddle. As the first American officer of the law in Taos County he had made a reputation by rounding up a great many cattle rustlers and horse thieves and by restoring much livestock to its legal owners. He looked Daniel up and down with a mild and weary curiosity.

"So you're Daniel Laird," he said at length. "Sit down."

Daniel sat.

"I heard you were looking for me," he said. "What do you want me for?"

"Don't you know?" Shinburn inquired.

Daniel shook his head.

Shinburn expressed his skepticism in a wry smile. He produced a plug of tobacco, offered it to Daniel, who refused, cut himself a chew with a pocket knife, stowed it in the corner of his face, and spoke judiciously.

"I reckon the best I can do is to take you across the plaza and turn you over to the plaintiff," he said. "I hope to God you and she can settle out of court. If you can take her off my hands, I'll sure thank you. She's been more nuisance than forty horse thieves. Let's go."

He led Daniel across the plaza to the old Fonda, which had been housing visitors to Taos for many years—a low, rambling adobe, built around a courtyard, with iron-barred windows and weeds growing out of its earthen roof. They passed through the hall which pierced the front and into the courtyard.

"You wait here," Shinburn told Daniel. He knocked on a door, was admitted and disappeared for about three minutes. Then he came out, nodded to Daniel, gesturing over his shoulder with his thumb.

"Go to it," he said, "and God be with you."

Inside the low-ceilinged room, dimly lit by a single window, they stood staring at each other, as though neither could quite believe in the other's existence. Betty was the first to recover.

"Sit down, Daniel," she said. "You look all tuckered out."

Daniel sat awkward and tongue-tied. He knew at once and instinctively that he had come to the end of his wandering, had found his fate, but as always he was tangled in his own inner conflicts. For him there could never be the undivided moment, the complete acceptance, the single mind. But he was bewildered also by the impression that he looked at another woman, that she had undergone some great and unaccountable change. She wore a plain gingham dress, like the wife of a ranchman, her cheeks were innocent of rouge and powder, her hair was pulled straight back from her face and bunched upon her neck. Her face was thinner and looked older, dominated wholly by her eyes, which held a troubled look. A slender, weary woman he saw, with something almost austere about her, and something fearful.

"I had to find you, Daniel," she said, speaking rapidly, almost breathlessly. "I don't know why. When I walked out on you that night I thought I was all done, honest I did. And then when I heard you had gone I knew I had to find you. I never thought I would go trailing after a man like a lost dog, but I did. I sold out for what I could get and took the stage to Santa Fe. I thought of course you would have to go there first. I put on this kind of a dress and a sunbonnet and talked nice and ignorant and told them you had done me wrong. It was the only way I could get them to hunt for you. A young fellow there in Santa Fe offered to marry me, even if I was in trouble, honest he did. But nobody had seen you or heard anything about you and I knew there would be no mistaking your looks. . . . It was a funny thing but the longer I hunted for you the more I had to find you, no matter what. I seemed a little crazy to myself. . . . When I came up here it was the same story for a long time and I began to think maybe you were dead. I camped on that Shinburn's trail; I just practically sat on his doorstep. He was the only man around with enough gumption to do anything and he didn't want to be bothered. He ain't interested in anything but livestock. But I wouldn't let him rest. If I had been a man he would have kicked me out long ago but you can't kick a woman. . . . Then finally he got a story from a sheep herder about a big gringo that walked across the mountains in two foot of snow. I knew it must be you because nobody else could do it and nobody else would try. . . ."

She stopped, breathless, her cheeks flushed, her lips parted, watching his unrevealing face. A look of something like terror came into her eyes.

"O my God!" she cried. "Don't you want me?"

For the first time now Daniel felt a great warmth inside him. This was not the woman who had flung him an impudent challenge and captivated his flesh, nor yet the provocative vision that had followed him into the wilderness and driven him out of it. In this moment she was only a fellow human who had a great need, who had uttered a cry for help. He rose and went and sat beside her, put his arm about her shoulders, kissed her lifted lips.

"Yes," he said, "I want you. I was a fool ever to try to deny it. You have been with me somehow all the time."

The instant he touched her she was transformed, confident again, possessive, running her hands over his face and through his hair, as though contact with him gave her new life.

"I'll take good care of you, Daniel," she said tenderly. "Don't you worry about a thing. You don't know it yet but I'm just what you need."

EPILOGUE

By JAMES LANE MORGAN

When I rode into the valley of Taos in the spring of 1906 I was going back to the past in a double sense. I was returning to the scenes of my own youth, and Taos at that time was perhaps as perfect a relic of a vanished world as could be found anywhere in America. As I rode across the little valley, green with its new-sprung crops and leafing cottonwoods, flashing with silver waters, perfumed by the great banks of blossoming wild plum along the ditches, I was aware this must be almost exactly what the mountain men had seen sixty years before when they returned each spring, eager for the arms of women, for bread and sugar and the white whisky of Turley's still after months in the wilderness. And there was the solid earthen town in the distance, squatting upon its low hill, just as it had been for a century. There are places so deeply imbued with the spirit of the past that change can touch them only lightly, and such a place, it seemed to me, was the valley of Taos.

It may surprise the reader that I had never seen this country since I left it the year after Ballard's death. There was no place for me on the grant after Blore's rise to power, but I had remained in the West for several years, leading a vagabond life as a hunter and prospector, simply because I could not bring myself to leave the mountains. I carried always a pan and rock hammer, I found a few pockets of gold-bearing quartz and bought a few claims and stock in others. I called myself a mining man and made a little money, but I knew I was evading my proper destiny. I knew what kept me in the West was a love of physical freedom, adventure and excitement. I knew I was hanging onto my youth because I had found it sweet. My adult business was back in New York, and there finally I returned, to assume the management of my father's property, to practice law and finally to become a judge, to marry and raise a family. I had been successful in a modest way, I had performed all the routines and obligations of a good citizen—and I had been haunted all those years by the memory of my life on the frontier, as some men are haunted by the memory of an early love which made life briefly more intense and vivid than it could ever become again. I had at once cultivated and assuaged my nostalgia for the mountains and the past by becoming an amateur historian, by collecting Western Americana, by writing monographs for the journals of historical societies. I had visited the West more than once, and I had always intended some time to return to Taos and the Dark River Valley, but I had postponed the day because I knew what a perilous thing it is for any man to go back to the places where he was young—to look upon the wrecks and relics of a vital period in his own life.

I was going back at last because my own researches made it necessary. I had long planned to write something about the Ballard grant and the Dark River Valley, and the significance of the story had grown upon me for years. I was impressed especially by the fact that the struggle to possess and dominate that little empire had produced men with a genuine capacity for leadership—men, it seemed to me, who might have played a part upon some much larger stage if the opportunity had been given them. Ballard was easily the greatest of them, but Blore, an inscrutable figure to me and touched with evil, had certainly been a man of great ability, and so had Tighe. I had met him only once, but I knew well the story of how he had tamed the grant single-handed. Daniel Laird was the most enigmatic of the four who had exercised some kind of power in the Dark River Valley, and to me the most interesting of them all—a man with a touch of genius who had never found the means of his own development, but had nevertheless somehow evolved his own set of values and remained faithful to it.

Laird was the only one of the four who still lived, and he not only lived but flourished. I had called upon him the year before at his ranch in the San Luis Valley of southern Colorado and we had spent a long evening talking about Ballard and the old days on the grant—about everything, in fact, except Daniel himself. He was not the kind of man who would tell you his own story, and I soon found that his serene reticence on that subject was impenetrable. I knew that after Blore had taken over Laird had assembled the ranchmen and made a famous speech in which he told them how they had all been cheated. I knew that Blore finally had somehow forced him out. Like all idealists he had won only the moral victory of refusing to compromise.

I knew a woman had played a part in his story and that he had married her, homesteaded in the San Luis Valley, and become the moderately prosperous owner of several hundred acres of alfalfa and a fine herd of white-faced Hereford cattle. More than that, he had become also a political figure of local note, for he sat in the state legislature and was known as its most uncompromising radical. First as a member of the Populist party and later as a follower of William Jennnings Bryan, he was always in the minority, often a minority of one, thundering in his mighty voice against the trusts and Wall Street, predicting the day when humble men who worked with their hands would rise in their organized power and smite the mighty. In a word, he was the same old Laird, the born champion of lost causes, the man with a vision of the future, the leader of the humble, the prophet of change. He had a good deal more intellectual sophistication now, but the same stubborn fidelity to his own lights, the same hatred of greed armed with authority, the same blind courage and bull-voiced eloquence. I think he never won a victory on the floor of the legislature, but he was unbeatable at the polls, partly because he could go into the Mexican precincts and completely charm the natives by addressing them in their own language and with a perfect inflection. He was said to be even more eloquent in Spanish than in English.

In appearance I found him little changed, except that his great shock of hair was nearly white. He was a good deal less shy than the man I remembered, but otherwise he seemed exactly the same fellow with whom I had gone fishing along the Dark River and eaten dinner in his cabin. Again he poured me a large jolt of whisky and took none himself and again he asked me so many questions that I found it hard to query him. Now as before he made the impression of a man at peace with himself, sustained by a love of life for its own sake.

No doubt Laird's public career was his own, but his worldly success was by common report ascribed almost wholly to his wife, whom I met at dinner the day I called upon him. She, like her husband, was a person with a legend, and I had heard a good deal about her. I was told that she had been a famous queen of the night life in Dodge City when it was the wildest track-end town in the West, that Blore had brought her to the Dark River Valley for reasons known only to himself, and that she had somewhat mysteriously emerged from that phase of her life as the wife of Daniel Laird. Apparently, she was about the only thing he had taken with him when he left the grant, and evidently she had proved to be an important asset, for her business ability was famous. It was said that Daniel never signed a paper or spent more than ten dollars without consulting her. His political career she regarded as a huge waste of time and energy, but with a certain good-humored indulgence. Her own life had been devoted largely to the raising of four sons, three of whom were already grown and the owners of ranches in the San Luis Valley, so that the Lairds were now the head of a veritable clan.

Betty Laird's story was a usual one, in that many of the dance-hall beauties of the Old West finally married ranchmen and became models of domestic propriety. Certainly there was nothing about her when I made her acquaintance to suggest a lurid past. I saw a small, quiet, gray-haired woman with careful manners, somewhat modified by an irreverent sense of humor. It was evident that she declined to take anyone seriously, including her famous husband. She had been heard to thank God that her children inherited his muscle and her own brains. Nevertheless, it was evident that these two were devoted to each other, and that they had a highly effective working partnership. Different as they were, both of them were rebels and individualists, so that perhaps they understood each other well enough.

— 2 —

I have been impressed all my life by the fact that no man can escape the inner drive of his destiny. Whatever kind of power is in him, that he must use, for better or worse, and even though it consume or destroy him. It was evident that Daniel Laird would be defying the mighty and defending the humble in his thunderous voice as long as breath was in him, and Clay Tighe had remained all his life a terror to the lawless, a man who imposed order by force and fear. The frontier needed such men and Tighe was no ordinary gunman. His whole career showed that he was a man with a genuine sense of justice, always ready to fight for his principles, and he had also some innate quality of power and authority that was hard to define. More than one man who had known him testified that he could stop trouble by his mere presence, without lifting either his hand or his voice, and that it was curiously hard to look him in the eye when he meant business. Moreover, he had no love of battle for its own sake, at least in his later years. When he retired to his Berenda ranch, north of the Dark River Valley, he let it be known that he was hanging up his gun—that from then on he was a cattleman and nothing more. He married a beautiful Mexican girl and raised a family, but he never found the peace he was seeking, never was able to go among his fellows unarmed without risking his life.

The late eighties were the period in which cattle rustling reached its height and was finally suppressed, partly by the law but largely by the action of organized vigilantes. Clay Tighe founded the first cattlemen's association in the Southwest, was its first president, and by reason of his talents and prestige, the leader in its struggle with the rustlers. A hard man but a just one, he would not countenance lynching, never shot a man unless he had to, dragged a great many rustlers into court and sent them to the penitentiary. Most of these were out again in a year or less so that his strict principles only multiplied his enemies. When he lit a candle one night to get a drink of water a rifle bullet smashed the window within an inch of his head. For years he did not dare to sit by a lighted window and in public he still followed his long-time custom of keeping his back to a wall.

There were no witnesses to his death except his murderers, but the story was recorded in tracks on sandy soil. He was driving alone in a buckboard across the open country east of the Dark River Valley when he slowed down to cross a narrow wash, fringed with sage and rabbit brush a few feet high. Rifles cracked at long range and Tighe fell backward into the bed of the vehicle. His spirited team ran away and brought his body home. Although he had been shot through the heart it was found that he had drawn his six-shooter and fired it once before he died.

— 3 —

Major Blore had died in Denver a few years before my visit to the West. If he had been alive I would have called upon him. I have no doubt he would have received me with impeccable politeness and told me nothing at all, for he was a man in whom a cold and deadly cunning hid behind an impenetrable surface. I knew of him only that he had returned to Denver after the second sale of the grant, a substantially richer man, and that he continued to grow richer to the day of his death. His cunning seemed unbeatable. He was one of those men of whom it is said that everything they touch turns to money.

He never married, but lived in a large house with a housekeeper whom he had brought from Virginia on one of his rare visits to the East. She was a very large girl, nearly a head taller than the Major, quite pretty in her buxom way, quite simple-minded and wholly devoted to her employer. In his later years Major Blore was afflicted by diabetes, which caused him to shrivel like a potato in the sun. He rarely appeared in public, but never missed a horse race or a horse show. One who saw him about 1900 described him as a tiny, frail-looking man, all of whose life seemed to be concentrated in his great blue eyes, which were as bright and hard and unrevealing as ever. For a long time before he died he was a house-bound invalid. It is said that his housekeeper used to pick him up in her arms like a baby and carry him to bed.

— 4 —

There were men in the Dark River Valley and elsewhere in the West who remembered Ballard, and all of these I intended to see and question, for none of them would live much longer. But there was only one survivor of those days, other than Laird, with whom I could claim a personal acquaintance, and she was the occasion of my visit to Taos. For there, in the old family homestead, Consuelo Ballard still lived, and she was still, to all accounts, a great lady.

The building of the railroad and the invasion of the Southwest by men and money from the East had destroyed the feudal society of the Mexican regime in little more than a generation. Some able individuals of the old families had made a place for themselves, but as a society the ricos were almost extinct and the country was littered with the crumbling remnants of their great earthen houses. Here in Taos their way of life had survived with less change than anywhere else in the state. The Coronels had declined in wealth and importance, but they still owned some thousands of sheep and valuable lands in the valley, and they were still patrons to the poor Mexicans who worked for them. The male head of the house, a nephew of Consuelo, was an able man who so little trusted the new regime that he never entered a bank, but kept his cash in an iron strong box and guarded it with a rifle. By common report Consuelo was the matriarchal head of the clan, greatly respected by the whole community, ministering to the poor just as she had done in the days when Ballard ruled the grant.

She received me in the long sala, the very room in which Ballard must have courted her, with the gracious dignity which I remembered as her distinguishing quality. She spoke perfect English in a voice which retained all of its richness and power, and she had nothing of the primitive provincialism of her male relatives. She would have been wholly equal to any society in the world.

Over thick chocolate and cigarettes we talked for hours, fumbling for common ground at first, but finally awakening a flood of memories that truly carried us both away and back through the years. "Do you remember?" We asked the question over and over, and the words were like a magic formula, for although we had known little of each other we had loved the same things. Between us we recreated the old house in the Dark River Valley, the roaring fires on the great hearths, the table that seated its hundred guests from all over the world, the dances and receptions, the daily arrival of the stagecoach with its various human cargo. Consuelo went further back than that and told me something of her early years in the valley, when the Arapahoe were a menace and grizzly bears raided their sheep herds. That, I am sure, had been the great epoch of her life and love. Her eyes shone and her voice was music when she spoke of it.

Of Jean Ballard she said little, and I had not expected that she would, but her last words, before she told me good-by, were about him.

"He was a great man," she said. "No one else could ever take his place. It was never the same after he died."

— 5 —

That, I knew from my own inquiries, was the exact truth. What Ballard had created died with him. Blore had sold the grant again within two years of Ballard's death and at an enormous profit. It was bought this time by a group of British capitalists and was one of the first large foreign investments in the American cattle business. Under this British regime the old house went through its last phase and had a last moment of glory before it fell into ruin. This was also the last time the dominion that Ballard had founded was ruled as a whole. A titled younger son came from England to take charge of the grant. He had the house done over in a style and with a magnificence never before seen in that part of the country. A grand piano was part of its furnishings and the wife of the baronet, a gifted musician, played Bach and Beethoven late at night, while Mexicans gathered outside to listen and coyotes answered in chorus from the hills. This lady also served tea under striped umbrellas on the lawn and her husband set up a cricket field. He astonished the natives by posting over the mountain trails on a flat saddle and scrutinizing them through a monocle. His operations in the livestock business did much to improve the local breed, for he imported registered bulls and the surrounding ranchers appropriated a large part of their offspring.

It came to be said the grant had a curse upon it, for nothing ever prospered there after Ballard's death, and the British regime soon came to an end in bankruptcy. The grant passed into the hands of another syndicate, a Dutch one this time, which formed a stock company and sold stock both in the United States and abroad. This concern employed a press agent who was an imaginative artist of no small power. I saw a brochure he prepared for the benefit of foreign investors. It showed the Dark River as a navigable stream, with steamboats tied up at a wharf and cultivated lands spreading to the horizon.

The Dutch company did build the dam that I had dreamed about and Blore had talked about, but it proved to be a shoddy job. In a spring of great freshets it washed away, sending a great wall of yellow water down the valley, with houses and wagons riding on its crest. Some irreverent spectators took ironic pleasure in the fact that for about twenty-four hours the Dark River looked as wide as it had in the company's advertising.

The future of the town was settled finally when the railroad passed it by, about twenty miles to the east, and did not even build a spur into the valley. The railroads then were the arbiters of destiny all over the West. Every town they touched was given new life and those they ignored were doomed.

— 6 —

When I left Taos I rode across the mountains to the Dark River Valley by the same trail Ballard must have followed more than half a century before, and I saw almost exactly what he must have seen. Since the building of railroads and highways the mountain trails were little used, so that the country was wild as ever, with not a human habitation visible to mar the beauty of the long forested ridges falling away to the prairie.

There in the mountains and there only did I briefly recover the illusion of a return to the past, for I was riding through the same country where I had spent so many days alone with a rifle or a fishing rod when I was twenty-six. It was so little changed that I could identify a great spruce in a canyon meadow where I had often stopped for lunch and a deep blue pool in which I had taken many a cooling plunge. I remember the thrill with which I watched a black-tail buck go bouncing through the down timber in twenty-foot leaps, and a flock of wild turkeys set their wings and sail across a canyon. I had always loved the mountains and I took pleasure in the fact that their massive resistance had saved something from the sweep of change, the corrosion of human greed.

So I came to Dark River, a sleepy little cowtown at the end of a bad dirt road. There I returned, with something of a jolt, to the dusty reality of the present, for the house Ballard built was now a ruin, the great cottonwood trees that had shaded it were dying of old age and neglect, the hollyhocks had run wild all over the dooryard. Nothing here was the same except the view when one looked eastward to mountains. Nor could I find anyone in the tiny town with whom I could claim an acquaintance, but I found half a dozen men who had been young when Ballard died and others who had heard about him from their parents. All of them loved to talk about the old days, had a curiously strong sense of the local past as a time somehow hallowed and significant. All of them knew about Major Blore, who had here achieved a posthumous fame as a figure almost diabolical, and Tighe and Laird were also remembered and had taken on somewhat legendary characters, as though Tighe's skill had grown with the years and Laird's voice was even louder in retrospect than it had been in fact. But the thing they all liked most to talk about was the open-handed magnificence of Ballard's establishment in its best years, when no man was ever turned away from his table and his wealth lay unguarded, as though all this had been a flowering of human life that deserved commemoration. "You'll never see anything like it again," was a phrase I heard several times, and it seemed a fitting epitaph for an epoch. Certainly the modern world, whatever its merits, seems a bit tight-fisted and calculating by comparison with that reckless and ample day.

To me the droning tales of these old-timers had the quality of elegy. I felt as though I were witnessing the process by which the past becomes a beloved myth, simplified in memory so that one may see the meanings that are always obscured by the noise and dust of the present. The sleepy inertia of the little town made its past seem truly heroic. In the days when I had known it and before, a great gust of passion and energy had struck this place and blown itself out and left in its wake the ruin of a proud house and a legend in the memories of aging men.

THE BUFFALO

by STEWART EDWARD WHITE

After Stewart Edward White died in 1946 his name was almost forgotten. His books, which were readily found on library shelves twenty years ago, began to disappear. Then slowly there came recognition again. An edition—The Saga of Andy Burnett—was prepared for teenagers, and it became a textbook. Paperback editions sold out as fast as they appeared on the stands. White was a prolific author, but nothing he did has so completely caught the flavor of the period with simplicity and clarity as have his Andy Burnett books. The best of these is The Long Rifle.

The little party of Mountain Men moved steadily toward the southwest. They were now four days out from Council Grove, where they had left the trace, known to all of them, that led toward the Rockies.

Those days had offered little but monotony. The grassland ran in long earth billows. The shallow troughs between their crests were wide. The cavalcade rode down the gentle slope; across the flat; up the other slope. From the hollow the sky line was definite. Andy Burnett, in his inexperience, could not rid himself of the feeling that, once the crest was attained, he should be able to see abroad for miles. But when he had mounted the summit he saw before him merely another billow of the earth.

There was no game outside a few bands of antelope, but smaller life was abundant. The brown grass of last year still stood; the green grass below it had not yet laid it low. Through it scurried rabbits and the littler rodents. Savannah sparrows and buntings swung from its blades; horned larks rose from its openings. Overhead sparrow hawks hung as though suspended, their wings vibrating, their sharp eyes cocked for a mouse or a bird. Curiously enough, in spite of the wide sweep of country, the scale of size was diminished. A coyote loping off looked as big as an elk: the cavalcate of horsemen were monstrous. This was due to the abundance of little things—the lack of tree or tiniest shrub, only the blades of grass.

These conditions, Andy found, made for modifications in life. There was now no fuel to be had, and little game. The company had to fall back largely on the meat it had dried or "jerked"—before reaching Council Grove. This, unleavened bread from the small store of flour, and coffee constituted the whole diet. The only possible fire was from the resinweed. It flared up hot, blazed for a few seconds, and was gone. It was not good fuel, but by constant attention the men managed to make it do for their simple cooking. Campfires were, of course, entirely out of the question.

"We'll git to the short grass purty quick," said Joe Crane. "Then there'll be a plenty of buffalo chips. And buffalo, if the critters ain't all moved north. I don't know how they act down thisaway."

The men no longer rode in as careless a formation as before reaching

Council Grove. They held together in a compact group, with the pack animals in the center. On approaching the crest of each of the earth billows someone trotted ahead to examine the next trough. The day's march was ended in midafternoon, the horses grazed under the eye of a mounted herdsman. At dark they were driven in and picketed close up to the camp. No guard was set for the first part of the night. Near one or two o'clock, however, Kelly aroused one of the sleepers who had been designated the night before. The man, instantly broad awake, shivering a little, arose in silence. Outside the horse herd he lay flat—or merely sat down if the terrain was favorable—his rifle at hand.

"Not one chance in a thousand for Injuns in this kentry," Joe told Andy. "Nothin' to bring 'em here. Only chance would be a party travelin' to git through, same as we are. But the p'int is, they wouldn't any Injuns be goin' through, 'less'n it was a war party on their way to raid the Kansas or Osages or mebbe to take a try at the Pawnees. And war parties is bad medicine, especially Comanche war parties. It's a slim chance, but when it comes to Injuns you take *no* chances."

Andy, as usual when Joe became instructive, showed his interest. Joe, encouraged, went on.

"Then they's scouts. Injuns is great hands to send out a scout or two just to look around. And they's always a young buck or two projectin' out on his own hook to pick up a sculp or so. You see, Andy, an Injun lad ain't got a show in the world till he can show one sculp. When they call him growed up they give him a powwow and a medicine dance; and then he's supposed to go out with his gang and not come back till he's got him an enemy sculp. Then he's a warrior. If he comes back without one, he just ranks wtih squaws, and the gals won't have nothin' to do with him. He has to go to work, and the women can order him around. I've knowed 'em to be away nigh a year before they had any luck. When they been out that long—or a good sight less—they're gittin' kind of desp'rate. They ain't so partic'lar whether it's an enemy sculp or not. All ha'r looks alike. That's one reason it don't pay to git keerless. Now you take the Crows. Crows in gin'ral has always been friendly to us Mountain Men. If you ever meet up with a Crow village, ride right in and make yoreself to home. And if you meet up with a real Crow war party, ride right up to them. Probably they'll try to git you to j'ine them for a leetle sport with the Arapahoes or Snakes or mebbe the Blackfeet. Though they don't tackle the Blackfeet much. But I'd hate like p'is'n to meet up with any of the young 'uns headin' home without no sculp to show. Good idee to look 'em over afore you declar' yoreself. If they look young and hungry and you don't see no ha'r on their leggin's, you cache!"

Joe grinned at Andy's interest.

"Crows is good people, too," he added. "You got nice black ha'r, Andy. Don't be gettin' keerless."

"Wagh!" agreed Fitz, who was listening.

"That's why they's liable to be some strays, even in this grass kentry," Joe concluded his instruction. " 'Course they won't bother us. An Injun's got sense, and twelve long rifles is too big odds. If we got keerless and scattered out, and lay around promiscuous, and left our horses stray, they might go back and tell the Old Man they's easy pickin's on the prairie."

"If I were an Indian I'd wait until we were all sound asleep, and then make a quick dash and kill the lot of us," suggested Andy, who had long been uneasy over the lack of precaution the first part of the night.

"If you was an Injun you'd act like an Injun," countered Joe good-naturedly. "An Injun never makes a move much afore daylight in the morning. That's one thing you can count on. There ain't many."

"Why is that?" asked Andy.

"Skeered," said Joe, "skeered of spirits. All the bad spirits prowl around night times. Shore they do! Don't the streams and waterfalls hush up at night? Don't the mountains throw big rocks all night?"

"Do they?" asked Andy.

"Shore they do! Snow quits melting. Water drops, and so the streams git small. Rocks that has been froze in gits loosened by the sun and takes a tumble when the ground freezes up again and gives 'em a push. You and I know that. But we ain't Injuns. Night's full of funny noises. All spirits. Why looka here, Andy; you take notice. You'll never see an Injun carryin' a grooved bar'l. What guns they got is all smooth-bore. That's one reason you kin stand up and let an Injun shoot at you, barrin' accidents, till further orders. They won't tech a rifled gun. For why? Because the bullet whines. More spirits! Wall, I ain't a-goin' to tell them ary different! So don't worry about no Injuns till long toward dawn. Then keep yore eyes shining."

Andy was learning fast. When his turn came to stand guard he knew enough to keep low, to silhouette the earth's surface as much as he could, to lie quiet, and to listen.

Before the party had left the long-grass country he had one exciting experience. That day they had come to the first sign of human activity— the haze of smoke from a distant grass fire.

"Oh, it ain't going to bother us none," Joe told him. "The old grass is too old and the new grass too green to burn fast. But it means somebody has sot her, and that means keep yore eyes shining."

They came up to the fire, which was eating its way very slowly forward in a long and irregular fringe of low flames, so low and narrow that an active man might easily leap across. Behind them the country, but slightly blackened, showed green with the new grass. It was a lazy fire. Its only activity was supplied by a swarm of birds that darted back and forth through the smoke, and chattered shrilly, apparently excited almost to lunacy by the catastrophic possibilities. In reality they were catching the insects driven up by the flames and stupefied with the smoke; and surely such abundance was enough to drive any hard-working bird into a frenzy.

The trappers camped that night to windward of the fire. As night came on the fire seemed to gain in power; though this was probably an illusion strengthened by the dusk. The eastern sky was for a time pink with the reflected light after sunset. Then the moon rose, blood-red in the smoke.

That night Andy stood the before-dawn watch. The fire fascinated him. In imagination it was an army outpost of campfires, extending miles to beyond the horizon; a serpent winding its crooked way; a slow tide coming in on a broken beach. Occasionally a clump of resinweed would catch and flare high, like a torch. As morning neared a breeze sprang up that quickly freshened to a wind. The flames rose like snakes rearing to look, bent flattened by a gust, reared again, throwing defiant sparks. From his place low to the ground Andy watched them, fascinated. Between the fire and the camp stood tall resinweed in bunches four or five feet high, bending in the rising wind. If the wind should change—But then, Andy remembered, these morning winds never did change. It was a beautiful sight. Andy found his eyes straying back to it constantly; and it was only by an effort of the will that he turned them to the shadowed west whence, if anywhere, danger might be expected. For a long time he peered vigilantly, then permitted himself another look toward the fascination of the flames.

His heart leaped to his throat. Dark figures, dozens of them, were darting here and there, stooping low, surrounding the little camp, firing the resinweed—from a clump of it the flames leaped upward with a roar.

"Indians! Indians!" cried Andy at the top of his lungs; and fired hastily at one of the crouching figures. As he flattened himself, reloading as Joe had taught him, he felt, rather than heard or saw, the sleeping men leap into action. In a moment he was conscious of a touch on his leg, and the Mountain Man hitched himself alongside.

"What did you see, lad?" Joe's low voice came to his ear.

"See them?" the boy's voice shook with excitement in spite of himself. "There! There! They're setting fire to the resinweed!"

For a moment the trapper peered in the direction Andy indicated. Then with a laugh he got to his feet.

"Stand up, boy, and take a look!" he advised aloud.

Andy stood up. He looked, and closed his eyes and looked again. The shadowy hurrying figures had vanished as though dismissed by magic. They had been an illusion evoked by his position so near the ground; the flames, hurried by the wind behind the swaying clumps, had conjured the appearance of crowds moving in the opposite direction. So vivid was the deception that Andy had to stoop again to convince himself. He accompanied Joe to the camp, burning with mortification.

The trappers, however, did not reproach him or laugh at him, for which he was absurdly grateful. Indeed they made no reference to the matter, but seemed to take the dissipation of the alarm quite as a matter of course. Kelly remarked that it was near dawn anyway, and they might as well cook up. They kindled their brief small fire of resinweed and set the coffeepot over it. The business of getting under way proceeded in usual train. Andy

obliterated himself. His face was still red with humiliation. Still no reference whatever was made to the affair. Only, when Andy had finished packing his pack animals and turned to mount his horse, he found neatly tied
to his saddle horn a clump of resinweed.

"Didn't want you to go off leavin' yore first sculp," said Joe.

The trappers' leathern faces were grave. Andy caught no faintest twinkle
in their eyes.

Abruptly the character of the country changed. The high luxuriant
grasses disappeared. Their place was taken by a short, curly growth so insignificant that after the lusher plains the prairies seemed almost barren.

"Buffalo grass," Andy was told. "Wuth two fer one of common grass."
Certainly the horses seemed to think so.

About this time the fuel problem was solved by quantities of dry buffalo
chips. Troughlike trails worn deep in the hard soil, round "wallows," broad
highways of trampled earth, the fairy rings of old herd formations further
attested the beasts' abundance. But these were all old signs.

One night Andy was awakened by a noise. It was not a loud noise, and
was very distant. There were a thousand nearer and louder that had not
disturbed him. But this was unusual. Andy had made this much progress
toward plainscraft; that his senses discriminated, even subconsciously. He
raised himself on his elbow, to find Joe also listening.

"Lobo wolf," whispered the trapper. The long, weird, mournful ulula-
tion again shivered across the moonight. "Good sign fer game. Them varmints don't bother with prairie dogs and rats and sich, like the coyotes.
Listen at him! In a minute he'll quit." Joe partly threw off his blanket
and filled his pipe. "Funny thing about wolves," he went on in a low voice,
once the tobacco was alight. None of the sleepers stirred. Joe's voice rang
no bell of alarm in that part of their consciousness that guarded. Any
one of them would have leaped to alertness at the smallest unwarranted
rustling. "Coyotes howl all the time. Wolves mostly tune up at midnight
and at daybreak; and, that's about all."

"I didn't know they were such a silent beast," whispered Andy.

"Oh, they bark, sort of short and snarling, 'most any time. But they
saves their howls. I like to hear him. Means meat. Buffalo, I hope. Perhaps
only elk. Or mebbe he's just scouting. I hear only one. I'd rather hear Old
Man Raven croak. He's the fellow don't git fur from supplies."

The howl of the wolf proved to be a reliable omen. The very next
morning Andy saw his first buffalo.

It was a lone bull. They came upon him at close range, and suddenly,
over the top of a low rise. He was ancient and thin, and the fur on his hide
was off in patches; but the hair of his head and shoulders was still long and
shaggy. He stood alone, at bay. A pack of gray wolves circled warily but
just out of reach of his lunge, their eyes ablaze with the eagerness of the
chase, trotting this way and that before the old warrior. The buffalo turned
constantly. His enemies were trying to get to his rear; to hamstring him.

Once down he would be at their mercy. He was trying in vain to face them all. Every once in a while one of the wolves darted in, snapped hastily at the old fellow's hindquarters, darted out again as he whirled in that direction.

So occupied were all concerned that not one of them noticed the men and horses, even when by common impulse they drew rein only ten or fifteen yards from the outside circumference of this strange battle. For some minutes the trappers leaned on the pommels, watching. It was evident the issue could not be long in doubt. Already the old buffalo was bleeding from a half-dozen shallow wounds where the sharp teeth of the wolves had snapped home. His sides heaved painfully. His tongue hung out, and a light foam blew away from his half-opened mouth. Each fresh attack he met more slowly, less certainly. The wolves were growing bolder, drawing closer their circle, darting in more frequently.

Kelly looked from one to the other of his companions.

"What say, boys? Shall we give them one?" he asked.

By way of assent the men leisurely dismounted. The flint-gunmen thumbed up the frizzens, shook in the priming powder.

"All ready?" said Kelly. "Let her go!"

A ragged volley rang out. A half-dozen of the marauders wilted or rolled over. One, caught at full speed by some sporting marksman, turned a complete somersault. The rest of the pack, surprised and bewildered, stopped short in full career, stared about them; seemed only slowly to realize the situation; only slowly to replace the eagerness of the kill with their customary sense of self-preservation. A few loped away; a few trotted. One or two even hesitated, snarled, bared their teeth. The trappers dropped the butts of their long rifles to earth, laughing in their silent fashion, immensely diverted.

Andy had welcomed Kelly's suggestion with a leap of joy. He had been the first afoot; the first to stand quiveringly eager for the word to fire. The wolf he had picked out as his mark had gone down satisfactorily. Now, while his companions stood in relish of the incident, he was hastily but methodically reloading. He was full of excitement and what might almost have been described as an indignant lust of battle. His sympathies had been strongly enlisted by the old buffalo's gallant stand. Nevertheless, in spite of his eagerness, he recharged the piece accurately, without mistake or false motion. The deerhorn charger he filled to the exact brim. The powder went into the barrel without the loss of a grain. The ball was precisely centered on the patch. He drove it home with the deft neat thrust from the wrist that seated it exactly, but without undue pressure. He capped the rifle without a fumble. He was quite unconscious of the fact that the trappers were watching him attentively.

The remainder of the pack had come together and were loping away across the prairie. But they were not yet wholly reconciled to the turn of events. Every few yards one or the other of them stopped, turned, half reared to look back. As Andy finished loading, one of them did just this. Only its head and its forward-pricked ears were visible above the fringe of grass. Still heated with his partisanship of what had been a losing battle, Andy steadied the long rifle, and as the bead, nestling clearly in the notch of the rear sight, came to rest, he pulled trigger.

"Good shot!" cried Kelly.

"Wagh!" cried several voices.

Andy looked around, awakened from his absorption, a little confused to find himself the center of attention. Joe Crane was capering about delightedly.

"I told you!" he addressed them all in general. "He makes them *come!*" He seemed suddenly informed with a pride of proprietorship in the boy. "And did you see him load! Spilled nary a grain and quicker'n ary rattle-snake coils. Forty rod, full, or I'm a horny toad. And I'll bet any of you a plew of beaver plumb atween the eyes!" He clapped Andy so heartily between the shoulder blades as almost to overset him, then tore away across the prairie to the dead wolf.

"Ef you kin do it thataway right along yo'll save yore ha'r yet, Andy," said Bill Williams.

Andy was embarrassed. He did not know where to turn. He tried to recover himself by setting about recharging his rifle.

Joe was back again waving the wolf scalp, his hands daubed with gore.

"Plumb atween the eyes!" he cried triumphantly. He rushed up to Andy and with a bloody forefinger smeared the boy's forehead. "That'll make ye wise like a wolf; and they's no animal wiser." He tore from Andy's saddle the withered bunch of resinweed, which Andy had been too proud to re-move, and in its place tied the wolf scalp. "Workin' up," said he with satis-faction. "You'll have real ha'r there yet!" He patted Andy again on the shoulder. "You make 'em *come!*" he repeated. A sudden thought checked him. "Has she got a name?" he inquired.

"What?" Andy found his voice, puzzled.

Joe laid his hand on the long rifle.

"The Boone gun," said Joe.

"I don't know. I suppose it must have. I never heard it."

"Well, she has now. Old Knock-'Em-Stiff, that's her!"

"Let's get on," said Kelly.

They mounted and turned away. The buffalo bull still stood in the middle of the trampled ground, his head low, his eyes fixed dully on the scattered bodies of his assailants. Andy looked back.

"What about him?" he asked.

"He's too old and stringy," returned Joe, misunderstanding the purport of the question. "Cast bull, druv out of the herd. Whar there's one there's others. We'll find fat cow shortly."

"But what will become of him? Will he get well?"

"Oh, the wolves'll git him tonight," replied the Mountain Man indifferently. "What you doin'?" he asked, as Andy dismounted.

The boy did not reply. Slowly he walked back to where the buffalo stood, his front still lowered in defiance of imaginary enemies. For several seconds he stood contemplating the forlorn old creature. Then for the third time he raised the rifle, for the third time the silvered bead came steadily to rest on its mark. At the crack of the piece the old bull sank forward on his knees; slowly rolled to its side; stretched out as though to rest, with a tired sigh.

"Now whatever did you do that for, Andy!" Joe demanded in astonishment as the boy remounted.

Andy did not reply. Thus he killed his first buffalo. For the moment he felt that he never wanted to kill another.

Not long afterward they saw a small band of twenty or thirty buffalo in the middle distance, showing black and immense upon the short grass; and soon afterward others and others of similar groups, until the whole extent of the plain to the north was dotted with them here and there. Andy had never conceived of wild game in such numbers; but his companions made light of his amazement. According to them he had not even begun to see buffalo. These few and scattered individuals were negligible.

As time to camp drew near, one of the men loped on ahead. Shortly they heard the distant faint *ping* of his rifle, and, turning in that direction, came upon him after a considerable ride seated on the carcass of a cow, smoking his pipe. He half apologized for taking them so far; the buffalo were scarce; this was the first cow he could find near water.

Andy hovered about the butchering, fascinated by the deftness with which they went at it. It was so different from the dressing of tame meat. Four of them heaved the carcass on its belly, spreading the legs to hold it in that position. Then one slit the hide along the spine, and the skin was peeled away on either side, so that it lay flat on the prairie, a spread mat beneath the carcass, protecting the meat from contamination by the earth. They cut out the tongue; they peeled away the hump and back strap, which they piled on the skin. One of the men carefully filled his canteen with blood from the body cavity. Andy experienced a slight heave at the stomach. Others skinned back and chopped off the leg bones.

"Guess that's about all," said Bill Williams.

With a mighty heave the body was rolled aside. Bill Williams, with his tomahawk, opened the ribs and from within carefully extracted certain tidbits. The whole they wrapped in the hide, slapped it across a pack, and moved a few hundred yards to the water spoken of by the hunter. It was murky and fouled by the beasts, undrinkable except as boiled with coffee, and then with a strong menagerie flavor. Andy controlled his squeamishness with difficulty; but times were to come when he was to remember the tepid nauseous stuff with longing. But the abandonment of so much good meat bothered him.

"Oh, we got enough for everybody," Joe assured him. "Yore eyes is gittin' bigger'n yore belly."

He could not comprehend Andy's idea of waste. There would be plenty more tomorrow. Later, when it seemed they might be running out of the herd, would be time enough to begin to save meat. When finally he understood the boy's point of view, he was amazed.

"Why, they's plenty buffalo," said he. He laughed a little at Andy as having been brought up on a farm with a few cattle. "You ain't seen buffalo yit," he assured the lad. "These is nothing." He tried to give Andy an idea. Not hundreds, nor thousands, but millions, moving across the wide-flung country like locusts. The earth black with them from horizon to horizon.

"I've traveled six days through them, movin' steady," said Joe, "solid pack. And then three days more of little bunches, like these yere, afore we got out onta clear plains agin. One time we couldn't move at all for three days. Too thick to break through. Had to roost top of a little rise. You'll see."

What did the few killed by man for his uses amount to? Nothing as compared to the stupendous natural waste incident to their mere numbers. Prairie fires in the dry of the year leaped on the fleeing herds like savage beasts and swept on, leaving the plains strewn with bodies, staggering with blind, singed victims. Stampedes trampled down the young and the weak by thousands. The ice of the rivers broke beneath their weight, and the swollen current of the spring thaws carried downstream, for days and days, a continuous line of the drowned.

"An old Nor'wester, name of MacDonnell, told me he counted atween seven and eight thousand drowned buffalo floatin' past his post; and then he got sick of countin' and quit," said Joe, "and of course that was just a few of the main herd that was out of luck."

And in addition wolves and coyotes always hovering about the herds to snatch down a calf or a yearling or to pounce upon some old lone bull, swarms of them. All of them made a living. In face of this orgy of nature's waste what effect the few hundreds or the few thousands appropriated by man, white or red, for his own uses? Or even the additional few thousands sacrificed, perhaps, to his wantonness?

"Why, if we all had a ton of powder and lead apiece," concluded Joe, "and done nothin' but shoot buffalo from now till Christmas time, we wouldn't make a dent in the outlyin' fringe of one herd! The man who eats brisket when he can git hump is just a tarnation fool. Wagh!"

Andy turned in his saddle to look back. He was amazed. The carcass had almost disappeared. Only a partly dismembered framework remained half visible through a black and flopping crowd of vultures. Other vultures soared and beat their wings just above. Still others, their wings held away from their bodies, sat upright on the ground, disgruntled or gorged. A dozen coyotes weaved restlessly back and forth. Joe, too, looked back; and laughed.

"Aint's much wasted thar!" said he.

They roasted the meat. Andy thought he had never tasted anything so delicious. Joe triumphed.

"What I tell you!" he cried. "That's *eatin'!*"

Andy sighed with repletion; eyed a choice bit uncertainly; gave up the idea.

"Couldn't get down another mouthful," he confessed. "Lord, I'm full! Guess I'll turn in!"

"No you don't!" cried Joe. "That's jist the first course to sort of take off the edge."

One of the men put over a pot of water to heat. Others busied themselves in cracking the leg bones and deftly extracting the marrow, which they dropped into the pot. The man who had filled his canteen with blood produced it and stirred in its contents.

"Git yore cups," cried the one who was doing the cooking, after about five minutes. "Next course!"

Andy tasted the mess gingerly and with misgivings.

"Why, it's good!" he cried surprised. The marrow had melted. The whole had cooked into a rich, well-flavored soup.

The remark was greeted by a general laugh. Under the stimulus of feast after comparative famine the customary silent gravity had broken into a comfortable and expansive good-fellowship. Even the dour and saturnine countenance of Bill Williams bore the slightly fatuous satisfaction of a well-fed baby. They filled their pipes and smoked awhile. A comfortable drowsiness seemed to fall upon their spirits. The smoldering little fire died to acrid coals. About as Andy was sinking to a doze of repletion, Fitz roused himself.

"Come on, boys, time for dessert," said he.

They stirred lazily to action. One coaxed up the fire. By its feeble light others, volunteers, set about further preparations. On the clean inner surface of the buffalo's skin they proceeded carefully to chop a portion of the backstrap into a fine hash. As soon as a sufficient quantity of this had been prepared they stuffed it into cleaned intestines, stuck them on sticks, and roasted them over the coals.

"Thar!" said Joe, proffering one of these sausages to Andy. "Stick that in yore face, and tell me if you ever tasted any better in yore settlemints!"

"I can't!" protested Andy. "I'm full way up to here!"

"Wagh! Eat!" commanded the trapper. "If yore goin' to be a Mountain Man you got to larn to swell yore belly out like a dawg."

"I'll be as sick as a dog if I do," Andy remonstrated. "I'm full, I tell you!"

"Wild meat'll never make you sick," said Joe emphatically. "You can starve for a week and then eat till yore skin cracks and nary a bellyache in a ton of it. It's tame meat makes you sick. Yere, ketch a holt!"

To his surprise Andy found room for more. And it, too, was delicious. But he was benumbed by food, dizzy with repletion. He rolled into his blankets and fell instantly deep into torpor.

But his sleep was sound and dreamless. Morning seemed to come instantly. He arose in its freshness full of energy and life.

"What I tell you?" cried Joe. "That's the stuff'll put ha'r on yore chest! Wagh!"

As they rode forward that day the groups of buffalo gradually became more numerous, until one could look in no direction without a sight of dozens of little bands, each in charge of its vigorous and truculent bull. When toward close of afternoon Andy learned that more meat was to be required, he eagerly petitioned to be appointed the hunter. His sporting blood was hot with the sight of so much game. Receiving the desired permission, he galloped ahead until he had placed a good interval between himself and his more slowly moving companions. Then he dismounted, tied his horse to an old skull, and set himself to a slow stalk of one of the little herds. He did so in approved fashion, with due concern for the light wind currents; and so, shortly, found himself lying flat in the short grass within a hundred yards of the animals. Some were lying down; some were afoot, grazing. One tremendous shaggy beast stood a few paces apart. He looked to be half again as big as any of the others.

His heart beating strongly from excitement, Andy thrust forward the long rifle, steadied its sights for a moment on the big beast's shoulder, and pulled trigger.

No result.

The buffalo did not budge a hair. Its companions continued to recline or to graze.

It did not seem possible to have missed completely at that distance, but there you were! Andy burned with mingled mortification and anger at himself. He reloaded in frantic haste, fearful that at any moment the buffalo would take alarm and depart. They did not. Again he took aim, more carefully this time. Again he fired. Again no apparent result.

After a moment the big buffalo seemed to awaken from his meditation. He curled his tail and began to walk slowly about. It began to look as though he had come to a reluctant conclusion that he was getting tired of being shot at; and was thinking of waking up his companions to a retreat. But as he turned Andy saw a thin froth of blood at his nostrils.

His heart leaped in a surge of new confidence as he drove the bullet down the barrel. Then he had not missed! He resolved that the next shot should finish the matter. By the time the reloading was finished the buffalo was showing signs of weakness. He staggered slightly. Andy arose to his feet; walked forward as quietly as he could. All heads turned toward him; every jaw stopped in mid-chew. For the space of time it took Andy to cover ten yards they stared incredulous. Then instantaneously they were all afoot and off in their strange clumsy-looking but swift gallop. One moment they were immobile; the next they were in full flight. Those lying down were no whit behind the others. They did not get up like a cow or a horse, but seemed fairly to spring afoot and off in one motion. Andy was completely surprised. He stared helplessly at the cloud of dust and the half-visible black forms weaving through it, unable to see anything clearly long enough to deliver a shot. The wounded buffalo had made off as spryly as the rest.

They ran for a quarter mile; then stopped, whirled, and looked back; stared for a moment; turned again and once more plunged into a gallop. In the course of their flight they had run near a number of other small herds. These had joined them. Still others, within easy distance to right or left, also set themselves in motion, paralleling the first. The movement spread, until in an incredibly brief span of time the whole plains were acrawl, and the dust clouds rose like smoke. Andy felt he had certainly started something!

Then his heart bounded with fresh hope. A single black speck had fallen behind its fleeing companions. It slowed to a walk. It lay down. The wounded bull!

The animal was evidently dying. Its nose already rested on the earth. Andy hurried forward eagerly. But when he was still at some distance, his quarry rose to its feet; stood for a moment uncertainly; then appeared to gather strength and made off. Andy's shot, hastily delivered at the distant and moving target, seemed to take no effect.

But the beast did not go as far this time. It slowed to a painful, plodding walk; at last lay down again.

Profiting by experience, Andy's second approach was more cautious. But there was no concealing cover, and the plain here was as flat as a board. Move as slowly as he might, he was still some hundred yards distant when again the buffalo rose to his feet. This time Andy took pains. He heard the bullet hit, and he was sure he had held steadily for the exact shot he had selected. But the shot had no other effect than to start the beast off more vigorously than ever.

Andy's blood was up. He set himself seriously to the task. In the next hour he got in four more shots, all at long range. He tried sneaking; he tried running as hard as he could, hoping to get into closer range. The last bullet did the trick—or the cumulative effect of them all. This time the buffalo did not rise again.

Andy reloaded and ran up. The beast was dead.

He came to himself. He stood alone, with his quarry, in the middle of an emptied plain. The sun had dipped almost to the horizon. Slowly his heart sank to dismay as he looked about him. He had not the remotest idea of the whereabouts of his horse; of the whereabouts of his companions; of the direction the chase had led him. Belatedly he realized

he should at least have noted its twists and turns; the sun was plain enough
in the sky. But he had not. Whether he was north, south, east, or west
of his original position he had no means of knowing. Nor could he even
remotely guess. He was lost, and lost aplenty; and he had not the least
idea of what to do about it. He cursed himself heartily for all kinds of
a fool. But that did no good. He sat down on the dead buffalo to think it
over.

For a time he came near to panic. Only by a strong effort of what might
be called subconscious common sense did he hold himself from rushing
off regardless. However, he hung onto himself. Here at least was meat. He
had his rifle, ammunition, flint and steel, a canteen of water. He would
not starve immediately. What he could do ultimately he did not know.
If he had had the faintest notion as to whether he was north or south of
the line of march, he might, by angling in the proper direction, have cut
in. But he had none.

By an effort of resolution he thrust aside all consideration of the appalling difficulties in the way of his mere survival. The thing to do was to
attend to the immediate. He slit the skin about the buffalo hump, and
rather bunglingly cut out a slab of meat. He twisted some grass into a tiny
nest in the center of which he deposited a bit of burning punk ignited by
the flint and steel. This he waved about in the air until it burst into flames.
More grass; little chips of fuel added gingerly—he had a tiny fire which
he nursed with care. The sun had almost touched the horizon. Night
hovered just beyond the rim of the world, ready to overflow, and with it
a mighty and appalling spirit of loneliness. Against it and its engulfing
terrors Andy had only the protection of his present tasks. He moved small
beneath them, executing them slowly, spreading them thin, postponing
the moment when he must front the gathering inimical forces. He did not
dare look about him lest he meet their faces. So he did not see Joe Crane,
leading his abandoned saddle horse, nor suspect his presence until the
Mountain Man spoke.

"Wall, bub," drawled Joe, "havin' a good time?"

Andy nearly leaped out of his skin. For a moment the reaction of
mingled emotions overwhelmed him. He could not speak. Strangely enough
this solution of his predicament had never occurred to him.

Crane leisurely dismounted, dropped the reins of his horse to the
ground, and walked over to the buffalo. He poked the toe of his moccasin
here and there in the shaggy fur.

"Put enough lead in him to sink a bull boat, didn't ye?" he commented casually. He continued his examination. A quizzical smile curled
his grave lips. "You shore picked you a good old tough one," said he.
"Wa'nt they no cows to be had?" He stopped to inspect Andy's butchering,
and straightened his back with every appearance of indignation. "What
do you mean by that!" he cried accusingly.

"What?" stammered Andy.

"Don't you know better than to cut good meat across the grain?" demanded Joe. "Whar you been brung up? My God, I never *see* sich ignorance!"

"I—I'm sorry; I didn't know," gulped Andy.

"Didn't know! Didn't know! I should say not!" grumbled Joe. "It's a crime to spile good meat thataway! Not that it's good meat—a tough old bull like that!" He fussed about for a moment or so longer, muttering to himself. Then he sat down on the buffalo and filled his pipe, watching the disconsolate Andy the while from beneath his bushy brows. "If I didn't know you had the makin's in you, Andy, I'd think you was a plumb fool." Said he after a moment, "Look at what you've gone and done! Fust off you leaves yore hoss whar ary redskin kin pick him up, and pick you up afterward. Then you picks you out the oldest and toughest bull in a herd of fat cows. Then you spatters him anywheres in his carcass regardless."

But Andy's reviving spirit interposed a mild objection to this.

"I hit him where I aimed," he muttered. "My rifle is too light." And indeed the bullet holes were well grouped behind the beast's shoulder.

"And whar did you aim?" Joe countered relentlessly. "Don't you know a buffalo's heart lies low? Looka here." He reached out and moved the animal's foreleg back and forth to expose a small bare spot just behind the shoulder. "Thar's yore mark. You kin see it when he steps. Yore rifle is heavy enough; thar's many a buffalo killed with balls lighter'n yours. Yo're shootin' too high."

"I didn't know," protested Andy.

"They's a lot of things you don't know. And then you goes chasin' him all over the prairie."

"I didn't want him to get away."

"Then why didn't you let him lay? If'n you chase a wounded animal he'll run fer miles. If'n you let him be, he'll lie down and all you have to do is to wait. Then you gits so busy I'm right on top of you afore you knows I'm yere. Supposin' I'd a-been an Injun? And then you finishes off by cuttin' meat across the grain!" Joe seemed to think this the greatest crime of all. He surveyed Andy severely, then relented a little. "You did know enough to send up a smoke," he conceded, "to find you by."

But Andy could not claim even this small credit.

"I didn't think of that," he confessed: "I was just going to cook me some meat."

"Wall"—Joe spat at the guilty fire—"if'n you'd only fell down a prairie-dog hole and broke yore leg, she'd have been complete!"

Andy was uncomfortably in the feeling of a small boy. He had to take thought to keep himself from shifting from one foot to the other. But as Joe continued placidly to smoke his pipe, and the sun continued to dip, he at last mustered up courage to ask a question.

"Oughtn't we to be getting back to find the others?" he suggested.

Joe grunted.

"They'll be along. No, you needn't bother to hunch up that fire. *They* got hoss track to follow."

Andy subsided.

A little later the trappers rode up. Each man dismounted and looked about him. Andy stood shrinkingly tense, awaiting comment on his performance. He knew that no detail escaped their slow, grave, expert scrutiny —the tough, stringly bull, the exposed position, the lack of water. But nobody said anything. They dismounted, unsaddled, hobbled the horses for the too brief ranging that could be permitted them before dark and the restrictions of the picket rope. Andy experienced a gush of gratitude for this forbearance.

But, it seemed, all did not take the situation with equal philosophy. Tilton, the man who in a fit of rage had killed his mule at the start of the expedition, was in a bad temper over the affair. His black looks shortly found a voice. He grumbled to himself as he moved about. Finally he began to express himself audibly. Addressing nobody in particular he gave his unbiased opinions.

Miles off the route! No water! No meat fit to eat! No chance to graze the horses! That's what comes of taking a greenhorn along! Why, he didn't even know enough to—

"You said enough, Red. You leave Andy be!" interposed Joe Crane steadily. "Mebbe he didn't know enough to—this-an'-that. But he does now. He larns; and that's more than I'll say for some."

"Meanin'?" demanded Tilton.

"You know the size of yore moccasins, and what fits yore feet." Joe sketched in the air the merest suggestion of the sign-language symbol for mule.

Tilton uttered a strangled bellow of rage, snatched his knife from its sheath. Joe bared his own blade.

But before they could come together Kelly, who had been lying on his side at some little distance, with one motion, like released whalebone, leaped between them.

"None of that!" he commanded sharply; and then, as they continued to press forward, he placed the palms of his hands against their chests and hurled them violently apart. It was a remarkable exhibition of agility and strength; for the belligerents staggered back like children.

Tilton was now foaming with rage. Given a split second he would have turned his attack on Kelly, who was unarmed. But the latter allowed him no split second.

"Stand still!" He did not raise his voice, but the command cracked like a rifle. "If you want to fight, there is the open prairie. But understand this: if you leave this camp for any such purpose, you needn't come back. I'll have no quarreling. And if there's any fighting among ourselves while this outfit is together, I'll be doing some of it." He held them for an appreciable time by sheer force of dominance.

Joe thrust his knife into his belt and turned away. Tilton's lowered red head shook back and forth sullenly, but he, too, reluctantly sheathed his blade. He muttered something about the mountains—"ain't through with me yet—"

"I don't care what you do when you get to the mountains," Kelly cut him short. "But as long as we're together I'll have no fighting among ourselves. We'll save that for the Comanches."

The other men made no comment. They had sat grave and impassive, aloof. No one could have guessed their opinions.

Nothing further was said. But the atmosphere was troubled. The psychic climate, so to speak, had changed.

Andy wrapped himself in his blanket. He was very low in his mind. In spite of his companions' forbearing tact, so little to be expected from such rough and direct characters, in spite of Joe's championship, it had been a miserable day. At any other time this first bivouac among the buffalo would have thrilled him to the core. Evidently the beasts had drifted back; or new bands had taken the places of those his awkwardness had driven away. The night was resonant. Bulls snorted; coyotes wailed like devils; wolves snarled and barked; ravens, not yet settled down for the night, screamed and croaked in a thousand voices. A surge of restless vitality arose from the darkened earth like an emanation. Calmness, the peace of night, had withdrawn to the remoteness of the stars, but it was not missed. The tumult of replacement excited like the beat of savage drums.

Andy, however, was encased in the complete insulation of his boyish chagrins. Over and over the events of the day thrust themselves upon him. He writhed beneath their recollection.

Alongside, Joe was disposing himself deliberately for the night. When he had settled down to his own satisfaction he turned his head in Andy's direction.

"Ain't nary wolf born wise," he observed. "Know a lot more'n you did this morning, don't ye, bub? That's somethin'. Funny thing is, Ben Tilton don't. Never will. That's about all the differ atween folks. Some larns; some don't."

Andy choked. He dared not trust his voice. He reached out his hand and timidly patted Joe's recumbent form.

"Wagh!" said the Mountain Man roughly. "Go to sleep and git ye a good rest. And don't never cut no more meat across the grain."

RENDEZVOUS

by A. B. GUTHRIE

A. B. Guthrie, Jr. is a phenomenon in American letters, being one of the first men to write wholly of the West and at the same time fully accepted in critical circles. His first important book was The Big Sky, *and it was so true to its background, its language rang so well on the ear, and its story flowed so cleanly that it was hailed as a masterpiece. One of the tests of a classic is that it does not have to be rewritten. Of* The Big Sky *this is so true that only a very brave writer would try to match it. In his next book,* The Way West, *Guthrie moved into a later period—the great westering. With* These Thousand Hills *Guthrie struck trouble in separating myth from history. In the excerpt from* The Big Sky *which follows, Guthrie captures the rendezvous with all of its madness and wild beauty.*

There was still snow above the Wind River plains, a deep snow with an old crust that skinned the front legs of the lead horse after he had broken through. Boone and Jim and Summers took turns breaking trail, so as to even the hurt among the horses. Loaded with furs and traps and bedding, the two pack animals followed along, one behind Boone and one behind Jim, and at the rear came Poordevil, riding the horse they had spared him and singing out "Hi-yi" every once in a while. Whenever Boone looked back Poordevil gave a big grin, showing the slot in his teeth. Sometimes he would pull out of the trail and lunge up alongside of Boone and grin again and say some fool thing just to hear his own voice. "Heap beaver heap quick betcha goddam." Down from the hills the plains looked almost dusty, and warm and quiet, as if below the reach of the winds that on the ridges were like a hand pushing into a man's face. Boone could see buffalo below, like a fluid stain on the tanned grass, and bunches of trees, and antelopes moving light and easy as birds. The sunlight lay yellow and soft on them all, seeming to have a warmth down there that it lost on the high places. Across the plains to the west the Wind River mountains climbed into snow banks.

Boone told himself they would find fur, traveling few and quiet this way. Big parties, like Jim Bridger's, put such a fright into beaver they wouldn't stir from their lodges or wouldn't come to medicine if they did. Even when the parties thought it was safe enough to split up, they left more beaver than they caught, what with one man holding a rifle and the other setting traps and both of them splashing along and maybe talking. A man took chances, hunting small; Indians might happen on him any day. If he kept his scalp, though, he got plews. And the risk wasn't so great with Summers along—not with a man along who could tell from the eye and ear of a horse or the set of a buffalo whether there was aught about. Boone figured he and Jim had got good themselves at smelling Indians; they wouldn't have their hair if they hadn't. He had seen men at rendezvous wouldn't know a war whoop if they heard one. Some of them were dead now, and others were bound to be, in time, if they didn't learn better, or if they didn't quit the mountains, as some of them were doing, and some true trappers, too. They had hurt the hunting, though, pushing up every trickle of water until there was hardly a place a man could feel was fresh any more.

It gave him a little pinch when he thought about them, about pork eaters from Canada and Missouri graybacks and Yankee traders and men from Kentucky and Tennessee moving in, traveling along streams and through passes that a man liked to think were his own, just as it gave him a pinch when he thought back to last year and remembered the white women that a couple of crazy preachers had brought to rendezvous on Horse Creek, bound on across to the Columbia. Damned if they weren't on wheels, those preachers and their women! He heard later they got a cart as far as the British post on the Boise. White women! And wheels! They figured to spoil a country, except that the woman would leave or die. Ask any hunter who had fought Indians and gone empty-stomached and like to froze, and he'd say it was no place for women, or for preachers, either, or farmers. And no place for wagons or carts, except maybe to bring trade goods as far as rendezvous. The rocks would knock them to pieces, and the rivers wash them down, and the sun shrivel the wheels apart. All the same, he got a pinch of misery, thinking, just as he had sometimes in Kentucky when he'd be out in the woods, feeling good that he was alone, with everything to himself, and then he would spy someone and it would all be spoiled, as if the country wasn't his any more, or the woods or the quiet.

Ahead of him, Jim's hair streamed from under his hat like a lick of fire. Jim let his hair hang long and loose, like Summers. For himself, Boone liked it better in a couple of plaits, like the Indians wore it, tied at the end with red cloth. He would get himself some new ribbons, come the rendezvous, and a new hunting shirt and leggings, with some hawks' bells and colored strings for the fringes. Buckskin got old and greasy in a year and lost its fringes, one by one, as a man needed laces for his moccasins. He would buy himself a new rifle, too, a percussion Hawken, about thirty-two balls to the pound; people were coming to see that cap and ball was better than a flintlock, just as he had always said. And he would play some hand and drink some whisky and have himself a squaw, and then he would be ready to go on. There wasn't any sense in staying when a man's beaver was spent.

Summers pulled up and swung his leg from across his horse and stood looking down at the plains, which seemed close but would take a spell to get to with the going like it was. Though spring was coming on, Summers still wore his old capote with the hood that came up from it and went over his head. He reached inside and got out a piece of roasted liver and began to munch while his eye traveled north and south and back again. Jim dismounted, too, and then Boone, and from the back Poordevil came galloping up and threw himself from his horse, showing off, and fell in the snow. Summers handed him a piece of liver when he got up. Poordevil grinned and bit into it and cleaned the slot with his tongue and took another bite.

Summers said, "This nigger's had enough of sagebrush fires and cold camps. That there timber looks good."

"It's like someone forgot to put a tree between the Powder and the Popo Agie," Jim said. "I aim to put my feet to a sure-enough fire and cook meat over quaking ash and set and set and eat and eat. It wears a body down, pullin' stems to keep a blaze."

Over nothing, Poordevil said, "Oh, goddam!" and laughed.

"You can't tell from what the nigger says what's bitin' him." Summers' gray eye was studying the Indian.

"He just talks to hear hisself, like a boy shootin' a new rifle at nothin'."

"All the same," Boone said, "he's comical. I wouldn't care no more for a bear cub."

Poordevil saw they were talking about him and felt big for it. He hit himself on the chest. "Hi-yi. Love whisky, me."

"Git on your medicine dog, you crazy bastard," Summers said. "We're goin' to kill us a bull and build a fire." Before he mounted he added, "We'll poke along the Popo Agie and the Wind and maybe up the Horn, dependin'. We'll catch beaver enough with the plews we got from fall, I'm thinkin'."

Jim faced half around to the north. "Reckon we'd fare better up a ways?"

"With Bridger's men thicker'n wolves around a hurt cow!"

Boone said, "Rendezvous is comin' soon enough, Jim. You'll see all them as is on Clark's Fork."

Summers said to Boone, "Ol' Red Head is a sociable nigger."

The horses stood slack in the snow, their eyes sad and lifeless, their ribs showing through the long winter hair.

"I'll break the way for a spell," Boone said, and stooped and examined the knees of his horse. "Come to Tar Springs, I'll doctor ye, Blackie," he promised. Blackie was a good horse, for all that he was ganted up now. Let the Indians have their white and spotted buffalo ponies; he would take a solid dark.

The bull Boone killed was young and fat enough, fatter than a cow would be now with a calf pulling on her and the grass scant yet. A couple of wolves loped up out of nowhere at the sound of the shot, and from a sky that didn't have a bird in it three crows came flapping. They lighted a little piece off and stepped back and forth, all the while keeping their sharp eyes on the butchering. The wolves rumped down to wait, their tongues hanging out and dripping, their gaze following the tenderloin and tongue and liver and marrowbone that Boone and Summers packed on the horses. The horses had come alive, now they were out of the snow, and kept cropping at the grass, eating it clear down into the dirt.

There was a good camping spot, with a small meadow almost shut in by the trees, near where the Wind and the Popo Agie joined to make the Horn. The four men pulled the saddles off and hobbled the horses with rawhide and turned them loose to graze. Summers took a long look around first, saying as he nearly always did, "It's a sight better to count ribs than tracks," and meaning it was better to keep a horse tied up and hungry than to turn him loose and let him get stolen by Indians.

Poordevil gathered wood, and Summers laid it and struck fire. In a little while all of them had sticks slanted over the blaze with chunks of liver on the ends. Jim had put a pot on the fire, too, into which he had cut pieces of bull meat.

Summers said, "Wisht we had some coffee," and Jim put in, "I hanker for salt," but straight meat and river water were good enough. They kept up a man's strength and never made him sick, no matter how much he ate, and made his blood good, too. A mountain man never got a running sore or a toothache or shook with a fever—or almost never, anyway. After a while he lost his taste for salt and bread and greens and such.

It was warmer down in the valley and clear of snow except where the trees grew thick and kept the wind and sun away. The sun was shining now, far off, giving only a touch of warmth when it lay on the back of a man's hand. It was making downward for the Wind River mountains that reared up, white where the snow lay and blue on the bare rock. From the west the wind was puffing.

After he had a bellyful Boone stretched out with his feet to the fire and his head on the saddle and slept. When he awakened the sun was near to the mountains, fixing soon to sink from sight.

"Jim went downstream, him and Poordevil," Summers informed him. Summers was spreading skins over some saplings to make a lodge.

"I'll point up, soon's I get my outfit on." He peeled off his leggings and got into a pair that had been cut off at the knees and pieced out with a blanket. There was nothing gave a trapper misery like hide drying tight on the legs, unless it was moccasins that hadn't been smoked enough and pinched a man so, drying out, that he had to cripple out of his bed at night and dip them in the water again. Boone's own moccasins were made from an old lodge skin that was half smoke itself.

There were beaver left all right. Boone saw cuttings along the stream and after a little came to a dam and peeked over. The pond lay smooth at first, and then a wedge of ripples started close to the bank and the point of it came toward him and sharpened into a head and turned and went the other way and sank into the water without a sound, leaving just the ripples running out and whispering along the banks.

Boone slipped along the shore, walking soft in the snow that lay old and coarse underneath the trees, keeping back from the ice that edged the pond where the water was shallow. When he found a likely place, he walked around it and went beyond and laid his traps down. He leaned his rifle against a bush, cut and sharpened a long, dry stick and cocked a trap, and then, carrying rifle and stick and trap, went to the spot he had chosen. He rested his rifle on the bank there, felt for footing on the fringe of ice, stepped on it once and then beyond it, into the water.

The water was cold—so cold it knotted the flesh, so cold it made a man wish for a larger stream where he could use a dugout and poke quietly along the banks, dry as could be. He lifted a foot out of the water, grunting a little with the cramp in it, and put it back and brought the other one up. After that, they didn't hurt him any more, feeling only dead and wooden in his moccasins. He felt the mud stiff and thick under his soles and saw bubbles rising around his ankles and smelled the sulphur smell they brought up.

He stooped and put the cocked trap in the water, so that the surface came a hand above the trigger, and let the chain out into deeper water until he came to the end of it. Then he slipped the stick through the ring in the chain and pushed the stick in the mud, putting all his weight to it. He tapped it next with his ax to make sure it was secure enough. Back at the bank he cut a willow twig and peeled it, and from his belt took the point of antelope horn he kept his medicine in. The medicine came to his nose, strong and gamy, as he took the stopper out. He dipped the twig in the medicine, restoppered his bottle and put it back, and stooped again and thrust the dry end of the twig into the mud between the jaws of the trap, so that the baited end stuck about four inches above the surface of the water. It wouldn't be long, he reckoned, until a beaver came to medicine. Backing up, he toed out the footprints his moccasins had left. With his hands he splashed water on the bank so as to drown out his scent. He reached out and got his rifle then and waded along the edge of the pond. When he came opposite his traps he stepped ashore.

By the time Boone had set four traps it had grown too dark to place the other two. He went back to camp with them, to find Summers and Jim and Poordevil eating boiled bull off pieces of bark, as the Snake Indians did. He found a chunk of bark himself and spooned meat on it and took the knife from his belt and ate. The spoon and kettle and one can, and the knives they wore, were all they had for cooking and eating since the Crows had paid them a visit in the fall.

"Beaver about," Jim said, and Boone nodded and went on chewing.

Summers was looking out into the closing darkness. He got up after a while, stiffly, and took his rifle. "Travel weather. I'm thinkin' we'll see Injuns any time. Best to bring in the horses and peg 'em close."

Poordevil said, "Medicine dogs all gone."

"Don't git to it afore it happens," Boone answered. "You mean medicine dogs'll be all gone."

"All gone. Goddam." He trailed along after Summers to bring the horses up.

Afterwards they all sat around the fire for a time, smoking and looking into it and not saying anything much. When his feet were dry Boone went into the lodge and laid himself down. He heard the others getting up and yawning and making a splatter on the ground before they came to bed, and then he didn't hear them any more, for the wind was flowing along with his dreams, flowing in the north country, rippling the grass, singing around lodges he had never seen till now.

The days were gone when a man could sleep as long as he wanted and get up lazy and eat some meat and lie down again, glad for warmth and a full stomach and even the ice that put the beaver out of reach. It wasn't quite sunup when Boone awakened, hearing the sharp chirp of a winter bird that spring was giving a voice to.

The others were sleeping, except for Summers who was sitting up and shivering a little. Poordevil was snoring a kind of whistling snore, as if the gap in his teeth gave a special sound to it. Every time the bird cheeped, he would stop and then start in again, maybe getting the cheep mixed up in his dreams. Jim's head was covered by his blanket. You would think he was a dead one, back in the settlements, lying there quiet with the cover over him from toe to scalp lock.

There was still some fire left, and some meat in the pot. Shaking in his buckskins, Boone threw some grass on the coals and nosed sticks over them. The flame came up, making him feel warmer just from the sight of it. The sun bulged up from the eastern hills, catching the Wind River mountains first and turning the snowbanks whiter than any cloud. Not a thing moved as far as Boone could tell, and not a noise sounded, except for Poordevil's whistling snore and the fire busy among the sticks. Even the bird had fallen silent. The wind itself was still now, blown over east and gone, and a man listening heard only his ears straining.

Boone set the pot by the fire and went to the horses, standing dull and patient, hobbled and tied to their picket lines. Blackie nickered and nosed Boone's shoulder as Boone bent over the knot.

When the horses were watered he tied them up again. They would have time to graze later after the morning hunt was over.

"Fair morning," Summers said when he came back. "Good thaw, though, or a rain, and the streams'll be too high for huntin'." He was looking west, to the snowbanks that looked clean-washed on the mountains.

They set out after they had eaten, Jim and Poordevil downstream and Boone up, and Summers across to the Wind.

The pond lay quiet as a sheet of ice. There was no sound in it or in all the woods, except for the quiet gurgle of water finding a small way around the dam. A fish nosed the surface while Boone watched, and the water riffled and lay flat again. From the dam he could see that his stick was gone, the stick he had forced into the mud to hold the trap. Sometimes a man worked so quiet he didn't do right. Like as not the beaver lay drowned in deep water now, and he would have to wade out and maybe swim for the plew and the twelve-dollar trap that held it. Only it wasn't once in a coon's age a beaver pulled loose on him, he sank his sticks that deep. He walked to the setting place, searching with his eyes for the stick floating and the ring of the chain around it. After a while he made out the float, lying free along the edge of ice, with the ring gone from it. A man couldn't tell where the beaver was, without he drowned quick, close to where the trap grabbed him. Boone waded out and looked into the water, following it while it got deeper and darker until the bottom was lost to his eye.

He straightened and shifted his rifle to the other hand, and stepped back toward shore to ease the ache in his legs, and then he heard a small noise in a clump of willows behind him, a bare whisper in the limbs. He looked around and saw the end of the chain, not knowing it for what it was, at first. He stooped and seized it and pulled her from the bushes, a young she in the prime. She crouched down when he had yanked her into the clear, not trying to run, but just crouching, looking at him while her nose trembled and a little shivering went over her.

"Got ye," he said, and cast about with his hand and picked up a dead stick big enough to kill her with.

He saw now that she had been at work on her leg. A little bit more and she would have chewed herself free. There were just the tendons holding, and a ragged flap of skin. The broken bone stuck out of the jaws of the trap, white and clean as a peeled root. Around her mouth he could see blood.

She looked at him, still not moving, still only with that little shaking, out of eyes that were dark and fluid and fearful, out of big eyes that liquid seemed to run in, out of eyes like a wounded bird's. They made him a little uneasy, stirring something that lay just beyond the edge of his mind and wouldn't come out where he could see it.

She let out a soft whimper as he raised the stick, and then the stick fell, and the eye that had been looking at him bulged out crazily, not looking at anything, not something alive and liquid any more, not something that spoke, but only a bloody eyeball knocked from its socket. It was only a beaver's eye all the time.

He skinned her, and cut off the tail and knifed out and tied the castor glands so they wouldn't leak and rolled them in the plew and reset his trap and went on. He got two more beaver. The fourth set was untouched. It was a good-enough morning.

Walking back to camp, he thought about rendezvous—and after. Jim wanted to hunt the Bear of the Sick River and head on south for the winter, to Taos, which people sometimes called Fernandez. A man couldn't tell what Summers would do, maybe not even Summers himself. Boone wondered whether Poordevil would want to go back to the Blackfeet. Thinking about the north country, of a sudden he knew what the beaver's eyes had put him in mind of.

Trapping or traveling, Jim Deakins watched the country for dust and the buffalo for movement, as any mountain man would. Winter and sum-

mer, the Blackfeet were pushing south from the Three Forks to war on
the Crows, and going on, a many a long camp from home, to rub out
white men as they trapped the streams and made over the passes. It wasn't
Indian sign he wanted to see, though; Bridger's men ought to come out of
the north any time now, pointed for rendezvous. Allen would be with them,
maybe, and Lanter and Hornsbeck and others that he had had himself a
time with before.

Hunting was all right, and wintering the way he and Boone and Summers had, but a man got lonesome finally and hankered for people and for
frolics. It was good to tell stories sometimes and to hear stories told and
to brag and to laugh over nothing and play horse while the whisky worked
in you, and to have the good feeling in the back of your head all the time
that when you were through talking and betting and drinking and wrestling
there would be an Indian girl waiting for you; and, afterwards, you would
lie quiet with her and hear the coyotes singing and the stream washing
and see the stars down close and feel the warmth of her, and the lonesome-
ness would all be gone, as if the world itself had come to set a spell with
you.

Take Boone, now. He never seemed to get lonesome or to want to see
folks, except once in a while for a squaw that he was through with almost
as quick as he got her. He was like an animal, like a young bull that traveled alone, satisfied just by earth and water and trees and the sky over
him. It was as if he talked to the country for company, and the country
talked to him, and as if that was enough. He found his fill of people quick;
he took his fill of whisky quicker, drinking it down like an Indian and
getting himself good and drunk while another man was just warming up.
Then one morning before rendezvous was more than half over he would
wake up and want to make off, to places where you wouldn't see a white
man in a coon's age.

Summers was the same in a way, but different, too, for Summers seemed
to live in his head a good part of the time, as if it was the years kept him
company. He would sit at the campfire and smoke or go about the horses
or tend to the skins, and a man would know that he was away back in his
mind, seeing old things, things that had happened long ago, before the
Mandan ever put out from St. Louis, seeing himself as a boy maybe in
Missouri or a young man down on the Platte. Summers liked company, all
right, and liked drinking and frolics as well as anybody, but in a quiet way,
as if nothing that happened now was as important as what had gone before. It was age getting him, likely; a man was lucky if he didn't grow too
old and have to think that the best of what was going to happen to him had
already happened. God was mighty mean in some ways, letting a body
get on to the point where he always hungered to turn back, making him
know he wasn't the man he had been, making his bed cold but keeping in
his mind the time when it wasn't. It was like a man was pushed backwards
down hill, seeing the top getting farther from him every day, but always

seeing it, always wishing he could go back. Sometimes God seemed pretty small.

Summers was in one of his spells now, just sitting and smoking and thinking, and saying only a word or two, and then only if spoken to first. Boone had dug a hole where the fire was and put a deer's head in it and raked the coals over. In the kettle there was meat cut small, cooking with wild onions that Jim had pulled, remembering food back in Kentucky.

"We might as well be gettin' on, with the water so high," Jim said. "Be rendezvous time before it goes down."

Summers asked "Reckon?" as if he wasn't listening.

Boone and Poordevil sat away from them a little. As Jim watched, Boone put his finger on his eye and Poordevil sounded the Indian word for it. Boone tried the word then, practicing with it until Poordevil smiled and bobbed his head that he had got it right.

Jim bent over the moccasin he was making, pulling a whang through the holes his awl had bored. Boone had got so's he spent a deal of time talking with Poordevil that way, learning the Blackfoot words for things.

The sun was coming down from overhead. They would eat and maybe sleep a little, and then it would be time to look at the traps again. Even with the water as high as it was, they caught a few beaver. It might be he would go out first and kill some meat. The cows were thin yet. Bull was better, or mountain sheep. There was a mess of mountain sheep on the shoulders of the Wind mountains—rams and ewes and lambs full of play. They leaped along slopes that would affright a bird, never falling, never hurting themselves.

Jim looked up from his work and let his eye go all around, and then he took to his feet and looked harder, at the buffalo running north of them.

Summers saw him and got up and looked, too, and reached over for the rifle he had leaned against a tree. He jerked his head as Boone lifted his glance. They stood watching, seeing the buffalo stream to the east, leaving a slow rising cloud behind them.

Without speaking, Summers moved off toward the horses and so started them all that way. The horses snorted as they trotted to them, and tried to shy off, rearing and plunging with the hobbles but making a poor out at getting away. Back at camp, the men threw saddles on them and led them into a patch of brush.

Summers squinted through the branches. The cloud that the buffalo had left was sinking, and at the tail end of it Jim could see horsemen coming through. "Can't tell," Summers said. "Injuns or hunters. They ain't like to sight our fire at this time of day without they ride close."

"Long Knives," Poordevil announced. "No Injuns."

"We'll see. Looks to be six or ten."

Except for Poordevil, who stood at the side of his horse without even his bow in his hand, they brought their saddle horses in front of them as the horsemen approached, looking over the backs of them and on through the branches with their rifles rested across their saddles. Summers' eye slid to Poordevil. "Can't figger how that nigger's lived so long."

If it was Long Knives it would be Bridger's men, Jim thought— Bridger's men making for rendezvous on the Seeds-kee-dee which some folks were calling the Green River now.

Summers relaxed. "Injuns don't carry rifles that way, I'm thinkin'." He stepped from the brush.

The horses pulled up short, and the riders swung their rifles on him until he shouted at them and fired his own weapon in the air. Jim fired his gun then, and heard Boone's go off next to him, and then there was a quick scattering of shots and voices shouting and hoofbeats thudding on the ground as the horsemen swept up.

"Dogged if it ain't Allen and Shutts and Reeson. How, Elbridge? How, Robinson?"

The men slid from their horses and shook hands around, yelling "Hi-yi," some of them, and strutting like Indians, making a show for all that their buckskins were worn and black with grease and the fringes down to nothing. One of the eight kept to his horse, though, a big, loose man whose slouched shoulders made a wide arch over his saddle horn. His eyes went around and fixed on Poordevil, as if Poordevil had done something against him. Still looking, he pulled off the handkerchief he had about his head, and Jim saw that a plume of hair grew solid white from a scar at the hair line in front.

"Ain't you gonna light, Streak?" Lanter asked. "Or are you gonna let your tail grow to that there mare?"

They all moved around, talking, telling about the winter, filling the quiet air with sound, all except the big man who still sat his horse with no smile on his face and no word in his mouth.

"Where's Bridger and the rest?" Summers asked.

"Comin' along. We took out ahead."

"How's Beaver?"

"We catched a few. The damn Blackfeet give us trouble again, a heap of it."

"Damn the goddam Injuns!" It was Streak speaking, speaking as he looked at Poordevil. "What's that one?"

Summers looked up but didn't answer right away, and Boone put in "Blackfoot" and looked afterwards as if he knew he shouldn't have said it.

"What!"

"More like a Poordevil," Summers said. "Let's smoke."

Streak got down off the horse and stood holding his gun. It was a smart rifle, decorated with brass tacks and a pattern of vermilion, as if he had just done fancying it up.

"We got ourselves a few plews," Summer was saying, talking to the rest but keeping the tail of his eye on Streak. "Not so many, though. It's poor doin's, account of floodwater."

Boone stood a little apart, listening.

"A goddam Blackfoot, is he?"

Lanter said, "No need actin' like a sore-tailed bear, Streak."

"This child'll rub that bastard out."

"You'll get kilt yourself." Boone had stepped in front of Streak, between him and Poordevil. Poordevil just stood there, not quite understanding, his eyes going around and his mouth open showing his broken jaw, and his crazy deerskin shirt hanging comical on him.

"By God!" Streak turned his head around to look at the others, who fell silent one by one and shifted a little, expecting trouble. "You hear what I did? Leave 'im alone, he says, leave 'im alone, us as've been fighting Blackfeet all winter. Leave 'im alone, like as if the Blackfeet didn't send Bodah under, like as if the Blackfeet ain't dogged us all along and put lead in some of us."

He turned on Boone, and his finger pointed to the scar on his hairline. "Whar you think I got this? From old age? Blackfeet, by God, years ago. Knicked my mare and knocked her over, the devils did, and took me for dead, lyin' there, but we raised runnin', me and my mare, afore they lifted my scalp."

"It wasn't Poordevil done it."

"One's like t'other, much as two peas."

Jim saw two of Bridger's men nodding as they agreed with Streak. The rest just stood there, waiting for what would happen next, their faces sober and their eyes sharp. Come a fight, he and Boone and Summers and Poordevil figured to get the worst of it, with eight on the other side.

Boone was looking Streak in the eye, giving him a sort of dark, wild look, the kind of look Jim had seen him give just before his temper broke. Boone was a sudden man, acting first and thinking after. Jim wondered that he held in so good now.

"This nigger can outrun, outdrink, outstud, and outfight any son of a bitch that sides with a Blackfoot. Stand out of my way! This hoss aims to raise h'ar."

Jim saw the look on Boone's face that meant he wouldn't stand any more. He saw the look and saw Summers slide between them, moving quick and easy like a young man. "Hold in, now. We aim to get along nice and sociable. I reckon we're plumb glad to see you. But we don't aim to have Poordevil kilt, not by anyone. Not by you, Streak, and not by any of the rest—you, Shutts, or you, Reeson, or Allen, or any of the rest if you're a mind to stand with Streak. If it's blood you want you'll have it, but some of it'll be yours, I'm thinkin'." His gaze fixed on Streak and then went to the others, and there wasn't anything in his face except quiet. Jim stepped over by him, his unloaded rifle in his hand, and there were the four of them together looking at the eight and waiting, four of them counting Poordevil, who had lost his foolish smile, Jim noticed as he moved, and stood quiet but sharp and alive, like an animal waiting for a man to make a move.

For a moment things seemed to hang, like a rock teetering on a slope, not knowing whether to roll or settle, and then Russell said easily, "I wouldn't fight Dick Summers for the whole damn Blackfoot Nation and the Rapahoes to boot." It was like the rock settling.

Lanter grunted. "Me neither. These here are friends. Y'hear, Streak?"

After a silence Streak gave in. "I wasn't fixin' to fight any but that Blackfoot. I'd like his scalp for my old leggin's. I would, now."

He let himself be turned around to the fire and sat down and by and by smoked with the rest, not like a man with a fright in him, but like one just waiting his time.

"We ain't fixed good for company," Summers said while he moved around the fire pushing wood into it.

"We got meat," Lanter said, "a sight of good bull meat—a little blue, maybe, but not as blue as some I've et." He got up, and Robinson with him, and went to one of the pack horses and came back carrying cuts of it.

The others got out their knives and carved themselves pieces and speared them on roasting sticks. Lanter, who looked as old as time and as weather-beaten as any rock, yelled as one of them bent over the meat. "Don't be cuttin' that meat ag'in the grain! Other way saves the blood and juice. Y'hear?"

The dark little man he spoke to looked up, his great eyes seeming to swim in his head, and nodded and went to work with his knife again.

"No more sense'n a fool hen, that greenhorn Spaniard," Lanter muttered. "He'd sp'ile young cow, he would." He watched his own cut beginning to sizzle over the fire. "Treat it right, nigh any meat is good."

"Savin' snake meat," Hornsbeck put in. "This nigger's throat plumb shuts up at snake meat. I et it onc't, after wreckin' a bull boat and losin' everything 'cept my hair, an' I do declare it were a long fight 'twixt my pore paunch and that there snake."

Lanter turned his stick. "Meat's meat, I say, bull or cow or snake or whatever. But man meat ain't proper meat to this child's way of thinkin'." He took his knife and cut a slice from his roast and spoke while his jaws worked on it. "I put tooth to man meat onc't, down with the Diggers, who made out it was jerked goat when they traded. Stringy, it was, and kind of white, and it grew in the mouth while a man chewed on it." He swallowed his mouthful. "It ain't proper doin's. It ain't now. This child's et skunk and goose cooked Injun style with the guts in and a roastin' stick pushed through from honker to hole, and raw fish and old moccasins when there was nothin' better, but my stomach is real delicate on man meat."

Poordevil had squatted by Boone, like a dog by its owner. His mouth was open, and through the hole in his teeth Jim could see his tongue lying pink and wet. As the meat browned, the men would carve off the outside, leaving the inside red and dripping to cook some more.

When the meat was gone Russell got up and stood waiting for the rest. "We best be getting on," he announced.

"How you pointin'?" Summers asked.

"To the Sweetwater and over. Come along."

Jim wanted to say "Sure," but Summers' gaze came to him and flicked on to Boone and Streak and Poordevil, and he said, "Reckon not, Russell. We can find us a few beaver yet, now the water's goin' down. Reckon we'll go up the Wind and over to Jackson's Hole and to rendezvous that way. We got time enough."

"We'll go on, then."

Streak turned in his saddle as they rode off and stared at Boone and then at Poordevil and hitched himself and went on. Jim figured he might as well have said he wasn't done yet.

Jim knew that Boone saw him, too, but Boone didn't say anything. He just watched the men ride away and by and by turned to Poordevil and put his fingers to his eye and said, *"No-waps-spa,"* and Poordevil bobbed his head.

Dick Summers pulled the hood over his head and brought his capote closer about him. There was no place in God's world where the wind blew as it did on the pass going over to Jackson's Hole. It came keen off the great high snow fields, wave on wave of it, tearing at a man, knocking him around, driving at his mouth and nose so that he couldn't breath in or out and had to turn his head and gasp to ease the ache in his lungs. A bitter stubborn wind that stung the face and watered the eye and bent the horses' heads and whipped their tails straight out behind them. A fierce, sad wind, crying in a crazy tumble of mountains that the Indians told many a tale about, tales of queer doings and spirit people and medicines strong and strange. The feel of it got into a man sometimes as he pushed deep into these dark hills, making him wonder, putting him on guard against things he couldn't lay his tongue to, making him anxious, in a way, for all that he didn't believe the Indians' stories. It flung itself on the traveler where the going was risky. It hit him in the face when he rounded a shoulder. It pushed against him like a wall on the reaches. Sometimes on a rise it seemed to come from everywhere at once, slamming at back and front and sides, so there wasn't a way a man could turn his head to shelter his face. But a body kept climbing, driving higher and farther into the wild heights of rock, until finally on the other side he would see the Grand Teton, rising slim and straight like a lodgepole pine, standing purple against the blue sky, standing higher than he could believe; and he would feel better for seeing it, knowing Jackson's Hole was there and Jackson's Lake and the dams he had trapped and the headwaters of the Seeds-kee-dee not so far away.

Summers bent his head into the wind, letting his horse make its own pace. Behind him plodded his pack horse, led by the lariat in his hand, and behind the pack horse came Boone and Jim and Poordevil and their animals.

It was known country to Summers, the Wind range was, and the ever-lasting snow fields and the Grand Teton that could come into sight soon, known country and old country to him now. He could remember when it was new, and a man setting foot on it could believe he was the first one, and a man seeing it could give names to it. That was back in the days of General Ashley and Provot and Jed Smith, the cool half-parson whom the Comanches had killed down on the Cimarron. It was as if everything was just made then, laid out fresh and good and waiting for a man to come along and find it.

It was all in the way a man thought, though, the way a young man thought. When the blood was strong and the heat high a body felt the earth was newborn like himself; but when he got some years on him he knew different; down deep in his bones he understood that everything was old, old as time, maybe—so old he wondered what folks had been on it before the Indians themselves, following up the waters and pitching their lodges on spots that he had thought were his alone and not shared by people who had gone before. It made a man feel old himself to know that younger ones coming along would believe the world was new, just as he had done, just as Boone and Jim were doing, though not so strong any more.

There rose the Grand Teton at last, so thin, seen from here, it didn't seem real. Summers pulled up to let the horses blow and felt the wind driving through to his skin and clear to his secret guts, with the keen touch of the snow fields in it. Boone yelled something to him, and Summers shook his head, and Boone cupped his hands around his mouth and yelled again, but sound wouldn't come against the wind; it blew backward down the pass, and Summers found himself wondering how far it would blow until it died out and was just one with the rush of air. He shook his head again, and Boone grinned and made a signal with his hand to show it didn't matter, and afterward tucked his chin around to the side to catch his breath. High to his left Summers could see a mountain sheep standing braced and looking, its head held high under the great load of horn. The trees grew twisted from cracks in the rock, grew leaning away from the wind, bowed and old-looking from the weight of it.

He let his gaze go to the back trail, to Boone and Jim and the horses standing hunched and sorry, their hair making patterns under the push of the wind. They were good boys, both, though different, brave and willing and wise to mountain ways. They were hivernans—winterers—who could smell an Indian as far as anybody and keep calm and shoot plumb center when the time came. Summers wondered, feeling a little foolish inside, that he still wanted to protect them, like an uncle or a pappy or somebody. It was Boone he felt most like protecting, because Boone thought simple and acted straight and quick. He didn't know how to get around a thing, how to talk his way out or to laugh trouble off, the way Jim did. Not that Jim was scared; he just had a slick way with him. Come finally to a fight, he didn't shy off. Boone, now, was dead certain to get himself into a battle at rendezvous with the man called Streak, and not in a play battle, either. It would be one or t'other, Summers was sure, and shook his head to get shut of the small black cloud at the back of it.

When they were going again his thoughts went back. As a man got older he felt different about things in other ways. He liked rendezvous still and to see the hills and travel the streams and all, but half the pleasure was in the remembering mind. A place didn't stand alone after a man had been there once. It stood along with the times he had had, with the thoughts he had thought, with the men he had played and fought and drunk with, so when he got there again he was always asking whatever became of so-and-so, asking if the others minded a certain time. It stood with the young him and the former feelings. A river wasn't the same once a man had camped by it. The tree he saw again wasn't the same tree if he had only so much as pissed against it. There was the first time and the place alone, and afterwards there was the place and the time and the man he used to be, all mixed up, one with the other.

Summers could go back in his mind and see the gentler country in Missouri State, and it was rich, too, if different—rich in remembered nests and squirrels and redbirds in the bush and fish caught and fowl shot, rich in soil turned and the corn rising higher than a boy's head, making a hidey-hole for him. He could go back there and live and be happy, he reckoned, as happy as a hoss could be with the fire going out of him and remembered things coming stronger and stronger into the mind.

Anyhow, he had seen the best of the mountains when the time was best. Beaver was poor doings now, and rendezvous was pinching out, and there was talk about farms over on the Columbia. Had a mountain man best close out, too? Had he best go back to his patch of land and get himself a mule and eat bread and hog meat and, when he felt like it, just send his mind back to the mountains?

Would he say goodbye to it all, except in his head? To rendezvous and hunting and set-tos with Indians and lonesome streams and high mountains and the great empty places that made a man feel like he was alone and cozy in the unspoiled beginnings of things? Could he fit himself back among people where he dassn't break wind without looking about first?

A man looking at things for the last time wanted to fix them in his head. He wanted to look separately at every tree and rock and run of water and to say goodbye to each and to tuck the pictures of them away so's they wouldn't ever be quite lost to him.

Jackson Lake and the wind down to a breath, the Three Tetons rising, the Hoary-Headed Fathers of the Snakes, and night and sleep and round-about to rendezvous, trapping a little as they went, adding to their packs, going on over the divide from the Snake to the headwaters of the Seeds-kee-dee, and then seeing from a distance the slow smoke of campfires rising, the men and motion, the lodges pitched around, the color that the blankets made and the horses grazing, and hearing Boone and Jim yelling and shooting off their rifles while they galloped ahead, drumming at the bellies of their horses. They made a sight, with feathers flying on them and ribbons and the horses' manes and tails woven and stuck with eagle plumes. A greenhorn would take them for sure-enough Indians.

Rendezvous again, 1837 rendezvous, but rendezvous of other times, too, rendezvous of 'thirty-two and 'twenty-six and before, rendezvous of all times, of men dead now, of squaws bedded with and left and forgotten, of whisky drunk and enjoyed and drained away, of plews that had become hats and the hats worn out.

Summers' horse began to lope, wanting to keep up with the others, but Summers held his rifle in front of him undischarged. A man got so he didn't care so much about putting on a show.

Boone felt Summers' gaze on him and, when he looked, saw it sink and fasten on the ground, as if Summers didn't want the thoughts he was think-ing to be found in his eyes.

Summers said, "This nigger couldn't hit a bull's hind end with a lodge-pole after five-six drinks."

"I ain't had too much," Boone answered after a silence. "I can walk a line or spit through a knothole." He drank from the can of whisky by his side. "It ain't true, anyways. You was some, now, yesterday, firin' offhand. You come off best."

"Didn't have more'n a swallow."

Summers and Jim were rumped down on either side of Boone. Poor-devil lay on the ground in front of them, snoring, the whites of his eyes glimmering through the parted lids and the spit running from one corner of his mouth and making a dark spot in the dirt.

"Reckon Poordevil thought he could drink the bar'l dry," Summers said.

"I ain't fixin' to drink no bar'l dry."

It was getting along in the afternoon, and over a ways from them a game of hand was starting up, now that the horse racing was about over for the day, and the shooting at a mark. The players set in a line on either side of the fire. While Boone watched they began to sing out and to beat with sticks on the dry poles they had put in front of them. Every man had his stake close to him. It was skins they were betting, mostly, and credit with the Company, and some trade goods and Indian makings and powder and ball, and sometimes maybe a rifle. They weren't worked up to the game yet. Come night, and they would be yelling and sweating and betting high, they and others sided across from other fires. A man could make out Streak easy, with his head bare and the sun catching at the white tuft of hair.

Up and down river Boone could catch sight of Indian lodges, moved in closer than usual to the white camp, maybe because the rendezvous was smaller. Nearer, horses were grazing, and still nearer the mountain men moved, talking and laughing and drinking and crowding up with some Indians at the log counter that Fitzpatrick had set the Company goods behind, under cover of skins. The tents of the Company men clustered around the store. In back of them, pack saddles and ropes and such were piled. The lodges of the free trappers, from where Boone looked on, were west of the others, away from the river. Behind the counter two clerks kept busy with their account books. In front of it a couple of white hunters showed they had a bellyful. They were dancing, Indian style, and by and by began to sing, patting their bellies with their open hands to make their voices shake, and ending with a big whoop.

Hi—hi—hi—hi,
Hi-i—hi-i—hi-i—hi-i,
Hi-ya—hi-ya—hi-ya—hi-ya,
Hi-ya—hi-ya—hi-ya—hi-ya,
Hi-ya—hi-ya—hi—hi.

The white men were Americans and French from Canada, mostly, but some were Spanish and some Dutch and Scotch and Irish and British. Everybody had arrived by now—the free trappers and the Company men and Indians from all over, coming by the Sweetwater and the Wind and over from the Snake and from Cache Valley to the south near the Great Lake, from Brown's Hole and New and Old Parks and the Bayou Salade, coming to wait for Tom Fitzpatrick and trade goods from the States. Just yesterday Fitzpatrick had pulled in, with only forty-five men and twenty carts drawn by mules, but bringing alcohol and tobacco and sugar and coffee and blankets and shirts and such, all the same. At the side of the counter two half-breeds were working a wedge press, already packing the furs for the trip back to St. Louis, making steady knocking noises as they drove the wedges in.

It wasn't any great shakes of a rendezvous—not like they used to have, with companies trying to outdo each other and maybe giving three pints for a good plew. Now there were just the American Fur Company and

Bridger and the rest of his old outfit working for it, and whisky cost four dollars and beaver went for four to five a pound, for all there wasn't much of it.

The Crows hadn't brought in more than a mite. They and the other tribes were restless and cranky; they talked about the white man hunting their grounds and about the Blackfeet warring on them and the traders putting low prices on fur and high ones on vermilion and blankets and strouding. They were crying—that's what they said—because the white brother took much and left little. The mountain men grumbled, too, trading pelts for half what they used to bring and hearing talk that maybe this was the last rendezvous.

It wasn't any great shakes of a rendezvous, but still it was all right; a man couldn't growl, not with whisky to be had and beaver still to be caught if he went careful, and the sky over him and the country clear to him any way he might want to travel.

Over his can of whisky Boone saw a little bunch of Crow girls coming on parade, dressed in bighorn skin white as milk and fancy with porcupine quills. Some of them would catch themselves a white man, and their pappies would get gifts of blankets or whisky or maybe a light fusee and powder and ball, and they would be glad to have a white brother in the family, and the white man would ride away from rendezvous with his squaw and keep her while she pleased him, and then he would up and leave her, and she would be plumb crazy for a while, taking on like kin had died, but after a while, like as not, she would find another mountaineer, or anyway an Indian, and so get all right again. Sometimes squaws got sure-enough dangerous when their men left them, especially if they left one to take up with another.

Boone saw that Jim's sharp eye had picked up the girls. "Them Crows are slick sometimes. They are, now," Jim said. He added, "And mighty obligin'."

"You ought to know," Summers said and smiled, looking at Jim as if he could see through him, looking at him with a little cloud in his eyes as if he wished he could go back to Jim's age. "Reckon maybe you should take one away with you, and not buzz yourself around like a bee in clover. They ain't after one-night rumpuses so much. Steady is what tickles 'em."

"Jim hankers for the whole damn tribe."

"You ain't so bad yourself, Boone, or didn't used to be. Can't figure you out. Bet you ain't had two women this spree. A body'd think you was still feared of catchin' a cold in your pants."

Some of the Crow girls were smart-looking, all right, and that went. A man didn't get to see so many Blackfoot girls, but there was one of them, if she kept coming along and grew up to her eyes, would make these other squaws look measly.

Boone said, "Must be there's a right smart more goat in you. I had enough colds so's not to be afraid."

The three of them sat for a while without speaking, watching Russell come lazing over from the store, smoking a pipe with a long stem.

"How, Russell."

"Hello," said Russell, and stopped and drew on his pipe while his eyes went over Poordevil. Poordevil didn't have anything on but a crotch cloth that came up under his belt and folded over and ended in red tassels. The sun lay on his brown body, catching flecks of old skin and making them shine. Russell put out his toe and poked Poordevil with it as if to see if he could rouse him. To Boone, Russell said, "He is't worth fighting about, he or any of the rest."

"I reckon I'll make up my own mind."

"As you please."

Russell was a proper man, and .educated, but a good hunter, so they said, and cool in a fix. "Too bad you arrived late," he said to Summers. "We had some excitement."

"I been hearin'."

"Such impudence! Those Bannock rascals coming in to trade but still refusing to give up the horses they had stolen!"

"Injuns think different from whites."

"You mean they don't think."

"Stealin's their way of fun," Summers explained.

"They'll have to learn better, even if the learning comes hard. We gave the Bannocks a lesson. Killed thirteen of them right here and chased after the rest and destroyed their village and shot some more during the three days we fought them. In the end they promised to be good Indians. Bloody business, but necessary."

"Maybe so."

"The only way to settle disputes with hostile Indians is with a rifle. It writes a treaty they won't forget."

"Maybe," Summers answered again.

"They'll sing small in a few years. A wave of settlers will wash over them. The country won't be held back by a handful of savages."

Boone said, "What 'ud settlers do out here?"

Russell gave him a look but didn't answer.

"Where you aim to fall-hunt?" Summers asked.

"Upper Yellowstone again, I guess. Fontanelle and Bridger are taking a hundred and ten men to Blackfoot country."

Boone asked, "Far as the Three Forks, or north of there?"

"I wouldn't think so. They're enough Blackfeet on the Gallatin and Madison and Jefferson without going farther."

Russell strolled off, still sucking on his pipe.

Boone drank again and then let himself back on his elbows, looking west, yonder to where the sun was about to roll behind the mountains. A current of air whispered by his ear, making a little singing sound. When it died down, the other noises came to him again—the hand players calling out and beating with their sticks, the Indian dogs growling over bones, the horses sneezing while they cropped the grass, and sometimes the Indian children yelling. The sun shed a kind of gentle shine, so that everything seemed soft and warm-colored—the river flowing, the butte hazy in the distance, the squaws with their bright blankets, the red and black and spotted horses stepping with their noses to the grass, the hills sharp against the sky and the sky blue, the lodges painted and pointed neat and the fire smoke rising slow, and high overhead a big hawk gliding.

It was funny, the way Jim and Summers had their eye out for him, not wanting him to frolic until he and Streak had had it out. Boone knew how much he could hold and still move quick and straight. He knew how much he could hold and it was a considerable—as much, maybe, as any man at rendezvous. He wasn't going to cut down on his fun—not much, anyway—just so's to be on guard. Besides, Streak hadn't acted up, not to him, or picked on Poordevil, though he had made his brags around, saying he didn't walk small for any man and would get himself a Black-foot yet, saying he could whip the likes of Caudill day or night, rain or shine, hot or cold or however. Summers allowed that Streak had held in because there wasn't any whisky in camp until yesterday.

Boone rested back on his elbows, feeling large and good, feeling the whisky warming his belly and spreading out, so that his arms and legs and neck all felt strong and pleasured, as if each had a happy little life of its own. This was the way to live, free and easy, with time all a man's own and none to say no to him. A body got so's he felt everything was kin to him, the earth and sky and buffalo and beaver and the yellow moon at night. It was better than being walled in by a house, better than breath-ing in spoiled air and feeling caged like a varmint, better than running after the law or having the law running after you and looking to rules all the time until you wondered could you even take down your pants without somebody's say-so. Here a man lived natural. Some day, maybe, it would all end, as Summers said it would, but not any ways soon—not so soon a body had to look ahead and figure what to do with the beaver gone and churches and courthouses and such standing where he used to stand all alone. The country was too wild and cold for settlers. Things went up and down and up again. Everything did. Beaver would come back, and fat prices, and the good times that old men said were going forever.

Poordevil groaned and opened one red eye and closed it quick, as if he wasn't up, yet, to facing things.

"How, Blackfoot."

Poordevil licked his lips. "Sick. God sick damn." He put his hand out, toward the can at Boone's side, and his eyes begged for a drink.

"First time I ever heerd goddam split," Jim said. "Seems on-religious."

"Not yet, you don't," Boone said to Poordevil. "Medicine first. Good medicine." He heaved himself up and went toward the fire and picked up the can he had set by it. It had water in it and a good splash of gall from the cow Summers had shot that morning. "Bitters. That's medicine now." He lifted the can and let his nose sample the rank smell of it. Before he handed it to the Indian he took a drink himself. "Here, Injun. Swaller away."

Poordevil sniffed of the bitters, like a dog at a heap of fresh dung, and brought up his upper lip in a curl that showed the gap between his teeth. He tilted the can and drank fast, his throat bobbing as he gulped. He threw the can from him and belched, and held out his hand for the whisky. He had a dull, silly, friendly look on his face like a man might expect to find on a no-account dog's if it so happened a dog could smile. Between the red lids his eyes looked misty, as if they didn't bring things to him clear.

Of a sudden Boone felt like doing something. That was the way it was with whisky. It lay in the stomach comfortable and peaceful for a time, and then it made a body get up and do. All around, the fires were beginning to show red, now that dark was starting to close in. Boone could see men moving around them, or sitting, and sometimes a camp kicker jerking a buffalo ham high from the fire to get off the ashes. There were talk and shouts and laughter and the chant and rattle of the hand players. It was a time when men let go of themselves, feeling full and big in the chest. It was a time to talk high, to make jokes and laugh and drink and fight, a time to see who had the fastest horse and the truest eye and the plumb-center rifle, a time to see who was the best man.

"I aim to move around," Boone said, and picked up his empty can.

"Last night you wasn't up to so much, Boone." It was Jim talking. "Me and Dick, we kep' our nose out of the strong water, just in case."

"Goddam it! You going to be dry all rendezvous? I ain't skeered."

Jim didn't answer, but Summers looked up with his little smile and said, "Not the whole livin' time, Boone. Just long enough, is all."

"Best get it over with right now, then."

Summers lifted himself and felt of the knife in his belt and took his rifle in his hand. "This nigger wouldn't say so, son. It's poor doin's, makin' up to trouble. Put out; we'll foller."

"Git up, Poordevil." Boone toed the Indian's ribs. "Whisky. Heap whisky."

Poordevil hoisted his tail in the air, like a cow getting up, and came to his feet staggering a little. "Love whisky, me. Love white brother."

"White brother love Poordevil," Jim said with his eyes on Boone. "Love Poordevil heap. He's bound to, ain't he, Dick, with whisky four dollars a pint? Nigh a plew a pint."

Poordevil put on a ragged cotton shirt that Boone had given him earlier.

"What's beaver for?" Boone asked, leading off toward the counter. "Just to spend, ain't it? For drinks and rifles and fixin's? You thinkin' to line your grave with it?"

All Jim answered was, "That Injun can drink a sight of whisky."

From the store they went to a fire that a dozen free trappers were sitting around, telling stories and drinking and cutting slices of meat from sides of ribs banked around the flames.

"Make way for a honest-to-God man," Summers ordered.

Boone put in, "Make way for three of 'em."

From the far side of the fire a voice said, "Summers' talk is just foolin', but that Caudill, now, he sounds like he sure enough believes it."

Boone squinted across and saw that the speaker was Foley, a long, strong, bony man with a lip that stuck out as if for a fight.

A little silence came on everybody. Boone stood motionless. "I ain't one to take low and go down, Foley. Make what you want out'n it."

There was the little silence again, and then Foley saying, "Plank your ass down, Caudill. You git r'iled too easy."

Summers lowered himself and put his can of whisky between his knees. "How," the other said now. "Move in and set."

Foley started the talk again. "Allen was sayin' as how he had a tool once would shoot around a corner."

"I did that. Right or left or up or down it would, and sharp or gentle, just accordin'. Hang me, I would have it yet, only one time I got 'er set wrong, and the ball made a plumb circle and came back to the bar'l like a chicken to roost. Knocked things all to hell."

"This child shot a kind of corner onc't," said Summers, "and I swear it saved my hair."

"So?"

Summers fired his pipe. "It was ten years ago, or nigh to it and the Pawnees was bad. They ketched me out alone, on the Platte, and there was a passel of 'em whoopin' and comin' at me. First arrow made wolf's meat of my horse, and there this nigger was, facin' up to a party as could take a fort."

Allen said, "I heerd you was kilt away back then, Dick. Sometimes be damned if you ain't like a dead one."

"Ain't near so dead as some, I'm thinkin'. It was lucky I had Patsy Plumb here with me." Summers patted the butt of his old rifle. "This here piece now, it don't know itself how far it can shoot. It scares me, sometimes, dogged if it don't, thinkin' how the ball goes on and on and maybe hit a friend in Californy, or maybe the governor of Indiana State. It took me a spell to get on to it, but after while I l'arn't I could kill a goat far as I could see him, only if he was humpin' I might have to face half-around to lead him enough. Yes, ma'am, I've fired at critters an' had time to load up ag'in afore ball and critter come together."

"Keeps you wore out, I'm thinkin', travelin' for your meat."

"That's a smart guess now. Well, here this child was, and the Pawnees comin', and just then I see a buffler about to make over a hill. He was that far away he didn't look no bigger'n a bug. I made the peace sign, quick and positive, and then I p'inted away yonder at the buffler, and the

Injuns stopped and looked while I up with Patsy. I knowed 'er inside out then, and I waited until the critter's tail switched out of sight over the hill, and then, allowin' for a breeze and a mite of dust in the air, I pulled trigger."

Summers had them all listening. It was as if his voice was a spell, as if his lined face with its topping of gray hair held their eyes and stilled their tongues. He puffed on his pipe, letting them wait, and took the pipe from his mouth and drank just a sip from his can of whisky.

"The Pawnees begun to holler again and prance around, but I helt 'em back with the peace sign and led 'em on, plumb over the hill. Took most of the day to git there. But just like this nigger knowed, there was Mr. Buffler, lyin' where the ball had dropped down on him. I tell you niggers, the Pawnees got a heap respectful. One after the other, they asked could they have meat and horns and hair, figgerin' it was big medicine for 'em, till there wasn't anything left of that bull except a spot on the ground, and dogged if some of the Pawnees didn't eat that!" Summers let a little silence come in before he spoke again. "I ain't never tried any long shots since."

"No?"

"I figger I ain't up to it. I swear I aimed to get that old bull through the heart, and there he was, plain gut-shot. Made me feel ashamed."

They laughed, and some clapped others on the back, and they dipped their noses into whisky, and their voices rang in the night while the dark gathered close around, making the fire like a little sun. In the light of it the men looked flat, as if they had only one side to them. The faces were like Indian faces, dark and weathered and red-lit now, and clean-shaved so as to look free of hair. Boone drank from his can and pushed closer to the fire, feeling the warmth of it wave out at him. Poordevil squatted behind him, seeming comfortable enough in his crotch cloth and cotton shirt. Around them were the keen night and the campfires blazing and the cries of men, good-sounding and cozy, but lost, too, in the great dark like a wolf howl rising and dying out to nothing.

"I reckon you two ain't the only ones ever shot a corner," Jim said. "Sharp or curve?"

"Sharp as could be. A plumb turnabout."

"It's Company firewater makes a man think things," Allen said. "He gets so he don't know goin' from comin'."

"In Bayou Salade it was, and we was forted up for the winter." Jim was getting to be a smart liar—as good as Summers, almost. "I took a look out one morning, and there not an arrer shot away was the biggest by-God painter a man ever see. 'Painter meat!' I says and grabbed up my rifle and leveled. The painter had got itself all stretched out, and lyin' so's only his head made a target. I aimed for the mouth, I did, and let 'er go, only I didn't take into account how quick that painter was."

Jim looked around the circle of faces. "He was almighty quick. The ball went in his mouth fair, and then that critter swapped ends, faster'n scat. I ain't hankered to look a painter in the tail since." Jim fingered his cheek gently. "That bullet grazed my face, comin' back."

The laughing and the lying went on, but of a sudden Boone found himself tired of it, tired of sitting and chewing and doing nothing. He felt a squirming inside himself, felt the whisky pushing him on. It was as if he had to shoot or run or fight, or else boil over like a pot. He saw Summers lift his can again and take the barest sip. Jim's whisky was untouched beside him. Goddam them, did they think they had to mammy him! Now was a good time, as good as any. The idea rose up in him, hard and sharp, like something a man had set his mind to before everything else. He downed his whisky and stood up. Summers looked around at him, his face asking a question.

"I'm movin' on."

Poordevil had straightened up behind him. Summers poked Jim and made a little motion with his head, and they both came to their feet.

Away from the fire Boone turned on them. "Christ Almighty! You nee'n to trail me. I aim to fix it so's you two dast take a few drams. Come on, Poordevil."

He turned on his heel and went on, knowing that Poordevil was at his back and Jim and Summers coming farther behind, talking so low he couldn't hear. He looked ahead, trying to make out Streak, and pretty soon he saw him, saw the white hair glinting in the firelight. The players chanted and beat on their poles, trying to mix up the other side, and the side in hand passed the cache back and forth, their hands moving this way and that and opening and closing until a man could only guess where the cache was.

The singing and the beating stopped after the guess was made, and winnings were pulled in and new bets laid while the plumstone cache changed sides.

Boone spoke above the whooping and the swearing. "This here's a Blackfoot Injun, name of Poordevil, and he's a friend of mine."

Some of the players looked up, holding up the bet making. Streak dragged his winnings in.

An older man, with a mouth like a bullet hole and an eye that seemed to have grown up squinting along a barrel, said, "Set, Caudill. Who gives a damn? Me, I had a pet skunk onc't, and it wasn't hardly ever he'd piss on a friend of mine, and when he did the friend like as not didn't stink no worse, but only fresher."

Lanter said, "Let's get on with the game."

"What happened to your skunk friend?" Jim asked.

"It was goin' on the second winter that I had him, and I was holed up with two old hunters, like o'Lanter here, and one night old No-Pee just up and left without givin' no reason at all."

"Likely his pride finally got the best of him," Lanter said.

" 'Twer'n't that. I figgered it out all right. Livin' close up with two hard cases like you, Lanter, his pore nose got so it just couldn't stand it no more."

Boone waited until the voices had quieted down. "I ain't aimin' to let no one pester Poordevil. Anyone's got such an idee, sing out!"

In front of him a man said, "Jesus Christ! My beaver's nigh drunk up already."

Streak's eyes lifted. His face was dark and his mouth tight and straight. A man couldn't tell whether he was going to fight or not. Boone met his gaze and held it, and a silence closed around them with eyes in it and faces waiting.

Streak got up, making out to move lazily. "The damn Blackfoot don't look so purty," he said to the man at his side. His glance rose to Boone. "How'll you have it?"

"Any way."

Streak left his rifle resting against a bush and moved out and came around the players. Boone handed his gun to Jim. Summers had stepped back, his rifle in the crook of his arm. Over at the side Poordevil grunted something in Blackfoot that Boone didn't understand.

Streak was a big man, bigger than he looked at first, and he moved soft and quick like a prime animal, his face closed up and set as if nothing less than a killing would be enough for him.

Boone waited, feeling the blood rise in him hot and ready, feeling something fierce and glad swell in his chest.

Streak bent over and came in fast and swung and missed and caught his balance and swung again before Boone could close with him. His fist struck like a club head, high on Boone's cheek. Boone grabbed for him, and the heavy fist struck again and again, and he kept driving into it, feeling the hurt of it like something good and satisfying, while his hands reached out and a dark light went to flashing in his head. He caught an arm and slipped and went down with Streak on top of him. A hand clamped on his throat and another clinched behind, and the two squeezed as if to pinch his head off. The fire circle around him, the fire and the players and Summers standing back with his rifle and Jim with his mouth open and his eyes squinched like he was hurting and Poordevil crouching as if about to dive in. They swung around him, mixed and cloudy, like something only half in the mind, while he threshed against the weight on him. He heard Streak's breath in his ear and his own wind squeaking in and out. He caught Streak's head in his hands and brought it down and ripped an ear with his teeth. Streak jerked the ear free, but in that instant Boone got a gulp of air, and the dizzy world steadied.

He had hold of Streak's wrist. He felt his own muscles swelling along his forearms as he called on his strength. It was as if his hands were something to order the power into. It came a little at a time, but steady and sure—a little and then a wait and then a little more, the hold on his throat barely slipping each time and then loosening more until he held

Streak's straining hands away. He called on all his strength and forced Streak's left arm straight, and then he dropped his grip on the other and whipped his free arm across and clamped it above Streak's elbow, straining the forearm back while he bore on the joint.

The arm cracked, going out of place, and Streak cried out and wrenched himself away and lunged to his feet, his face black and twisted and his left arm hanging crooked. As he came in again, his good arm raised, Boone caught the dark flicker of a knife and heard Jim's quick cry of warning.

He hadn't time to get out his own blade. As he twisted away, the knife came down and cut through his shirt, and the bite of it along his arm was like the bite of fire. He snatched at the wrist and caught it. Above the whistle of their lungs Summers' voice came: "By God, he asked for it!"

His hands fought the wrist, the knuckles, the clutched fingers, and caught a thumb and bent it back. He jerked the hand around under his chest and saw it weakening, one finger and another letting up like something dying and the handle coming into sight. The knife slipped out and fell in the grass. Boone snatched it up, holding to Streak with his other hand. A word stuttered on the man's lips, and the campfire showed a sudden look of fear in his face, a look of such fear that a man felt dirtied seeing it. The eyes flicked wide, flicked and fluttered and came wide again and closed slow as Boone wrenched the knife free and drove it in again.

Boone pushed with his hand. Streak fell over backwards, making a soft thump as he hit, and lay on his back, twitching, with the knife upthrust from his chest.

Poordevil let out a whoop and began to caper around, and Jim joined in, dancing with his knees high and yelling, "Hi-ya!"

Summers' rifle still was in the crook of his arm. "I'm thinking the trouble's over," he said, and nobody answered until Lanter spoke up with "Let's git on with the game. The parade's done passed. Any of you niggers want to take Streak's place?" Boone heard him add under his breath, "That damn Caudill's strong as any bull."

Boone turned to Summers. "Maybe you're ready to wet your dry now?"

" 'Pears like a time for it, after we doctor you."

"It ain't no more'n a scratch. To hell with it! Let's have some fun."

Summers looked at the long cut on Boone's arm. "Reckon it won't kill ye, at that."

The men went back to playing hand, leaving Streak's body lying. Closed out from the firelight by the rank of players, it was a dark lump on the ground, like a sleeper. A man had to look sharp to see the knife sticking from it.

Boone passed it again, near daylight, after he had drunk he didn't recollect how much whisky and had had himself a woman and won some beaver. There was the taste of alcohol in his mouth, and the gummy taste of Snake tobacco. He held his arm still at his side, now that the wound had started to stiffen. He felt fagged out and peaceful, with every hunger fed except that one hankering to point north. With day coming on the land, the world was like a pond clearing. From far off on a butte came the yipping of coyotes. Suddenly a squaw began to cry out, keening for a dead Bannock probably, her voice rising lonely and thin in the halfnight. A man could just see the nearest lodges, standing dark and dead. There was dew on the grass, and a kind of dark mist around Streak's carcass, which lay just as it had before, except that some Indian had lifted the hair, thinking that that plume of white would make a fancy prize.

Summers took one last look from the little rise on which he and Boone and Jim stood.

The camp had begun to stir now that morning was flooding over the sky. Squaws were laying fires and fixing meat to cook, and so were the white hunters and Company *engagés* who didn't have a woman to do the squaw's work. He and Boone and Jim hadn't taken up with the squaws so much as the others, except for a time or two. As far as Summers knew, they hadn't fathered a child either, not anywhere, though like as not they had. Already one Indian was at the counter, probably asking for whisky. Summers saw a squaw come poking out of a lodge and after her two half-breed children, whom the French called *brulés* on account of their burned look. He wondered whether even the squaw knew who their pappy was. Farther off, horses were running, bucking and kicking up and nipping at one another in the early chill. The sun touched the tops of the hills, but lower down the dark lay yet. Against the morning sky the mountains were still dead, waiting for day to get farther along before they came to life.

"Me," said Jim, "I'd wait and go east with the furs."

Summers didn't answer, but it went through his mind again that he didn't want to go back with anybody. He wanted to be by himself, to go along alone with the emptiness that was in him, to look and listen and see and smell, to say goodbye a thousand times and, saying it, maybe to find that the hurt was gone. He wanted to hear water at night and the wind in the trees, to take the mountains and the brown plains sharp and lasting into his mind, to kill a buffalo and cook the *boudins* by his own small fire, feeling the night press in around him, seeing the stars wink and the dipper steady, and everything saying goodbye, goodbye.

Goodbye, Dick Summers. Goodbye, you old nigger, you. We mind the time you came to us, young and green and full of sap. We watched you grow into a proper mountain man. We saw you learning, trapping and fighting and finding trails, and going around then proud-breasted like a young rooster, ready for a frolic or a fracas, your arm strong and your wind sound and the squaws proud to have you under a robe. But new times are a-coming now, and new people, a heap of them, and wheels rolling over the passes, carrying greenhorns and women and maybe children, too, and plows. The old days are gone and beaver's through. We'll see a sight of change, but not you, Dick Summers. The years have fixed you. Time to go now. Time to give up. Time to sit back and remember. Time for a chair and a bed. Time to wait to die. Goodbye, Dick. Goodbye, Old Man Summers.

"We didn't do so bad," Boone said, "what with beaver so trapped out and the price what it was."

Summers wondered whether he had done bad or good. He had saved his hair, where better men had lost theirs. He had seen things a body never would forget and done things that would stay in the mind as long as time. He had lived a man's life, and now it was at an end, and what had he to show for it? Two horses and a few fixin's and a letter of credit for three hundred and forty-three dollars. That was all, unless you counted the way he had felt about living and the fun he had had while time ran along unnoticed. It had been rich doings, except that he wondered at the last, seeing everything behind him and nothing ahead. It was strange about time; it slipped under a man like quiet water, soft and unheeded but taking a part of him with every drop—a little quickness of the muscles, a little sharpness of the eye, a little of his youngness, until by and by he found it had taken the best of him almost unbeknownst. He wanted to fight it then, to hold it back, to catch what had been borne away. It wasn't that he minded going under, it wasn't he was afraid to die and rot and forget and be forgotten; it was that things were lost to him more and more—the happy feeling, the strong doing, the fresh taste for things like drink and women and danger, the friends he had fought and funned with, the notion that each new day would be better than the last, good as the last one was. A man's later life was all a long losing, of friends and fun and hope, until at last time took the mite that was left of him and so closed the score.

"Wisht you'd change your mind," Boone said. "It'll be fat doin's up north, Dick."

Fat doings! Jim and Boone wouldn't understand until they got old. They wouldn't know that a man didn't give up the life but that it was the other way about. What if the doings were fat? What if beaver grew plenty again and the price high? He had seen times right here on the Seeds-kee-dee when beaver were so thick a hunter shot them from the bank, and so dear that a good pack fetched nigh a thousand dollars. Such doings wouldn't put spring in a man's legs or take the stiffness from his joints. They wouldn't make him a proper mountain man again.

Settlers and Indians

THE RAID

by ALAN LEMAY

The captivity narrative has long been an American genre. The first stories of men and women captured by Indians are to be found in memoirs of the Colonial period. In the early nineteenth century there appeared another type of captivity, that of the Algerine captivities. This was obviously fertile ground for the novelist and many fiction writers have worked it. LeMay appeared to abandon the field of Western writing for many years after writing several minor works, then returned to it with a sense of this-is-what-it-was-like more completely developed than almost any other writer. In The Searchers *he caught the slow horror of the wait for the Indian raid and the suddenness of its surprise and the feeling of how it must have been living with the threat of the raid hanging over every action. In his next novel,* The Unforgiven, *he reversed the story and used as his heroine an Indian girl who grew up as part of a settler's family,*

Supper was over by sundown, and Henry Edwards walked out from the house for a last look around. He carried his light shotgun, in hopes the rest of the family would think he meant to pick up a sage hen or two —a highly unlikely prospect anywhere near the house. He had left his gun belt on its peg beside the door, but he had sneaked the heavy six-gun itself into his waistband inside his shirt. Martha was washing dishes in the wooden sink close by, and both their daughters—Lucy, a grown-up seventeen, and Debbie, just coming ten—were drying and putting away. He didn't want to get them all stirred up; not until he could figure out for himself what had brought on his sharpened dread of the coming night.

"Take your pistol, Henry," Martha said clearly. Her hands were busy, but her eyes were on the holster where it hung empty in plain sight, and she was laughing at him. That was the wonderful thing about Martha. At thirty-eight she looked older than she was in some ways, especially her hands. But in other ways she was a lot younger. Her sense of humor did that. She could laugh hard at things other people thought only a little bit funny, or not funny at all; so that often Henry could see the pretty sparkle of the girl he had married twenty years back.

He grunted and went out. Their two sons were on the back gallery as he came out of the kitchen. Hunter Edwards, named after Martha's family, was nineteen, and as tall as his old man. He sat on the floor, his head lolled back against the adobe, and his mind so far away that his mouth hung open. Only his eyes moved as he turned them to the shotgun. He said dutifully, "Help you, Pa?"

"Nope."

Ben, fourteen, was whittling out a butter paddle. He jumped up, brushing shavings off his blue jeans. His father made a Plains-Indian sign—a fist pulled downward from in front of his shoulder, meaning "sit-stay." Ben went back to his whittling.

"Don't you forget to sweep them shavings up," Henry said.

"I won't, Pa."

They watched their father walk off, his long, slow-looking steps quiet in his flat-heeled boots, until he circled the corrals and was out of sight.

"What's he up to?" Ben asked. "There ain't any game out there. Not short of the half mile."

Hunter hesitated. He knew the answer but, like his father, he didn't want to say anything yet. "I don't know," he said at last, letting his voice sound puzzled. Within the kitchen he heard a match strike. With so much clear light left outside, it was hard to believe how shadowy the kitchen was getting, within its thick walls. But he knew his mother was lighting a lamp. He called softly, "Ma . . . Not right now."

His mother came to the door and looked at him oddly, the blown-out match smoking in her hand. He met her eyes for a moment, but looked away again without explaining. Martha Edwards went back into the kitchen, moving thoughtfully; and no light came on. Hunter saw that his father was in sight again, very far away for the short time he had been gone. He was walking toward the top of a gentle hill northwest of the ranch buildings. Hunter watched him steadily as long as he was in sight. Henry never did go clear to the top. Instead he climbed just high enough to see over, then circled the contour to look all ways, so that he showed himself against the sky no more than he had to. He was at it a long time.

Ben was staring at Hunter. "Hey. I want to know what—"

"Shut up, will you?"

Ben looked astonished, and obeyed.

From just behind the crest of the little hill, Henry Edwards could see about a dozen miles, most ways. The evening light was uncommonly clear, better to see by than the full glare of the sun. But the faint roll of the prairie was deceptive. A whole squadron of cavalry could probably hide itself at a thousand yards, in a place that looked as flat as a parade ground. So he was looking for little things—a layer of floating dust in the branches of the mesquite, a wild cow or an antelope disturbed. He didn't see anything that meant much. Not for a long time.

He looked back at his house. He had other things, the stuff he worked with—barn, corrals, stacks of wild hay, a shacky bunkhouse for sleeping extra hands. But it was the house he was proud of. Its adobe walls were three and four feet thick, so strong that the first room they had built had for a long time been called the Edwards Fort. They had added on to it since, and made it even more secure. The shake roof looked burnable, but it wasn't, for the shakes were laid upon two feet of sod. The outside doors were massive, and the windows had heavy battle shutters swung inside.

And the house had luxuries. Wooden floor. Galleries—some called them porches, now—both front and back. Eight windows with glass. He had made his family fairly comfortable here, at long last, working patiently with his hands through the years when there was no money, and no market for cows, and nothing to do about it but work and wait.

He could hardly believe there had been eighteen years of that kind of hanging on. But they had come out here that long ago—the same year Hunter had been born—drawn by these miles and miles of good grass, free to anyone who dared expose himself to the Kiowas and Comanches. It hadn't looked so dangerous when they first came, for the Texas Rangers had just punished the Wild Tribes back out of the way. But right after that the Rangers were virtually disbanded, on the thrifty theory that the Federal Government was about to take over the defense. The Federal troops did not come. Henry and Martha held on and prayed. One year more, they told each other again and again . . . just another month . . . only until spring. . . . So the risky years slid by, while no military help appeared. Their nearest neighbors, the Pauleys, were murdered off by a Comanche raid, without survivors except a little boy less than two years old; and they heard of many, many more.

Six years of that. Then, in 1857, Texas gave up waiting, and the Rangers bloomed again. A tough line of forts sprang up—McKavitt, Phantom Hill, Bell's Stockade. The little strongholds were far strung out, all the way from the Salt Fork to the Rio Grande, but they gave reassurance nonetheless. The dark years of danger were over; they had lasted out, won through to years of peace and plenty in which to grow old— or so they thought for a little while. Then the War Between the States drained the fighting men away, and the Kiowas and Comanches rose up singing once more, to take their harvest.

Whole counties were scoured out and set back to wilderness in those war years. But the Edwardses stayed, and the Mathisons, and a few more far-spread, dug-in families, holding the back door of Texas, driving great herds of longhorns to Matagordas for the supply of the Confederate troops. And they waited again, holding on just one year more, then another, and one more yet.

Henry would have given up. He saw no hope that he would ever get a foothold out here again, once he drew out, but he would gladly have sacrificed their hopes of a cattle empire to take Martha and their children to a safer place. It was Martha who would not quit, and she had a will that could jump and blaze like a grass fire. How do you take a woman back to the poverty of the cotton rows against her will? They stayed.

The war's end brought the turn of fortune in which they had placed their faith. Hiring cowboys on promise, borrowing to provision them, Henry got a few hundred head into the very first drive to end-of-track at Abilene. Now, with the war four years past, two more drives had paid off. And this year he and Aaron Mathison, pooling together, had sent north more than three thousand head. But where were the troops that peace should have released to their defense? Bolder, wilder, stronger every year, the Comanches and their Kiowa allies punished the range. Counties that had survived the war were barren now; the Comanches had struck the outskirts of San Antonio itself.

Once they could have quit and found safety in a milder land. They couldn't quit now, with fortune beyond belief coming into their hands. They were as good as rich—and living in the deadliest danger that had overhung them yet. Looking back over the years, Henry did not know how they had survived so long; their strong house and everlasting watchfulness could not explain it. It must have taken miracles of luck, Henry knew, and some mysterious quirks of Indian medicine as well, to preserve them here. If he could have seen, in any moment of the years they had lived here, the endless hazards that lay ahead, he would have quit that same minute and got Martha out of there if he had had to tie her.

But you get used to unresting vigilance, and a perpetual danger becomes part of the everyday things around you. After a long time you probably wouldn't know how to digest right, any more, if it altogether went away. All that was behind could not explain, exactly, the way Henry felt tonight. He didn't believe in hunches, either, or any kind of spirit warnings. He was sure he had heard, or seen, or maybe even smelled some sign so small he couldn't remember it. Sometimes a man's senses picked up dim warnings he didn't even recognize. Like sometimes he had known an Indian was around, without knowing what told him, until a little later the breeze would bring the smell of the Indian a little stronger—a kind of old-buffalo-robe smell—which of course had been the warning before he knew he smelled anything. Or sometimes he knew horses were coming before he could hear their hoofs; he supposed this came by a tremor of the ground so weak you didn't know you felt it, but only knew what it meant.

He became aware that he was biting his mustache. It was a thin blond mustache, trailing downward at the corners of his mouth, so that it gave his face a dour look it didn't have underneath. But it wasn't a chewed mustache, because he didn't chew it. Patiently he studied the long sweep of the prairie, looking steadily at each quadrant for many minutes. He was sorry now that he had let Amos go last night to help the Mathisons chase cow thieves; Amos was Henry's brother and a rock of strength. It should have been enough that he let Martin Pauley go along. Mart was the little boy they had found in the brush, after the Pauley massacre, and raised as their own. He was eighteen now, and given up to be the best shot in the family. The Mathisons hadn't been satisfied anyway. Thought he should send Hunter, too, or else come himself. You can't ever please everybody.

A quarter mile off a bedded-down meadow lark sprang into the air, circled uncertainly, then drifted away. Henry became motionless, except for his eyes, which moved continually, casting the plain. Five hundred yards to the right of the spot where the meadow lark had jumped, a covey of quail went up.

Henry turned and ran for the house.

Martin Pauley had found this day a strange one almost from the start. Twelve riders had gathered to trail some cow thieves who had bit into the Mathisons'; and the queer thing about it was that five out of the twelve soon disagreed with all the others as to what they were following.

Aaron Mathison, who owned the run-off cattle, was a bearded, calm-eyed man of Quaker extraction. He had not been able to hold onto the part of his father's faith which forswore the bearing of arms, but he still prayed, and read the Bible every day. Everything about the Mathison place was either scrubbed, or raked, or whitewashed, but the house was cramped and sparely furnished compared to the Edwards'. All the money Aaron could scrape went into the quality of his livestock. Lately he had got his Lazy Lightning brand on ten head of blood bulls brought on from Kansas City. These had been held, by the chase-'em-back method, with a small herd on the Salt Crick Flats. This was the herd that was gone.

They picked up the churned trail of the stolen herd shortly after dawn, and followed it briskly, paced by the light-riding Mathison boys on their good horses. Martin Pauley lagged back, dogging it in the early hours. He had a special grouch of his own because he had looked forward to a visit with Laurie Mathison before they set out. Laurie was eighteen, like himself—straight and well boned, he thought, in terms he might have used to judge a filly. Lately he had caught her unwary gray eyes following him, now and then, when he was around the Mathisons'. But not this morning.

Laurie had been flying around, passing out coffee and quickgrab break-fast, with two of the Harper boys and Charlie MacCorry helping her on three sides—all of them clowning, and cutting up, and showing off, till there was no way to get near. Martin Pauley was a quiet boy, dark as an Indian except for his light eyes; he never did feel he cut much of a figure among the blond and easy-laughing people with whom he was raised. So he had hung back, and never did get to talk to Laurie. She ran out to his stirrup, and said, "Hi," hardly looking at him as she handed him a hunk of hot meat wrapped in bread—no coffee—and was gone again. And that was the size of it.

For a while Martin kept trying to think of something cute he might have said. Didn't think of a thing. So he got bored with himself, and took a wide unneedful swing out on the flank. He was casting the prairie rest-lessly, looking for nothing in particular, when presently he found some-thing that puzzled him and made him uneasy.

Mystified, he crossed the trail and swung wide on the other flank to take a look at the ground over there; and here he found Amos, doing the same thing. Amos Edwards was forty, two years older than his brother Henry, a big burly figure on a strong but speedless horse. He was some different from the rest of the Edwards family. His heavy head of hair was darker, and probably would have been red-brown, except that it was un-brushed, without any shine to it. And he was liable to be pulled back into his shell between rare bursts of temper. Just now he was riding lumpily, hands in his pockets, reins swinging free from the horn, while he guided his horse by unnoticeable flankings with the calves of his legs and two-ounce shifts of weight. Martin cleared his throat a few times, hoping Amos would speak, but he did not.

"Uncle Amos," Martin said, "you notice something almighty fishy about this trail?"

"Like what?"

"Well, at the jump-off I counted tracks of twelve, fifteen ponies working this herd. Now I can't find no more than four, five. First I supposed the rest had pushed on ahead, and their trails got tromp out by cows—"

"That's shrewd," Amos snubbed him. "I never would have thunk of it."

"—only, just now I find me a fit-up where two more ponies forked off— and they sure didn't push on ahead. They turned back."

"Why?"

"Why? Gosh, Uncle Amos—how the hell should I know? That's what itches me."

"Do me one thing," Amos said. "Drop this 'Uncle' foolishness."

"Sir?"

"You don't have to call me 'Sir,' neither. Nor 'Grampaw,' neither. Nor 'Methuselah,' neither. I can whup you to a frazzle."

Martin was blanked. "What should I call you?"

"Name's Amos."

"All right. Amos. You want I should mosey round and see what the rest of 'em think?"

"They'll tell you the same." He was pulled back in his shell, fixing to bide his time.

It was straight-up noon, and they had paused to water at a puddle in a coulee, before Amos made his opinion known. "Aaron," he said in tones most could hear, "I'd be relieved to know if all these boys realize what we're following here. Because it ain't cow thieves. Not the species we had in mind."

"How's this, now?"

"What we got here is a split-off from an Indian war party, running wild loose on a raid." He paused a moment, then finished quietly. "Maybe you knowed that already. In case you didn't, you know it now. Because I just told you."

Aaron Mathison rubbed his fingers through his beard and appeared to consider; and some of the others put in while he did that. Old Mose Harper pointed out that none of the thieves had ridden side by side, not once on the trail, as the tracks showed plain. Indians and dudes rode single file—Indians to hide their numbers, and dudes because the horses felt like it—but white men rode abreast in order to gab all the time. So the thieves were either Indians or else not speaking. One t'other. This contribution drew partly hidden smiles from Mose Harper's sons.

Young Charlie MacCorry, a good rough-stock rider whom Martin resented because of his lively attentions to Laurie Mathison, spoke of noticing that the thieves all rode small unshod horses, a whole lot like buffalo ponies. And Lije Powers got in his two cents. Lije was an old-time buffalo hunter, who now lived by wandering from ranch to ranch, "stopping by." He said now that he had "knowed it from the fust," and allowed that what they were up against was a "passel of Caddoes."

Those were all who took any stock in the theory.

Aaron Mathison reasoned in even tones that they had no real reason to think any different than when they had started. The northeasterly trend of the trail said plainly that the thieves were delivering the herd to some beef contractor for one of the Indian Agencies—maybe old Fort Towson. Nothing else made any sense. The thieves had very little start; steady riding should force a stand before sundown tomorrow. They had only to push on, and all questions would soon be answered.

"I hollered for a back track at the start," Amos argued. "Where's the main war party these here forked off from? If they're up ahead, that's one thing. But if they're back where our families be—"

Aaron bowed his head for several moments, as if in prayer; but when his head came up he was looking at Amos Edwards with narrowed eyes. He spoke gently, slipping into Quakerish phrasings; and Martin Pauley, who had heard those same soft tones before, knew the argument was done. "Thee can turn back," Aaron said. "If thee fears what lies ahead or what lies behind, I need thee no more."

He turned his horse and rode on. Two or three hesitated, but ended by following him.

Amos was riding with his hands in his pockets again, letting his animal keep up as it chose; and Martin saw that Amos had fallen into one of his deadlocks. This was a thing that happened to Amos repeatedly, and it seemed to have a close relationship with the shape of his life. He had served two years with the Rangers, and four under Hood, and had twice been up the Chisholm Trail. Earlier he had done other things—bossed a bull train, packed the mail, captained a stage station—and he had done all of them well. Nobody exactly understood why he always drifted back, sooner or later, to work for his younger brother, with never any understanding as to pay.

What he wanted now was to pull out of the pursuit and go back. If he did turn, it could hardly be set down to cowardice. But it would mark him as unreliable and self-interested to an unforgivable degree in the eyes of the other cowmen. A thing like that could reflect on his whole family, and tend to turn the range against them. So Amos sat like a sack of wheat, in motion only because he happened to be sitting on a horse, and the horse was following the others.

His dilemma ended unexpectedly.

Brad Mathison, oldest of Aaron's boys, was ranging far ahead. They saw him disappear over the saddle of a ridge at more than two miles. Immediately he reappeared, stopped against the sky, and held his rifle over his head with both hands. It was the signal for "found." Then he dropped from sight beyond the ridge again.

Far behind him, the others put the squeeze to their horses, and lifted into a hard run. They stormed over the saddle of the ridge, and were looking down into a broad basin. Some scattered bunches of red specks down there were cattle grazing loose on their own. Aaron Mathison, with his cowman's eyes, recognized each speck that could be seen at all as an individual animal of his own. Here was the stolen herd, unaccountably dropped and left.

Brad was only about a mile out on the flats, but running his horse full stretch now toward the hills beyond the plain.

"Call in that damn fool," Amos said. He fired his pistol into the air, so that Brad looked back.

Aaron spun his horse in close circles to call in his son. Brad turned reluctantly, as if disposed to argue with his father, but came trotting back. Now Aaron spotted something fifty yards to one side, and rode to it for a closer look. He stepped down, and the others closed in around him. One of the young blood bulls lay there, spine severed by the whack of an axe. The liver had been ripped out, but no other meat taken. When they had seen this much, most of the riders sat and looked at each other. They barely glanced at the moccasin prints, faint in the dustfilm upon the baked ground. Amos, though, not only dismounted, but went to his knees; and Martin Pauley stooped beside him, not to look wise, but trying to find out what Amos was looking for. Amos jabbed the carcass with his thumb. "Only nine, ten hours old," he said. Then, to Lije Powers, "Can you tell what moccasins them be?"

Lije scratched his thin beard. "Injuns," he said owlishly. He meant it for a joke, but nobody laughed. They followed Mathison as he loped out to meet his son.

"I rode past five more beef kills," Brad said when they came together. He spoke soberly, his eyes alert upon his father's face. "All these down here are heifers. And all killed with the lance. Appears like the lance wounds drive deep forward from just under the short ribs, clean through to the heart. I never saw that before."

"I have," Lije Powers said. He wanted to square himself for his misfire joke. "Them's Comanche buffler hunters done that. Ain't no others left can handle a lance no more."

Some of the others, particularly the older men, were looking gray and bleak. The last five minutes had taken them ten years back into the past, when every night of the world was an uncertain thing. The years of watchfulness and struggle had brought them some sense of confidence and security toward the last; but now all that was struck away as if they had their whole lives to do over again. But instead of taking ten years off their ages it put ten years on.

"This here's a murder raid," Amos said, sending his words at Aaron like rocks. "It shapes up to scald out either your place or Henry's. Do you know that now?"

Aaron's beard was sunk on his chest. He said slowly, "I see no other likelihood."

"They drove your cattle to pull us out," Amos hammered it home. "We've give 'em free run for the last sixteen hours!"

"I question if they'll hit before moonrise. Not them Comanche." Lije spoke with the strange detachment of one who has seen too much for too long.

"Moonrise! Ain't a horse here can make it by midnight!"

Brad Mathison said through his teeth, "I'll come almighty close!" He wheeled his pony and put it into a lope.

Aaron bellowed, "Hold in that horse!" and Brad pulled down to a slamming trot.

Most of the others were turning to follow Brad, talking blasphemies to their horses and themselves. Charlie MacCorry had the presence of mind to yell, "Which place first? We'll be strung out twenty mile!"

"Mathison's is this side!" Mose Harper shouted. Then to Amos over his shoulder, "If we don't fight there, we'll come straight on!"

Martin Pauley was scared sick over what they might find back home, and Laurie was in his mind too, so that the people he cared about were in two places. He was crazy to get started, as if haste could get him to both places at once. But he made himself imitate Amos, who unhurriedly pulled off saddle and bridle. They fed grain again, judging carefully how much their animals would do best on, and throwing the rest away. The time taken to rest and feed would get them home quicker in the end.

By the time they crossed the saddleback the rest of the riders were far spaced, according to the judgment of each as to how his horse might best be spent. Amos branched off from the way the others took. Miles were important, now, and they could save a few by passing well west of Mathison's. Amos had already made up his mind that he must kill his horse in this ride; for they had more than eighty miles to go before they would know what had happened—perhaps was happening now—to the people they had left at home.

Henry Edwards stood watching the black prairie through a loophole in a batten shutter. The quartering moon would rise late; he wanted to see it coming, for he believed now that all the trouble they could handle would be on them with the moon's first light. The dark kitchen in which the family waited was closed tight except for the loopholes. The powder smoke was going to get pretty thick in here if they had to fight. Yet the house was becoming cold. Any gleam of light would so hurt their chances that they had even drawn the coals from the firebox of the stove and drowned them in a tub.

The house itself was about as secure as a house could be made. The loopholed shutters, strap-hinged on the inside, were heavy enough to stop a 30-30, if not a buffalo slug, and the doors were even better. Nine or ten rifles could hold the place forever against anything but artillery. As few as seven would have their hands full against a strong war party, but should hold.

There lay the trouble and the fear. Henry did not have seven. He had himself, and his two sons, and Martha. Hunter was a deadly shot, and Ben, though only fourteen, would put in a pretty fair job. But Martha couldn't shoot any too well. Most likely she would hold fire until the last scratch, in hopes the enemy would go away. And Lucy . . . Lucy might do for a lookout someplace, but her dread of guns was so great she would be useless even to load. Henry had made her strap on a pistol, but he doubted if she could ever fire it, even to take her own life in event of capture.

And then there was Deborah. The boys had been good shots at eight; but Debbie, though pushing ten, seemed so little to Henry that he hadn't let her touch a weapon yet. You don't see your own children grow unless there's a new one to remind you how tiny they come. In Henry's eyes, Debbie hadn't changed in size since she was brand new, with feet no bigger than a fingertip with toes.

Four rifles, then, or call it three and a half, to hold two doors and eight shuttered windows, all of which could be busted in.

Out in the work-team corral a brood mare gave a long whinny, then another after a moment's pause. Everyone in the kitchen held his breath, waiting for the mare's call to be answered. No answer came, and after a while, when she whinnied again, Henry drew a slow breath. The mare had told him a whole basket of things he didn't want to know. Strange ponies were out there, probably with stud horses among them; the mare's nose had told her, and the insistence of her reaction left no room for doubt. They were Indian ridden, because loose ponies would have answered, and horses ridden by friends would have been let to answer. The Indians were Comanches, for the Comanches were skillful at keeping their ponies quiet. They wove egg-size knots into their rawhide hacka-mores, so placed that the pony's nostrils could be pinched if he so much as pricked an ear. This was best done from the ground, so Henry judged that the Comanches had dismounted, leaving their ponies with horse holders. They were fixing to close on foot—the most dangerous way there was.

One thing more. They were coming from more than one side, because none would have approached downwind, where the mare could catch their scent, unless they were all around. A big party, then, or it would not have split up. No more hope, either, that the Comanches meant only to break fence on the far side of the corrals to run the stock off. This was a full-scale thing, with all the chips down, tonight.

Lucy's voice came softly out of the dark. "Debbie?" Then more loudly, with a note of panic, "Debbie! Where are you?" Everyone's voice sounded eery coming out of the unseen.

"Here I am." They heard the cover put back on the cookie crock at the far end of the room.

"You get back on your pallet, here! And stay put now, will you?"

Long ago, hide-hunting at the age of eighteen, Henry and two others had fought off more than twenty Kiowas from the shelter of nothing more than a buffalo wallow. They had fought with desperation enough, believing they were done for; but he couldn't remember any such sinking of the heart as he felt now behind these fort-strong walls. Little girls in the house —that's what cut a man's strings, and made a coward of him, every bit as bad as if the Comanches held them hostage already. His words were steady, though, even casual, as he made his irrevocable decision.

"Martha. Put on Debbie's coat."

A moment of silence; then Martha's single word, breathy and uncertain: "Now?"

"Right now. Moon's fixing to light us up directly." Henry went into a front bedroom, and quietly opened a shutter. The sash was already up to cut down the hazard of splintering glass. He studied the night, then went and found Martha and Debbie in the dark. The child was wearing moccasins, and hugged a piece of buffalo robe.

"We're going to play the sleep-out game," he told Debbie. "The one where you hide out with Grandma. Like you know? Very quiet, like a mouse?" He was sending the little girl to her grandmother's grave.

"I know." Debbie was a shy child, but curiosly unafraid of the open prairie or the dark. She had never known her grandmother, or seen death, but she had been raised to think the grave on the hill a friendly thing. Sometimes she left little picnic offerings up there for Grandma.

"You keep down low," Henry said, "and you go quietly, quietly along the ditch. Then up the hill to Grandma, and roll up in your robe, all snug and cozy."

"I remember how." They had practiced this before, and even used it once, under a threat that blew over.

Henry couldn't tell from the child's whisper whether she was frightened or not. He supposed she must be, what with the tension that was on all of them. He picked her up in his arms and carried her to the window he had opened. Though he couldn't see her, it was the same as if he could. She had a little triangular kitty-cat face, with very big green eyes, which you could see would be slanting someday, if her face ever caught up to them. As he kissed her, he found tears on her cheek, and she hugged him around the neck so hard he feared he would have to pull her arms away. But she let go, and he lifted her through the window.

"Quiet, now—stoop low—" he whispered in her ear. And he set her on the ground outside.

Amos pulled up at the top of a long rise ten miles from home; and here Martin Pauley, with very little horse left under him, presently caught up. On the south horizon a spot of fire was beginning to show. The glow bloomed and brightened; their big stacks of wild hay had caught and were going up in light. The east rim still showed nothing. The raiders had made their choice and left Mathison's alone.

For a moment or two Martin Pauley and Amos Edwards sat in silence. Then Amos drew his knife and cut off the quirt, called a romal, that was braided into his long reins. He hauled up his animal's heavy head; the quirt whistled and snapped hard, and the horse labored into a heavy, rocking run.

Martin stepped down, shaking so hard all over that he almost went to his knees. He reset his saddle, and as he mounted again his beat-out pony staggered, almost pulled over by the rider's weight. Amos was out of sight. Mart got his pony into an uncertain gallop, guiding the placement of its awkwardly slung hoofs by the light of the high moon. It was blowing in a wind-broke roar, and when a patch of foam caught Martin in the teeth he tasted blood in it. Yet the horse came nearer to getting home than Martin could have hoped. Half a mile from the house the animal stumbled in a shallow wash and came down heavily. Twice the long head swung up in an effort to rise, but flailed down again. Martin drew his six-gun and put a bullet in the pony's head, then dragged his carbine from the saddle boot and went on, runing hard.

The hay fires and the wooden barn had died down to bright beds of coals, but the house still stood. Its shingles glowed in a dozen smoldering patches where torches had been thrown onto the roof, but the sod beneath them had held. For a moment a great impossible hope possessed Martin, intense as a physical pain. Then, while he was still far out, he saw a light come on in the kitchen as a lamp was lighted inside. Even at the distance he could see that the light came through a broken door, hanging skew-jawed on a single hinge.

Martin slowed to a walk, and went toward the house unwillingly. Little flames still wandered across the embers of the hay stacks and the barn, sending up sparks which hung idly on the quiet air; and the house itself showed against the night in a dull red glow. On the back gallery lay a dead pony, tail to the broken door. Probably it had been backed against the door to break the bar. By the steps Amos' horse was down, knees folded under. The heavy head was nodded lower and lower, the muzzle dipping the dust; it would never get up.

Martin stepped over the legs of the dead Comanche pony and went into the kitchen, walking as though he had never learned to walk, but had to pull each separate string. Near the door a body lay covered by a sheet. Martin drew back the limp muslin, and was looking into Martha's face. Her lips were parted a little, and her open eyes, looking straight up, appeared perfectly clear, as if she were alive. Her light hair was shaken loose, the lamplight picking out the silver in it. Martha had such a lot of hair that it was hardly noticeable, at first, that she had been scalped.

Most of the batten shutters had been smashed in. Hunter Edwards lay in a heap near the splintered hall door, his empty hands still clawed as if grasping the duck gun that was gone. Ben had fallen in a tangled knot by the war window, his gangly legs sprawled. He looked immature and undersized as he lay there, like a skinny small boy.

Martin found the body of Henry Edwards draped on its back across the broad sill of a bedroom window. The Comanche knives had done eery work upon his body. Like Martha, Henry and both boys had been scalped. Martin gently straightened the bodies of Henry, and Hunter, and Ben, then found sheets to put over them, as Amos had done for Martha. Martin's hands were shaking, but he was dry-eyed as Amos came back into the house.

When Martin had got a good look at his foster uncle, he was afraid of him. Amos' face was wooden, but such a dreadful light shone from behind the eyes that Martin thought Amos had gone mad. Amos carried something slim and limp in his arms, clutched against his chest. As Amos passed the lamp, Martin saw that the thing Amos carried had a hand, and that it was Martha's hand. He had not drawn down the sheet that covered Martha far enough to see that the body lacked an arm. The Comanches did things like that. Probably they had tossed the arm from one to another, capering and whooping, until they lost it in the dark.

"No sign of Lucy. Or Deborah," Amos said. "So far as I could find in the lack of light." The words were low and came unevenly, but they did not sound insane.

Martin said, "We used to practice sending Debbie up the hill to Grandma's grave—"

"I been up. They sent her there. I found her bit of buffalo robe. But Debbie's not up there. Not now."

"You suppose Lucy—" Martin let the question trail off, but they had worked so much together that Amos was able to answer.

"Can't tell yet if Lucy went up with Debbie to the grave. Not till daylight comes on."

Amos had got out another sheet and was tearing it into strips. Martin knew Amos was making bandages to fix up their people as decently as he could. His hands moved methodically, going through the motions of doing the next thing he ought to do, little as it mattered. But at the same time Amos was thinking about something else. "I want you to walk to he Mathisons'. Get them to hook their buckboard, and bring their women on. . . . Martha should have clean clothes put on."

Probably Amos would have stripped and bathed the body of his brother's wife, and dressed it properly, if there had been no one else to do it. But not if a walk of fifteen miles would get it done a more proper way. Martin turned toward the door without question.

"Wait. Pull off them boots and get your moccasins on. You got a long way to go." Martin obeyed that, too. "Where's them pegs you whittled out? I figure to make coffins out of the shelves."

"Behind the woodbox. Back of the range." Martin started off into the night.

Martin Pauley was eight miles on the way to Mathisons' when the first riders met him. All ten who had ridden the day before were on their way over, riding fresh Mathison horses and leading spares. A buckboard, some distance back, was bringing Mrs. Mathison and Laurie, who must no longer be left alone with a war party on the loose.

The fore riders had been pressing hard, hoping against hope that someone was left alive over there. When they had got the word from Martin, they pulled up and waited with him for the buckboard. Nobody pestered at him for details. Laurie made a place for him beside her on the buckboard seat, and they rode in silence, the team at a good trot.

After a mile or two Laurie whimpered, "Oh, Martie . . . Oh, Martie . . ." She turned toward him, rested her forehead against the shoulder of his brush jacket, and there cried quietly for a little while. Martin sat slack and still, nothing left in him to move him either toward her or away from her. Pretty soon she straightened up, and rode beside him in silence, not touching him any more.

Dawn was near when they got to the house. Amos had been hard at work. He had laid out his brother Henry and the two boys in one bedroom, and put their best clothes on them. He had put Martha in another room, and Mrs. Mathison and Laurie took over there. All the men went to work, silently, without having to be told what to do. These were lonely, self-sufficient people, who saw each other only a few times a year, yet they worked together well, each finding for himself the next thing that needed to be done. Some got to work with saw, boxplane, auger, and pegs, to finish the coffins Amos had started, while others made coffee, set up a heavy breakfast, and packed rations for the pursuit. They picked up and sorted out the litter of stuff the Indians had thrown about as they looted, put everything where it had belonged, as nearly as they could guess, scrubbed and sanded away the stains, just as if the life of this house were going to go on.

Two things they found in the litter had a special meaning for Martin Pauley. One was a sheet of paper upon which Debbie had tried to make a calendar a few weeks before. Something about it troubled him, and he couldn't make out what it was. He remembered wishing they had a calendar, and very dimly he recalled Debbie bringing this effort to him. But his mind had been upon something else. He believed he had said, "That's nice," and "I see," without really seeing what the little girl was showing him. Debbie's calendar had not been hung up; he couldn't remember seeing it again until now. And now he saw why. She had made a mistake, right up at the top, so the whole thing had come out wrong. He turned vaguely to Laurie Mathison, where she was washing her hands at the sink.

"I . . ." he said. "It seems like . . ."

She glanced at the penciled calendar. "I remember that. I was over here that day. But it's all right. I explained to her."

"Explained what? What's all right?"

"She made a mistake up here, so it all—"

"Yes, I see that, but—"

"Well, when she saw she had spoiled it, she ran to you. . . ." Her gray eyes looked straight into his. "You and I had a fight that day. Maybe it was that. But—you were always Debbie's hero, Martie. She was—she's still just a baby, you know. She kept saying—" Laurie compressed her lips.

"She kept saying what?"

"Martie, I made her see that—"

He took Laurie by the arms hard. "Tell me."

"All right. I'll tell you. She kept saying, 'He didn't care at all.' "

Martin let his hands drop. "I wasn't listening," he said. "I made her cry, and I never knew."

He let her take the unlucky sheet of paper out of his hand, and he never saw it again. But the lost day when he should have taken Debbie in his arms, and made everything all right, was going to be with him a long time, a peg upon which he hung his grief.

The other thing he found was a miniature of Debbie. Miniatures had been painted of Martha and Lucy, too, once when Henry took the three of them to Fort Worth, but Martin never knew what became of those. Debbie's miniature, goldframed in a little plush box, was the best of the three. The little triangular face and the green eyes were very true, and suggested the elfin look that went with Debbie's small size. He put the box in his pocket.

They laid their people deep under the prairie sod beside Grandma. Aaron Mathison read from the Bible and said a prayer, while Martin, Amos, and the six others chosen for the pursuit stood a little way back from the open graves, holding their saddled horses.

It wasn't a long service. Daylight had told them that Lucy must have been carried bodily from the house, for they found no place where she had set foot to the ground. Debbie, the sign showed, had been picked up onto a running horse after a pitifully short chase upon the prairie. There was hope, then, that they still lived, and that one of them, or even both, might be recovered alive. Most of Aaron's amazing vitality seemed to have drained out of him, but he shared the cracking strain that would be upon them all so long as the least hope lasted. He made the ritual as simple and as brief as he decently could. "Man that is born of woman . . ."

Those waiting to ride feared that Aaron would get carried away in the final prayer, but he did not. Martin's mind was already far ahead on the trail, so that he heard only the last few words of the prayer, yet they stirred his hair. "Now may the light of Thy countenance be turned away from the stubborn and the blind. Let darkness fall upon them that will not see, that all Thy glory may light the way of those who seek . . . and all Thy wisdom lead the horses of the brave. . . . Amen."

It seemed to Martin Pauley that old Aaron, by the humility of his prayer, had invited eternal damnation upon himself, if only the search for Lucy and Debbie might succeed. His offer of retribution to his God was the only word that had been spoken in accusation or in blame, for the error of judgment that had led the fighting men away.

Amos must have had his foot in the stirrup before the end of the prayer, for he swung into the saddle with the last "Amen," and led off without a word. With Martin and Amos went Brad Mathison, Ed Newby, Charlie MacCorry, Mose Harper and his son Zack, and Lije Powers, who thought his old-time prairie wisdom had now come into its own, whether anybody else thought so or not. Those left behind would put layers of boulders in the graves against digging varmints, and set up the wooden crosses Martin Pauley had sectioned out of the house timbers in the last hours of the dark.

At the last moment Laurie Mathison ran to Martin where he sat already mounted. She stepped up lightly upon the toe of his stirruped boot, and kissed him hard and quickly on the mouth. A boldness like that would have drawn a blast of wrath at another time, but her parents seemed unable to see. Aaron still stood with bowed head beside the open graves; and Mrs. Mathison's eyes were staring straight ahead into a dreadful loneliness. The Edwardses, Mathisons, and Pauleys had come out here together. The three families had sustained each other while the Pauleys lived, and after their massacre the two remaining families had looked to each other in all things. Now only the Mathisons were left. Mrs. Mathison's usually mild and kindly face was bleak, stony with an insupportable fear. Martin Pauley would not have recognized her, even if he had been in a mood to notice anything at all.

He looked startled as Laurie kissed him, but only for a second. He seemed already to have forgotten her, for the time being, as he turned his horse.

Out in the middle of a vast, flat plain, a day's ride from anything, lay a little bad-smelling marsh without a name. It covered about ten acres and had cat-tails growing in it. Tules, the Mexicans called the cat-tails; but at that time certain Texans were still fighting shy of Mexican ways. Nowhere around was there a river, or a butte, or any landmark at all, except that nameless marsh. So that was how the "Fight at the Cat-tails" got its foolish-sounding name.

Seven men were still with the pursuit as they approached the Cat-tail fight at sundown of their fifth day. Lije Powers had dropped out on the occasion of his thirty-ninth or fortieth argument over interpretation of sign. He had found a headdress, a rather beautiful thing of polished heifer horns on a browband of black and white beads. They were happy to see it, for it told them that some Indian who still rode was wounded and in bad shape, or he would never have left it behind. But Lije chose to make an issue of his opinion that the headdress was Kiowa, and not Comanche —which made no difference at all, for the two tribes were allied. When they got tired of hearing Lije talk about it, they told him so, and Lije branched off in a huff to visit some Mexican hacienda he knew about somewhere to the south.

They had found many other signs of the punishment the Comanches had taken before the destruction of the Edwards family was complete. More important than other dropped belongings—a beaded pouch, a polished ironwood lance with withered scalps on it—were the shallow stone-piled Indian graves. On each lay the carcass of a horse of the Edwards' brand, killed in the belief that its spirit would carry the Comanche ghost. They had found seven of these burials. Four in one place, hidden behind a hill, were probably the graves of Indians killed outright at the ranch; three more, strung out at intervals of half a day, told of wounded who had died in the retreat. In war, no Indian band slacked its pace for the dying. Squaws were known to have given birth on the backs of traveling ponies, with no one to wait for them or give help. The cowmen could not hope that the wounded warriors would slow the flight of the murderers in the slightest.

Amos kept the beaded pouch and the heifer-born headdress in his saddlebags; they might help identify the Comanche killers someday. And for several days he carried the ironwood lance stripped of its trophies. He was using it to probe the depth of the Indian graves, to see if any were shallow enough so that he could open them without falling too far back. Probably he hoped to find something that would give some dead warrior a name, so that someday they might be led to the living by the unwilling dead. Or so Martin supposed at first.

But he could not help seeing that Amos was changing. Or perhaps he was seeing revealed, a little at a time, a change that had come over Amos suddenly upon the night of the disaster. At the start Amos had led them at a horse-killing pace, a full twenty hours of their first twenty-four. That was because of Lucy, of course. Often Comanches cared for and raised captive white children, marrying the girls when they were grown, and taking the boys into their families as brothers. But grown white women were raped unceasingly by every captor in turn until either they died or were "thrown away" to die by the satiated. So the pursuers spent themselves and their horseflesh unsparingly in that first run; yet found no sign, as their ponies failed, that they had gained ground upon the fast-traveling Comanches. After that Amos set the pace cagily at a walk until the horses recovered from that first all-out effort, later at a trot, hour after hour, saving the horses at the expense of the men. Amos rode relaxed now, wasting no motions and no steps. He had the look of a man resigned to follow this trail down the years, as long as he should live.

And then Amos found the body of an Indian not buried in the ground, but protected by stones in a crevice of a sandstone ledge. He got at this one—and took nothing but the scalp. Martin had no idea what Amos believed about life and death; but the Comanches believed that the spirit of a scalped warrior had to wander forever between the winds, denied entrance to the spirit land beyond the sunset. Amos did not keep the scalp, but threw it away on the prairie for the wolves to find.

Another who was showing change was Brad Mathison. He was always the one ranging farthest ahead, the first to start out each morning, the most reluctant to call it a day as the sun went down. His well-grained horses—they had brought four spares and two pack mules—showed it less than Brad himself, who was turning hollow-eyed and losing weight. During the past year Brad had taken to coming over to the Edwardses to set up with Lucy—but only about once every month or two. Martin didn't believe there had been any overpowering attachment there. But now that Lucy was lost, Brad was becoming more involved with every day that diminished hope.

By the third day some of them must have believed Lucy to be dead; but Brad could not let himself think that. "She's alive," he told Martin Pauley. Martin had said nothing either way. "She's got to be alive, Mart." And on the fourth day, dropping back to ride beside Mart, "I'll make it up to her," he promised himself. "No matter what's happened to her, no matter what she's gone through. I'll make her forget." He pushed his horse forward again, far into the lead, disregarding Amos' cussing.

So it was Brad, again, who first sighted the Comanches. Far out in front he brought his horse to the edge of a rimrock cliff; then dropped from the saddle and led his horse back from the edge. And now once more he held his rifle over his head with both hands, signaling "found."

The others came up on the run. Mart took their horses as they dismounted well back from the edge, but Mose Harper took the leads from Mart's hands. "I'm an old man," Mose said. "Whatever's beyond, I've seen it afore—most likely many times. You go on up."

The cliff was a three-hundred-foot limestone wall, dropping off sheer, as if it might be the shoreline of a vanished sea. The trail of the many Comanche ponies went down this precariously by way of a talus break.

Twenty miles off, out in the middle of the flats, lay a patch of haze, shimmering redly in the horizontal light of the sunset. Some of them now remembered the cat-tail marsh that stagnated there, serving as a waterhole. A black line, wavering in the ground heat, showed in front of the marsh haze. That was all there was to see.

"Horses," Brad said. "That's horses, there at the water!"

"It's where they ought to be," Mart said. A faint reserve, as of disbelief in his luck, made the words come slowly.

"Could be buffler," Zack Harper said. He was a shag-headed young man, the oldest son of Mose Harper. "Wouldn't look no different."

"If there was buffalo there, you'd see the Comanche runnin' 'em," Amos stepped on the idea.

"If it's horses, it's sure a power of 'em."

"We've been trailin' a power of 'em."

They were silent awhile, studying the distant pen scratch upon the world that must be a band of livestock. The light was failing now as the sunset faded.

"We better feed out," Brad said finally. He was one of the youngest there, and the veteran plainsmen were usually cranky about hearing advice from the young; but lately they seemed to listen to him anyway. "It'll be dark in an hour and a half. No reason we can't jump them long before daylight, with any kind of start."

Ed Newby said, "You right sure you want to jump all them?"

Charlie MacCorry turned to look Ed over. "Just what in hell you think we come here for?"

"They'll be took unawares," Amos said. "They're always took unawares. Ain't an Indian in the world knows how to keep sentries out once the night goes cold."

"It ain't that," Ed answered. "We can whup them all right. I guess. Only thing . . . Comanches are mighty likely to kill any prisoners they've got, if they're jumped hard enough. They've done it again and again."

Mart Pauley chewed a grass blade and watched Amos. Finally Mart said, "There's another way. . . ."

Amos nodded. "Like Mart says. There's another way." Mart Pauley was bewildered to see that Amos looked happy. "I'm talking about their horses. Might be we could set the Comanch' afoot."

Silence again. Nobody wanted to say much now without considering a long while before he spoke.

"Might be we can stampede them ponies, and run off all the whole bunch," Amos went on. "I don't believe it would make 'em murder anybody—that's still alive."

"This thing ain't going to be too easy," Ed Newby said.

"No," Amos agreed. "It ain't easy. And it ain't safe. If we did get it done, the Comanch' should be ready to deal. But I don't say they'll deal. In all my life, I ain't learned but one thing about an Indian: Whatever you know you'd do in his place—he ain't going to do that. Maybe we'd still have to hunt them Comanches down, by bunches, by twos, by ones."

Something like a bitter relish in Amos' tone turned Mart cold. Amos no longer believed they would recover Lucy alive—and wasn't thinking of Debbie at all.

"Of course," Charlie MacCorry said, his eyes on a grass blade he was picking to shreds, "you know, could be every last one of them bucks has his best pony on short lead. Right beside him where he lies."

"That's right," Amos said. "That might very well be. And you know what happens then?"

"We lose our hair. And no good done to nobody."

"That's right."

Brad Mathison said, "In God's name, will you try it, Mr. Edwards?"

"All right."

Immediately Brad pulled back to feed his horses, and the others followed more slowly. Mart Pauley still lay on the edge of the rimrock after the others had pulled back. He was thinking of the change in Amos. No deadlock now, no hesitation in facing the worst answer there could be. No hope, either, visible in Amos' mind that they would ever find their beloved people alive. Only that creepy relish he had heard when Amos spoke of killing Comanches.

And thinking of Amos' face as it was tonight, he remembered it as it was that worst night of the world, when Amos came out of the dark, into the shambles of the Edwards' kitchen, carrying Martha's arm clutched against his chest. The mutilation could not be seen when Martha lay in the box they had made for her. Her face looked young, and serene, and her crossed hands were at rest, one only slightly paler than the other. They were worn hands, betraying Martha's age as her face did not, with little random scars on them. Martha was always hurting her hands. Mart thought, "She wore them out, she hurt them, working for us."

As he thought that, the key to Amos' life suddenly became plain. All his uncertainties, his deadlocks with himself, his labors without pay, his perpetual gravitation back to his brother's ranch—they all fell into line. As he saw what had shaped and twisted Amos' life, Mart felt shaken up; he had lived with Amos most of his life without ever suspecting the truth. But neither had Henry suspected it—and Martha least of all.

Amos was—had always been—in love with his brother's wife.

Amos held them where they were for an hour after dark. They pulled saddles and packs, fed out the last of their grain, and rubbed down the horses with wads of dry grass. Nobody cooked. The men chewed on cold meat and lumps of hard frying-pan bread left from breakfast. All of them studied the shape of the hills a hundred miles beyond, taking a line on the

Comanche camp. That fly speck, so far out upon the plain, would be easy to miss in the dark. When the marsh could no longer be seen they used the hill contours to take sights upon the stars they knew, as each appeared. By the time the hills, too, were swallowed by the night, each had star bearings by which he could find his way.

Mose Harper mapped his course by solemnly cutting notches in the rim of the hat. His son Zack grinned as he watched his father do that, but no one else thought it comical that Mose was growing old. All men grew old unless violence overtook them first; the plains offered no third way out of the predicament a man found himself in, simply by the fact of his existence on the face of the earth.

Amos was still in no hurry as he led off, sliding down the talus break by which the Comanches had descended to the plain. Once down on the flats, Amos held to an easy walk. He wanted to strike the Comanche horse herd before daylight, but when he had attacked he wanted dawn to come soon, so they could tell how they had come out, and make a finish. There must be no long muddle in the dark. Given half a chance to figure out what had happened, the war party would break up into singles and ambushes, becoming almost impossible to root out of the short grass.

When the moon rose, very meager, very late, it showed them each other as black shapes, and they could make out their loose pack and saddle stock following along, grabbing jawfuls of the sparse feed. Not much more. A tiny dolloping whisk of pure movement, without color or form, was a kangaroo rat. A silently vanishing streak was a kit fox. About midnight the coyotes began their clamor, surprisingly near, but not in the key that bothered Mart; and a little later the hoarse, deeper howling of a loafer wolf sounded for a while a great way off. Brad Mathison drifted his pony alongside Mart's.

"That thing sound all right to you?"

Mart was uncertain. One note had sounded a little queer to him at one point, but it did not come again. He said he guessed it sounded like a wolf.

"Seems kind of far from timber for a loafer wolf. This time of year, anyway," Brad worried. "Known 'em to be out here, though," he answered his own complaint. He let his horse drop back, so that he could keep count of the loose stock.

After the loafer wolf shut up, a dwarf owl, such as lives down prairie dog holes, began to give out with a whickering noise about a middle distance off. Half a furlong farther on another took it up, after they had left the first one silent behind, and later another as they came abreast. This went on for half an hour, and it had a spooky feel to it because the owls always sounded one at a time, and always nearby. When Mart couldn't stand it any more he rode up beside Amos.

"What you think?" he asked, as an owl sounded again.

Amos shrugged. He was riding with his hands in his pockets again, as Mart had often seen him ride before, but there was no feel of dead-lock or uncertainty about him now. He was leading out very straight, sure of his direction, sure of his pace.

"Hard to say," he answered.

"You mean you don't know if that's a real owl?"

"It's a real something. A noise don't make itself."

"I know, but that there is an easy noise to make. You could make it, or—"

"Well, I ain't."

"—or I could make it. Might be anything."

"Tell you something. Every critter you ever hear out here can some-times sound like an awful poor mimic of itself. Don't always hardly pay to listen to them things too much."

"Only thing," Mart stuck to it, "these here all sound like just one owl, follering along. Gosh, Amos. I question if them things ever travel ten rods from home in their life."

"Yeah. I know. . . . Tell you what I'll do. I'll make 'em stop, being's they bother you." Amos pushed his lips out and sounded an owl cry—not the cry of just any owl, but an exact repeat of the one they had just heard.

No more owls whickered that night.

As Mart let his pony drop back, it came almost to a stop, and he realized that he was checking it, unconsciously holding back from what was ahead. He wasn't afraid of the fighting—at least, he didn't think he was afraid of it. He wanted more than anything in the world to come to grips with the Comanches; of that he felt perfectly certain. What he feared was that he might prove to be a coward. He tried to tell himself that he had no earthly reason to doubt himself, but it didn't work. Maybe he had no earthly reason, but he had a couple of unearthly ones, and he knew it. There were some strange quirks inside of him that he couldn't under-stand at all.

One of them evidenced itself in the form of an eery nightmare that he had had over and over during his childhood. It was a dream of utter darkness, at first, though after a while the darkness seemed to redden with a dim, ugly glow, something like the redness you see through your lids when you look at the sun with closed eyes. But the main thing was the sound—a high, snarling, wailing yammer of a great many voices, re-peatedly receding, then rising and swelling again; as if the sound came nearer in search of him, then went past, only to come back. The sound filled him with a hideous, unexplained terror, though he never knew what made it. It seemed the outcry of some weird semihuman horde—perhaps of ghoulish and inicimal dead who sought to consume him. This went on and on, while he tried to scream, but could not; until he woke shiver-ing miserably, but wet with sweat. He hadn't had this nightmare in a long time, but sometimes an unnatural fear touched him when the coyotes sung in a certain way far off on the sand hills.

Another loony weakness had to do with a smell. This particularly worried him tonight, for the smell that could bring an unreasoning panic into him was the faintly musky, old-leather-and-fur smell of Indians. The queer thing about this was that he felt no fear of the Indians themselves. He had seen a lot of them, and talked with them in the fragments of sign language he knew; he had even made swaps wtih some of them—mostly Caddoes, the far-wandering peddlers of the plains. But if he came upon a place where Indains had camped, or caught a faint scent of one down the wind, the same kind of panic could take hold of him as he felt in the dream. If he failed to connect this with the massacre he had survived, it was perhaps because he had no memory of the massacre. He had been carried asleep into the brush, where he had presently wakened lost and alone in the dark; and that was all he knew about it firsthand. Long after, when he had learned to talk, the disaster had been explained to him, but only in a general way. The Edwardses had never been willing to talk about it much.

And there was one more thing that could cut his strings; it had taken him unawares only two or three times in his life, yet worried him most of all, because it seemed totally meaningless. He judged this third thing to be a pure insanity, and wouldn't let himself think about it at all, times it wasn't forced on him without warning.

So now he rode uneasily, dreading the possibility that he might go to pieces in the clutch, and disgrace himself, in spite of all he could do. He began preaching to himself, inaudibly repeating over and over admonishments that unconsciously imitated Biblical forms. "I will go among them. I will prowl among them in the night. I will lay hands upon them; I will destroy them. Though I be cut in a hundred pieces, I will stand against them. . . ." It didn't seem to do any good.

He believed dawn could be no more than an hour off when Brad came up to whisper to him again. "I think we gone past."

Mart searched the east, fearing to see a graying in the sky too soon. But the night was still very dark, in spite of the dying moon. He could feel a faint warm breath of air upon his left cheek. "Wind's shifted to the south," he answered. "What little there is. I think Amos changed his line. Wants to come at 'em up wind."

"I know. I see that. But I think———"

Amos had stopped, and was holding up his hand. The six others closed up on him, stopped their horses and sat silent in their saddles. Mart couldn't hear anything except the loose animals behind, tearing at the grass. Amos rode on, and they traveled another fifteen minutes before he stopped again.

This time, when the shuffle of their ponies' feet had died, a faint sound lay upon the night, hard to be sure of, and even harder to believe. What

they were hearing was the trilling of frogs. Now, how did they get way
out here? They had to be the little green fellows that can live anywhere
the ground is a little damp, but even so—either they had to shower down
in the rare rains, like the old folks said, or else this march had been here
always, while the dry world built up around.

Amos spoke softly. "Spread out some. Keep in line, and guide on me.
I'll circle close in as I dare."

They spread out until they could just barely see each other, and rode
at the walk, abreast of Amos as he moved on. The frog song came closer,
so close that Mart feared they would trample on Indians before Amos
turned. And now again, listening hard and straining their eyes, they rode
for a long time. The north star was on their right hand for a while. Then
it was behind them a long time. Then on their left, then ahead. At last it
was on their right again, and Amos stopped. They were back where they
started. A faint gray was showing in the east; their timing would have
been perfect, if only what they were after had been here. Mose Harper
pushed his horse in close. "I rode through the ashes of a farm," he said to
Amos. "Did you know that? I thought you was hugging in awful close."

"Hush, now," Amos said. "I'm listening for something."

Mose dropped his tone. "Point is, them ashes showed no spark. Amos,
them devils been gone from here all night."

"Catch up the loose stock," Amos said. "Bring 'em in on short lead."

"Waste of time," Mose Harper argued. "The boys are tard, and the
Comanches is long gone."

"Get that loose stuff in," Amos ordered again, snapping it this time.
"I want hobbles on 'em all—and soon!"

Mart was buckling a hobble on a pack mule when Brad dropped on
one knee beside him to fasten the other cuff. "Look out yonder," Brad
whispered. "When you get a chance."

Mart stood up, following Brad's eyes. A faint grayness had come
evenly over the prairie, as if rising from the ground, but nothing showed a
shadow yet. Mart cupped his hands over his eyes for a moment, then looked
again, trying to look beside, instead of straight at, an unevenness on the
flat land that he could not identify. But now he could not see it at all.

He said, "For a minute I thought—but I guess not."

"I swear something showed itself. Then took down again."

"A wolf, maybe?"

"I don't know. Something funny about this, Mart. The Comanch' ain't
been traveling by night nor laying up by day. Not since the first hundred
miles."

Now followed an odd aimless period, while they waited, and the light
imperceptibly increased. "They're out there," Amos said at last. "They're
going to jump us. There's no doubt of it now." Nobody denied it, or made
any comment. Mart braced himself, checking his rifle again and again.
"I got to hold fast," he kept telling himself. "I got to do my share of the

work. No matter what." His ears were beginning to ring. The others stood about in loose meaningless positions, not huddled, not restless, but motionless, and very watchful. When they spoke they held their voices low.

Then Amos' rifle split the silence down the middle, so that behind lay the quiet night, and ahead rose their hour of violence. They saw what Amos had shot at. A single file of ten Comanches on wiry buffalo ponies had come into view at a thousand yards, materializing out of the seemingly flat earth. They came on at a light trot, ignoring Amos' shot. Zack Harper and Brad Mathison fired, but weren't good enough either at the range.

"Throw them horses down!" Amos shouted. "Git your backs to the marsh and tie down!" He snubbed his pony's muzzle back close to the horn, picked up the off fetlock, and threw the horse heavily. He caught one kicking hind foot, then the other, and pig-tied them across the fore cannons. Some of the others were doing the same thing, but Brad was in a fight with his hotblood animal. It reared eleven feet tall, striking with fore hoofs, trying to break away. "Kill that horse!" Amos yelled. Obediently Brad drew his six-gun, put a bullet into the animal's head under the ear, and stepped from under as it came down.

Ed Newby still stood, his rifle resting ready to fire across the saddle of his straddling horse. Mart lost his head enough to yell, "Can't you throw him? Shall I shoot him, Ed?"

"Leave be! Let the Comanch' put him down."

Mart went to the aid of Charlie MacCorry, who had tied his own horse down all right and was wrestling with a mule. They never did get all of the animals down, but Mart felt a whole lot better with something for his hands to do. Three more of the Comanche single-file columns were in sight now, widely spread, trotting well in hand. They had a ghostly look at first, of the same color as the prairie, in the gray light. Then detail picked out, and Mart saw the bows, lances bearing scalps like pennons, an occasional war shield carried for the medicine in its painted symbols as much as for the bullet-deflecting function of its iron-tough hide. Almost half the Comanches had rifles. Some trader, standing on his right to make a living, must have taken a handsome profit putting those in Comanche hands.

Amos' rifle banged again. One of the lead ponies swerved and ran wild as the rider rolled off into the grass. Immediately, without any other discernible signal, the Comanches leaned low on their ponies and came on at a hard run. Two or three more of the cowmen fired, but without effect.

At three hundred yards the four Comanche columns cut hard left, coming into single loose line that streamed across the front of the defense. The cowmen were as ready as they were going to be; they had got themselves into a ragged semicircle behind their tied-down horses, their backs to the water. Two or three sat casually on their down horses, estimating the enemy.

"May as well hold up," Mose Harper said. His tone was as pressureless as a crackerbox comment. "They'll swing plenty close, before they're done."

"I count thirty-seven," Ed Newby said. He was still on his feet behind his standing horse.

Amos said, "I got me a scalp out there, when I git time to take it."

"Providin'," Mose Harper tried to sound jocular, "they don't leave your carcass here in the dirt."

"I come here to leave Indian carcasses in the dirt. I ain't made no change of plan."

They could see the Comanche war paint now as the warriors rode in plain sight across their front. Faces and naked bodies were striped and splotched in combinations of white, red, and yellow; but whatever the pattern, it was always ponited up wtih heavy accents of black, the Comanche color for war, for battle, and for death. Each warrior always painted up the same, but it was little use memorizing the paint patterns, because you never saw an Indian in war paint except when you couldn't lay hands on him. No use remembering the medicine shields, either, for these, treated as sacred, were never out of their deerskin cases until the moment of battle. Besides paint the Comanches wore breech clouts and moccasins; a few had horn or bear-claw headdresses. But these were young warriors, without the great eagle-feather war bonnets that were the pride of old war chiefs, who had tallied scores of coups. The ponies had their tails tied up, and were ridden bareback, guided by a single jaw rein.

Zack Harper said, "Ain't that big one Buffalo Hump?"

"No-that-ain't-Buffler-Hump," his father squelched him. "Don't talk so damn much."

The Comanche leader turned again and circled in. He brought his warriors past the defenders within fifty yards, ponies loosely spaced, racing full out. Suddenly, from every Comanche throat burst the screaming war cry; and Mart was paralyzed by the impact of that sound, stunned and sickened as by a blow in the belly with a rock. The war cries rose in a high unearthly yammering, wailing and snarling, piercing to his backbone to cut off every nerve he had. It was not exactly the eery sound of his terror-dream, but it was the spirit of that sound, the essence of its meaning. The muscles of his shoulders clenched as if turned to stone, and his hands so vised upon his rifle that it rattled, useless, against the saddle upon which it rested. And at the same time every other muscle in his body went limp and helpless.

Amos spoke into his ear, his low tone heavy wtih authority but unexcited. "Leave your shoulders go loosc. Make your shoulders slack, and your hands will take care of theirselves. Now help me git a couple!"

That worked. All the rifles were sounding now from behind the tied-down horses. Mart breathed again, picked a target, and took aim. One Comanche after another was dropping from sight behind his pony as he came opposite the waiting rifles; they went down in order, like ducks in a shooting gallery, shamming a slaughter that wasn't happening. Each Comanche hung by one heel and a loop of mane on the far side of his pony and fired under the neck, offering only one arm and part of a painted face for target. A pony somersaulted, its rider springing clear unhurt, as Mart fired.

The circling Comanches kept up a continuous firing, each warrior reloading as he swung by, then coming past to fire again. This was the famous Comanche wheel, moving closer wtih every turn, chewing into the defense like a racing grindstone, yet never committing its force beyond possibility of a quick withdrawal. Bullets buzzed over, whispering "Cousin," or howled in ricochet from dust-spouts short of the defenders. A lot of whistling noises were arrows going over. Zack Harper's horse screamed, then went into a heavy continuous groaning.

Another Indain pony tumbled end over end; that was Amos' shot. The rider took cover behind his dead pony before he could be killed. Here and there another pony jerked, faltered, then ran on. A single bullet has to be closely placed to bring a horse down clean.

Amos said loud through his teeth, "The horses, you fools! Get them horses!" Another Comanche pony slid on its knees and stayed down, but its rider got behind it without hurt.

Ed Newby was firing carefully and unhurriedly across his standing horse. The buzzbees made the horse switch its tail, but it stood. Ed said, "You got to get the shoulder. No good to gut-shot 'em. You fellers ain't leading enough." He fired again, and a Comanche dropped from behind his running horse with his brains blown out. It wasn't the shot Ed was trying to make, but he said, "See how easy?"

Fifty yards out in front of him Mart Pauley saw a rifle snake across the quarters of a fallen pony. A horn headdress rose cautiously, and the rifle swung to look Mart square in the eye. He took a snap shot, aiming between the horns, which disappeared, and the enemy rifle slid unfired into the short grass.

After that there was a letup, while the Comanches broke circle and drew off. Out in front of the cowmen lay three downed ponies, two dead Comanches, and two live ones, safe and dangerous behind their fallen horses. Amos was swearing softly and steadily to himself. Charlie MacCorry said he thought he goosed one of them up a little bit, maybe, but didn't believe he convinced him.

"Good God almighty," Brad Mathison broke out, "there's got to be some way to do this!"

Mose Harper scratched his beard and said he thought they done just fine that trip. "Oncet when I was a little shaver, with my pa's bull wagons, a couple of hundred of 'em circled us all day long. We never did get 'em whittled down very much. They just fin'y went away. . . . You glued to the ground, Zack? Take care that horse!"

Zack got up and took a look at his wounded horse, but didn't seem to know what to do. He stood staring at it, until his father walked across and shot it.

Mart said to Amos. "Tell me one thing. Was they hollering like that the time they killed my folks?"

Amos seemed to have to think that over. "I wasn't there," he said at last. "I suppose so. Hard to get used to, ain't it?"

"I don't know," Mart said shakily, "if I'll ever be able to get used to it."

Amos looked at him oddly for some moments. "Don't you let it stop you," he said.

"It won't stop me."

They came on again, and this time they swept past at no more than ten yards. A number of the wounded Comanche ponies lagged back to the tail of the line, their riders saving them for the final spurt, but they were still in action. The Comanches made this run in close bunches; the attack became a smother of confusion. Both lead and arrows poured fast into the cowmen's position.

Zack whimpered, "My God—there's a million of 'em!" and ducked down behind his dead horse.

"Git your damn head up!" Mose yelled at his son. "Fire into 'em!" Zack raised up and went to fighting again.

Sometime during this run Ed Newby's horse fell, pinning Ed under it, but they had no time to go to him while this burst of the attack continued. An unhorsed Comanche came screaming at Amos with clubbed rifle, and so found his finish. Another stopped at least five bullets as a compadre tried to rescue him in a flying pickup. There should have been another; a third pony was down out in front of them, but nobody knew where the rider had got to. This time as they finished the run the Comanches pulled off again to talk it over.

All choices lay with the Comanches for the time being. The cowmen got their backs into the job of getting nine hundred pounds of horse off Ed Newby. Mose Harper said, "How come you let him catch you, Ed?"

Ed Newsby answered through set teeth. "They got my leg—just as he came down—"

Ed's leg was not only bullet-broken, but had doubled under him, and got smashed again by the killed horse. Amos put the shaft of an arrow between Ed's teeth, and the arrowwood splintered as two men put their weight into pulling the leg straight.

A party of a dozen Comanches, mounted on the fastest of the Indian ponies, split off from the main bunch and circled out for still another sweep.

"Hold your fire," Amos ordered. "You hear me? Take cover—but let 'em be!"

Zack Harper, who had fought none too well, chose this moment to harden. "Hold hell! I aim to get me another!"

"You fire and I'll kill you," Amos promised him; and Zack put his rifle down.

Most took to the ground as the Comanches swept past once more, but Amos stood up, watching from under his heavy brows, like a staring ox. The Indians did not attack. They picked up their dismounted and their dead; then they were gone.

"Get them horses up!" Amos loosed the pigging string and got his own horse to its feet.

"They'll scatter now," Mose Harper said.

"Not till they come up with their horse herd, they won't!"

"Somebody's got to stay with Ed," Mose reminded them. "I suppose I'm the one to do that—old crip that I be. But some of them Comanch' might circle back. You'll have to leave Zack with me."

"That's all right."

"And I need one fast man on a good horse to get me help. I can't move him. Not with what we got here."

"We all ought to be back," Amos objected, "in a couple of days."

"Fellers follering Comanches don't necessarily ever come back. I got to have either Brad Mathison or Charlie MacCorry."

"You get Mathison, then," Charlie said. "I'm going on."

Brad whirled on Charlie in an unexpected blast of temper. "There's a quick way to decide it," he said, and stood braced, his open hand ready above his holster.

Charlie MacCorry looked Brad in the eye as he spat at Brad's boots and missed. But after that he turned away.

So three rode on, following a plume of dust already distant upon the prairie. "We'll have the answer soon," Amos promised. "Soon. We don't dast let 'em lose us now."

Mart Pauley was silent. He didn't want to ask him what three riders could do when they caught up with the Comanches. He was afraid Amos didn't know.

They kept the feather of dust in sight all day, but in the morning, after a night camp without water, they failed to pick it up. The trail of the Comanche war party still led westward, broad and plain, marked at intervals with the carcasses of buffalo ponies wounded at the Cat-tails. They pushed on, getting all they could out of their horses.

This day, the second after the Fight at the Cat-tails, became the strangest day of the pursuit before it was done, because of something unexplained that happened during a period while they were separated.

A line of low hills, many hours away beyond the plain, began to shove up from the horizon as they rode. After a while they knew the Comanches they followed were already into that broken country where pursuit would be slower and more treacherous than before.

"Sometimes it seems to me," Amos said, "them Comanches fly with their elbows, carrying the pony along between their knees. You can nurse a horse along till he falls and dies, and you walk on carrying your saddle. Then a Comanche comes along, and gets that horse up, and rides it twenty miles more. Then eats it."

"Don't we have any chance at all?"

"Yes. . . . We got a chance." Amos went through the motions of spitting, with no moisture in his mouth to spit. "And I'll tell you what it be. An Indian will chase a thing until he thinks he's chased it enough. Then he quits. So the same when he runs. After while he figures we must have quit, and he starts to loaf. Seemingly he never learns there's such a thing as a critter that might just keep coming on."

As he looked at Amos, sitting his saddle like a great lump of rock— yet a lump that was somehow of one piece with the horse—Mart Pauley was willing to believe that to have Amos following you could be a deadly thing with no end to it, ever, until he was dead.

"If only they stay bunched," Amos finished, and it was a prayer; "if only they don't split and scatter . . . we'll come up to 'em. We're bound to come up."

Late in the morning they came to a shallow sink, where a number of posthole wells had been freshly dug among the dry reeds. Here the trail of the main horse herd freshened, and they found the bones of an eaten horse, polished shiny in a night by the wolves. And there was the Indian smell, giving Mart a senseless dread to fight off during their first minutes in this place.

"Here's where the rest of 'em was all day yesterday," Amos said when he had wet his mouth; "the horse guards, and the stole horses, and maybe some crips Henry shot up. And our people—if they're still alive."

Brad Mathison was prone at a pothole, dipping water into himself with his tin cup. but he dropped the cup to come up with a snap. As he spoke, Mart Pauley heard the same soft tones Brad's father used when he neared an end of words. "I've heard thee say that times enough," Brad said.

"What?" Amos asked, astonished.

"Maybe she's dead," Brad said, his bloodshot blue eyes burning steadily into Amos' face. "Maybe they're both dead. But if I hear it from thee again, thee has chosen me—so help me God!"

Amos stared at Brad mildly, and when he spoke again it was to Mart Pauley. "They've took an awful big lead. Them we fought at the Cat-tails must have got here early last night."

"And the whole bunch pulled out the same hour," Mart finished it.

It meant they were nine or ten hours back—and every one of the Comanches was now riding a rested animal. Only one answer to that—

such as it was: They had to rest their own horses, whether they could spare time for it or not. They spent an hour dipping water into their hats; the ponies could not reach the little water in the bottom of the posthole wells. When one hole after another had been dipped dry they could only wait for the slow seepage to bring in another cupful, while the horses stood by. After that they took yet another hour to let the horses crop the scant bunch grass, helping them by piling grass they cut with their knives. A great amount of this work gained only the slightest advantage, but none of them begrudged it.

Then, some hours beyond the posthole wells, they came to a vast sheet of rock, as flat and naked as it had been laid down when the world was made. Here the trail ended, for unshod hoofs left no mark on the barren stone. Amos remembered this reef in the plain. He believed it to be about four miles across by maybe eight or nine miles long, as nearly as he could recall. All they could do was split up and circle the whole ledge to find where the trail came off the rock.

Mart Pauley, whose horse seemed the worst beat out, was sent straight across. On the far side he was to wait, grazing within sight of the ledge, until one of the others came around to him; then both were to ride to meet the third.

Thus they separated. It was while they were apart, each rider alone with his tiring horse, that some strange thing happened to Amos, so that he became a mystery in himself throughout their last twenty-four hours together.

Brad Mathison was first to get around the rock sheet to where Mart Pauley was grazing his horse. Mart had been there many hours, yet they rode south a long way before they sighted Amos, waiting for them far out on the plain.

"Hasn't made much distance, has he?" Brad commented.

"Maybe the rock slick stretches a far piece down this way."

"Don't look like it to me."

Mart didn't say anthing more. He could see for himself that the reef ended in a couple of miles.

Amos pointed to a far-off landmark as they came up. "The trail cuts around that hump," he said, and led the way. The trail was where Amos had said it would be, a great welter of horse prints already blurred by the wind. But no other horse had been along here since the Comanches passed long before.

"Kind of thought to see your tracks here," Brad said.

"Didn't come this far."

Then where the hell had he been all this time? If it had been Lije Powers, Mart would have known he had sneaked himself a nap. "You lost a bed blanket," Mart noticed.

"Slipped out of the strings somewhere. I sure ain't going back for it now." Amos was speaking too carefully. He put Mart in mind of a man half stopped in a fist fight, making out he was unhurt so his opponent wouldn't know, and finish him.

"You feel all right?" he asked Amos.

"Sure. I feel fine." Amos forced a smile, and this was a mistake, for he didn't look to be smiling. He looked as if he had been kicked in the face. Mart tried to think of an excuse to lay a hand on him, to see if he had a fever; but before he could think of anything Amos took off his hat and wiped sweat off his forehead with his sleeve. That settled that. A man doesn't sweat with the fever on him.

"You look like you et something," Mart said.

"Don't know what it could have been. Oh, I did come on three-four rattlesnakes." Seemingly the thought made Amos hungry. He got out a leaf of jerky, and tore strips from it with his teeth.

"You sure you feel—"

Amos blew up, and yelled at him. "I'm all right, I tell you!" He quirted his horse, and loped out ahead.

They off-saddled in the shelter of the hump. A northering wind came up when the sun was gone; its bite reminded them that they had been riding deep into the fall of the year. They huddled against their saddles, and chewed corn meal. Brad walked across and stood over Amos. He spoke reasonably.

"Looks like you ought to tell us, Mr. Edwards." He waited, but Amos didn't answer him. "Something happened while you was gone from us today. Was you laid for? We didn't hear no guns, but . . . Be you hiding an arrow hole from us by any chance?"

"No," Amos said. "There wasn't nothing like that."

Brad went back to his saddle and sat down. Mart laid his bedroll flat, hanging on by the upwind edge, and rolled himself up in it, coming out so that his head was on the saddle.

"A man has to learn to forgive himself," Amos said, his voice unnaturally gentle. He seemed to be talking to Brad Mathison. "Or he can't stand to live. It so happens we be Texans. We took a reachin' holt, way far out, past where any man has right or reason to hold on. Or if we didn't, our folks did, so we can't leave off, without giving up that they were fools, wasting their lives, and wasted in the way they died."

The chill striking up through Mart's blankets made him homesick for the Edwards' kitchen, like it was on winter nights, all warm and light, and full of good smells, like baking bread. And their people—Mart had taken them for granted, largely; just a family, people living alone together, such as you never thought about, especially, unless you got mad at them. He had never known they were dear to him until the whole thing was busted up forever. He wished Amos would shut up.

"This is a rough country," Amos was saying. "It's a country knows how to scour a human man right off the face of itself. A Texan is nothing but a human man way out on a limb. This year, and next year, and maybe for a hundred more. But I don't think it'll be forever. Someday this country will be a fine good place to be. Maybe it needs our bones in the ground before that time can come."

Mart was thinking of Laurie now. He saw her in a bright warm kitchen like the Edwards', and he thought how wonderful it would be living in the same house with Laurie, in the same bed. But he was on the empty prairie without any fire—and he had bedded himself on a sharp rock, he noticed now.

"We've come on a year when things go hard," Amos talked on. "We get this tough combing over because we're Texans. But the feeling we get that we fail, and judge wrong, and go down in guilt and shame—that's because we be human men. So try to remember one thing. It wasn't your fault, no matter how it looks. You got let in for this just by being born. Maybe there never is any way out of it once you're born a human man, except straight across the coals of hell."

Mart rolled out to move his bed. He didn't really need that rock in his ribs all night. Brad Mathison got up, moved out of Amos' line of sight, and beckoned Mart with his head. Mart put his saddle on his bed, so it wouldn't blow away, and walked out a ways with Brad on the dark prairie.

"Mart," Brad said when they were out of hearing, "the old coot is just as crazy as a bedbug fell in the rum."

"Sure sounds so. What in all hell you think happened?"

"God knows. Maybe nothing at all. Might be he just plainly cracked. He was wandering around without rhyme or principle when we come on him today."

"I know."

"This puts it up to you and me," Brad said. "You see that, don't you? We may be closer the end than you think."

"What you want to do?"

"My horse is standing up best. Tomorrow I'll start before light, and scout on out far as I can reach. You come on as you can."

"My horse got a rest today," Mart began.

"Keep saving him. You'll have to take forward when mine gives down."

"All right." Mart judged that tomorrow was going to be a hard day to live far behind on a failing pony. Like Brad, he had a feeling they were a whole lot closer to the Comanches than they had any real reason to believe.

They turned in again. Though they couldn't know it, until they heard about it a long time after, that was the night Ed Newby came out of his delirium, raised himself for a long look at his smashed leg, then put a bullet in his brain.

By daylight Brad Mathison was an hour gone. Mart hadn't known how Amos would take it, but there was no fuss at all. They rode on in silence, crossing chains of low hills, with dry valleys between; they were beginning to find a little timber, willow and cottonwood mostly along the dusty streambeds. They were badly in need of water again; they would have to dig for it soon. All day long the big tracks of Brad Mathison's horse led on, on top of the many-horse trample left by the Comanche herd; but he was stirring no dust, and they could only guess how far he must be ahead.

Toward sundown Amos must have begun to worry about him, for he sent Mart on a long swing to the north, where a line of sand hills offered high ground, to see what he could see. He failed to make out any sign of Brad; but, while he was in the hills alone, the third weird thing that could unstring him set itself in front of him again. He had a right to be nerveraw at this point, perhaps; the vast emptiness of the plains had taken on a haunted, evilly enchanted feel since the massacre. And of course they were on strange ground now, where all things seemed faintly odd and wrong, because unfamiliar. . . .

He had dismounted near the top of a broken swell, led his horse around it to get a distant view without showing himself against the sky. He walked around a ragged shoulder—and suddenly froze at sight of what stood on the crest beyond. It was nothing but a juniper stump; not for an instant did he mistake it for anything else. But it was in the form of similar stumps he had seen two or three times before in his life, and always with the same unexplainable effect. The twisted remains of the juniper, blackened and sand-scoured, had vaguely the shape of a man, or the withered corpse of a man; one arm seemed upraised in a writhing gesture of agony, or perhaps of warning. But nothing about it explained the awful sinking of the heart, the terrible sense of inevitable doom, that overpowered him each of the times he encountered this shape.

An Indian would have turned back, giving up whatever he was about; for he would have known the thing for a medicine tree with a powerful spirit in it, either telling him of a doom or placing a doom upon him. And Mart himself more or less believed that the thing was some kind of a sign. An evil prophecy is always fulfilled, if you put no time limit upon it; fulfilled quite readily, too, if you are a child counting little misfortunes as disasters. So Mart had the impression that this mysteriously upsetting kind of an encounter had always been followed by some dreadful, unforeseeable thing.

He regarded himself as entirely mature now, and was convinced that to be filled with cowardice by the sight of a dead tree was a silly and unworthy thing. He supposed he ought to go and uproot that desolate twist of wood, or whittle it down, and so master the thing forever. But even to move toward it was somehow impossible to him, to a degree that such a move was not even thinkable. He returned to Amos feeling shaken and sickish, unstrung as much by doubt of his own soundness as by the sense of evil prophecy itself.

The sun was setting when they saw Brad again. He came pouring off a long hill at four miles, raising a restless dust. "I saw her!" he yelled, and hauled up sliding. "I saw Lucy!"

"How far?"

"They're camped by a running crick—they got fires going—look, you can see the smoke!" A thin haze lay flat in the quiet air above the next line of hills.

"Ought to be the Warrior River," Amos said. "Water in it, huh?"

"Didn't you hear what I said?" Brad shouted. "I tell you I saw Lucy— I saw her walking through the camp—"

Amos' tone was bleak. "How far off was you?"

"Not over seventy rod. I bellied up a ridge this side the river, and they was right below me!"

"Did you see Debbie?" Mart got in.

"No, but—they got a bunch of baggage; she might be asleep amongst that. I counted fifty-one Comanch'— What you unsaddling for?"

"Good a place as any," Amos said. "Can't risk no more dust like you just now kicked up. Come dark we'll work south, and water a few miles below. We can take our time."

"Time?"

"They're making it easy for us. Must think they turned us back at the Cat-tails, and don't have to split up. All we got to do is foller to their village—"

"Village? You gone out of your mind?"

"Let 'em get back to their old chiefs and their squaws. The old chiefs have gone cagy; a village of families can't run like a war party can. For all they know——"

"Look—look——" Brad hunted desperately for words that would fetch Amos back to reality. "Lucy's there! I saw her—can't you hear? We got to get her out of there!"

"Brad," Amos said, "I want to know what you saw in that camp you thought was Lucy."

"I keep telling you I saw her walk——"

"I heard you!" Amos' voice rose and crackled this time. *"What* did you see walk? Could you see her yellow hair?"

"She had a shawl on her head. But——"

"She ain't there, Brad."

"God damn it, I tell you, I'd know her out of a million——"

"You saw a buck in a woman's dress," Amos said. "They're game to put anything on 'em. You know that."

Brad's sun-polished blue eyes blazed up as they had at the pothole water, and his tone went soft again. "Thee lie," he said. "I've told thee afore——"

"But there's something I ain't told you," Amos said. "I found Lucy yesterday. I buried her in my own saddle blanket. With my own hands by the rock. I thought best to keep it from you long's I could."

The blood drained from Brad's face, and at first he could not speak. Then he stammered, "Did they—was she——"

"Shut up!" Amos yelled at him. "Never ask me what more I seen!"

Brad stood as if knocked out for half a minute more; then he turned to his horse, stiffly, as if he didn't trust his legs too well, and he tightened his cinch.

Amos said, "Get hold of yourself! Grab him, Mart!" Brad stepped into the saddle, and the gravel jumped from the hoofs of his horse. He leveled out down the Comanche trail again, running his horse as if he would never need it again.

"Go after him! You can handle him better than me."

Mart Pauley had pulled his saddle, vaulted bareback onto the sweaty withers, and in ten jumps opened up all the speed his beat-out horse had left. He gained no ground on Brad, though he used up what horse he had in trying to. He was chasing the better horse—and the better rider, too, Mart supposed. They weighed about the same, and both had been on horses before they could walk. Some small magic that could not be taught or learned, but had been born into Brad's muscles, was what made the difference. Mart was three furlongs back as Brad sifted into the low hills.

Up the slopes Mart followed, around a knob, and onto the down slope, spurring his wheezing horse at every jump. From here he could see the last little ridge, below and beyond as Brad had described it, with the smoke of Comanche campfires plain above it. Mart's horse went to its knees as he jumped it into a steep ravine, but he was able to drag it up.

Near the mouth of the ravine he found Brad's horse tied to a pin-oak scrub; he passed it, and rode on into the open, full stretch. Far up the last ridge he saw Brad climbing strongly. He looked back over his shoulder, watching Mart without slowing his pace. Mart charged through a dry tributary of the Warrior and up the ridge, his horse laboring gamely as it fought the slope. Brad stopped just short of the crest, and Mart saw him tilt his canteen skyward; he drained it unhurriedly, and threw it away. He was already on his belly at the crest as Mart dropped from his horse and scrambled on all fours to his side.

"God damn it, Brad, what are you doing?"

"Get the hell out of here. You ain't wanted."

Down below, at perhaps four hundred yards, half a hundred Comanches idled about their business. They had some piled mule packs, a lot of small fires in shallow fire holes, and parts of at least a dozen buffalo down there. The big horse herd grazed unguarded beyond. Most of the bucks were throwing chunks of meat into the fires, to be snatched out and bolted as soon as the meat blackened on the outside. No sign of pickets. The Comanches relied for safety upon their horsemanship and the great empty distances of the prairies. They didn't seem to know what a picket was.

Mart couldn't see any sign of Debbie. And now he heard Brad chamber a cartridge.

"You'll get Debbie killed, you son-of-a-bitch!"

"Get out of here, I said!" Brad had his cheek on the stock; he was aiming into the Comanche camp. He took a deep breath, let it all out, and lay inert, waiting for his head to steady for the squeeze. Mart grabbed the rifle, and wrenched it out of line.

They fought for possession, rolling and sliding down the slope. Brad rammed a knee into Mart's belly, twisted the rifle from his hands, and broke free. Mart came to his feet before Brad, and dived to pin him down. Brad braced himself on one hand, and with the other swung the rifle by the grip of the stock. Blood jumped from the side of Mart's head as the barrel struck. He fell backward, end over end; then went limp, rolled slackly down the hill, and lay still where he came to rest.

Brad swore softly as he settled himself into firing position again. Then he changed his mind and trotted northward, just behind the crest of the ridge.

Mart came to slowly, without memory or any idea of where he was. Sight did not return to him at once. His hands groped, and found the rocky ground on which he lay; and next he recognized a persistent rattle of gunfire and the high snarling of Comanche war cries, seemingly some distance away. His hands went to his head, and he felt clotting blood. He reckoned he had got shot in the head, and was blind, and panic took him. He struggled up, floundered a few yards without any sense of balance, and fell into a dry wash. The fall knocked the wind out of him, and when he had got his breath back his mind had cleared enough so that he lay still.

Some part of his sight was coming back by the time he heard a soft footstep upon sand. He could see a shadowy shape above him, swimming in a general blur. He played possum, staring straight up with unwinking eyes, waiting to lose his scalp.

"Can you hear me, Mart?" Amos said.

He knew Amos dropped to his knees beside him. "I got a bullet in my brain," Mart said. "I'm blind."

Amos struck a match and passed it before one eye and then the other. Mart blinked and rolled his head to the side. "You're all right," Amos said. "Hit your head, that's all. Lie still till I get back!" He left, running.

Amos was gone a long time. The riflery and the war cries stopped, and the prairie became deathly still. For a while Mart believed he could sense a tremor in the ground that might mean the movement of many horses; then this faded, and the night chill began to work upward out of the ground. But Mart was able to see the winking of the first stars when he heard Amos coming back.

"You look all right to me," Amos said.

"Where's Brad?"

Amos was slow in answering. "Brad fit him a one-man war," he said at last. "He skirmished 'em from the woods down yonder. Now, why from there? Was he trying to lead them off you?"

"I don't know."

"Wha'd you do? Get throwed?"

"I guess."

"Comanches took him for a Ranger company, seemingly. They're long gone. Only they took time to finish him first."

"Was he scalped?"

"Now, what do you think?"

After he had found Mart, Amos had backed off behind a hill and built a signal fire. He slung creosote bush on it, raised a good smoke, and took his time sending puff messages with his saddle blanket.

"Messages to who?"

"Nobody, damn it. No message, either, rightly—just a lot of different-size hunks of smoke. Comanches couldn't read it, because it didn't say nothing. So they upped stakes and rode. It's all saved our hair, once they was stirred up."

Mart said, "We better go bury Brad."

"I done that already." Then Amos added one sad, sinister thing. "All of him I could find."

Mart's horse had run off with the Comanche ponies, but they still had Brad's horse and Amos'. And the Comanches had left them plenty of buffalo meat. Amos dug a fire pit, narrow but as deep as he could reach, in the manner of the Wichitas. From the bottom of this, his cooking fire could reflect only upon its own smoke, and he didn't put on stuff that made any. When Mart had filled up on buffalo meat he turned wrong side out, but an hour later he tried again, and this time it stuck.

"Feel like you'll be able to ride come daylight?"

"Sure I'll ride."

"I don't believe we got far to go," Amos said. "The Comanch' been acting like they're close to home. We'll come up to their village soon. Maybe tomorrow."

Mart felt much better now. "Tomorrow," he repeated.

Tomorrow came and went, and showed them they were wrong. Now at last the Comanche war party split up, and little groups carrying two or three horses to the man ranged off in ten directions. Amos and Mart picked one trail at random and followed it with all tenacity as it turned and doubled, leading them in far futile ways. They lost it on rock ledges, in running water, and in blown sand, but always found it again, and kept on.

Another month passed before all trails became one, and the paired scratches of many travois showed they were on the track of the main village at last. They followed it northeast, gaining ground fast as the trail grew fresh.

"Tomorrow," Amos said once more. "All hell can't keep them ahead of us tomorrow."

That night it snowed.

By morning the prairie was a vast white blank; and every day for a week more snow fell. They made some wide, reaching casts and guesses, but the plains were empty. One day they pushed their fading horses in a two-hour climb, toiling through drifts to the top of a towering butte. At its craggy lip they set their gaunted horses in silence, while their eyes swept the plain for a long time. The sky was dark that day, but near the ground the air was clear; they could see about as far as a man could ride through that clogging snow in a week. Neither found anything to say, for they knew they were done. Mart had not wept since the night of the massacre. Then he had suffered a blinding shock, and an inconsolable, aching grief so great he had never expected to cry again. But now as he faced the emptiness of a world that was supposed to have Debbie in it, yet was blank to its farthest horizons, his throat began to knot and hurt. He faced away to hide from Amos the tears he could no longer hold back; and soon after that he started his horse slowly back down that long, long slope, lest Amos hear the convulsive jerking of his breath and the snuffling of tears that ran down inside his nose.

They made an early, snowbound camp, with no call to hurry any more or stretch the short days. "This don't change anything," Amos said doggedly. "Not in the long run. If she's alive, she's safe by now, and they've kept her to raise. They do that time and again with a little child small enough to be raised their own way. So . . . we'll find them in the end; I promise you that. By the Almighty God, I promise you that! We'll catch up to 'em, just as sure as the turning of the earth!"

But now they had to start all over again in another way.

FLAME ON THE FRONTIER

by DOROTHY JOHNSON

Dorothy Johnson is one of the few women to have written seriously and well about the West. About a decade ago she published a slight paperback volume, Indian Country, *a collection of deceptively simple stories. When* The Hanging Tree *was published, there was no question that this second collection was equally as good as the first. In Dorothy Johnson's stories there is more undersatnding of the emotions of the Westerner of the nineteenth century than almost anyone else has brought to the subject. Her writing is sharp and pointed, poignant and meaningful, and almost every one of her stories says something about the West in a way it has not been said before. More interested in people than in history or background, she is one of the few fiction writers who can recreate her place and period, without recourse to the trappings and symbols of the myth.*

On Sunday morning, wearing white man's sober clothing, a Sioux chief named Little Crow attended the church service at the Lower Agency and afterward shook hands with the preacher. On Sunday afternoon, Little Crow's painted and feathered Santee Sioux swooped down on the settlers in bloody massacre. There was no warning. . . .

Hannah Harris spoke sharply to her older daughter, Mary Amanda. "I've told you twice to get more butter from the spring. Now step! The men want to eat."

The men—Oscar Harris and his two sons, sixteen and eighteen—sat in stolid patience on a bench in front of the cabin, waiting to be called to the table.

Mary Amanda put down the book she had borrowed from a distant neighbor and went unwillingly out of the cabin. She liked to read and was proud that she knew how, but she never had another book in her hands as long as she lived. Mary Amanda Harris was, on that day in August in 1862, just barely thirteen years old.

Her little sister Sarah tagged along down to the spring for lack of anything better to do. She was healthily hungry, and the smell of frying chicken had made her fidget until her mother had warned, "Am I going to have to switch you?"

The two girls wrangled as they trotted down the accustomed path.

"Now what'd you come tagging for?" demanded Mary Amanda. She wanted to stay, undisturbed, in the world of the book she had been reading.

Sarah said,"I guess I got a right to walk here as good as you."

She shivered, not because of any premonition but simply because the air was cool in the brush by the spring. She glanced across the narrow creek and saw a paint-striped face. Before she could finish her scream, the Indian had leaped the creek and smothered her mouth.

At the cabin they heard that single, throat-tearing scream instantly muffled. They knew what had to be done; they had planned it, because this day might come to any frontier farm.

Hannah Harris scooped up the baby boy, Willie, and hesitated only to cry out, "The girls?"

The father, already inside the cabin, handed one rifle to his eldest son as he took the other for himself. To Jim, who was sixteen, he barked, "The axe, boy."

Hannah knew what she had to do—run and hide—but that part of the plan had included the little girls, too. She was to take the four younger children, including the dull boy, Johnny. She was too sick with the meaning of that brief scream to be able to change the plan and go without the girls.

But Oscar roared, "Run for the rushes! You crazy?" and broke her paralysis. With the baby under one arm she began to run down the hill to a place by the river where the rushes grew high.

The only reason Hannah was able to get to the rushes with her two youngest boys was that the men, Oscar and Jim and Zeke, delayed the Indians for a few minutes. The white men might have barricaded themselves in the cabin and stood off the attackers for a longer period, but the approaching Indians would have seen that frantic scuttling into the rushes.

Oscar and Jim and Zeke did not defend. They attacked. With the father going first, they ran toward the spring and met the Indians in the brush. Fighting there, they bought a little time for the three to hide down by the river, and they paid for it with their lives.

Hannah, the mother, chose another way of buying time. She heard the invaders chopping at whatever they found in the cabin. She heard their howls as they found clothing and kettles and food. She stayed in the rushes as long as she dared, but when she smelled the smoke of the cabin burning, she knew the Indians would be ranging out to see what else might be found.

Then she thrust the baby into Johnny's arms and said fiercely, "You take care of him and don't you let him go until they kill you."

She did not give him any instructions about how to get to a place of safety. There might be no such place.

She kissed Johnny on the forehead and she kissed the baby twice, because he was so helpless and because he was, blessedly, not crying.

She crawled to the left, far to the left of the children, so that she would not be seen coming directly from their hiding place. Then she came dripping up out of the rushes and went shrieking up the hill straight toward the Indians.

When they started down to meet her, she hesitated and turned. She ran, still screaming, toward the river, as if she were so crazed she did not know what she was doing. But she knew. She knew very well. She did exactly what a meadowlark will do if its nest in the grass is menaced—she came into the open, crying and frantic, and lured the pursuit away from her young.

But the meadowlark acts by instinct, not by plan. Hannah Harris had to fight down her instinct, which was to try to save her own life.

As the harsh hands seized her, she threw her arm across her eyes so as not to see death. . . .

Of the two girls down at the spring, only Sarah screamed. Mary Amanda did not have time. A club, swung easily by a strong arm, cracked against her head.

Sarah Harris heard the brief battle and knew her father's voice, but she did not have to see the bodies, a few yards away on the path through the brush. One of the Indians held her without difficulty. She was a thin little girl, nine years old.

Mary Amanda was unconscious and would have drowned except that her guard pulled her out of the creek and laid her, face down, on the gravel bank.

The girls never saw their cabin again. Their captors tied their hands behind them and headed back the way they had come to rejoin the war party. The girls were too frightened to cry or speak. They stumbled through the brush.

Mary Amanda fell too many times. Finally she gave up and lay still, waiting to die, sobbing quietly. Her guard grunted and lifted his club.

Sarah flew at him shrieking. Her hands were tied, but her feet were free and she could still run.

"Don't you hurt my sister!" she scolded. "Don't you do it, I say!" She bowed her head and bunted him.

The Indian, who had never had anything to do with white people except at a distance, or in furious flurries of raiding, was astonished by her courage, and impressed. All he knew of white girls was that they ran away, screaming, and then were caught. This one had the desperate, savage fury of his own women. She chattered as angrily as a bluejay. (Bluejay was the name he gave her, the name everyone called her, in the years she lived and grew up among the Sioux.)

She had knocked the wind out of him, but he was amused. He jerked the older girl, Mary Amanda, to her feet.

The mother, Hannah, was taken along by the same route, about a mile behind them, but she did not know they were still alive. One of them she saw again six years later. The other girl she never saw again.

For hours she went stumbling, praying, "Lord in thy mercy, make them kill me fast!"

When they did not, she let hope flicker, and when they camped that night, she began to ask timidly, "God, could you help me get away?"

She had no food that night, and no water. An Indian had tied her securely.

The following day her captors caught up with a larger party, carrying much loot and driving three other white women. They were younger than Hannah. That was what saved her.

When she was an old woman, she told the tale grimly: "I prayed to the Lord to let me go, and He turned the Indians' backs on me and I went into the woods, and that was how I got away."

She did not tell how she could still hear the piercing shrieks of the other white women, even when she was far enough into the woods so that she dared to run.

She blundered through the woods, hiding at every sound, praying to find a trail, but terrified when she came to one, for fear there might be Indians around the next bend. After she reached the trail and began to follow it, she had a companion, a shaggy yellow dog.

For food during two days she had berries. Then she came upon the dog eating a grouse he had killed, and she stooped, but he growled.

"Nice doggie," she crooned. "Nice old Sheppy!"

She abased herself with such praise until—probably because he had caught other game and was not hungry—he let her take the tooth-torn, dirt-smeared remnants. She picked off the feathers with fumbling fingers, washed the raw meat in the creek and ate it as she walked.

She smelled wood smoke the next morning and crawled through brush until she could see a clearing. She saw white people there in front of a cabin, and much bustling. She heard children crying and the authoritative voices of women. She stood up then and ran, screaming, toward the cabin, with the dog jumping and barking beside her.

One of the hysterical women there seized a rifle and fired a shot at Hannah before a man shouted, "She's white!" and ran out to meet her.

There were sixteen persons in the cramped cabin or near it—refugees from other farms. Hannah Harris kept demanding, while she wolfed down food, "Ain't anybody seen two little girls? Ain't anybody seen a boy and a baby?"

Nobody had seen them.

The draggled-skirted women in the crowded cabin kept busy with their children, but Hannah Harris had no children any more—she who had had four sons and two daughters. She dodged among the refugees, beseeching, "Can't I help with something? Ain't there anything I can do?"

A busy old woman said with sharp sympathy, "Miz Harris, you go lay down some place. Git some sleep. All you been through!"

Hannah Harris understood that there was no room for her there. She stumbled outside and lay down in a grassy place in the shade. She slept, no longer hearing the squalling of babies and the wrangling of the women.

Hannah awoke to the crying of voices she knew and ran around to the front of the cabin. She saw two men carrying a stretcher made of two shirts buttoned around poles. A bundle sagged on the stretcher, and a woman was trying to lift it, but it cried with two voices.

Johnny lay there, clutching the baby, and both of them were screaming.

Kneeling, she saw blood on Johnny's feet and thought with horror. "Did the Injuns do that?" Then she remembered, "No, he was barefoot when we ran."

He would not release the baby, even for her. He was gaunt, his ribs showed under his tattered shirt. His eyes were partly open, and his lips were drawn back from his teeth. He was only half conscious, but he still had strength enough to clutch his baby brother, though the baby screamed with hunger and fear.

Hannah said in a strong voice, "Johnny, you can let go now. You can let Willie go. Johnny, this is your mother talking."

With a moan, he let his arms go slack.

For the rest of his life, and he lived another fifty years, he suffered from nightmares and often awoke screaming.

With two of her children there Hannah Harris was the equal of any woman. She pushed among the others to get to the food, to find cloth for Johnny's wounded feet. She wrangled with them, defending sleeping space for her children.

For a few months she made a home for her boys by keeping house for a widower named Lincoln Bartlett, whose two daughters had been killed at a neighbor's cabin. Then she married him.

The baby, Willie, did not live to grow up, in spite of the sacrifices that had been made for him. He died of diphtheria. While Link Bartlett dug a little grave, Hannah sat, stern but dry-eyed, on a slab bench, cradling the still body in her arms.

The dull boy, Johnny, burst out hoarsely, "It wasn't no use after all, was it?" and his mother understood.

She told him strongly, "Oh, yes, it was! It was worth while, all you did. He's dead now, but he died in my arms, with a roof over him. I'll know where he's buried. It ain't as if the Indians had butchered him some place that I'd never know."

She carried the body across the room and laid it tenderly in the box that had been Willie's bed and would be his coffin. She turned to her other son and said, "Johnny, come sit on my lap."

He was a big boy, twelve years old, and he was puzzled by this invitation, as he was puzzled about so many things. Awkwardly he sat on her knees, and awkwardly he permitted her to cuddle his head against her shoulder.

"How long since your mother kissed you?" she asked, and he mumbled back, "Don't know."

She kissed his forehead. "You're my big boy. You're my Johnny."

He lay in her arms for a while, tense and puzzled. After a while, not knowing why it was necessary to cry, he began to sob, and she rocked him back and forth. She had no tears left.

Johnny said something then that he had thought over many times, often enough to be sure about it. "It was him that mattered most, I guess."

Hannah looked down at him, shocked.

"He was my child and I loved him," she said. "It was him I worried about. . . . But it was you I trusted."

The boy blinked and scowled. His mother bowed her head.

"I never said so. I thought you knowed that. When I give him to you that day, Johnny boy, I put more trust in you than I did in the Lord God."

That was a thing he always remembered—the time his mother made him understand that for a while he had been more important than God.

The Harris sisters were sold twice, the second time to a Sioux warrior named Runs Buffalo, whose people ranged far to the westward.

Bluejay never had to face defeat among the Indians. The little girl who had earned her name by scolding angrily had the privileges of a baby girl. She was fed and cared for like the Indian children, and she had more freedom and less scolding than she had had in the cabin that was burned. Like the other girls, she was freer than the boys. Her responsibility would not begin for three or four years. When the time came, she would be taught to do the slow, patient work of the women, in preparation for being a useful wife. But while she was little, she could play.

While the boys learned to shoot straight and follow tracks, while they tested and increased their endurance and strength, the little girls played and laughed in the sun. Bluejay did not even have a baby to look after, because she was the youngest child in the lodge of Runs Buffalo. She was the petted one, the darling, and the only punishment she knew was what she deserved for profaning holy objects. Once at home she had been switched by her father for putting a dish on the great family Bible. In the Indian village, she learned to avoid touching medicine bundles or sacred shields and to keep silent in the presence of men who understood religious mysteries.

Mary Amanda, stooped over a raw buffalo hide, scraping it hour after hour with tools of iron and bone, because that was women's work and she was almost a woman, heard familiar shrill arguments among the younger girls, the same arguments that had sounded in the white settlement, and in the same language: "You're it!" . . . "I am not!"

That much the little Indian girls learned of English. Sarah learned Sioux so fast that she no longer needed English and would have stopped speaking it except that her older sister insisted.

Mary Amanda learned humility through blows. To her, everything about the Indians was contemptible. She learned their language simply to keep from being cuffed by the older women, who were less shocked at her ignorance of their skills than at her unwillingness to learn the work that was a woman's privilege to perform. She sickened at the business of softening hides with a mixture of clay and buffalo manure. If she had been more docile, she might have been an honored daughter in the household. Instead, she was a sullen slave. Mary Amanda remembered what Sarah often forgot: that she was white. Mary Amanda never stopped hoping that they would be rescued. The name the Indians gave her was The Foreigner.

When she tried to take Sarah aside to talk English, the old woman of the household scolded.

Mary Amanda spoke humbly in Sioux. "Bluejay forgets to talk like our own people. I want her to know how to talk."

The old woman growled, "You are Indians," and Mary Amanda answered, "It is good for Indians to be able to talk to white people."

The argument was sound. A woman interpreter would never be permitted in the councils of chiefs and captains, but who could tell when the skill might be useful? The girls were allowed to talk together, but Sarah preferred Sioux.

When The Foreigner was sixteen years old she had four suitors. She knew what a young man meant by sending a gift to the lodge and later standing out in front, blanket-wrapped and silent.

When the young man came, Mary Amanda pretended not to notice, and the old woman pretended with her, but there was chuckling in the lodge as everyone waited to see whether The Foreigner would go out, perhaps to bring in water from the creek.

Her little sister teased her. "Go on out. All you have to do is let him put his blanket around you and talk. Go on. Other girls do."

"Indian girls do," Mary Amanda answered sadly. "That ain't the way boys do their courting back home."

The tall young men were patient. Sometimes as many as three at once stood out there through twilight into darkness, silent and waiting. They were eligible, respected young men, skilled in hunting and taking horses, proved in courage, schooled in the mysteries of protective charms and chanted prayer. All of them had counted coup in battle.

Mary Amanda felt herself drawn toward the lodge opening. It would be so easy to go out!

She asked Sarah humbly, "Do you think it's right, the way they buy their wives? Of course, the girl's folks give presents to pay back."

Sarah shrugged. "What other way is there? . . . If it was me, I'd go out fast enough. Just wait till I'm older!" She reminded her sister of something it was pleasanter to forget. "They don't have to wait for you to make up your mind. They could sell you to an old man for a third wife."

When Mary Amanda was seventeen, a man of forty, who had an aging wife, looked at her with favor, and she made her choice. On a sweet summer evening she arose from her place in the tepee and, without a word to anyone, stooped and passed through the lodge opening. She was trembling as she walked past Hawk and Grass Runner and eluded their reaching hands. She stopped before a young man named Snow Mountain.

He was as startled as the family back in the tepee. Courting The Foreigner had become almost a tradition with the young men, because she seemed unattainable and competition ruled their lives. He wrapped his blanket around her and felt her heart beating wildly.

He did not tell her she was pretty. He told her that he was brave and cunning. He told her he was a skilled hunter, his lodge never lacked for meat. He had many horses, most of them stolen from the Crows in quick, desperate raids.

Mary Amanda said, "You give horses to buy what you want. Will Runs Buffalo give presents to you in return?"

That was terribly important to her. The exchange of gifts was in itself the ceremony. If she went to him with no dowry, she went without honor.

"I cannot ask about that," he said. "My mother's brother will ask."

But Runs Buffalo refused.

"I will sell the white woman for horses," he announced. "She belongs to me. I paid for her."

Mary Amanda went without ceremony, on a day in autumn, to the new lodge of Snow Mountain. She went without pride, without dowry. The lodge was new and fine, she had the tools and kettles she needed, and enough robes to keep the household warm. But all the household things were from his people, not hers. When she cried, he comforted her.

For her there was no long honeymoon of lazy bliss. Her conscience made her keep working to pay Snow Mountain for the gifts no one had given him. But she was no longer a slave, she was queen in her own household. An old woman, a relative of his mother, lived with them to do heavy work. Snow Mountain's youngest brother lived with him, helping to hunt and butcher and learning the skills a man needed to know.

Mary Amanda was a contented bride—except when she remembered that she had not been born an Indian. And there was always in her mind the knowledge that many warriors had two wives, and that often the two wives were sisters.

"You work too hard," Snow Mountain told her. "Your little sister does not work hard enough."

"She is young," The Foreigner reminded him, feeling that she should apologize for Bluejay's shortcomings.

Snow Mountain said, "When she is older, maybe she will come here."

Afterward she knew he meant that in kindness. But thinking of Sarah as her rival in the tepee, as her sister-wife, froze Mary Amanda's heart. She answered only, "Bluejay is young."

Sarah Harris, known as Bluejay, already had two suitors when she was only fourteen. One of them was only two or three years older than she was, and not suitable for a husband; he had few war honors and was not very much respected by anyone except his own parents. The other was a grown man, a young warrior named Horse Ears, very suitable and, in fact, better than the flighty girl had any right to expect.

When Sarah visited in her sister's lodge, she boasted of the two young men.

Mary Amanda cried out, "Oh, no! You're too young to take a man. You could wait two years yet, maybe three. Sarah, some day you will go back home."

Two years after the massacre, the first rumor that the Harris girls were alive reached the settlement, but it was nothing their mother could put much faith in. The rumor came in a roundabout way, to Link Bartlett, Hannah's second husband, from a soldier at the fort, who had it from another soldier, who had it from a white trader, who heard it from a Cheyenne. And all they heard was that two white sisters were with a Sioux village far to the westward. Rumors like that drifted in constantly. Two hundred women had been missing after that raid.

Two more years passed before they could be fairly sure that there were really two white sisters out there and that they were probably the Harrises.

After still another year, the major who commanded the army post nearest the settlement was himself convinced, and negotiations began for their ransom.

Link Bartlett raised every cent he could—he sold some of his best land —to buy the gifts for that ransom.

In the sixth year of the captivity, a cavalry detachment was ordered out on a delicate diplomatic mission—to find and buy the girls back, if possible.

Link Bartlett had his own horse saddled and was ready to leave the cabin, to go with the soldiers, when Hannah cried harshly, "Link, don't you go! Don't go away and leave me and the kids!"

The children were dull Johnny and a two-year-old boy, named Lincoln, after his father, the last child Hannah ever had.

Link tried to calm her. "Now, Hannah, you know we planned I should go along to see they got back all right—if we can find 'em at all."

"I ain't letting you go," she said. "If them soldiers can't make out without you, they're a poor lot." Then she jarred him to his heels. She said, almost gently, "Link, if I was to lose you, I'd die."

That was the only time she ever hinted that she loved him. He never asked for any more assurance. He stayed at home because she wanted him there.

Mary Amanda's son was half a year old when the girls first learned there was hope of their being ransomed.

The camp crier, walking among the lodges, wailed out the day's news so that everyone in the village would know what was planned: "Women, stay in the camp. Keep your children close to you where they will be safe. There is danger. Some white soldiers are camped on the other side of the hills. Three men will go out to talk to them. The three men are Runs Buffalo, Big Moon and Snow Mountain."

Mary Amanda did not dare ask Snow Mountain anything. She watched him ride out with the other men, and then she sat on the ground in front of his tepee, nursing her baby. Bluejay came to the lodge and the two girls sat together in silence as the hours passed.

The men from the Sioux camp did not come back until three days later.

When Snow Mountain was ready to talk, he remarked, "The white soldiers came to find out about two white girls. They will bring presents to pay if the white girls want to go back."

Mary Amanda answered, "O-o-oh," in a sigh like a frail breeze in prairie grass.

There was no emotion in his dark, stern face. He looked at her for a long moment, and at the baby. Then he turned away without explanation. She called after him, but he did not answer. She felt the dark eyes staring, heard the low voices. She was a stranger again, as she had not been for a long time.

Nothing definite had been decided at the parley with the white soldiers, the girls learned. The soldiers would come back sometime, bringing presents for ransom, and if the presents were fine enough, there would be talk and perhaps a bargain. Mary Amanda felt suddenly the need to prepare Sarah for life in the settlement. She told her everything she could remember that might be useful.

"You'll cook over a fire in a fireplace," she said, "and sew with thread, and you'll have to learn to knit."

Bluejay whimpered, "I wish you could come, too."

"He wouldn't let me go, of course," Mary Amanda answered complacently. "He wouldn't let me take the baby, and I wouldn't leave without *him*. You tell them I got a good man. Be sure to tell them that."

At night, remembering the lost heaven of the burned cabin, remembering the life that was far away and long ago, she cried a little. But she did not even consider begging Snow Mountain to let her go. She had offended him, but when he stopped brooding they would talk again. He had not said anything to her since he had tested her by telling her the ransom had been offered.

He did not even tell her that he was going away. He gave orders to the old woman in the lodge and discussed plans with his younger brother, but he ignored his wife. Five men were going out to take horses from the Crows, he said. Mary Amanda shivered.

Before he rode away with his war party, he spent some time playing with the baby, bouncing the child on his knee, laughing when the baby laughed. But he said nothing to Mary Amanda, and the whole village knew that he was angry and that she deserved his anger.

Her hands and feet were cold as she watched him go, and her heart was gnawed by the fear that was part of every Indian woman's life: "Maybe he will never come back."

Not until the white soldiers had come back to parley again did she understand how cruelly she had hurt him.

She dreamed of home while they waited for news of the parley, and she tried to make Bluejay dream of it.

"You'll have to do some things different there, but Ma will remind you. I'll bet Ma will cry like everything when she sees you coming." Mary

Amanda's eyes flooded with tears, seeing that meeting. "I don't remember she ever did cry," she added thoughtfully, "but I guess she must have sometimes. . . . Ma must have got out of it all right. Who else would be sending the ransom? Oh, well, sometime I'll find out all about it from Snow Mountain. . . . I wonder if she got Johnny and Willie away from the cabin safe. Tell her I talked about her lots. Be sure to tell Ma that, Sarah. Tell her how cute my baby is."

Bluejay, unnaturally silent, dreamed with her wide-eyed, of the reunion, the half-forgotten heaven of the settlement.

"Tell her about Snow Mountain," Mary Amanda reminded her sister. "Be sure to do that. How he's a good hunter, so we have everything we want, and more. And everybody respects him. Tell her he's good to me and the baby. . . . But, Sarah, don't ever say he steals horses. They wouldn't understand, back home. . . And don't ever let on a word about scalps. If they say anything about scalps, you say our people here don't do that."

"They do, though," Sarah reminded her flatly. "It takes a brave man to stop and take a scalp off when somebody's trying to kill him."

Looking at her Mary Amanda realized that Sarah didn't even think taking scalps was bad, so long as your own people did it and didn't have it done to them.

"You're going to have to forget some things," she warned with a sigh.

While the parley was still on, Big Moon, the medicine priest, came to the lodge where The Foreigner bent over her endless work. He was carrying something wrapped in buckskin.

"Tell them the names of the people in your lodge before you came to the Sioux," he said shortly as he put down the buckskin bundle. "They are not sure you are the women they want."

In the bundle were sheets of paper and a black crayon.

Sarah came running. She sat fascinated as Mary Amanda wrote carefully on the paper: "Popa, Moma, Zeke, Jim, Johny, Wily."

Mary Amanda was breathless when she finished. She squeezed Sarah's arm. "Just think, you're going to go home!"

Sarah nodded, not speaking. Sarah was getting scared.

The following day, the ransom was paid and brought into camp. Then The Foreigner learned how much she had offended Snow Mountain.

Big Moon brought fine gifts to the lodge, and piled them inside—a gun, powder and percussion caps and bullets, bolts of cloth, mirrors and beads and tools and a copper kettle.

"The Foreigner can go now," he said.

Mara Amanda stared. "I cannot go back to the white people. I am Snow Mountain's woman. This is his baby."

"The gifts pay also for the baby," Big Moon growled. "Snow Mountain will have another wife, more sons. He does not need The Foreigner. He has sold her to the white man."

Mary Amanda turned pale. "I will not go with the white men," she said angrily. "When Snow Mountain comes back, he will see how much The Foreigner's people cared for her. They have sent these gifts as her dowry."

Big Moon scowled. "Snow Mountain may not come back. He had a dream, and the dream was bad. His heart is sick, and he does not want to come back."

As a widow in the Sioux camp, her situation would be serious. She could not go back to her parents' home, for she had no parents. But neither could she leave the camp now to go back to the settlement and never know whether Snow Mountain was alive or dead. Sarah stood staring at her in horror.

"I will wait for him," Mary Amanda said, choking. "Will Big Moon pray and make medicine for him?"

The fierce old man stared at her, scowling. He knew courage when he saw it, and he admired one who dared to gamble for high stakes.

"All these gifts will belong to Big Moon," she promised, "if Snow Mountain comes back."

The medicine priest nodded and turned away. "Bluejay must come with me," he said briefly. "I will take her to the white soldiers and tell them The Foreigner does not want to come."

She watched Sarah walk away between the lodges after the medicine priest. She waved good-bye, and then went into the lodge. The old woman said, "Snow Mountain has a good wife. . . ."

Ten days passed before the war party came back. Mary Amanda waited, hardly breathing, as they brought Snow Mountain into camp tied on a travois, a pony drag.

Big Moon said, "His shadow is gone out of his body. I do not know whether it will come back to stay."

"I think it will come back to stay," said The Foreigner, "because I have prayed and made a sacrifice."

At the sound of her voice, Snow Mountain opened his eyes. He lay quiet in his pain, staring up at her, not believing. She saw tears on his dark cheeks.

Her name was always The Foreigner, but for the rest of her life she was a woman of the Santee Sioux.

Sarah Harris, who had been called Bluejay, was hard to tame, they said in the settlement. Her mother fretted over her heathen ways. The girl could not even make bread!

"I can tan hides," Sarah claimed angrily. "I can butcher a buffalo and make pemmican. I can pitch a tepee and pack it on a horse to move."

But those skills were not valued in a white woman, and Sarah found the settlement not quite heaven. She missed the constant talk and laughter of the close-pitched tepees. She had to learn a whole new system of polite behavior. There was dickering and trading and bargaining, instead of a proud exchanging of fine gifts. A neighbor boy slouching on a bench outside the cabin, talking to her stepfather while he got up courage to ask whether Sarah was at home, was less flattering as a suitor than a young warrior, painted and feathered, showing off on a spotted horse. Sometimes Sarah felt that she had left heaven behind her.

But she never went back to it. When she was seventeen, she married the blacksmith, Herman Schwartz, and their first baby was born six months later.

Sarah's oldest child was six and her second child was three when the Indian man appeared at the door of her cabin and stood silently peering in.

"Git out of here!" she cried, seizing the broom.

He answered in the Sioux tongue, "Bluejay has forgotten."

She gave Horse Ears a shrill welcome in his own language and the three-year-old started to cry. She lifted a hand for an accustomed slap but let it fall. Indian mothers did not slap their children.

But she was not Indian any more, she recollected. She welcomed Horse Ears in as a white woman does an invited guest. In her Sunday-company voice she chattered politely. It was her privilege because she was a white woman. No need any more for the meek silence of the Indian woman.

She brought out bread and butter and ate with him. That was her privilege, too.

"My sister?" she asked.

He had not seen The Foreigner for a long time. He had left that village.

"Does Bluejay's man make much meat?" Horse Ears asked. "Is he a man with many honors in war?"

She laughed shrilly. "He makes much meat. He has counted coup many times. We are rich."

"I came to find out those things," he answered. "In my lodge there is only one woman."

She understood, and her heart leaped with the flattery. He had traveled far, and in some danger, to find out that all was well with her. If it was not, there was refuge in his tepee. And not only now, she realized, but any time, forever.

A shadow fell across the threshold; a hoarse voice filled the room. "What's that bloody Injun doing here?" roared Sarah's husband. "Are you all right?"

"Sure, we're all right," she answered. "I don't know who he is. He was hungry."

His eyes narrowed with anger, "Is he one of them you used to know?"

Her body tensed with fear. "I don't know him, I told you!"

Her husband spoke to the Indian in halting Sioux, but Horse Ears was wise. He did not answer.

"Git out!" the blacksmith ordered, and the Indian obeyed without a word.

As Sarah watched him go down the path, without turning, she wished fervently that she could tell him good-bye, could thank him for coming. But she could not betray him by speaking.

Herman Schwartz strode toward her in silent, awesome, blazing fury. She did not cringe; she braced her body against the table. He gave her a blow across the face that rocked her and blinded her.

She picked up the heavy iron skillet.

"Don't you ever do that again or I'll kill you," she warned.

He glared at her with fierce pride, knowing that she meant what she said.

"I don't reckon I'll have to do it again," he said complacently. "If I ever set eyes on that savage again, I'll kill him. You know that, don't you, you damn squaw?"

She shrugged. "Talk's cheap."

As she went down to the spring for a bucket of water, she was singing.

Her girlhood was gone, and her freedom was far behind her. She had two crying children and was pregnant again. But two men loved her, and both of them had just proved it.

Forty years later, her third child was elected to the state legislature, and she went, a frightened, white-haired widow, to see him there. She was proud, but never so proud as she had been on a summer day three months before he was born.

THE BRIDE COMES
TO YELLOW SKY

by STEPHEN CRANE

Stephen Crane was the bantam cock of American literature. Self-educated, aggressive, bright and quick, he made his way to the top of American letters while still in his twenties and burnt himself out before he was thirty. One of the first American writers to call a spade something other than an agricultural instrument, he bullied his way to attention with his forthright, naturalistic novel, Maggie, A Girl of the Streets, *followed by* The Red Badge of Courage. *He subsequently wrote other novels, numerous short stories, as well as two volumes of poetry, covered several wars as a correspondent, married a whorehouse madam, and moved to England where he was lionized by Henry James and Joseph Conrad.*

The great Pullman was whirling onward with such dignity of motion that a glance from the window seemed simply to prove that the plains of Texas were pouring eastward. Vast flats of green grass, dull-hued spaces of mesquit and cactus, little groups of frame houses, woods of light and tender trees, all were sweeping into the east, sweeping over the horizon, a precipice.

A newly married pair had boarded this coach at San Antonio. The man's face was reddened from many days in the wind and sun, and a direct result of his new black clothes was that his brick-coloured hands were constantly performing in a most conscious fashion. From time to time he looked down respectfully at his attire. He sat with a hand on each knee, like a man waiting in a barber's shop. The glances he devoted to other passengers were furtive and shy.

The bride was not pretty, nor was she very young. She wore a dress of blue cashmere, with small reservations of velvet here and there, and with steel buttons abounding. She continually twisted her head to regard her puff sleeves, very stiff, straight, and high. They embarrassed her. It was quite apparent that she had cooked, and that she expected to cook, duti-fully. The blushes caused by the careless scrutiny of some passengers as she had entered the car were strange to see upon this plain, under-class countenance, which was drawn in placid, almost emotionless lines.

They were evidently very happy. "Ever been in a parlor-car before?" he asked, smiling with delight.

"No," she answered; "I never was. It's fine, ain't it?"

"Great! And then after a while we'll go forward to the diner, and get a big lay-out. Finest meal in the world. Charge a dollar."

"Oh, do they?" cried the bride. "Charge a dollar? Why, that's too much—for us—ain't it, Jack?"

"Not this trip, anyhow," he answered bravely. "We're going to go the whole thing."

Later he explained to her about the trains. "You see, it's a thousand miles from one end of Texas to the other; and this train runs right across it, and never stops but four times." He had the pride of an owner. He pointed out to her the dazzling fittings of the coach; and in truth her eyes opened wider as she contemplated the sea-green figured velvet, the shining brass, silver, and glass, the wood that gleamed as darkly brilliant as the surface of a pool of oil. At one end a bronze figure sturdily held a support for a separated chamber, and at convenient places on the ceiling were frescos in olive and silver.

To the minds of the pair, their surroundings reflected the glory of their marriage that morning in San Antonio; this was the environment of their new estate; and the man's face in particular beamed with an elation that made him appear ridiculous to the Negro porter. This individual at times surveyed them from afar with an amused and superior grin. On other occasions he bullied them with skill in ways that did not make it exactly plain to them that they were being bullied. He subtly used all the manners of the most unconquerable kind of snobbery. He oppressed them; but of this oppression they had small knowledge, and they speedily forgot that infrequently a number of travelers covered them with stares of derisive enjoyment. Historically there was supposed to be something infinitely humorous in their situation.

"We are due in Yellow Sky at 3:42," he said, looking tenderly into her eyes.

"Oh, are we?" she said, as if she had not been aware of it. To evince surprise at her husband's statement was part of her wifely amiability. She took from a pocket a little silver watch; and as she held it before her, and stared at it with a frown of attention, the new husband's face shone.

"I bought it in San Anton' from a friend of mine," he told her gleefully.

"It's seventeen minutes past twelve," she said, looking up at him with a kind of shy and clumsy coquetry. A passenger, noting this play, grew excessively sardonic, and winked at himself in one of the numerous mirrors.

At last they went to the dining-car. Two rows of Negro waiters, in glowing white suits, surveyed their entrance with the interest, and also the equanimity, of men who had been forewarned. The pair fell to the lot of a waiter who happened to feel pleasure in steering them through their meal. He viewed them with the manner of a fatherly pilot, his countenance radiant with benevolence. The patronage, entwined with the ordinary deference, was not plain to them. And yet, as they returned to their coach, they showed in their faces a sense of escape.

To the left, miles down a long purple slope, was a little ribbon of mist where moved the keening Rio Grande. The train was approaching it at an angle, and the apex was Yellow Sky. Presently it was apparent that, as the distance from Yellow Sky grew shorter, the husband became commensurately restless. His brick-red hands were more insistent in their prominence. Occasionally he was even rather absent-minded and far-away when the bride leaned forward and addressed him.

As a matter of truth, Jack Potter was beginning to find the shadow of a deed weigh upon him like a leaden slab. He, the town marshal of Yellow Sky, a man known, liked, and feared in his corner, a prominent person, had gone to San Antonio to meet a girl he believed he loved, and there, after the usual prayers, had actually induced her to marry him, without consulting Yellow Sky for any part of the transaction. He was now bringing his bride before an innocent and unsuspecting community.

Of course people in Yellow Sky married as it pleased them, in accordance with a general custom; but such was Potter's thought of his duty to his friends, or of their idea of his duty, or of an unspoken form which does not control men in these matters, that he felt he was heinous. He had committed an extraordinary crime. Face to face with this girl in San Antonio, and spurred by his sharp impulse, he had gone headlong over all the social hedges. At San Antonio he was like a man hidden in the dark. A knife to sever any friendly duty, any form, was easy to his hand in that remote city. But the hour of Yellow Sky—the hour of daylight—was approaching.

He knew full well that his marriage was an important thing to his town. It could only be exceeded by the burning of the new hotel. His friends could not forgive him. Frequently he had reflected on the advisability of telling them by telegraph, but a new cowardice had been upon him. He feared to do it. And now the train was hurrying him toward a scene of amazement, glee, and reproach. He glanced out of the window at the line of haze swinging slowly in toward the train.

Yellow Sky had a kind of brass band, which played painfully, to the delight of the populace. He laughed without heart as he thought of it. If the citizens could dream of his prospective arrival with his bride, they would parade the band at the station and escort them, amid cheers and laughing congratulations, to his adobe home.

He resolved that he would use all the devices of speed and plainscraft in making the journey from the station to his house. Once within that safe citadel, he could issue some sort of vocal bulletin, and then not go among the citizens until they had time to wear off a little of their enthusiasm.

The bride looked anxiously at him. "What's worrying you, Jack?"

He laughed again. "I'm not worrying, girl; I'm only thinking of Yellow Sky."

She flushed in comprehension.

A sense of mutual guilt invaded their minds and developed a finer tenderness. They looked at each other with eyes softly aglow. But Potter often laughed the same nervous laugh; the flush upon the bride's face seemed quite permanent.

The traitor to the feelings of Yellow Sky narrowly watched the speeding landscape. "We're nearly there," he said.

Presently the porter came and announced the proximity of Potter's home. He held a brush in his hand, and, with all his airy superiority gone, he brushed Potter's new clothes as the latter slowly turned this way and that way. Potter fumbled out a coin and gave it to the porter, as he had seen others do. It was a heavy and musclebound business, as that of a man shoeing his first horse.

The porter took their bag, and as the train began to slow they moved forward to the hooded platform of the car. Presently the two engines and their long string of coaches rushed into the station of Yellow Sky.

"They have to take water here," said Potter, from a constricted throat and in mournful cadence, as one announcing death. Before the train stopped his eye had swept the length of the platform, and he was glad and astonished to see there was none upon it but the station-agent, who, with a slightly hurried and anxious air, was walking toward the water-tanks. When the train had halted, the porter alighted first, and placed in position a little temporary step.

"Come on, girl," said Potter, hoarsely. As he helped her down they each laughed on a false note. He took the bag from the Negro, and bade his wife cling to his arm. As they slunk rapidly away, his hang-dog glance perceived that they were unloading the two trunks, and also that the station-agent, far ahead near the baggage-car, had turned and was running toward him, making gestures. He laughed, and groaned as he laughed, when he noted the first effect of his marital bliss upon Yellow Sky. He gripped his wife's arm firmly to his side, and they fled. Behind them the porter stood, chuckling fatuously.

II

The California express on the Southern Railway was due at Yellow Sky in twenty-one minutes. There were six men at the bar of the Weary Gentleman saloon. One was a drummer who talked a great deal and rapidly; three were Texans who did not care to talk at that time; and two were Mexican sheep-herders, who did not talk as a general practice in the Weary Gentleman saloon. The barkeeper's dog lay on the board walk that crossed in front of the door. His head was on his paws, and he glanced drowsily here and there with the constant vigilance of a dog that is kicked on occasion. Across the sandy street were some vivid green grass-plots, so wonderful in appearance, amid the sands that burned near them in a blazing sun, that they caused a doubt in the mind. They exactly resembled the grass mats used to represent lawns on the stage. At the cooler end of the railway station, a man without a coat sat in a tilted chair and smoked his pipe. The fresh-cut bank of the Rio Grande circled near the town, and there could be seen beyond it a great plum-coloured plain of mesquit.

Save for the busy drummer and his companions in the saloon, Yellow Sky was dozing. The new-comer leaned gracefully upon the bar, and recited many tales with the confidence of a bard who has come upon a new field.

"—and at the moment that the old man fell downstairs with the bureau in his arms, the old woman was coming up with two scuttles of coal, and of course—"

The drummer's tale was interrupted by a young man who suddenly appeared in the open door. He cried: "Scratchy Wilson's drunk, and has turned loose with both hands." The two Mexicans at once set down their glasses and faded out of the rear entrance of the saloon.

The drummer, innocent and jocular, answered: "All right, old man. S'pose he has? Come in and have a drink, anyhow."

But the information had made such an obvious cleft in every skull in the room that the drummer was obliged to see its importance. All had become instantly solemn. "Say," said he, mystified, "what is this?" His three companions made the introductory gesture of eloquent speech; but the young man at the door forestalled them.

"It means, my friend," he answered, as he came into the saloon, "that for the next two hours this town won't be a health resort."

The barkeeper went to the door, and locked and barred it; reaching out of the window, he pulled in heavy wooden shutters, and barred them. Immediately a solemn, chapel-like gloom was upon the place. The drummer was looking from one to another.

"But say," he cried, "what is this, anyhow? You don't mean there is going to be a gun-fight?"

"Don't know whether there'll be a fight or not," answered one man, grimly; "but there'll be some shootin'—some good shootin'."

The young man who had warned them waved his hand. "Oh, there'll be a fight fast enough, if any one wants it. Anybody can get a fight out there in the street. There's a fight just waiting."

The drummer seemed to be swayed between the interest of a foreigner and a perception of personal danger.

"What did you say his name was?" he asked.

"Scratchy Wilson," they answered in chorus.

"And will he kill anybody? What are you going to do? Does this happen often? Does he rampage around like this once a week or so? Can he break in that door?"

"No; he can't break down that door," replied the barkeeper. "He's tried it three times. But when he comes you'd better lay down on the floor, stranger. He's dead sure to shoot at it, and a bullet may come through."

Thereafter the drummer kept a strict eye upon the door. The time had not yet been called for him to hug the floor, but as a minor precaution, he sidled near to the wall. "Will he kill anybody?" he said again.

The men laughed low and scornfully at the question.

"He's out to shoot, and he's out for trouble. Don't see any good in experimentin' with him."

"But what do you do in a case like this? What do you do?"

A man responded: "Why, he and Jack Potter—"

"But," in chorus the other men interrupted, "Jack Potter's in San Anton'."

"Well, who is he? What's he got to do with it?"

"Oh, he's the town marshal. He goes out and fights Scratchy when he gets on one of these tears."

"Wow!" said the drummer, mopping his brow. "Nice job he's got."

The voices had toned away to mere whisperings. The drummer wished to ask further questions, which were born of an increasing anxiety and bewilderment; but when he attempted them, the men merely looked at him in irritation and motioned him to remain silent. A tense waiting hush was upon them. In the deep shadows of the room their eyes shone as they listened for sounds from the street. One man made three gestures at the barkeeper; and the latter, moving like a ghost, handed him a glass and a bottle. The man poured a full glass of whisky, and set down the bottle noiselessly. He gulped the whisky in a swallow, and turned again toward the door in immovable silence. The drummer saw that the barkeeper, without a sound, had taken a Winchester from beneath the bar. Later he saw this individual beckoning to him, so he tiptoed across the room.

"You better come with me back of the bar."

"No, thanks," said the drummer, perspiring; "I'd rather be where I can make a break for the back door."

Whereupon the man of bottles made a kindly but peremptory gesture. The drummer obeyed it, and, finding himself seated on a box with his head below the level of the bar, balm was laid upon his soul at sight of various zinc and copper fittings that bore a resemblance to armor-plate. The barkeeper took a seat comfortably upon an adjacent box.

"You see," he whispered, "this here Scratchy Wilson is a wonder with a gun—a perfect wonder; and when he goes on the war-trail, we hunt our holes—naturally. He's about the last one of the old gang that used to hang out along the river here. He's a terror when he's drunk. When he's sober he's all right—kind of simple—wouldn't hurt a fly—nicest fellow in town. But when he's drunk—whoo!"

There were periods of stillness. "I wish Jack Potter was back from San Anton'," said the barkeeper. "He shot Wilson up once—in the leg—and he would sail in and pull out the kinks in this thing."

Presently they heard from a distance the sound of a shot, followed by three wild yowls. It instantly removed a bond from the men in the darkened saloon. There was a shuffling of feet. They looked at each other. "Here he comes," they said.

III

A man in a maroon-colored flannel shirt, which had been purchased for purposes of decoration, and made principally by some Jewish women on the East Side of New York, rounded a corner and walked into the middle of the main street of Yellow Sky. In either hand the man held a long, heavy, blue-black revolver. Often he yelled, and these cries rang through a semblance of a deserted village, shrilly flying over the roofs in a volume that seemed to have no relation to the ordinary vocal strength of a man. It was as if the surrounding stillness formed the arch of a tomb over him. These cries of ferocious challenge rang against walls of silence. And his boots had red tops with gilded imprints, of the kind beloved in winter by little sledding boys on the hillsides of New England.

The man's face flamed in a rage begot of whisky. His eyes, rolling, and yet keen for ambush, hunted the still doorways and windows. He walked with the creeping movement of the midnight cat. As it occurred to him, he roared menacing information. The long revolvers in his hands were as easy as straws; they were moved with an electric swiftness. The little fingers of each hand played sometimes in a musician's way. Plain from the low collar of the shirt, the cords of his neck straightened and sank, straightened and sank, as passion moved him. The only sounds were his terrible invitations. The calm adobes preserved their demeanor at the passing of this small thing in the middle of the street.

There was no offer of fight—no offer of fight. The man called to the sky. There were no attractions. He bellowed and fumed and swayed his revolvers here and everywhere.

The dog of the barkeeper of the Weary Gentleman saloon had not appreciated the advance of events. He yet lay dozing in front of his master's door. At sight of the dog, the man paused and raised his revolver humorously. At sight of the man, the dog sprang up and walked diagonally away, with a sullen head, and growling. The man yelled, and the dog broke into a gallop. As it was about to enter an alley, there was a loud noise, a whistling, and something spat the ground directly before it. The dog screamed, and, wheeling in terror, galloped headlong in a new direction. Again there was a noise, a whistling, and sand was kicked viciously before it. Fear-stricken, the dog turned and flurried like an animal in a pen. The man stood laughing, his weapons at his hips.

Ultimately the man was attracted by the closed door of the Weary Gentleman saloon. He went to it and, hammering with a revolver, demanded drink.

The door remaining imperturbable, he picked a bit of paper from the walk, and nailed it to the framework with a knife. He then turned his back contemptuously upon this popular resort and, walking to the opposite side of the street and spinning there on his heel quickly and lithely, fired at the bit of paper. He missed it by a half-inch. He swore at himself, and went away. Later he comfortably fusilladed the windows of his most intimate friend. The man was playing with this town; it was a toy for him.

But still there was no offer of fight. The name of Jack Potter, his ancient antagonist, entered his mind, and he concluded that it would be a glad thing if he should go to Potter's house, and by bombardment induce him to come out and fight. He moved in the direction of his desire, chanting Apache scalp-music.

When he arrived at it, Potter's house presented the same still front as had the other adobes. Taking up a strategic position, the man howled a challenge. But this house regarded him as might a great stone god. It gave no sign. After a decent wait, the man howled further challenges, mingling with them wonderful epithets.

Presently there came the spectacle of a man churning himself into deepest rage over the immobility of a house. He fumed at it as the winter wind attacks a prairie cabin in the North. To the distance there should have gone the sound of a tumult like the fighting of two hundred Mexicans. As necessity bade him, he paused for breath or to reload his revolvers.

IV

Potter and his bride walked sheepishly and with speed. Sometimes they laughed together shamefacedly and low.

"Next corner, dear," he said finally.

They put forth the efforts of a pair walking bowed against a strong wind. Potter was about to raise a finger to point the first appearance of the new home when, as they circled the corner, they came face to face with a man in a maroon-colored shirt, who was feverishly pushing cartridges into a large revolver. Upon the instant the man dropped his revolver to the ground and, like lightning, whipped another from its holster. The second weapon was aimed at the bridegroom's chest.

There was a silence. Potter's mouth seemed to be merely a grave for his tongue. He exhibited an instinct to at once loosen his arm from the woman's grip, and he dropped the bag to the sand. As for the bride, her face had gone as yellow as old cloth. She was a slave to hideous rites, gazing at the apparitional snake.

The two men faced each other at a distance of three paces. He of the revolver smiled with a new and quiet ferocity.

"Tried to sneak up on me," he said. "Tried to sneak up on me!" His eyes grew more baleful. As Potter made a slight movement, the man thrust his revolver venomously forward. "No; don't you do it, Jack Potter. Don't you move a finger toward a gun just yet. Don't you move an eyelash. The time has come for me to settle with you, and I'm goin' to do it my own way, and loaf along with no interferin'. So if you don't want a gun bent on you, just mind what I tell you."

Potter looked at his enemy. "I ain't got a gun on me, Scratchy," he said. "Honest, I ain't." He was stiffening and steadying, but yet somewhere at the back of his mind a vision of the Pullman floated: the sea-green figured velvet, the shining brass, silver, and glass, the wood that gleamed as darkly brilliant as the surface of a pool of oil—all the glory of the marriage, the environment of the new estate. "You know I fight when it comes to fighting, Scratchy Wilson; but I ain't got a gun on me. You'll have to do all the shootin' yourself."

His enemy's face went livid. He stepped forward, and lashed his weapon to and fro before Potter's chest. "Don't you tell me you ain't got no gun on you, you whelp. Don't tell me no lie like that. There ain't a man in Texas ever seen you without no gun. Don't take me for no kid." His eyes blazed with light, and his throat worked like a pump.

"I ain't takin' you for no kid," answered Potter. His heels had not moved an inch backward. "I'm taking' you for a damn fool. I tell you I ain't got a gun, and I ain't. If you're goin' to shoot me up, you better begin now; you'll never get a chance like this again."

So much enforced reasoning had told on Wilson's rage; he was calmer. "If you ain't got a gun, why ain't you got a gun?" he sneered. "Been to Sunday-school?"

"I ain't got a gun because I've just come from San Anton' with my wife. I'm married," said Potter. "And if I'd thought there was going to be any galoots like you prowling around when I brought my wife home, I'd had a gun, and don't you forget it."

"Married!" said Scratchy, not at all comprehending.

"Yes, married. I'm married," said Potter, distinctly.

"Married?" said Scratchy. Seemingly for the first time, he saw the drooping, drowning woman at the other man's side. "No!" he said. He was like a creature allowed a glimpse of another world. He moved a pace backward, and his arm, with the revolver, dropped to his side. "Is this the lady?" he asked.

"Yes; this is the lady," answered Potter.

There was another period of silence.

"Well," said Wilson at last, slowly, 'I s'pose it's all off now."

"It's all off if you say so, Scratchy. You know I didn't make the trouble." Potter lifted his valise.

"Well, I 'low it's off, Jack," said Wilson. He was looking at the ground. "Married!" He was not a student of chivalry; it was merely that in the presence of this foreign condition he was a simple child of the earlier plains. He picked up his starboard revolver, and, placing both weapons in their holsters, he went away. His feet made funnel-shaped tracks in the heavy sand.

THE WIND AND
THE SNOW OF WINTER

by WALTER VAN TILBURG CLARK

If there is a single book which shows the growth of the Western myth to the level of art, it is The Ox-Bow Incident *by Walter Van Tilburg Clark. Using the same materials as Owen Wister and Zane Grey, Clark wrote a morality tale in the medieval tradition which probed deeply into the entire concept of Frontier law and justice. Nothing else written on the subject has the meaning and depth of this novel, and at the same time, very few books on the West possess its authenticity. "The Wind and the Snow of Winter" has much the same tone as Steinbeck's "Leader of the People," an honest sadness about a world which is dying and about how little this death means to those who were not a part of it.*

It was near sunset when Mike Braneen came onto the last pitch of the old wagon road which had led into Gold Rock from the east since the Comstock days. The road was just two ruts in the hard earth, with sagebrush growing between them, and was full of steep pitches and sharp turns. From the summit it descended even more steeply into Gold Rock, in a series of short switchbacks down the slope of the canyon. There was a paved highway on the other side of the pass now, but Mike never used that. Cars coming from behind made him uneasy, so that he couldn't follow his own thoughts long, but had to keep turning around every few minutes, to see that his burro, Annie, was staying out on the shoulder of the road, where she would be safe. Mike didn't like cars anyway, and on the old road he could forget about them and feel more like himself. He could forget about Annie too, except when the light, quick tapping of her hoofs behind him stopped. Even then he didn't really break his thoughts. It was more as if the tapping were another sound from his own inner machinery, and when it stopped he stopped too, and turned around to see what she was doing. When he began to walk ahead again at the same slow, unvarying pace, his arms scarcely swinging at all, his body bent a little forward from the waist, he would not be aware that there had been any interruptoin of the memory or the story that was going on in his head. Mike did not like to have his stories interrupted except by an idea of his own, something to do with his prospecting, or the arrival of his story at an actual memory which warmed him to closer recollection or led into a new and more attractive story.

An intense, golden light, almost liquid, fanned out from the peaks above him and reached eastward under the gray sky, and the snow which occasionally swarmed across this light was fine and dry. Such little squalls had been going on all day, and still there was nothing like real snow down, but only a fine powder which the wind swept along until it caught under the brush, leaving the ground bare. Yet Mike Braneen was not deceived. This was not just a flurrying day; it was the beginning of winter. If not tonight, then tomorrow, or the next day, the snow would begin which shut off the mountains, so that a man might as well be on a great plain for all he could see, perhaps even the snow which blinded a man at once and blanketed the desert in an hour. Fifty-two years in this country had made Mike Braneen sure about such things, although he didn't give much thought to them, but only to what he had to do because of them. Three nights before he had been awakened by a change in the wind. It was no longer a wind born in the near mountains, cold with night and altitude, but a wind from far places, full of a damp chill which got through his blankets and into his bones. The stars had still been clear and close above the dark humps of the mountains, and overhead the constellations had moved slowly in full panoply, unbroken by any invisible lower darkness; yet he had lain there half awake for a few minutes, hearing the new wind beat the brush around him, hearing Annie stirring restlessly and thumping in her hobble. He had thought drowsily, "Smells like winter this time," and then, "It's held off a long time this year, pretty near the end of December." Then he had gone back to sleep, mildly happy because the change meant he would be going back to Gold Rock. Gold Rock was the other half of Mike Braneen's life. When the smell of winter came he always started back for Gold Rock. From March or April until the smell of winter he wandered slowly about among the mountains, anywhere between the White Pines and the Virginias, with only his burro for company. Then there would come the change, and they would head back for Gold Rock.

Mike had traveled with a good many burros during that time, eighteen or twenty, he thought, although he was not sure. He could not remember them all, but only those he had had first, when he was a young man and always thought most about seeing women when he got back to Gold Rock, or those with something queer about them, like Baldy, who'd had a great pale patch, like a bald spot, on one side of his belly, or those who'd had something queer happen to them, like Maria. He could remember just how it had been that night. He could remember it as if it were last night. It had been in Hamilton. He had felt unhappy, because he could remember Hamilton when the whole hollow was full of people and buildings, and everything was new and active. He had gone to sleep in the hollow shell of the Wells Fargo Building, hearing an old iron shutter banging against the wall in the wind. In the morning Maria had been gone. He had followed the scuffing track she made on account of her loose hobble, and it had led far up the old snow gullied road to Treasure Hill, and then ended at one of the black shafts that opened like mouths right at the edge of the road. A man remembered a thing like that. There weren't many burros that foolish. But burros with nothing particular about them were hard to remember—especially those he'd had in the last twenty years or so, when he had gradually stopped feeling so personal about them and had begun to call all the jennies Annie and all the burros Jack.

The clicking of the little hoofs behind him stopped, and Mike stopped too, and turned around. Annie was pulling at a line of yellow grass along the edge of the road.

"Come on, Maria," Mike said patiently. The burro at once stopped pulling at the dead grass and came on up toward him, her small black nose working, the ends of the grass standing out on each side of it like whiskers. Mike began to climb again, ahead of her.

It was a long time since he had been caught by a winter, too. He could not remember how long. All the beginnings ran together in his mind, as if they were all the beginning of one winter so far back that he had almost forgotten it. He could still remember clearly, though, the winter he had stayed out on purpose, clear into January. He had been a young man then, thirty-five or forty or forty-five, somewhere in there. He would have to stop and try to bring back a whole string of memories about what had happened just before, in order to remember just how old he had been, and it wasn't worth the trouble. Besides, sometimes even that system didn't work. It would lead him into an old camp where he had been a number of times, and the dates would get mixed up. It was impossible to remember any other way, because all his comings and goings had been so much alike. He had been young, anyhow, and not much afraid of anything except running out of water in the wrong place; not even afraid of the winter. He had stayed out because he'd thought he had a good thing, and he had wanted to prove it. He could remember how it felt to be out in the clear winter weather on the mountains, the piñon trees and the junipers weighted down with feathery snow, and making sharp blue shadows on the white slopes. The hills had made blue shadows on one another too, and in the still air his pick had made the beginning of a sound like a bell's. He knew he had been young, because he could remember taking a day off now and then, just to go tramping around those hills, up and down the white and through the blue shadows, on a kind of holiday. He had pretended to his common sense that he was seriously prospecting, and had carried his hammer, and even his drill along, but he had really just been gallivanting, playing colt. Maybe he had been even younger than thirty-five, though he could still be stirred a little, for that matter, by the memory of the kind of weather which had sent him gallivanting. High-blue weather, he called it. There were two kinds of high-blue weather, besides the winter kind, which didn't set him off very often, spring and fall. In the spring it would have a soft, puffy wind and soft, puffy white clouds which made separate shadows that traveled silently across hills that looked soft too. In the fall it would be still, and there would be no clouds at all in the blue, but there would be something in the golden air and the soft, steady sunlight on the mountains that made a man as uneasy as the spring blowing, though in a different way, more sad and not so excited. In the spring high-blue a man had been likely to think about women he had slept with, or wanted to sleep with, or imaginary women made up with the help of newspaper

pictures of actresses or young society matrons, or of the old oil paintings
in the Lucky Boy Saloon, which showed pale, almost naked women against
dark, sumptuous backgrounds—women with long hair or braided hair,
calm, virtuous faces, small hands and feet, and ponderous limbs, breasts,
and buttocks. In the fall high-blue, though it had been much longer since
he had seen a woman, or heard a woman's voice, he was more likely to
think about old friends, men, or places he had heard about, or places he
hadn't seen for a long time. He himself thought most often about Goldfield
the way he had last seen it in the summer in 1912. That was as far south
as Mike had ever been in Nevada. Since then he had never been south of
Tonopah. When the high-blue weather was past, though, and the season
worked toward winter, he began to think about Gold Rock. There were
only three or four winters out of the fifty-two when he hadn't gone home
to Gold Rock, to his old room at Mrs. Wright's, up on Fourth Street, and
to his meals in the dining room at the International House, and to the
Lucky Boy, where he could talk to Tom Connover and his other friends,
and play cards, or have a drink to hold in his hand while he sat and
remembered.

This journey had seemed a little different from most, though. It had
started the same as usual, but as he had come across the two vast valleys,
and through the pass in the low range between them, he hadn't felt quite
the same. He'd felt younger and more awake, it seemed to him, and yet,
in a way, older too, suddenly older. He had been sure that there was plenty
of time, and yet he had been a little afraid of getting caught in the storm.
He had kept looking ahead to see if the mountains on the horizon were
still clearly outlined, or if they had been cut off by a lowering of the clouds.
He had thought more than once how bad it would be to get caught out
there when the real snow began, and he had been disturbed by the first
flakes. It had seemed hard to him to have to walk so far too. He had kept
thinking about distance. Also the snowy cold had searched out the regions
of his body where old injuries had healed. He had taken off his left mitten
a good many times, to blow on the fingers which had been frosted the
year he was sixty-three, so that now it didn't take much cold to turn them
white and stiffen them. The queer tingling, partly like an itch and partly
like a pain, in the patch on his back that had been burned in that old
powder blast was sharper than he could remember its ever having been
before. The rheumatism in his joints, which was so old a companion that
it usually made him feel no more than tight-knit and stiff, and the place
where his leg had been broken and torn when that ladder broke in '97
ached, and had a pulse he could count. All this made him believe that he
was walking more slowly than usual, although nothing, probably not even
a deliberate attempt, could actually have changed his pace. Sometimes he
even thought, with a moment of fear, that he was getting tired.

On the other hand, he felt unusually clear and strong in his mind. He
remembered things with a clarity which was like living them again—nearly

all of them events from many years back, from the time when he had been really active and fearless and every burro had had its own name. Some of these events, like the night he had spent in Eureka with the little brown-haired whore, a night in the fall in 1888 or '89, somewhere in there, he had not once thought of for years. Now he could remember even her name. Armandy, she had called herself: a funny name. They all picked names for their business, of course, romantic names like Cecily or Rosamunde or Belle or Claire, or hard names like Diamond Gert or Horseshoe Sal, or names that were pinned on them, like Indian Kate or Roman Mary, but Armandy was different.

He could remember Armandy as if he were with her now, not the way she had behaved in bed; he couldn't remember anything particular about that. In fact he couldn't be sure that he remembered anything about that at all. There were others he could remember more clearly for the way they had behaved in bed, women he had been with more often. He had been with Armandy only that one night. He remembered little things about being with her, things that made it seem good to think of being with her again. Armandy had a room upstairs in a hotel. They could hear a piano playing in a club across the street. He could hear the tune, and it was one he knew, although he didn't know its name. It was a gay tune that went on and on the same, but still it sounded sad when you heard it through the hotel window, with the lights from the bars and hotels shining on the street, and the people coming and going through the lights, and then, beyond the lights, the darkness where the mountains were. Armandy wore a white silk dress with a high waist, and a locket on a gold chain. The dress made her look very brown and like a young girl. She used a white powder on her face, that smelled like violets, but this could not hide her brownness. The locket was heart-shaped, and it opened to show a cameo of a man's hand holding a woman's hand very gently, just their fingers laid out long together, and the thumbs holding, the way they were sometimes on tombstones. There were two little gold initials on each hand, but Armandy would never tell what they stood for, or even if the locket was really her own. He stood in the window, looking down at the club from which the piano music was coming, and Armandy stood beside him, with her shoulder against his arm, and a glass of wine in her hand. He could see the toe of her white satin slipper showing from under the edge of her skirt. Her big hat, loaded with black and white plumes, lay on the dresser behind them. His own leather coat, with the sheepskin lining, lay across the foot of the bed. It was a big bed, with a knobby brass foot and head. There was one oil lamp burning in the chandelier in the middle of the room. Armandy was soft-spoken, gentle, and a little fearful, always looking at him to see what he was thinking. He stood with his arms folded. His arms felt big and strong upon his heavily muscled chest. He stood there, pretending to be in no hurry, but really thinking eagerly about what he would do with Armandy, who had something about her which tempted him to be cruel. He stood there, with his chin down into his heavy, dark beard, and watched a man come riding down the middle of the street from the west. The horse was a fine black, which lifted its head and feet with pride. The man sat very straight, with a high rein, and something about his clothes and hat made him appear to be in uniform, although it wasn't a uniform he was wearing. The man also saluted friends upon the sidewalks like an officer, bending his head just slightly, and touching his hat instead of lifting it. Mike Braneen asked Armandy who the man was, and then felt angry because she could tell him, and because he was an important man who owned a mine that was in bonanza. He mocked the airs with which the man rode, and his princely greetings. He mocked the man cleverly, and Armandy laughed and repeated what he said, and made him drink a little of her wine as a reward. Mike had been drinking whisky, and he did not like wine anyway, but this was not the moment in which to refuse such an invitation.

Old Mike remembered all this, which had been completely forgotten for years. He could not remember what he and Armandy had said, but he remembered everything else, and he felt very lonesome for Armandy, and for the room with the red, figured carpet and the brass chandelier with oil lamps in it, and the open window with the long tune coming up through it, and the young summer night outside on the mountains. This loneliness was so much more intense than his familiar loneliness that it made him feel very young. Memories like this had come up again and again during these three days. It was like beginning life over again. It had tricked him into thinking, more than once, "Next summer I'll make the strike, and this time I'll put it into something safe for the rest of my life, and stop this fool wandering around while I've still got some time left"—a way of thinking which he had really stopped a long time before.

It was getting darker rapidly in the pass. When a gust of wind brought the snow against Mike's face so hard that he noticed the flakes felt larger, he looked up. The light was still there, although the fire was dying out of it, and the snow swarmed across it more thickly. Mike remembered God. He did not think anything exact. He did not think about his own relationship to God. He merely felt the idea as a comforting presence. He'd always had a feeling about God whenever he looked at a sunset, especially a sunset which came through under a stormy sky. It had been the strongest feeling left in him until these memories like the one about Armandy had begun. Even in this last pass his strange fear of the storm had come on him again a couple of times, but now that he had looked at the light and thought of God it was gone. In a few minutes he would come to the summit and look down into his lighted city. He felt happily hurried by this anticipation.

He would take the burro down and stable her in John Hammersmith's shed, where he always kept her. He would spread fresh straw for her, and see that the shed was tight against the wind and snow, and get a measure of grain for her from John. Then he would go up to Mrs. Wright's house at the top of Fourth Street, and leave his things in the same room he always had, the one in front, which looked down over the roofs and chimneys of his city, and across at the east wall of the canyon, from which the sun rose late. He would trim his beard with Mrs. Wright's shears, and shave the upper part of his cheeks. He would bathe out of the blue bowl and pitcher, and wipe himself with the towel with yellow flowers on it, and dress in the good dark suit and the good black shoes with the gleaming box toes, and the good black hat which he had left in the chest in his room. In this way he would perform the ceremony which ended the life of the desert and began the life of Gold Rock. Then he would go down to the International House, and greet Arthur Morris in the gleaming bar, and go into the dining room and eat the best supper they had, with fresh meat and vegetables, and new-made pie, and two cups of hot clear coffee. He would be served by the plump blond waitress who always joked with him, and gave him many little extra things with his first supper, including the drink which Arthur Morris always sent in from the bar.

At this point Mike Braneen stumbled in his mind, and his anticipation wavered. He could not be sure that the plump blond waitress would serve him. For a moment he saw her in a long skirt, and the dining room of the International House, behind her, had potted palms standing in the corners, and was full of the laughter and loud, manly talk of many customers who wore high vests and mustaches and beards. These men leaned back from tables covered with empty dishes. They patted their tight vests and lighted expensive cigars. He knew all their faces. If he were to walk down the aisle betwen the tables on his side they would all speak to him. But he also seemed to remember the dining room with only a few tables, with oilcloth on them instead of linen, and with moody young men sitting at them in their work clothes—strangers who worked for the highway department, or were just passing through, or talked mining in terms which he did not understand or which made him angry.

No, it would not be the plump blond waitress. He did not know who it would be. It didn't matter. After supper he would go up Canyon Street under the arcade to the Lucky Boy Saloon, and there it would be the same as ever. There would be the laurel wreaths on the frosted glass panels of the doors, and the old sign upon the window, the sign that was older than Tom Connover, almost as old as Mike Braneen himself. He would open the door and see the bottles and the white women in the paintings, and the card table in the back corner and the big stove and the chairs along the wall. Tom would look around from his place behind the bar.

"Well, now," he would roar, "look who's here, boys. Now will you believe it's winter?" he would roar at them.

Some of them would be the younger men, of course, and there might even be a few strangers, but this would only add to the dignity of his reception, and there would also be his friends. There would be Henry Bray with the gray walrus mustache, and Mark Wilton and Pat Gallagher. They would all welcome him loudly.

"Mike, how are you, anyway?" Tom would roar, leaning across the bar to shake hands with his big, heavy, soft hand with the diamond ring on it. "And what'll it be, Mike? The same?" he'd ask, as if Mike had been in there no longer ago than the night before.

Mike would play that game too. "The same," he would say.

Then he would really be back in Gold Rock; never mind the plump blond waitress.

Mike came to the summit of the old road and stopped and looked down. For a moment he felt lost again, as he had when he'd thought about the plump blond waitress. He had expected Canyon Street to look much brighter. He had expected a lot of orange windows close together on the other side of the canyon. Instead these were only a few scattered lights across the darkness, and they were white. They made no communal glow upon the steep slope, but gave out only single white needles of light, which pierced the darkness secretly and lonesomely, as if nothing could ever pass from one house to another over there. Canyon Street was very dark too. There it went, the street he loved, steeply down into the bottom of the canyon, and down its length there were only the few street lights, more than a block apart, swinging in the wind and darting about that cold, small light. The snow whirled and swooped under the nearest street light below.

"You are getting to be an old fool," Mike Braneen said out loud to himself, and felt better. This was the way Gold Rock was now, of course, and he loved it all the better. It was a place that grew old with a man, that was going to die sometime too. There could be an understanding with it.

He worked his way slowly down into Canyon Street, with Annie slipping and checking behind him. Slowly, with the blown snow behind them, they came to the first built-up block and passed the first dim light showing through a smudged window under the arcade. They passed the dark places after it, and the second light. Then Mike Braneen stopped in the middle of the street, and Annie stopped beside him, pulling her rump in and turning her head away from the snow. A highway truck, coming down from the head of the canyon, had to get way over onto the wrong side of the street to pass them. The driver leaned out as he went by, and yelled, "Pull over, Pop. You're in town now."

Mike Braneen didn't hear him. He was staring at the Lucky Boy. The Lucky Boy was dark, and there were boards nailed across the big window that had shown the sign. At last Mike went over onto the boardwalk to look more closely. Annie followed him, but stopped at the edge of the walk and scratched her neck against a post of the arcade. There was the other sign, hanging crossways under the arcade, and even in that gloom Mike could see that it said Lucky Boy and had a Jack of Diamonds painted on it. There was no mistake. The Lucky Boy sign, and others like it under the arcade, creaked and rattled in the wind.

There were footsteps coming along the boards. The boards sounded hollow, and sometimes one of them rattled. Mike Braneen looked down slowly from the sign and peered at the approaching figure. It was a man wearing a sheepskin coat with the collar turned up around his head. He was walking quickly, like a man who knew where he was going, and why, and where he had been. Mike almost let him pass. Then he spoke.

"Say, fella—"

He even reached out a hand as if to catch hold of the man's sleeve, though he didn't touch it. The man stopped and asked, impatiently, "Yeah?" and Mike let the hand down again slowly.

"Well, what is it?" the man asked.

"I don't want anything," Mike said. "I got plenty."

"Okay, okay," the man said. "What's the matter?"

Mike moved his hand toward the Lucky Boy. "It's closed," he said.

"I see it is, Dad," the man said. He laughed a little. He didn't seem to be in quite so much of a hurry now.

"How long has it been closed?" Mike asked.

"Since about June, I guess," the man said. "Old Tom Connover, the guy that ran it, died last June."

Mike waited for a moment. "Tom died?" he asked.

"Yup. I guess he'd just kept it open out of love of the place anyway. There hasn't been any real business for years. Nobody cared to keep it open after him."

The man started to move on, but then he waited, peering, trying to see Mike better.

"This June?" Mike asked finally.

"Yup. This last June."

"Oh," Mike said. Then he just stood there. He wasn't thinking anything. There didn't seem to be anything to think.

"You knew him?" the man asked.

"Thirty years," Mike said. "No, more'n that," he said, and started to figure out how long he had known Tom Connover, but lost it, and said, as if it would do just as well, "He was a lot younger than I am, though."

"Hey," said the man, coming closer, and peering again. "You're Mike Braneen, aren't you?"

"Yes," Mike said.

"Gee, I didn't recognize you at first. I'm sorry."

"That's all right," Mike said. He didn't know who the man was, or what he was sorry about.

He turned his head slowly and looked out into the street. The snow was coming down heavily now. The street was all white. He saw Annie with her head and shoulders in under the arcade, but the snow settling on her rump.

"Well, I guess I'd better get Molly under cover," he said. He moved toward the burro a step, but then halted.

"Say, fella—"

The man had started on, but he turned back. He had to wait for Mike to speak.

"I guess this about Tom's mixed me up."

"Sure," the man said. "It's tough, an old friend like that."

"Where do I turn up to get to Mrs. Wright's place?"

"Mrs. Wright?"

"Mrs. William Wright," Mike said. "Her husband used to be a foreman in the Aztec. Got killed in the fire."

"Oh," the man said. He didn't say anything more, but just stood there, looking at the shadowy bulk of old Mike.

"She's not dead too, is she?" Mike asked slowly.

"Yeah, I'm afraid she is, Mr. Braneen," the man said. "Look," he said more cheerfully. "It's Mrs. Branley's house you want right now, isn't it? Place where you stayed last winter?"

Finally Mike said, "Yeah. Yeah, I guess it is."

"I'm going up that way. I'll walk up with you," the man said.

After they had started Mike thought that he ought to take the burro down to John Hammersmith's first, but he was afraid to ask about it. They walked on down Canyon Street, with Annie walking along beside them in the gutter. At the first side street they turned right and began to climb the steep hill toward another of the little street lights dancing over a crossing. There was no sidewalk here, and Annie followed right at their heels. That one street light was the only light showing up ahead.

When they were halfway up to the light Mike asked, "She die this summer too?"

The man turned his body half around, so that he could hear inside his collar.

"What?"

"Did she die this summer too?"

"Who?"

"Mrs. Wright," Mike said.

The man looked at him, trying to see his face as they came up toward the light. Then he turned back again, and his voice was muffled by the collar.

"No, she died quite a while ago, Mr. Braneen."

"Oh," Mike said finally.

They came up onto the crossing under the light, and the snow-laden wind whirled around them again. They passed under the light, and their three lengthening shadows before them were obscured by the innumerable tiny shadows of the flakes.

EARLY MARRIAGE

by CONRAD RICHTER

Very few authors have been able to catch the tone of the folk tale in their writing. Stephen Vincent Benet is one who did, MacKinley Kantor is another. But perhaps none has done this more successfully than Conrad Richter. Coming to the writing of fiction late in life, Richter has established a reputation which in time will place him beside Willa Cather as one of the few real artists. Every word, every phrase falls into place with the deceptive carelessness of infinite pain. Each of his books has this quality of mastery, and it has brought him both the Pulitzer Prize and the National Book Award. "Early Marriage" from his book, Early Americana, *reads like a tale an old frontier woman might tell her grandchildren.*

For two days the leathery face of Asa Putman had been a document in cipher to anyone who could read the code. Since Saturday but one traveler had passed his solitary post, a speck of adobe and picket corrals lost on the vast, sandy stretch of the Santa Ana plain. Far as the eye could see from his doorway, the rutted El Paso trail, unfenced, gutterless, innocent of grading, gravel, culverts, or telephone poles, imprinted only by iron tires, the hoofs of horses and oxen, sheep and cattle, and the paw of the loping lobo wolf, lay with dust unraised.

Ordinarily, there were freighters with cracking whips and trailers rumbling on behind. Army trains to and from the forts set up their tents for the night beyond the springs. The private coaches of Santa Fe and Colorado merchants, of cattle kings and Government officials, stopped long enough for the Putman children to admire the ladies, the magnificent woodwork, and the luxurious cushions inside. Trail herds of gaunt red steers bawled for the water in the earthen tank, and pairs and companies of horsemen rode up and down.

But since Saturday not even a solitary buckboard from the far settlements in the Cedar country had called for supplies or letters. Only a girl from the Blue Mesa had ridden in for her and her neighbors' mail. She had eaten dinner with the Putmans, refused to stay overnight and started her long ride home.

A stranger from the East would have spoken about the stillness, the deadly waiting, and asked uneasily why Uncle Gideon hadn't come as promised. But in the Putman household it was not mentioned.

Asa deliberately busied himself about the post, filling the bin beneath the counter with navy beans and green coffee, leafing through the packet of letters in the drawer, and making a long rite out of feeding the occupants of the picket corrals—four horses of which were fresh for the next stage.

Rife, just turned fifteen, carried water and gathered cow chips in an old hide dragged by a rope to his saddle horn. Ignacita, the Mexican house-

324

keeper, spat sharply on her heavy irons in the torrid kitchen and kept glancing over her shoulder and out of the open door and windows.

And Nancy Belle, going on seventeen, packed and repacked the high, iron-bound trunk that her father had bought for her at Santa Fe and sang softly to herself in the way that women sang fifty and sixty years ago.

Saturday she was being married at Gunstock, two hundred miles away —five days' journey in a wagon, four in a saddle or buckboard.

For six months she had thought of little else. The almanac fell apart at June as naturally as her mother's Bible did at the Twenty-third Psalm. So often had she run her finger down the page that anyone might tell from the worn line of type the very day she and Stephen Dewee would be man and wife. The Dewees lived four hundred miles west across the territory in the Beaverhead country. She and Stephen were taking a mountain ranch near his people, and for the wedding they had compromised on Gunstock, nearly equidistant from both families and convenient to friends scattered up and down the Rio Grande.

She had lighted a candle in the dusk, when a figure appeared reluctantly in her doorway. Asa Putman had never been at ease in his daughter's bedroom. A tall, rawhide man in an unbuttoned, sagging vest, he was visibly embarrassed by any furnishings that suggested refinement. Invariably he kept his hat on in the house. He had it on now, a flat top and a flat brim, not so much like the Western hats you see now. Nancy Belle knew that her mother's people had never forgiven him for bringing his young wife and their two small children to this lonely post, at the mercy of outlaws and the worse Apaches.

Tonight she could see that something bothered him. He gave her a sidewise glance, so sharp and characteristic.

"I don't expect, Nancy Belle, you could put off your weddin'?"

The girl stood quietly gazing at him with a face like the tintype of her mother. But under her sedate gray dress, with tight waist and full skirts to the instep, she had frozen. She looked much older than her years. Her air of gentlefolk and her wide-apart gray eyes came from her mother. But the chin, tipped up with resolute fearlessness, was her father's.

"No, papa!" Her two clear words held all the steady insistence of the desert.

"I figured how you'd feel," he nodded, avoiding her eyes. "I just wanted to put it up to you. I'd 'a' covered the *jornada* on foot to be on time at my own weddin', but I didn't have to count on Gideon to hold me up."

"Are you telling me, papa, that you can't go to Gunstock tomorrow?" Her voice remained quiet, but a coldness had seized her. Of all the people she had visualized at her wedding, the one next to Stephen she could least spare was the tall, grave figure of her father.

"I reckon I kind of can't, Nancy Belle," he said soberly. "Rife could tend to the stage all right and do the feedin'. But they's men come to this post no boy can handle." He shifted his position. "I figured once on closin' up the post till I got back. But the stage is comin' and the mail. And the freighters count on me for feed and grub. Then I got to protect my own property and the mail and freight for the Cedar country that's in the storage room."

"I know," Nancy Belle said steadily. "I can get to Gunstock all right."

Far back in her father's assaying eyes, she fancied she saw a glint of pride.

"You're pretty nigh a woman now, Nancy Belle. And Rife's a good slice of a man. It's a straight trail to the Rio Grande, once you turn at the old post. Both you and Rife's been over it before. Of course, I'd like to be at the weddin', but the boy can tell me about it." He went to the window. "Rife!" he called.

Nancy Belle's brother came in presently. A slight boy, with his father's blue eyes, he seldom made a fuss over anything, even when he shot a stray duck on the tank or when they braked down the last cedar hill into Santa Fe with all the open doors of the plaza shops in sight. And when his father told him now, he showed neither enthusiasm nor regret—merely straightened.

"Sure. I can take you, Nancy Belle," he said.

Something pulled under his sister's tight basque. She remembered the long miles they would have in the wagon, the camps at lonely places, the ugly shadow ever hovering over the outposts of this frontier country, and the blight that, since Saturday, seemed to have fallen on the trail. Her eyes swam. Now, at the last minute, she yielded.

"If you'll let me ride, papa, I'll wait another day for Uncle Gideon," she promised.

Her father's eyes moved to the ruffled red calico curtains at the shadeless windows.

"I don't hardly count on Gideon comin' any more, Nancy Belle. Besides, it's too long in the saddle to Gunstock—especially for a girl to get married. You'd be plumb wore out, and you wouldn't have your trunk. You couldn't get dressed for your weddin'."

He turned thoughtfully and went out, Rife close behind. Nancy Belle could hear her father's tones, slow and grave, coming from near one of the picket corrals.

It was too far to catch the words; but when they came in, she saw that her brother's features looked a little pale under the tan.

"You better get some sleep, Nancy Belle," her father said. "You and Rife are startin' before daylight. If Gideon comes, I'll ride after."

They had scarcely gone from the room when Ignacita came in from the kitchen, her black eyes glittering over a pile of freshly starched white in her arms.

"Nancy Belle, *chinita!*" she whispered, plucking at the girl's sleeve. "You don't say to your *papacito* I talk to you! I have promise I don't scare you. But I can't see you go so far in the wildness alone, *pobrecita!* Sometimes people go safe from one place to the other, oh, *si!* But sometimes, *chinita,* they don't come back! You have not the oldness like Ignacita. Ay, I tell you these old eyes have see men and women quartered from a tree like sheep or maybe tied over a stove like I don't have the words to say to you."

Nancy Belle did not answer except to lay, one by one, the ironed pieces in her trunk—a bride's muslin underwear trimmed with red and blue feather stitching; long petticoats stiffly flounced with ruffles, and nightgowns long in the sleeve and high in the neck, with ruffles at wrist and throat. The Mexican woman went on hoarsely. The girl folded away her winter's cashmere dress, buttoned up the front and with a white fichu. She unwrapped and wrapped again in crumpled white tissue the red slippers the old gentleman on the stage had sent her as a wedding present from Philadelphia.

When Ignacita had left, she opened her keepsake box covered with colored shells. The mirror on the inside lid turned back a face as calm as the little golden clouds that hung of an evening over the east to catch the desert sunset. But after she had undressed and put on her nightdress, for a long time she was aware of the soft pound of her heart faintly swaying the bed on its rawhide springs.

At the first sound of Ignacita's hand on the kitchen stove, Nancy Belle sprang out of bed. She dressed on the brown pool of burro skin, the only carpet on her adobe floor. Through the west window she could see the morning star burning like a brilliant candle. It hung, she told herself, over Gunstock and the Beaverhead, where Stephen, at this moment, in their new log ranch house, lay thinking about her.

They ate in the kitchen by lamplight. She had never been so conscious of every detail—the great white cups and saucers, the familiar steel knives, the homy smell of the scorched paper lamp-shade, the unreadable eyes of her father, Rife, and Ignacita.

Asa Putman himself carried out the trunk. There was already hay in the wagon, a gunny sack of oats, food in a canned-tomato box and utensils in another, a water-keg, bed roll tied in a wagon sheet, an ax, a bridle, and her own side-saddle, made to order over a man's tree. Her eyes caught the gleam of a rifle leaning up against the seat in the lantern-light. Tethered to the rear of the wagon stood her saddle mare, Fancy, with pricked-up ears. She was going along to their new ranch home. Nancy Belle felt that she was still among intimate things, but outside the little circle of light lay darkness and the unknown.

When she said good-by to her father, he kissed her—something he had not done for years.

"You haven't changed your mind, Nancy Belle?" he asked.

She climbed quickly up over the wheel to the spring seat of the wagon before he might see that she was crying. Rife swung up like a monkey on the other side and pushed the rifle into the crevice behind the seat cushion. The lines tautened and the wagons lurched.

"*Dios* go with you safe to your husband, Nancy Belle!" she heard Ignacita cry after her.

The morning star had set. They moved into a world of silent blackness. Nancy Belle could not see how the horses remained on the trail. When she looked back, the only light in all these square miles of black, unfriendly earth was the yellow window of her father's post.

It was almost a vision, golden and far away, like all beautiful things. She didn't trust herself to look again.

Two hours later the wagon was a lonely speck of boat rocking in an illimitable sage-green sea beneath the sun. The canvas wagon sheet fastened over the bows was a kind of sail, and eastward the sandy water did not stop rolling till it washed up at the foot of the faintly blue ramparts of the distant Espiritu Range.

Just before they turned west on the cross trail to the Rio Grande, a heavy wagon with a yoke of oxen in front and a cow behind toiled round the crumbling adobe walls of the old, abandoned post house. A bearded man and a thin woman with a white face sat on the seat. She held a baby in her arms, and three black-eyed children peered from under the wagon sheet.

The bearded man saluted and stopped his willing team. Rife did likewise. The woman spoke first. Her tongue was swift and slightly acid.

"You better turn around and follow us if you want to save your hair!" she called. "Yesterday a sheep-herder told us he saw—"

A sharp word from the bearded man caused her to relapse into sullen silence. He asked Rife where he might be going, then climbed down to the trail and said he wanted to talk to him a little. The boy followed reluctantly behind his wagon. Nancy Belle could hear the bearded man's tones coming slow and grave like her father's, while the woman made silent and horribly expressive lip language.

Rife came back, walking stiffly. The bearded man climbed up beside the woman.

"They got to go on," he told her in a low tone, then saluted with his whip. "Good luck, boy! And you, miss!"

Rife raised his whip in stiff acknowledgment. The wagons creaked apart. Nancy Belle saw in front of her the trail to the Rio Grande, little more than a pair of wheel tracks, that lost itself on the lonely plain. Rife seemed relieved that she did not ask what the bearded man had said. But it was enough for her not to be able to forget the woman's fearful signs and mouthings and the horror in the curious eyes of the staring children.

Sister and brother talked very little. Nancy Belle saw her brother's eyes keep sweeping the country, scanning the horizons. Bunches of bear grass that might have been feathers pinioned his blue gaze, and clumps of cane cactus that seemed to hold pointing gun barrels. At arroyos thick with chamiso and Apache plume she could see his feet tighten on the footboard. Once he pulled out the rifle, but it was only a herd of antelopes moving across the desert page.

They camped for the night when the sun was still high. Nancy Belle asked no questions as the boy drove far off the trail into a grassy *cañada*. She sang softly to herself as she fried the salt side bacon and put the black coffee-pot to boil.

Rife hobbled Anton Chico and the Bar X horse and staked out Fancy close to the wagon.

She pretended not to notice when, before dark, he poured earth on the fire till not a spark or wisp of smoke remained. Out of one eye she watched him climb the side of the *cañada* and stand long minutes sweeping the country from the ridge, a slight, tense figure against the sullen glow of the sunset.

"It's all right," he said when he came down. "You can go to bed."

"What's all right?" she asked him.

"The horses," he said, turning away, and Nancy Belle felt a stab of pain that so soon this boy must bear a man's responsibilities and tell a man's lies.

She prayed silently on her blankets spread on the hay in the wagon box, and lay down with her head on the side-saddle, her unread Testament in her hand. She heard Rife unroll his camp bed on the ground beneath the wagon. It was all very strange and hushed without her father. Just to feel the Testament in her hand helped to calm her and to remember the day at the post when she had first met Stephen.

Her father had never let her come in contact with the men of the trail. Always, at the first sign of dust cloud on the horizon, he would tell both children to heap up the chip-box, fill the water-buckets and carry saddles and bridles into the house. But this day Asa Putman and Rife had gone to Fort Sumner. And to Nancy Belle, Uncle Gideon could seldom say no.

It had been a very hot day. She had been sitting in the shade of the earthen bank of the tank, moving her bare feet in the cool water, watching the ripples in the hot south wind. The leaves of the cottonwoods clashed overhead, and she heard nothing until she looked up, and there was a young man on a blue-gray horse, with dust clinging to his hat brim and mustache. His eyes were direct as an eagle's. Firm lines modeled his lean face. But what she noticed most at the time was the little bow tie on his dark shirt.

Instantly she had tucked her bare, wet legs under her red dress. Her face burned with shame, but the young stranger talked to her about her father coolly, as if she, a girl of fifteen, had not been caught barefooted. Then he did what in her mind was a noble thing. When Uncle Gideon came out, he magnificently turned his back for her to run into the house and pull on shoes and stockings.

She thought of Stephen constantly next day and the next. She had grown a little used to the journey without her father now—the still, uncertain nights under the wagon sheet, sitting, lying, listening, waiting; the less uncertain days with the sun on the endless spaces; her never-quiet perch on the high spring seat under the slanted bow; the bumps, creaks, and lumberings of the wagon; the sand sifting softly over the red, turning wheels; all afternoon the sun in their faces; ahead the far haze and heat waves in which were still lost Gunstock and the Rio Grande. Almost she had forgotten the bearded man with the oxen and the curious, detached horror in the eyes of his children.

Since morning of the third day their progress had been slower. The trail seemed level, except for the heavy breathing of the horses. But when Nancy Belle glanced back she could see the steady grade they had been climbing. Abruptly, in mid-afternoon, she found that the long, blue Espiritu Range had disappeared, vanished behind a high pine-clad hill which was its southernmost beginning. It was like the lizard that swallowed itself, a very real lizard. At this moment they were climbing over the lizard's tail.

"Cedars!" Rife said briefly, pointing with the whip to dark sprawling growths ahead.

"You breathe deep up here!" Nancy Belle drank in the light air.

Rife took a sniff, but his blue eyes never ceased to scan the high, black-thatched hill under whose frowning cliff they must pass.

"Soon we can see the Gunstock Mountains," Nancy Belle said.

"And Martin Cross's cabin," Rife nodded. "It's the last water to the Rio Grande."

"He's a nice old man," Nancy Belle ventured casually. "It would be nice to camp by his cabin tonight and talk."

The boy inclined his head. After a few moments he started to whistle softly. At the first cedar Nancy Belle leaped off the moving wagon and climbed back with an evergreen branch. The twig, crushed in her hand, smelled like some store in Santa Fe.

They gained the summit. A breeze was sweeping here from the southwest, and the horses freshened. But Rife had suddenly stopped whistling and Nancy Belle's sprig of cedar lay on her lap. The frowning cliff of the pine-clad hill was still there. But Martin Cross's cabin had turned to a desolate mound of ashes. As they stared, a gust of wind sent wisps of smoke scurrying from the mound, and a red eye opened to watch them from the embers. Nancy Belle felt an uncontrollable twitching in the hair roots at the base of her scalp.

Where Martin Cross's eastbound wheel tracks met the trail, Rife reluctantly halted the horses and wet his air-dried lips.

"The water keg's dry, and the horses. If papa was here, he'd drive over."

"I'm the oldest." Nancy Belle found her voice steady. "I'll ride over. There might be something we can do."

The boy rose quickly. His eyes seemed to remember something his father had said.

"You can drive the wagon over if I wave."

He had thrown her the lines and slipped back through the canvas-covered tunnel of wagon box, picking up Fancy's bridle and the rifle. Barebacked he rode toward the smoldering ashes at the foot of that frowning hill. The chestnut mare's tail and mane streamed like something gold in the wind.

When she looked back to the trail, her eyes were pinioned by a light object in the wheel track ahead of the Bar X horse. It was a long gray feather. Instantly she told herself that it had come from some wild turkey Martin Cross had shot, and yet never had air anywhere become so suddenly horrible and choking as in this canyon.

Rife did not signal her to drive over. She saw him come riding back at full speed. The mare was snorting. As he stopped her at the wagon, her chestnut head kept turning back toward what had once been a cabin. Rife slipped the lead rope about her neck and climbed into the seat with the rifle in his hands.

"The water—you wouldn't want it!" he said thickly. His cheeks, she noticed, were the color of *yeso*.

"Rife"—Nancy Belle touched his arm when she had driven down the canyon—"what did you see at the cabin?"

The boy sat deaf and rigid beside her, eyes staring straight ahead. She saw that his young hands were still tortured around the barrel of his rifle.

Far down on the pitch-dark mesa she stopped the horses in the trail and listened. There were no stars, not a sound but the flapping of the wagon sheet in the wind and the clank of coffee-pot and water-bucket under the wagon. Half standing on the footboard, she guided the team off the trail in the intense blackness. Her swift hands helped the trembling boy stake out the mare and hobble the team. They did not light a lantern. Rife declined to eat. Nancy Belle chewed a few dry mouthfuls.

The wind came drawing out of the blackness with a great shaft. It hissed through the grass, sucked and tore at the wagon sheet, and whistled through the spokes and brake rigging. Rife did not take his bed roll under the wagon tonight. He drew the ends of the wagon sheet together and lay down in the wagon box near his sister. For a long time they were silent. When she heard his heavy breathing, she lifted the rifle from his chest.

The storm grew. Sand began pelting against the canvas and sifted into the wagon box. An invisible cloud of choking dust found its way into eyes, mouth, ears, and lungs. Nancy Belle laid down the rifle a moment to pull a blanket over the face of the boy. He tossed and muttered pitifully, but he slept on.

Magically the rain, when it came, stopped the sand and dust. The girl drank in the clean-washed air. At daylight she slipped out to the ground. The mesa, stretching away in the early light, touched here and there with feathers of mist, would have been beautiful except for a sharp new loneliness. The horses were gone!

At her exclamation, Rife appeared from the wagon box. His shame at having slept through the night was quickly overshadowed by their misfortune.

Together they found where Fancy's stake had been pulled out and dragged. Yards farther on they could tell by Anton Chico's tracks that his hobbles had parted.

Nancy Belle made her brother come back to the wagon and stuff his pockets with cold biscuits and antelope jerky. She said she would have a hot breakfast ready when he returned. The horses, perhaps, were just down in some draw where they had drifted from the wind.

When he had gone with the rifle, she filled the coffee-pot from a clearing water-hole in the nearest arroyo. She fried potatoes and onions in the long-handled skillet. And when he did not come, she set fresh biscuits in the Dutch oven. Each biscuit held a square of salt side bacon in its top, and as it baked, the fat oozed down and incased it in a kind of glazed tastiness.

At noon she thought she heard a shot. Nowhere could she see him on the endless sweep of mesa. By late afternoon she was still alone. She read her Testament and wondered how many women over the world had read it in hours like this. Sitting in the shadow of the wagon, facing the direction in which he had gone, she looked up every few minutes. But all her eyes could find were cloud shadows racing across the lonely face of the mesa. All she could hear were the desolate cries from the unseen lark sparrows.

Darkness, stillness settled down on the empty land. She climbed back into the wagon and sat on the chuck-box, hands rigid on her knees. Again and again she convinced herself that the horses could not have been driven off or she would have seen the drivers' tracks. When wild, sharp barks shattered the stillness and set wires jerking in her limbs, she talked to herself steadily, but a little meaninglessly, of the post—on and on as the darkness was filled with the ringing and counter-ringing of shrill, cracked yappings—not long tones like a dog's, but incredibly short syllables rising, rising in a mad eternal scale and discord.

"I wish papa had given me two of the chairs," she repeated. "Mamma said they were post oak from Texas. She said they had got white from scrubbing. I liked the laced rawhide seats with the hair left on. It made them soft to sit on. The seats in the parlor were black. And the ones in the kitchen were red. But I liked the brockle one in my room best."

The insane din around the wagon had become terrific. There were only two or three of the animals, Nancy Belle guessed, but they threw their voices and echoes together to make a score.

"When I was little I liked to go in the storage room," her voice went on, scarcely intelligible to her own ears. "It was dark and cool, and smelled of burlap and kerosene and whisky, and sweetish with brown sugar. I can see the fat sacks of green coffee. And the round tins of kerosene had boards on the side. The flour-sacks were printed: 'Rough and Ready' in red letters. Mamma once used to make our underwear out of the sacking. I can smell the salt side bacon in the gunny sacks."

She could tell from the sounds that one of the animals was running insanely back and forth near the wagon tongue. She had never noticed before that they yelped both when breathing in and out. Suddenly came silence. It warned her. Instinctively she felt for the ax.

"Nancy Belle!" a boy's far, anxious voice called from the darkness.

She hallooed and leaned out over the tailboard. Three shadowy forms were coming across the mesa in the starlight. Never had horses looked so good.

"Were you scared?" Rife greeted. "Anything bother you?"

"Nothing," Nancy Belle said. "Just coyotes."

"I had to give Fancy her head after it got dark." He slid wearily to the ground. "She brought us straight back to the wagon."

Nancy Belle had wanted to put her arms around her brother. Now she hugged the mare instead. Rife ate fresh biscuits and a tin plate of cold potatoes. He drank several tin cups of coffee. Nancy Belle had slipped the oats-laden gunny-sack *morrals* over the horses' heads.

"I had to walk halfway to the mountain," Rife said.

"Just help hitch up; then you can sleep all night," she promised.

It rained again heavily toward midnight. Flashes of lightning lit the drenched plain. For minutes at a time, quivering fingers of blue phosphorescence stood on the ears of the toiling horses. At dawn Nancy Belle still held the reins as the mud-splashed wagon crawled through a world bathed in early purple splendor.

Four days they had been crossing a hundred and seventy miles of desolate plain. Now the end waited in sight. To the west lay a land broken and tumbled by a mighty hand. Hill shouldered hill and range peered over range, all indescribably violet except where peaks tipped by the unseen sun were far-off flaming towers of copper.

It was a new land, her promised land, Stephen's land, Nancy Belle told herself, where nobody burned cow chips, but snapping cedar and pine, where cold water ran in the wooded canyons, and the eye, weary of one flat circle the horizon round, had endless geometric designs to refresh the retina.

She sang softly as the wagon lumbered to the edge of a long, shallow valley, brown and uninhabited, running north and south, and desolate except for a winding ribbon that was white with sky and narrowly bordered with green.

"Rife!" Nancy Belle cried. "The Rio Grande!"

An hour afterwards they pulled out of the sun into the shade of the long cottonwood *bosque*. Nancy Belle wasn't singing now. Where she remembered wide sandbars glistening with sky and tracked by waterfowl, a chocolate-red flood rolled. Where had been the island, tops of tule and scrub willow swung to and fro with the current.

Anton Chico and the Bar X horse stopped of their own accord in the trail, ears pricked forward at the swirling brown wash. While Rife turned the three horses loose to graze, Nancy Belle silently fried bacon and made coffee. When she had washed skillet and tin dishes in the river, the boy had wired the wagon box to the brake rigging. Now he was tying securely one end of his rope to the center of the coupling pole under the wagon. The other end she knew he would fasten to the inadequate upper horn of the side-saddle.

"I wouldn't mind the river if I just had my own saddle," he mourned.

They hitched up the team silently. Rife cinched the side-saddle on Fancy and straddled it, the single stirrup useless to a man. Nancy Belle climbed into the wagon and picked up the lines. The other bank looked as far away as the Espiritu Range from the post. She wanted to say something to her brother—some last word, in case they didn't make it. But all she did was cluck her tongue to the horses.

Gingerly, one slow foot at a time, the team moved down the trail into the water.

"Give 'em their heads!" Rife called from the right rear.

Nancy Belle held a rein in each hand. The red channel water came to the wagon tongue, covered it, reached the horses' bellies. The team wanted to stop. Nancy Belle swung her whip, a stick tipped with a long rawhide lash. The wagon went on. The collars of both horses kept dipping, but never entirely out of sight. Still barely wading, the slow team reached the firmer footing of the island.

Two-thirds of the river still rolled in front of the wagon. The west bank did not seem to have grown much closer, but the east bank behind them had moved far away. The team had to be whipped into the violent current. The water churned white through the wagon wheels. Suddenly both horses appeared to stumble and drop out of sight. Their heads came up wildly, spray blowing from their nostrils. The muddy water hid their legs, but by their bobbing motions Nancy Belle knew that they were swimming.

"Keep 'em pointed up the river!" Rife shouted.

Already she felt the wagon floating. It swung downstream with the current; then Rife's rope from Fancy's saddle snubbed it. The team was snorting with every breath. The Bar X horse swam high in the water, his withers and part of his back out of the chocolate current. But all she could see of Anton Chico were his nose and ears.

Down between her ankles she saw water in the wagon box. She thought of the hemstitched sheets at the bottom of her trunk, the towels and pillowcases crocheted with shell lace. Her blue velvet corduroy dress was probably wet already, and all the cunning print aprons with dust caps to match. River water couldn't hurt the little yellow creamer, sugar bowl, and covered butter dish that had been her mother's. And the gingham dresses could be washed. What worried her were her wedding dress and the keepsake box, especially the tintypes, one of which was Rife in a child's suit edged with black braid, his brand-new hat on his knee.

An older Rife was shouting something behind her now. She couldn't catch the words. Then she found what it was. The neck and withers of Anton Chico raised suddenly out of the water and both horses were scrambling up the steep bank below the ford. Only quick work with the lines saved the wagon from turning over. Safe and blowing on the high bank, the dripping horses shook themselves like puppies.

Nancy Belle couldn't go on until she had opened the trunk and appraised the damage. Rife unsaddled Fancy and drove on with the refreshed team. Behind his slight back in the wagon box, the girl changed to her blue velvet corduroy, which was hardly wet at all. Then she combed her hair and rolled into a cranny of her trunk the old felt hat that had been too large for her father.

A half-dozen riders met the wagon some miles down the Gunstock Canyon. All of them, Nancy Belle noticed, carried guns. Stephen wore a new white shirt and a gray hat with curled brim she had not seen before. He stood in his stirrups and swung her down in front of him on the saddle, where he kissed her. She had never felt his lips press into such a straight line.

"Papa couldn't come," she said. "So Rife brought me."

She felt Stephen's rigid arm around her.

"We just got in from the Beaverhead ourselves."

"He means they never get any news out in the Beaverhead or he'd 'a' come further east to meet you!" Uncle Billy Williams put in. He had a lovable, squeaky voice. "The Apaches been breakin' loose again. Funny you didn't hear anything over in your country."

Nancy Belle gave him an inscrutable look with her gray eyes. Uncle Billy pulled out his bandanna and blew his nose.

"They got my old friend Judge Hower and his wife and kid in a buggy on the Upper Espiritu. The man that found what they did to 'em, they say, cried like a baby."

"That's all right, Uncle Billy," Stephen said in a gentle voice.

Nancy Belle glanced at Rife. Her brother's face looked gray, the eyes staring as when he had ridden in the late afternoon sunlight from the smoking ashes of Martin Cross's cabin.

Nearly fifty people, gathered in the big parlor upstairs at the hotel, greeted Nancy Belle. An old man whose young black eyes twinkled out of a bearded face said he was glad to see that she had her "hair on straight." Rife stopped with the trunk before driving to the livery, and Stephen's mother showed Nancy Belle to a room to dress.

The guests stopped talking when she came into the parlor in her white wedding dress. Her basque came to a point in the front and back. It fitted like a glove. The silk undershirt came to her instep, and the ruffled overskirt to her knees. She had parted her hair from side to side and brushed the bangs down on her forehead. She felt very light-headed. The wagon still seemed to be jerking under her.

She glimpsed Rife gazing at her, a rapt expression in his reticent blue eyes. She was glad to see that he had brushed his hair. The brass swinging lamp had been lighted and the dark woodwork of the parlor festooned with evergreen branches. White streamers from the wall met in a papier-mâché bell in one corner. She noticed two children peering eagerly from the dark hall.

Stephen came to her, very straight in a long coat and stand-up collar with a black tie. He led her up beneath the papier-mâché bell. In a sibilant, church-like whisper, the Gunstock preacher made sure of her full name. Then he coughed and began the ceremony. He had a deep voice, but Nancy Belle didn't hear all of the service. Her mind kept going back to a tall, grave man in a lonely adobe post on the wide Santa Ana plain. And after she had said: "I do," her lips moved, but she was not praying for Stephen, her husband.

The Miners

THE ILIAD OF SANDY BAR

by BRET HARTE

In the Yukon territory today there live two old Italians who came over the White Pass more than half a century ago. One is known as "Old Nick" and his neighbor, who lives several hundred yards away, is called "The Other Nick." They have so seldom left their gold claims that they haven't learned English, and being the only Italian-speaking persons in the area, they can talk only to each other. However, sometime before World War I, they cabined together for a month, and in the years since they have not spoken to each other. It is not that they are enemies, but, as one Yukon pioneer explains it, "they said all they had to say to each other." It is this spirit of the lonely men who live on gold claims until they are "bushed"— made strange in their own ways—which Bret Harte captures in this short story.

Before nine o'clock it was pretty well known all along the river that the two parties of the "Amity Claim" had quarreled and separated at daybreak. At that time the attention of their nearest neighbor had been attracted by the sounds of altercations and two consecutive pistol-shots. Running out, he had seen dimly in the gray mist that rose from the river the tall form of Scott, one of the partners, descending the hill toward the cañon; a moment later, York, the other partner, had appeared from the cabin, and walked in an opposite direction toward the river, passing within a few feet of the curious watcher. Later it was discovered that a serious China-man, cutting wood before the cabin, had witnessed part of the quarrel. But John was stolid, indifferent, and reticent. "Me choppee wood, me no fightee," was his serene response to all anxious queries. "But what did they *say, John?*" John did not *sabe*. Colonel Starbottle deftly ran over the various popular epithets which a generous public sentiment might accept as reasonable provocation for an assault. But John did not recognize them. "And this yer's the cattle," said the Colonel, with some severity, "that some thinks oughter be allowed to testify agin a White Man! Git—you heathen!"

Still the quarrel remained inexplicable. That two men, whose amiability and grave tact had earned for them the title of "The Peacemakers," in a community not greatly given to the passive virtues,—that these men, singu-larly devoted to each other, should suddenly and violently quarrel, might well excite the curiosity of the camp. A few of the more inquisitive visited the late scene of conflict, now deserted by its former occupants. There was no trace of disorder or confusion in the neat cabin. The rude table was arranged as if for breakfast; the pan of yellow biscuit still sat upon that hearth whose dead embers might have typified the evil passions that had raged there but an hour before. But Colonel Starbottle's eye, albeit some-what bloodshot and rheumy, was more intent on practical details. On ex-amination, a bullet-hole was found in the doorpost, and another nearly opposite in the casing of the window. The Colonel called attention to the fact that the one "agreed with" the bore of Scott's revolver, and the other

with that of York's derringer. "They must hev stood about yer," said the
Colonel, taking position; "not more'n three feet apart, and—missed!"
There was a fine touch of pathos in the falling inflection of the Colonel's
voice, which was not without effect. A delicate perception of wasted opportunity thrilled his auditors.

But the Bar was destined to experience a greater disappointment. The
two antagonists had not met since the quarrel, and it was vaguely rumored
that, on the occasion of a second meeting, each had determined to kill the
other "on sight." There was, consequently, some excitement—and, it is
to be feared, no little gratification—when, at ten o'clock, York stepped
from the Magnolia Saloon into the one long straggling street of the camp,
at the same moment that Scott left the blacksmith's shop at the forks of
the road. It was evident, at a glance, that a meeting could only be avoided
by the actual retreat of one or the other.

In an instant the doors and windows of the adjacent saloons were filled
with faces. Heads unaccountably appeared above the river banks and from
behind boulders. An empty wagon at the cross-road was suddenly crowded
with people, who seemed to have sprung from the earth. There was much
running and confusion on the hillside. On the mountain-road, Mr. Jack
Hamlin had reined up his horse and was standing upright on the seat of
his buggy. And the two objects of this absorbing attention approached
each other.

"York's got the sun," "Scott'll line him on that tree," "He's waiting to
draw his fire," came from the cart; and then it was silent. But above this
human breathlessness the river rushed and sang, and the wind rustled the
tree-tops with an indifference that seemed obtrusive. Colonel Starbottle
felt it and in a moment of sublime preoccupation, without looking around,
waved his cane behind him warningly to all Nature, and said, "Shu!"

The men were now within a few feet of each other. A hen ran across
the road before one of them. A feathery seed vessel, wafted from a wayside
tree, fell at the feet of the other. And, unheeding this irony of Nature, the
two opponents came nearer, erect and rigid, looked in each other's eyes,
and—passed!

Colonel Starbottle had to be lifted from the cart. "This yer camp is
played out," he said gloomily, as he affected to be supported into the
Magnolia. With what further expression he might have indicated his feelings it was impossible to say, for at that moment Scott joined the group.
"Did you speak to me?" he asked of the Colonel, dropping his hand, as if
with accidental familiarity, on that gentleman's shoulder. The Colonel,
recognizing some occult quality in the touch, and some unknown quantity
in the glance of his questioner, contented himself by replying, "No, sir,"
with dignity. A few rods away, York's conduct was as characteristic and
peculiar. "You had a mighty fine chance; why didn't you plump him?"
said Jack Hamlin, as York drew near the buggy. "Because I hate him,"
was the reply, heard only by Jack. Contrary to popular belief, this reply

was not hissed between the lips of the speaker, but was said in an ordinary tone. But Jack Hamlin, who was an observer of mankind, noticed that the speaker's hands were cold and his lips dry, as he helped him into the buggy, and accepted the seeming paradox with a smile.

When Sandy Bar became convinced that the quarrel between York and Scott could not be settled after the usual local methods, it gave no further concern thereto. But presently it was rumored that the "Amity Claim" was in litigation, and that its possession would be expensively disputed by each of the partners. As it was well known that the claim in question was "worked out" and worthless, and that the partners whom it had already enriched had talked of abandoning it but a day or two before the quarrel, this proceeding could only be accounted for as gratuitous spite. Later, two San Francisco lawyers made their appearance in this guileless Arcadia, and were eventually taken into the saloons, and—what was pretty much the same thing—the confidences of the inhabitants. The results of this unhallowed intimacy were many subpoenas; and, indeed, when the "Amity Claim" came to trial, all of Sandy Bar that was not in compulsory attendance at the county seat came there from curiosity. The gulches and ditches for miles around were deserted. I do not propose to describe that already famous trial. Enough that, in the language of the plaintiff's counsel, "it was one of no ordinary significance, involving the inherent rights of that untiring industry which had developed the Pactolian resources of this golden land"; and, in the homelier phrase of Colonel Starbottle, "a fuss that gentlemen might hev settled in ten minutes over a social glass, ef they meant business; or in ten seconds with a revolver, ef they meant fun." Scott got a verdict, from which York instantly appealed. It was said that he had sworn to spend his last dollar in the struggle.

In this way Sandy Bar began to accept the enmity of the former partners as a lifelong feud, and the fact that they had ever been friends was forgotten. The few who expected to learn from the trial the origin of the quarrel were disappointed. Among the various conjectures, that which ascribed some occult feminine influence as the cause was naturally popular in a camp given to dubious compliment of the sex. "My word for it, gentlemen," said Colonel Starbottle, who had been known in Sacramento as a Gentleman of the Old School, "there's some lovely creature at the bottom of this." The gallant Colonel then proceeded to illustrate his theory by divers sprightly stories, such as Gentlemen of the Old School are in the habit of repeating, but which, from deference to the prejudices of gentlemen of a more recent school, I refrain from transcribing here. But it would appear that even the Colonel's theory was fallacious. The only woman who personally might have exercised any influence over the partners was the pretty daughter of "old man Folinsbee," of Poverty Flat, at whose hospitable house—which exhibited some comforts and refinements rare in that crude civilization—both York and Scott were frequent visitors. Yet into this charming retreat York strode one evening a month after the quarrel, and, beholding Scott sitting there, turned to the fair hostess with the abrupt query, "Do you love this man?" The young woman thus addressed returned that answer—at once spirited and evasive—which would occur to most of my fair readers in such an emergency. Without another word, York left the house. "Miss Jo" heaved the least possible sigh as the door closed on York's curls and square shoulders, and then, like a good girl, turned to her insulted guest. "But would you believe it, dear?" she afterwards related to an intimate friend, "the other creature, after glowering at me for a moment, got up on its hind legs, took its hat, and left too; and that's the last I've seen of either."

The same hard disregard of all other interests or feelings in the gratification of their blind rancor characterized all their actions. When York purchased the land below Scott's new claim, and obliged the latter, at a great expense, to make a long détour to carry a "tail-race" around it, Scott retaliated by building a dam that overflowed York's claim on the river. It was Scott who, in conjunction with Colonel Starbottle, first organized that active opposition to the Chinamen which resulted in the driving off of York's Mongolian laborers; it was York who built the wagon-road and established the express which rendered Scott's mules and pack-trains obsolete; it was Scott who called into life the Vigilance Committee which expatriated York's friend, Jack Hamlin; it was York who created the "Sandy Bar Herald," which characterized the act as "a lawless outrage" and Scott as a "Border Ruffian"; it was Scott, at the head of twenty masked men, who, one moonlight night, threw the offending "forms" into the yellow river, and scattered the types in the dusty road. These proceedings were received in the distant and more civilized outlying towns as vague indications of progress and vitality. I have before me a copy of the "Poverty Flat Pioneer" for the week ending August 12, 1856, in which the editor, under the head of "County Improvements," says: "The new Presbyterian Church on C Street, at Sandy Bar, is completed. It stands upon the lot formerly occupied by the Magnolia Saloon, which was so mysteriously burnt last month. The temple, which now rises like a Phoenix from the ashes of the Magnolia, is virtually the free gift of H. J. York, Esq., of Sandy Bar, who purchased the lot and donated the lumber. Other buildings are going up in the vicinity, but the most noticeable is the 'Sunny South Saloon,' erected by Captain Mat. Scott, nearly opposite the church. Captain Scott has spared no expense in the furnishing of this saloon, which promises to be one of the most agreeable places of resort in old Tuolumne. He has recently imported two new first-class billiard-tables with cork cushions. Our old friend, 'Mountain Jimmy,' will dispense liquors at the bar. We refer our readers to the advertisement in another column. Visitors to Sandy Bar cannot do better than give 'Jimmy' a call." Among the local items occurred the following: "H. J. York, Esq., of Sandy Bar, has offered a reward of $100 for the detection of the parties who hauled away the steps of the new Presbyterian Church, C Street,

Sandy Bar, during divine service on Sabbath evening last. Captain Scott adds another hundred for the capture of the miscreants who broke the magnificent plate-glass windows of the new saloon on the following evening. There is some talk of reorganizing the old Vigilance Committee at Sandy Bar."

When, for many months of cloudless weather, the hard, unwinking sun of Sandy Bar had regularly gone down on the unpacified wrath of these men, there was some talk of mediation. In particular, the pastor of the church to which I have just referred—a sincere, fearless, but perhaps not fully enlightened man—seized gladly upon the occasion of York's liberality to attempt to reunite the former partners. He preached an earnest sermon on the abstract sinfulness of discord and rancor. But the excellent sermons of the Rev. Mr. Daws were directed to an ideal congregation that did not exist at Sandy Bar,—a congregation of beings of unmixed vices and virtues, of single impulses, and perfectly logical motives, of preternatural simplicity, of childlike faith, and grown-up responsibilities. As unfortunately the people who actually attended Mr. Daws's church were mainly very human, somewhat artful, more self-excusing than self-accusing, rather good-natured, and decidedly weak, they quietly shed that portion of the sermon which referred to themselves, and accepting York and Scott—who were both in defiant attendance—as curious examples of those ideal beings above referred to, felt a certain satisfaction—which, I fear, was not altogether Christian-like—in their "raking-down." If Mr. Daws expected York and Scott to shake hands after the sermon, he was disappointed. But he did not relax his purpose. With that quiet fearlessness and determination which had won for him the respect of men who were too apt to regard piety as synonymous with effeminacy, he attacked Scott in his own house. What he said has not been recorded, but it is to be feared that it was part of his sermon. When he had concluded, Scott looked at him, not unkindly, over the glasses of his bar, and said, less irreverently than the words might convey, "Young man, I rather like your style; but when you know York and me as well as you do God Almighty, it'll be time to talk."

And so the feud progressed; and so, as in more illustrious examples, the private and personal enmity of two representative men led gradually to the evolution of some crude, half-expressed principle or belief. It was not long before it was made evident that those beliefs were identical with certain broad principles laid down by the founders of the American Constitution, as expounded by the statesmanlike A., or were the fatal quicksands on which the ship of state might be wrecked, warningly pointed out by the eloquent B. The practical result of all which was the nomination of York and Scott to represent the opposite factions of Sandy Bar in legislative councils.

For some weeks past the voters of Sandy Bar and the adjacent camps had been called upon, in large type, to "RALLY!" In vain the great pines at the cross-roads—whose trunks were compelled to bear this and other legends—moaned and protested from their windy watch-towers. But one day, with fife and drum and flaming transparency, a procession filed into the triangular grove at the head of the gulch. The meeting was called to order by Colonel Starbottle, who, having once enjoyed legislative functions, and being vaguely known as "war-horse," was considered to be a valuable partisan of York. He concluded an appeal for his friend with an enunciation of principles, interspersed with one or two anecdotes so gratuitously coarse that the very pines might have been moved to pelt him with their cast-off cones as he stood there. But he created a laugh, on which his candidate rode into popular notice; and when York rose to speak, he was greeted with cheers. But, to the general astonishment, the new speaker at once launched into bitter denunciation of his rival. He not only dwelt upon Scott's deeds and example as known to Sandy Bar, but spoke of facts connected with his previous career hitherto unknown to his auditors. To great precision of epithet and directness of statement, the speaker added the fascination of revelation and exposure. The crowd cheered, yelled, and were delighted; but when this astounding philippic was concluded, there was a unanimous call for "Scott!" Colonel Starbottle would have resisted this manifest impropriety, but in vain. Partly from a crude sense of justice, partly from a meaner craving for excitement, the assemblage was inflexible; and Scott was dragged, pushed, and pulled upon the platform. As his frowsy head and unkempt beard appeared above the railing, it was evident that he was drunk. But it was also evident, before he opened his lips, that the orator of Sandy Bar—the one man who could touch their vagabond sympathies (perhaps because he was not above appealing to them)—stood before them. A consciousness of this power lent a certain dignity to his figure, and I am not sure but that his very physical condition impressed them as a kind of regal unbending and large condescension. Howbeit, when this unexpected Hector arose from this ditch, York's myrmidons trembled. "There's naught, gentlemen," said Scott, leaning forward on the railing,—"there's naught as that man hez said as isn't true. I *was* run outer Cairo; I *did* belong to the Regulators; I *did* desert from the army; I *did* leave a wife in Kansas. But thar's one thing he didn't charge me with, and maybe he's forgotten. For three years, gentlemen, I was that man's pardner!" Whether he intended to say more, I cannot tell; a burst of applause artistically rounded and enforced the climax, and virtually elected the speaker. That fall he went to Sacramento, York went abroad, and for the first time in many years distance and a new atmosphere isolated the old antagonists.

With little of change in the green wood, gray rock, and yellow river, but with much shifting of human landmarks and new faces in its habitations, three years passed over Sandy Bar. The two men, once so identified with its character, seemed to have been quite forgotten. "You will never return to Sandy Bar," said Miss Folinsbee, the "Lily of Poverty Flat," on meeting York in Paris, "for Sandy Bar is no more. They call it Riverside now; and the new town is built higher up on the river bank. By the bye, 'Jo' says that Scott has won his suit about the 'Amity Claim,' and that he lives in the old cabin, and is drunk half his time. Oh, I beg your pardon," added the lively lady, as a flush crossed York's sallow cheek; "but, bless me, I really thought that old grudge was made up. I'm sure it ought to be."

It was three months after this conversation, and a pleasant summer evening, that the Poverty Flat coach drew up before the veranda of the Union Hotel at Sandy Bar. Among its passengers was one, apparently a stranger, in the local distinction of well-fitting clothes and closely shaven face, who demanded a private room and retired early to rest. But before sunrise next morning he arose, and, drawing some clothes from his carpet-bag, proceeded to array himself in a pair of white duck trousers, a white duck overshirt, and straw hat. When his toilet was completed, he tied a red bandana handkerchief in a loop and threw it loosely over his shoulders. The transformation was complete. As he crept softly down the stairs and stepped into the road, no one would have detected in him the elegant stranger of the previous night, and but few have recognized the face and figure of Henry York, of Sandy Bar.

In the uncertain light of that early hour, and in the change that had come over the settlement, he had to pause for a moment to recall where he stood. The Sandy Bar of his recollection lay below him, nearer the river; the buildings around him were of later date and newer fashion. As he strode toward the river, he noticed here a schoolhouse and there a church. A little farther on, the "Sunny South" came in view, transformed into a restaurant, its gilding faded and its paint rubbed off. He now knew where he was; and running briskly down a declivity, crossed a ditch, and stood upon the lower boundary of the "Amity Claim."

The gray mist was rising slowly from the river, clinging to the tree-tops and drifting up the mountain-side until it was caught among these rocky altars, and held a sacrifice to the ascending sun. At his feet the earth, cruelly gashed and scarred by his forgotten engines, had, since the old days, put on a show of greenness here and there, and now smiled forgivingly up at him, as if things were not so bad after all. A few birds were bathing in the ditch with a pleasant suggestion of its being a new and special provision of Nature, and a hare ran into an inverted sluice-box as he approached, as if it were put there for that purpose.

He had not yet dared to look in a certain direction. But the sun was now high enough to paint the little eminence on which the cabin stood. In spite of his self-control, his heart beat faster as he raised his eyes toward it. Its window and door were closed, no smoke came from its adobe chimney, but it was else unchanged. When within a few yards of it, he picked up a broken shovel, and shouldering it with a smile, he strode toward the door and knocked. There was no sound from within. The smile died upon his lips as he nervously pushed the door open.

A figure started up angrily and came toward him,—a figure whose blood-shot eyes suddenly fixed into a vacant stare, whose arms were at first out-stretched and then thrown up in warning gesticulation,—a figure that sud-denly gasped, choked, and then fell forward in a fit.

But before he touched the ground, York had him out into the open air and sunshine. In the struggle, both fell and rolled over on the ground. But the next moment York was sitting up, holding the convulsed frame of his former partner on his knee, and wiping the foam from his inarticulate lips. Gradually the tremor became less frequent and then ceased, and the strong man lay unconscious in his arms.

For some moments York held him quietly thus, looking in his face. Afar, the stroke of a woodman's axe—a mere phantom of sound—was all that broke the stillness. High up the mountain, a wheeling hawk hung breathlessly above them. And then came voices, and two men joined them.

"A fight?" No, a fit; and would they help him bring the sick man to the hotel?

And there for a week the stricken partner lay, unconscious of aught but the visions wrought by disease and fear. On the eighth day at sunrise he rallied, and opening his eyes, looked upon York and pressed his hand; and then he spoke:—

"And it's you. I thought it was only whiskey."

York replied by only taking both of his hands, boyishly working them backward and forward, as his elbow rested on the bed, with a pleasant smile.

"And you've been abroad. How did you like Paris?"

"So, so! How did *you* like Sacramento?"

"Bully!"

And that was all they could think to say. Presently Scott opened his eyes again.

"I'm mighty weak."

"You'll get better soon."

"Not much."

A long silence followed, in which they could hear the sounds of wood-chopping, and that Sandy Bar was already astir for the coming day. Then Scott slowly and with difficulty turned his face to York and said,—

"I might hev killed you once."

"I wish you had."

They pressed each other's hands again, but Scott's grasp was evidently failing. He seemed to summon his energies for a special effort.

"Old man!"

"Old chap."

"Closer!"

York bent his head toward the slowly fading face.

"Do ye mind that morning?"

"Yes."

A gleam of fun slid into the corner of Scott's blue eyes as he whispered,—

"Old man, thar *was* too much saleratus in that bread!"

It is said that these were his last words. For when the sun, which had so often gone down upon the idle wrath of these foolish men, looked again upon them reunited, it saw the hand of Scott fall cold and irresponsive from the yearning clasp of his former partner, and it knew that the feud of Sandy Bar was at an end.

AN ODYSSEY OF THE NORTH

by JACK LONDON

The spirit of adventure captured Jack London young and held him most of his life. And so it was natural that he rode with the flood of gold hunters into the Yukon, but just short of the gold-fields he stopped for a time to earn his living as a guide over the White Horse Rapids. Here he met the drifters, prospectors, get-rich-quick operators and all the rest who were drawn to the creeks of the Klondike River and Dawson City. Although London wrote other tales of the gold country, in this story he captured the aspects of the long hunt and the emptiness of the cold frontier. His people, who live far from law and civilization, take on a quality of unreality in a world unbelievably harsh.

I

The sleds were singing their eternal lament to the creaking of the harnesses and the tinkling bells of the leaders; but the men and dogs were tired and made no sound. The trail was heavy with new-fallen snow, and they had come far, and the runners, burdened with flintlike quarters of frozen moose, clung tenaciously to the unpacked surface and held back with a stubbornness almost human. Darkness was coming on, but there was no camp to pitch that night. The snow fell gently through the pulseless air, not in flakes, but in tiny frost crystals of delicate design. It was very warm—barely ten below zero—and the men did not mind. Beyers and Bettles had raised their ear flaps, while Malemute Kid had even taken off his mittens.

The dogs had been fagged out early in the afternoon, but they now began to show new vigor. Among the more astute there was a certain restlessness—an impatience at the restraint of the traces, an indecisive quickness of movement, a sniffing of snouts and pricking of ears. These became incensed at their more phlegmatic brothers, urging them on with numerous sly nips on their hinder quarters. Those, thus chidden, also contracted and helped spread the contagion. At last the leader of the foremost sled uttered a sharp whine of satisfaction, crouching lower in the snow and throwing himself against the collar. The rest followed suit. There was an ingathering of back bands, a tightening of traces; the sleds leaped forward, and the men clung to the gee poles, violently accelerating the uplift of their feet that they might escape going under the runners. The weariness of the day fell from them, and they whooped encouragement to the dogs. The animals responded with joyous yelps. They were swinging through the gathering darkness at a rattling gallop.

"Gee! Gee!" the men cried, each in turn, as their sleds abruptly left the main trail, heeling over on single runners like luggers on the wind.

Then came a hundred yards' dash to the lighted parchment window, which told its own story of the home cabin, the roaring Yukon stove, and the steaming pots of tea. But the home cabin had been invaded. Three-score huskies chorused defiance, and as many furry forms precipitated themselves upon the dogs which drew the first sled. The door was flung open, and a man, clad in the scarlet tunic of the Northwest Police, waded knee-deep among the furious brutes, calmly and impartially dispensing soothing justice with the butt end of a dog whip. After that the men shook hands; and in this wise was Malemute Kid welcomed to his own cabin by a stranger.

Stanley Prince, who should have welcomed him, and who was responsible for the Yukon stove and hot tea aforementioned, was busy with his guests. There were a dozen or so of them, as nondescript a crowd as ever served the Queen in the enforcement of her laws or the delivery of her mails. They were of many breeds, but their common life had formed of them a certain type—a lean and wiry type, with trail-hardened muscles, and sun-browned faces, and untroubled souls which gazed frankly forth, clear-eyed and steady. They drove the dogs of the Queen, wrought fear in the hearts of her enemies, ate of her meager fare, and were happy. They had seen life, and done deeds, and lived romances; but they did not know it.

And they were very much at home. Two of them were sprawled upon Malemute Kid's bunk, singing chansons which their French forebears sang in the days when first they entered the Northwest land and mated with its Indian women. Bettles' bunk had suffered a similar invasion, and three or four lusty *voyageurs* worked their toes among its blankets as they listened to the tale of one who had served on the boat brigade with Wolseley when he fought his way to Khartoum. And when he tired, a cowboy told of courts and kings and lords and ladies he had seen when Buffalo Bill toured the capitals of Europe. In a corner two half-breeds, ancient comrades in a lost campaign, mended harnesses and talked of the days when the Northwest flamed with insurrection and Louis Riel was king.

Rough jests and rougher jokes went up and down, and great hazards by trail and river were spoken of in the light of commonplaces, only to be recalled by virture of some grain of humor or ludicrous happening. Prince was led away by these uncrowned heroes who had seen history made, who regarded the great and the romantic as but the ordinary and the incidental in the routine of life. He passed his precious tobacco among them with lavish disregard, and rusty chains of reminiscence were loosened, and forgotten odysseys resurrected for his especial benefit.

When conversation dropped and the travelers filled the last pipes and unlashed their tight-rolled sleeping furs, Prince fell back upon his comrade for further information.

"Well, you know what the cowboy is," Malemute Kid answered, beginning to unlace his moccasins; "and it's not hard to guess the British blood in his bed partner. As for the rest, they're all children of the *coureurs du bois*, mingled with God knows how many other bloods. The two turning in by the door are the regulation 'breeds' or *Boisbrules*. That lad with the worsted breech scarf—notice his eyebrows and the turn of his jaw— shows a Scotchman wept in his mother's smoky tepee. And that hand- some-looking fellow putting the capote under his head is a French half- breed—you heard him talking; he doesn't like the two Indians turning in next to him. You see, when the 'breeds' rose under Riel the full-bloods kept the peace, and they've not lost much love for one another since."

"But I say, what's that glum-looking fellow by the stove? I'll swear he can't talk English. He hasn't opened his mouth all night."

"You're wrong. He knows English well enough. Did you follow his eyes when he listened? I did. But he's neither kith nor kin to the others. When they talked their own patois you could see he didn't understand. I've been wondering myself what he is. Let's find out."

"Fire a couple of sticks into the stove!" Malemute Kid commanded, raising his voice and looking squarely at the man in question.

He obeyed at once.

"Had discipline knocked into him somewhere," Prince commented in a low tone.

Malemute Kid nodded, took off his socks, and picked his way among recumbent men to the stove. There he hung his damp footgear among a score or so of mates.

"When do you expect to get to Dawson?" he asked tentatively.

The man studied him a moment before replying. "They say seventy-five mile. So? Maybe two days."

The very slightest accent was perceptible, where there was no awkward hesitancy or groping for words.

"Been in the country before?"

"No."

"Northwest Territory?"

"Yes."

"Born there?"

"No."

"Well, where the devil were you born? You're none of these." Malemute Kid swept his hand over the dog drivers, even including the two policemen who had turned into Prince's bunk. "Where did you come from? I've seen faces like yours before, though I can't remember just where."

"I know you," he irrelevantly replied, at once turning the drift of Malemute Kid's questions.

"Where? Ever see me?"

"No; your partner, him priest, Pastilik, long time ago. Him ask me if I see you, Malemute Kid. Him give me grub. I no stop long. You hear him speak 'bout me?"

"Oh! you're the fellow that traded the otter skins for the dogs?"

The man nodded, knocked out his pipe, and signified his disinclination for conversation by rolling up in furs. Malemute Kid blew out the slush lamp and crawled under the blankets with Prince.

"Well, what is he?"

"Don't know—turned me off, somehow, and then shut up like a clam. But he's a fellow to whet your curiosity. I've heard of him. All the coast wondered about him eight years ago. Sort of mysterious, you know. He came down out of the North, in the dead of winter, many a thousand miles from here, skirting Bering Sea and traveling as though the devil were after him. No one ever learned where he came from, but he must have come far. He was badly travel-worn when he got food from the Swedish missionary on Golovin Bay and asked the way south. We heard of this afterward. Then he abandoned the shore line, heading right across Norton Sound. Terrible weather, snowstorms and high winds, but he pulled through where a thousand other men would have died, missing St. Michaels and making the land at Pastilik. He'd lost all but two dogs, and was nearly gone with starvation.

"He was so anxious to go on that Father Roubeau fitted him out with grub; but he couldn't let him have any dogs, for he was only waiting my arrival to go on a trip himself. Mr. Ulysses knew too much to start on without animals, and fretted around for several days. He had on his sled a bunch of beautifully cured otter skins, sea otters, you know, worth their weight in gold. There was also at Pastilik an old Shylock of a Russian trader, who had dogs to kill. Well, they didn't dicker very long, but when the Strange One headed south again, it was in the rear of a spanking dog team. Mr. Shylock, by the way, had the otter skins. I saw them, and they were magnificent. We figured it up and found the dogs brought him at least five hundred apiece. And it wasn't as if the Strange One didn't know the value of sea otter; he was an Indian of some sort, and what little he talked showed he'd been among white men.

"After the ice passed out of the sea, word came up from Nunivak Island that he'd gone in there for grub. Then he dropped from sight, and this is the first heard of him in eight years. Now where did he come from? and what was he doing there? and why did he come from there? He's Indian, he's been nobody knows where, and he's had discipline, which is unusual for an Indian. Another mystery of the North for you to solve, Prince."

"Thanks awfully, but I've got too many on hand as it is," he replied.

Malemute Kid was already breathing heavily; but the young mining engineer gazed straight up through the thick darkness, waiting for the strange orgasm which stirred his blood to die away. And when he did sleep, his brain worked on, and for the nonce he, too, wandered through the white unknown, struggled with the dogs on endless trails, and saw men live, and toil, and die like men.

The next morning, hours before daylight, the dog drivers and policemen pulled out for Dawson. But the powers that saw to Her Majesty's interests and ruled the destinies of her lesser creatures gave the mailmen little rest for a week later they appeared at Stuart River, heavily burdened with letters for Salt Water. However, their dogs had been replaced by fresh ones; but, then, they were dogs.

The men had expected some sort of a layover in which to rest up; besides, this Klondike was a new section of the Northland, and they had wished to see a little something of the Golden City where dust flowed like water and dance halls rang with never-ending revelry. But they dried their socks and smoked their evening pipes with much the same gusto as on their former visit, though one or two bold spirits speculated on desertion and the possibility of crossing the unexplored Rockies to the east, and thence, by the Mackenzie Valley, of gaining their old stamping grounds in the Chippewyan country. Two or three even decided to return to their homes by that route when their terms of service had expired, and they began to lay plans forthwith, looking forward to the hazardous undertaking in much the same way a city-bred man would to a day's holiday in the woods.

He of the Otter Skins seemed very restless, though he took little interest in the discussion, and at last he drew Malemute Kid to one side and talked for some time in low tones. Prince cast curious eyes in their direction, and the mystery deepened when they put on caps and mittens and went outside. When they returned, Malemute Kid placed his gold scales on the table, weighed out the matter of sixty ounces, and transferred them to the Strange One's sack. Then the chief of the dog drivers joined the conclave, and certain business was transacted with him. The next day the gang went on upriver, but He of the Otter Skins took several pounds of grub and turned his steps back toward Dawson.

"Didn't know what to make of it," said Malemute Kid in response to Prince's queries; "but the poor beggar wanted to be quit of the service for some reason or other—at least it seemed a most important one to him, though he wouldn't let on what. You see, it's just like the army: he signed for two years, and the only way to get free was to buy himself out. He couldn't desert and then stay here, and he was just wild to remain in the country. Made up his mind when he got to Dawson, he said; but no one knew him, hadn't a cent, and I was the only one he'd spoken two words with. So he talked it over with the lieutenant-governor, and made arrangements in case he could get the money from me—loan, you know. Said he'd pay back in the year, and, if I wanted, would put me onto something rich. Never'd seen it, but knew it was rich.

"And talk! why, when he got me outside he was ready to weep. Begged and pleaded; got down in the snow to me till I hauled him out of it. Palavered around like a crazy man. Swore he's worked to this very end for years and years, and couldn't bear to be disappointed now. Asked him what end, but he wouldn't say. Said they might keep him on the other half of the trail and he wouldn't get to Dawson in two years, and then it would be too late. Never saw a man take on so in my life. And when I said I'd let him have it, had to yank him out of the snow again. Told him to consider it in the light of a grubstake. Think he'd have it? No sir! Swore he'd give me all he found, make me rich beyond the dreams of avarice, and all such stuff. Now a man who puts his life and time against a grubstake ordinarily finds it hard enough to turn over half of what he finds. Something behind all this, Prince; just you make a note of it. We'll hear of him if he stays in the country————"

"And if he doesn't?"

"Then my good nature gets a shock, and I'm sixty some odd ounces out."

The cold weather had come on with the long nights, and the sun had begun to play his ancient game of peekaboo along the southern snow line ere aught was heard of Malemute Kid's grubstake. And then, one bleak morning in early January, a heavily laden dog train pulled into his cabin below Stuart River. He of the Otter Skins was there, and with him walked a man such as the gods have almost forgotten how to fashion. Men never talked of luck and pluck and five-hundred-dollar dirt without bringing in the name of Axel Gunderson; nor could tales of nerve or strength or daring pass up and down the campfire without the summoning of his presence. And when the conversation flagged, it blazed anew at mention of the woman who shared his fortunes.

As has been noted, in the making of Axel Gunderson the gods had remembered their old-time cunning and cast him after the manner of men who were born when the world was young. Full seven feet he towered in his picturesque costume which marked a kind of Eldorado. His chest, neck, and limbs were those of a giant. To bear his three hundred pounds of bone and muscle, his snowshoes were greater by a generous yard than those of other men. Rough-hewn, with rugged brow and massive jaw and unflinching eyes of palest blue, his face told the tale of one who knew but the law of might. Of the yellow of ripe corn silk, his frost-incrusted hair swept like day across the night and fell far down his coat of bearskin. A vague tradition of the sea seemed to cling about him as he swung down the narrow trail in advance of the dogs; and he brought the butt of his dog whip against Malemute Kid's door as a Norse sea rover, on southern foray, might thunder for admittance at the castle gate.

Prince bared his womanly arms and kneaded sour-dough bread, casting, as he did so, many a glance at the three guests—three guests the like of which might never come under a man's roof in a lifetime. The Strange One, whom Malemute Kid had surnamed Ulysses, still fascinated him; but his interest chiefly gravitated between Axel Gunderson and Axel Gunderson's wife. She felt the day's journey, for she had softened in comfortable cabins during the many days since her husband mastered the wealth of frozen pay streaks, and she was tired. She rested against his great breast like a slender flower against a wall, replying lazily to Malemute Kid's good-natured banter, and stirring Prince's blood strangely with an occasional sweep of her deep, dark eyes. For Prince was a man, and healthy, and had seen few women in many months. And she was older than he, and an Indian besides. But she was different from all native wives he had met: she had traveled—had been in his country among others, he gathered from the conversation; and she knew most of the things the women of his own race knew, and much more that it was not in the nature of things for them to know. She could make a meal of sun-dried fish or a bed in the snow; yet she teased them with tantalizing details of many-course dinners, and caused strange internal dissensions to arise at the mention of various quondam dishes which they had well-nigh forgotten. She knew the ways of the moose, the bear, and the little blue fox, and of the wild amphibians of the Northern seas; she was skilled in the lore of the woods and the streams, and the tale writ by man and bird and beast upon the delicate snow crust was to her an open book; yet Prince caught the appreciative twinkle in her eye as she read the Rules of the Camp. These rules had been fathered by the Unquenchable Bettles at a time when his blood ran high, and were remarkable for the terse simplicity of their humor. Prince always turned them to the wall before the arrival of ladies; but who could suspect that this native wife—— Well, it was too late now.

This, then, was the wife of Axel Gunderson, a woman whose name and fame had traveled with her husband's, hand in hand, through all the Northland. At table, Malemute Kid baited her with the assurance of an old friend, and Prince shook off the shyness of first acquaintance and joined in. But she held her own in the unequal contest, while her husband, slower in wit, ventured naught but applause. And he was very proud of her; his every look and action revealed the magnitude of the place she occupied in his life. He of the Otter Skins ate in silence, forgotten in the merry battle; and long ere the others were done he pushed back from the table and went out among the dogs. Yet all too soon his fellow travelers drew on their mittens and parkas and followed him.

There had been no snow for many days, and the sleds slipped along the hard-packed Yukon trail as easily as if it had been glare ice. Ulysses led the first sled; with the second came Prince and Axel Gunderson's wife; while Malemute Kid and the yellow-haired giant brought up the third.

"It's only a hunch, Kid," he said, "but I think it's straight. He's never been there, but he tells a good story, and shows a map I heard of when I was in the Kootenay country years ago. I'd like to have you go along; but he's a strange one, and swore point-blank to throw it up if anyone was brought in. But when I come back you'll get first tip, and I'll stake you next to me, and give you a half share in the town site besides.

"No! no!" he cried, as the other strove to interrupt. "I'm running this, and before I'm done it'll need two heads. If it's all right, why, it'll be a second Cripple Creek, man; do you hear?—a second Cripple Creek! It's quartz, you know, not placer; and if we work it right we'll corral the whole thing—millions upon millions. I've heard of the place before, and so have you. We'll build a town—thousands of workmen—good water-ways—steamship lines—big carrying trade—light-draught steamers for head reaches—survey a railroad, perhaps—sawmills—electric-light plant —do our own banking—commercial company—syndicate—— Say! just you hold your hush till I get back!"

The sleds came to a halt where the trail crossed the mouth of Stuart River. An unbroken sea of frost, its wide expanse stretched away into the unknown east. The snowshoes were withdrawn from the lashings of the sleds. Axel Gunderson shook hands and stepped to the fore, his great webbed shoes sinking a fair half yard into the feathery surface and packing the snow so the dogs should not wallow. His wife fell in behind the last sled, betraying long practice in the art of handling the awkward footgear. The stillness was broken with cheery farewells; the dogs whined; and He of the Otter Skins talked with his whip to a recalcitrant wheeler.

An hour later the train had taken on the likeness of a black pencil crawling in a long, straight line across a mighty sheet of foolscap.

II

One night, many weeks later, Malemute Kid and Prince fell to solving chess problems from the torn page of an ancient magazine. The Kid had just returned from his Bonanza properties and was resting up preparatory to a long moose hunt. Prince, too, had been on creek and trail nearly all winter, and had grown hungry for a blissful week of cabin life.

"Interpose the black knight, and force the king. No, that won't do. See, the next move——"

"Why advance the pawn two squares? Bound to take it in transit, and with the bishop out of the way——"

"But hold on! That leaves a hole, and——"

"No; it's protected. Go ahead! You'll see it works."

It was very interesting. Somebody knocked at the door a second time before Malemute Kid said, "Come in." The door swung open. Something staggered in. Prince caught one square look and sprang to his feet. The horror in his eyes caused Malemute Kid to whirl about; and he, too, was startled, though he had seen bad things before. The thing tottered blindly toward them. Prince edged away till he reached the nail from which hung his Smith & Wesson.

"My God! what is it?" he whispered to Malemute Kid.

"Don't know. Looks like a case of freezing and no grub," replied the Kid, sliding away in the opposite direction. "Watch out! It may be mad," he warned, coming back from closing the door.

The thing advanced to the table. The bright flame of the slush lamp caught its eye. It was amused, and gave voice to eldritch cackles which betokened mirth. Then, suddenly, he—for it was a man—swayed back, with a hitch to his skin trousers, and began to sing a chantey, such as men lift when they swing around the capstan circle and the sea snorts in their ears:

> *"Yan-kee ship come down de ri-ib-er,*
>   *Pull! my bully boys! Pull!*
> *D'yeh want—to know de captain ru-uns her?*
>   *Pull! my bully boys! Pull!*
> *Jon-a-than Jones ob South Caho-li-in-a,*
>   *Pull! my bully—"*

He broke off abruptly, tottered with a wolfish snarl to the meat shelf, and before they could intercept was tearing with his teeth at a chunk of raw bacon. The struggle was fierce between him and Malemute Kid; but his mad strength left him as suddenly as it had come, and he weakly surrendered the spoil. Between them they got him upon a stool, where he sprawled with half his body across the table. A small dose of whiskey strengthened him, so that he could dip a spoon into the sugar caddy which Malemute Kid placed before him. After his appetite had been somewhat cloyed, Prince, shuddering as he did so, passed him a mug of weak beef tea.

The creature's eyes were alight with a somber frenzy, which blazed and waned with every mouthful. There was very little skin to the face. The face, for that matter, sunken and emaciated, bore little likeness to human countenance. Frost after frost had bitten deeply, each depositing its stratum of scab upon the half-healed scar that went before. This dry, hard surface was of a bloody-black color, serrated by grievous cracks wherein the raw red flesh peeped forth. His skin garments were dirty and in tatters, and the fur of one side was singed and burned away, showing where he had lain upon his fire.

Malemute Kid pointed to where the sun-tanned hide had been cut away, strip by strip—the grim signature of famine.

"Who—are—you?" slowly and distinctly enunciated the Kid.

The man paid no heed.

"Where do you come from?"

"Yan-kee ship come down de ri-ib-er," was the quavering response.

"Don't doubt the beggar came down the river," the Kid said, shaking him in an endeavor to start a more lucid flow of talk.

But the man shrieked at the contact, clapping a hand to his side in evident pain. He rose slowly to his feet, half leaning on the table.

"She laughed at me—so—with the hate in her eye; and she—would—not—come."

His voice died away, and he was sinking back when Malemute Kid gripped him by the wrist and shouted, "Who? Who would not come?"

"She, Unga. She laughed, and struck at me, so, and so. And then——"

"Yes?"

"And then——"

"And then what?

"And then he lay very still in the snow a long time. He is—still in—the—snow."

The two men looked at each other helplessly.

"Who is in the snow?"

"She, Unga. She looked at me with the hate in her eye, and then——"

"Yes, yes."

"And then she took the knife, so; and once, twice—she was weak. I traveled very slow. And there is much gold in that place, very much gold."

"Where is Unga?" For all Malemute Kid knew, she might be dying a mile away. He shook the man savagely, repeating again and again, "Where is Unga? Who is Unga?"

"She—is—in—the—snow."

"Go on!" The Kid was pressing his wrist cruelly.

"So—I—would—be—in—the   snow—but—I—had—a—debt—to—pay. It—was—heavy—I—had—a—debt—to—pay—a—debt—to—pay I —had——" The faltering monosyllables ceased as he fumbled in his pouch, and drew forth a buckskin sack. "A—debt—to—pay—five——pounds—of—gold—grub—stake—Male—e—mute—Kid—I——" The exhausted head dropped upon the table; nor could Malemute Kid rouse it again.

"It's Ulysses," he said quietly, tossing the bag of dust on the table. "Guess it's all day with Axel Gunderson and the woman. Come on, let's get him between the blankets. He's Indian; he'll pull through and tell a tale besides."

As they cut his garments from him, near his right breast could be seen two unhealed, hard-lipped knife thrusts.

III

"I will talk of the things which were in my own way; but you will understand. I will begin at the beginning, and tell of myself and the woman, and, after that, of the man."

He of the Otter Skins drew over to the stove as do men who have been deprived of fire and are afraid the Promethean gift may vanish at any moment. Malemute Kid picked up the slush lamp and placed it so its light might fall upon the face of the narrator. Prince slid his body over the edge of the bunk and joined them.

"I am Naass, a chief, and the son of a chief, born between a sunset and a rising, on the dark seas, in my father's oomiak. All of a night the men toiled at the paddles, and the women cast out the waves which threw in upon us, and we fought with the storm. The salt spray froze upon my mother's breast till her breath passed with the passing of the tide. But I—I raised my voice with the wind and the storm, and lived.

"We dwelt in Akatan——"

"Where?" asked Malemute Kid.

"Akatan, which is in the Aleutians; Akatan, beyond Chignik, beyond Kardalak, beyond Unimak. As I say, we dwelt in Akatan, which lies in the midst of the sea on the edge of the world. We farmed the salt seas for the fish, the seal, and the otter; and our homes shouldered about one another on the rocky strip between the rim of the forest and the yellow beach where our kayaks lay. We were not many, and the world was very small. There were strange lands to the east—islands like Akatan; so we thought all the world was islands and did not mind.

"I was different from my people. In the sands of the beach were the crooked timbers and wave-warped planks of a boat such as my people never built; and I remember on the point of the island which overlooked the ocean three ways there stood a pine tree which never grew there, smooth and straight and tall. It is said the two men came to that spot, turn about, through many days, and watched with the passing of the light. These two men came from out of the sea in the boat which lay in pieces on the beach. And they were white like you, and weak as the little children when the seal have gone away and the hunters come home empty. I know of these things from the old men and the old women, who got them from their fathers and mothers before them. These strange white men did not take kindly to our ways at first, but they grew strong, what of the fish, and the oil, and fierce. And they built them each his own house, and took the pick of our women, and in time children came. Thus he was born who was to become the father of my father's father.

"As I said, I was different from my people, for I carried the strong, strange blood this white man who came out of the sea. It is said we had other laws in the days before these men; but they were fierce and quarrelsome, and fought with our men till there were no more left who dared to fight. Then they made themselves chiefs, and took away our old laws and gave us new ones, insomuch that the man was the son of his father, and not his mother, as our way had been. They also ruled that the son, first-born, should have all things which were his father's before him, and that the brothers and sisters should shift for themselves. And they gave us other laws. They showed us new ways in the catching of fish and the killing of bear which were thick in the woods; and they taught us to lay by bigger stores for the time of famine. And these things were good.

"But when they had become chiefs, and there were no more men to face their anger, they fought, these strange white men, each with the other.

And the one whose blood I carry drove his seal spear the length of an arm through the other's body. Their children took up the fight, and their children's children; and there was great hatred between them, and black doings, even to my time, so that in each family but one lived to pass down the blood of them that went before. Of my blood I was alone; of the other man's there was but a girl, Unga, who lived with her mother. Her father and my father did not come back from the fishing one night; but afterward they washed up to the beach on the big tides, and they held very close to each other.

"The people wondered, because of the hatred between the houses, and the old men shook their heads and said the fight would go on when children were born to her and children to me. They told me this as a boy, till I came to believe, and to look upon Unga as a foe, who was to be the mother of children which were to fight with mine. I thought of these things day by day, and when I grew to a stripling I came to ask why this should be so. And they answered, 'We do not know, but that in such way your fathers did.' And I marveled that those which were to come should fight the battles of those that were gone, and in it I could see no right. But the people said it must be, and I was only a stripling.

"And they said I must hurry, that my blood might be the older and grow strong before hers. This was easy, for I was head man, and the people looked up to me because of the deeds and the laws of my fathers, and the wealth which was mine. Any maiden would come to me, but I found none to my liking. And the old men and the mothers of maidens told me to hurry, for even then were the hunters bidding high to the mother of Unga; and should her children grow strong before mine, mine would surely die.

"Nor did I find a maiden till one night coming back from the fishing. The sunlight was lying, so, low and full in the eyes, the wind free, and the kayaks racing with the white seas. Of a sudden the kayak of Unga came driving past me, and she looked upon me, so, with her black hair flying like a cloud of night and the spray wet on her cheek. As I say, the sunlight was full in the eyes, and I was a stripling; but somehow it was all clear, and I knew it to be the call of kind to kind. As she whipped ahead she looked back within the space of two strokes—looked as only the woman Unga could look—and again I knew it as the call of kind. The people shouted as we ripped past the lazy oomiaks and left them far behind. But she was quick at the paddle, and my heart was like the belly of a sail, and I did not gain. The wind freshened, the seat whitened, and, leaping like the seals on the windward breech, we roared down the golden pathway of the sun."

Naass was crouched half out of his stool, in the attitude of one driving a paddle, as he ran the race anew. Somewhere across the stove he beheld the tossing kayak and the flying hair of Unga. The voice of the wind was in his ears, and its salt beat fresh upon his nostrils.

"But she made the shore, and ran up the sand, laughing, to the house of her mother. And a great thought came to me that night—a thought worthy of him that was chief over all the people of Akatan. So, when the moon was up, I went down to the house of her mother, and looked upon the goods of Yash-Noosh, which were piled by the door—the goods of Yash-Noosh, a strong hunter who had it in mind to be the father of the children of Unga. Other young men had piled their goods there and taken them away again; and each young man had made a pile greater than the one before.

"And I laughed to the moon and the stars, and went to my own house where my wealth was stored. And many trips I made, till my pile was greater by the fingers of one hand than the pile of Yash-Noosh. There were fish, dried in the sun and smoked; and forty hides of the hair seal, and half as many of the fur, and each hide was tied at the mouth and big bellied with oil; and ten skins of bear which I killed in the woods when they came out in the spring. And there were beads and blankets and scarlet cloths, such as I got in trade from the people who lived to the east, and who got them in trade from the people who lived still beyond in the east. And I looked upon the pile of Yash-Noosh and laughed, for I was head man in Akatan, and my wealth was greater than the wealth of all my young men, and my fathers had done deeds, and given laws, and put their names for all time in the mouths of the people.

"So, when the morning came, I went down to the beach, casting out of the corner of my eye at the house of the mother of Unga. My offer yet stood untouched. And the women smiled, and said sly things one to the other. I wondered, for never had such a price been offered; and that night I added more to the pile, and put beside it a kayak of well-tanned skins which never yet had swam in the sea. But in the day it was yet there, open to the laughter of all men. The mother of Unga was crafty, and I grew angry at the shame in which I stood before my people. So that night I added till it became a great pile, and I hauled up my oomiak, which was of the value of twenty kayaks. And in the morning there was no pile.

"Then made I preparation for the wedding, and the people that lived even to the east came for the food of the feast and the potlatch token. Unga was older than I by the age of four suns in the way we reckoned the years. I was only a stripling; but then I was a chief, and the son of a chief, and it did not matter.

"But a ship shoved her sails above the floor of the ocean, and grew larger with the breath of the wind. From her scuppers she ran clear water, and the men were in haste and worked hard at the pumps. On the bow stood a mighty man, watching the depth of the water and giving commands with a voice of thunder. His eyes were of the pale blue of the deep waters, and his head was maned like that of a sea lion. And his hair was yellow, like the straw of a southern harvest or the manila rope yarns which sailormen plait.

"Of late years we had seen ships from afar, but this was the first to come to the beach of Akatan. The feast was broken, and the women and children fled to the houses, while we men strung our bows and waited with spears in hand. But when the ship's forefoot smelled the beach the strange men took no notice of us, being busy with their own work. With the falling of the tide they careened the schooner and patched a great hole in her bottom. So the women crept back, and the feast went on.

"When the tide rose, the sea wanderers kedged the schooner to deep water and then came among us. They bore presents and were friendly; so I made room for them, and out of the largeness of my heart gave them tokens such as I gave all the guests, for it was my wedding day, and I was head man in Akatan. And he with the mane of the sea lion was there, so tall and strong that one looked to see the earth shake with the fall of his feet. He looked much and straight at Unga, with his arms folded, so, and stayed till the sun went away and the stars came out. Then he went down to his ship. After that I took Unga by the hand and led her to my own house. And there was singing and great laughter, and the women said sly things, after the manner of women at such times. But we did not care. Then the people left us alone and went home.

"The last noise had not died away when the chief of the sea wanderers came in by the door. And he had with him black bottles, from which we drank and made merry. You see, I was only a stripling, and had lived all my days on the edge of the world. So my blood became as fire, and my heart as light as the froth that flies from the surf to the cliff. Unga sat silent among the skins in the corner, her eyes wide, for she seemed to fear. And he with the mane of the sea lion looked upon her straight and long. Then his men came in with bundles of goods, and he piled before me wealth such as was not in all Akatan. There were guns, both large and small, and powder and shot and shell, and bright axes and knives of steel, and cunning tools, and strange things the like of which I had never seen. When he showed me by sign that it was all mine, I thought him a great man to be so free; but he showed me also that Unga was to go away with him in his ship. Do you understand?—that Unga was to go away with him in his ship. The blood of my fathers flamed hot on the sudden, and I made to drive him through with my spear. But the spirit of the bottles had stolen the life from my arm, and he took me by the neck, so, and knocked my head against the wall of the house. And I was made weak like a newborn child, and my legs would no more stand under me. Unga screamed, and she laid hold of the things of the house with her hands, till they fell all about us as he dragged her to the door. Then he took her in his great arms, and when she tore at his yellow hair laughed with a sound like that of the big bull seal in the rut.

"I crawled to the beach and called upon my people, but they were afraid. Only Yash-Noosh was a man, and they struck him on the head with an oar, till he lay with his face in the sand and did not move. And

they raised the sails to the sound of their songs, and the ship went away
on the wind.

"The people said it was good, for there would be no more war of the
bloods in Akatan; but I said never a word, waiting till the time of the
full moon, when I put fish and oil in my kayak and went away to the
east. I saw many islands and many people, and I, who had lived on the
edge, saw that the world was very large. I talked by signs; but they had
not seen a schooner nor a man with the mane of a sea lion, and they
pointed always to the east. And I slept in queer places, and ate odd things,
and met strange faces. Many laughed, for they thought me light of head;
but sometimes old men turned my face to the light and blessed me, and
the eyes of the young women grew soft as they asked me of the strange
ship, and Unga, and the men of the sea.

"And in this manner, through rough seas and great storms, I came to
Unalaska. There were two schooners there, but neither was the one I
sought. So I passed on to the east, with the world growing ever larger,
and in the island of Unamok there was no word of the ship, nor in
Kadiak, nor in Atognak. And so I came one day to a rocky land, where
men dug great holes in the mountain. And there was a schooner, but not
my schooner, and men loaded upon it the rocks which they dug. This I
thought childish, for all the world was made of rocks; but they gave me
food and set me to work. When the schooner was deep in the water, the
captain gave me money and told me to go; but I asked which way he went,
and he pointed south. I made signs that I would go with him, and he
laughed at first, but then, being short of men, took me to help work the
ship. So I came to talk after their manner, and to heave on ropes, and
to reef the stiff sails in sudden squalls, and to take my turn at the wheel.
But it was not strange, for the blood of my fathers was the blood of the
men of the sea.

"I had thought it an easy task to find him I sought, once I got among
his own people; and when we raised the land one day, and passed between
a gateway of the seat to a port, I looked for perhaps as many schooners as
there were fingers to my hands. But the ships lay against the wharves for
miles, packed like so many little fish; and when I went among them to
ask for a man with the mane of a sea lion, they laughed, and answered me
in the tongues of many peoples. And I found that they hailed from the
uttermost parts of the earth.

"And I went into the city to look upon the face of every man. But they
were like the cod when they run thick on the banks, and I could not count
them. And the noise smote upon me till I could not hear, and my head
was dizzy with much movement. So I went on and on, through the lands
which sang in the warm sunshine; where the harvests lay rich on the
plains; and where great cities were fat with men that lived like women,
with false words in their mouths and their hearts black with the lust

of gold. And all the while my people of Akatan hunted and fished, and were happy in the thought that the world was small.

"But the look in the eyes of Unga coming home from the fishing was with me always, and I knew I would find her when the time was met. She walked down quiet lanes in the dusk of the evening, or led me chases across the thick fields wet with the morning dew, and there was a promise in her eyes such as only the woman Unga could give.

"So I wandered through a thousand cities. Some were gentle and gave me food, and others laughed, and still others cursed; but I kept my tongue between my teeth, and went strange ways and saw strange sights. Sometimes I, who was a chief and the son of a chief, toiled for men—men rough of speech and hard as iron, who wrung gold from the sweat and sorrow of their fellow men. Yet no word did I get of my quest till I came back to the sea like a homing seal to the rookeries. But this was at another part, in another country which lay to the north. And there I heard dim tales of the yellow-haired sea wanderer, and I learned that he was a hunter of seals, and that even then he was abroad on the ocean.

"So I shipped on a seal schooner with the lazy Siwashes, and followed his trackless trail to the north where the hunt was then warm. And we were away weary months, and spoke many of the fleet, and heard much of the wild doings of him I sought; but never once did we raise him above the sea. We went north, even to the Pribilofs, and killed the seals in herds on the beach, and brought their warm bodies aboard till our scuppers ran grease and blood and no man could stand upon the deck. Then were we chased by a ship of slow steam, which fired upon us with great guns. But we put on sail till the sea was over our decks and washed them clean, and lost ourselves in a fog.

"It is said, at this time, while we fled with fear at our hearts, that the yellow-haired sea wanderer put in to the Pribilofs, right to the factory, and while the part of his men held the servants of the company, the rest loaded ten thousand green skins from the salt houses. I say it is said, but I believe; for in the voyages I made on the coast with never a meeting the northern seas rang with his wildness and daring, till the three nations which have lands there sought him with their ships. And I heard of Unga, for the captains sang loud in her praise, and she was always with him. She had learned the ways of his people, they said, and was happy. But I knew better—knew that her heart harked back to her own people by the yellow beach of Akatan.

"So, after a long time, I went back to the port which is by a gateway of the sea, and there I learned that he had gone across the girth of the great ocean to hunt for the seal to the east of the warm land which runs south from the Russian seas. And I, who was become a sailorman, shipped with men of his own race, and went after him in the hunt of the seal. And there were few ships off that new land; but we hung on the flank of the seal pack and harried it north through all the spring of the year. And when the cows were heavy with pup and crossed the Russian line, our men grumbled and were afraid. For there was much fog, and every day men were lost in the boats. They would not work, so the captain turned the ship back toward the way it came. But I knew the yellow-haired sea wanderer was unafraid, and would hang by the pack, even to the Russian Isles, where few men go. So I took a boat, in the black of night, when the lookout dozed on the fo'c'slehead, and went alone to the warm, long land. And I journeyed south to meet the men by Yeddo Bay, who are wild and unafraid. And the Yoshiwara girls were small, and bright like steel, and good to look upon; but I could not stop, for I knew that Unga rolled on the tossing floor by the rookeries of the north.

"The men by Yeddo Bay had met from the ends of the earth, and had neither gods nor homes, sailing under the flag of the Japanese. And with them I went to the rich beaches of Copper Island, where our salt piles became high with skins. And in that silent sea we saw no man till we were ready to come away. Then one day the fog lifted on the edge of a heavy wind, and there jammed down upon us a schooner, with close in her wake the cloudy funnels of a Russian man-of-war. We fled away on the beam of the wind, with the schooner jamming still closer and plunging ahead three to our two. And upon her poop was the man with the mane of the sea lion, pressing the rails under with the canvas and laughing in his strength of life. And Unga was there—I knew her on the moment—but he sent her below when the cannon began to talk across the sea. As I say, with three feet to our two, till we saw the rudder lift green at every jump— and I swinging on to the wheel and cursing, with my back to the Russian shot. For we knew he had it in mind to run before us, that he might get away while we were caught. And they knocked our masts out of us till we dragged into the wind like a wounded gull; but he went on over the edge of the sky line—he and Unga.

"What could we? The fresh hides spoke for themselves. So they took us to a Russian port, and after that to a lone country, where they set us to work in the mines to dig salt. And some died, and—and some did not die."

Naass swept the blanket from his shoulders, disclosing the gnarled and twisted flesh, marked with the unmistakable striations of the knout. Prince hastily covered him, for it was not nice to look upon.

"We were there a weary time and sometimes men got away to the south, but they always came back. So, when we who hailed from Yeddo Bay rose in the night and took the guns from the guards, we went to the north. And the land was very large, with plains, soggy with water, and great forests. And the cold came, with much snow on the ground, and no man knew the way. Weary months we journeyed through the endless forest—I do not remember, now, for there was little food and often we lay down to die. But at last we came to the cold sea, and but three were left to look upon it. One had shipped from Yeddo as captain, and he knew in his head the lay of the great lands, and of the place where men may cross from one to the other on the ice. And he led us—I do not know, it was so long—till there were but two. When we came to that place we found five of the strange people which live in that country, and they had dogs and skins, and we were very poor. We fought in the snow till they died, and the captain died, and the dogs and skins were mine. Then I crossed on the ice, which was broken, and once I drifted till a gale from the west put me upon the shore. And after that, Golovin Bay, Pastilik, and the priest. Then south, south, to the warm sunlands where first I wandered.

"But the sea was no longer fruitful, and those who went upon it after the seal went to little profit and great risk. The fleets scattered, and the captains and the men had no word of those I sought. So I turned away from the ocean which never rests, and went among the lands, where the trees, the houses, and the mountains sit always in one place and do not move. I journeyed far, and came to learn many things, even to the way of reading and writing from books. It was well I should do this, for it came upon me that Unga must know these things, and that someday, when the time was met—we—you understand, when the time was met.

"So I drifted, like those little fish which raise a sail to the wind but cannot steer. But my eyes and my ears were open always, and I went among men who traveled much, for I knew they had but to see those I sought to remember. At last there came a man, fresh from the mountains, with pieces of rock in which the free gold stood to the size of peas, and he had heard, he had met, he knew them. They were rich, he said, and lived in the place where they drew the gold from the ground.

"It was in a wild country, and very far away; but in time I came to the camp, hidden between the mountains, where men worked night and day, out of the sight of the sun. Yet the time was not come. I listened to the talk of the people. He had gone away—they had gone away—to England, it was said, in the matter of bringing men with much money together to form companies. I saw the house they had lived in; more like a palace, such as one sees in the old countries. In the nighttime I crept in through a window that I might see in what manner he treated her. I went from room to room, and in such way thought kings and queens must live, it was all so very good. And they all said he treated her like a queen, and many marveled as to what breed of woman she was for there was other blood in her veins, and she was different from the women of Akatan, and no one knew her for what she was. Aye, she was a queen; but I was a chief, and the son of a chief, and I had paid for her an untold price of skin and boat and bead.

"But why so many words? I was a sailorman, and knew the way of the ships on the seas. I followed to England, and then to other countries. Sometimes I heard of them by word of mouth, sometimes I read of them in the papers; yet never once could I come by them, for they had much

money, and traveled fast, while I was a poor man. Then came trouble upon
them, and their wealth slipped away one day like a curl of smoke. The
papers were full of it at the time; but after that nothing was said, and I
knew they had gone back where more gold could be got from the ground.

"They had dropped out of the world, being now poor, and so I wandered
from camp to camp, even north to the Kootenay country, where I picked
up the cold scent. They had come and gone, some said this way, and some
that, and still others that they had gone to the country of the Yukon. And
I went this way, and I went that, ever journeying from place to place, till
it seemed I must grow weary of the world which was so large. But in the
Kootenay I traveled a bad trail, and a long trail, with a breed of the
Northwest, who saw fit to die when the famine pinched. He had been to
the Yukon by an unknown way over the mountains, and when he knew
his time was near gave me the map and the secret of a place where he
swore by his gods there was much gold.

"After that all the world began to flock into the north. I was a poor
man; I sold myself to be a driver of dogs. The rest you know. I met him
and her in Dawson. She did not know me, for I was only a stripling, and
her life had been large, so she had no time to remember the one who had
paid for her an untold price.

"So? You bought me from my term of service. I went back to bring
things about in my own way, for I had waited long, and now that I had
my hand upon him was in no hurry. As I say, I had it in mind to do my
own way, for I read back in my life, through all I had seen and suffered,
and remembered the cold and hunger of the endless forest by the Russian
seas. As you know, I led him into the east—him and Unga—into the east
where many have gone and few returned. I led them to the spot where the
bones and the curses of men lie with the gold which they may not have.

"The way was long and the trail unpacked. Our dogs were many and
ate much; nor could our sleds carry till the break of spring. We must come
back before the river ran free. So here and there we cached grub, that our
sleds might be lightened and there be no chance of famine on the back
trip. At the McQuestion there were three men, and near them we built
a cache, as also did we at the Mayo, where was a hunting camp of a dozen
Pellys which had crossed the divide from the south. After that, as we went
on into the east, we saw no men; only the sleeping river, the moveless
forest, and the White Silence of the North. As I say, the way was long and
the trail unpacked. Sometimes, in a day's toil, we made no more than eight
miles, or ten, and at night we slept like dead men. And never once did
they dream that I was Naass, head man of Akatan, the righter of wrongs.

"We now made smaller caches, and in the nighttime it was a small
matter to go back on the trail we had broken and change them in such
way that one might deem the wolverines the thieves. Again there be places
where there is a fall to the river, and the water is unruly, and the ice makes
above and is eaten away beneath. In such a spot the sled I drove broke

through, and the dogs; and to him and Unga it was ill luck, but no more. And there was much grub on that sled, and the dogs the strongest. But he laughed, for he was strong of life, and gave the dogs that were left little grub till we cut them from the harnesses one by one and fed them to their mates. We would go home light, he said, traveling and eating from cache to cache, with neither dogs nor sleds; which was true, for our grub was very short, and the last dog died in the traces the night we came to the gold and the bones and the curses of men.

"To reach that place—and the map spoke true—in the heart of the great mountains, we cut ice steps against the wall of a divide. One looked for a valley beyond, but there was no valley; the snow spread away, level as the great harvest plains, and here and there about us mighty mountains shoved their white heads among the stars. And midway on that strange plain which should have been a valley the earth and the snow fell away, straight down toward the heart of the world. Had we not been sailormen our heads would have swung round with the sight, but we stood on the dizzy edge that we might see a way to get down. And on one side, and one side only, the wall had fallen away till it was like the slope of the decks in a topsail breeze. I do not know why this thing should be so, but it was so. 'It is the mouth of hell,' he said; 'let us go down.' And we went down.

"And on the bottom there was a cabin, built by some man, of logs which he had cast down from above. It was a very old cabin, for men had died there alone at different times, and on pieces of birch bark which were there we read their last words and their curses. One had died of scurvy; another's partner had robbed him of his last grub and powder and stolen away; a third had been mauled by a bald-faced grizzly; a fourth had hunted for game and starved—and so it went, and they had been loath to leave the gold, and had died by the side of it in one way or another. And the worthless gold they had gathered yellowed the floor of the cabin like in a dream.

"But his soul was steady, and his head clear, this man I had led thus far. 'We have nothing to eat,' he said, 'and we will only look upon this gold, and see whence it comes and how much there be. Then we will go away quick, before it gets into our eyes and steals away our judgment. And in this way we may return in the end, with more grub, and possess it all.' So we looked upon the great vein, which cut the wall of the pit as a true vein should, and we measured it, and traced it from above and below, and drove the stakes of the claims and blazed the trees in token of our rights. Then, our knees shaking with lack of food, and a sickness in our bellies, and our hearts chugging close to our mouths, we climbed the mighty wall for the last time and turned our faces to the back trip.

"The last stretch we dragged Unga between us, and we fell often, but in the end we made the cache. And lo, there was no grub. It was well done, for he thought it the wolverines, and damned them and his gods in the one breath. But Unga was brave, and smiled, and put her hand in his, till I turned away that I might hold myself. 'We will rest by the fire,' she said, 'till morning, and we will gather strength from our moccasins.' So we cut the tops of our moccasins in strips, and boiled them half of the night, that we might chew them and swallow them. And in the morning we talked of our chance. The next cache was five days' journey; we could not make it. We must find game.

" 'We will go forth and hunt,' he said.

" 'Yes,' said I, 'we will go forth and hunt.'

"And he ruled that Unga stay by the fire and save her strength. And we went forth, he in quest of the moose and I to the cache I had changed. But I ate little, so they might not see in me such strength. And in the night he fell many times as he drew into camp. And I, too, made to suffer great weakness, stumbling over my snowshoes as though each step might be my last. And we gathered strength from our moccasins.

"He was a great man. His soul lifted his body to the last; nor did he cry aloud, save for the sake of Unga. On the second day I followed him, that I might not miss the end. And he lay down to rest often. That night he was near gone; but in the morning he swore weakly and went forth again. He was like a drunken man, and I looked many times for him to give up, but his was the strength of the strong, and his soul the soul of a giant, for he lifted his body through all the weary day. And he shot two ptarmigan, but would not eat them. He needed no fire; they meant life; but his thought was for Unga, and he turned toward camp. He no longer walked, but crawled on hand and knee through the snow. I came to him, and read death in his eyes. Even then it was not too late to eat of the ptarmigan. He cast away his rifle and carried the birds in his mouth like a dog. I walked by his side, upright. And he looked at me during the moments he rested, and wondered that I was so strong. I could see it, though he no longer spoke; and when his lips moved, they moved without sound. As I say, he was a great man, and my heart spoke for softness; but I read back in my life, and remembered the cold and hunger of the endless forest by the Russian seas. Besides, Unga was mine, and I had paid for her an untold price of skin and boat and bead.

"And in this manner we came through the white forest, with the silence heavy upon us like a damp sea mist. And the ghosts of the past were in the air and all about us; and I saw the yellow beach of Akatan, and the kayaks racing home from the fishing, and the houses on the rim of the forest. And the men who had made themselves chiefs were there, the law-givers whose blood I bore and whose blood I had wedded in Unga. Aye, and Yash-Noosh walked with me, the wet sand in his hair, and his war spear, broken as he fell upon it, still in his hand. And I knew the time was met, and saw in the eyes of Unga the promise.

"As I say, we came thus through the forest, till the smell of the camp smoke was in our nostrils. And I bent above him, and tore the ptarmigan from his teeth. He turned on his side and rested, the wonder mounting in his eyes, and the hand which was under slipping slow toward the knife at his hip. But I took it from him, smiling close in his face. Even then he did not understand. So I made to drink from black bottles, and to build high upon the snow a pile of goods, and to live again the things which happened on the night of my marriage. I spoke no word, but he understood. Yet was he unafraid. There was a sneer to his lips, and cold anger, and he gathered new strength with the knowledge. It was not far, but the snow was deep, and he dragged himself very slow. Once he lay so long I turned him over and gazed into his eyes. And sometimes he looked forth, and sometimes death. And when I loosed him he struggled on again. In this way we came to the fire. Unga was at his side on the instant. His lips moved without sound; then he pointed at me, that Unga might understand. And after that he lay in the snow, very still, for a long while. Even now is he there in the snow.

"I said no word till I had cooked the ptarmigan. Then I spoke to her, in her own tongue, which she had not heard in many years. She straightened herself, so, and her eyes were wonder-wide, and she asked who I was, and where I had learned that speech.

" 'I am Naass,' I said.

" 'You?' she said. 'You?' And she crept close that she might look upon me.

" 'Yes,' I answered; 'I am Naass, head man of Akatan, the last of the blood, as you are the last of the blood.'

"And she laughed. By all the things I have seen and the deeds I have done may I never hear such a laugh again. It put the chill to my soul, sitting there in the White Silence, alone with death and this woman who laughed.

" 'Come!' I said, for I thought she wandered. 'Eat of the food and let us be gone. It is a far fetch from here to Akatan.'

"But she shoved her face in his yellow mane, and laughed till it seemed the heavens must fall about our ears. I had thought she would be overjoyed at the sight of me, and eager to go back to the memory of old times, but this seemed a strange form to take.

" 'Come!' I cried, taking her strong by the hand. 'The way is long and dark. Let us hurry!'

" 'Where?' she asked, sitting up, and ceasing from her strange mirth.

" 'To Akatan,' I answered, intent on the light to grow on her face at the thought. But it became like his, with a sneer to the lips, and cold anger.

" 'Yes,' she said; 'we will go, hand in hand, to Akatan, you and I. And we will live in the dirty huts, and eat of the fish and oil, and bring forth a spawn—a spawn to be proud of all the days of our life. We will forget the world and be happy, very happy. It is good, most good. Come! Let us hurry. Let us go back to Akatan.'

"And she ran her hand through his yellow hair, and smiled in a way which was not good. And there was no promise in her eyes.

"I sat silent, and marveled at the strangeness of woman. I went back to the night when he dragged her from me and she screamed and tore at his hair—at his hair which now she played with and would not leave. Then I remembered the price and the long years of waiting; and I gripped her close, and dragged her away as he had done. And she held back, even as on that night, and fought like a she-cat for its whelp. And when the fire was between us and the man, I loosed her, and she sat and listened. And I told her of all that lay between, of all that had happened to me on strange seas, of all that I had done in strange lands; of my weary quest, and the hungry years, and the promise which had been mine from the first. Aye, I told all, even to what had passed that day between the man and me, and in the days yet young. And as I spoke I saw the promise grow in her eyes, full and large like the break of dawn. And I read pity there, the tenderness of woman, the love, the heart and the soul of Unga. And I was a stripling again, for the look was the look of Unga as she ran up the beach, laughing, to the home of her mother. The stern unrest was gone, and the hunger, and the weary waiting. The time was met. I felt the call of her breast, and it seemed there I must pillow my head and forget. She opened her arms to me, and I came against her. Then, sudden, the hate flamed in her eye, her hand was at my hip. And once, twice, she passed the knife.

" 'Dog!' she sneered, as she flung me into the snow. 'Swine!' And then she laughed till the silence cracked, and went back to her dead.

"As I say, once she passed the knife, and twice; but she was weak with hunger, and it was not meant that I should die. Yet was I minded to stay in that place, and to close my eyes in the last long sleep with those whose lives had crossed with mine and led my feet on unknown trails. But there lay a debt upon me which would not let me rest.

"And the way was long, the cold bitter, and there was little grub. The Pellys had found no moose, and had robbed my cache. And so had the three white men, but they lay thin and dead in their cabin as I passed. After that I do not remember, till I came here, and found food and fire—much fire."

As he finished, he crouched closely, even jealously, over the stove. For a long while the slush lamp shadows played tragedies upon the wall.

"But Unga!" cried Prince, the vision still strong upon him.

"Unga? She would not eat of the ptarmigan. She lay with her arms about his neck, her face deep in his yellow hair. I drew the fire close, that she might not feel the frost, but she crept to the other side. And I built a fire there; yet it was litle good, for she would not eat. And in this manner they still lie up there in the snow."

"And you?" asked Malemute Kid.

"I do not know; but Akatan is small, and I have little wish to go back and live on the edge of the world. Yet is there small use in life. I can go to Constantine, and he will put irons upon me, and one day they will tie a piece of rope, so, and I will sleep good. Yet—no; I do not know."

"But, Kid," protested Prince, "this is murder!"

"Hush!" commanded Malemute Kid. "There be things greater than our wisdom, beyond our justice. The right and the wrong of this we cannot say, and it is not for us to judge."

Naass drew yet closer to the fire. There was a great silence, and in each man's eyes many pictures came and went.

Badmen and Cattlemen

THE FOOL'S HEART

by EUGENE MANLOVE RHODES

Eugene Manlove Rhodes was a cowboy and a rancher. He smelled of cows and, as J. Frank Dobie says, so do his characters. The author of a number of novels, none of them are as good as his short stories. But in spite of a self-conscious attempt to create serious works of art, Rhodes retained much of the plain range simplicity which he tried to shed, and it was when he was not working at being an artist that he wrote his best stories. He had an ear for dialect and an understanding of what a cowboy might do in a given situation. In West is West, Good Men and True, *and* Once in the Saddle, *he was both influenced by the myth of the West and by the West he knew. His strength comes in those moments when he is able to capture the actual and eschew the myth. "Gene" Rhodes has arrived and must be taken into account here.*

I

Charley Ellis did not know where he was; he did not know where he was going; he was not even cheered by any hope of damnation. His worldly goods were the clothes he wore, the six-shooter on his thigh, the horse between his legs, and his saddle, bridle and spurs. He had no money; no friends closer than five hundred miles. Therefore, he whistled and sang; he sat jauntily; his wide hat took on the cant joyous; he cocked a bright eye appreciatively at a pleasant world—a lonesome world just now, but great fun.

By years, few-and-twenty; by size, of the great upper-middle class; blond, tanned, down-cheeked. Add a shock of tow-colored hair, a pug nose of engaging impudence—and you have the inventory.

All day he had ridden slowly across a dreary land of rolling hills, north-ward and ever northward; a steepest, interminable gray ridge of lime-stone on his right, knife-sharp, bleak and bare; the vast black bulk of San Mateo on the west; and all the long day the rider had seen no house, or road, or any man.

One thing troubled him a little: his big roan horse was road-weary and had lost his aforetime pleasing plumpness. He had also lost a shoe to-day and was intending to be very tenderfooted at once.

Charley was pleased, then, topping a hill, to observe that somebody had chopped a deep notch into the stubborn limestone ridge; and to see, framed in that tremendous notch, a low square of ranch buildings on a high tableland beyond. A dark and crooked chasm lay between—Ellis could see only the upper walls of it, but the steep angle of the sides gave the depth.

A deep and broad basin fell away before his feet. Westward it broke into misty branches between ridges blue-black with pine. Plainly the waters of these many valleys drained away through the deep-notched chasm.

It was late. The valley was dark with shadow. Beyond, the lonely ranch loomed high and mysterious in a blaze of the dying sunlight. Ellis felt his blood stir and thrill to watch it higher and higher above him as he followed down a plunging ridge. Higher and higher it rose; another downward step and it was gone.

Ellis led his horse now, to favor the unshod foot on the stony way. He came to a road in the valley; the road took him to a swift and noisy stream, brawling, foaming-white and narrow.

They drank; they splashed across.

A juniper stood beside the road. To it was nailed a signboard, with the rudely painted direction:

BOX O RANCH, FIVE MILES

Below was a penciled injunction:

Don't Try the Box Canon. It's Fenced.
Too rough Anyway. Keep to the Road.

"Vinegaroan, you old skeesicks," said Charley, "I'm goin' to leave you here and hoof it in. Good grass here and you're right tired. Besides that foot of yours'll be ruined with a little more of these rocks. I'll hustle a shoe and tack it on in the morning." He hung the saddle high in the juniper—for range cattle prefer a good sixty-dollar saddle to other feed. Tents and bedding are nutritious but dry. A line of washing has its points for delicate appetites; boots make dainty tidbits; harness is excellent—harness is the good old stand-by—harness is worthy of high praise, though buckle-y; but for all-round merit, wholesome, substantial, piquant, the saddle has no equal. Bridle and blankets are the customary relishes for the saddle, but the best cattle often omit them.

Charley hobbled old Vinegaroan and set out smartly, hobbling himself in his high-heeled boots. As the dim road wound into the falling dusk he regaled himself with the immortal saga of Sam Bass:

"Sam Bass he came from Indiana—it was his native state;
He came out here to Texas, and here he met his fate.
Sam aways drank good liquor and spent his money free,
And a kinder-hearted fellow you'd seldom ever see!"

II

The Box O Ranch stands on a bone-dry mesa, two miles from living water. It is a hollow square of adobe; within is a mighty cistern, large enough to store the filtered rain water from all the roofs. The site was chosen for shelter in Indian times; there is neither hill nor ridge within gunshot. One lonely cedar fronts the house, and no other tree is in sight; for that one tree the ranch was built there and not in another place. A mile away you come to the brink of Nogales Cañon, narrow and deep and dark; a thousand feet below the sunless waters carve their way to the far-off river. The ranch buildings and corrals now mark one corner of a fenced pasture, three miles square; the farther cliffs of Nogales Cañon make the southern fence.

The great mesas pyramid against the west, step on step; on that heaven-high pedestal San Mateo Peak basks in the sun, a sleeping lion. But the wonder and beauty of San Mateo are unprized. San Mateo is in America.

Two men came to the Box O in the glare of afternoon—a tall man, great of bone and coarse of face, hawk-nosed; a shorter man and younger, dark, thin-lipped, with little restless eyes, grey and shifting. He had broad eyebrows and a sharp thin nose.

A heavy revolver swung at the tall man's thigh—the short man had an automatic; each had a rifle under his knee. They were weary and thirst-parched; the horses stumbled as they walked—they were streaked and splashed with the white salt of sweat, caked with a mire of dust and lather, dried now by the last slow miles, so that no man might know their color.

The unlocked house lay silent and empty; the stove was cold; the dust of days lay on the table. "Good enough!" croaked the shorter man. "Luck's with us."

He led the way to the cistern. They drank eagerly, prudently; they sluiced the stinging dust from face and neck and hair.

"Ain't it good?" said the short man.

"Huh! That wasn't such a much. Wait till you're good and dry once— till your lips crack to the quick and your tongue swells black."

"Never for mine! I'm for getting out of this. I'm hunting the rainiest country I can find; and I stay there."

"If we get away! What if we don't find fresh horses in the pasture? There's none in sight."

"Reed's always got horses in the pasture. They're down in the cañon, where the sun hasn't dried up the grass. Oh, we'll get away, all right!

"They've got to track us, Laxon—and we've left a mighty crooked trail. They can't follow our trail at night and the Angel Gabriel couldn't guess where we are headed for."

"You don't allow much for chance? Or for—anything else? We sure don't deserve to get away," said Laxon.

He led his horse in, took off the bridle and pumped up a bucket of water. The poor beast drank greedily and his eyes begged for more.

"Not now, Bill. Another in ten minutes," he said in answer to a feeble nickering. He unsaddled; he sighed at the scalded back. "I'll douse a few bucketfuls on you quick as your pard gets his."

He turned his head. The younger man leaned sullenly against the wall. He had not moved. Laxon's face hardened. It was an ugly and brutal face at best—the uglier that he was slightly cross-eyed. Now it was the face of a devil.

"You worthless cur, get your horse! I thought you was yellow when you killed poor Mims last night—and now I know it! No need of it—not a bit. We could 'a' got his gun and his box of money without. Sink me to hell if I've not half a mind to give you up! If I was sure they'd hang you first I'd do it!"

"Don't let's quarrel, Jess. I'll get the horse, of course," said Moss wearily. "I'm just about all in—that's all. I could sleep a week!"

"Guess your horse ain't tired, you swinc! I ought to kick you through the gate! Quarrel? You! Wish you'd try it. Wish you'd just raise your voice at me! Sleep, says he! Sleep, when somebody may drop in on us any time! All the sleep you get is the next hour. We ride to-night and sleep all day to-morrow in some hollow of the deep hills over beyond the Divide. No more daylight for us till we strike the Gila."

Moss made no answer. Laxon hobbled stiffly into the house and brought back canned tomatoes, corned beef and a butcher knife. They wolfed their food in silence.

"Sleep now, baby!" said Laxon. "I'll stand watch."

He spread the heavy saddle blankets in the sun; he gave the horses water, a little at a time, until they had their fill; with a gunny sack and pail he washed them carefully. Their sides were raw with spurring; there were ridges and welts where a doubled rope had lashed.

A cruel day to the northward two other horses lay stark and cold by Bluewater Corral; a cruel night beyond Bluewater the paymaster of the Harqua Hala Mine lay by the broken box of his trust, with a bullet in his heart.

Laxon found a can of baking powder and sprinkled it on the scalded backs.

"Pretty hard lines, Bill," he said, with a pat for the drooping neck. "All that heft of coin heaped up behind the cantle—that made it bad. Never mind! You'll come out all right—both of you."

His thoughts went back to those other horses at Bluewater. He had shot them at sunrise. He could not turn them loose to drink the icy water and die in agony; he could not stay; he could not shut them in the corral to endure the agony of thirst until the pursuit came up—a pursuit that so easily might lose the trail in the rock country and never come to Bluewater. It had been a bitter choice.

He built a fire and investigated the chuck room; he put on the coffee pot, took a careful look across the mesa and came back to Moss. The hour was up.

Moss slept heavily; his arms sprawled wide, his fingers jerking; he moaned and muttered in his sleep; his eyes were sunken and on his cheek the skin was stretched skulltight. The watcher was in less evil case; his reserves of stored-up vitality were scarcely touched as yet. Conscious of this, his anger for the outworn man gave way to rough compassion; the hour had stretched to nearly two before he shook the sleeper's shoulder.

"Come, Moss! You're rested a little and so's your horse. I've got some good hot coffee ready for you. Get a cup of that into your belly and you'll be as good as new. Then you go drive all the horses up out of the pasture —just about time before dark. While you're gone I'll cook a hot supper, bake up a few pones of bread for us to take along, and pack up enough other truck to do us. I'd go, but you're fifty pounds lighter'n me. Besides, you know the pasture."

"Oh, I'll go," said Moss as he drank his coffee. "There's a little corral down in the bottom. Guess I can ease a bunch in there and get me a new mount. The rest'll be easy."

"We'll pick out the likeliest, turn the others out and throw a scare into 'em," said Laxon. "We don't want to leave any fresh horses for them fellows, if they come. And, of course, they'll come."

"Yes, and they'll have a time finding out which is our tracks. I'll just leave this money here, and the rifle," said Moss in the corral. "That'll be so much weight off, anyway." He untied a slicker from behind the saddle. Unrolling it he took out an ore sack and tossed it over beside Laxon's saddle; it fell with a heavy clink of coins. "Say, Jess! Look over my doin' the baby act a while ago, will you? I should have taken care of my horse, of course—poor devil; but I was all in—so tired I hardly knew what I was about." He hesitated. "And—honest, Jess—I thought Mims was going after his gun."

"Guess I didn't sense how tired you was," said Jess, and there was relief in his voice. "Let it all slide. We're in bad and we got to stick together—us two."

At sundown Moss drove back twelve head of saddle stock. He had caught a big range sorrel at the horse pen in the cañon.

"This one'll do for me," he announced as he swung down.

"I'll take the big black," said Laxon. "Trot along now and eat your supper. I'll be ready by the time you're done. I've got our stuff all packed —and two canteens. Say, Moss, I've got two bed blankets. I'm goin' to carry my share of grub behind my saddle. My sack of money I'll wad up in my blanket and sling it across in front of me. See? We don't want any more sore-backed horses. You'd better do the same."

"All right!" said Moss. "You fix it up while I eat."

Laxon roped and saddled the black, and tied one of the grub sacks behind the cantle; he made a neat roll of his own sack of money and the blanket and tied it across behind the horn. Then he fixed his partner's money sack and grub sack the same way and thrust the rifle into the scabbard. He opened the outer gate of the corral and let the loose horses out on the eastern mesa.

"Hike, you! We'll fall in behind you in a pair of minutes and make you burn the breeze! . . . Now for Bill, the very tired horse, and we'll be all ready to hit the trail."

Bill was lying down in a corner. Laxon stirred him up and led him by the foretop out through the pasture gate. The saddle-house door opened noiselessly; Moss steadied his automatic against the doorframe and waited.

"You go hunt up your pardner, old Bill. You and him orter be good pals from now on. So long! Good luck!" said Laxon. He closed the gate.

Moss shot him between the shoulder blades. Laxon whirled and fell on his face; the swift automatic crackled. Laxon rose to his elbow, riddled and torn; bullet after bullet crashed through his body. He shot the sorrel horse between the eyes; the black reared up and broke his rope. As he fell backward a ball from Laxon's forty-five pierced his breast; falling, another shot broke his neck. Then Laxon laughed—and died.

III

White, frantic, cursing, the trapped murderer staggered out from his ambush. Shaking horribly he made sure that Laxon was dead.

"The squint-eyed devil!" he screamed.

He ran to the outer gate. The band of freed horses was close by and unalarmed, but twilight was deepening fast. What was to be done must be done quickly.

He set the outer gate open. He bridled old Bill and leaped on, bare-backed; with infinite caution he made a wide circle beyond the little bunch of horses and worked them slowly toward the gate.

They came readily enough and, at first, it seemed that there would be no trouble; but at the gate they stopped, sniffed, saw those dim, mysterious forms stretched out at the further side, huddled, recoiled and broke away in a little, slow trot.

Moss could not stop them. Poor old Bill could only shuffle. The trot became a walk; they nibbled at the young grass.

Once he turned them back, but before they reached the gate they edged away uneasily. Twilight was done. Twice he turned them back. All the stars were out and blazing clear; a cool night breeze sprang up. Nearing the gate the horses sniffed the air; they snorted, wheeled and broke away; the trot became a gallop, the gallop a run.

Moss slipped the bridle off and walked back to the corral. His whole body was shaking in a passion of rage and fear.

He drank deeply at the cistern; he reloaded the automatic; he went to the dead horses. Whatever came, he would not abandon that money. After all, there was a chance. He would keep the notes with him; he would hide the gold somewhere in the rocky cliffs of the cañon; he would

climb out over the cliffs, where he would leave no track to follow; he
would keep in the impassable hills, hiding by day; he would carry food
and water; he would take the rifle and first time he saw a horseman alone
he would have a horse.

Eagerly he untied the two treasure sacks and emptied one into the
other. He started for the house. Then his heart stopped beating. It was
a voice, faint and far away:

> *"Rabbit! Rabbit! Tail mighty white!*
> *Yes, good Lord—he'll take it out o' sight!*

In a frenzy of fear the murderer dropped his treasure and snatched up
the rifle. He ran to the gate and crouched in the shadow. His hair stood up;
his heart pounded at his ribs; his knees knocked together.

> *"Rabbit! Rabbit! Ears mighty long!*
> *Yes, good Lord—you set 'em on wrong!*
> *Set 'em on wrong!"*

It was a gay young voice, coming from the westward, nearer and
nearer. Slinking in the shadows, Moss came to the corner. In the starlight
he saw a man very near now, coming down the road afoot, singing as he
came:

> *"Sam Bass he came from Indiana—it was his native state."*

From the west? His pursuers would be coming from the north along
his track—they would not be singing, and there would be more than one.
Why was this man afoot? With a desperate effort of the will Moss pulled
himself together. He slipped back into the kitchen and lit the lamp. He
threw dry sticks on the glowing coals—they broke into a crackling flame;
the pleasant tingling incense of cedar filled the room. He dabbed at his
burning face with a wet towel; he smoothed his hair hastily. Drawn, pale
and haggard, the face in the glass gave him his cue—he was an invalid.

Would the man never come? He felt the mounting impulse to struggle
no longer—to shriek out all the ghastly truth; to give up—anything, so he
might sleep and die and rest. But he had no choice; he must fight on.
Someway he must use this newcomer for his need. But why afoot? Why
could not the man have a horse? Then his way would have been so easy.
His throat and mouth were dust-dry—he drank deep of the cool water
and felt new life steal along his veins.

Then—because he must busy himself to bridge the dreadful interval—
he forced his hands to steadiness; he filled and lit a pipe.

"Hello, the house!"

Moss threw open the door; the dancing light leaped out against the dark. Along that golden pathway a man came, smiling.

"Hello yourself, and see how you like it! You're late. Turn your horse in the corral while I warm up supper for you."

IV

"I left my horse back up the road. I just love to walk," said Charley. At the door he held up a warning hand. "Before I come in, let's have a clear understanding. No canned corn goes with me. I don't want anybody even to mention canned corn."

"Never heard of it," said Moss. "Sit ye down. How'd fried spuds, with onions and bacon, suit you?"

"Fine and dandy! Anything but ensilage." Ellis limped to a box by the fire and painfully removed a boot. "Cracky! Some blisters!"

Moss bent over the fire.

"You're not from round these parts, are you?" he asked. He raked out coal for the coffeepot and put the potatoes to warm.

"Nope. From Arizona—lookin' for work. What's the show to hook up with this outfit?"

"None. Everybody gone to the round-up. Oh, I don't live here myself. I'm just a-stayin' round for my health." . . . If I could only get to this man's horse—if I could leave this man in the trap! The pursuit must be here by to-morrow. Steady! I must feel my way. . . . "Horse played out?"

"No; but he's right tired and he lost the shoe off his nigh forefoot to-day. Stake me to a new shoe, of course?"

"Sure!" . . . But this man will tell his story. I can never get away on a tired horse—they will overtake me; they will be here tomorrow. Shall I make it seem that Laxon and this man have killed each other? No; there will still be his tracks where he came—mine where I leave. How then? . . . "Sorry I can't let you have a horse to get yours. Just set myself afoot about sunset. Had all the saddle horses in the corral—saw a coyote—ran out to shoot at him—did you hear me, mister: I didn't get your name. Mine's Moss."

"Ellis—Charley Ellis. No; I was 'way over behind that hill at sundown. You're sure looking peaked and pale, Mr. Moss."

"It's nothing—weak heart," said Moss. The heavy brows made a black bar across his white face. . . . How then? I will stay here. I will be the dupe, the scapegoat—this man shall take my place, shall escape, shall be killed resisting arrest. . . . "Just a little twinge. I'm used to it. Where was I? Oh, yes—the horses. Well, I didn't shut the gate good. It blew open and away went my horses to the wild bunch. Idiotic, wasn't it? And I was planning to make a start tonight, ten mile or so, on a little hunting trip.

That reminds me—I got a lot of bread baked up and it's out in my pack. You wash up and I'll go get it. There's the pan." . . . This man Ellis was the murderer! I left my horse. Ellis stole away while I was asleep. He tried to escape on my horse. He can't get far; the horse is about played out. When I woke and missed Ellis I found the dead man in the corral!

The black thought shaped and grew. He hugged it to his heart as he took bread from the pack sacks; he bettered it as he hid the sack of money. He struck a match and picked out a sheaf of five-dollar bills; he tore them partway across, near one corner, perhaps an inch. Then he took one bill from the torn package, crumpled it up and wadded it in his pocket, putting the others back in the sack.

Next, he found the empty ore-sack, the one that had carried Laxon's half of the plunder. With a corner of it he pressed lightly over the dead man's back, so that a tiny smear of drying blood showed on the sack.

Then he took the bread and hurried to the house, dropping the ore sack outside the door. It was swiftly done. Ellis was just combing his hair when his host returned.

"There! Coffee's hot and potatoes will be in a jiffy. Sit up. Where'd you say you left your horse?"

"Where the wagon road crosses the creek west of the Box Cañon— where there's a sign nailed to a tree."

"Which sign? There's several—different places."

" 'Five miles to the Box O Ranch,' it says."

"Hobbled your horse, I reckon?"

"Yep. Wasn't really no need of hobbling, either—he won't go far. Some gaunted up, he is. He'll be glad when I get a job. And I'll say this for old Vinegaroan—he's a son-of-a-gun to pitch; but he don't put on. When he shows tired he's tired for fair. Only for his wild fool ways, he'd be the best horse I ever owned. But, then, if it hadn't been for them wild fool ways the V R wouldn't never 'a' let me got my clutches on him. They never raised a better horse, but he was spoiled in breaking. He thinks you want him to buck. Don't mean no harm by it."

"I see! Roan horse, branded 'V R' and some devilish; you might say he named himself."

"That's it."

"What is he—red roan?"

"Naw—blue roan. Mighty fine looker when he's fat—the old scoundrel!"

"Old horse? Or is that just a love name?"

Charley laughed.

"Just a love name. He's seven years old."

Moss poured the coffee and dished up the potatoes.

"There! She's ready—pitch in! I'll take a cup of coffee with you. Big horse?"

"Fifteen hands. Say, this slumgullion tastes mighty ample after—you

know—fodder. Last night I stayed in a little log shack south of the peak."
Moss interrupted.

"How many rooms? So I can know whose house it was."

"Two rooms—'HG' burned on the door. 'Chas. J. Graham, Cañada Alamosa," stenciled on the boxes. No one at home but canned corn and flour and coffee. Night before at the Anchor X Ranch. No one at home. Note sayin' they'd gone to ship steers at Magdalena. Didn't say nothing about goin' after chuck—but I know. There wasn't one cussed thing to eat except canned corn—not even coffee. Blest if I've seen a man for three days. Before that I laid up a couple of days with an old Mexican, right on the tiptop of the Black Range—hunting, and resting up my horse."

"I knowed a V R brand once, up North," said Moss reflectively. "On the hip for mares, it was; thigh for geldings; side for cattle."

"That one's on the Gila—Old Man Hearn—shoulder for horses; hip for cattle."

"Let me fill your cup," said Moss. "Now I'll tell you what—I wish you could lay up with me. I'd be glad to have you. But if you want work bad, and your horse can make eighteen or twenty miles by noon to-morrow, I think you can catch onto a job. They're meetin' at Rosedale to-morrow to start for the north round-up. This country here has done been worked. They'll light out after dinner and make camp about twenty-five miles north. You follow back the road you came here for about a mile. When the road bends to come here, at the head of the draw, you bear off to the left across the mesa, northwestlike. In six or eight miles you'll hit a plain road from the river, running west, up into the mountains. That'll take you straight to Rosedale."

"Well! I'll have to be up and doin', then, and catch'em before they move. Much obliged to you! Think I'm pretty sure of a job?"

"It's a cinch. Them V Cross T cattle are a snaky lot, and they never have enough men."

"Look here! Stake me to a number-one shoe and some nails, will you? Loan me a rasp and a hammer? I'll stick the tools up in the tree where the sign is. Clap a shoe on at daylight and shack along while it's cool. I'll make it by ten o'clock or later."

"But you'll stay all night?"

"No—we might oversleep. I'll chin with you a while and then hike along back and sleep on my saddle blankets. Then I'll be stirrin' soon in the mawnin'."

"Well, I'm sorry to see you go; but you know your own business. No more? Smoke up, then?" He tossed papers and tobacco across. "Say, I want you to send a Mex boy down here with a horse, so I can drive my runaways in off the flat. Don't forget!"

"I'll not. May I have a bucket and wash up these blistered feet of mine before I hike?"

"Sure you can! Sit still; I'll get the water. I'll rustle round and see if some of the boys ain't left some clean socks too; and I'll wrap you up a parcel of breakfast."

"Well, this is luck!" declared Charley a little later, soaking his feet luxuriantly and blowing smoke rings while his host busied himself packing a lunch. "A job, horseshoe, socks, supper and breakfast—and no canned corn! I'll do somebody else a good turn sometime—see if I don't! I wasn't looking for much like this a spell back, either. About an hour by sun, I was countin' on maybe makin' supper on a cigarette and a few verses of The Boston Burglar—unless I could shoot me a cottontail at sundown—most always you can find a rabbit at sundown. Then I sighted this dizzy old ranch peekin' through the gap at me. Bing! Just look at me now! Nobody's got nothin' on me! Right quaint, ain't it? What a difference a few hours'll make—the things that's waitin for a fellow and him not knowin' about it!"

Moss laughed.

"Well, I got to be steppin'," said Charley.

"Hold on! I'm not done with you yet. That's a good pair of boots you've got there—but they'll be just hell on those blistered feet. How'd you like to swap for my old ones? Sevens, mine are."

"So's mine. Why, I'll swap with you. Yours'll be a sight easier on me. I'm no great shakes on walking, me."

"Why, man, did you think I meant to swap even? Your boots are worth ten dollars—almost new—and mine just hang together. I wouldn't take a mean advantage of you like that. Come! I'll make you an offer: Give me your boots and your forty-five, with the belt and scabbard, for my automatic, with its rigging and five dollars, and I'll throw in my boots."

"Shucks! You're cheating yourself! Trade boots and guns even—that'll be fair enough." Charley unbuckled his spurs.

"Don't be silly! Take the money. It's a long time till pay day. I've been all along that long road, my boy. If you're broke—I'm just guessing that, because I've been broke myself—why, you don't want to ask for an advance the first thing."

"I'll tell you what, then—swap spurs too. That'll make about an even break."

"Nonsense! Keep your spurs. You don't want these old petmakers of mine. They'd be a hoodoo to a cowboy. Take the money, son. I wish it was more. I've got plenty enough, but not here. If you feel that way about it, call it a loan and pay it back when you're flush. Better still, pass it on to somebody else that needs it."

Charley surrendered.

"I'll take it, then—that way. You're all right, Mr. Moss! Try on your new boots and see how they fit."

"Fine as silk! Couldn't be better if they was made to order," said Moss. "Good boots. That's always the way with you young fellows. Every cent goes for a fancy outfit. Bet you've got a fire-new saddle—and you without a copper cent in your pocket."

"Well, purty nigh it," admitted Charley, grinning. "Set me back fifty-four pesos less'n a year ago. But she's a daisy."

"Swell fork?"

Charley snorted.

"Swell fork nothin'! No, sir; I don't need no roll. I ride'em slick—take off my spurs and grease my heels! I been throwed, of course—everybody has—but I never clawed leather yet and I don't need no swell fork!"

Moss smiled indulgently.

"Well, I must right you out for horseshoein'. You stay here and rest up. Number one shoe, I think you said?"

He came back with the horseshoe and tools, bringing also the discarded ore sack, now bulging with a liberal feed of corn.

"For Vinegaroan, with my love!" he said, laughing, and clapping Ellis on the shoulder.

A lump came into Charley's throat.

"I reckon you're a real-for-certain white man, Mr. Moss. If old Vinega-roan could talk he'd sure thank you. I'm going now and let you go to bed. You don't look so clean beat out as you did, but you look right tired. *Adiós!* And I hope to meet up with you again."

"Oh, you'll see me again! Good-by!"

They shook hands. Charley shouldered his pack and limped sturdily along the starlit road, turning once for a shouted "Good-by!" Moss waved a hand from the lighted doorway; a gay song floated back to him:

> *Ada! Ada! Open that do',*
> *Ada!*
> *Ada! Ada! Open that do',*
> *This mawnin'.*
> *Ada! Ada! Open that do',*
> *Or I'll open it with a fohty-fo'*
> *This mawnin'!"*

"Oh, yes! you'll see me again!" said Moss, smiling evilly. Then he closed the door. "Tired?" he said. "Tired? I've got to sleep if I swing for it."

V

BOX O RANCH, August fifth.
Statement of Elmer Moss

My name is Elmer Moss. I left Florence, Arizona, three weeks ago looking for work. I did not find a place and drifted on to this ranch. I stayed here a week or two, six years ago, when George Sligh worked here.

Last night my horse was pretty well give out and had lost a shoe; so I left him at the crossing of Nogales Creek, west of the pasture fence, and walked in.

I got in soon after dark and found a man who said his name was Charley Ellis, and that he was working here. He was a fellow, with rather a pleasant face. He was about my size, with light hair and blue eyes and a pug nose. He made me welcome. Said he couldn't say about work, but for me to stay here till the boss came back. We talked quite late.

I woke up early in the morning. Ellis was not in his bed. I supposed he had gone to wrangle horses out of the pasture and I went back to sleep, for I was very tired from riding a slow horse. I woke again after a while and got up. Ellis was not back yet. I went out into the corral. And there I found a dead man. He was shot all to pieces—I don't know how many times. There were two dead horses, both shot and both saddled.

I found the boot tracks where Ellis had gone back the way I came. He is trying to get away on my horse and leave me with a murdered man on my hands to explain.

I was so scared I didn't know what to do. I went out in the pasture to the rim, where I could see all over the cañon. If I could have got a horse I would have run away. There wasn't a horse in sight except one. That one was close up under the rimrock. He had been ridden almost to death. He wouldn't have carried me five miles. After I came back I found another one, in worse shape than the first, outside the corral gates. I let him in and gave him water and hay. There were horsetracks of all sizes round the corral.

I don't know what to do. I don't know what has happened here. It may be a week before anybody comes. If anyone comes today, or while the tracks are fresh that I made coming and that Ellis made going away, I'm all right. The story is all there, plain as print. My boots are new and his was all worn out. There's no chance for mistake. And my horse has lost a shoe from his left forefoot; so he will be easy tracked. And he's badly jaded—he can't go fast. If anybody comes to-day they can trail him up and catch him easy. If no one comes to-day I'm a goner.

I just now went and spread a tarp over the dead man. He was laughing when he died. He's laughing yet—and his eyes are wide open. It's horrible! Left everything else just as it was. Am writing this now, and taking my time at it, to get everything straight while there's no one to get me rattled and all mixed up. And in case I go out of my head. Or get hold of a horse somehow and try to get away. No, I won't try to run away. If I did it would be just the same as confessing that I was the murderer. If they caught me I'd hang sure.

Nothing can save me except the straight truth. And that won't help me none unless somebody comes along to-day. This man Ellis was about my size—but I told you that before. He wore blue overalls, pretty badly faded, and a gray flannel shirt. I didn't notice his hat; he didn't have it on much. I saw a revolver belt under his pillow and it's gone now; but I didn't see the gun.

That made me think. I went back and looked round everywhere to see where Ellis had reloaded his gun. I found fresh shells—nine of them, thirty-twos, automatic shells, smokeless, rimless—scattered over the floor of the saddle room just as an automatic would throw them. He killed his man from ambush. I went back and looked at the dead man. He was shot in the back twice anyway. Hit six times in all, as near as I could see. I couldn't bear to touch him. He looked terrible, laughing that way—and I'm about to break down. There was a hole in his neck about the size a thirty-two would make.

There was a six-shooter in the sand near his hand with three empty shells in it. Them shells was what killed the horses—after the dead man was first shot, I reckon. I covered him up again. I see now that I shouldn't have gone near him. I see now—too late—that I never should have made one single foot-track in that corral. If I had only known—if I had only thought in time—the tracks in there would have cleared me. All I had to do was to stay out. But how could I think of that?

Later: There is a tree in front of the house and I have started a grave there. If no one comes by sundown I'll bury the poor fellow. I will rig up some sort of a sled and put the body on it and make the give-out pony drag it out to the grave.

The work of digging has done me good and steadied my nerves. I am half done and now I am able to set a little. I will go back and finish it now.

Later—ten o'cock: Thank God! When the grave was done and I climbed out I saw a big dust off in the north coming this way. I am saved! They are closer now and coming very fast—ten or twelve men on horseback. I have looked over this statement carefully and don't think I have forgotten anything. This is the truth and nothing but the truth, so help me God.

I want to make one thing straight: Moss is not my right name. I have used that name for nine years. I was of good family and had my chance in life; but I was wild. Whatever happens I will bring no more disgrace to the name. I shall stick to Elmer Moss. If it had rained and washed the tracks out—if the wind had covered them with sand—what a shape I would be in now! They are quite close. I am leaving my gun on these sheets of paper. I am going out to meet them.

"That's all," said Tom Hall.

No one answered. Every man drew a long, deep breath—almost a sigh. There was a shuffling of feet.

The dark looks that had been bent on Moss, where he sat leaning heavily on the table, were turned long since to pity and rough friendliness.

A dozen stern-faced men were crowded in the kitchen—a little white and sick, some of them from what they had seen in the corral.

Each man looked at the others. Young Broyles let his hand rest lightly on Moss' shoulder. Then Old Man Teagardner frowned into his beard and spoke:

"Your story sounds like the truth, Mr. Moss," he said. "The boot-tracks going away from here are the same tracks we found in Bluewater Pens, and these two played-out horses came from Bluewater. If you're telling the truth you've been up against it hard. Still, you must be held as a prisoner—for the present, at least, till we find your man. And we'll want you to answer a few questions. What kind of a horse did you have?"

"A blue roan, V R brand, thin, fifteen hands high, no shoe on left forefoot, seven or eight years old. Saddle nearly new," answered Moss dully.

Then he raised his head and his voice swelled to sudden anger:

"You can ask me questions any time—you got me. Why don't you go after Ellis? That's your business! He's getting farther away every minute. Of course you'll keep me prisoner. What do you take me for—a fool? S'pose I'd think you'd find a man in the shape I'm in and let him go foot-loose as soon as he said: "Please, mister, I didn't do it? Send some of your gang after Ellis and I'll answer all the fool questions you can think up."

"Son," said Teagardner evenly, "your party won't get away. We've sent men or messages all over the country and everybody's forwarded it on. Every man not accounted for will be held on suspicion. Some of the boys will go in a little while; but, ten to one, your man Ellis is caught now—or killed. Say, boys, let's get out where we can get a breath of air."

"He won't fight, I tell you!" urged Moss as he followed his questioners outdoors. "He'll be as innocent as a lamb. If he don't ooze away without bein' seen his play is to saw it off onto me."

"All the more reason, then, why you should answer our questions."

"Questions!" cried Moss bitterly. "I wish somebody'd answer me a few. Who was that dead man? What did Ellis kill him for? Who was your gang lookin' for?"

"We don't know the dead man's name. None of us ever seen him before," said Cook. "We've followed them for two days. Robbery and murder. Now one has killed the other for his share of the stolen money."

"Then you didn't know the man you was after? But," said Moss, "this man may have got killed himself for reasons of his own. He may have nothing to do with your bank robbers. There was all sorts of shod horse-tracks leading away from the gate—I saw 'em this morning. Maybe that was the outfit you're after."

Teagardner stroked his long white beard and motioned the others to silence. Said he:

"Some of us'll follow 'em up, to be sure—but them was only saddle horses that they turned out, I judge—so us fellows couldn't get 'em. As I figure it out, that's how come your Ellis 'man to be in the fix he was. He shot his pardner and his pardner set him afoot before he died. So, when you come, Ellis left you to hold the sack. . . . Well! Cal, you and Hall pick out two other men to suit yourselves, and follow Ellis up. Watch close for any sign of him hiding out the money. He dassent keep it with him. We'll look for it here. Made your choice?"

"These two sticks'll do us, Uncle Ben."

"All right, then; get a mouthful to eat first and take something with you. I'll see you before you start. Broyles, you and Dick take the trail of that bunch of saddle horses after dinner. Bring 'em back—or see where they went to. It's just barely possible that there's been two separate gangs on the warpath here; but I judge not. I judge them's just saddle horses. Sam, you and Spike cook dinner. You other chaps make some sort of a coffin. Keep Moss with you. After while we'll all turn to and see if Ellis hid the money here."

"Now, whatever happens, you fellows get that man alive—*sabe?* No shooting. I ain't quite satisfied. Moss, he tells a straight-enough story and everything seems to back him up so far; but this man Ellis—where does he get off? If he comes along peaceful and unsuspicious—why, he's guilty and playin' foxy, layin' it all onto Moss. If he's scared it hangs him; if he keeps his upper lip right he's brazening it out, and we hang him for that. If he fights you he's guilty; if he hides out that proves he's guilty. If he gets clean away that's absolute proof. Any game where a man hasn't got one chance to win don't look just right."

Young Broyles burst into the room.

"See what I found! It was out in the corral, in the sand. I kicked at that ore sack layin' there by the dead horses—and I kicked up this! Nineteen five-dollar bills, done up like a pack of envelopes."

"They're all torn—see? and they're usually put up in hundred-dollar bunches, aren't they?" said Hall. "There's one gone—maybe."

"Yes," said Cal eagerly; "and that ore sack—there was two of 'em likely, and after the murder Ellis put all the stuff into one and dropped this bundle doin' it! Say! We ought to call Moss."

"I'll tell him," said Teagardner.

"But how'd them bills get torn? And where's the other one?" demanded Cal.

Hall shrugged his shoulders. "How'd I know? Come on, fellows—let's hike!"

Dinner was eaten; Broyles and Dick departed on their search; the coffin was made; and the dead man was laid in it.

"Shall you bury him now?" asked Moss.

"I hope so!" said Spike with a shudder.

"Me, too," echoed Sam. "I can't stand that awful laugh on his face. Let's get him out of sight, Uncle Ben."

"No. We want Ellis to see him, for one thing. Then again the sheriff may come and he may want to take charge. Besides, I think maybe we'll bury the murderer here and take this one to San Marcial."

Moss licked his lips.

"Put them both in one grave—why not? It's deep enough," suggested Cook. "They killed old Mims—let them talk it over together."

"Only one man shot Mims," said Teagardner. "This poor fellow may not have been the one. The man that killed him—his own pardner—the man that shot him in the back from behind a 'dobe wall, and then left an innocent man to stand for it—that's the man killed Mims. I don't think we've any right to force such company on this dead man. Come on! Let's get to work."

They dragged the dead horses far out on the plain; they piled sand where the blood pools had been; roof and wall and floor, they ransacked the house, outbuildings and the stables for the stolen money.

"You're forgetting one thing," said Moss. "As I am still your prisoner I am naturally still under suspicion. I may be the murderer after all and Ellis may be the victim—as, of course, he'll claim to be. Somebody ought to follow my track where I walked out to the rim this morning."

Teagardner eyed him, with mild reproach.

"Set your mind at rest, Mr. Moss. We're taking all bets. We did exactly that while you were resting just before dinner. You didn't take a step that isn't accounted for. You didn't ride one of the give-out horses down in the cañon and hide it there, either. And it will be the same with Ellis. That money will be found. We need it—as evidence."

"Well, if you've done looking I'd like to rest—to go to sleep if I can. I'm done!"

"Yes—you look fagged out. No wonder—you've been under a strain. It's blistering hot—we'll all go out to the grave, under that tree. It's the only cool place round here. Bring some water, you boys."

"Nice pleasant place for a sleep," suggested Sam, with a nervous giggle, at the grave side. "What's the matter with the shady side of the house?"

"No air," said Moss. "This suits me."

Teagardner sat on a stone and gazed long into the grave, smoking placidly. He was a very old man—tough and sturdy and straight and tall for all that. Long and long ago, Teagardner had been an oldtimer here. Half a lifetime since—at an age when most are content to become spectators—he had fared forth to new ventures, after a quarter century in Australia and the Far East—Hong-Kong last—he had come back to the land of his youth—to die.

If Napoleon, at eighty, had come back from St. Helena, some such position might have been his as was Uncle Ben's. Legend and myth had grown about his name, wild tales of the wild old days—the days when he had not been the Old Man, or everybody's Uncle Ben, but strong among the strongest. The chase had passed his way that morning and he had taken horse, despite his seven-and-seventy years, with none to say him nay.

"It is a deep grave—and the soil is tough," he said, raising his eyes at last. "You have been a miner, Mr. Moss?"

"After a fashion—yes."

"You must have worked hard digging this."

"I did. It seemed to do me good. I was nervous and excited. Shucks! I was scared—that's the kind of nervous I was."

"You say you rode across from Arizona. Where did you stay night before last?"

"In a two-room log house under San Mateo Peak, to the south; H. G. Ranch—or it has been once, for them letters are branded on the door. No one was there."

Spike nodded. "Charley Graham's. Charley, he's at the round-up."

"Well, I'm right sorry he wasn't there, as things turned out; but if you'll send a man over to-morrow he'll find the corn cans I opened—and some flour and coffee, and nothing else—only my horse's tracks and the shoe he lost somewhere on the road. That'll prove my alibi, all right—at least, as far as your bank robbery's concerned. The greenbacks you found seem to hook these two other gentlemen up with that."

"We'll send a man there all right, if needed. And it wasn't a bank that was robbed—it was a mine—a paymaster," said Uncle Ben.

"Well, you didn't tell me."

"No; I didn't tell you. And the night before that?"

"I stayed at the Anchor X Ranch. No one there, either. If your man goes that far he'll get canned corn straight—not even coffee to go with it. And he'll find a note to the effect that the oufit has gone to ship a bunch of steers at Magdalena."

Again Teagardner's quiet eye went round the circle and again the prisoner's story was confirmed.

"That's right. They load up to-day. Aw, let the man sleep, Uncle Ben. He's giving it to you straight."

But Uncle Ben persisted.

"And before that? You must have seen some man, somewhere, some-time."

Moss shook his head impatiently.

"For nearly a week before that I camped with an old Mexican hunter, on the divide south of Chloride, letting my horse rest up and hunting deer. Leastwise he hunted and I went along for company. I didn't have any rifle and he wouldn't lend me his. His name was Delfin Something-or-Other, and he lived in Springerville, he said. Say, old man, you make me tired! Am I to blame because no one lives in this accursed country? By George! If I could have taken a long look ahead I'd have hired me a witness and carried him with me."

"If we could take a long look ahead—or a short one—we'd be greatly surprised, some of us," Teagardner answered, without heat. "There—go to sleep, all of you. I slept last night. I'll call you when it's time."

He changed his seat to a softer one on the fresh mound of earth; he twisted his long gray beard and looked down into the grave. Moss watched him through narrowed lids. Then fatigue claimed him, stronger than horror or hate or fear, and he fell asleep.

VI

"You chuckle-headed idiots!" gasped Charley Ellis.

"Oh, that's all right too," said Tom Hall. "Some folks is too smart for their own good. You keep still."

Three men held Charley, one by each arm and one by the collar. His eyes were flashing; he was red with anger and considerably the worse for wear, having just made a sincere and conscientious attempt to break the neck of Mr. Moss—an almost successful attempt. It had taken more than three men to pull him off. Moss, white and smiling, mopped his bruised face beyond the coffin and the open grave; the sun setting between the clouds threw a red, angry light over all.

"Quiet having been resumed," observed Teagardner patiently "let us pass on to unfinished business. Tom, we've been so all-fired busy explainin' the situation to Mr. Ellis that we haven't got your report yet. Spit it out!"

"Uncle Ben, this Ellis is the man we want," said Tom Hall. "We found where he'd tacked a shoe on the horse—of course Moss couldn't know that. We tracked him a ways toward Rosedale and then we met these three Rosedale men coming back with him. They told him they was holdin' everybody and gathered him in. He made no objection—handed over his gun without a word. It was an automatic thirty-two. Horse and saddle just as Moss described 'em, all right—and this ore sack tied on the saddle besides."

Uncle Ben shook his head.

"It won't do, Tom. Everything is as Moss told it—but everything is just as Ellis tells it, too. So far as I can see they've got only one horse, one saddle and one interestin' past between them."

"You blithering, blistering, gibbering, fat-headed fools!" said Charley pleasantly. "If you'd told me about what Moss said I would 'a' told you to leave my horse and let Moss try his hand at describin' him. He's got one white hoof; he's been cut with barbed wire; and my saddle's been sewed up with buckskin where the linin's ripped. Moss couldn't have told you that. Did you give me a fair chance for my life? No, sir; you come blunderin' in and let Moss look 'em all over—pretendin' to be petting old Vinegaroan. I wasn't mistrustin' anything like this. They said there'd been trouble and they was makin' all strangers account for themselves. That seemed reasonable enough and I wasn't worrying."

"We've got only your word for that," sneered Sam. "I reckon Moss could have told us all about it if we had asked him."

"And maybe again he couldn't—Ellis is right," said Hall soberly. "He didn't get an even break. I'm sorry."

"What about the ore sack?"

"Boy's," said Uncle Ben, "you're going at this all wrong. Mr. Ellis says he took feed in that sack—that's reasonable. And that he kept the sack by him counts in his favor, I think."

"So do I," said Cal. "And I'll swear that if he had any money in it he must 'a' eat the bills and flung the coins away, one piece at a time. He never hid it after he left this house—that's sure. I know every inch of ground he's been over and my eyes is pretty near out from reading sign. I even went on, to make sure, after we met the Rosedale men, clear to where he met them and loped all the way back to catch up with 'em."

"How about this then?" cried Spike triumphantly. He was one of those who held Ellis. "I just took it out of his pocket."

It was a new five-dollar bill, and it was torn. Teagardner produced the package of bills. The tears matched exactly.

A horrible snarl burst from a dozen throats. They crowded and jostled, Moss with the rest; hands reached out to clutch at the prisoner.

"Hang him! Hang him!"

"Stand back! Stand back, you blind fools! I'll shoot the next man that touches him!" shouted Teagardner. "Stand back."

"You'll hang nobody, you howling dogs!" said Ellis coolly. "We stand just where we did before—my word against Moss'."

"Exactly!" said Uncle Ben. "Have a little sense, can't ye? Cook if you was this man, and guilty, how would you say you got this bill?"

"I'd say Moss gave it to me, of course."

"And you, Spike, if you knew positively that Ellis was innocent—then how did he get this bill?"

"He must have got it from Moss," said Spike reluctantly.

Charley laughed. "Well, that's where I got it—when we traded boots and guns, like I was tellin' you."

"You're a damned liar!"

No one was holding Charley's foot. It now caught Moss squarely in the breast and hurled him over the mound of earth and almost into the grave.

"Old gentleman—Uncle Ben, as they call you"—said Charley then, "you seem to have charge here, and you're old enough to have a real idea once in a while. There's just as much against Moss as against me, and no more—isn't there?"

"Precisely—up to date."

"Well, then, why aren't we treated the same? Why am I held this way while he goes free?"

"That's right!" said Cal.

"Hold Moss, a couple of you," said Uncle Ben. "Now, Mr. Ellis, look here!" He pushed aside the unnailed coffin lid to show the dead man's face. "Do you know this man?"

"Hell, he's laughing! No; I never saw him before. What's he laughing at? What's the joke?"

"He is laughing at his murderer."

"Well, I know who that is," said Charley. "And that's more than the rest of you do."

Teagardner replaced the lid.

"All we know—yet—is that he is either laughing at you or laughing at Moss. Your stories exactly offset each other. What are we going to do next? Understand me—there'll be nobody hanged till he's proved guilty."

"Keep us!" said Charley. "Watch us night and day! Chain us together with every chain on the ranch. One of us is a liar. Send some of your men along the back track till you find where the liar's story don't fit with the certain truth. I can describe every little trifling thing at the ranches where I stayed; I can tell what my old Mexican hunter looks like, if you can find him. Can Moss?"

"Son," said Teagardner, "you've got the right idea, and your plan would work—if we had to do it; but we don't have to do it. You've overlooked one thing. There's two ends to every lie—and one end of this lie is on this side of the murder. If we find the money where you hid it after you left here—you swing, Ellis. If we find it here at the ranch—why, either of you may have hid it. Everything that's happened at the ranch may have been done by either of you two men—everything but one."

He turned a slow eye on Moss, who stood by the coffin, white and trembling, with a man at each arm. His voice rang—measured, stern and hard.

"Everything but one," he repeated. "Ellis had nothing to do with one thing. . . . Moss dug the grave. And the grave is too deep. I always thought the grave was too deep. Jump into the grave, Sam, and see why Moss made it so deep!"

Moss dropped to his knees; his guards held him up; they forced him forward to the edge of the grave. A shudder ran through the crowd; they swayed forward; the last ray of the sun fell on them in a golden shaft. Sam leaped into the grave.

"Moss dug his grave too deep—because he was afraid somebody might want to make it a little deeper," said Teagardner. "Ground solid there? Try the other end."

Sam found loose earth at the other end. He shoveled furiously; he came to a package wrapped in slickers. He threw it up. They slashed the cords; they unrolled the slickers; at the grave's edge they poured the blood-bought money at the murderer's feet.

THE LONE STAR RANGER

by ZANE GREY

It is really not important whether Zane Grey's books have sold six million copies. He is the most widely read author who ever wrote about the West. With melodrama and a sentimental manner, he was able to attract readers and now, many years after his death, he continues to hold them spellbound. A dentist turned novelist, Zane Grey was a one-man literary factory, turning out books on all phases of the West. There are those who scorn what he wrote and there are those who look back and point to one or more of his works as being his best. Was it Under the Tonto Rim, The Vanishing American, Riders of the Purple Sage, The Lone Star Ranger *or any of a dozen others? His best does not compare with the work of many who have written of the West since, but Grey has his place in Western fiction history.*

How long Duane was traveling out of that region he never knew. But he reached familiar country and found a rancher who had before befriended him. He had food and sleep; and in a couple of weeks he was himself again.

When the time came for Duane to ride away on his endless trail his friend reluctantly imparted the information that some thirty miles south, near the village of Shirley, there was posted at a certain cross-road a reward for Buck Duane dead or alive. Duane had heard of such notices, but he had never seen one. His friend's reluctance and refusal to state for what particular deed this reward was offered roused Duane's curiosity. He had never been any closer to Shirley than this rancher's home. Doubtless some post-office burglary, some gun-shooting scrape had been attributed to him. And he had been accused of worse deeds. Abruptly Duane decided to ride over there and find out who wanted him dead or alive, and why.

As he started south on the road he reflected that this was the first time he had ever deliberately hunted trouble. Introspection awarded him this knowledge; during that last terrible flight on the lower Nueces and while he lay abed recuperating he had changed. A fixed, immutable, hopeless bitterness abided with him. He had reached the end of his rope. All the power of his mind and soul were unavailable to turn him back from his fate. That fate was to become an outlaw in every sense of the term, to be what he was credited with being—that is to say, to embrace evil. He had never committed a crime. He wondered now was crime close to him? He reasoned finally that the desperation of crime had been forced upon him, if not its motive; and that if driven, there was no limit to his possibilities. He understood now many of the hitherto inexplicable actions of certain noted outlaws—why they had returned to the scene of the crime that had outlawed them; why they took such strangely fatal chances; why life was no more to them than a breath of wind; why they rode straight into the jaws of death to confront wronged men or hunting rangers, vigilantes, to laugh in their very faces. It was such bitterness as this that drove these men.

Toward afternoon, from the top of a long hill, Duane saw the green fields and trees and shining roofs of a town he considered must be Shirley. And at the bottom of the hill he came upon an intersecting road. There was a placard nailed on the crossroad sign-post. Duane drew rein near it and leaned close to read the faded print. $1000 REWARD FOR BUCK DUANE DEAD OR ALIVE. Peering closer to read the finer, more faded print, Duane learned that he was wanted for the murder of Mrs. Jeff Aiken at her ranch near Shirley. The month September was named, but the date was illegible. The reward was offered by the woman's husband, whose name appeared with that of a sheriff's at the bottom of the placard.

Duane read the thing twice. When he straightened he was sick with the horror of his fate, wild with passion at those misguided fools who could believe that he had harmed a woman. Then he remembered Kate Bland, and, as always when she returned to him, he quaked inwardly. Years before word had gone abroad that he had killed her, and so it was easy for men wanting to fix a crime to name him. Perhaps it had been done often. Probably he bore on his shoulders a burden of numberless crimes.

A dark, passionate fury possessed him. It shook him like a storm shakes the oak. When it passed, leaving him cold, with clouded brow and piercing eye, his mind was set. Spurring his horse, he rode straight toward the village.

Shirley appeared to be a large, pretentious country town. A branch of some railroad terminated there. The main street was wide, bordered by trees and commodious houses, and many of the stores were of brick. A large plaza shaded by giant cottonwood trees occupied a central location.

Duane pulled his running horse and halted him, plunging and snorting, before a group of idle men who lounged on benches in the shade of a spreading cottonwood. How many times had Duane seen just that kind of lazy shirt-sleeved Texas group! Not often, however, had he seen such placid, lolling, good-natured men change their expression, their attitude so swiftly. His advent apparently was momentous. They evidently took him for an unusual visitor. So far as Duane could tell, not one of them recognized him, had a hint of his identity.

He slid off his horse and threw the bridle.

"I'm Buck Duane," he said. "I saw that placard—out there on a sign-post. It's a damn lie! Somebody find this man Jeff Aiken. I want to see him."

His announcement was taken in absolute silence. That was the only effect he noted, for he avoided looking at these villagers. The reason was simple enough; Duane felt himself overcome with emotion. There were tears in his eyes. He sat down on a bench, put his elbows on his knees and his hands to his face. For once he had absolutely no concern for his fate. This ignominy was the last straw.

Presently, however, he became aware of some kind of commotion among these villagers. He heard whisperings, low, hoarse voices, then the shuffle of rapid feet moving away. All at once a violent hand jerked his gun from its holster. When Duane rose a guant man, livid of face, shaking like a leaf, confronted him with his own gun.

"Hands up, thar, you Buck Duane!" he roared, waving the gun.

That appeared to be the cue for pandemonium to break loose. Duane opened his lips to speak, but if he had yelled at the top of his lungs he could not have made himself heard. In weary disgust he looked at the guant man, and then at the others, who were working themselves into a frenzy. He made no move, however, to hold up his hands. The villagers surrounded him, emboldened by finding him now unarmed. Then several men lay hold of his arms and pinioned them behind his back. Resistance was useless even if Duane had had the spirit. Some one of them fetched his halter from his saddle, and with this they bound him helpless.

People were running now from the street, the stores, the houses. Old men, cowboys, clerks, boys, ranchers came on the trot. The crowd grew. The increasing clamor began to attract women as well as men. A group of girls ran up, then hung back in fright and pity.

The presence of cowboys made a difference. They split up the crowd, got to Duane, and lay hold of him with rough, businesslike hands. One of them lifted his fists and roared at the frenzied mob to fall back, to stop the racket. He beat them back into a circle; but it was some little time before the hubbub quieted down so a voice could be heard.

"—shut up, will you-all?" he was yelling. "Give us a chance to hear somethin'. Easy now—soho. There ain't nobody goin' to be hurt. Thet's right; everybody quiet now. Let's see what's come off."

This cowboy, evidently one of authority, or at least one of strong personality, turned to the gaunt man, who still waved Duane's gun.

"Abe, put the gun down," he said. "It might go off. Here, give it to me. Now, what's wrong? Who's this roped gent, an' what's he done?"

The gaunt fellow, who appeared now about to collapse, lifted a shaking hand and pointed.

"Thet thar feller—he's Buck Duane!" he panted.

An angry murmur ran through the surrounding crowd.

"The rope! The rope! Throw it over a branch! String him up!" cried an excited villager.

"Buck Duane! Buck Duane!"

"Hang him!"

The cowboy silenced these cries.

"Abe, how do you know this fellow is Buck Duane?" he asked, sharply.

"Why—he said so," replied the man called Abe.

"What!" came the exclamation, incredulously.

"It's a tarnal fact," panted Abe, waving his hands importantly. He was an old man and appeared to be carried away with the significance of his deed. "He like to rid' his hoss right over us-all. Then he jumped off, says he was Buck Duane, an' he wanted to see Jeff Aiken bad."

This speech caused a second commotion as noisy though not so enduring as the first. When the cowboy, assisted by a couple of his mates, had restored order again some one had slipped the noose-end of Duane's rope over his head.

"Up with him!" screeched a wild-eyed youth.

The mob surged closer was shoved back by the cowboys.

"Abe, if you ain't drunk or crazy tell thet over," ordered Abe's interlocutor.

With some show of resentment and more of dignity Abe reiterated his former statement.

"If he's Buck Duane how'n hell did you get hold of his gun?" bluntly queried the cowboy.

"Why—he set down thar—an' he kind of hid his face on his hand. An' I grabbed his gun an' got the drop on him."

What the cowboy thought of this was expressed in a laugh. His mates likewise grinned broadly. Then the leader turned to Duane.

"Stranger, I reckon you'd better speak up for yourself," he said.

That stilled the crowd as no command had done.

"I'm Buck Duane, all right," said Duane, quietly. "It was this way—"

The big cowboy seemed to vibrate with a shock. All the ruddy warmth left his face; his jaw began to bulge; the corded veins in his neck stood out in knots. In an instant he had a hard, stern, strange look. He shot out a powerful hand that fastened in the front of Duane's blouse.

"Somethin' queer here. But if you're Duane you're sure in bad. Any fool ought to know that. You mean it, then?"

"Yes."

"Rode in to shoot up the town, eh? Same old stunt of you gunfighters? Meant to kill the man who offered a reward? Wanted to see Jeff Aiken bad, huh?"

"No," replied Duane. "Your citizen here misrepresented things. He seems a little off his head."

"Reckon he is. Somebody is, that's sure. You claim Buck Duane, then, an' all his doings?"

"I'm Duane; yes. But I won't stand for the blame of things I never did. That's why I'm here. I saw that placard out there offering the reward. Until now I never was within half a day's ride of this town. I'm blamed for what I never did. I rode in here, told who I was, asked somebody to send for Jeff Aiken."

"An' then you set down an' let this old guy throw your own gun on you?" queried the cowboy in amazement.

"I guess that's it," replied Duane.

"Well, it's powerful strange, if you're really Buck Duane."

A man elbowed his way into the circle.

"It's Duane. I recognize him. I seen him in more'n one place," he said. "Sibert, you can rely on what I tell you. I don't know if he's locoed or what. But I do know he's the genuine Buck Duane. Any one who'd ever seen him onct would never forget him."

"What do you want to see Aiken for?" asked the cowboy Sibert.

"I want to face him, and tell him I never harmed his wife."

"Why?"

"Because I'm innocent, that's all."

"Suppose we send for Aiken an' he hears you an' doesn't believe you; what then?"

"If he won't believe me—why, then my case's so bad—I'd be better off dead."

A momentary silence was broken by Sibert.

"If this isn't a queer deal! Boys, reckon we'd better send for Jeff."

"Somebody went fer him. He'll be comin' soon," replied a man.

Duane stood a head taller than that circle of curious faces. He gazed out above and beyond them. It was in this way that he chanced to see a number of women on the outskirts of the crowd. Some were old, with hard faces, like the men. Some were young and comely, and most of these seemed agitated by excitement or distress. They cast pitying glances upon Duane as he stood there with that noose round his reck. Women were more human than men, Duane thought. He met eyes that dilated, seemed fascinated at his gaze, but were not averted. It was the old women who were voluble, loud in expression of their feelings.

Near the trunk of the cottonwood stood a slender woman in white. Duane's wandering glance rested upon her. Her eyes were riveted upon him. A soft-hearted woman, probably, who did not want to see him hanged!

"Thar comes Jeff Aiken now," called a man, loudly.

The crowd shifted and trampled in eagerness.

Duane saw two men coming fast, one of whom, in the lead, was of stalwart build. He had a gun in his hand, and his manner was that of fierce energy.

The cowboy Sibert thrust open the jostling circle of men.

"Hold on, Jeff," he called, and he blocked the man with the gun. He spoke so low Duane could not hear what he said, and his form hid Aiken's face. At that juncture the crowd spread out, closed in, and Aiken and Sibert were caught in the circle. There was a pushing forward, a pressing of many bodies, hoarse cries and flinging hands—again the insane tumult was about to break out—the demand for an outlaw's blood, the call for a wild justice executed a thousand times before on Texas's bloody soil.

Sibert bellowed at the dark encroaching mass. The cowboys with him beat and cuffed in vain.

"Jeff, will you listen?" broke in Sibert, hurriedly, his hand on the other man's arm.

Aiken nodded coolly. Duane, who had seen many men in perfect control of themselves under circumstances like these, recognized the spirit that dominated Aiken. He was white, cold, passionless. There were lines of bitter grief deep round his lips. If Daune ever felt the meaning of death he felt it then.

"Sure this's your game, Aiken," said Sibert. "But hear me a minute. Reckon there's no doubt about this man bein' Buck Duane. He seen the placard out at the cross-roads. He rides in to Shirley. He says he's Buck Duane an' he's lookin' for Jeff Aiken. That's all clear enough. You know how these gunfighters go lookin' for trouble. But here's what stumps me. Duane sits down there on the bench and lets old Abe Strickland grab his gun an' get the drop on him. More'n that, he gives me some strange talk about how, if he couldn't make you believe he's innocent, he'd better be dead. You see for yourself Duane ain't drunk or crazy or locoed. He doesn't strike me as a man who rode in here huntin' blood. So I reckon you'd better hold on till you hear what he has to say."

Then for the first time the drawn-faced, hungry-eyed giant turned his gaze upon Duane. He had intelligence which was not yet subservient to passion. Moreover, he seemed the kind of man Duane would care to have judge him in a critical moment like this.

"Listen," said Duane, gravely, with his eyes steady on Aiken's, "I'm Buck Duane. I never lied to any man in my life. I was forced into outlawry. I've never had a chance to leave the country. I've killed men to save my own life. I never intentionally harmed any woman. I rode thirty miles to-day—deliberately to see what this reward was, who made it, what for. When I read the placard I went sick to the bottom of my soul. So I rode in here to find you—to tell you this: I never saw Shirley before today. It was impossible for me to have—killed your wife. Last September I was two hundred miles north of here on the upper Nueces. I can prove that. Men who know me will tell you I couldn't murder a woman. I haven't any idea why such a deed should be laid at my hands. It's just that wild border gossip. I have no idea what reasons you have for holding me responsible. I only know—you're wrong. You've been deceived. And see here, Aiken. You understand I'm a miserable man. I'm about broken, I guess. I don't care any more for life, for anything. If you can't look me in the eyes, man to man, and believe what I say—why, by God! you can kill me!"

Aiken heaved a great breath.

"Buck Duane, whether I'm impressed or not by what you say needn't matter. You've had accusers, justly or unjustly, as will soon appear. The thing is we can prove you innocent or guilty. My girl Lucy saw my wife's assailant."

He motioned for the crowd of men to open up.

"Somebody—you, Sibert—go for Lucy. That'll settle this thing."

Duane heard as a man in an ugly dream. The faces around him, the hum of voices, all seemed far off. His life hung by the merest thread. Yet he did not think of that so much as of the brand of a woman-murderer which might be soon sealed upon him by a frightened, imaginative child.

The crowd trooped apart and closed again. Duane caught a blurred image of a slight girl clinging to Sibert's hand. He could not see distinctly. Aiken lifted the child, whispered soothingly to her not to be afraid. Then he fetched her closer to Duane.

"Lucy, tell me. Did you ever see this man before?" asked Aiken, huskily and low. "Is he the one—who came in the house that day—struck you down—and dragged mama—?"

Aiken's voice failed.

A lightning flash seemed to clear Duane's blurred sight. He saw a pale, sad face and violet eyes fixed in gloom and horror upon his. No terrible moment in Daune's life ever equaled this one of silence—of suspense.

"It ain't him!" cried the child.

Then Sibert was flinging the noose off Duane's neck and unwinding the bonds round his arms. The spellbound crowd awoke to hoarse exclamations.

"See there, my locoed gents, how easy you'd hang the wrong man," burst out the cowboy, as he made the rope-end hiss. "You-all are a lot of wise rangers. Haw! haw!"

He freed Duane and thrust the bone-handled gun back in Duane's holster.

"You Abe, there. Reckon you pulled a stunt! But don't try the like again. And, men, I'll gamble there's a hell of a lot of bad work Buck Duane's named for—which all he never done. Clear away there. Where's his hoss? Duane, the road's open out of Shirley."

Sibert swept the gaping watchers aside and pressed Duane toward the horse, which another cowboy held. Mechanically Duane mounted, felt a lift as he went up. Then the cowboy's hard face softened in a smile.

"I reckon it ain't uncivil of me to say—hit that road quick!" he said, frankly.

He led the horse out of the crowd. Aiken joined him, and between them they escorted Duane across the plaza. The crowd appeared irresistibly drawn to follow.

Aiken paused with his big hand on Duane's knee. In it, unconsciously probably, he still held the gun.

"Duane, a word with you," he said. "I believe you're not so black as you've been painted. I wish there was time to say more. Good-by. May God help you further as he did this day!"

Duane said good-by and touched the horse with his spurs.

"So long, Buck!" called Sibert, with that frank smile breaking warm over his brown face; and he held his sombrero high.

GUNSMOKE

A TELEVISION SCRIPT

by JOHN MESTON

Motion pictures took the Western to heart because the land and movement were beautiful on the screen. It is more difficult to understand how the Western started on radio where a few sound effects—gunshot, hoofbeats—were all that was available to evoke the wide open spaces. But the conditioned audience needed no more and Gunsmoke *became a success on radio. Those who avoided the usual Western story, the Zane Grey or Hopalong Cassidy, turned to* Gunsmoke. *With the advent of television,* Gunsmoke *became visual. Despite far-fetched attempts at originality, the only thing which distinguishes one program from another is the quality of its stories. Produced with care and written with simplicity and earthiness,* Gunsmoke *has been consistently outstanding.*

EXT. MARSHAL'S OFFICE—MED SHOT (DAY)

(Matt is half-dozing in a chair on the porch. There are two empty chairs. Chester comes out of the office, sees him, and joins him.

CHESTER: Mind if I set here and help you watch the street, Mr. Dillon?
MATT: *(comes to)*: Huh?
CHESTER: *(sits)*: I've got spring fever, I guess.
MATT: Everybody feels lazy these days.
CHESTER: It'll change soon enough.
MATT: It will?
CHESTER: As soon the first trail herd of the season hits Dodge.
MATT: Oh . . .
CHESTER: Them Texans—they're just born trouble makers. They're bad enough at home, but they're worse away from it.
MATT: Mmm . . . let's see—you spent some ten years there, didn't you? Almost like home to you, I'd say.
CHESTER: Well now, that just proves I know what I'm talking about.

(Sound of horse approaching.)

MATT: *(looks offstage)*: Here comes a Texan now, Chester. Look at his rig.

ANGLE TO INCLUDE STREET AND HORSE

(Riding down the street—with a center-fire rig—is PHIL JACKS. He's a Texas cowboy about thirty. He's tough, but straight-forward, honest, decent. He's just ridden up the trail and it's been a mean trip—he's sore about everything, and with every right to be. He sees the Marshal's office and rides over.)

CHESTER: That's a Texan, all right. What do you suppose he's doing here?
MATT: Looking for somebody to shoot, according to you.

(Jacks dismounts, ties.)

MATT: (*cont'd*) Know him, Chester?

CHESTER (*shakes his head*): Most everybody I knew in Texas has been hung by now.

MED SHOT

(*as Jacks walks up to them.*)

JACKS: I'm looking for Matt Dillon.

MATT: My name.

JACKS: I'm Phil Jacks. I'm with a herd of three thousand San Saba cattle about five days' drive from here. The name of the trail boss is Dolph Quince.

MATT: Dolph Quince was here last year. Give him my regards.

JACKS: You give them to him, Marshal.

MATT: Sure. He'll be here in about five days, you say. . . .

JACKS: If we don't run into no more trouble. He said for you to ride back with me, Marshal.

MATT: Oh? Did he say why?

JACKS: He just said for me to ride into Dodge and find you.

MATT: Can you tell me what this's all about?

JACKS: It's about Kansas, Marshal.

MATT: What?

JACKS: We don't like it.

CHESTER: Well, for heaven's sake, if you don't like it why don't you stay in Texas, instead of coming up here and drinking and shooting and getting people's backs up, and . . .

JACKS: I haven't even said hello to you, mister.

CHESTER: Good—let's leave it that way.

MATT: Chester . . . what's got into you anyway?

ANOTHER ANGLE

CHESTER: Well, the first herd ain't even over the horizon and already there's trouble. (*to Jacks*): Why don't you people drive your old mossy-haired steers to California, anyway?

JACKS: (*half-smile*): Why'd *you* leave Texas, mister?

CHESTER: What . . .

JACKS (*laughs*): You're all riled cause you don't like Kansas any better'n anybody else does.

CHESTER: I don't like Texas either.

JACKS: Texas is sure rough on women and dogs, ain't it?

CHESTER (*laughs*): Now by golly, I ain't heard that since . . .

JACKS: You left Texas.

CHESTER: All right—you got me pegged. . . . I'll shut up.

MATT: Now we're getting someplace.

JACKS: Ready to go, Marshal?

MED SHOT

(*Matt gets up, takes a look at Jacks.*)

MATT: Dolph Quince is a good man. He wouldn't have sent you here without a reason. (*to Chester*): Suppose you take Jacks over to Delmonico's for a good feed. He looks like he could use it. I've got some business and I'll meet you back here in an hour or so.

(*Chester gets up, extends his hand to Jacks.*)

CHESTER: My name's Chester Good.

(*They shake.*)

CHESTER (*cont'd*): The restaurant's just down the street.
JACKS: Okay.

ANOTHER ANGLE

(*They start off.*)

MATT: Don't shoot him, Chester. I'll never find that herd alone.
JACKS: I'm gonna buy him a drink first, Marshal—temper him down a little.
CHESTER: Now that's not a bad idea at all. Take your pick, Jacks—we have a goodly number of very choice saloons here in Dodge . . .

DISSOLVE TO:

EXT. PRAIRIE—MED LONG SHOT (DAY)

(*Matt, Chester and Jacks are riding across the prairie. Matt carries a rifle in his saddle.*)

MED SHOT

(*Jacks points toward a small rise ahead.*)

JACKS: My guess is we'll be able to see them from the top of that rise.
CHESTER: I sure hope so. Another day of this'd kill me.
MATT: Aren't you riding back with us, Chester?
CHESTER: What?
MATT: Well, if it's a hundred miles here, it's a hundred miles back.
CHESTER: Oh . . . I kinda forgot about that.
JACKS: Three thousand head of cattle leave so much dust, you'll never see them miles, Chester.
CHESTER: Maybe not, but I'll sure know they're there.

(*Jacks laughs.*)

ANOTHER ANGLE

(*They ride up the rise and at the top they pull up. Jacks points offstage.*)

JACKS: There they are.
CHESTER: By golly.

STOCK SHOT—CATTLE TRAILING
BACK TO SCENE

(*as they watch.*)

CHESTER: That's a powerful big herd, Jacks.
JACKS: Yeah.
CHESTER: Worth a lot of money.
JACKS: If we get it to Dodge, it will be.

(*Matt gives him a look, then—*)

MATT: Where'll we find Dolph Quince?
JACKS: The cook'll have camp set up somewhere by now. We find him,
    Quince'll ride in sooner or later.
MATT: Okay.

(*Chester is looking at the cattle offstage.*)

CHESTER: All them steaks—my . . .

STOCK SHOT—CATTLE ON TRAIL
MED SHOT

(*Matt and party start down the slope.*)

DISSOLVE TO:

EXT. COW CAMP—FULL SHOT (DAY)

(*This is a big camp—cowboys, chuck wagon, fire, remuda in b.g.,
men riding in and out, saddles, gear, etc. The cook, the dirtiest man
in camp, has supper ready and is hollering at the men to come and
get it. Drinking coffee near the fire with a couple of men is* DOLPH
QUINCE. *Quince is in his forties, a big man with the easy authority
of one who's used to it and knows his business. He has bearing and
dignity. There's a general air about all the men of smoldering anger
. . . sullenness . . . suspicion. . . . CAMERA PANS from camp to
prairie, and we see Matt, Chester and Jacks riding up.*)

MED SHOT

(*They ride up and stop not far from the camp. Jacks points toward
Quince.*)

JACKS: That's Dolph Quince by that fire, Marshal.
MATT: Yeah.
JACKS: Chester and I'll take your horse.
MATT: Okay.

(*Matt dismounts, hands reins to Jacks.*)

JACKS: We'll turn them in with the remuda.
MATT: Thanks.

(Matt starts toward Quince. Chester and Jacks ride toward the remuda.)

ANGLE ON FIRE

As Matt comes up to Quince. The other men grow quiet and wander off.)

QUINCE: Well, hello, Marshal.
MATT: How are you, Quince?

(They shake hands.)

QUINCE: Things could be better, Marshal.
MATT: Oh . . . ?
QUINCE: There's fresh meat in camp. Ask the cook for a plate.
MATT: Thanks.
QUINCE: Here . . . I'll go with you. I need some more coffee.

MOVING SHOT

(As they walk to the chow line. Again the men grow quiet as Matt approaches, and move away.)

QUINCE: You like buffalo veal? One of the boys roped and shot a calf this morning.
MATT: I like it fine.
QUINCE: I *guess* it was buffalo that scared our horses last night.
MATT: Buffalo?
QUINCE: Anyway, the whole remuda broke loose.

(Matt looks at him, but waits his time. They step up to the cook.)

MED SHOT

QUINCE: Give this man a plate of meat, cook.
COOK: Okay, Quince.

(The cook gives Matt a dirty look, but dishes up a plate for him.)

MATT: Thanks.
QUINCE: Coffee, too—and fill this.

(He holds out his cup. The cook fetches Matt a cup, too.)

QUINCE *(cont'd)*: A nester woman come to the bedground before daylight this morning. Had a boy with her, driving a wagon. Asked if we had any little calves that'd been dropped during the night.
MATT: She probably picks up calves from all the herds.

QUINCE: We'd have to get rid of them, anyway. So I let her have them—even if she was a Kansan.

MATT: Oh. Where was her husband?

QUINCE: Dead, according to the boy.

MATT: I see.

QUINCE: If it'd been a Kansas man asked for calves, I don't think I could've talked these boys into allowing it.

MATT: That so?

QUINCE: It sure is, Marshal. We can set down over here.

(They walk off, camera following.)

MED SHOT

(Quince leads him to a spot a little away from everybody.)

QUINCE: This'll do.

(They sit. As they talk, Matt eats. Quince says nothing, and after a moment, Matt speaks casually.)

MATT: Tell me, Quince—You seen any Kansas Jayhawkers around?

QUINCE: How'd you know?

MATT: Just a guess.

(Quince speaks with controlled anger and bitterness.)

QUINCE: Two nights ago, some of them Jayhawkers managed to sneak up on Snyder when he was out on guard. That's him right there.

(He points offstage.)
SNYDER, *a cowboy in his late teens, stands by the fire with his coffee —glum, silent.)*

BACK TO SCENE

QUINCE: They stripped him and flogged him, Marshal, and then stampeded the cattle. We had our hands full for the next few hours or we might've caught up with them.

MATT: Mmm . . . Any trouble since then, Quince?

QUINCE: Not yet.

MATT: Quince, the ordinary Kansan hates Jayhawkers as much as you do. They're nothing but shifty, murderous criminals. They got started on the Missouri border during the War . . . and they got the taste of blood in their mouths, and now . . . well . . . it's like they've got no place to go.

QUINCE: We'll show them a place.

MATT: They're bandits, that's all. You've got bandits in Texas, but that doesn't make every Texan a bandit, does it?

QUINCE: It's kinda hard to make the men see that, Marshal.
MATT: I know.

ANOTHER ANGLE

(*Jacks comes up with a plate and a cup of coffee.*)

JACKS: I'll join you, if you don't mind.
QUINCE: Sit down, Jacks.
MATT: Where's Chester?
JACKS: He run into a fella he knew from last season—they're over there swapping lies.

(*Jacks sits down . . . starts eating.*)

QUINCE: I been complaining to the Marshal about our welcome here.
JACKS (*irony*): Oh, it ain't such a problem, maybe—I've heard of trail drivers buying off Jayhawkers at two or three dollars a head. Let's see . . . with three thousand head that'd cost us around six or nine thousand dollars.
QUINCE: I'm paying nobody nothing.
JACKS: They ain't asked us yet. But I'll kill the first one I see anyway, so . . .
MATT: But maybe they won't bother you again.

CLOSER ANGLE

QUINCE: Marshal, every dollar I've got's in those cattle, and all the money my relatives and friends could raise, too. We've come a long way from the San Saba and we're almost to Dodge. I'd kinda hate to lose now.
MATT: Well, Quince, I don't quite know what I can do.
QUINCE: What about the Army?
MATT: They're up north chasing Indians.
QUINCE: Sure. Well, Marshal, one reason I wanted you to come down here was to ride with us a few days—get acquainted with the men a little. They're in a bad temper and when they hit Dodge they're gonna be looking for Kansas scalps. It could get real bloody.
MATT: I'll ride with you.
QUINCE: I figured you would. You see, Marshal, the way we look at it, the good citizens of Dodge are out to fleece us anyway . . . and on top of that they hire gunfighters to shoot us as soon as we kick up our heels a little. All in all, it kinda makes for bad feeling.
MATT: There's some misunderstanding on both sides.
QUINCE: You and I know that—but they don't.
JACKS: Oh, say, Quince, I near forgot . . .
QUINCE: What?
JACKS: A stranger rode up to the remuda . . . asked for a job. I told him to eat first.

QUINCE: A job? Now? He must be crazy. Where is he?

MED SHOT

(*Jacks puts down his plate, stands up.*)

JACKS: He's right over there. I'll get him.

(*He walks off.*)

MATT: I'd like to stand a guard tonight, Quince.

QUINCE: Oh, there's no need for that, Marshal.

MATT: If I'm riding with you, I'll do my share of the work.

QUINCE: All right. You go out with the last watch. The wrangler'll give you a night horse.

MATT: Okay.

ANOTHER ANGLE

(*Jacks comes back with* CARL STUDER. *Studer is thirty-five, a seedy, thin-faced, shifty individual.*)

JACKS: Here he is, Quince. (*to Studer*): This here's Dolph Quince, the trail boss.

STUDER: Mr. Quince . . .

QUINCE: Your name?

STUDER: Studer . . . Carl Studer.

QUINCE: You lost, Studer?

STUDER: I . . . I don't know what you mean?

QUINCE: Well, do you know we're only four days' drive out of Dodge?

STUDER: Sure . . . but . . . I was wondering if you could use a hand?

QUINCE: For four days?

STUDER: That'd help.

QUINCE: You must be awful hungry, Studer.

STUDER: I guess I am.

QUINCE: All right . . . we'll feed you from here to Dodge . . . if you work. But I won't pay you nothing—I ain't got the money and I don't need a hand anyway.

STUDER: Sure grateful to you, Mr. Quince.

(*He starts off. Quince stops him.*)

QUINCE: Wait a minute—where're you from, Studer?

STUDER: Colorado.

QUINCE: Then you ain't a Kansan?

STUDER: No sir.

QUINCE: Good. Then maybe the boys won't tear you apart. You'll ride the fourth watch tonight, Studer.

STUDER: Yes sir.

(*He walks off.*)

MED. SHOT

(Matt and Quince both look after him.)

QUINCE: Now there's the sort of man spends his whole miserable life just looking for salt pork and sundown.

MATT: If that's all he's looking for.

QUINCE: What do you mean?

MATT: Oh, it's just an old habit of mine, Quince. I guess I wouldn't still be alive if I trusted everybody on first sight.

QUINCE: You don't trust this fella?

MATT: He's probably all right. But, still—I'd keep him in camp unless it's daylight.

QUINCE: You mean . . .

MATT: Don't put him on night guard, Quince.

QUINCE: Well, all right. But, Marshal, I always thought I led a hard life . . . till now. I think you beat me.

MATT: I get shot at more than you, that's all.

QUINCE: Maybe that's it. Well—

ANOTHER ANGLE

(He stands up. Matt follows.

QUINCE *(cont'd)*: You'd better hole up early tonight, Marshal. You'll be out singing to them cow brutes in a few hours.

MATT: Sure.

QUINCE: Breakfast's at four o'clock.

MATT: Okay.

QUINCE: You'll find it don't take long to stay all night in this camp.

(Matt laughs. Quince walks off. Matt picks up his plate and cup and starts toward the chuckwagon.)

DISSOLVE TO:

STOCK SHOT—CATTLE . . . MEN RIDING HERD (NIGHT)

EXT. CAMP ANGLE ON REMUDA (DAY)

(It's early morning. A couple of men are roping mounts out of the remuda, several more are saddling up. Camera pans to Matt and three or four cowboys riding in from guard. They ride up, dismount. All of the men's attitudes toward Matt has changed some—to respect and being a little more friendly. The men saddling up ad lib brief hellos to him. A cowboy who rode in with him nods toward the chuck wagon offstage.)

COWBOY: Smell that coffee, Marshal?

MATT: I sure do.

COWBOY: That's the best thing about riding the last watch—you get fresh coffee.

MATT: Then let's get to it.

COWBOY: You bet.

(*They unsaddle and turn their horses into the remuda.*)

ANGLE ON CHUCK WAGON AND FIRE

(*A few men are standing around the fire, including Chester, Jacks and Quince. Matt and Cowboy walk into scene. They ad lib hellos.*)

COWBOY: I'll fetch you some coffee, Marshal.

MATT: I'll get it.

COWBOY: No trouble.

(*He walks off. Quince gives Matt a look, smiles.*)

QUINCE: There's one down, anyway.

MATT: He thinks I know every girl in Dodge is all.

JACKS: Don't you?

MATT: Chester's your man, for that.

CHESTER: Sure—I spend all my time with the ladies. They love it cause I'm so rich and all.

JACKS: That's the impression you give me the first time I saw you. Come on . . . let's get some coffee.

CHESTER: Okay.

(*They walk off.*)

CLOSER ANGLE

MATT: Well, no trouble last night, Quince.

QUINCE: I kinda wish there had been.

MATT: What?

QUINCE: It's like fighting Indians, Marshal—when you can't see them, you worry more'n when they're coming at you.

MATT: I know what you mean. (*nods offstage*): Did you keep him off guard?

(*Quince looks.*)
(*Studer is sitting off by himself.*)

BACK TO SCENE

QUINCE: Yeah. He don't look like much of a hand to me, anyway. I don't know why I let him hang around—never did have no use for ragtails like him.

(*Cowboy walks into scene with the coffee.*)

COWBOY: Here you go, Marshal.

MATT (*takes it*): Thanks.

QUINCE: We're traveling out, Marshal—I'll see you with the herd.

MATT: I'll be along directly, Quince.

(*Quince nods, and walks off.*)

COWBOY: Say, Marshal . . . I was just thinking—

MATT: Mmmm?

COWBOY: There's another little gal I remember—Polly something . . . kinda dark-haired, slim . . . worked over at that Lady Gay place. . . .

(*Matt smiles as the Cowboy goes on.*)

COWBOY: You must know her. Real nice gal . . . didn't seem to mind talking to a raggedy trail hand at all. All them gals ain't like that, are they? This one . . . she seemed different. . . .

DISSOLVE TO:

STOCK SHOT—CATTLE ON TRAIL

EXT. PRAIRIE MED. SHOT (DAY)

(*Jacks and Chester and Matt are riding alongside the herd offstage, slowly.*)

CHESTER: Land's sakes . . . we'll never get to Dodge this rate.

JACKS: We gotta get to Dodge, Chester—you owe me a drink.

CHESTER: And I'll glady buy it . . . gladly. I'm going on up ahead—I can't see nothing through all them cattle. Look at them—

STOCK—CATTLE

BACK TO SCENE

CHESTER (*cont'd*): I like riding point better'n this.

JACKS: Don't get lost.

CHESTER: Not likely. See you later, Mr. Dillon.

MATT: Sure, Chester.

(*Chester rides off.*)

JACKS: He's a good man, Marshal.

MATT: The best.

ANOTHER ANGLE

(*Quince rides up to them. They pull up for a moment.*)

QUINCE: Well, how's it feel to be a trail hand again, Marshal?

MATT: Nothing to it if I could sleep all winter like you.

QUINCE: When would you spend your money?

JACKS (*to Quince*): I already offered to trade jobs with him. You know where I found him in Dodge?

QUINCE: Hanging a horsethief, I hope.

JACKS: Not hardly. He was setting idle in a chair, taking in the sun like an old man.

QUINCE: Don't let it fool you, Jacks. I've seen him move. But look, you two—you crossed the Cimarron yesterday. What's it like?

MATT: The water's gone down. You won't have any trouble.

QUINCE: I was also thinking about the sand.

JACKS: It was sound where we crossed, Quince.

QUINCE: Then we'll cross the same place. Jacks, you go up ahead and ride point and lead us to it.

JACKS: Okay.

(*He starts off.*)

QUINCE: Pick up that new fella, Studer, on the way.

JACKS: I don't need him.

QUINCE: I want him up front where I can see him.

JACKS: All right.

(*He rides off.*)

MED. SHOT

(*They look toward the herd offstage.*)

MATT: Your cattle are in good shape, considering the walk they've had.

QUINCE: Yeah . . . but they're kinda triggered up. It's the heat. Look how they trail. . . .

STOCK SHOT—CATTLE
BACK TO MATT, QUINCE

MATT: Well, maybe nothing'll blow them off.

QUINCE: The Cimarron worries me some. First crossing I tried last year when I came up, had a quicksand bottom that'd bog a saddle blanket.

MATT: Lose many cattle?

QUINCE: Thirty head. Couldn't even dig their tails out.

MATT: You know, Quince, I sometimes wonder if it's worth it to you, driving cattle up here.

QUINCE: Texas is bankrupt, Marshal. The War broke us. All we got is these mossy-horned cattle.

MATT: Sure. But maybe there'll be an easier way someday.

QUINCE: The railroad? We'd starve waiting for it.

MATT (*nods*): Anyway, this San Saba herd of yours is the first to reach Dodge this year. Prices are high. You ought to profit twenty dollars a head.

QUINCE: We ain't reached Dodge yet, Marshal.

MATT: No. . . .

ANOTHER ANGLE

> (*They start riding.*)

QUINCE: Them Jayhawking devils can still scatter this herd.
MATT: Well, maybe you've seen the last of them.
QUINCE: Maybe. . . .

> (*The sound of a shot is heard up ahead.*)

QUINCE: What's that?

> (*Another shot.*)

MATT: Come on. . . .

> (*They boot their horses and ride.*)

FULL SHOT

> (*They ride hard. Jacks' horse, unmanned, comes into scene. Then Jacks, lying on the ground, badly wounded, Chester's horse is in background, and Chester is kneeling by Jacks. Matt and Quince ride up.*)

MED SHOT

CHESTER: Studer shot him—right in the back!

> (*Quince jumps off his horse, goes to Jacks.*)

MATT: I'm going after him, Quince . . .
CHESTER: I'll get my horse.

> (*Chester hurries off after his horse.*)

QUINCE: Get him, Marshal—get him alive! (*looks offstage*): Hey!

> (*Matt looks.*)
> (*Studer is riding toward the cattle, offstage, shouting and waving a blanket, and if he can manage it, also firing his sixgun.*)

BACK TO SCENE

> (*Quince looks toward the cattle offstage.*)

QUINCE: He's stampeding them!
MATT: I'll get him . . .

> (*Matt starts off.*)

STOCK—CATTLE STAMPEDE
MED. LONG SHOT

> (*Matt followed by Chester is riding after Studer . . . who changes his direction and rides toward a small hill, firing back at his pur-*)

suers as he goes. Then a couple of mounted figures appear at the top of the hill and fire their sixguns at Matt and Chester. One of them is JAY, *about thirty-five, a ruffian. Matt pulls his rifle and still at full speed fires a couple of shot at Studer. Studer is hit and falls . . . dead. Then Matt fires a couple at the men beyond and they disappear behind the hill. Matt signals to Chester and they pull up near Studer.*)

MED SHOT

(*Studer lies still.*)

CHESTER: He looks dead to me . . .
MATT: Yeah. . . . You stay here—I'm going after those other two.
CHESTER: Yessir. But you be careful—there might be more of them over there.
MATT: I hope there are.

(*Matt rides toward the hill, camera following him.*)

ANOTHER ANGLE

(*When Matt approaches the top of the hill, he jumps off his horse, rifle in hand. Just then a Jayhawker suddenly appears at the top of the hill and snaps a shot off at Matt. Matt fires his rifle without raising it to his shoulder and the Jayhawker falls . . . dead.*)

MED SHOT

(*Matt goes to the top of the hill, cautiously looks over.*)
(*Down the hill a couple of hundred yards, one man is getting mounted, the other, Jay, is running toward his horse which is some distance off.*

FULL SHOT

(*Matt stands up and yells down at the men.*)

MATT: Hold it, you men . . .

(*The first man swings into his saddle, jerks his horse around and fires a couple of shots at Matt. Matt aims carefully and shoots him out of his saddle . . . dead. Jay gives up trying to reach his horse and drops down behind a boulder.*)

ANOTHER ANGLE

(*Matt, rifle in hand, walks slowly down the hill toward Jay. About a hundred yards from him he stops. Jay calls out from cover.*)

JAY: That's far enough, Mister.
MATT: Throw your gun out and stand up. . . .
JAY: Not likely. You go on back.

MATT: You're forgetting I've got a rifle.
JAY: But you're in pistol range now.
MATT: Then start shooting, mister.

(*Matt slowly walks forward.*)

MED. SHOT

(*Jay is growing mighty nervous.*)

JAY: Stop right there, I tell you . . .

(*Matt takes a few more steps, then stops.*)

MATT: All right, fella, put down and come forward.
JAY: Wait—listen to me . . .
MATT: I'm listening . . .
JAY: All I want is my horse and I'll get out of here. I promise we won't bother you no more.
MATT: You sure won't. You're all dead. All but you, mister.
JAY: Just let me get my horse . . .
MATT: You've stampeded that herd twice . . . you stripped and flogged a man the other night—what makes you think I'd let you ride off now?
JAY: I ain't giving up . . .
MATT: Look—I'm not a trail driver . . . I'm a United States Marshal. Give up and I promise you there'll be no lynching. You'll get a fair trial.
JAY: No . . .
MATT: If you don't, you'll die—right where you are.

(*Matt starts walking slowly forward again.*)

JAY: Lemme go—I'm warning you . . .
MATT: I can kill you any time, Mister . . . any time. . . .
JAY: Stop . . .
MATT: Don't make me do it . . .

(*Matt continues toward him.*)

ANOTHER ANGLE

(*Jay suddenly raises up, snaps a shot off at Matt. Matt fires almost simultaneously—and Jay pitches forward . . . dead. Matt walks up to him, and looks down at him.*)

MATT: You just had to try it, didn't you . . . ?

(*At the sound of approaching horses, Matt turns.*)

FULL SHOT

(*Quince and Snyder come over the hill and ride down to Matt.*)

MED SHOT

(*Quince takes a look around.*)

QUINCE: You leave a bloody trail, Marshal.

MATT: Yeah. . . .

QUINCE: I sent Chester to help stop the cattle . . . but I brought Snyder with me. After the whipping they gave him the other night, I kinda figured he deserved to be in on this.

SNYDER: I guess I'm too late. Looks like you've taken care of all of them.

MATT: Be glad you don't have to kill a man, son.

SNYDER: I don't think I'd of minded, Marshal.

MATT: Yeah . . . I know.

QUINCE: Too bad you couldn't have got *one* of them alive, Marshal.

MATT: I had no choice.

QUINCE: No . . .

MATT: Tell me—how's Jacks?

QUINCE: Dead.

MATT: Oh. . . . He was a good man.

QUINCE (*nods*): The boys'll have the lead cattle turned by now. We'll let them mill around for an hour and then graze them out.

MATT: Snyder—I left my horse over the rise there—would you get him for me?

SNYDER: Sure, Marshal.

(*He rides off.*)

ANOTHER ANGLE

(*Quince studies the battle scene a moment.*)

QUINCE: Looks like you walked right down onto this man, Marshal.

MATT: I was trying to take him alive—like you asked.

QUINCE: Well, I guess I just wanted to hang him myself. Anyway, I'm glad he's dead.

MATT: When you can spare a couple of men, we oughta dig some graves.

QUINCE: Sure. And Marshal—we'll be burying Jacks, too. I'm wondering if you might know how to do it . . . proper, I mean. A prayer or something, maybe.

MATT: I'll try, Quince.

QUINCE: Thanks. I'll get back to the cattle.

MATT: Sure.

(*Quince rides off.*)

MED. SHOT

(*Matt glances at Jay, then starts walking toward the hill. Snyder tops it, leading Matt's horse.*)

DISSOLVE TO:

STOCK SHOT—CATTLE GRAZING
MED. LONG SHOT—PRAIRIE

(*Half a dozen cowboys ride slowly toward the camp offstage. Camera pans to another group—and then to the camp.*)

FULL SHOT—CAMP

(*The Cook has a fire going and coffee. A few men ride in . . . sober and quiet. A little distance from the chuck wagon Jacks lies wrapped in a blanket—and a couple of men are just finishing digging the grave. Snyder stands near the grave, watching. Matt and Chester are by the fire.*)

ANGLE ON GRAVE

(*As the men finish digging. They've been spelling each other off and the one in the hole climbs out. They look at the grave and then at Jacks in his blanket.*)

ANGLE ON QUINCE

(*as he rides in from the cattle. He rides up to the camp near the fire, dismounts. Cowboy steps up.*

COWBOY: I'll take him, Quince.
QUINCE: Thanks.

(*Cowboy leads the horse off. Quince steps up to Matt and Chester.*)

MED. FULL SHOT

MATT: How're the cattle?
QUINCE: The cattle are fine. (*glances toward grave*): You thought of something to say?
MATT (*nods*): I guess.

(*Quince addresses the men scattered about.*)

QUINCE: Men . . .

(*He starts toward the grave, Matt and Chester follow and the men drift toward it, too.*)

ANGLE ON GRAVE

(*as the men gather. A couple of them pick up Jacks' body, move it to the grave, and lower it. As the diggers start to throw earth in, Matt and Quince remove their hats . . . the others follow suit. They watch in silence as the grave is filled. Then the diggers step back . . . and Quince glances at Matt. Matt steps forward. He thinks a moment and then begins . . . haltingly. It's a long time since he's heard much less said the words.*

MATT: "We brought nothing into this world, neither may we carry anything out of this world. The Lord giveth, and the Lord taketh away. . . ."

(He stops . . . trying to remember what follows. Chester speaks quietly:)

CHESTER: "Even as it pleaseth the Lord . . ."
MATT: ". . . Even as it pleaseth the Lord, so cometh things to pass. Blessed be the name of the Lord." Amen.
CAST: Amen. . . .

(After a moment, the men begin to move away. Chester with them.)

ANOTHER ANGLE

(Snyder stands staring at the grave.)

MATT: Oh . . . Snyder.
SNYDER: Yeah . . . ?
MATT: Would you do something for me?

(Snyder steps up.)

SNYDER: What?
MATT: Well, I smuggled a quart of wagonyard whiskey out of Dodge when I rode down here. The cook's got it hid in the chuckwagon.
SNYDER: Oh . . . ?
MATT: Its' not much, but it'll cut the alkali in your drinking water. Get it and pass it around, will you?
QUINCE: That's a fine idea, Marshal.

(Snyder nods, starts off.)

SNYDER: All as wants a drink of the Marshal's whiskey get on over to the chuckwagon.

MED. SHOT

(The men stop, ad lib their pleasure, but quietly, and go with Snyder.)

ANGLE ON MATT, QUINCE

(Quince steps up.)

QUINCE: There's time when a drink's good for a man's soul, Marshal. I guess this is one of them.
MATT: I think Jacks would approve.
QUINCE: He would. Uh . . . by the way, Marshal, the boys all know how you handled them Jayhawkers.

MATT: Oh . . .

QUINCE: They feel some better about things.

MATT: Good.

QUINCE: Course it don't mean they ain't gonna hurrah Dodge some when we get there.

MATT: And I'm going to give them a pretty free hand.

QUINCE (smiles): Come on—we got a drink coming out of that bottle, too.

(They start toward the chuck wagon.)

FADE OUT:

STAGE TO LORDSBURG

by ERNEST HAYCOX

From the beginning the Western was destined for the movies. The Great Train Robbery *and* The Squaw Man *gave birth to a film tradition which is still evolving. For years the stories were as simple and obvious as the poorest dime novel. "Meanwhile, back at the ranch," and "They went thataway" were used so often that hearing them today evokes a smile. An old movie hand himself, Ernest Haycox, author of hundreds of short stories, wrote "Stage to Lordsburg." Recreated for the screen, it became* Stagecoach. *The characters were no longer simon-pure, but* Stagecoach *and a half-dozen other films of equal quality gave a new vitality to the Western film and gained it new respect from critical audiences.*

This was one of those years in the Territory when Apache smoke signals spiraled up from the stony mountain summits and many a ranch cabin lay as a square of blackened ashes on the ground and the departure of a stage from Tonto was the beginning of an adventure that had no certain happy ending. . . .

The stage and its six horses waited in front of Weilner's store on the north side of Tonto's square. Happy Stuart was on the box, the ribbons between his fingers and one foot teetering on the brake. John Strang rode shotgun guard and an escort of ten cavalrymen waited behind the coach, half asleep in their saddles.

At four-thirty in the morning this high air was quite cold, though the sun had begun to flush the sky eastward. A small crowd stood in the square, presenting their final messages to the passengers now entering the coach. There was a girl going down to marry an infantry officer, a whisky drummer from St. Louis, an Englishman all length and bony corners and bearing with him an enormous sporting rifle, a gambler, a solid-shouldered cattleman on his way to New Mexico and a blond young man upon whom both Happy Stuart and the shotgun guard placed a narrow-eyed interest.

This seemed all until the blond man drew back from the coach door; and then a girl known commonly throughout the Territory as Henriette came quietly from the crowd. She was small and quiet, with a touch of paleness in her cheeks and her quite dark eyes lifted at the blond man's unexpected courtesy, showing surprise. There was this moment of delay and then the girl caught up her dress and stepped into the coach.

Men in the crowd were smiling but the blond one turned, his motion like the swift cut of a knife, and his attention covered that group until the smiling quit. He was tall, hollow-flanked, and definitely stamped by the guns slung low on his hips. But it wasn't the guns alone; something in his face, so watchful and so smooth, also showed his trade. Afterwards he got into the coach and slammed the door.

Happy Stuart kicked off the brakes and yelled, "Hi!" Tonto's people were calling out their last farewells and the six horses broke into a trot

428

and the stage lunged on its fore and aft springs and rolled from town with dust dripping off its wheels like water, the cavalrymen trotting briskly behind. So they tipped down the long grade, bound on a journey no stage had attempted during the last forty-five days. Out below in the desert's distance stood the relay stations they hoped to reach and pass. Between lay a country swept empty by the quick raids of Geronimo's men.

The Englishman, the gambler and the blond man sat jammed together in the forward seat, riding backward to the course of the stage. The drummer and the cattleman occupied the uncomfortable middle bench; the two women shared the rear seat. The cattleman faced Henriette, his knees almost touching her. He had one arm hooked over the door's window sill to steady himself. A huge gold nugget slid gently back and forth along the watch chain slung across his wide chest and a chunk of black hair lay below his hat. His eyes considered Henriette, reading something in the girl that caused him to show her a deliberate smile. Henriette dropped her glance to the gloved tips of her fingers, cheeks unstirred.

They were all strangers packed closely together, with nothing in common save a destination. Yet the cattleman's smile and the boldness of his glance were something as audible as speech, noted by everyone except the Englishman, who sat bolt upright with his stony indifference. The army girl, tall and calmly pretty, threw a quick side glance at Henriette and afterwards looked away with a touch of color. The gambler saw this interchange of glances and showed the cattleman an irritated attention. The whisky drummer's eyes narrowed a little and some inward cynicism made a faint change on his lips. He removed his hat to show a bald head already beginning to sweat; his cigar smoke turned the coach cloudy and ashes kept dropping on his vest.

The blond man had observed Henriette's glance drop from the cattleman; he tipped his hat well over his face and watched her—not boldly but as though he were puzzled. Once her glance lifted and touched him. But he had been on guard against that and was quick to look away.

The army girl coughed gently behind her hand, whereupon the gambler tapped the whisky drummer on the shoulder. "Get rid of that." The drummer appeared startled. He grumbled, "Beg pardon," and tossed the smoke through the window.

All this while the coach went rushing down the ceaseless turns of the mountain road, rocking on its fore and aft springs, its heavy wheels slamming through the road ruts and whining on the curves. Occasionally the strident yell of Happy Stuart washed back. "Hi, Nellie! By God—!" The whisky drummer braced himself against the door and closed his eyes.

Three hours from Tonto the road, making a last round sweep, let them down upon the flat desert. Here the stage stopped and the men got out to stretch. The gambler spoke to the army girl, gently: "Perhaps you would find my seat more comfortable." The army girl said "Thank you," and changed over. The cavalry sergeant rode up to the stage, speaking to Happy Stuart.

"We'll be goin' back now—and good luck to ye."

The men piled in, the gambler taking the place beside Henriette. The blond man drew his long legs together to give the army girl more room, and watched Henriette's face with a soft, quiet care. A hard sun beat fully on the coach and dust began to whip up like fire smoke. Without escort they rolled across a flat earth broken only by cacti standing against a dazzling light. In the far distance, behind a blue heat haze, lay the faint suggestion of mountains.

The cattleman reached up and tugged at the ends of his mustache and smiled at Henriette. The army girl spoke to the blond man. "How far is it to the noon station?" The blond man said courteously: "Twenty miles." The gambler watched the army girl with the strictness of his face relaxing, as though the run of her voice reminded him of things long forgotten.

The miles fell behind and the smell of alkali dust got thicker. Henriette rested against the corner of the coach, her eyes dropped to the tips of her gloves. She made an enigmatic, disinterested shape there; she seemed past stirring, beyond laughter. She was young, yet she had a knowledge that put the cattleman and the gambler and the drummer and the army girl in their exact places; and she knew why the gambler had offered the army girl his seat. The army girl was in one world and she was in another, as everyone in the coach understood. It had no effect on her for this was a distinction she had learned long ago. Only the blond man broke through her indifference. His name was Malpais Bill and she could see the wildness in the corners of his eyes and in the long crease of his lips; it was a stamp that would never come off. Yet something flowed out of him toward her that was different than the predatory curiosity of other men; something unobtrusively gallant, unexpectedly gentle.

Upon the box Happy Stuart pointed to the hazy outline two miles away. "Injuns ain't burned that anyhow." The sun was directly overhead, turning the light of the world a cruel brass-yellow. The crooked crack of a dry wash opened across the two deep ruts that made this road. Johnny Strang shifted the gun in his lap. "What's Malpais Bill ridin' with us for?"

"I guess I wouldn't ask him," returned Happy Stuart and studied the wash with a troubled eye. The road fell into it roughly and he got a tighter grip on his reins and yelled: "Hang on! Hi, Nellie! God damn you, hi!" The six horses plunged down the rough side of the wash and for a moment the coach stood alone, high and lonely on the break, and then went reeling over the rim. It struck the gravel with a roar, the front wheels bouncing and the back wheels skewing around. The horses faltered but Happy Stuart cursed at his leaders and got them into a run again. The horses lunged up the far side of the wash two and two, their muscles bunching and the soft dirt flying in yellow clouds. The front wheels struck solidly and something cracked like a pistol shot; the stage rose out of the wash, teetered crosswise and then fell ponderously on its side, splintering the coach panels.

Johnny Strang jumped clear. Happy Stuart hung to the handrail with one hand and hauled on the reins with the other; and stood up while the passengers crawled through the upper door. All the men, except the whisky drummer, put their shoulders to the coach and heaved it upright again. The whisky drummer stood strangely in the bright sunlight shaking his head dumbly while the others climbed back in. Happy Stuart said, "All right, brother, git aboard."

The drummer climbed in slowly and the stage ran on. There was a low, gray dobe relay station squatted on the desert dead ahead with a scatter of corrals about it and a flag hanging limp on a crooked pole. Men came out of the dobe's dark interior and stood in the shade of the porch gallery. Happy Stuart rolled up and stopped. He said to a lanky man: "Hi, Mack. Where's the God-damned Injuns?"

The passengers were filing into the dobe's dining room. The lanky one drawled: "You'll see 'em before tomorrow night." Hostlers came up to change horses.

The little dining room was cool after the coach, cool and still. A fat Mexican woman ran in and out with the food platters. Happy Stuart said: "Ten minutes," and brushed the alkali dust from his mouth and fell to eating.

The long-jawed Mack said: "Catlin's ranch burned last night. Was a troop of cavalry around here yesterday. Came and went. You'll git to the Gap tonight all right but I do' know about the mountains beyond. A little trouble?"

"A little," said Happy, briefly, and rose. This was the end of rest. The passengers followed, with the whisky drummer straggling at the rear, reaching deeply for wind. The coach rolled away again, Mack's voice pursuing them. "Hit it a lick, Happy, if you see any dust rollin' out of the east."

Heat had condensed in the coach and the little wind fanned up by the run of the horses was stifling to the lungs; the desert floor projected its white glitter endlessly away until lost in the smoky haze. The cattleman's knees bumped Henriette gently and he kept watching her, a celluloid toothpick drooped between his lips. Happy Stuart's voice ran back, profane and urgent, keeping the speed of the coach constant through the ruts. The whisky drummer's eyes were round and strained and his mouth was open and all the color had gone out of his face. The gambler observed this without expression and without care; and once the cattleman, feeling the sag of the whisky drummer's shoulder, shoved him away. The Englishman sat bolt upright, staring emotionlessly at the passing desert. The army girl spoke to Malpais Bill: "What is the next stop?"

"Gap Creek."

"Will we meet soldiers there?"

He said: "I expect we'll have an escort over the hills into Lordsburg."

And at four o'clock of this furnace-hot afternoon the whisky drummer made a feeble gesture with one hand and fell forward into the gambler's lap.

The cattleman shrugged his shoulders and put a head through the window, calling up to Happy Stuart: "Wait a minute." When the stage stopped everybody climbed out and the blond man helped the gambler lay the whisky drummer in the sweltering patch of shade created by the coach. Neither Happy Stuart nor the shotgun guard bothered to get down. The whisky drummer's lips moved a little but nobody said anything and nobody knew what to do—until Henriette stepped forward.

She dropped to the ground, lifting the whisky drummer's shoulders and head against her breasts. He opened his eyes and there was something in them that they could all see, like relief and ease, like gratefulness. She murmured: "You are all right," and her smile was soft and pleasant, turning her lips maternal. There was this wisdom in her, this knowledge of the fears that men concealed behind their manners, the deep hungers that rode them so savagely, and the loneliness that drove them to women of her kind. She repeated, "You are all right," and watched this whisky drummer's eyes lose the wildness of what he knew.

The army girl's face showed shock. The gambler and the cattleman looked down at the whisky drummer quite impersonally. The blond man watched Henriette through lids half closed, but the flare of a powerful interest broke the severe lines of his cheeks. He held a cigarette between his fingers; he had forgotten it.

Happy Stuart said: "We can't stay here."

The gambler bent down to catch the whisky drummer under the arms. Henriette rose and said, "Bring him to me," and got into the coach. The blond man and the gambler lifted the drummer through the door so that he was lying along the back seat, cushioned on Henriette's lap. They all got in and the coach rolled on. The drummer groaned a little, whispering: "Thanks—thanks," and the blond man, searching Henriette's face for every shred of expression, drew a gusty breath.

They went on like this, the big wheels pounding the ruts of the road while a lowering sun blazed through the coach windows. The mountain bulwarks began to march nearer, more definite in the blue fog. The cattleman's eyes were small and brilliant and touched Henriette personally, but the gambler bent toward Henriette to say: "If you are tired—"

"No," she said. "No. He's dead."

The army girl stifled a small cry. The gambler bent nearer the whisky drummer, and then they were all looking at Henriette; even the Englishman stared at her for a moment, faint curiosity in his eyes. She was remotely smiling, her lips broad and soft. She held the drummer's head with both her hands and continued to hold him like that until, at the swift fall of dusk, they rolled across the last of the desert floor and drew up before Gap Station.

The cattleman kicked open the door and stepped out, grunting as his stiff legs touched the ground. The gambler pulled the drummer up so that Henriette could leave. They all came out, their bones tired from the shaking. Happy Stuart climbed from the box, his face a gray mask of alkali and his eyes bloodshot. He said: "Who's dead?" and looked into the coach. People sauntered from the station yard, walking with the indolence of twilight. Happy Stuart said, "Well, he won't worry about tomorrow," and turned away.

A short man with a tremendous stomach shuffled through the dusk. He said: "Wasn't sure you'd try to git through yet, Happy."

"Where's the soldiers for tomorrow?"

"Other side of the mountains. Everybody's chased out. What ain't forted up here was sent into Lordsburg. You men will bunk in the barn. I'll make out for the ladies somehow." He looked at the army girl and he appraised Henriette instantly. His eyes slid on to Malpais Bill standing in the background and recognition stirred him then and made his voice careful. "Hello, Bill. What brings you this way?"

Malpais Bill's cigarette glowed in the gathering dusk and Henriette caught the brief image of his face, serene and watchful. Malpais Bill's tone was easy, it was soft. "Just the trip."

They were moving on toward the frame house whose corners seemed to extend indefinitely into a series of attached sheds. Lights glimmered in the windows and men moved around the place, idly talking. The unhitched horses went away at a trot. The tall girl walked into the station's big room, to face a soldier in a disheveled uniform.

He said: "Miss Robertson? Lieutenant Hauser was to have met you here. He is at Lordsburg. He was wounded in a brush with the Apaches last night."

The tall army girl stood very still. She said: "Badly?"

"Well," said the soldier, "yes."

The fat man came in, drawing deeply for wind. "Too bad—too bad. Ladies, I'll show you the rooms, such as I got."

Henriette's dove-colored dress blended with the background shadows. She was watching the tall army girl's face whiten. But there was a strength in the army girl, a fortitude that made her think of the soldier. For she said quietly, "You must have had a bad trip."

"Nothing—nothing at all," said the soldier and left the room. The gambler was here, his thin face turning to the army girl with a strained expression, as though he were remembering painful things. Malpais Bill had halted in the doorway, studying the softness and the humility of Henriette's cheeks. Afterwards both women followed the fat host of Gap Station along a narrow hall to their quarters.

Malpais Bill wheeled out and stood indolently aganst tihe wall of this desert station, his glance quick and watchful in the way it touched all the men loitering along the yard, his ears weighing all the night-softened voices. Heat died from the earth and a definite chill rolled down the mountain hulking so high behind the house. The soldier was in his saddle, murmuring drowsily to Happy Stuart.

"Well, Lordsburg is a long ways off and the dam' mountains are squirm-in' with Apaches. You won't have any cavalry escort tomorrow. The troops are all in the field."

Malpais Bill listened to the hoofbeats of the soldier's horse fade out, remembering the loneliness of a man in those dark mountain passes, and went back to the saloon at the end of the station. This was a low-ceilinged shed with a dirt floor and whitewashed walls that once had been part of a stable. Three men stood under a lantern in the middle of this little place, the light of the lantern palely shining in the rounds of their eyes as they watched him. At the far end of the bar the cattleman and the gambler drank in taciturn silence. Malpais Bill took his whisky when the bottle came, and noted the barkeep's obscure glance. Gap's host put in his head and wheezed, "Second table," and the other men in here began to move out. The barkeep's words rubbed together, one tone above a whisper. "Better not ride into Lordsburg. Plummer and Shanley are there."

Malpais Bill's lips were stretched to the long edge of laughter and there was a shine like wildness in his eyes. He said, "Thanks, friend," and went into the dining room.

When he came back to the yard night lay wild and deep across the desert and the moonlight was a frozen silver that touched but could not dissolve the world's incredible blackness. The girl Henriette walked along the Tonto road, swaying gently in the vague shadows. He went that way, the click of his heels on the hard earth bringing her around.

Her face was clear and strange and incurious in the night, as though she waited for something to come, and knew what it would be. But he said: "You're too far from the house. Apaches like to crawl down next to a settlement and wait for strays."

She was indifferent, unafraid. Her voice was cool and he could hear the faint loneliness in it, the fatalism that made her words so even. "There's a wind coming up, so soft and good."

He took off his hat, long legs braced, and his eyes were both attentive and puzzled. His blond hair glowed in the fugitive light.

She said in a deep breath: "Why do you do that?"

His lips were restless and the sing and rush of strong feeling was like a current of quick wind around him. "You have folks in Lordsburg?"

She spoke in a direct, patient way as though explaining something he should have known without asking. "I run a house in Lordsburg."

"No," he said, "it wasn't what I asked."

"My folks are dead—I think. There was a massacre in the Superstition Mountains when I was young."

He stood with his head bowed, his mind reaching back to fill in that gap of her life. There was a hardness and a rawness to this land and little sympathy for the weak. She had survived and had paid for her survival, and looked at him now in a silent way that offered no explanations or apologies for whatever had been said; she was still a pretty girl with the dead patience of all the past years in her eyes, in the expressiveness of her lips.

He said:" Over in the Tonto Basin is a pretty land. I've got a piece of a ranch there—with a house half built."

"If that's your country why are you here?"

His lips laughed and the rashness in him glowed hot again and he seemed to grow taller in the moonlight. "A debt to collect."

"That's why you're going to Lordsburg? You will never get through collecting those kind of debts. Everybody in the Territory knows you. Once you were just a rancher. Then you tried to wipe out a grudge and then there was a bigger one to wipe out—and the debt kept growing and more men are waiting to kill you. Someday a man will. You'd better run away from the debts."

His bright smile kept constant, and presently she lifted her shoulders with resignation. "No," she murmured, "you won't run." He could see the sweetness of her lips and the way her eyes were sad for him; he could see in them the patience he had never learned.

He said, "We'd better go back," and turned her with his arm. They went across the yard in silence, hearing the undertone of men's drawling talk roll out of the shadows, seeing the glow of men's pipes in the dark corners. Malpais Bill stopped and watched her go through the station door; she turned to look at him once more, her eyes all dark and her lips softly sober, and then passed down the narrow corridor to her own quarters. Beyond her window, in the yard, a man was murmuring to another man: "Plummer and Shanley are in Lordsburg. Malpais Bill knows it." Through the thin partition of the adjoining room she heard the army girl crying with a suppressed, uncontrollable regularity. Henriette stared at the dark wall, her shoulders and head bowed; and afterwards returned to the hall and knocked on the army girl's door and went in.

Six fresh horses fiddled in front of the coach and the fat host of Gap Station came across the yard swinging a lantern against the dead, bitter black. All the passengers filed sleep-dulled and miserable from the house. Johnny Strang slammed the express box in the boot and Happy Stuart gruffly said: "All right, folks."

The passengers climbed in. The cattleman came up and Malpais Bill drawled: "Take the corner spot, mister," and got in, closing the door.

The Gap host grumbled: "If they don't jump you on the long grade you'll be all right. You're safe when you get to Al Schrieber's ranch." Happy's bronze voice shocked the black stillness and the coach lurched forward, its leather springs squealing.

They rode for an hour in this complete darkness, chilled and uncomfortable and half asleep, feeling the coach drag on a heavy-climbing grade. Gray dawn cracked through, followed by a sunless light rushing all across the flat desert now far below. The road looped from one barren shoulder to another and at sunup they had reached the first bench and were slamming full speed along a boulder-strewn flat. The cattleman sat in the forward corner, the left corner of his mouth swollen and crushed, and when Henriette saw that her glance slid to Malpais Bill's knuckles. The army girl had her eyes closed, her shoulders pressing against the Englishman, who remained bolt upright with the sporting gun between his knees. Beside Henriette the gambler seemed to sleep, and on the middle bench Malpais Bill watched the land go by with a thin vigilance.

At ten they were rising again, with juniper and scrub pine showing on the slopes and the desert below them filling with the powdered haze of another hot day. By noon they reached the summit of the range and swung to follow its narrow rock-ribbed meadows. The gambler, long motionless, shifted his feet and caught the army girl's eyes.

"Schrieber's is directly ahead. We are past the worst of it."

The blond man looked around at the gambler, making no comment; and it was then that Henriette caught the smell of smoke in the windless air. Happy Stuart was cursing once more and the brake blocks began to cry. Looking through the angled vista of the window panel Henriette saw a clay and rock chimney standing up like a gaunt skeleton against the day's light. The house that had been there was a black patch on the ground, smoke still rising from pieces that had not been completely burnt.

The stage stopped and all the men were instantly out. An iron stove squatted on the earth, with one section of pipe stuck upright to it. Fire licked lazily along the collapsed fragments of what had been a trunk. Beyond the location of the house, at the foot of a corral, lay two nude figures grotesquely bald, with delicate knife slashes marking their bodies. Happy Stuart went over there and had his look; and came back.

"Schriebers. Well—"

Malpais Bill said: "This morning about daylight." He looked at the gambler, at the cattleman, at the Englishman who showed no emotion. "Get back in the coach." He climbed to the coach's top, flattening himself full length there. Happy Stuart and Strang took their places again. The horses broke into a run.

The gambler said to the army girl: "You're pretty safe between those two fellows," and hauled a .44 from a back pocket and laid it over his lap. He considered Henriette more carefully than before, his taciturnity breaking. He said: "How old are you?"

Her shoulders rose and fell, which was the only answer. But the gambler said gently, "Young enough to be my daughter. It is a rotten world. When I call to you, lie down on the floor."

The Englishman had pulled the rifle from between his knees and laid it across the sill of the window on his side. The cattleman swept back the skirt of his coat to clear the holster of his gun.

The little flinty summit meadows grew narrower, with shoulders of gray rock closing in upon the road. The coach wheels slammed against the stony ruts and bounced high and fell again with a jar the springs could not soften. Happy Stuart's howl ran steadily above this rattle and rush. Fine dust turned all things gray.

Henriette sat with her eyes pinned to the gloved tips of her fingers, remembering the tall shape of Malpais Bill cut against the moonlight of Gap Station. He had smiled at her as a man might smile at any desirable woman, with the sweep and swing of laughter in his voice; and his eyes had been gentle. The gambler spoke very quietly and she didn't hear him until his fingers gripped her arm. He said again, not raising his voice: "Get down."

Henriette dropped to her knees, hearing gunfire blast through the rush and run of the coach. Happy Stuart ceased to yell and the army girl's eyes were round and dark. The walls of the canyon had tapered off. Looking upward through the window on the gambler's side, Henriette saw the weaving figure of an Apache warrior reel nakedly on a calico pony and rush by with a rifle raised and pointed in his bony elbows. The gambler took a cool aim; the stockman fired and aimed again. The Englishman's sporting rifle blasted heavy echoes through the coach, hurting her ears, and the smell of powder got rank and bitter. The blond man's boots scraped the coach top and round small holes began to dimple the paneling as the Apache bullets struck. An Indian came boldly abreast the coach and made a target that couldn't be missed. The cattleman dropped him with one shot. The wheels screamed as they slowed around the sharp ruts and the whole heavy superstructure of the coach bounced high into the air. Then they were rushing downgrade.

The gambler said quietly, "You had better take this," handing Henriette his gun. He leaned against the door with his small hands gripping the sill. Pallor loosened his cheeks. He said to the army girl: "Be sure and keep between those gentlemen," and looked at her with a way that was desperate and forlorn and dropped his head to the window's sill.

Henriette saw the bluff rise up and close in like a yellow wall. They were rolling down the mountain without brake. Gunfire fell off and the crying of the Indians faded back. Coming up from her knees then she saw the desert's flat surface far below, with the angular pattern of Lordsburg vaguely on the far borders of the heat fog. There was no more firing and Happy Stuart's voice lifted again and the brakes were screaming on the wheels, and going off, and screaming again. The Englishman stared out of the window sullenly; the army girl seemed in a deep desperate dream; the cattleman's face was shining with a strange sweat. Henriette reached over to pull the gambler up, but he had an unnatural weight to him and slid into the far corner. She saw that he was dead.

At five o'clock that long afternoon the stage threaded Lordsburg's narrow streets of dobe and frame houses, came upon the center square and stopped before a crowd of people gathered in the smoky heat. The passengers crawled out stiffly. A Mexican boy ran up to see the dead gambler and began to yell his news in shrill Mexican. Malpais Bill climbed off the top, but Happy Stuart sat back on his seat and stared taciturnly at the crowd. Henriette noticed then that the shotgun messenger was gone.

A gray man in a sleazy white suit called up to Happy. "Well, you got through."

Happy Stuart said: "Yeah. We got through."

An officer stepped through the crowd, smiling at the army girl. He took her arm and said, "Miss Robertson, I believe. Lieutenant Hauser is quite all right. I will get your luggage—"

The army girl was crying then, definitely. They were all standing around, bone-weary and shaken. Malpais Bill remained by the wheel of the coach, his cheeks hard against the sunlight and his eyes riveted on a pair of men standing under the board awning of an adjoining store. Henriette observed the manner of their waiting and knew why they were here. The blond man's eyes, she noticed, were very blue and flame burned brilliantly in them. The army girl turned to Henriette, tears in her eyes. She murmured: "If there is anything I can ever do for you—"

But Henriette stepped back, shaking her head. This was Lordsburg and everybody knew her place except the army girl. Henriette said formally, "Good-by," noting how still and expectant the two men under the awning remained. She swung toward the blond man and said, "Would you carry my valise?"

Malpais Bill looked at her, laughter remote in his eyes, and reached into the luggage pile and got her battered valise. He was still smiling as he went beside her, through the crowd and past the two waiting men. But when they turned into an anonymous and dusty little side street of the town, where the houses all sat shoulder to shoulder without grace or dignity, he had turned sober. He said: "I am obliged to you. But I'll have to go back there."

They were in front of a house no different from its neighbors; they had stopped at its door. She could see his eyes travel this street and comprehend its meaning and the kind of traffic it bore. But he was saying in that gentle, melody-making tone:

"I have watched you for two days." He stopped, searching his mind to find the thing he wanted to say. It came out swiftly. "God made you a woman. The Tonto is a pretty country."

Her answer was quite barren of feeling. "No. I am known all through the Territory. But I can remember that you asked me."

He said: "No other reason?" She didn't answer but something in her eyes pulled his face together. He took off his hat and it seemed to her he was looking through this hot day to that far-off country and seeing it fresh and desirable. He murmured: "A man can escape nothing. I have got to do this. But I will be back."

He went along the narrow street, made a quick turn at the end of it, and disappeared. Heat rolled like a heavy wave over Lordsburg's house-tops and the smell of dust was very sharp. She lifted her valise, and dropped it and stood like that, mute and grave before the door of her dismal house. She was remembering how tall he had been against the moonlight at Gap Station.

There were four swift shots beating furiously along the sultry quiet, and a shout, and afterwards a longer and longer silence. She put one hand against the door to steady herself, and knew that those shots marked the end of a man, and the end of a hope. He would never come back; he would never stand over her in the moonlight with the long gentle smile on his lips and with the swing of life in his casual tone. She was thinking of all that humbly and with the patience life had beaten into her. . . .

She was thinking of all that when she heard the strike of boots on the street's packed earth; and turned to see him, high and square in the muddy sunlight, coming toward her with his smile.

OPEN WINTER

by H. L. DAVIS

H. L. Davis, like a number of other writers about the West, had a well-developed sense of humor. Sophisticated, his comedy is also less raucous. His humor shows itself in Honey in the Horn, *which won him a Pulitzer Prize, in* Beulah Land *and other novels as well as his short stories. An Oregonian, Davis portrayed a section of country generally slighted, and with a sense of actuality that had nothing whatever to do with Western myth. He was a realist and the kind of story-teller who might have written with equal authority about any other section of the country. In "Open Winter," from his story collection* Team Bells Woke Me, *he reveals the difference between his native state and other sections of the West.*

I

The drying east wind, which always brought hard luck to Eastern Oregon at whatever season it blew, had combed down the plateau grasslands through so much of the winter that it was hard to see any sign of grass ever having grown on them. Even though March had come, it still blew, drying the ground deep, shrinking the watercourses, beating back the clouds that might have delivered rain, and grinding coarse dust against the fifty-odd head of work horses that Pop Apling, with young Beech Cartwright helping, had brought down from his homestead to turn back into their home pasture while there was still something left of them.

The two men, one past sixty and the other around sixteen, shouldered the horses through the gate of the home pasture about dark, with lights beginning to shine out from the little freighting town across Three Notch Valley, and then they rode for the ranch house, knowing even before they drew up outside the yard that they had picked the wrong time to come. The house was too dark, and the corrals and outbuildings too still, for a place that anybody lived in.

There were sounds, but they were of shingles flapping in the wind, a windmill running loose and sucking noisily at a well that it had already pumped empty, a door that kept banging shut and dragging open again. The haystacks were gone, the stackyard fence had dwindled to a few naked posts, and the entire pasture was as bare and as hard as a floor all the way down into the valley.

The prospect looked so hopeless that the herd horses refused even to explore it, and merely stood with their tails turned to the wind, waiting to see what was to happen to them next.

Old Apling went poking inside the house, thinking somebody might have left a note or that the men might have run down to the saloon in town for an hour or two. He came back, having used up all his matches and stopped the door from banging, and said the place appeared to have been handed back to the Government, or maybe the mortgage company.

"You can trust old Ream Gervais not to be any place where anybody wants him," Beech said. He had hired out to herd for Ream Gervais over the winter. That entitled him to be more critical than old Apling, who had merely contracted to supply the horse herd with feed and pasture for the season at so much per head. "Well, my job was to help herd these steeds while you had 'em, and to help deliver 'em back when you got through with 'em, and here they are. I've put in a week on 'em that I won't ever git paid for, and it won't help anything to set around and watch 'em try to live on fence pickets. Let's git out."

Old Apling looked at the huddle of horses, at the naked slope with a glimmer of light still on it, and at the lights of the town twinkling in the wind. He said it wasn't his place to tell any man what to do, but that he wouldn't feel quite right to dump the horses and leave.

"I agreed to see that they got delivered back here, and I'd feel better about it if I could locate somebody to deliver 'em to," he said. "I'd like to ride across to town yonder, and see if there ain't somebody that knows something about 'em. You could hold 'em together here till I git back. We ought to look the fences over before we pull out, and you can wait here as well as anywhere else."

"I can't, but go ahead," Beech said. "I don't like to have 'em stand around and look at me when I can't do anything to help 'em out. They'd have been better off if we'd turned 'em out of your homestead and let 'em run loose on the country. There was more grass up there than there is here."

"There wasn't enough to feed 'em, and I'd have had all my neighbors down on me for it," old Apling said. "You'll find out one of these days that if a man aims to live in this world he's got to git along with the people in it. I'd start a fire and thaw out a little and git that pack horse unloaded, if I was you."

He rode down the slope, leaning low and forward to ease the drag of the wind on his tired horse. Beech heard the sound of the road gate being let down and put up again, the beat of hoofs in the hard road, and then nothing but the noises around him as the wind went through its usual process of easing down for the night to make room for the frost. Loose boards settled into place, the windmill clacked to a stop and began to drip water into a puddle, and the herd horses shifted around facing Beech, as if anxious not to miss anything he did.

He pulled off some fence pickets and built a fire, unsaddled his pony and unloaded the pack horse, and got out what was left of a sack of grain and fed them both, standing the herd horses off with a fence picket until they had finished eating.

That was strictly fair, for the pack horse and the saddle pony had worked harder and carried more weight than any of the herd animals, and the grain was little enough to even them up for it. Nevertheless, he felt mean at having to club animals away from food when they were hungry, and they crowded back and eyed the grain sack so wistfully that he carried it inside the yard and stored it down in the root cellar behind the house, so it wouldn't prey on their minds. Then he dumped another armload of fence pickets onto the fire and sat down to wait for old Apling.

The original mistake, he reflected, had been when old Apling took the Gervais horses to feed at the beginning of winter. Contracting to feed them had been well enough, for he had nursed up a stand of bunch grass on his homestead that would have carried an ordinary pack of horses with only a little extra feeding to help out in the roughest weather. But the Gervais horses were all big harness stock, they had pulled in half starved, and they had taken not much over three weeks to clean off the pasture that old Apling had expected would last them at least two months. Nobody would have blamed him for backing out on his agreement then, since he had only undertaken to feed the horses, not to treat them for malnutrition.

Beech wanted him to back out of it, but he refused to, said the stockmen had enough troubles without having that added to them, and started feeding out his hay and insisting that the dry wind couldn't possibly keep up much longer, because it wasn't in Nature.

By the time it became clear that Nature had decided to take in a little extra territory, the hay was all fed out, and, since there couldn't be any accommodation about letting the horses starve to death, he consented to throw the contract over and bring them back where they belonged.

The trouble with most of old Apling's efforts to be accommodating was that they did nobody any good. His neighbors would have been spared all their uneasiness if he had never brought in the horses to begin with. Gervais wouldn't have been any worse off, since he stood to lose them anyway; the horses could have starved to death as gracefully in November as in March, and old Apling would have been ahead a great deal of carefully accumulated bunch grass and two big stacks of extortionately valuable hay. Nobody had gained by his chivalrousness; he had lost by it, and yet he liked it so well that he couldn't stand to leave the horses until he had raked the country for somebody to hand the worthless brutes over to.

Beech fed sticks into the fire and felt out of patience with a man who could stick to his mistakes even after he had been cleaned out by them. He heard the road gate open and shut, and he knew by the draggy-sounding plod of old Apling's horse that the news from town was going to be bad.

Old Apling rode past the fire and over to the picket fence, got off as if he was trying to make it last, tied his horse carefully as if he expected the knot to last a month, and unsaddled and did up his latigo and folded his saddle blanket as if he was fixing them to put in a show window. He remarked that his horse had been given a bait of grain in town and wouldn't need feeding again, and then he began to work down to what he had found out.

"If you think things look bad along this road, you ought to see that town," he said. "All the sheep gone and all the ranches deserted and no

trade to run on and their water threatenin' to give out. They've got a little
herd of milk cows that they keep up for their children, and to hear 'em
talk you'd think it was an ammunition supply that they expected to stand
off hostile Indians with. They said Gervais pulled out of here around a
month ago. All his men quit him, so he bunched his sheep and took 'em
down to the railroad, where he could ship in hay for 'em. Sheep will be a
price this year, and you won't be able to buy a lamb for under twelve
dollars except at a fire sale. Horses ain't in much demand. There's been
a lot of 'em turned out wild, and everybody wants to get rid of 'em."

"I didn't drive this bunch of pelters any eighty miles against the wind
to git a market report," Beech said. "You didn't find anybody to turn 'em
over to, and Gervais didn't leave any word about what he wanted done
with 'em. You've probably got it figured out that you ought to trail 'em
a hundred and eighty miles to the railroad, so his feelings won't be hurt,
and you're probably tryin' to study how you can work me in on it, and
you might as well save your time. I've helped you with your accommodation jobs long enough. I've quit, and it would have been a whole lot better
for you if I'd quit sooner."

Old Apling said he could understand that state of feeling, which didn't
mean that he shared it.

"It wouldn't be as much of a trick to trail down to the railroad as a
man might think," he said, merely to settle a question of fact. "We
couldn't make it by the road in a starve-out year like this, but there's old
Indian trails back on the ridge where any man has got a right to take livestock whenever he feels like it. Still, as long as you're set against it, I'll
meet you halfway. We'll trail these horses down the ridge to a grass patch
where I used to corral cattle when I was in the business, and we'll leave
'em there. It'll be enough so they won't starve, and I'll ride on down and
notify Gervais where they are, and you can go where you please. It
wouldn't be fair to do less than that, to my notion."

"Ream Gervais triggered me out of a week's pay," Beech said. "It ain't
much, but he swindled you on that pasture contract too. If you expect me
to trail his broken-down horses ninety miles down this ridge when they
ain't worth anything, you've turned in a poor guess. You'll have to think
of a better argument than that if you aim to gain any ground with me."

"Ream Gervais don't count in this," old Apling said. "What does he
care about these horses, when he ain't even left word what he wants done
with 'em? What counts is you, and I don't have to think up any better
argument, because I've already got one. You may not realize it, but you
and me are responsible for these horses till they're delivered to their
owner, and if we turn 'em loose here to bust fences and overrun that town
and starve to death in the middle of it, we'll land in the pen. It's against the
law to let horses starve to death, did you know that? If you pull out of
here I'll pull out right along with you, and I'll have every man in that

town after you before the week's out. You'll have a chance to git some action on that pistol of yours, if you're careful."

Beech said he wasn't intimidated by that kind of talk, and threw a couple of handfuls of dirt on the fire, so it wouldn't look so conspicuous. His pistol was an old single-action relic with its grips tied on with fish line and no trigger, so that it had to be operated by flipping the hammer. The spring was weak, so that sometimes it took several flips to get off one shot. Suggesting that he might use such a thing to stand off any pack of grim-faced pursuers was about the same as saying that he was simple-minded. As far as he could see, his stand was entirely sensible, and even humane.

"It ain't that I don't feel sorry for these horses, but they ain't fit to travel," he said. "They wouldn't last twenty miles. I don't see how it's any worse to let 'em stay here than to walk 'em to death down that ridge."

"They make less trouble for people if you keep 'em on the move," old Apling said. "It's something you can't be cinched for in court, and it makes you feel better afterwards to know that you tried everything you could. Suit yourself about it, though. I ain't beggin' you to do it. If you'd sooner pull out and stand the consequences, it's you for it. Before you go, what did you do with that sack of grain?"

Beech had half a notion to leave, just to see how much of that dark threatening would come to pass. He decided that it wouldn't be worth it. "I'll help you trail the blamed skates as far as they'll last, if you've got to be childish about it," he said. "I put the grain in a root cellar behind the house, so the rats wouldn't git into it. It looked like the only safe place around here. There was about a half a ton of old sprouted potatoes ricked up in it that didn't look like they'd been bothered for twenty years. They had sprouts on 'em—" He stopped, noticing that old Apling kept staring at him as if something was wrong. "Good Lord, potatoes ain't good for horse feed, are they? They had sprouts on 'em a foot long!"

Old Apling shook his head resignedly and got up. "We wouldn't ever find anything if it wasn't for you," he said. "We wouldn't ever git any good out of it if it wasn't for me, so maybe we make a team. Show me where that root cellar is, and we'll pack them spuds out and spread 'em around so the horses can git started on 'em. We'll git this herd through to grass-land yet, and it'll be something you'll never be ashamed of. It ain't every-body your age gits a chance to do a thing like this, and you'll thank me for holdin' you to it before you're through."

II

They climbed up by an Indian trail onto a high stretch of tableland, so stony and scored with rock breaks that nobody had ever tried to cultivate it, but so high that it sometimes caught moisture from the atmosphere that the lower elevations missed. Part of it had been doled out among the Indians as allotment lands, which none of them ever bothered to lay claim to, but the main spread of it belonged to the nation, which was too busy to notice it.

The pasture was thin, though reliable, and it was so scantily watered and so rough and broken that in ordinary years nobody bothered to bring stock onto it. The open winter had spoiled most of that seclusion. There was no part of the trail that didn't have at least a dozen new bed grounds for lambed ewes in plain view, easily picked out of the landscape because of the little white flags stuck up around them to keep sheep from straying out and coyotes from straying in during the night. The sheep were pasturing down the draws out of the wind, where they couldn't be seen. There were no herders visible, not any startling amount of grass, and no water except a mud tank thrown up to catch a little spring for one of the camps.

They tried to water the horses in it, but it had taken up the flavor of sheep, so that not a horse in the herd would touch it. It was too near dark to waste time reasoning with them about it, so old Apling headed them down into a long rock break and across it to a tangle of wild cherry and mountain mahogany that lasted for several miles and ended in a grass clearing among some dwarf cottonwoods with a mud puddle in the center of it.

The grass had been grazed over, though not closely, and there were sheep tracks around the puddle that seemed to be fresh, for the horses, after sniffing the water, decided that they could wait a while longer. They spread out to graze, and Beech remarked that he couldn't see where it was any improvement over the tickle-grass homesteads.

"The grass may be better, but there ain't as much of it, and the water ain't any good if they won't drink it," he said. "Well, do you intend to leave 'em here, or have you got some wrinkle figured out to make me help trail 'em on down to the railroad?"

Old Apling stood the sarcasm unresistingly. "It would be better to trail 'em to the railroad, now that we've got this far," he said. "I won't ask you to do that much, because it's outside of what you agreed to. This place has changed since I was here last, but we'll make it do, and that water ought to clear up fit to drink before long. You can settle down here for a few days while I ride around and fix it up with the sheep camps to let the horses stay here. We've got to do that, or they're liable to think it's some wild bunch and start shootin' 'em. Somebody's got to stay with 'em, and I can git along with these herders better than you can."

"If you've got any sense, you'll let them sheep outfits alone," Beech said. "They don't like tame horses on this grass any better than they do wild ones, and they won't make any more bones about shootin' 'em if they find out they're in here. It's a hard place to find, and they'll stay close on account of the water, and you'd better pull out and let 'em have it themselves. That's what I aim to do."

"You've done what you agreed to, and I ain't got any right to hold you any longer," old Apling said. "I wish I could. You're wrong about them sheep outfits. I've got as much right to pasture this ridge as they have, and they know it, and nobody ever lost anything by actin' sociable with people."

"Somebody will before very long," Beech said. "I've got relatives in the sheep business, and I know what they're like. You'll land yourself in trouble, and I don't want to be around when you do it. I'm pullin' out of here in the morning, and if you had any sense you'd pull out along with me."

There were several things that kept Beech from getting much sleep during the night. One was the attachment that the horses showed for his sleeping place; they stuck so close that he could almost feel their breath on him, could hear the soft breaking sound that the grass made as they pulled it, the sound of their swallowing, the jar of the ground under him when one of the horses changed ground, the peaceful regularity of their eating, as if they didn't have to bother about anything so long as they kept old Apling in sight.

Another irritating thing was old Apling's complete freedom from uneasiness. He ought by rights to have felt more worried about the future than Beech did, but he slept, with the hard ground for a bed and his hard saddle for a pillow and the horses almost stepping on him every minute or two, as soundly as if the entire trip had come out exactly to suit him and there was nothing ahead but plain sailing.

His restfulness was so hearty and so unjustifiable that Beech couldn't sleep for feeling indignant about it, and got up and left about daylight to keep from being exposed to any more of it. He left without waking old Apling, because he saw no sense in a leave-taking that would consist merely in repeating his common-sense warnings and having them ignored, and he was so anxious to get clear of the whole layout that he didn't even take along anything to eat. The only thing he took from the pack was his ramshackle old pistol; there was no holster for it, and, in the hope that he might get a chance to use it on a loose quail or prairie chicken, he stowed it in an empty flour sack and hung it on his saddle horn, a good deal like an old squaw heading for the far blue distances with a bundle of diapers.

III

There was never anything recreational about traveling a rock desert at any season of the year, and the combination of spring gales, winter chilliness and summer drought all striking at once brought it fairly close to hard punishment. Beech's saddle pony, being jaded at the start with overwork and underfeeding and no water, broke down in the first couple of miles, and got so feeble and tottery that Beech had to climb off and lead him, searching likely-looking thickets all the way down the gully in the hope of finding some little trickle that he wouldn't be too finicky to drink.

The nearest he came to it was a fair-sized rock sink under some big half-budded cottonwoods that looked, by its dampness and the abundance of fresh animal tracks around it, as if it might have held water recently, but of water there was none, and even digging a hole in the center of the basin failed to fetch a drop.

The work of digging, hill climbing and scrambling through brush piles raised Beech's appetite so powerfully that he could scarcely hold up, and a little above where the gully opened into the flat sagebrush plateau, he threw away his pride, pistoled himself a jack rabbit, and took it down into the sagebrush to cook, where his fire wouldn't give away which gully old Apling was camped in.

Jack rabbit didn't stand high as a food. It was considered an excellent thing to give men in the last stages of famine, because they weren't likely to injure themselves by eating too much of it, but for ordinary occasions it was looked down on, and Beech covered his trail out of the gully and built his cooking fire in the middle of a high stand of sagebrush, so as not to be embarrassed by inquisitive visitors.

The meat cooked up strong, as it always did, but he ate what he needed of it, and he was wrapping the remainder in his flour sack to take along with him when a couple of men rode past, saw his pony, and turned in to look him over.

They looked him over so closely and with so little concern for his privacy that he felt insulted before they even spoke.

He studied them less openly, judging by their big gallon canteens that they were out on some long scout.

One of them was some sort of hired hand, by his looks; he was broad-faced and gloomy-looking, with a fine white horse, a flower-stamped saddle, an expensive rifle scabbarded under his knee, and a fifteen-dollar saddle blanket, while his own manly form was set off by a yellow hotel blanket and a ninety-cent pair of overalls.

The other man had on a store suit, a plain black hat, fancy stitched boots, and a white shirt and necktie, and rode a burr-tailed Indian pony and an old wrangling saddle with a loose horn. He carried no weapons in sight, but there was a narrow strap across the lower spread of his necktie which indicated the presence of a shoulder holster somewhere within reach.

He opened the conversation by inquiring where Beech had come from, what his business was, where he was going and why he hadn't taken the county road to go there, and why he had to eat jack rabbit when the country was littered with sheep camps where he could get a decent meal by asking for it?

"I come from the upper country," Beech said, being purposely vague about it. "I'm travelin', and I stopped here because my horse give out. He won't drink out of any place that's had sheep in it, and he's gone short of water till he breaks down easy."

"There's a place corralled in for horses to drink at down at my lower camp," the man said, and studied Beech's pony. "There's no reason for you to bum through the country on jack rabbit in a time like this. My herder can take you down to our water hole and see that you get fed and put to work till you can make a stake for yourself. I'll give you a note. That pony looks like he had Ream Gervais' brand on him. Do you know anything about that herd of old work horses he's been pasturing around?"

"I don't know anything about him," Beech said, sidestepping the actual question while he thought over the offer of employment. He could have used a stake, but the location didn't strike him favorably. It was too close to old Apling's camp, he could see trouble ahead over the horse herd, and he didn't want to be around when it started. "If you'll direct me how to find your water, I'll ride on down there, but I don't need anybody to go with me, and I don't need any stake. I'm travelin'."

The man said there wasn't anybody so well off that he couldn't use a stake, and that it would be hardly any trouble at all for Beech to get one. "I want you to understand how we're situated around here, so you won't think we're any bunch of stranglers," he said. "You can see what kind of a year this has been, when we have to run lambed ewes in a rock patch like this. We've got five thousand lambs in here that we're trying to bring through, and we've had to fight the blamed wild horses for this pasture since the day we moved in. A horse that ain't worth hell room will eat as much as two dozen sheep worth twenty dollars, with the lambs, so you can see how it figures out. We've got 'em pretty well thinned out, but one of my packers found a trail of a new bunch that came up from around Three Notch within the last day or two, and we don't want them to feel as if we'd neglected them. We'd like to find out where they lit. You wouldn't have any information about 'em?"

"None that would do you any good to know," Beech said. "I know the man with that horse herd, and it ain't any use to let on that I don't, but it wouldn't be any use to try to deal with him. He don't sell out on a man he works for."

"He might be induced to," the man said. "We'll find him anyhow, but I don't like to take too much time to it. Just for instance, now, suppose you knew that pony of yours would have to go thirsty till you gave us a few directions about that horse herd? You'd be stuck here for quite a spell, wouldn't you?"

He was so pleasant about it that it took Beech a full minute to realize that he was being threatened. The heavy-set herder brought that home to him by edging out into a flank position and hoisting his rifle scabbard so it could be reached in a hurry. Beech removed the cooked jack rabbit from his flour sack carefully, a piece at a time, and, with the same mechanical thoughtfulness, brought out his triggerless old pistol, cut down on the pleasant-spoken man, and hauled back on the hammer and held it poised.

"That herder of yours had better go easy on his rifle," he said, trying to keep his voice from trembling. "This pistol shoots if I don't hold back the hammer, and if he knocks me out I'll have to let go of it. You'd better watch him, if you don't want your tack drove. I won't give you no directions about that horse herd, and this pony of mine won't go thirsty for it, either. Loosen them canteens of yours and let 'em drop on the ground. Drop that rifle scabbard back where it belongs, and unbuckle the straps and let go of it. If either of you tries any funny business, there'll be one of you to pack home, heels first."

The quaver in his voice sounded childish and undignified to him, but it had a more businesslike ring to them than any amount of manly gruffness. The herder unbuckled his rifle scabbard, and they both cast loose their canteen straps, making it last as long as they could while they argued with him, not angrily, but as if he was a dull stripling whom they wanted to save from some foolishness that he was sure to regret. They argued ethics, justice, common sense, his future prospects, and the fact that what he was doing amounted to robbery by force and arms and that it was his first fatal step into a probably unsuccessful career of crime. They worried over him, they explained themselves to him, and they ridiculed him.

They managed to make him feel like several kinds of a fool, and they were so pleasant and concerned about it that they came close to breaking him down. What held him steady was the thought of old Apling waiting up the gully.

"That herder with the horses never sold out on any man, and I won't sell out on him," he said. "You've said your say and I'm tired of holdin' this pistol on cock for you, so move along out of here. Keep to open ground, so I can be sure you're gone, and don't be in too much of a hurry to come back. I've got a lot of things I want to think over, and I want to be let alone while I do it."

IV

He did have some thinking that needed tending to, but he didn't take time for it. When the men were well out of range, he emptied their canteens into his hat and let his pony drink. Then he hung the canteens and the scabbarded rifle on a bush and rode back up the gully where the horse camp was, keeping to shaly ground so as not to leave any tracks. It was harder going up than it had been coming down.

He had turned back from the scene of his run-in with the two sheepmen about noon, and he was still a good two miles from the camp when the sun went down, the wind lulled and the night frost began to bite at him so hard that he dismounted and walked to get warm. That raised his appetite again, and, as if by some special considerateness of Nature, the cottonwoods around him seemed to be alive with jack rabbits heading down into the pitch-dark gully where he had fooled away valuable time trying to find water that morning.

They didn't stimulate his hunger much; for a time they even made him feel less like eating anything. Then his pony gave out and had to rest, and, noticing that the cotonwoods around him were beginning to bud out, he remembered that peeling the bark off in the buding season would fetch out a foamy, sweet-tasting sap which, among children of the plateau country, was considered something of a delicacy.

He cut a blaze on a fair-sized sapling, waited ten minutes or so, and touched his finger to it to see how much sap had accumulated. None had; the blaze was moist to his touch, but scarcely more so than when he had whittled it.

It wasn't important enough to do any bothering about, and yet a whole set of observed things began to draw together in his mind and form themselves into an explanation of something he had puzzled over: the fresh animal tracks he had seen around the rock sink when there wasn't any water; the rabbits going down into the gully; the cottonwoods in which the sap rose enough during the day to produce buds and got driven back at night when the frost set in. During the day, the cottonwoods had drawn the water out of the ground for themselves; at night they stopped drawing it, and it drained out into the rock sink for the rabbits.

It all worked out so simply that he led his pony down into the gully to see how much there was in it, and, losing his footing on the steep slope, coasted down into the rock sink in the dark and landed in water and thin mud up to his knees. He led his pony down into it to drink, which seemed litle enough to get back for the time he had fooled away on it, and then he headed for the horse camp, which was all too easily discernible by the plume of smoke rising, white and ostentatious, against the dark sky from old Apling's campfire.

He made the same kind of entrance that old Apling usually affected when bringing some important item of news. He rode past the campfire and pulled up at a tree, got off deliberately, knocked an accumulation of dead twigs from his hat, took off his saddle and bridle and balanced them painstakingly in the tree fork, and said it was affecting to see how widespread the shortage of pasture was.

"It generally is," old Apling said. "I had a kind of a notion you'd be back after you'd had time to study things over. I suppose you got into some kind of a rumpus with some of them sheep outfits. What was it? Couldn't you git along with them, or couldn't they hit it off with you?"

"There wasn't any trouble between them and me," Beech said. "The only point we had words over was you. They wanted to know where you was camped, so they could shoot you up, and I didn't think it was right to tell 'em. I had to put a gun on a couple of 'em before they'd believe I meant business, and that was all there was to it. They're out after you now, and they can see the smoke of this fire of yours for twenty miles, so they ought to be along almost any time now. I thought I'd come back and see you work your sociability on 'em."

"You probably kicked up a squabble with 'em yourself," old Apling said. He looked a little uneasy. "You talked right up to 'em, I'll bet, and slapped their noses with your hat to show 'em that they couldn't run over you. Well, what's done is done. You did come back, and maybe they'd have jumped us anyway. There ain't much that we can do. The horses have got to have water before they can travel, and they won't touch that seep. It ain't cleared up a particle."

"You can put that fire out, not but what the whole country has probably seen the smoke from it already," Beech said. "If you've got to tag after these horses, you can run 'em off down the draw and keep 'em to the brush where they won't leave a trail. There's some young cottonwood bark that they can eat if they have to, and there's water in a rock sink under some big cottonwood trees. I'll stay here and hold off anybody that shows up, so you'll have time to git your tracks covered."

Old Apling went over and untied the flour-sacked pistol from Beech's saddle, rolled it into his blankets, and sat down on it. "If there's any holdin' off to be done, I'll do it," he said. "You're a little too high-spirited to suit me, and a little too hasty about your conclusions. I looked over that rock sink down the draw today, and there wasn't anything in it but mud, and blamed little of that. Somebody had dug for water, and there wasn't none."

"There is now," Beech said. He tugged off one of his wet boots and poured about a pint of the disputed fluid on the ground. "There wasn't any in the daytime because the cottonwoods took it all. They let up when it turns cold, and it runs back in. I waded in it."

He started to put his boot back on. Old Apling reached out and took it, felt of it inside and out, and handed it over as if performing some ceremonial presentation.

"I'd never have figured out a thing like that in this world," he said. "If we git them horses out of here, it'll be you that done it. We'll bunch 'em and work 'em down there. It won't be no picnic, but we'll make out to handle it somehow. We've got to, after a thing like this."

Beech remembered what had occasioned the discovery, and said he would have to have something to eat first. "I want you to keep in mind that it's you I'm doin' this for," he said. "I don't owe that old groundhog of a Ream Gervais anything. The only thing I hate about this is that it'll look like I'd done him a favor."

"He won't take it for one, I guess," old Apling said. "We've got to git these horses out because it'll be a favor to you. You wouldn't want to have it told around that you'd done a thing like findin' that water, and then have to admit that we'd lost all the horses anyhow. We can't lose 'em. You've acted like a man tonight, and I'll be blamed if I'll let you spoil it for any childish spite."

They got the horses out none too soon. Watering them took a long time, and when they finally did consent to call it enough and climb back up the side hill, Beech and old Apling heard a couple of signal shots from the direction of their old camping place, and saw a big glare mount up into the sky from it as the visitors built up their campfire to look the locality over. The sight was almost comforting; if they had to keep away from a pursuit, it was at least something to know where it was.

V

From then on they followed a grab-and-run policy, scouting ahead before they moved, holding to the draws by day and crossing open ground only after dark, never pasturing over a couple of hours in any one place, and discovering food value in outlandish substances—rock lichens, the sprouts of wild plum and serviceberry, the moss of old trees and the bark of some young ones—that neither they nor the horses had ever considered fit to eat before. When they struck Boulder River Canyon they dropped down and toenailed their way along one side of it where they could find grass and water with less likelihood of having trouble about it.

The breaks of the canyon were too rough to run new-lambed sheep in, and they met with so few signs of occupancy that old Apling got overconfident, neglected his scouting to tie back a break they had been obliged to make in a line fence, and ran the horse herd right over the top of a camp where some men were branding calves, tearing down a cook tent and part of a corral and scattering cattle and bedding from the river all the way to the top of the canyon.

By rights, they should have sustained some damage for that piece of carelessness, but they drove through fast, and they were out of sight around a shoulder of rimrock before any of the men could get themselves picked up. Somebody did throw a couple of shots after them as they were pulling into a thicket of mock orange and chokecherry, but it was only with a pistol, and he probably did it more to relieve his feelings than with any hope of hitting anything.

They were so far out of range that they couldn't even hear where the bullets landed.

Neither of them mentioned that unlucky run-in all the rest of that day. They drove hard, punished the horses savagely when they lagged, and kept them at it until, a long time after dark, they struck an old rope ferry that crossed Boulder River at a place called, in memory of its original founders, Robbers' Roost.

The ferry wasn't a public carrier, and there was not even any main road down to it. It was used by the ranches in the neighborhood as the only means of crossing the river for fifty miles in either direction, and it was tied in to a log with a good solid chain and padlock. It was a way to cross, and neither of them could see anything else but to take it.

Beech favored waiting for daylight for it, pointing out that there was a ranch light half a mile up the slope, and that if anybody caught them hustling a private ferry in the dead of night they would probably be taken for criminals on the dodge. Old Apling said it was altogether likely, and drew Beech's pistol and shot the padlock apart with it.

"They could hear that up at that ranch house," Beech said. "What if they come pokin' down here to see what we're up to?"

Old Apling tossed the fragments of padlock into the river and hung the pistol in the waistband of his trousers. "Let 'em come," he said. "They'll go back again with their fingers in their mouths. This is your trip, and you put in good work on it, and I like to ruined the whole thing stoppin' to patch an eighty-cent fence so some scissorbill wouldn't have his feelings hurt, and that's the last accommodation anybody gits out of me till this is over with. I can take about six horses at a trip, it looks like. Help me to bunch 'em."

Six horses at a trip proved to be an overestimate. The best they could do was five, and the boat rode so deep with them that Beech refused to risk handling it. He stayed with the herd, and old Apling cut it loose, let the current sweep it across into slack water, and hauled it in to the far bank by winding in its cable on an old homemade capstan. Then he turned the horses into a counting pen and came back for another load.

He worked at it fiercely, as if he had a bet up that he could wear the whole ferry rig out, but it went with infernal slowness, and when the wind began to move for daylight there were a dozen horses still to cross and no place to hide them in case the ferry had other customers.

Beech waited and fidgeted over small noises until, hearing voices and the clatter of hoofs on shale far up the canyon behind him, he gave way, drove the remaining horses into the river, and swam them across, letting himself be towed along by his saddle horn and floating his clothes ahead of him on a board.

He paid for that flurry of nervousness before he got out. The water was so cold it paralyzed him, and so swift it whisked him a mile downstream before he could get his pony turned to breast it. He grounded on a gravel bar in a thicket of dwarf pillows, with numbness striking clear to the center of his diaphragm and deadening his arms so he couldn't pick his clothes loose from the bundle to put on. He managed it, by using his teeth and elbows, and warmed himself a little by driving the horses afoot through the brush till he struck the ferry landing.

It had got light enough to see things in outline, and old Apling was getting ready to shove off for another crossing when the procession came lumbering at him out of the shadows. He came ashore, counted the horses into the corral to make sure none had drowned, and laid Beech under all the blankets and built up a fire to limber him out by. He got breakfast and got packed to leave, and he did some rapid expounding about the iniquity of risking the whole trip on such a wild piece of foolhardiness.

"That was the reason I wanted you to work this boat," he said. "I could have stood up to anybody that come projectin' around, and if they wanted trouble I could have filled their order for 'em. They won't bother us now, anyhow; it don't matter how bad they want to."

"I could have stood up to 'em if I'd had anything to do it with," Beech said. "You've got that pistol of mine, and I couldn't see to throw rocks. What makes you think they won't bother us? You know it was that brandin' crew comin' after us, don't you?"

"I expect that's who it was," old Apling agreed. "They ought to be out after the cattle we scattered, but you can trust a bunch of cowboys to pick out the most useless things to tend to first. I've got that pistol of yours because I don't aim for you to git in trouble with it while this trip is on. There won't anybody bother us because I've cut all the cables on the ferry, and it's lodged downstream on a gravel spit. If anybody crosses after us within fifty miles of here, he'll swim, and the people around here ain't as reckless around cold water as you are."

Beech sat up. "We got to git out of here," he said. "There's people on this side of the river that use that ferry, you old fool, and they'll have us up before every grand jury in the country from now on. The horses ain't worth it."

"What the horses is worth ain't everything," old Apling said. "There's a part of this trip ahead that you'll be glad you went through. You're entitled to that much out of it, after the work you've put in, and I aim to see that you git it. It ain't any use tryin' to explain to you what it is. You'll notice it when the time comes."

VI

They worked north, following the breaks of the river canyon, finding the rock breaks hard to travel, but easy to avoid observation in, and the grass fair in stand, but so poor and washy in body that the horses had to spend most of their time eating enough to keep up their strength so they could move.

They struck a series of gorges, too deep and precipitous to be crossed at all, and had to edge back into milder country where there were patches of plowed ground, some being harrowed over for summer fallow and others venturing out with a bright new stand of dark-green wheat.

The pasture was patchy and scoured by the wind, and all the best parts of it were under fence, which they didn't dare cut for fear of getting in trouble with the natives. Visibility was high in that section; the ground lay open to the north as far as they could see, the wind kept the air so clear that it hurt to look at the sky, and they were never out of sight of wheat ranchers harrowing down summer fallow.

A good many of the ranchers pulled up and stared after the horse herd as it went past, and two or three times they waved and rode down toward the road, as if they wanted to make it an excuse for stopping work. Old Apling surmised that they had some warning they wanted to deliver against trespassing, and he drove on without waiting to hear it.

They were unable to find a camping place anywhere among those wheat fields, so they drove clear through to open country and spread down for the night alongside a shallow pond in the middle of some new grass not far enough along to be pastured, though the horses made what they could out of it. There were no trees or shrubs anywhere around, not even sagebrush. Lacking fuel for a fire, they camped without one, and since there was no grass anywhere except around the pond, they left the horses unguarded, rolled in to catch up sleep, and were awakened about daylight by the whole herd stampeding past them at a gallop.

They both got up and moved fast. Beech ran for his pony, which was trying to pull loose from its picket rope to go with the bunch. Old Apling ran out into the dust afoot, waggling the triggerless old pistol and trying to make out objects in the half-light by hard squinting. The herd horses fetched a long circle and came back past him, with a couple of riders clouting along behind trying to turn them back into open country. One of the riders opened up a rope and swung it, the other turned in and slapped the inside flankers with his hat, and old Apling hauled up the old pistol, flipped the hammer a couple of rounds to get it warmed up, and let go at them twice.

The half darkness held noise as if it had been a cellar. The two shots banged monstrously, Beech yelled to old Apling to be careful who he shot at, and the two men shied off sideways and rode away into the open country. One of them yelled something that sounded threatening in tone as they went out of sight, but neither of them seemed in the least inclined to bring on any general engagement. The dust blew clear, the herd horses came back to grass, old Apling looked at the pistol and punched the two exploded shells out of it, and Beech ordered him to hand it over before he got in trouble with it.

"How do you know but what them men had a right here?" he demanded sternly. "We'd be in a fine jack pot if you'd shot one of 'em and it turned out he owned this land we're on, wouldn't we?"

Old Apling looked at him, holding the old pistol poised as if he was getting ready to lead a band with it. The light strengthened and shed a rose-colored radiance over him, so he looked flushed and joyous and lifted

up. With some of the dust knocked off him, he could have filled in easily
as a day star and son of the morning, whiskers and all.

"I wouldn't have shot them men for anything you could buy me!" he
said, and faced north to a blue line of bluffs that come up out of the
shadows, a blue gleam of water that moved under them, a white steamboat that moved upstream, glittering as the first light struck it. "Them
men wasn't here because we was trespassers. Them was horse thieves,
boy! We've brought these horses to a place where they're worth stealin',
and we've brought 'em through! The railroad is under them bluffs, and
that water down there is the old Columbia River!"

They might have made it down to the river that day, but having it in
sight and knowing that nothing could stop them from reaching it, there
no longer seemed any object in driving so unsparingly. They ate breakfast
and talked about starting, and they even got partly packed up for it. Then
they got occupied with talking to a couple of wheat ranchers who pulled
in to inquire about buying some of the horse herd; the drought had run
up wheat prices at a time when the country's livestock had been allowed
to run down, and so many horses had been shot and starved out that they
were having to take pretty much anything they could get.

Old Apling swapped them a couple of the most jaded herd horses for
part of a haystack, referred other applicants to Gervais down at the railroad, and spent the remainder of the day washing, patching clothes and
saddlery, and watching the horses get acquainted once more with a conven-
tional diet.

The next morning a rancher dropped off a note from Gervais urging
them to come right on down, and adding a kind but firm admonition
against running up any feed bills without his express permission. He made
it sound as if there might be some hurry about catching the horse market
on the rise, so they got ready to leave, and Beech looked back over the
road they had come, thinking of all that had happened on it.

"I'd like it better if old Gervais didn't have to work himself in on the
end of it," he said. "I'd like to step out on the whole business right now."

"You'd be a fool to do that," old Apling said. "This is outside your work
contract, so we can make the old gopher pay you what it's worth. I'll
want to go in ahead and see about that and about the money that he owes
me and about corral space and feed and one thing and another, so I'll want
you to bring 'em in alone. You ain't seen everything there is to a trip
like this, and you won't unless you stay with it."

VII

There would be no ending to this story without an understanding of
what that little river town looked like at the hour, a little before sundown
of a windy spring day, when Beech brought the desert horse herd down

into it. On the wharf below town, some men were unloading baled hay from a steamboat, with some passengers watching from the saloon deck, and the river beyond them hoisting into white-capped peaks that shone and shed dazzling spray over the darkening water.

A switch engine was handling stock cars on a spur track, and the brakeman flagged it to a stop and stood watching the horses, leaning into the wind to keep his balance while the engineer climbed out on the tender to see what was going on.

The street of the town was lined with big leafless poplars that looked as if they hadn't gone short of moisture a day of their lives; the grass under them was bright green, and there were women working around flower beds and pulling up weeds, enough of them so that a horse could have lived on them for two days.

There was a Chinaman clipping grass with a pair of sheep shears to keep it from growing too tall, and there were lawn sprinklers running clean water on the ground in streams. There were stores with windows full of new clothes, and stores with bright hardware, and stores with strings of bananas and piles of oranges, bread and crackers and candy and rows of hams, and there were groups of anxious-faced men sitting around stoves inside who came out to watch Beech pass and told one another hopefully that the back country might make a good year out of it yet, if a youngster could bring that herd of horses through it.

There were women who hauled back their children and cautioned them not to get in the man's way, and there were boys and girls, some near Beech's own age, who watched him and stood looking after him, knowing that he had been through more than they had ever seen and not suspecting that it had taught him something that they didn't know about the things they saw every day. None of them knew what it meant to be in a place where there were delicacies to eat and new clothes to wear and look at, what it meant to be warm and out of the wind for a change, what it could mean merely to have water enough to pour on the ground and grass enough to cut down and throw away.

For the first time, seeing how the youngsters looked at him, he understood what that amounted to. There wasn't a one of them who wouldn't have traded places with him. There wasn't one that he would have traded places with, for all the haberdashery and fancy groceries in town. He turned down to the corrals, and old Apling held the gate open for him and remarked that he hadn't taken much time to it.

"You're sure you had enough of that ridin' through town?" he said. "It ain't the same when you do it a second time, remember."

"It'll last me," Beech said. "I wouldn't have missed it, and I wouldn't want it to be the same again. I'd sooner have things the way they run with us out in the high country. I'd sooner not have anything be the same a second time."

THE LEADER OF THE PEOPLE

by JOHN STEINBECK

It is said that to be great an artist need have created only one masterpiece; the rest of his works became unimportant. Probably an even better measure of an artist is that the argument revolves about which of his works is the masterpiece. Some people hold with John Steinbeck's very early books about the Salinas Valley, some with Grapes of Wrath, *and some with* The Sea of Cortes. *"The Leader of the People" is from* The Red Pony, *one of those slight volumes which so sharply prove the strength of Steinbeck as a writer. And of all the rich parts of this story, none is a greater commentary on contemporary America than the very pointed: "The westering has gone out of the people."*

On Saturday afternoon Billy Buck, the ranch-hand, raked together the last of the old year's haystack and pitched small forkfuls over the wire fence to a few mildly interested cattle. High in the air small clouds like puffs of cannon smoke were driven eastward by the March wind. The wind could be heard whishing in the brush on the ridge crests, but no breath of it penetrated down into the ranch-cup.

The little boy, Jody, emerged from the house eating a thick piece of buttered bread. He saw Billy working on the last of the haystack. Jody tramped down scuffing his shoes in a way he had been told was destructive to good shoe-leather. A flock of white pigeons flew out of the black cypress tree as Jody passed, and circled the tree and landed again. A half-grown tortoise-shell cat leaped from the bunkhouse porch, galloped on stiff legs across the road, whirled and galloped back again. Jody picked up a stone to help the game along, but he was too late, for the cat was under the porch before the stone could be discharged. He threw the stone into the cypress tree and started the white pigeons on another whirling flight.

Arriving at the used-up haystack, the boy leaned against the barbed wire fence. "Will that be all of it, do you think?" he asked.

The middle-aged ranch-hand stopped his careful raking and stuck his fork into the ground. He took off his black hat and smoothed down his hair. "Nothing left of it that isn't soggy from ground moisture," he said. He replaced his hat and rubbed his dry leathery hands together.

"Ought to be plenty mice," Jody suggested.

"Lousy with them," said Billy. "Just crawling with mice."

"Well, maybe, when you get all through, I could call the dogs and hunt the mice."

"Sure, I guess you could," said Billy Buck. He lifted a forkful of the damp ground-hay and threw it into the air. Instantly three mice leaped out and furrowed frantically under the hay again.

Jody sighed with satisfaction. Those plump, sleek, arrogant mice were doomed. For eight months they had lived and multiplied in the haystack. They had been immune from cats, from traps, from poison and from

Jody. They had grown smug in their security, overbearing and fat. Now the time of disaster had come; they would not survive another day.

Billy looked up at the top of the hills that surrounded the ranch. "Maybe you better ask your father before you do it," he suggested.

"Well, where is he? I'll ask him now."

"He rode up to the ridge ranch after dinner. He'll be back pretty soon." Jody slumped against the fence post. "I don't think he'd care."

As Billy went back to his work he said ominously, "You'd better ask him anyway. You know how he is."

Jody did know. His father, Carl Tiflin, insisted upon giving permission for anything that was done on the ranch, whether it was important or not. Jody sagged farther against the post until he was sitting on the ground. He looked up at the little puffs of wind-driven cloud. "Is it like to rain, Billy?"

"It might. The wind's good for it, but not strong enough."

"Well, I hope it don't rain until after I kill those damn mice." He looked over his shoulder to see whether Billy had noticed the mature profanity. Billy worked on without comment.

Jody turned back and looked at the side-hill where the road from the outside world came down. The hill was washed with lean March sunshine. Silver thistles, blue lupins and a few poppies bloomed among the sage bushes. Halfway up the hill Jody could see Doubletree Mutt, the black dog, digging in a squirrel hole. He paddled for a while and then paused to kick bursts of dirt out between his hind legs, and he dug with an earnestness which belied the knowledge he must have had that no dog had ever caught a squirrel by digging in a hole.

Suddenly, while Jody watched, the black dog stiffened, and backed out of the hole and looked up the hill toward the cleft in the ridge where the road came through. Jody looked up too. For a moment Carl Tiflin on horseback stood out against the pale sky and then he moved down the road toward the house. He carried something white in his hand.

The boy started to his feet. "He's got a letter," Jody cried. He trotted away toward the ranch house, for the letter would probably be read aloud and he wanted to be there. He reached the house before his father did, and ran in. He heard Carl dismount from his creaking saddle and slap the horse on the side to send it to the barn where Billy would unsaddle it and turn it out.

Jody ran into the kitchen. "We got a letter!" he cried.

His mother looked up from a pan of beans. "Who has?"

"Father has. I saw it in his hand."

Carl strode into the kitchen then, and Jody's mother asked, "Who's the letter from, Carl?"

He frowned quickly. "How did you know there was a letter?"

She nodded her head in the boy's direction. "Big-Britches Jody told me."

Jody was embarrassed.

His father looked down at him contemptuously. "He *is* getting to be a Big-Britches," Carl said. "He's minding everybody's business but his own. Got his big nose into everything."

Mrs. Tiflin relented a little. "Well, he hasn't enough to keep him busy. Who's the letter from?"

Carl still frowned on Jody. I'll keep him busy if he isn't careful." He held out a sealed letter. "I guess it's from your father."

Mrs. Tiflin took a hairpin from her head and slit open the flap. Her lips pursed judiciously. Jody saw her eyes snap back and forth over the lines. "He says," she translated, "he says he's going to drive out Saturday to stay for a little while. Why, this is Saturday. The letter must have been delayed." She looked at the postmark. "This was mailed day before yesterday. It should have been here yesterday." She looked up questioningly at her husband, and then her face darkened angrily. "Now what have you got that look on you for? He doesn't come often."

Carl turned his eyes away from her anger. He could be stern with her most of the time, but when occasionally her temper arose, he could not combat it.

"What's the matter with you?" she demanded again.

In his explanation there was a tone of apology Jody himself might have used. "It's just that he talks," Carl said lamely. "Just talks."

"Well, what of it? You talk yourself."

"Sure I do. But your father only talks about one thing."

"Indians!" Jody broke in excitedly. "Indians and crossing the plains!"

Carl turned fiercely on him. "You get out, Mr. Big-Britches! Go on, now! Get out!"

Jody went miserably out the back door and closed the screen with elaborate quietness. Under the kitchen window his shamed, downcast eyes fell upon a curiously shaped stone, a stone of such fascination that he squatted down and picked it up and turned it over in his hands.

The voices came clearly to him through the open kitchen window. "Jody's damn well right," he heard his father say. "Just Indians and crossing the plains. I've heard that story about how the horses got driven off about a thousand times. He just goes on and on, and he never changes a word in the things he tells."

When Mrs. Tiflin answered her tone was so changed that Jody, outside the window, looked up from his study of the stone. Her voice had become soft and explanatory. Jody knew how her face would have changed to match the tone. She said quietly, "Look at it this way, Carl. That was the big thing in my father's life. He led a wagon train clear across the plains to the coast, and when it was finished, his life was done. It was a big thing to do, but it didn't last long enough. Look!" she continued, "it's as though he was born to do that, and after he finished it, there wasn't anything more for him to do but think about it and talk about it. If there'd been any farther west to go, he'd have gone. He's told me so himself. But at last there was the ocean. He lives right by the ocean where he had to stop."

She had caught Carl, caught him and entangled him in her soft tone.

"I've seen him," he agreed quietly. "He goes down and stares off west over the ocean." His voice sharpened a little. "And then he goes up to the Horseshoe Club in Pacific Grove, and he tells people how the Indians drove off the horses."

She tried to catch him again. "Well, it's everything to him. You might be patient with him and pretend to listen."

Carl turned impatiently away. "Well, if it gets too bad, I can always go down to the bunkhouse and sit with Billy," he said irritably. He walked through the house and slammed the front door after him.

Jody ran to his chores. He dumped the grain to the chickens without chasing any of them. He gathered the eggs from the nests. He trotted into the house with the wood and interlaced it so carefully in the wood-box that two armloads seemed to fill it to overflowing.

His mother had finished the beans by now. She stirred up the fire and brushed off the stove-top with a turkey wing. Jody peered cautiously at her to see whether any rancor toward him remained. "Is he coming today?" Jody asked.

"That's what his letter said."

"Maybe I better walk up the road to meet him."

Mrs. Tiflin clanged the stove-lid shut. "That would be nice," she said. "He'd probably like to be met."

"I guess I'll just do it then."

Outside, Jody whistled shrilly to the dogs. "Come on up the hill," he commanded. The two dogs waved their tails and ran ahead. Along the roadside the sage had tender new tips. Jody tore off some pieces and rubbed them on his hands until the air was filled with the sharp wild smell. With a rush the dogs leaped from the road and yapped into the brush after a rabbit. That was the last Jody saw of them, for when they failed to catch the rabbit, they went back home.

Jody plodded on up the hill toward the ridge top. When he reached the little cleft where the road came through, the afternoon wind struck him and blew up his hair and ruffled his shirt. He looked down on the little hills and ridges below and then out at the huge green Salinas Valley. He could see the white town of Salinas far out in the flat and the flash of its windows under the waning sun. Directly below him, in an oak tree, a crow congress had convened. The tree was black with crows all cawing at once.

Then Jody's eyes followed the wagon road down from the ridge where he stood, and lost it behind a hill, and picked it up again on the other side. On that distant stretch he saw a cart slowly pulled by a bay horse. It disappeared behind the hill. Jody sat down on the ground and watched the place where the cart would reappear again. The wind sang on the hilltops and the puff-ball clouds hurried eastward.

Then the cart came into sight and stopped. A man dressed in black dismounted from the seat and walked to the horse's head. Although it was so far away, Jody knew he had unhooked the check-rein, for the horse's head dropped forward. The horse moved on, and the man walked slowly up the hill beside it. Jody gave a glad cry and ran down the road toward them. The squirrels bumped along off the road, and a road-runner flirted its tail and raced over the edge of the hill and sailed out like a glider.

Jody tried to leap into the middle of his shadow at every step. A stone rolled under his foot and he went down. Around a little bend he raced, and there, a short distance ahead, were his grandfather and the cart. The boy dropped from his unseemly running and approached at a dignified walk.

The horse plodded stumble-footedly up the hill and the old man walked beside it. In the lowering sun their giant shadows flickered darkly behind them. The grandfather was dressed in a black broadcloth suit and he wore kid congress gaiters and a black tie on a short, hard collar. He carried his black slouch hat in his hand. His white beard was cropped close and his white eyebrows overhung his eyes like moustaches. The blue eyes were sternly merry. About the whole face and figure there was a granite dignity, so that every motion seemed an impossible thing. Once at rest, it seemed the old man would be stone, would never move again. His steps were slow and certain. Once made, no step could ever be retraced; once headed in a direction, the path would never bend nor the pace increase nor slow.

When Jody appeared around the bend, Grandfather waved his hat slowly in welcome, and he called, "Why, Jody! Come down to meet me, have you?"

Jody sidled near and turned and matched his step to the old man's step and stiffened his body and dragged his heels a little. "Yes, sir," he said. "We got your letter only today."

"Should have been here yesterday," said Grandfather. "It certainly should. How are all the folks?"

"They're fine, sir." He hesitated and then suggested shyly, "Would you like to come on a mouse hunt tomorrow, sir?"

"Mouse hunt, Jody?" Grandfather chuckled. "Have the people of this generation come down to hunting mice? They aren't very strong, the new people, but I hardly thought mice would be game for them."

"No, sir. It's just play. The haystacks gone. I'm going to drive out the mice to the dogs. And you can watch, or even beat the hay a little."

The stern, merry eyes turned down on him. "I see. You don't eat them, then. You haven't come to that yet."

Jody explained, "The dogs eat them, sir. It wouldn't be much like hunting Indians, I guess."

"No, not much—but then later, when the troops were hunting Indians and shooting children and burning teepees, it wasn't much different from your mouse hunt."

They topped the rise and started down into the ranch cup, and they lost the sun from their shoulders. "You've grown," Grandfather said. "Nearly an inch, I should say."

"More," Jody boasted. "Where they mark me on the door, I'm up more than an inch since Thanksgiving even."

Grandfather's rich throaty voice said, "Maybe you're getting too much water and turning to pith and stalk. Wait until you head out, and then we'll see."

Jody looked quickly into the old man's face to see whether his feelings should be hurt, but there was no will to injure, no punishing nor putting-in-your-place light in the keen blue eyes. "We might kill a pig," Jody suggested.

"Oh, no! I couldn't let you do that. You're just humoring me. It isn't the time and you know it."

"You know Riley, the big boar, sir?"

"Yes. I remember Riley well."

"Well, Riley ate a hole into that same haystack, and it fell down on him and smothered him."

·"Pigs do that when they can," said Grandfather.

"Riley was a nice pig, for a boar, sir. I rode him sometimes, and he didn't mind."

A door slammed at the house below them, and they saw Jody's mother standing on the porch waving her apron in welcome. And they saw Carl Tiflin walking up from the barn to be at the house for the arrival.

The sun had disappeared from the hills by now. The blue smoke from the house chimney hung in flat layers in the purpling ranch-cup. The puff-ball clouds, dropped by the falling wind, hung listlessly in the sky.

Billy Buck came out of the bunkhouse and flung a wash basin of soapy water on the ground. He had been shaving in mid-week, for Billy held Grandfather in reverence, and Grandfather said that Billy was one of the few men of the new generation who had not gone soft. Although Billy was in middle age, Grandfather considered him a boy. Now Billy was hurrying toward the house too.

When Jody and Grandfather arrived, the three were waiting for them in front of the yard gate.

Carl said, "Hello, sir. We've been looking for you."

Mrs. Tiflin kissed Grandfather on the side of his beard, and stood still while his big hand patted her shoulder. Billy shook hands solemnly, grinning under his straw moustache. "I'll put up your horse," said Billy, and he led the rig away.

Grandfather watched him go, and then, turning back to the group, he said as he had said a hundred times before, "There's a good boy. I knew his father, old Muletail Buck. I never knew why they called him Mule-tail except he packed mules."

Mrs. Tiflin turned and led the way into the house. "How long are you going to stay, Father? Your letter didn't say."

"Well, I don't know. I thought I'd stay about two weeks. But I never stay as long as I think I'm going to."

In a short while they were sitting at the white oilcloth table eating their supper. The lamp with the tin reflector hung over the table. Outside the dining-room windows the big moths battered softly against the glass.

Grandfather cut his steak into tiny pieces and chewed slowly. "I'm hungry," he said. "Driving out here got my appetite up. It's like when we were crossing. We all got so hungry every night we could hardly wait to let the meat get done. I could eat about five pounds of buffalo meat every night."

"It's moving around does it," said Billy. "My father was a government packer. I helped him when I was a kid. Just the two of us could about clean up a deer's ham."

"I knew your father, Billy," said Grandfather. "A fine man he was. They called him Mule-tail Buck. I don't know why except he packed mules."

"That was it," Billy agreed. "He packed mules."

Grandfather put down his knife and fork and looked around the table. "I remember one time we ran out of meat—" His voice dropped to a curious low sing-song, dropped into a tonal groove the story had worn for itself. "There was no buffalo, no antelope, not even rabbits. The hunters couldn't even shoot a coyote. That was the time for the leader to be on the watch. I was the leader, and I kept my eyes open. Know why? Well, just the minute the people began to get hungry they'd start slaughtering the team oxen. Do you believe that? I've heard of parties that just ate up their draft cattle. Started from the middle and worked toward the ends. Finally they'd eat the lead pair, and then the wheelers. The leader of a party had to keep them from doing that."

In some manner a big moth got into the room and circled the hanging kerosene lamp. Billy got up and tried to clap it between his hands. Carl struck with a cupped palm and caught the moth and broke it. He walked to the window and dropped it out.

"As I was saying," Grandfather began again, but Carl interrupted him. "You'd better eat some more meat. All the rest of us are ready for our pudding."

Jody saw a flash of anger in his mother's eyes. Grandfather picked up his knife and fork. "I'm pretty hungry, all right," he said. "I'll tell you about that later."

When supper was over, when the family and Billy Buck sat in front of the fireplace in the other room, Jody anxiously watched Grandfather. He saw the signs he knew. The bearded head leaned forward; the eyes lost their sternness and looked wonderingly into the fire; the big lean fingers laced themselves on the black knees. "I wonder," he began, "I just wonder whether I ever told you how those thieving Piutes drove off thirty-five of our horses."

"I think you did," Carl interrupted. "Wasn't it just before you went up into the Tahoe country?"

Grandfather turned quickly toward his son-in-law. "That's right. I guess I must have told you that story."

"Lots of times," Carl said cruelly, and he avoided his wife's eyes. But he felt the angry eyes on him, and he said, " 'Course I'd like to hear it again."

Grandfather looked back at the fire. His fingers unlaced and laced again. Jody knew how he felt, how his insides were collapsed and empty. Hadn't Jody been called a Big-Britches that very afternoon? He arose to heroism and opened himself to the term Big-Britches again. "Tell about Indians," he said softly.

Grandfather's eyes grew stern again. "Boys always want to hear about Indians. It was a job for men, but boys want to hear about it. Well, let's see. Did I ever tell you how I wanted each wagon to carry a long iron plate?"

Everyone but Jody remained silent. Jody said, "No. You didn't."

"Well, when the Indians attacked, we always put the wagons in a circle and fought from between the wheels. I thought that if every wagon carried a long plate with rifle holes, the men could stand the plates on the outside of the wheels when the wagons were in the circle and they would be protected. It would save lives and that would make up for the extra weight of the iron. But of course the party wouldn't do it. No party had done it before and they couldn't see why they should go to the expense. They lived to regret it, too."

Jody looked at his mother, and knew from her expression that she was not listening at all. Carl picked at a callus on his thumb and Billy Buck watched a spider crawling up the wall.

Grandfather's tone dropped into its narrative groove again. Jody knew in advance exactly what words would fall. The story droned on, speeded up for the attack, grew sad over the wounds, struck a dirge at the burials on the great plains. Jody sat quietly watching Grandfather. The stern blue eyes were detached. He looked as though he were not very interested in the story himself.

When it was finished, when the pause had been politely respected as the frontier of the story, Billy Buck stood up and stretched and hitched his trousers. "I guess I'll turn in," he said. Then he faced Grandfather. "I've got an old powder horn and a cap and ball pistol down to the bunkhouse. Did I ever show them to you?"

Grandfather nodded slowly. "Yes, I think you did, Billy. Reminds me of a pistol I had when I was leading the people across." Billy stood politely until the little story was done, and then he said, "Good night," and went out of the house.

Carl Tiflin tried to turn the conversation then. "How's the country between here and Monterey? I've heard it's pretty dry."

"It is dry," said Grandfather. "There's not a drop of water in the Laguna

Seca. But it's a long pull from '87. The whole country was powder then, and in '61 I believe all the coyotes starved to death. We had fifteen inches of rain this year."

"Yes, but it all came too early. We could do with some now." Carl's eye fell on Jody. "Hadn't you better be getting to bed?"

Jody stood up obediently. "Can I kill the mice in the old haystack, sir?"

"Mice? Oh! Sure, kill them all off. Billy said there isn't any good hay left."

Jody exchanged a secret and satisfying look with Grandfather. "I'll kill every one tomorrow," he promised.

Jody lay in his bed and thought of the impossible world of Indians and buffaloes, a world that had ceased to be forever. He wished he could have been living in the heroic time, but he knew he was not of heroic timber. No one living now, save possibly Billy Buck, was worthy to do the things that had been done. A race of giants had lived then, fearless men, men of a staunchness unknown in this day. Jody thought of the wide plains and of the wagons moving across like centipedes. He thought of Grandfather on a huge white horse, marshaling the people. Across his mind marched the great phantoms, and they marched off the earth and they were gone.

He came back to the ranch for a moment, then. He heard the dull rushing sound that space and silence make. He heard one of the dogs, out in the doghouse, scratching a flea and bumping his elbow against the floor with every stroke. Then the wind arose again and the black cypress groaned and Jody went to sleep.

He was up half an hour before the triangle sounded for breakfast. His mother was rattling the stove to make the flames roar when Jody went through the kitchen. "You're up early," she said. "Where are you going?"

"Out to get a good stick. We're going to kill the mice today."

"Who is 'we'?"

"Why, Grandfather and I."

"So you've got him in it. You always like to have someone in with you in case there's blame to share."

"I'll be right back," said Jody. "I just want to have a good stick ready for after breakfast."

He closed the screen door after him and went out into the cool blue morning. The birds were noisy in the dawn and the ranch cats came down from the hill like blunt snakes. They had been hunting gophers in the dark, and although the four cats were full of gopher meat, they sat in a semi-circle at the back door and mewed piteously for milk. Doubletree Mutt and Smasher moved sniffing along the edge of the brush, performing the duty with rigid ceremony, but when Jody whistled, their heads jerked up and their tails waved. They plunged down to him, wriggling their skins and yawning. Jody patted their heads seriously, and moved on to the weathered scrap pile. He selected an old broom handle and a short piece of inch-square scrap wood. From his pocket he took a shoelace and tied the ends of the sticks loosely together to make a flail. He whistled his new weapon through the air and struck the ground experimentally, while the dogs leaped aside and whined with apprehension.

Jody turned and started down past the house toward the old haystack ground to look over the field of slaughter, but Billy Buck, sitting patiently on the back steps, called to him, "You better come back. It's only a couple of minutes till breakfast."

Jody changed his course and moved toward the house. He leaned his flail against the steps. "That's to drive the mice out," he said. "I'll bet they're fat. I'll bet they don't know what's going to happen to them today."

"No, nor you either," Billy remarked philosophically, "nor me, nor anyone."

Jody was staggered by this thought. He knew it was true. His imagination twitched away from the mouse hunt. Then his mother came out on the back porch and struck the triangle, and all thoughts fell in a heap.

Grandfather hadn't appeared at the table when they sat down. Billy nodded at his empty chair. "He's all right? He isn't sick?"

"He takes a long time to dress," said Mrs. Tiflin. "He combs his whiskers and rubs up his shoes and brushes his clothes."

Carl scattered sugar on his mush. "A man that's led a wagon train across the plains has got to be pretty careful how he dresses."

Mrs. Tiflin turned on him. "Don't do that, Carl! Please don't!" There was more of threat than of request in her tone. And the threat irritated Carl.

"Well, how many times do I have to listen to the story of the iron plates, and the thirty-five horses? That time's done. Why can't he forget it, now it's done?" He grew angrier while he talked, and his voice rose. "Why does he have to tell them over and over? He came across the plains. All right! Now it's finished. Nobody wants to hear about it over and over."

The door into the kitchen closed softly. The four at the table sat frozen. Carl laid his mush spoon on the table and touched his chin with his fingers.

Then the kitchen door opened and Grandfather walked in. His mouth smiled tightly and his eyes were squinted. "Good morning," he said, and he sat down and looked at his mush dish.

Carl could not leave it there. "Did—did you hear what I said?"

Grandfather jerked a little nod.

"I don't know what got into me, sir. I didn't mean it. I was just being funny."

Jody glanced in shame at his mother, and he saw that she was looking at Carl, and that she wasn't breathing. It was an awful thing that he was doing. He was tearing himself to pieces to talk like that. It was a terrible thing to him to retract a word, but to retract it in shame was infinitely worse.

Grandfather looked sidewise. "I'm trying to get right side up," he said gently. "I'm not being mad. I don't mind what you said, but it might be true, and I would mind that."

"It isn't true," said Carl. "I'm not feeling well this morning. I'm sorry I said it."

"Don't be sorry, Carl. An old man doesn't see things sometimes. Maybe you're right. The crossing is finished. Maybe it should be forgotten, now it's done."

Carl got up from the table. "I've had enough to eat. I'm going to work. Take your time, Billy!" He walked quickly out of the dining-room. Billy gulped the rest of his food and followed soon after. But Jody could not leave his chair.

"Won't you tell any more stories?" Jody asked.

"Why, sure I'll tell them, but only when—I'm sure people want to hear them."

"I like to hear them, sir."

"Oh! Of course you do, but you're a little boy. It was a job for men, but only little boys like to hear about it."

Jody got up from his place. "I'll wait outside for you, sir. I've got a good stick for those mice."

He waited by the gate until the old man came out on the porch. "Let's go down and kill the mice now," Jody called.

"I think I'll just sit in the sun, Jody. You go kill the mice."

"You can use my stick if you like."

"No, I'll just sit here a while."

Jody turned disconsolately away, and walked down toward the old hay-stack. He tried to whip up his enthusiasm with thoughts of the fat juicy mice. He beat the ground with his flail. The dogs coaxed and whined about him, but he could not go. Back at the house he could see Grandfather sitting on the porch, looking small and thin and black.

Jody gave up and went to sit on the steps at the old man's feet.

"Back already? Did you kill the mice?"

"No, sir. I'll kill them some other day."

The morning flies buzzed close to the ground and the ants dashed about in front of the steps. The heavy smell of sage slipped down the hill. The porch boards grew warm in the sunshine.

Jody hardly knew when Grandfather started to talk. "I shouldn't stay here, feeling the way I do." He examined his strong old hands. "I feel as though the crossing wasn't worth doing." His eyes moved up the side-hill and stopped on a motionless hawk perched on a dead limb. "I tell those old stories, but they're not what I want to tell. I only know how I want people to feel when I tell them.

"It wasn't Indians that were important, nor adventures, nor even getting out here. It was a whole bunch of people made into one big crawling beast. And I was the head. It was westering and westering. Every man wanted something for himself, but the big beast that was all of them wanted only westering. I was the leader, but if I hadn't been there, someone else would have been the head. The thing had to have a head.

"Under the little bushes the shadows were black at white noonday. When we saw the mountains at last, we cried—all of us. But it wasn't getting here that mattered, it was movement and westering.

"We carried life out here and set it down the way those ants carry eggs. And I was the leader. The westering was as big as God, and the slow steps that made the movement piled up and piled up until the continent was crossed.

"Then we came down to the sea, and it was done." He stopped and wiped his eyes until the rims were red. "That's what I should be telling instead of stories."

When Jody spoke, Grandfather started and looked down at him. "Maybe I could lead the people some day," Jody said.

The old man smiled. "There's no place to go. There's the ocean to stop you. There's a line of old man along the shore hating the ocean because it stopped them."

"In boats I might, sir."

"No place to go, Jody. Every place is taken. But that's not the worst —no, not the worst. Westering has died out of the people. Westering isn't a hunger any more. It's all done. Your father is right. It is finished." He laced his fingers on his knee and looked at them.

Jody felt very sad. "If you'd like a glass of lemonade I could make it for you."

Grandfather was about to refuse, and then he saw Jody's face. "That would be nice," he said. "Yes, it would be nice to drink a lemonade."

Jody ran into the kitchen where his mother was wiping the last of the breakfast dishes. "Can I have a lemon to make a lemonade for Grandfather?"

His mother mimicked— "And another lemon to make a lemonade for you."

"No, ma'am. I don't want one."

"Jody! You're sick!" Then she stopped suddenly. "Take a lemon out of the cooler," she said softly. "Here, I'll reach the squeezer down to you."